WHITE PAWN

ҩ⭑ҩ

Book 1 of the
Kestrel Harper Saga

ҩ⭑ҩ

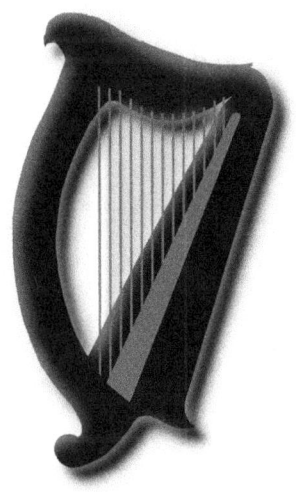

Tamara Brigham

꧁*꧂

For Amanda and Rachel, who tolerated the hours I spent writing
and
For Stardust, for the parting gift of inspiration.

꧁*꧂

⥺Chapter 1⥤

The Kármár winds had always been an omen of change. How appropriate that they should blow this night, for surely by morning, nothing would be the same in Enesfel again. General Guthrie McHador, his weathered face rimmed by waves of light brown hair, watched the monarch sleeping, lost in his own thoughts of what had been and what lay ahead. His shoulders ached from the cold. He knew he should have closed the window hours ago; the frigid Kármár had brought snow early to Enesfel this year and was pushing through the small window onto the ledge and the stone floor beneath it. But King Innis had forbidden closing it and the general, as the King's most loyal supporter, would have done anything the old monarch asked of him, even if that request seemed likely to hasten the man's death. As frail and weary as King Innis was, however, the general doubted that closing the window would have given the man even one extra minute of life.

He was on the cusp of death.

The sharp cries of a woman in labor had finally died away in the adjoining room and were replaced by the welcome sounds of an infant crying. The King relaxed his grip on Guthrie's hand with a relieved smile, proving he had not been asleep as the general had thought, and fell into a light doze. Guthrie stood after his hand was free, intending to close the window now that the King slept, to keep any more snow from blowing into the room. He stood, his movements stiff, and went to the window.

"Lord McHador?"

"Yes?" He turned towards the midwife who stood in the doorway to the queen's chamber, realizing as he spoke that he was standing at the window still without having closed it.

Before the woman could say more, more sounds of pain erupted beyond that open door. Guthrie grimaced and closed his eyes. No complications, he thought, looking to see if the old man had stirred. Thankfully, the King still slept, but it would not last long. The last thing the monarch needed was for his beloved third wife to endure complications.

The midwife curtsied. "There are twins, milord. The first child is a fine, healthy daughter. Her Majesty is doing very well; there is no cause for concern or alarm."

No cause for concern, he thought with a snort, watching her scamper back to assist the attending physician. That sixty-eight-year-old Innis Lachlan and his forty-four-year-old wife Cordelia had conceived a child was incredible enough. That there could be twins was a miracle. A girl. The King had always longed for a daughter to spoil in the midst of numerous sons. How unfortunate that his wish should be granted when he would not be able to enjoy the little girl. Thank k'Ádhá, the general thought to himself, it had not been another prince. The five Enesfel had were more than enough.

His attention shifted outside onto the suffocating, oppressive storm clouds high overhead. Adjusting his burgundy wool cape to keep the night chill from seeping in around his neck, he tried to force his thoughts away from their grim path and onto his men, particularly those chosen for duty on this miserable night. But the sounds of the queen's labor kept pushing into his head, demanding notice, and he was unable to concentrate on anything else.

"Where are you, Ártur?" he muttered into the darkness. The King's coughing began again, like the sound of nails rattling within a metal pail, and the worried general returned to the bedside. "Why did he send you home?"

There was no need to ask that question. The general knew why. The King did not want the Elyri healer to watch him die, did not want Ártur to be accused of his death afterwards. Guthrie also knew that, even if Ártur were here, he would be unable to change the course of the night's events. He might be able to delay the inevitable, but he could not change it. As Mormer, the Teren physician employed by the King, had said earlier this evening, it was unlikely the King would live through the night. Swallowing the hard lump in his throat, Guthrie resisted the call of the wine carafe at the bedside. He could not afford to lose control as he had over Jezeel's death. Enesfel depended on him to be strong, as did King Innis.

As if aware of the general's thoughts, the ancient ruler coughed again, opened his eyes, and said, "One drink will not kill you…"

"No…but I will not be able to stop at one," the general admitted, knowing himself too well.

"I admire your willpower…" The King's cracked voice caught, his words interrupted by a particularly staccato cry from his wife, and the old man's eyes flicked back and forth between the doorway and his general. "Still, Guthrie? What is…?"

He closed his battle-scarred hands around the King's to offer the man reassurance. "There is no cause for alarm, My Liege. The midwife says there are twins; the first is a healthy daughter…"

"A daughter…" Smiling wanly, the King pushed himself to sitting and nodded his thanks as Guthrie adjusted the pillows behind him to prop him up. The general did not need words to explain the flashes of emotion that flickered across the King's face. He had been ten years old when he had entered King Innis' employment and had been by his side ever since. He had served first as page, then as almost son, and finally as general, advisor, and closest of friends. The only person who knew the monarch more completely was the woman giving birth in the other room.

The King once again reached for the general's hand and Guthrie offered it gladly. If either of them had believed that knowing tonight would likely be their final moments together would make the parting easier, everything about this night had conspired to prove them wrong. Lingering in their private musings, in memories of times and places lost to history, they listened to the birthing cries until jarred out of those thoughts by the door opening between the rooms. The night was silent at last, and Mormer entered the royal bedchamber, wiping his hands on the smock he wore. He glanced at the window, seemed prepared to chastise someone for leaving it open, but instead he bowed and allowed his face to regain a more professional composure before he spoke.

"Your Majesty, the Lady has given birth to healthy twins. A daughter and a son." He said the last word as if he might be punished for bringing yet another prince into the Lachlan dynasty. "They are resting comfortably; there were no complications."

"I want to see them."

"You should not be…" the physician started. But the King was already struggling to get out of bed and the general was right there to assist him.

The King swayed as he got to his feet, but leaning on the general steadied him. "Or what?" he croaked. "Out with it, physician. Stay in bed or I shall die? Will walking a few feet and sitting in a chair beside my wife make such a difference in how long I shall remain in this world?" Rather than wait for an answer, he began the tedious shuffling journey towards the queen's chamber. Guthrie heard the doctor sigh, though he doubted Innis did. Nor did he think that the doctor heard the King mutter beneath his breath, "I would like to see my children…for them to see me…at least one time."

The doctor said nothing further and obligingly assisted the general in getting the King to his wife's bedside. The remains of dozens of candles and several lanterns littered the room, but most of them had been extinguished to allow the queen and children to sleep. As soon as he was settled in the gilded, high-backed chair beside the bed, the King shooed both men away and took the first tiny infant from the midwife's arms. Mormer departed as bid, but Guthrie lingered beyond the doorway, near enough to be of service should it be required, but out of sight and immediate hearing range of any conversation between the royal couple.

Rubbing the back of his neck, he stared at the King's empty bed, feeling a sense of foreboding. He could hear the midwife moving around the room, fussing over mother and children and exchanging one child in the King's arms for the other. The tense, sinking knot in the general's stomach was relieved by the unmistakable sound of the King's laughter, a sound both joyous and heartbreaking. Enjoy the children, the general thought as he swallowed back the encroaching tears. You deserve that much, My Liege.

Both he and the King knew that these children would not likely see the throne of Enesfel. There were too many heirs before them, heirs who would someday have families of their own if they did not already. While the twins would have every blessing their position could afford them, there would undoubtedly be troubled times ahead as the elder heirs fought and bickered over the throne. Guthrie could not help but wonder what lay in store for these two defenseless children and for the kingdom itself.

He remained where he was even after the midwife had extinguished all but one of the candles and left the room for the night. The general saw no reason to enter or intrude; it would make no difference if the King slept in the chair, with his wife, or in his own bed, so Guthrie merely waited for orders from his King. He was soldier enough to

ॐ ॐ

remain at his station until further notice, even if that meant standing against the wall outside of the queen's room all night.

An unexpected shiver ran through his body and he tilted his head towards the open door, thinking he had heard something within the room. He heard nothing now and began to relax once more until the feeling came again, this time followed by a quiet voice.

"Lord McHador? Are you still there?" It was the queen.

To the general's perceptions, both rooms seemed suddenly darker, colder. A burst of icy air rushed past as he turned to enter the queen's room, moving past him into the King's chamber, towards the open window. Closing his eyes against the sudden faintness and dizzying nausea, the general tried to speak, to answer his queen's summons, but his throat constricted around the words and refused to allow sound to pass.

He knew. He wanted to run from the room, away from the inevitability that threatened to drown him. Instead, he squared his shoulders and willed his leaden feet to move, stopping only when he reached the side of the queen's bed. She was holding her husband's skeletal hand; the babes slept in their cradle. The King's head hung forward, his chin resting on his chest as if he had fallen asleep. The general did not want to hear her say what he already knew, and so he squatted down in front of the chair and held his hand before the King's face. There was nothing.

"Shall I call for Mormer?" he finally succeeded in asking as his hand fell to his side.

The queen pushed a stray wisp of blond behind her ear. "There is no need of that, I think…"

"The children…?"

He did not look at her, could not look at anything except the King's still open eyes, but he sensed her movement as she propped herself up enough to look towards her children. "Do you believe his presence will harm them?"

It was an old superstition, one he had heard from the time he was a very small boy, regarding the need to remove the dead from the presence of the living before the living were infected, tainted in some way. But it was a superstition the general did not believe. He had spent his share of time amongst the dead on the battlefield and elsewhere, and not once had he seen anything bad happen as a result that could not be explained by some other earthly or manmade act. "I...no, milady..."

This time, the movement on the bed resulted in the queen placing the King's hand on his lap and a gentle tug on the general's arm. Guthrie looked at her then, still fighting back tears.

"Leave him be," she murmured. "To everyone else, it will appear that he has died in his sleep during the night. He is where he wished to be...and I am happy with him here. Since you were near...were his best friend...I thought you should be the first to know, but no one else needs to tonight."

"Yes, my queen...thank you." He had to force himself into the role of servant in order to retain some semblance of calm as he closed the monarch's eyes and rose to his feet. "Is there anything I can do for you? Anything you need?"

"Go to bed, Guthrie." She had the most beautiful smile, even when it was a grieving one. Guthrie had never had any doubts or questions about why the King had loved her so deeply. "Sleep will no doubt elude us, but it is best if you are not here when he is found...and I would like to be alone with him awhile longer."

The general bowed stiffly. "Very well, my queen. Goodnight then, and...congratulation on the birth. May the three of you be blessed."

"Thank you."

He lingered in the doorway long enough to watch her rise painfully from the bed and sit on the floor in front of Innis, putting her head in his lap and closing her eyes. The tableau in the dim candle light wrenched at his heart. He forced himself to turn away, and with the same grim determination he wore into battle, marched to his own room without looking back. During that entire walk he fought the despair of realizing that from this night forth, his decisions would be his own. King Innis could no longer guide him as he had for so many years. Guthrie wondered if this was what it felt like to grow up.

Would he wake in the morning to discover this night had been a dream? He prayed it was so, but knew that such a wish would require sleeping, and as the queen had said, sleep was likely to elude each of them this night. Guthrie had no intentions of trying. Once in his own dark room, he went to the window, opened it, and stared outside once more. The cloud cover seemed to have thinned; the storm appeared to be passing. Was that an illusion too? For the moment, the general was uncertain as to what was real and what was not.

He was never consciously aware of daybreak; it was the sounds of servants passing in the corridor that caused him to realize that the outside world was brighter. After a deep sigh, he left the window, changed into clean garments, and folded the dirty ones with care as was his habit. By the time someone brought his morning meal, the snowfall was a whisper and patches of faint dusky blue poked through the clouds. The Kármár had blown themselves out; whatever changes they heralded had been wrought during the darkness and remained to be revealed by the light of this new day. It would only be a matter of time before someone discovered and reported the King's death. Then any hopes of forgetting, of denying this night had come to pass, would be lost.

Bracing himself for what was to come, Guthrie resumed staring through the window, lost in the memories of much happier times.

ޮ*ً

Leafless skeletons swayed before the Kármár's wrath, knocking their thin arms against the stone and mortar walls of the house as the pane glass windows strained to keep out the cold and snow. The craggy

ޮ Ƿ ً

mountains around Bhryell sheltered the small valley town from the worst weather; if the drifts of powder white that built against the exterior walls of the boy's home were any indication, he was grateful he was not living anywhere west of the Llaethlágárá.

Kavan had heard the adults talking earlier about how the snows had come too soon this year, how the premature frost had killed much of the year's final harvest. Cold rains had fallen steadily for several weeks prior, heralding that destruction, and the snow had been coming down for days. Very few ventured outdoors, preferring what little warmth the hearth fires could provide over the bitter wet weather. The hope the people clung to was that an early winter might mean an early spring, but it seemed to him a common perception that, before this winter ended, much more than the final harvest would be lost. The Kármár would indeed bring change, and this year, it would not likely be good.

The boy looked up abruptly, staring into the dwindling fire on the hearth but not truly seeing it. What he did see, what he sensed, were things he did not quite comprehend. Sorrow. Chaos. Hope. As surely as he knew his own name, he was certain that Enesfel's great King was dead and that somewhere another had been born. Twins, but he knew not where they were, or how he knew this to be true. A word came to mind, or a name perhaps, Arlan, but it belonged to no one he knew and held no meaning. It was only a word, a word connected to the images and impressions he had been shown, but he had no idea what any of it meant. Bewildered, he rose and went to the window. Little could be seen through the swirling snow so he watched the flakes fall instead. It was the distraction of darkness that he wanted most to help clear his head.

Pushing his white hair from his eyes, he pondered the connection between the death and the births, certain there was one. He was equally certain that what he had witnessed were actual events, not flashes of fancy and imagination. Glancing at the staircase behind him, he considered waking his family, but he was still a child, unproven and untrained in Elyri ways, and he doubted that anyone would believe him. Only Ártur would, and thus it would be best, he decided, to await his cousin's return home. Ártur would have news from Rhidam, if there was any, and he would be able to prove the truth…and perhaps even explain it.

Kavan wanted that proof himself.

With a shrug of resignation, he settled again on the plush woven rug and tried unsuccessfully to refocus on his book. Too many unsettling things had happened to him in the last three days; this was only the latest oddity to plague him. Based on what he knew of his people, he presumed that the Elyri gifts were awakening within him, as they did in all of his kind. But he also knew how his uncle frowned upon such gifts, and it made him wary of speaking up, of revealing himself to them, or anyone. He was afraid of their rejection. Afraid of the power.

Looking down into the palm of his white hand, he watched with fascination as a small flame sprang to life there, glimmering and flickering as a candle but burning nothing.

"Kavan?" A woman's voice called from the top of the stairs but Kavan did not respond other than to quickly douse the flame. She came into the room to find him reading before the fire, dressed in the simple white robe he preferred over everything else. "Kavan, you should be in bed."

He looked at her with an expression she might have called tortured if she had seen it on an older child or adult. On Kavan's delicate young features, she did not know what to call it, but she did find it unsettling. "I am almost finished with this section, aene Dháná. May I finish?"

"What are you reading so intently that it has kept you up?" Knowing how much her nephew enjoyed reading, it did not surprise her to find him thus occupied. After some resistance from him, she took the book and studied it. It was not a small volume; it was three and a half inches thick, bound in handsome dark leather, and appeared in excellent condition despite its obvious age. Though unable to read the text, she did recognize one word on its cover and her eyes widened in disbelief. "Where did you get this, Kavan?"

The boy began to say something, stopped, and then rubbed one hand across his tired eyes. He had intended to keep the book a secret, but perhaps it was better that she question that than the handlight she seemed not to have noticed. "Ártur found it in Rhidam. He gave it to me during his last visit. I have read it twelve times. Please, let me finish."

"If you have read it twelve times in the past four months, you already know what it says."

Her words were true, but it did not sway him. "Please?"

She closed the book. "Tomorrow. To bed with you," she continued before he could protest, "or I shall not return this to you until the next time Ártur is home."

Frustrated, Kavan sighed, uncoiled gracefully to his feet, and started towards the stairs, pausing to glance back, hoping his aunt would change her mind and give the book back to him.

Dháná shook her head and waited until he was out of sight before examining the book further. Saint Kóráhm, or Heretic Kóráhm as he was more frequently called, was a forbidden topic of conversation amongst the leaders of the Faith. Not forbidden by any written law, but rather by a sense of mutual discomfort and awkwardness. He was discussed even less by the Faithful, who had little interest in discussing the merits or faults of a man long dead. Most copies of Kóráhm's writings had been destroyed centuries ago, so her son finding one intact was no small feat. She supposed it was normal for Kavan to be curious about the man whose name he bore, but why he would want to read a philosophical and religious treatise once, let alone a dozen times, was incomprehensible to her. She flipped through the pages, trying to read a few sporadic passages, but she, like the majority of Elyri, was not fluent in the ancient High language and what little she could decipher was certainly not easy reading, especially for any child Kavan's age.

But she had long ago realized that Kavan was hardly typical.

If her husband found the book in his home it would be burned and Kavan would be severely punished. Ártur would likely be as well, possibly banished from his home if his father was of a mind to do so. Dhàná considered keeping it away from Kavan, removing it from the house. She did not have the heart to disappoint the boy, however; Kavan asked so little of anyone, and what harm could there truly be in a book? She would return it to him with the warning to keep it out of Tám's sight, and she would remind her son that bringing such material into Tám MacLyr's house was ill-considered.

Sighing with weariness and the weight such a decision placed on her shoulders, she stirred the fire once more before returning upstairs where she paused long enough to put the book beneath Kavan's pillow, careful not to rouse the already sleeping boy.

❧Chapter 2❧

Prince Donal Lachlan toyed absently with the sausage on his platter as he stared at the random pattern of ice crystals on the window glass. If he had built a fire, as his squire had suggested, the glass would have been clear, but he had arrived late last night from his three-month tour of duty on the Enesfel-Hatu border and had not wanted to trouble the staff either with building one for him or with the necessity of cleaning the hearth this morning. This particular billeting room was rarely used and he saw no point in dirtying it any more than he already had. Sleeping there had only meant that he did not have to wake his wife with his late arrival. He would see her soon enough, and be properly clean and adorned when he did so.

Prince Bowen would chide him for the ignoble concern for the comforts of the serving staff or even for those of his wife, but Donal did not care. Chivalry, grace, and respect were as much a part of the eldest Lachlan prince as breathing.

Pushing the barely touched tray away, he wrapped the heavy wool blanket around his bare shoulders with one hand. His distracted gaze never left the window.

He had awakened late this morning, feeling more drained than when he had retired, only now that weariness was accompanied by an

ill-feeling in his stomach. His head throbbed in the rhythm of galloping hoof beats and a slight metallic taste filled his mouth. He craved
strong drink and was in sore need of a bath and shave, but all of those
things would have to wait until he was in his own rooms. It only required that he move from the bed he sat in.

He could not bring himself to do it.

Once more he glanced down at his morning meal. It had already
been cold by the time he awoke and it held no appeal for him. Perhaps,
he wondered, he should have allowed the servant who had come for
the tray to take it away. Eating had seemed like a good idea then, however, as he had hoped it would remove the bitter taste in his throat and
mouth, but when the servant made casual mention of the birth of the
twins, Prince Donal lost what little appetite he thought he had. He had
been staring at the window ever since.

It was troublesome enough to have new siblings at the age of
thirty-six. But twins? Another prince? It meant more in-fighting, and
Prince Donal was sorely tired of in-fighting. He rubbed his temples
with calloused thumbs and closed his eyes. If there was any consolation he could have in this, it was that his duty on the battlefield would
mean he would likely have little contact with the new children. He
planned to take full advantage of that.

Noises in the corridor distracted him enough that his thoughts
turned to dressing. The blanket fell away with a dull sound as he stood
and crossed the room to the dresser where his squire had laid out fresh
clothes some time earlier. The prince balked at the notion of donning
clean clothes in his current unwashed state, but those he had worn yesterday, indeed for the last several days, had already been taken away
for cleaning. There was a wash basin, towel, and shaving necessities
on the dresser, however, and though the water was cold he chose to
make due. It was not the first time he had been forced to bathe in cold
water.

Smiling slightly, the prince turned his face this way and that as he studied his reflection in the mirror. The six days' growth on his cheeks and chin was a nice start towards a beard that would please both his father and his wife. A beard would make him look more like Innis. More like the majority of historical Lachlan kings.

He shuddered and grimaced at the thought. No, he did not want that, did not want there to be any small hint that might cause his great father to believe his eldest son had changed his mind about his place within the dynasty. With a shaky hand, he reached for the razor, prepared to do away with the traitorous facial hair, but distant wailing, echoing through the castle halls, made him pause as his hand closed around it. He knew that sort of wail better than he cared to. Dropping the razor, he hastened to pull on his trousers and then struggled with his still damp boots. The wailing drew closer, a single voice joined by others in chorus. As he cursed his uncooperative footwear, a single sharp knock sounded on the door.

"Who is it?" he barked, expecting his wife or one of his brothers, or even his squire, but hoping it was Ártur MacLyr. He wanted to see the healer, his best friend, before seeing anyone else this morning. Instead, the door opened to reveal the stalwart bulk of the King's General who looked as though he had gotten very little sleep himself. With a frown, Prince Donal stared at him, his boot half on. Guthrie McHador had never come to his room before and rarely spoke directly to Donal except in the arena of battle.

The prince could not think of any way that the man's presence here could be good.

The general bowed, giving the prince the chance to gain his composure and finish pulling on his boots before speaking. Though he liked this prince, better than any of the others in fact, he had never been comfortable with him outside of battle. In combat, Prince Donal placed himself at the general's disposal, trusting his experience and behaving like any other soldier would with their commander. Here, in this arena, neither man felt quite sure where they stood with one another. It made for awkward moments such as this.

Boots on at last, Prince Donal stood up and grabbed the clean tunic from the dresser, casting a questioning glance at the general as he did so. Guthrie interpreted that as permission to speak and cleared his throat as he bowed again.

"Pardon the intrusion, My Liege. I would have come sooner, but the servants informed me you were asleep; I waited for word that you were awake before coming. I am here to place myself at your disposal."

With a grunt, the prince pulled the tunic over his head. "And to tell me what the commotion is about I hope. The twins?"

With a faint, but heavy-hearted smile, Guthrie answered, "Are doing well, milord."

"Lady Cordelia then?" The tunic seemed to cling to his broad chest and he struggled to pull it down. "The hours after birthing are…"

"She is also well, though understandably exhausted after such an ordeal. The birth went on far into the night and early morning hours."

"Indeed, indeed." The prince turned towards the mirror, finished adjusting his tunic, and ran his large hands through his hair to tidy it as best he could. The general said no more, waiting for further cues from the prince. Finally, more to hide his nervousness than out of any real annoyance, the prince snapped, "Well…what then? Out with it. Do not tell me the turmoil in the halls is for nothing. Where is Ártur? What is wrong?"

The prince did not miss the way the general dropped his gaze or the way the man's hands clenched at his side. Donal's frown deepened.

"Your father sent Ártur home to his family when the storm hit. As for…" Guthrie swallowed hard and forced himself to meet the other man's gaze. "I suggest Your Majesty finish dressing and come with me."

"Very well, sir, if you insist, but…" The words stopped and it was Prince Donal's turn to try to swallow past the lump in his throat as the realization hit. "Your maj…my fath…?"

The general sighed. He wanted to leave the room, longed to do anything that would keep him from uttering words he dreaded saying aloud. Speaking the truth made the reality impossible to pretend away. But instead of leaving, he squared his shoulders and took a deep breath. "He was found seated at the Lady's bedside this morning by the servants. He passed in his sleep; Lord Nelsen found no indication of foul play. As the eldest son, the throne is yours, milord. I have come to bring you the news and," he paused, "offer whatever assistance I may."

He watched as the uncrowned King sank onto the side of the bed and rubbed his face with both hands. Prince Donal was five years his senior; they had grown up together and were more peers in some ways than prince and general. Donal Lachlan was one of the most capable soldiers in Enesfel's cavalry and had served in that capacity since the moment he could ride and fight efficiently. A soldier's life and career were rarely long; he was not the only person to expect that King Innis would outlive him. He had not been close to his father since the King had pushed him to accept the role of heir-apparent; Donal had fought all of his life to push that title away. It was why he had become a soldier. But he respected the great man, however, because Innis could do the one thing that Donal could not fathom. He had ruled a kingdom.

Being responsible for a squadron of men in combat seemed to him a much different, much easier, thing. Being king was a responsibility he neither wanted nor felt capable of shouldering.

It had not helped that King Innis had worked hard to keep the seriousness of his health from his sons. It had been intended to prevent premature bickering over the throne, but hiding the truth had left Prince Donal unprepared for the burden suddenly thrust on him.

Voice as soft and soothing as he could manage, the general continued, "Your father had every faith in your ability to rule, milord, though he knew it would not be easy for you to accept this duty. Of all of his sons, you are the best equipped, the best suited, for the throne. As I was in his service, so shall I be in yours, if you will have me. I am quite certain that you will be as successful in this as you have always been in battle." Donal Lachlan was a survivor.

It was something he saw in the general's eyes, felt in the man's deep voice, which gave the prince the strength to force himself to his feet. He was grateful for Guthrie's assistance when his trembling fingers refused to hook the clasp of his cloak. The luxurious warmth of the fabric and fur did little to dispel the chill in his soul, however, and the previously sick feeling in his stomach had turned into a sour knot. "I appreciate any aid you can offer. Father trusted you, and your leadership in the field was always sound and timely. I trusted you in combat…and Father has relied on you all of these years…I shall continue to do so. Has the bo…has he been taken from the Lady's room?"

"I am sure he has been, as he was near the children. Lord Nelsen likely has the body in state."

"When will Ártur…?" His voice trailed into silence. There was little the Elyri healer could do to change the course of events, little he could have done to stave off the inevitable death of the ancient monarch, but Prince Donal would feel more at ease if his friend were here beside him.

Guthrie's shoulders hitched. "I do not know, milord. I am sure he will return in a few days, but I was not privy to…"

"No, you wouldn't have been." The prince knew that his father often kept private counsel with the healer, as Donal himself did. With a nervous tug at his cloak to settle it evenly across his shoulders, he continued, "I suppose he must be buried before reading his final testament, if he made one…which he must have done with the hope of new children before him. Have they been named?"

"Deidre Agnes and Arlan Trebor."

The sick feeling in the prince's stomach threatened to dislodge. It took several deep breaths and a few rough swallows to stifle the reflex. Then Prince Donal bit the inside of his lip and strode into the corridor. His father had given each of his son's names that he hoped would influence their personalities. Names that would, he hoped, mold them, shape them into men that he, and Enesfel, could be proud of. In Donal's eyes, few of them had lived up to the potential of their names. Prince Arlan was the pledge, and that he bore the family name Trebor indicated a favoritism no other son carried. Or perhaps the late King had simply run out of names. Six princes certainly required a number of names.

Not that he feared this infant. Unlike his other brothers, this child would never fight him for the throne. It was possible that Donal would be dead before Prince Arlan came of age, and it was likely, given the number of heirs before him, that this youngest Lachlan prince would never rule.

But his name was a reminder of the chaos Innis foresaw, the chaos Prince Donal knew was already being birthed as the news of the King's passing spread through the castle and throughout Rhidam.

It was a damp, chilly climb up the narrow, circular stairs to the King's chamber on the third floor. The prince muttered as he climbed, adjusting his cloak further to block out the cold that tried to creep in along his neck. The occasional burning torches in the wall sconces allowed them to find their way, but he wished he had brought a lamp. It might have dispelled the gloom that tried to claw and cling to him. The sound of wailing grew fainter as they neared their destination, and the eeriness of the silence in the dim passage felt more chilling than the temperature of the air. The general opened the door for him into the nearly empty corridor at the top of the staircase.

Inhaling to calm himself, the prince paused long enough to note that there were few servants here. He would have preferred more activity, perhaps more wailing to break the silence, but even that would have been an uncomfortable and unbearable reminder of the plague that had claimed his two-year-old daughters, Gwenyr and Ilka, six years earlier. For all of his Elyri knowledge, skill, and power, Ártur had not been able to save them. It was further proof that the healer would not have been able to save King Innis from death either.

The late King's room was cold, the window still open from the night before. Guthrie chided himself for not closing it and he wondered why none of the servants had done so either. He took a step towards the window as Mormer Nelsen came out of the queen's room. Their eyes met before the physician gave a small, polite bow to Prince Donal and then continued into the corridor without speaking to either of them.

Having long ago reached an understanding with each other, the prince did not think to reprimand the physician for what could have been perceived as a lack of respect. He did not care if the man was there or not, and the Teren doctor stayed out of his way as much as possible. Donal watched Guthrie close the window and then, after another calming, steadying breath, he entered his stepmother's room where it was quiet and barely lit. It was much the way he recalled the room being when he had learned of the death of his daughters. The shadows cast on the walls by the two bedside candles writhed as if in pain.

Even the shadows mourned the King's passing.

The Queen Mother motioned him into the room, watching him but not speaking. Following the tilt of her head, he approached the cradle against the far wall. He could not name his fears but he knew that feeling of discomfort that nested in his soul too well after more than a decade of war. It was why he could not look at the empty chair at the bedside. He squatted down beside the cradle to look at the children more closely. Opposites. Sable and flaxen.

"That is Deidre," the woman behind him said as he touched the blond child's pink cheek.

A sister. A sister after all of these years. A sister younger than his daughters. A sister young enough to be his daughter. It was insane.

To avoid the surge of tears, he turned his attention to the other child and gently touched the dark hair. "Then this is Arlan."

He thought he heard a soft chuckle from his stepmother but without looking at her, he could not verify it. At that moment, he could not bring himself to look away from his youngest brother, swaddled in crimson linen and wool. He wondered if he had looked like this as an infant.

"His name is not meant to trouble you. Innis hoped he would be as good for Enesfel as you will be."

The prince stood and straightened his clothes. "I had no idea you had faith in my judgment and abilities." He could sense the general standing beyond the doorway and wondered if he should have sent the man away or if he should have invited him in. Either way, he knew the general had heard the rough break in his voice as he spoke. Did Guthrie McHador think him weak for being unable to control his grief?

The queen grasped his rough hand and squeezed it gently. "I have watched your career as closely as your father ever did. We both know what you are capable of when you wish to be."

"He never spoke of my accomplishments, or failures…neither criticized nor praised…"

"He did not know how. You know he was never a competent speaker, either in public or in private. But he thrived on General McHador's reports of your deeds." The prince heard the fondness with which she spoke of the general and caught the way she looked to the doorway as she spoke. She might not be able to see him, but she knew the general was there too. The two had been friends for as many years as she had lived in Rhidam as queen. "Your father was proud of you and believed you capable; in your heart you know that. Regardless of your arguments to the contrary, he knew you would accept this responsibility when the time came. If he had thought you unfit or truly unwilling…"

"You know I do not want this."

She nodded. "But you will do it."

Donal sank down on the side of the bed, treasuring the fact that she treated him as her son. He had not known his own mother, who had died shortly after his birth, and Innis' second wife had been a stranger to him. "There is no choice, milady…"

Again she squeezed his hand. "You could abdicate the throne to Farrell. He would gladly accept it."

The thought made Donal cringe; he cleared his throat and nodded with a groan. "But it would be the downfall of all Father worked to accomplish; it would be a step backwards for Enesfel."

"Likely so," she agreed, "but there was a time when naming Farrell his heir did cross your father's mind. But he knew, just as you know, that Farrell would not be up to the challenges of ruling, not now, perhaps not ever. And he knew you might challenge Farrell for the right to rule. A civil war would be costly for everyone. And you are the rightful heir, the first son, his favorite child…like him in many ways. He loved you dearly, even if he poorly showed it. In the end, he wanted you to have your due."

"Milady…" His faithless voice cracked again.

The queen leaned forward and kissed his cheeks. "You will be a good king, Donal," she murmured. "The people will place their faith in you as your father has done, if you give them the chance."

Donal sat, motionless, absorbing the woman's comfort, until at last he dried his cheeks of the tears that graced them. The weight of indecision had been lifted, though exactly how and when that had happened he could not say. It enabled him to stand after kissing the woman's forehead as tenderly as she had kissed him. "I am sorry for your loss, milady."

She tried to smile at him as she said, "It is everyone's loss, but through it, we have gained you. Go in peace, My Liege. The kingdom awaits your guidance."

He hovered there, gazing into her deep blue eyes that held both sorrow and strength, and then he strode from the room with more determination in his posture and step than he had felt minutes before. He passed the general, who followed without a word back down the twisted stairway from which they had come.

This time, they turned down a different corridor and emerged from the stairwell into the Grand Hall. Each of the royal banners of burgundy and amber, with the black Lachlan eagle emblazoned upon them, was rolled up in mourning. Without them, the Hall looked every bit of what it was, a centuries-old castle hall, dark and smoky, with more history in the cracks and crevices than could ever be gleaned by living here. Nineteen Lachlan kings had reigned from these halls before Donal, a handful of Nethite princes, and an unknown number of Elyri nobles and others before that. Nineteen Lachlan kings, their families, their retainers, servants, and advisors, had lived and died within these walls. Eighteen of those kings had stood before the moment he faced, and though he was not superstitious, he found himself silently asking those predecessors for the strength to face what lay before him.

Most of the torches and lamps in the Hall were unlit; only those at the far end of the chamber burned, drawing attention to the platform on which King Innis lay, entombed in glass for viewing. The royal colors did hang there, marking with respect the ruler he had once been.

Around the platform, the other princes were gathered. All of them. It surprised Donal to see it, as rarely were they all in Rhidam at the same time. Rarer still was it that they should all be gathered in the same room without their father demanding it. Perhaps Mormer had recently placed the King for viewing, as Donal could not imagine most of his siblings staying any longer than they had to.

Of the four, only mouse-haired Girvin was weeping. Donal recognized the movements as Cordelia's oldest child wiped his eyes, his cheeks, his nose, and then his eyes again. Prince Farrell stood apart from the rest as usual, more interested in conversing with a passing chambermaid than with paying respects to his sire. He did not even notice Donal's arrival and might as well have been in another room. To Donal, it appeared Farrell had been on his way out when the girl had entered, and it was her presence that had detained him.

Eight-year-old Owain was making a determined effort to touch the glass casing, or perhaps to touch the man behind it, only to have the older Prince Bowen, who held his other hand and looked as though he would rather be anywhere else, scold each attempt. Donal sighed; his father would be grieved, but not surprised, to see his sons this way. Judging from the sudden tension in Guthrie's posture, the prince decided that the general thought so too.

Hearing footsteps, Prince Bowen looked over his shoulder at the two approaching men. Pulling Owain by the hand, he dragged the boy with him and stopped in front of Donal without acknowledging the general's presence.

"What will it be, brother?"

Jaw tightening at the venom lacing the other man's voice, Donal glanced at Owain who, at eight, was too young to be concerned with the death of a man he had hardly known. The boy was still staring at Innis with an unfathomable expression on his face. Prince Donal scowled and looked back at Bowen. "If it matters to you…"

"Of course it matters. We need to know to whom we owe fealty."

Donal's eyes narrowed. "It is my duty, to Enesfel and to Father, and I will…"

"Why endanger Enesfel with your apathy? Why not give the throne to Farrell, who at least has the desire for it?"

"Give the throne to that?" Donal gestured towards their brother who still conversed with the serving girl, whispering near her ear with his hand on her arm in a too intimate fashion. Donal could not see her face, but knowing Farrell as he did, he wagered she was blushing. "You would like that, wouldn't you? Someone you can manipulate." If the accusation offended Bowen, he did not express it. "I do not think such a choice would be wise. Despite his age, Farrell has much growing up to do."

Prince Bowen shrugged, running his free hand over his close-cropped blond hair. Donal smiled; though Innis' third son hoped Donal would pass up the throne, he had not expected it in this moment. At last Bowen decided that this was neither the time nor place for a confrontation; he pulled Owain by the arm as he turned, jerking the boy into motion. "Point taken, brother. Come, Owain. There is nothing to see here. We will come back later."

It was only when those two were out of his sight that Prince Donal relaxed. If there was some discreet way to dispose of Bowen, he would gladly consider it. Bowen's only ambition was to rule, by any means, but he was basically a coward in Donal's eyes and seemed to lack the creative genius to find his way to the throne without violence. Donal would watch his back, however, for he had no doubt that, for all of Bowen's slowness and lack of subtlety, he would find ways to attempt to seize the throne. It would require ridding Enesfel of both Donal and Prince Farrell, but the heir-apparent had no doubt that Bowen would try.

With only Prince Girvin standing beside the glass case, Donal approached the platform, ignoring the younger man's presence. His attention was focused inward, on his own discomfort and thoughts. He had hoped to convince himself that his father slept beneath that glass, but the presence of the others, and the braided black silk cord draped over the glass which tradition held would bind a man's spirit to the body until the burial, refused to offer Donal that comfort.

King Innis was dead.

The uncrowned King wanted to weep, swear, or kick something, but all he could do was stare at his father's unmoving body and pray that no one chose to speak to him. It would be unthinkable for him to weep like a woman or child in public. He believed he had to stay strong, put on the battle mask he had worn often in order to move forward and follow his duty. But that was proving harder and harder to do the longer he stared at the old man's wizened features.

A gleeful screech from the far end of the Hall punctuated the silence, where Prince Owain had scampered back into the room and leapt onto Farrell's back. Prince Farrell spun the boy around several times before depositing him in a jumble on the stone floor, both of them laughing happily. Prince Donal clenched his fists, marginally aware that within him the sudden flash of anger had displaced the nearly overwhelming despair.

The eldest Lachlan prince had no true siblings. Those he should have had either died at birth or shortly after. Farrell and Bowen were the progeny of King Innis' second wife. Girvin and the twins were Queen Cordelia's children. He had no difficulty recognizing them as legitimate siblings. Marriage had made them brothers, bound them as family.

Prince Owain was different.

Not that the boy could be blamed for the circumstances of his birth, but Prince Donal hated both him and Bowen for the lies surrounding his life. While he had lived, King Innis would allow no harm to befall the boy he believed to be his son. As king, Donal felt free to at last cleanse the family of this rot, for he knew that Prince Owain was no more King Innis' son than General McHador was.

Spinning away from his father's gray form, the prince motioned for the general to follow him. They strode from the Grand Hall, into the State Room, where he waited for the general to close the door.

"How soon may we hold the coronation?" he asked brusquely.

"Traditionally," explained the general, "not until after the burial. However…you are King. You may do as you see fit and necessary to secure the kingdom's welfare."

Glancing in the direction of the Grand Hall, though unable to see Prince Owain through the closed door, Donal wondered if the general was aware of his thoughts and desires. It would not surprise him, as Guthrie's experience around the Lachlans had honed his instincts to their moods, particularly those of the late King and the King-elect. Would the general support his choices, Donal wondered as he paced the length of the room, his mind racing with possibilities and questions? His steps quickened as the questions came faster and his anger grew more pronounced, until he forced himself to stop moving, closed his eyes, and willed his mind to cease racing. "I suppose the children must be presented first. We can do that this afternoon if the Lady is well enough. Will you see that preparations are made?"

Guthrie had not moved, had not questioned the furious pacing, recognizing Donal's attempts to find clear-headedness. It was not his place to interfere, to question a King, even though Innis had often encouraged his questions. Donal was not Innis and Guthrie understood his place. "I will, milord."

"Can we get a message to Ártur?"

"You know there are no other Elyri in the keep, milord, but I will see if there are any in Rhidam who might be able to get a message to him. But, if I may say so, even if he can be located, it may be many days before he can come, due to the storm, and even in this cold, the body will not keep indefinitely."

Prince Donal was not surprised that the general had anticipated his wishes. Guthrie McHador knew his reluctance to take up the mantle of monarch. "I know…but I must try," he said wearily. "See that the crypt is readied and that he is prepared for burial tomorrow…weather permitting. We can read his final statement at that time. Make arrangements for the coronation to take place in one week. That should give us time to be certain the storm has passed and time for guests to arrive to attend if they wish." He smiled lamely, wondering if anyone but the usual court hangers-on would come to witness his ascension to the throne. Attending would mean acknowledging that a much-loved King was gone. Prince Donal could not imagine the people of Enesfel letting King Innis go that easily. "See to the preparations, Lord General. Speak to Lord Transk if you require assistance, as I would like him to stay on at court. I will be in my chambers should anyone have need of me prior to the presentation, but make certain no one does. I want to bathe from my journey, and I would rather not see anyone except my wife…or Ártur."

"Yes, milord. As you wish." The general bowed and remained that way until the soon to be King had left the State Room. Guthrie followed, stepping into the Grand Hall and casting a long glance at the deceased. He did not need to move any closer, to see the man again. He had already said his farewell. It was hard enough to know Innis was there, hard to admit he was gone.

But it was a little easier than it had been last night.

"I will do my best to see that he rules well and long, my friend. I swear it."

ஒChapter 3ॐ

The fresh powdery snow puffed upward before his boots as the solitary figure trudged from the village náós towards one of the larger houses at the northern edge of Bhryell. Little could be heard at this hour, only the whisper of the wind and occasional domestic noises from the homes he passed. He enjoyed the hush after the chaos he had endured over the last several days, but it was not silence that he longed for. As he neared his destination, his ears latched onto that one sound he longed most to hear, the pleasing notes of brass harp strings. He smiled in spite of the cold and the heaviness in his heart and quickened his pace. He had waited too long to hear that sound again, too long to come home.

He did not knock on the door of his father's house as he entered, as there was no need. This was home, no matter how long he had been away from Bhryell. The pale child who sat before the fire looked up at him with a rare, wide smile as his hands fell away from the instrument on his lap. The volume of Saint Kóráhm lay beside him, mostly covered by the folds of his white robe. The older man gestured and removed his cloak as the boy obliged, resuming the song he had been playing. After hanging the cloak on a hook on the wall to the side of the door, Ártur sat on the floor studying his cousin, reveling in his much-missed company, wondering why Kavan seemed different to him. It had only been a matter of months since he had last seen the boy, and yet in some subtle way, it felt as though it had been much longer.

His scrutiny was intense enough that he was not immediately aware of the song ending. It was only when the brilliant green eyes met his with equal intensity that he flinched and blinked. Kavan lowered his gaze as though chastised, and Ártur clasped the smaller shoulder warmly. "Don't," he murmured. Kavan had done nothing wrong, and the healer did not want the boy to ever feel that he had. "You have improved greatly since I was last home. You have not neglected your practice."

"Of course not…though aendhá would rather I be in the shop with him or playing with the other children." Kavan traced the polished wood with his fingers and added, "I do not want to make harps; I want to play them." The issue of playing with the other children remained unaddressed.

"Play them you should if your present skill is any indication of what the future holds for you. He will see that in time." His voice faded off with the last word, however. He knew his father well enough to know that Tám's acceptance of anything that was different, anything out of the ordinary, would never be that simple. Hopefully, the healer thought to himself, Kavan had not yet become jaded enough to realize that. "You have been reading?"

Kavan shifted his knee and robe to keep the book completely covered. He had not realized it had been visible and knew how dangerous that could be. But with his cousin, he had no such fears. "I have read it nearly thirteen times." He grinned at Ártur's suppressed laughter. "Have you found others?"

The healer shook his head. "No, but I am still looking. As I said before, do not get your hopes up, Kavan. I was lucky to stumble upon that one. If I find others, you know I will bring them to you." He let his head fall back and his eyes close as he absorbed the lulling warmth of the fire. "Is there any other news?"

"Elys has been here nearly every day, asking about your return."

Kavan paused. "You have been to see her?"

"Not yet. I had a few medical visits I had promised to make after I arrived in Bhryell two nights past, now I am here. If I stopped to see her first," he chuckled, "it could be days before I got to see you. I have felt a deep need to hear you play again. King Innis is…"

"He is dead."

The healer's head snapped up and he stared at Kavan with shock. The boy shrugged and looked away, losing himself in the dancing tongues of fire on the hearth. In a quieter voice, Kavan continued, "It happened last night. I…saw it…or felt it…or…I…I was reading…and then I just knew. He is dead…isn't he?"

Ártur could not at first find words. Kavan should not know about the King's condition, as no one outside of Rhidam would know yet, but perhaps the grief etched on Ártur's face told the story. More likely, however, was something the healer suddenly sensed in his cousin. He was beginning to recognize why Kavan seemed different, but how could it be? The boy was barely seven years old; Elyri abilities usually did not manifest themselves for at least another year or two, yet Kavan was, it seemed, reading his cousin's emotions and perhaps his thoughts.

Spluttering, he replied, "He was not when I left Rhidam, but he was dying…has been dying for some time. I did not expect it to come so soon…" He coughed in sudden surprise. "You say you saw it?"

Kavan looked at his hands, wondering how to explain and worrying that he should not. If anyone could help him, however, if there was anyone he could trust, it was his cousin. Finally, he murmured, "It happened like a blink, like a picture in my mind, something I could see but not with my eyes. There was an old man in an amber night robe, slumped in a chair, his hands folded in his lap. I don't know how

I knew it…but I know he was dead. There was a fair-haired woman in a nearby bed; I could hear babies crying, two of them. I could smell blood and candle wax and sweat. There was so much detail…the smells, the sounds…it was as if I was standing in the room with them. I don't know how I know it was King Innis, but I am certain it was."

"May I?" Ártur reached for Kavan's hands hesitantly, leery of what he might discover, but there was no hesitancy in Kavan's acceptance of the offer. Instead, there was desperation in the way he clutched the healer's hands, a need for reassurance, a need to know there was not something wrong with him. "Yes, remember what I taught you. You do not need to do anything except relax."

The process took only a few seconds, less time than Ártur expected because the boy's mind was instantly blank and open to him. Such was normally a difficult feat for an undisciplined mind, yet Kavan did it as if he had been doing it for years. When he refocused on the boy's face, Ártur knew the truth. The boy's mind was attuning itself to the energies around him. His psychic gifts were awakening. Not awakening, Ártur corrected himself. The young mind was as focused and attuned as an untrained Elyri could be.

And he had llánec. The Sight.

He touched Kavan's face with an awe and reverence that made the boy pull back uncomfortably.

"How long have you…?"

"Ártur!"

His question interrupted, the intimacy he felt with Kavan undercut, the healer looked up at his mother as she burst into the room and rushed to hug him. He pushed to his feet to meet her, feeling a sudden, wide chasm erupt between himself and his young cousin. Accepting his mother's embrace, he forced himself to focus on her rather than the empty feeling within. Though her pale red hair was beginning to gray at the temples, she still looked very nearly his age.

"We were not expecting you. How good of you to come. I shall make up your bed and…"

Extricating himself from her grasp, he ran his hand through his hair. "I shall not be able to stay, I'm afraid. I am due back in Rhidam promptly…"

"But you have only just arrived. Why must you…?"

He knew his mother was disappointed but he felt duty-bound to return to Rhidam. "King Innis was…" he glanced at Kavan, "is dead, bhyne, and the queen has borne his heirs. They will be looking for me."

Dháná saw the sidelong glance between cousins and shuddered. She had known for several days that the change had begun in her nephew, but she had tried to ignore the signs. Such an early showing of ability would not please her husband and she had to admit it frightened her too. She watched the boy silently fingering the harp strings, and then looked at her son.

"llánec," Ártur murmured, awe in his voice. "I read him. He saw the King's death…"

Dháná's face lost color. "You know what this will mean…?"

The healer grimaced, not wanting to think about his father or discuss it in front of Kavan. "Many in Rhidam will desire my presence, and I suspect Prince Donal will wish to continue my employment. If not…the infants deserve my attention until I am properly dismissed. Besides…I should attend the final rite…"

"May I attend?" Kavan's voice was small and he did not look at either adult as he spoke. He did not need to. He felt keenly their surprise at his request and anticipated the questions that would be asked. To his relief, before Dháná could ask them, Ártur came to his defense.

"It would be good for him to attend, to see Rhidam. I was younger than he when aendhá Rístyrd took me. The pr…King…is no threat to us. This may be the safest time, the only time, he will have to go until he is much older."

"But the old woman said…"

The healer rolled his eyes, a look that cut her statement short. "It may have been the paranoid ramblings of a dying woman. The plague did that, made the dying delusional. Besides, how will we know when the right time comes? We cannot keep him confined to Bhryell forever. Perhaps this is a sign. It is the first reason he has had to go…and if he is to ever…we must take the chance. I will watch over him. No harm will come to him, and I shall bring him home directly after the coronation."

Dháná wrung her hands. Kavan was toying with the hem of his sleeve but she knew he was listening, even if he appeared not to be. He always listened. He knew nothing of the woman they spoke of, and even if he longed to know more, he would never consider interrupting them. He was the most polite, well-mannered child she knew and she loved him as though he were her third son. She knew how much the cousins adored each other and how much it would mean to her son to take Kavan with him. And perhaps, she sighed, trying to give a confident smile, giving Kavan a few days in Rhidam would give her a chance to decide how to tell Tám that their nephew was in need of training.

"Very well," she relented with a sigh. "Kavan, you may go. Ártur, tend him closely; I want nothing to happen to him. You must eat before you go, however. Your father and brother will want to see you before you leave us again."

It was several hours later before Ártur successfully pried away from his family and began trudging back through the snow towards Hes Índári Náós with Kavan following behind. Ártur did not begrudge his family their time; indeed, he treasured it too, as he saw them too rarely since accepting the appointment as Royal Healer in the Enesfel court. His mother worried for his safety amongst the Teren, and his father wanted his son to remain in Elyriá where he felt their people belonged. His brother Sámel cared little either way as long as his brother was happy, as sometimes happened between siblings far apart in age. Ártur shared little in common with his brother except parentage. He felt more a brother to Kavan, whom he had seen come into the world as a newborn infant.

He fretted as he walked. If the weather in Enesfel was as bad as it had been when he left, he and Kavan might not reach their destination by nightfall. If what Kavan had seen was accurate, and Ártur had little reason to doubt it, he knew he was needed in Rhidam. If not now, he would be as soon as Prince Donal received word of his father's death and returned from the Enesfel-Hatu border. If Ártur did not reach the castle before nightfall, the gate would be closed and he would have to wait for entrance until morning, an idea he did not relish. He might be safe enough in one of Rhidam's inns, but this time he had Kavan's comfort and welfare to consider. He could take care of himself, but how could he best protect Kavan outside the secure castle grounds?

"I have never been in the k'rylagthé," Kavan was saying, breathless with excitement and the effort of keeping up with Ártur in the deep snow. "How do they work? Are they difficult to use? Where will it take us?"

Noting that Kavan had used the High Elyri word rather than the vernacular, and wondering where he had learned it, Ártur laughed softly. "So many questions, sínréc…"

"How do you learn to use it? How will we…?"

"Kavan." The boy fell silent, but the healer ruffled his hair and chuckled before pushing open the door of the náós. "They are a means of travel, much like any other. If you know how to use them, they are not difficult, and they can take you anywhere you wish to go…within reason. You can only travel between Gates, not to places that do not have one."

The náós was empty, the gdhededhá out on some errand. The interior of Bhryell's center of worship was dim enough that Kavan was tempted to use the handlight if only to show Ártur he could do it. He chose not to, however, and instead quietly followed his cousin up the aisle to the front of the room.

"Is there a map that tells where they are? Where they go?" Kavan's steps faltered when he realized his cousin was entering the k'dhín bhólibh, the room where wrongs were spoken to those who could absolve them. He had been in that tiny closet of a room with his aunt and with Ártur and had previously attributed the peculiar sensations that pricked his skin and mind to be caused by the holiness of the place and occasion. He had never before considered that those sensations could have some other cause. That perhaps he had been aware of the world's intangible power much longer than anyone would believe.

"No, it is a matter of practice and…" The healer looked at Kavan, noting the hesitancy. He would have thought little of it, as most novices hesitated before such a demonstration, but he could see on the child's face that there was more to Kavan's reluctance than a fear of the unknown. "Kavan?"

The boy shook his head, held his place for the span of a few more heart beats, and then stepped into the enclosure. There was no hesitancy then, as he held out his hands. He might be puzzled and troubled, but Kavan was not afraid.

As the healer began the process that would operate the Gate, Kavan watched a pale mist form and wrap around them. Soon Ártur was obscured from view, but Kavan could feel him there, both with his hands and with his other senses. Since he could no longer see anything, he closed his eyes, to focus on the power. The darkness behind his lids revealed numerous small pinpoints of light visible only to his mind's eye. The air hummed and tickled, his head buzzed, and he felt as though he was floating on gentle waves. He realized that one of those points was growing steadily nearer, and after a blinding flash, all sensation ceased, leaving only the feel of solid ground beneath his feet.

Kavan waited for his stomach to catch up with him, feeling queasy and disoriented when he opened his eyes, but Ártur tugged his hand and lead him out of the k'dhín bhólibh into a towering chamber that the boy knew belonged to a great náós even though he had never seen it before. It was older, dustier than the náós in Bhryell, and most certainly larger. Where the multitude of crowned arches had once been inlaid with gold and silver gilt, they had long ago been stripped bare as high as a man could reach. The colored window glass had been broken out, scavenged for other uses, and the windows were boarded over to keep the elements out. There were no longer benches or tables, and what wood remained in the structure had been carved on by both men and rats. Still, to Kavan's eyes, the architecture did not need those embellishments to be beautiful. Its Elyri-built majesty spoke for itself despite the decay.

He pulled free of his cousin's hand and crossed to the marble altar, circling it several times as he examined its dusty, etched exterior. He did not need to touch it to feel the faint power radiating from it. It was another of those oddities he had recently begun to experience. No doubt, the altar remained intact simply because it was too heavy and would be too awkward, and noticeable, to carve away and move in sections. A stone image of Dhágdhuán the Intercessor burning on the pyre filled the wall behind the altar, his cold dark eyes gazing with sadness over the empty expanse of a room. Kavan felt an overpowering aura of abandonment; the building was alive with it. He shivered and quickly rejoined Ártur, glancing back several times as though he were being followed.

"Why does no one come here, Ártur? Surely there is no place more beautiful in all of Rhidam."

The healer shrugged. "Only the Elyri who come through Rhidam use it, but even that is far too rare I'm afraid. The Faith among Teren was driven out centuries ago…when Neth conquered Enesfel. King Innis wanted to restore the náós, restore the Faith, but the ongoing war with Hatu gave him time for little else during his reign. And in truth, he was unable to persuade any gdhededhá to come to Enesfel."

Man and boy stepped into the mid-afternoon sunlight to be dazzled by the brightness of the snow. Ártur was relieved that the storm had passed and that his fears of not reaching the castle had been for naught. From the position of the sun, Kavan knew that only a few minutes had passed since they had stood in Bhryell. He was amazed enough to want to try the Gate himself. As Ártur lifted him onto his shoulders, Kavan asked, "Will you show me how to work the k'rylagthé?"

He did not see the healer's raised brow. "I do not know how to teach it…and I doubt you will be able to master it yet, but yes, I will try to show you." He suspected that, by the time they were ready to return to Bhryell, Kavan would forget the request. It would spare him the embarrassment of trying to teach it and failing.

The healer carried Kavan down the gentle incline of the street into the midst of the clutter of houses and shops that formed the city of Rhidam. Kavan could feel the eyes of many upon them as they passed, some curious, a few openly hostile, but no one spoke to them. Though he had never been amongst Teren, had never met anyone other than Elyri, Kavan refused to stare in return. It would not be polite, and he had no desire to draw any of that sensed animosity to them. In the distance, the circular towers of the stronghold rose above the rooftops like gloomy shadows against the afternoon sky. Kavan kept his eyes focused there until all that kept them from the castle was the gatehouse, the ice-filled moat, and the tall stone bailey laden with snow. The steel reinforced oak gate was shut tight and there was an absence of activity as they neared the raised bridge. Not unusual perhaps, the boy mused as Ártur set him down and whistled. If the King had indeed died, it would be reason enough to bar the keep to the outside world.

"Who goes there?" someone barked with annoyance before a grizzled face peered out through a tiny window. "Lord MacLyr! It's about time!"

The man could be heard hurrying down the steps as the wooden gate began to creak open and the drawbridge was lowered for passage. He emerged through a door at the rear of the tower and reached for the healer's hands with a curious glance at Kavan. "Everyone has been asking about you. You have heard about the King?"

"Yes," Ártur replied with a shiver. Having outside confirmation of Kavan's vision was disconcerting. "I came as soon as I heard."

"Prince Donal is seeking audience with you and asked that if you arrived to send you to him at once."

"The prince is here already?" Ártur had not expected that.

"Indeed; he arrived late last evening. Come, in with you, sir."

"Thank you." Taking Kavan's hand, the healer passed through the gate, across the bridge to the inner gate, and across the courtyard, mulling over what coincidence had brought Prince Donal home on the night of his father's death. The snow was not as deep here because the outer walls and the moat kept the drifts from blowing in. Inside the entrance hall, the wooden double doors of the Grand Hall were closed. Rather than open them, Ártur stomped the snow from his feet, encouraged Kavan to do likewise, and then traveled the corridor to the left. It eventually opened into the Grand Hall which was vacant except for the royal throne and the glass box at the front of it. Despite having been told that the prince wanted to see him, beside that box was where the healer wanted to be, and over the distance it took to get to it, he did not realize he had released Kavan's hand. He did not even know if Kavan was still following.

The late King's countenance did not reflect pain or suffering; his passing appeared to have been peaceful. Ártur refused to ask himself what would have happened if he had remained in Rhidam. His presence would not have stayed the death of the man who had been his employer since he had first become a healer fourteen years ago. Ártur had known when he left for Bhryell that it was possible the King would die before he returned to Rhidam. The two had parted with that knowledge in mind, but the healer had hoped it would not come to pass until he could return to the King's side.

"King Innis?" asked Kavan quietly, having taken his time to join his cousin whom he knew wanted a moment alone with the king. The healer's only response was a nod. Kavan moved closer and studied the man within the glass, seeing him in reality for the first time. The white of his sparse hair, his broad jaw and cheeks that made his face appear too wide, and the frailty of his frame were all emphasized by the emaciation of long-term illness. On the outside, there were no visible differences Kavan could see between this Teren and the Elyri. King Innis was the first Teren Kavan had been able to examine up close and he wanted to touch him, to feel whether the man's skin felt the same, if his hair felt the same. Kavan wanted to know what death felt like. With the glass between them, however, he could not, but still he touched his fingertips to the smooth surface as if tracing the outlines of the King's face, allowing a sensation of peace, calm, and happiness to fill him. Not having expected to feel anything, the boy was startled, but not enough to remove his hand from the glass. He allowed those sensations to wash over him for several minutes before whispering, "He was happy when he died. At peace. I hope my death is like this."

Ártur started to ask what Kavan meant by such a peculiar observation but the echo of heavy footsteps came into the Hall, recognizable ones that made the healer turn to face their maker with an expression of relief.

When their eyes met, the heavier built man tried to smile. "Lord MacLyr. It is good that you have made it back."

"Sooner than expected, yes. It appears I'm not the only one who did so." He took the man's offered hand. "General McHador, this is my cousin, Kavan Cliáth. Kavan, this is Lord General Guthrie McHador."

The bearded man cocked an eyebrow. "I never knew you were related to the Cliáths. If that were common knowledge, I wager you would have garnished a remarkable amount of influence..."

"I believe I have enough of that, General," Ártur replied. Influence of any sort meant more eyes turned on him, and any Elyri outside of Elyriá knew better than to attract that much attention.

"Yes," the general nodded, "I imagine you do." He offered his hand to Kavan and was pleased when the boy took it in a firm grasp. "Welcome to Rhidam, Master Cliáth. It is good to have you here, though unfortunate that it could not be under better circumstances."

"Thank you, sir," Kavan said with a bow of his head as he tried to close the unexpected rush of images from the man's mind that passed through that handshake.

Unaware that anything unusual had transpired, the general turned his attention back to Ártur and said, "We were unable to send for you; he passed during the night and we could find no Elyri to send word. We were not expecting your quick return to Rhidam."

He was fishing for details without directly asking questions. It was not that the healer mistrusted the general; he had merely grown accustomed to keeping the details of Elyri ability to himself. "I came as soon as I could. The prince is here? How is he taking this?"

"He arrived during the night. He does not like it, but he knows there are few viable options available. His sense of moral and familial obligation does not give him any. He will do what he must; he has never shirked responsibility before, no matter how distasteful, but..." He clenched his hands behind his back and glanced at the late King. He had been studying the boy at Ártur's side, intrigued by something he could not pinpoint, but when that scrutiny was returned, it took all of the general's willpower not to move away. Looking elsewhere was easier. "But it won't be easy for him," he finally murmured.

"It has started already."

It was not a question. "Neither Prince Farrell nor Prince Girvin cares one wit about the throne, but the King wasn't dead nine hours before Prince Bowen began to attack Donal's integrity. I've had to break up several squabbles amongst men who have sided with one prince over the other. I have no doubt that Prince Bowen will begin making bids for the throne within a fortnight. When the children were presented earlier, the tension between the two princes was so thick everyone could feel it."

Ártur sighed. "We knew it would happen."

"I know…but I wish it could have waited for a few more days, at least until the King is buried."

"I would never expect Prince Bowen to be anything but difficult. Why should he show respect in death when he spared little in life?"

"Indeed," Guthrie agreed. He stepped away from Kavan, using the excuse of touching the glass to put distance between himself and the boy. The child's green eyes unnerved him, even when he was not looking directly at the general. "You did not prepare the queen for twins; the King was pleased to hear it."

Ártur gave Kavan another quick glance. "It is not unheard of for there to be no indications of twins, should their life signs be synchronized. I detected nothing…but twins are common in the Lachlan dynasty, as well as in the Queen's family. Sons?"

"A daughter and a son. He finally got the princess he desired…when he was unable to enjoy her. I wager she will be richly spoiled. Thank goodness," Guthrie snorted, "there was only one son. Enesfel has enough princes."

The healer nodded. "That is very true. Did he get to see the children at least?"

"The moment Lord Nelsen and the midwife said all was well, he insisted on going to the Lady's bedside. He would have been nowhere else. He held them both once and then fell asleep in the chair with the

Lady's hand clasped in his. I was there when he…passed…in his sleep…but the Lady chose to leave him undisturbed until the servants came." Talking about Innis' death was not easy, but he suspected he would have to tell his story many more times over the next few days. Perhaps he would find the telling less difficult each time.

With a reassuring hand on the general's shoulder, Ártur caught Kavan's gaze, this time a much less quick or cursory glance than before. An old man slumped in a chair at a bedside. Kavan had indeed seen the King's death. It should not be possible, but it was. Beneath Kavan's unwavering gaze and the realization that his cousin was more than a mere boy, the healer felt very small. A shiver ran up his spine and he looked quickly away.

"At least he is at peace. No more concerns over his feuding progeny. I suppose Prince…King…Donal is not, however. I should announce my arrival, see if he needs anything."

Guthrie gestured to the doorway he had entered through. "Come. See the children first. The queen will be disappointed if you do not and you know the King will demand most of your attention as soon as he knows you are here."

"That is so," the healer conceded. "Come, Kavan."

They walked only a short distance down a quiet corridor before coming to a steep, cold stairwell. The darkness there was marred by the smoky glare of the torches lining the passage at intervals of about ten feet. The only sounds therein were their footfalls on the stone and the rustle of their clothing, sounds that to Kavan seemed louder than they should have been. He was relieved when they emerged from the stairwell into a long hall.

There was a young boy further down the corridor who stopped, seemingly startled by their arrival and appeared ready to bolt in fear. Kavan was equally surprised, as he had not anticipated seeing another child in the castle.

"Pardon, Prince Owain," Guthrie started with a bow, giving the boy respect since he got little from anyone else.

"I was on my way to the kitchen," the boy spoke hastily as if afraid of being reprimanded, as if he needed an excuse and permission to move around within his own home. He took a few slow steps forward, staring at Kavan in a way that suggested he had never seen another child his own age at close proximity.

Ártur motioned the tow-headed prince to come closer. "Prince Owain, this is my cousin, Kavan."

Not knowing how he was expected to respond or what he was expected to do, Kavan followed the first instinct to surface. He bowed, leaving his eyes on the prince to see if his actions were appropriate. Prince Owain appeared stunned for a moment, as if he had never had anyone bow to him, and then gave a short awkward laugh. "You do not need to bow to me; I'm not the King. I'm just a boy. We could be friends…if you wish…" His offer was hesitant and Kavan suspected the prince expected rejection. "You could come to the kitchen with me…"

Ártur smiled. He had known Prince Owain the child's whole life and he knew how lonely the boy was. He also knew that his cousin socialized little with children his own age in Bhryell, and the healer hoped this meeting would be advantageous for both boys. "Go if you wish, Kavan, but do not go far."

"I wish to see the babes…" Kavan felt he had a vested interest in those children. He needed to know if what he had seen within his mind matched reality.

"Then let us see them!" Prince Owain exclaimed, leading them into the queen's chamber with a gesture for them to be quiet. The youngest Prince did not knock before opening the door, which caused the queen to look up from her bed in surprise.

"Owain! You should not…"

The blonde boy dropped to one knee before she finished, blushing and trembling in what appeared to be fear. Kavan's first impulse was to step in front of him, to shield him from unforeseen blows or harsh words. But before he took a step, it was the general who spoke and negated any confrontation that might have erupted. "Pardon the intrusion, milady. Healer MacLyr has returned and has come to see the children before he attends the King. This is his kinsman, Kavan Cliáth."

With Prince Owain seemingly forgotten, she extended her hand to the healer, who bowed and lightly kissed the ring she wore. "Your return is welcome, Lord MacLyr. And Master Cliáth, it is an honor to have you in Rhidam."

Though not expecting the boy to respond in kind, she was pleased when he mimicked Ártur's actions. She smiled at him warmly, released his hands, and then closed her eyes with a sigh as the healer placed his hands on her stomach.

Kavan enjoyed watching his cousin work, knowing he would never carry that particular Elyri talent, but this time he stayed back respectfully, aware that although Prince Owain had gotten to his feet, his demeanor was no less cowed. He glanced at the prince, tried to reassure him with a smile, but the prince kept his eyes on the floor and did not see it.

When his examination was complete, Ártur met the queen's gaze with a private smile, conveying that everything was as it should be, that she was in good health and would recover quickly. With her own relieved expression, she indicated the cradle. "You have heard?"

The healer turned towards the children. "Yes, Lord McHador told me…there were no signs of twins, but I am pleased for you." He knelt beside the cradle for a closer examination.

The infants were both small, as was to be expected of twins. He was surprised, but also pleased, that she had successfully carried them to term and borne them without incident or complication. It held promise for the continued health of all three of them. The girl child did not stir as he picked her up, unwrapped her, and laid his hand on her tiny pink chest. Kavan moved closer, his need to see the children driving him. The room was as he had believed it would be, how his mind's eye had seen it, and he knew the children would be too.

"She is healthy and beautiful," said Ártur with a smile as he wrapped her in the blanket once again and nestled her in the cradle.

The boy child was awake and squirmed and fussed when his skin was exposed to the cool air. The healer repeated his inspection, both with his eyes and with his healing senses. "Also fit and healthy. His Majesty would be proud of them both, and of you, My Queen."

Kavan had never seen anyone as small and delicate in his short life as the two newborns were. The young prince's hand was flailing as though reaching for something, and Kavan impulsively touched it, only to flinch in surprise at the static sensation caused by the skin to skin contact. He glanced at his cousin, who smiled and did not seem to notice anything unusual. Kavan scowled and tried to pry his finger free without hurting the child who had grasped him so firmly.

The young prince who matched his vision exactly was intent on holding on.

"It appears he likes you, Master Cliáth," the queen said with a smile. "That is good. I…" She paused and looked from the healer to the general, and lastly to Prince Owain. "Owain, would you please show Master Cliáth the grounds? I have matters to discuss with Lord MacLyr."

The prince's face brightened with relief. Not only could he escape the room, and spend time with the other boy, he was apparently avoiding punishment. "Come, Kavan. I shall take you to the kitchen first…"

Kavan looked at his cousin, not particularly wanting to leave, but the healer was already pulling the tiny hand from his finger. Reluctantly, Kavan followed the tugging on his arm, passing by the general who held the door open for the boys and began to follow them out of the room.

"I shall leave you to your discussion," Guthrie said to the queen and healer.

"Do not depart in haste, Lord McHador. Come in; close the door," the queen said in a low voice. "What I have to discuss concerns you as well."

"As you wish." The general closed the door as asked and remained in the room, watching the woman adjust her pillows behind her as she sat up further against the headboard.

"I wish to speak with you regarding the future of the twins. I am not a young woman. I may not always be able to tend them…nor may you, Lord General, as willing as you might be to undertake their care. Your duty to the kingdom may take you from us far too early…" There was a note of pain in those words, as if the thought of his death disturbed her, and she shook her head when the general began to protest. She turned her eyes to the healer. "If it becomes necessary, Lord Healer, I want you to take the children with you to Elyriá…"

"Milady," the healer said in a quavering voice as he bowed. "I have never reared children…and I am home so rarely it would be impractical…not to mention it would not be proper for royal children to be…"

She interrupted him with narrowed blue eyes. "I do not care about the properness of it, Healer. I care only about their welfare. If the day comes that they are not safe in their own home, I suspect it will be the day when you too are no longer safe here. You are to be married soon, are you not? That will do. If you find duty disallows you to assume guardianship, you will find someone else in Elyriá who can care for them. This is not open for discussion. My mind is made up…as was Innis'. He is not here to protect them, and Donal may not always be able to if Bowen has his way. Do not allow Bowen, or anyone else, to harm them, is that understood, gentlemen? They must be protected."

Ártur bowed again, accepting her wishes readily enough, already considering possibilities for appropriate guardians although praying it never came to that. It was not his place to challenge her, and he could easily understand her fears, particularly where Prince Bowen was concerned. And if it had been King Innis' wish, Ártur would accept his employer's dying request and obey it.

The general, however, was not easily swayed. Ártur could feel the tension between the two stubborn individuals as they stared at one another without speaking. Not even the late King would have argued with Cordelia when she was in this frame of mind; he had loved her too dearly and had given her everything she had ever asked of him. The general, on the other hand, was use to standing firm in his conviction and was never easily moved, not even by the late King. Ártur kept his eyes downcast, remaining in his bow as he waited for whatever decision would be reached between the two.

Although no words passed, the tension in the room gradually subsided until at last the queen said, "I wish to rest. You are both dismissed…and again Lord MacLyr, welcome back."

From the tone of her voice, Ártur could not tell which of the two had triumphed, and the general's face was composed and unreadable. "Thank you, milady," the healer said with a bow. He did not know the outcome of the stand-off and felt perhaps it was in his best interest not to know.

❧Chapter 4❧

In the smoky warmth of the castle kitchen, sitting on tall wooden stools out of the way of the staff who were bustling about preparing for the castle's next meal, Kavan and Prince Owain shared a morsel of rye bread and flagon of milk leftover from the day's offering. Kavan listened to the youngest prince's stories of life for an eight-year-old prince in the royal court of Enesfel, but he said very little. He imagined that his life in Bhryell would seem dull to the prince, especially since it consisted of little more than playing his harp, reading, swimming when he could, sometimes sweeping and cleaning in the harp crafter's shop for his uncle and cousin, and attending religious services with his caretakers. Most children he knew in Bhryell thought him strange and he saw no reason to believe that this prince would think any differently.

"May I ask you a question?"

Kavan blinked and refocused on the prince, realizing his mind had begun to drift into music. "Of course," he replied.

The prince shifted awkwardly but any nervousness he felt did not keep him from asking, "Have you always been…white?"

Looking at his hands, Kavan bit his lip to stop its trembling. Just once he would like for a stranger to overlook the fact that his skin was the color of pristine snow. He knew it was too much to ask for, but he hoped for it nonetheless. His heart wanted to reply but he did not trust his voice.

Prince Owain slumped on the stool, his face dark with dismay. Kavan watched him, seeing a boy who, despite his tales of excitement, was used to being ignored, one who was accustomed to having the adults in his life pay little attention to him and who had no one his own age to share with. The question had, Kavan believed, been more an effort to talk than anything malicious or cruel.

Those realizations enabled Kavan to swallow the bitter lump in his throat and reply, "I was born this way."

The prince did not smile, as though he understood how difficult that admission must be, but his eyes shown with gratitude for Kavan's willingness to answer. "I would have liked to be born like that," he murmured.

Then people would notice you and pay attention, Kavan thought without voicing the words.

They finished eating in silence, Kavan aware that he was being scrutinized as if the prince was looking for something. Because such scrutiny was something he was used to, he showed no reaction to it. He had barely swallowed the last of his milk when Owain, apparently onto a change of topic, jumped off his stool and said, "Come with me to the courtyard."

"I should not go far…"

The prince giggled. "It is not far; it is the courtyard. You came through it when you arrived. It will be safe. Soon it will be dark and then we must be inside, but there is room to play there. Don't be afraid."

Kavan gave him a quizzical look as he put the cup on the counter and got up. Play? He was not sure he knew how to play. Though he had watched Bhryell's children do it, he had never been invited to join them as far as he could recall, and thus he had no memory of ever playing before. "Why should I be afraid?" he asked, hoping to hide that lack of skill. "I only wish not to be improper…"

"You will not be punished for going to the courtyard if that's your concern. I go there all the time." The prince tugged on his sleeve and continued, "Are you coming?"

Deciding that the prince was likely right, that there was no harm in going back to the courtyard, Kavan followed the stocky blonde outside where it was indeed beginning to grow dark. Though apprehensive about what sort of play would be required, and afraid of failure or ridicule from Owain, the possibility of making a single friend seemed worth the risk. No other child had reached out to him, had looked on him without fear or apprehension, and he was latching on to the only one who had.

The courtyard was empty of palace staff, save for the soldiers at the perimeter, leaving a wide open space for running, something Kavan knew was often a part of play. He stopped beside the prince and looked around as Owain was doing; both boys spotted the dark shape huddled against the wall inside the front gate at the same instance. A beggar, Kavan guessed, someone huddled beneath a stained and worn woolen blanket meant to fend off the winter chill. It seemed odd to Kavan that a beggar should be within the castle walls, that the soldiers at the gate, and around the courtyard, were ignoring the person. Perhaps it was a relative of one of the staff, he mused, waiting to be taken home when their work was complete for the day.

But it was the solid object leaning against the hunched shape that attracted Kavan's attention. A wrinkled hand rested on a wooden frame that could only belong to a small harp. No simple beggar then, Kavan decided, as the prince giggled and whispered, "Watch this!"

Owain ran across the courtyard and snatched the instrument from beneath the figure's hand, causing the beggar to look up with a squawk. The dirty brown blanket fell away to reveal the face of an ancient man with unusual deep violet eyes, who flailed about in his effort to reach the young thief and the prize he had stolen.

Horrified by such an unwarranted action, Kavan followed and to his surprise caught the prince quickly enough to pull the instrument from his hands. Though large in comparison to the boy holding it, the instrument was, in fact, quite small, a quarter scale harp, he believed, of the sort favored by traveling minstrels.

He was given no chance to examine it or return it to its owner. Prince Owain, interpreting Kavan's actions as part of the game, laughed again and tugged the blanket from the beggar's shoulders against the old man's protests and attempts to scramble after it. The prince, however, danced out of the beggar's reach, laughing all the while.

"Fool!" hissed Kavan. "Why are you…?"

The prince paused in his game to stare at Kavan in unexpected amazement. He had not anticipated that the other boy might not like this game. "You cannot call me a fool," he said petulantly. "I am a prince, heir to the throne of…"

"And these are probably the only things he owns," Kavan scolded, finding the sound of the growl in his voice to be unnatural. "Why bully the less fortunate? He was not harming…"

Ignoring statements that did not suit him, the prince grunted, "He is not supposed to be here. He is expelled for trespassing every day, but still he comes back." He wrapped the blanket around himself like a cloak, in a gesture that struck Kavan as arrogant.

"Give the blanket back." Kavan was already holding the harp towards the man, who, in his efforts to reach the prince and the blanket, did not move to take what Kavan offered.

"He's blind," Prince Owain sneered as if that justified his actions. Whether to comply with Kavan's demand or because he was bored with it, the prince dropped the blanket beyond the beggar's reach. The old man heard it hit the stones and crawled to find it. Kavan, with the harp in one hand, took a step towards the blanket to assist; with his attention divided he was not expecting to have the prince seize the instrument from him or kick at the beggar's arm, a move that caused the precariously balanced, emaciated figure to crumple sideways to the pavement.

There was no thought to what Kavan did next. In the same instant, he went from staring at the beggar, dumbfounded, to shoving the prince into the wall to get him far away from the old man. Owain, in his surprise, allowed the harp to clatter to the stones.

Not having anticipated a physical confrontation from the smaller, slighter, younger boy, Prince Owain gasped, "It's only a harp! Don't be foolish…"

"Foolish?" Kavan cried, caught in the grips of unfamiliar emotions without recognizing Owain's hurt or confusion. "I'll…"

He threw Owain to the ground, the unexpectedness of the move the only reason he was able to succeed. The prince quickly recovered from that surprise, however, and the wrestling that ensued resulted in the bulkier boy gaining the upper hand. The beggar called for them to stop fighting, but Kavan's only interests were self-preservation and retrieving the harp that the prince had accidentally kicked and sent skittering across the courtyard.

Where were the guards, the servants, Kavan wondered as he struggled, not to regain the upper hand but rather to disengage from the fight. Why did no one come to the sounds of the old man's shouting and fighting in the courtyard? As quickly as the questions came to mind, however, Kavan decided, as the prince's fist caught the side of his face, that it might be best if no one came. Fighting with a prince could not be a wise choice. Kavan was certain he would be punished for doing so, Ártur might lose his position, and his aunt and uncle would never allow Kavan out of Bhryell again.

Finally, he pulled free, the effort causing the prince to tumble backward and land awkwardly on his left arm with a cry of pain. Both boys scrambled to their feet, and Kavan, in his inexperience, made the mistake of thinking the fight was over. The prince grabbed a fallen tree branch and set chase, eventually cornering Kavan against the side of an outbuilding.

"You cannot hurt me! I am a prince!"

He brought the branch down on Kavan's shoulder. Kavan cowered, not knowing how to protect himself from such an attack, or if he should. He had started this altercation after all. Other boys his age might know how to fight back, having made sport of such battles in play. Kavan was defenseless.

Or so he believed. A hot prickling sensation began to bubble deep within the pit of his being, an unpleasant feeling that Kavan neither recognized nor understood. Trapped in that corner, he could not run from the blows, nor was he able to escape that burning inside of him, and when it erupted, all he could do was watch the prince jerk away, drop the stick, and fall to his knees clutching his head as he moaned. Though he was crying, there was no physical injury that Kavan could see.

Cautiously, Kavan approached, wary that it was a trick. He reached out to offer assistance, but Prince Owain was suddenly on his feet shouting, "Don't! Stay away from me! You…you're a…leave me alone!" And with that, the prince ran back into the castle, weaving and staggering and still clutching his head.

Kavan knew he must have done something, understanding instinctively that the prince's pain was connected to that burning prickle that was gone from within him. What Kavan did not understand was what he had done or how. Whatever it was, there would be a reprimand, either from Ártur, or the King, or at least his uncle. With that sobering realization in mind, causing his shoulders to sag, Kavan retrieved the harp and inspected it for damage as he carried it back to its owner.

The instrument turned out to be a Cliáthan, one of his family's designs. It was made of some dense black wood that Kavan had never seen before, unpainted or varnished and unusually heavy. He could not recall seeing his uncle or cousin working with wood of this type, which meant it was likely much older than Kavan. The instrument's frame was shaped like a kestrel with raised wings, the brass strings filling those wings beautifully. Such a frame meant it was a custom made instrument; there was likely nothing else like it in the entire world. It was priceless, in Kavan's eyes, for that reason alone. He placed it in the old man's gnarled hands, reluctant to let the instrument go without playing it, and arranged the shreds of blanket around his shoulders.

"Thank you," said the beggar in a voice that, though cracked, sounded younger than his skeletal figure warranted.

Kavan shrugged before realizing the gesture could not be seen. "I am sorry for what he did…"

The man's hand rested on Kavan's and the boy blinked at the jolt of power that passed between them. "I am an easy target," the beggar said, "and he seeks the attention. He has done it before. But you? Why such kindness for an old man…?"

"Why not? Kindness is far better than cruelty, is it not?" That he could have chosen to ignore the man did not occur to him as an option. Kavan fished in the pocket of his white robe for the two silver sónás he carried and placed the coins in the man's palm. "Your harp is not damaged; I checked it myself. Keep these for the trouble we caused, sir. Perhaps if he is always cruel to you, you should consider taking rest elsewhere."

Rather than wait for a reply, Kavan ran inside, wanting to escape the memories of that fight, unaware that the unseeing violet eyes of the smiling beggar stared in the direction of his running footsteps until he was no longer within hearing range.

As Kavan followed the twists and turns of the castle corridors, he quickly discovered he had no idea where he should go. He saw no guards or wandering servants who might be able to direct him to wherever his cousin was. He recalled going up two flights of stairs to reach the level of the queen's chambers, and hoping that Ártur might still be on that level if it housed other bed chambers, he found the stairs and climbed. On the third floor, he crept through the corridors, listening for Ártur's voice but never hearing it. He was beginning to despair of finding his way when he came upon a wooden door with the image of the burning pyre inlayed upon it. Kavan breathed a sigh of relief. Surely if Ártur knew of this room, he would think to look for Kavan there if the boy was gone too long.

The broad metal hinges popped and the oak groaned as the door was opened. Inside, the benches and much of the floor were dust covered, but as a single tallow candle burned on the altar, Kavan knew that someone had come here not long before. There was no one here now, however, and the silence of the small náós had a welcoming calm. If he waited, perhaps whoever had lit the candle would return and take him to Ártur.

Kavan approached the altar and touched the top with reverence as he circled behind it to kneel in the shadows where he felt safest. The fingers of his right hand touched his forehead, his breast over his heart, and finally his lips as he gazed at the dusty image of Dhágdhuán above him. He was surprised that, for all of Enesfel's purported disbelief in the ancient Faith, this icon remained intact within the home of the royal family.

His body hurt all over from the beating the prince had given him. He hoped any bruises would be gone by the time he returned home. Unfamiliar with that sort of pain, alone here where no one would see him, Kavan let himself seek comfort in crying. Ártur would scold him for starting a fight, as surely the prince would tell it that way, leaving out his own actions that were the precursor to Kavan's. Kavan would never seek to displace the blame, however. If asked, he would tell the truth, tell everything as it had happened, and admit to being the first to resort to physical force. He was berating himself for his foolishness, shifting from one side to another to find a more comfortable kneeling position, when he finally heard the door scrape open.

It was not Ártur's footsteps he heard, however, and the unfamiliar sound made him shiver nervously. Expecting castigation, he waited until the sound ceased before summoning the courage to peer around the altar with the hopes of being able to escape the room and whoever had invaded it. That the person might be able to take him to Ártur was no longer a consideration. The man in soldier's clothing who knelt at the altar with his hands covering his face appeared sad, not a threat, but Kavan saw no way to get around him to the door without being noticed, and taking the risk did not seem wise. At the moment, his instincts were the last one's he trusted.

Deciding that if he returned to his prayers long enough, he would remain hidden until the man was gone, he began to withdraw behind the altar again. Either his movement alerted the stranger to his presence, or else the man had simply sensed he was no longer alone because he lifted his head and stared directly at Kavan, hazel eyes brightening when they met his.

"Kneel with me, blessed one," the man commanded with a note of desperation in his voice.

No one had ever asked Kavan for anything like that before. Frozen in place as his thoughts scrambled to make sense of what he saw and heard, he whispered, "Sir?"

The man managed to smile, though it did not dispel the melancholy on his face. "Good…you do speak. I thought perhaps you were a spirit. You look to be one of great holiness…as though you belong to this place. I fear I do not. It has been too many years since I have knelt here…or anywhere…and I fear I may say or do something wrong."

Kavan hesitated before crawling cautiously to kneel before the man who took Kavan's small hands in his. The boy looked away from the broad face long enough to inspect the gnarled, battle-worn hands, wondering why he saw flashes of war within his head as he held them.

"Pray with me. Pray for me, blessed one."

"I am not..." No one had ever called him blessed, and he could not decide if the label scared him or made him feel good. He did not, however, feel blessed.

The man continued, "My father has left me a burden I do not wish to bear, one I do not know how to carry. It is my duty, and I will do what I must, but I do not want it. If I must accept this...I desire the wisdom and guidance that he possessed."

"Was he a wise man? A holy man?"

The soldier appeared ashamed. "I do not know. I did not know him as well as I should have. But I do know he believed there was something guiding his actions, and I want that same guidance. I need it. I thought perhaps..." He paused to look around the disused room. "If anyone can tell me what I must do to obtain it, a divine messenger such as you surely can."

Kavan shook his head, deciding then that blessed he could accept, but never divine. "I am not divine, sir...nor a messenger...but I will pray with you if you wish."

Despite Kavan's look of alarm, the soldier nodded and squeezed the small hands more tightly. "Please." His belief in whatever he thought Kavan was had not been dispelled by the boy's protests.

The desperation in the request and the man's tone encouraged Kavan to pray aloud for spiritual guidance for him, for grace, understanding, forgiveness, and strength of character, despite the awkwardness he felt in doing so. And though he did not voice his thoughts for himself, he prayed too for all of those things, not feeling worthy after the fight but feeling he desperately needed them.

Eventually, the soldier pulled his hands free, wiped his cheeks, and rose to his feet with a more peaceful expression behind the turmoil of his unshaven face then he had possessed previously.

"Such a childlike grace and faith in your words. You are indeed blessed. I have never before believed in záryph, but you being sent to me was a sign I shall not forget."

"Sir, I am not…"

But the soldier was already striding away after a kiss on Kavan's silver-white hair, and the boy leaned back, still on his knees, watching the door close. Had he been wrong to allow the stranger to believe he was something he was not? After much thought, he decided he had not been given the chance to express otherwise, and if it gave the unhappy soldier faith and peace to believe he had spoken with a záryph, then not saying otherwise was likely worthwhile.

For a long time, Kavan stared into the shadows, facing the altar, no longer thinking about anything, until the door opened again, this time bringing familiar footsteps. Ártur did not speak as he knelt, nor did Kavan. Only when the boy found the courage to look up into the healer's face with troubled eyes did Ártur voice his thoughts.

"You have made a lasting impression on Enesfel's royalty and we have only been here three hours." He waited for Kavan to say something, but all he received from the boy was a silent plea for understanding. "The queen has asked to speak to you and would like you to play for her if a harp can be found." He paused again as the boy's head bobbed in agreement. "More importantly, however…what did you do to Prince Owain?"

Kavan swallowed hard and barely resisted hanging his head. "I do not know," he whispered.

Ártur held back his retort. If Kavan knew, he would say. The boy was disturbingly honest, too honest in the healer's opinion. He could see the bruises scattered across the ivory of Kavan's face and the dirt on his robe, but there were no serious visible injuries. "Prince Owain burst into the queen's chambers yelling about white-faced demons for some reason." At Kavan's pained expression and the rise of tears in his green eyes, Ártur touched his arm sympathetically. "What happened?"

Kavan stared at his knees, hesitating long enough to form the words he wanted. "After going to the kitchen, we went to the courtyard; he said it was allowed. There was a blind beggar there…with a harp…the oldest Cliáthan quarter-scale I have ever seen…I even got to hold it!"

Seeing the start of annoyance on his cousin's face, Kavan reined in the enthusiasm over the harp, silently glad that Ártur remained patient. "Prince Owain took it from him. I took it away, tried to give it back, but the prince took his blanket…kicked him…and we started to fight. I…I started it. I pushed him into the wall and scolded him. He started hitting me with a branch then I felt a prickling burning here…" he indicated the area beneath his diaphragm. "He kept hitting me…and then it was like…something clawing out of me…then he fell down, holding his head…and when I tried to help him, he ran away." With a near silent whisper and unshed tears, Kavan asked, "What happened, Ártur? What did I do?"

"May I read you?"

Kavan scowled. "To learn if I am telling the truth?"

"No, sínréc. I believe you, but I cannot know what you did until I can see for myself. I need to learn more by looking within you."

The boy reluctantly offered his hands, but the healer took only one and placed his other hand on Kavan's chest. Minutes ticked past as Kavan tried to follow the course of his cousin's searching. When the larger hands fell away, Ártur could only shake his head in disbelief. He did not know which surprised him more, that Kavan had gotten into a fight over a beggar and a harp, or the power he displayed that had ended it.

Striving to keep his emotion out of his voice, Ártur said, "I have examined you both thoroughly; there is no doubt in my diagnosis...though I do not know how it can be so. I believe you have used a form of a seldom taught discipline known as sídysá."

"What is that?"

The healer sat instead of kneeling any longer. He did not expect such an explanation to be a short one with a child as young as Kavan. Such disciplines were best explained by bhydáni, but Kavan deserved an answer, and Ártur was the only one here to give it. He did not believe it should wait until they returned to Bhryell. "Energy is gathered and directed in a sharp, brutal, cohesive burst...like a fist of power, like an explosion. When the discipline was more widely known, it was most often used as an attack on another mind, capable of creating pain, brain damage, or even death if the attacker was skilled enough."

The boy's face could not lose color, but the expression on it was the same as if he had. "Did I harm the prince? Is he going to...die?"

Ártur shook his head and squeezed Kavan's shoulder. "You gave him a headache. A rather bad headache, but he should be over it by morning. I made sure he will sleep tonight, which is the best thing for him. There was not enough power behind what you did, nor was it focused enough, to do permanent damage, but even a protected Elyri mind like mine would have experienced pain from it. sídysá is an advanced technique, one that I have never seen appear naturally and one that is rarely taught. It is too dangerous, particularly against a Teren's untrained and unprotected mind. I do not know how to do it. I do not know anyone who does, though I am certain at least a few bhydáni must. It appears," he sighed and raked his hand through his short, pale red hair, "that you have a built-in defense mechanism, one that could prove deadly if not harnessed."

Not yet thinking about the ramifications of a built-in defense mechanism, Kavan took a breath and decided this was the best time to reveal the other oddities he had discovered. "That is not all I can do, Ártur."

The healer looked surprised but recovered quickly. "Of course not. You have llánec…"

Kavan shook his head. "Other things. If I do not shut them out, I hear thoughts, like voices, particularly aendhá Tám's. His are loud and hurt my head. I had to learn to shut them out because I could not sleep. I caught sunlight once, in my hands, but I have not tried to do it again. I can feel power when I touch the altar in the náós…any náós…"

With each ability he confessed, Kavan watched his cousin's surprise deepen. "And I can do this."

The small tongue of flame that sparked in the small white palm was brighter than any Ártur had seen from a novice. It took the healer many moments to find his voice. This could not be. It was not normal.

"Handlights," he started, "are almost an inborn ability. It takes little knowledge to create them and is usually one of the first disciplines we're taught…although it generally requires a fair amount of practice to use it so quickly and efficiently…" The corners of his mouth quirked up in response to the touch of pride in Kavan's eyes. "Hearing thoughts is not an uncommon gift either, the ability usually requires physical contact and rarely functions as clearly as what you have experienced. And I have never known anyone who has learned to shut them out on their own…though it is clearly possible." He looked Kavan over, running one hand through the boy's hair before cupping his chin. "We will need to do something about this when we return home. Such an early manifestation of talent demands training…before someone gets hurt."

That demand, however, would be hard to fulfill. Tám MacLyr was one of a fair number of Elyri who held their natural abilities with distrust and disdain. He had ceased his own training as soon as he had been allowed to as a child and had done his best to encourage his children to do likewise. Ártur, as a healer, had been exempt from that, for it was unimaginable to any Elyri to not train a child with the healing gifts, but Ártur's two siblings had both trained only as long as they had to. Such an early display of power in Kavan would not please Tám. Another argument between the healer and his father was in the offing and Kavan would be the center of it.

Not liking that thought, not wanting Kavan to feel guilty or responsible for something beyond his control, Ártur promptly changed the subject. "I met King Donal in the corridor. It seems he came here to gather his wits after our earlier discussion and encountered a záryph that sounded, to me, suspiciously like you."

Blushing, Kavan looked away, hiding his face. He would have behaved differently if he had known whom he was dealing with. "I could not find my way back to you so when I found this place, I decided you would find me here if I stayed put. I was praying when he came in; I thought he was a soldier…"

"And he is…or was…a better soldier could not be found in all the land, save for General McHador. That is why he is finding this transition difficult. He told me you prayed with him, and that he was touched by whatever you said. I believe you may have reached him in a way that no one else, even me, has been able to do. Today has been difficult for him and as he does not need the embarrassment tonight of learning you are quite mortal, I think I shall keep the truth to myself. He will find out tomorrow anyhow."

The healer got to his feet and helped Kavan to stand. "Why does he not want to be King? I thought all princes want to be kings," he murmured as they started towards the room Ártur used when he was at court.

"Just as you do not want to be a harp-maker like your father, so Donal does not want to be a King. He would rather remain a soldier. He never expected to outlive his father and is ill-prepared for this unexpected change."

Neither spoke again until they reached the door to the bedroom. "He will be a good King," Kavan said at last, his tone reflecting none of the doubt that Ártur and the others were feeling about the future of Enesfel.

"I hope so. We all do. But things will not be the same."

Kavan nodded. "They never are. Will it be dangerous for you here?"

Ártur swallowed hard and tightened his grip on Kavan's hand as he opened the chamber door. "I cannot say. I do not know. We will learn soon enough, I imagine."

⮰Chapter 5⮰

The late morning air was beginning to warm as staff and family gathered around the Lachlan family crypt at the rear of the castle. King Donal stood closest to the stone slab on which his father's body rested, keeping his eyes focused anywhere but on the body itself. Prince Bowen glared at him from across the crowd, still expecting Donal to capitulate, still expecting that his half-brother did not have the fortitude to follow through with the coronation or the duties of kingship. The prince knew Donal would never give the throne to him outright, but passing the throne to the more easily manipulated Farrell would have suited Bowen fine.

It was with a sigh of disappointment that the new King admitted to himself that his advisors were right. The longer they waited to put the late King to rest, the more difficult it would be for him, and thus the kingdom, to move forward. There were matters that needed to be dealt with promptly, and for him to hesitate in initiating his own rule would be looked upon as weakness by the other sovereignties. And there were things Donal wanted to do, things he had shared with the healer and the general, that were best not put off. No matter that his actions would further alienate Bowen. The middle prince despised his eldest brother as it was; further hatred would be of little consequence to the King.

Between the King and the healer, Kavan watched the proceedings in a way that told Donal the child missed nothing important. He had not felt embarrassed to learn that his záryph was his best friend's cousin; the boy radiated too much wisdom and goodness in the King's eyes for that. Instead, he took the boy aside and thanked him for his kindness. Later, when he heard about the incident between Kavan and Prince Owain, he reassured Kavan that he held no one but Owain responsible. He could not fathom, when looking into the deep green innocent eyes, that this boy could have started a fight with the volatile youngest Lachlan.

The military drums began their slow, steady dirge as six well-groomed and polished soldiers began the procession past the royal family and the body. The sunlight was incapable of changing the cold and gray appearance of the dead man's face. The King looked at his father, seeing no life in the bony hands that were folded over the barreled chest, and issued a sigh of defeat. He was King; it was irrefutable.

Lords and ladies and servants shuffled past, paying respects to the deceased by laying gifts of coin, flowers, personal trinkets and written prayers around the man. General McHador was last, laying the late King's sword on the man's chest and wrapping the lifeless fingers around the hilt. That done, Donal anointed the body with sweetly scented oil, a medicinal balm from deep inside Hatu intended to slow decay, and the blessed water meant to ease the King's way into the afterlife. It was the first time the new King had touched his father's body, and the first time in many years, he realized, he had touched the man at all. The contact was made more difficult by the eyes around him that watched him expectantly, waiting, he believed, to see him fail. Only once did he falter, but a glance at the child at Ártur's side enabled the King to continue. Strangely, he did not find that odd. As he circled the body, one of the six soldiers recounted the noble deeds and accomplishments of the dead in a singsong chant, which continued after Donal was finished and returned to his place at the front of the crowd beside his wife.

When the chanter finally fell silent, leaving only the rat-tat of the drums filling the day's silent spaces, the six soldiers took places alongside the body and slid the pallet into place within the crypt. The bronze marker bearing the King's name was already prepared and mounted to mark his place alongside those other Lachlans who had gone before. In time, his bones would join his ancestors in the sepulcher beneath their feet. The new King watched, feeling nauseous and restless until a small hand slipped into his. When he looked at the boy beside him, he let out the breath he had not realized he was holding. Kavan's tears mirrored the questions the King wanted to have answered. How could one believe in eternity when this act of interment seemed so final? Where was Innis now? How did the living continue their lives shouldering such a burden?

This child seemed to understand his fears, his sorrows, and the dilemmas he faced in a way that no one else did and that made Donal relax. Believing he was understood made the unanswered questions easier to bear as they waited for the heavy thud of the marble and metal sealing his father away from his reach. When the soldiers stepped back, the drummers stopped playing and the new King of Enesfel led the collection of men and women into the Grand Hall.

The lords, nobles, and merchants who had been able to reach Rhidam in time for the burial gathered to hear what their late monarch's last wishes had been, some hoping for their piece of the man and his wealth, others hoping to find some small bit of power or position in his passing. Cordelia was seated at the front of the room with an aura of subtle defiance around her, and Donal nodded, agreeing with her distaste for the petty vultures and politicians who preyed on the deceased. King Innis had been much loved by his subjects, but that did not stop some from hoping to benefit from his passing. Hopefully, Donal thought to himself, his father had seen that all were dealt with as they deserved.

The King assumed his place on a chair near the throne. Until the coronation, which was still days away, the throne would, by custom, remain empty, covered with a burgundy and amber shroud. For Donal, not sitting there was preferred, and to further ease his discomfort he brought Kavan with him and gathered the boy onto his lap, much to the dismay and amazement of many. He did his best to ignore the gawkers as the late King's Chamberlain, Sir Edard Transk, mounted the platform where the body had been only hours before, and began to read the last written testament of King Innis Trebor Lachlan.

Kavan listened to the rhetoric, trying to decipher the Trade words he did not yet know, watching the members of the royal family and others in the audience, wondering, as they were, why the King had wanted him on his lap when he was neither family nor Teren. It had been a long time since he had sat on his aunt's lap, longer still since he had sat on anyone else's, but the awkwardness of it was set aside in favor of whatever benefit the new king found in the sharing. It was a political statement, perhaps, or for personal reassurance, but either way, it gave Kavan a unique perspective on the events that he would not otherwise have had.

There was nothing unusual in the manifesto, only Innis' wishes for the new King and the kingdom. Everything the popular monarch had owned was left, as was tradition, to his eldest son and heir and his wife, who were to share with the others children as seemed fitting so long as each was taken care of and provided for. There were admonitions to each of his sons, instructing them to cooperate with each other for the good of Enesfel. Prince Girvin nodded throughout, still weeping and trying to dry his cheeks with a long since soaked kerchief. Prince Owain glared at Kavan with undisguised jealousy, while Prince Farrell appeared not to be paying attention. He was seated beside a young noblewoman, whispering to her and playing with her fingers suggestively in a way that made Donal scowl. Prince Bowen's face was blank, revealing no hint of agreement or rejection of his father's wishes, though he, at least, did appear to be listening. Of all of them, only Donal found the courage to smile, a smile that, to Kavan seemed curiously out of place and forced.

The disappointed gathering, having gotten nothing monetary or material from the late King, dissipated after Lord Transk left the platform. The King helped Kavan gently from his lap and strode off to speak with the chamberlain. The aura in the room had shifted into something Kavan found abrasive and heavy, and he disliked the looks that passed between his cousin and the general when the King dismissed the chamberlain and motioned for Prince Bowen to follow him into the State Room. Since Kavan did not believe he would receive answers if he asked the questions burning in his mind, and since it seemed that the adults had forgotten his presence, he turned his attention to the wall tapestries, listening for clues as to what was transpiring and trying to shut out the unpleasantness he felt in the air.

"What does Your Majesty want with me?" Prince Bowen quipped with a smirk as he stepped through the State Room door, closed it, and leaned against its frame. The room was sparse though elegant, containing only a long table made of heavy walnut, the two dozen matching chairs with crimson and amber cushions, and a matching cabinet containing books, parchment, pens and ink, and wine. The prince made note that his brother used the table to keep distance between them, the King moving to the farthest side of the room, and his smirk deepened.

"I thought it best not to make my first decree public."

The hair on the back of Prince Bowen's neck stood at attention. Those were not the sort of words he expected to hear from a man who appeared afraid of him and Donal's icy tone did little to assure him.

"Decree, My King?" he asked coolly, hoping his brother was about to denounce his claim to the throne though doubting it was so. "What sort of decree would require me...?"

"Enough." The King snorted and waved his hand, cutting his brother short. "Do you think me daft? Enough of secrets and evasiveness between us. It is time we speak plainly with one another."

Bowen snorted back. "I have no secrets."

But the King, knowing better, took a step closer, emboldened by Bowen's defensive tone. Bowen scowled. "Owain is not our father's son. We both know it. I am ashamed to call him, and the one who sired him..." he paused to let those words linger in the air between them, "brothers. The lies have disgraced the name of Lachlan for too long. It is time to bring them to an end."

The only reaction he received was a twitch at the corner of Bowen's mouth. The King had expected Bowen would be difficult, if not impossible, to break, but he was determined to do it. "I present you with three options regarding his, and your, future. I can expose you and his mother as the liars you are...which I hardly think will be beneficial to your reputation. Or I can deny him the right to rule in Enesfel and send both Owain and Ula away..."

Prince Bowen, feigning boredom as he scratched at his elbow, asked, "What if I choose to accept neither of those choices?"

The King's eyes narrowed as he closed the distance by another two strides. "I will imprison all three of you for treason and bar you and Owain and all of your heirs from ever sitting on Enesfel's throne."

"Imprison a child?" Prince Bowen laughed, a strained sound that belied his tension. "Do you think your subjects will look favorably upon a King who imprisons a child?"

Refusing to be baited, Donal continued. "House imprisonment is always an option until he is older. Do not think I have considered this matter lightly. It is my right to deal with traitors in any way I deem fitting. Eight years you have deceived the Crown and the land, and some day even Owain will know the truth. I will take no chances with the security of this kingdom; I will no longer claim him as a brother. If you accept their banishment, they will leave Enesfel and not return under penalty of death. They will, at least, live…and you might be able to salvage your reputation. Or allow them to remain and I will expose all of you. The choice is yours, Bowen."

"When do you want…?"

The words were barely out of his mouth before the King replied, "Now."

Prince Bowen wanted to pace, but instead, he continued to glare at his brother who neither flinched nor spoke again. The King held his ground, moving only after several minutes of silence to fold his arms across his chest in a gesture that looked, to Bowen, like one of arrogance and triumph. Only then did Bowen square his shoulders, break the gaze between them, and turn to stare out of the window. It was as clear a signal of defeat as any the King could have hoped for, and both knew it.

With gravel in his voice, the prince asked, "When must they leave?" Though Bowen could not see it, he could feel the King's suppressed smile.

"After the coronation. Owain's absence would be questioned. I will make it known that they are on a visit to Ula's family since Neth is the most logical place for her to go. What explanation you offer when they do not return I will leave up to you, but if that explanation turns to accusations against the Crown, or against our father, you will be imprisoned. And if you disobey me, if they are not gone the day after the coronation, or are discovered to still reside in Enesfel, all three of you will bear my wrath."

With his back to the King, Prince Bowen asked, "If I do this…send them away…my name remains clear of this matter?"

The King had nothing to lose by agreeing to that condition. It was the only way to get what he wanted. "Agreed."

Bowen did not bow. He would never bow to his brother when he had only rarely bowed to their father. Jaw clenched, he muttered a terse, "Yes, My Liege," and then stormed out of the room, roughly grabbing Owain by the arm as he passed and dragging the boy with him across the Hall. Pensive looks were exchanged between the two men remaining in the room but it was several minutes before the King joined them wearing an expression of relief.

"He agreed."

Kavan, standing against the wall where he could see everyone, felt the relief in his cousin and the general as well, but some undercurrent in the room caused him to bite his lip and look at the floor.

"He had no choice if he wished to keep his reputation from further tarnish," the King continued. "That he chose not to take the risk proves to me his guilt. They will leave the day after the coronation, and in exchange for his compliance, none of this will ever be made public and his name will remain out of it. Documents of ineligibility have already been drafted. They require three signatures of witness, but I am making it four; there may come a time when your signature, Ártur, might be considered invalid, but I am asking you to sign it as a personal favor to me."

The healer was far from pleased; Kavan could feel it without looking at his cousin. Despite his misgivings, however, the elder Elyri bowed and murmured, "As you wish, My Liege," words that left a bitter burn in Kavan's belly.

His acceptance brought the King further relief. "Lord General, bring Chamberlain Transk and Duke Niall to the State Room. Both will stay on in their current posts; they will still be on the grounds. Ártur and I will meet you there. The four of you will sign the writ and that will be the end of the matter. Ártur, you will be here for the coronation?"

It was both a question and a command, and the healer bowed again. "If Your Lordship wishes it, I would be nowhere else."

Donal's hand gripped the man's slender shoulder. "You know I do. I also desire that you stay on as court physician, for the Queen Mother, the children and myself. We need your support." His smile turned upon Kavan, but it faltered as he noted the boy's dark, perplexed expression. Feeling that he had done what was best for the kingdom, he could not understand why that young expression caused him to feel guilty, and since he could not afford to dwell on it then, he pushed the feeling aside and offered Kavan his hand. He was pleased that the boy accepted the gesture with a solid, unhesitating grip. "You are welcome in Rhidam and the castle any time, young Cliáth. I believe your face and company will be a much-needed blessing to all of us in the days ahead."

"Yes, Sire," Kavan murmured with a bow, although his feelings did not agree with that sentiment at all.

❧*☙

As if to avail himself of whatever blessings he felt the boy offered, the King did his best to fill Kavan's time in Rhidam with the wonders and splendors of the life of nobility, in the castle, around the grounds, and in Rhidam. One morning they rode out of the city in the company of Ártur and many guards, making a great arc around the city to give Kavan a sense of the size of one of the Teren's largest municipalities. During that ride, he gifted the boy with a well-balanced dagger and when they stopped to share the noon meal in a bright, sunlit grove, he taught Kavan how to throw it. The aptitude Kavan showed for that skill unsettled the monarch, as the first several tries to hit a target showed success of varying degrees, but that unsettled feeling did not stop Donal from showering the Elyri boy with attention. They read together, discussed history and philosophy, and sat together, with Ártur nearby, every evening meal in the Banquet Hall. No harp was located, however, thus Kavan was unable to play for the royal family as requested. Undaunted, the King procured from him a promise that, should Kavan ever return to Rhidam, he was to bring his harp and play for the royal family then. It was a promise Kavan had no difficulty making.

That the King spent much time with the boy, after years of touting his dislike for young children, was perplexing to many. If anyone thought the behavior odd, or potentially damaging to Donal's rule, they did not voice those thoughts within Kavan's hearing. Not that he would have paid heed to such talk. He liked the King and enjoyed sharing intelligent discourse with someone other than his cousin. Few in Bhryell realized how advanced he was intellectually, and those who did treated him as precocious or avoided him. Having a King acknowledge his thoughts as worthy of attention made Kavan feel less alone and as less of an oddity.

This night, however, the King was occupied with preparations for tomorrow's coronation and Kavan was bored of watching Ártur read at his bedroom desk. The twins, whom Kavan had spent more time with, reading to, talking to, or rocking them in their cradles, were sleeping, and Prince Owain continued to avoid him since that first badly ended encounter. Normally content to entertain himself with books when there was no music to be enjoyed or made, tonight Kavan wanted something else to occupy his time. He wanted a harp. He wanted home.

From the third floor window where he stood, he gazed at the náos spires for some time, wishing he had been given the opportunity to explore that ancient building. There had been no chance, however, and in a few days he knew the opportunity would be lost. If he had been in Bhryell, he would have considered going there alone, but he knew it was not safe for an Elyri child to be alone in the streets of Rhidam. Restlessly, he decided that if he could not go there he at least had to get out of the room, and so he left the window and picked up his cloak from the chair where it hung.

The healer glanced at him with a smile as Kavan left the room. By now he held no concern that Kavan would get lost on the grounds, and any fears he had of Kavan being in danger had been dispelled by the King's fondness for his cousin. With Kavan in Rhidam, Ártur felt more at peace in his work than ever before. For Ártur, King Donal was right. Having Kavan in Rhidam was a blessing.

As he had done nearly every evening in Rhidam, Kavan returned expectantly to the courtyard but there had been no further sign of the blind beggar. It appeared that the old man had taken Kavan's words to heart and had found somewhere more peaceful to rest out of Prince Owain's reach. But Kavan had hoped to see the compelling man once more if only to ask permission to play that harp a single time. This was the first time Kavan had been kept away from the instrument he adored, and he was, to his surprise, miserable because of it. This night was no different than the others; Kavan made a casual circle of the entire courtyard but the man with the violet eyes was not there. His longing for a harp to play would go unsatisfied until he returned home.

Prince Owain, however, was there, having come into the courtyard during Kavan's musings to angrily kick a small wooden ball over the cobbled surface. Kavan tried to give him a wide berth, but when it appeared that the prince was staying near the doors, Kavan realized he would have to move closer in order to go inside. Perhaps, he decided, this was his opportunity to apologize. Recalling vividly the beating he had gotten at the blonde boy's hand, he approached with caution.

When their eyes met, Kavan could see in the blue ones that he was not the only one afraid. It made him rethink his fear. Owain, after several moments of not moving, scooped up his ball and started to back towards the door without taking his eyes off of Kavan.

"I am sorry," Kavan said softly, finding the position of needing to apologize for the first time to be an awkward one. "What happened…it was not intentional. I did not know what was happening…or how to stop it. I did not mean to hurt you."

The prince began to say something but then bit his lip and shrugged his shoulders. "It is your fault I have to leave."

"Leave?" Confused, Kavan took a small step forward, the impulse to help, to comfort, welling up strong within him.

Sullenly, Owain looked at the ground and shuffled his feet. Now that he was face to face with Kavan, the younger boy did not seem as frightening as he had to the prince over the last several days. "Bowen says Mother and I must go away. He says it is not safe for us in Rhidam…and I thought it was because of our fight…and what you did."

Kavan now understood the undertones of the dialogue between the King, the general, and Ártur the day of the burial. Feeling that it would only make things worse for Owain if the prince knew the truth, and seeing no other benefit in speaking of what he suspected, Kavan shook his head and asked, "Where are you going?"

"To my mother's family…in Neth."

Neth. The word made Kavan shiver. To many, Neth was the scourge of the Five Sovereignties, a land ruled by constant turmoil, upheaval, violence, and prejudice. For an Elyri especially, it was the worst imaginable place to go. "Maybe if I speak with the King…"

Something dark and jealous flashed in the prince's eyes and Kavan swallowed back the rest of his words. It had not occurred to him that Owain might want the King's attention too. As abruptly as that look came, however, it bled off and the prince sighed. "He is the one making us go." He looked at the ball in his hands and thus missed the look of regret that settled on Kavan's face. "Here…take this," he said, presenting the ball to Kavan. "Keep it."

"I…thank you…" Kavan began, but as soon as the ball was out of Owain's hands, the other boy turned and ran inside without looking back, leaving Kavan perplexed and sad.

Alone in the courtyard, Kavan pondered what had been said and what had not before he closed his fist around the ball and returning to the room he shared with Ártur. His cousin was still reading by the dim candlelight at the desk where Kavan had left him. He looked up as Kavan entered, but when the boy sat on the edge of the bed, rolling the ball from one hand to the other in silence, the healer returned to his reading.

"Ártur?" the boy eventually asked after undressing and crawling beneath the blankets.

"Yes?" Ártur's head remained bent over the book and Kavan stared at the ceiling for several more moments.

"Why is King Donal making Prince Owain leave Enesfel?"

That pulled the healer's attention away from reading, as he scowled at his cousin. "How do you know about that?"

There were many answers Kavan could have given, but honesty seemed best. "I suspected it before, on the day of the burial...from the way you, the general, and the King were behaving...from the things that were said. I did not...believe...I had heard right. It did not make sense. But the prince has confirmed it...he told me he had to leave." Kavan propped himself up on one elbow to look at his cousin. "It isn't my fault, is it? Because of what I did?"

The healer shifted uncomfortably. He had not thought that Kavan might grasp the intricacies of the unspoken dialogue between himself, Guthrie, and the King on the day of the burial. If he had, he would have sent Kavan elsewhere. It was a testimony to how little he knew about the boy. But it was too late to try to pass off Owain's departure as a simple visit to relatives. He did not want to lie to Kavan, and he believed if he tried, Kavan would see through his attempt.

"No. This has nothing to do with you," he finally said with a sigh.

"He says he is not safe here. Is he in danger?"

"No..." His thoughts were swirling, scrambling for answers to the questions he knew were coming. Kavan was not going to drop the subject and Ártur did not have the stomach to silence him.

"Then why, Ártur? What has he done? What has his mother done? He is unhappy about leaving. It is not fair of the King to send his brother away if he does not want to go. This is the only home he's ever known..."

"Kavan..." Ártur closed the book. "The task of ruling a kingdom is never simple. Sometimes a ruler must do unpopular things on behalf of the kingdom. Prince Owain is not...things are not as they appear on the surface. If Owain and his mother are allowed to stay, the King feels the kingdom will be at risk. I can explain it no better than that. The King has forbidden those of us who know of this to speak of it. You should not know as much as you do, but I suspect he did not think you would be this perceptive. I must insist that you speak of this to no one else. Prince Owain and his mother are going to her family's home, and that is the end of it. There will be enough gossip as it is; do not add to it." He turned back to his book, considering the topic at rest.

Though he nodded in agreement and acceptance of those terms, Kavan wrapped his arms around himself with a violent shiver and murmured, "Sending him to Neth is a bad idea. It will bring Enesfel much grief one day."

Ártur's head snapped around and his gaze fixed on Kavan. The boy's tone, his words, and even his posture were troublesome. He might have thought nothing of it, but knowing that Kavan had the Sight, the healer was prepared to take anything Kavan said very seriously. Afraid of the answer, he asked, "Why? What do you see?"

Surprised that Ártur would quickly accept what Kavan himself did not yet understand, the boy shrugged. "I...it is only a feeling...that sending Prince Owain to Neth is the wrong thing to do...that it will have dire consequences in the end."

Many minutes later, when Ártur was able to break away from Kavan's intense gaze, he absently closed his book for a second time and went out of the room. Kavan, alone with his thoughts, stared into the bright tongue of flame that appeared in his palm, lost to the peculiar feelings gripping him. Only when the sound of his cousin's footsteps returned did he look up and the handlight flicker out. Ártur's expression told him enough.

"The King will not let them stay."

The healer set the large, flat wooden box he carried on the desk and then seemed to crumple as he sank onto the edge of the bed. "No. Why should he? He does not believe in llánec as I do. There have been no prophets in Enesfel for centuries…and even those in Elyriá doubt the accuracy and existence of the Sight. Donal has no reason to believe me. He knows I do not think he should send them to Neth, but his decision is set. They will leave Rhidam as planned. All we can do is pray you are wrong."

Kavan rubbed his eyes. "I will try…but I do not think I am wrong, Ártur." He leaned back into the pillows, wondering why he believed his feelings with such certainty. The more he saw of political workings, the less he liked them. Why, he wondered, must it be hard for a man to believe the truth?

Dizziness swept over him, and glad he was already lying down, he groaned and curled up on his side as images paraded through his mind. He recognized Rhidam's Grand Hall, but not the black-bearded individual kneeling before the throne at what appeared to be a coronation. Coming on the heels of the premonition of disaster, Kavan could not imagine what this might mean.

"Kavan?" Unfamiliar with the effects of the Sight, Ártur laid his hand on the boy's forehead. There was no apparent fever, but the contact was enough to show the healer the last lingering moments of the images in his cousin's head.

"It is nothing…" Kavan whispered. To anyone else, those images would likely be nothing. For Kavan, however, they left the distinct impression that he would not be kept as far from a life amongst kings and courts as he hoped.

Ártur knew better than to believe it was nothing. It was something important, but as he did not understand what he saw either, he chose not to pursue an explanation Kavan could not give. "I have something for you," he said soothingly, hoping to take Kavan's mind off of whatever he had seen. "Donal asked me to give this to you."

From the desk, he picked up the box he had brought in and carried it to the bed as Kavan sat up. It was a crude, battered case that could have contained anything, but what he found within made Kavan gasp. With shaky hands, Kavan reached for the small, black wood, kestrel shaped brass-strung harp, identical to that which the blind beggar had possessed. He would not have believed the ancient man would have parted with such a priceless possession until he touched it and was bombarded with imagery of the harp's final moments before being placed inside its rudimentary housing. Those flashes gave Kavan no doubt that this was the same instrument.

The healer gave a low whistle and ran his fingers down the wet-looking wood. "May I?" he asked. It was Kavan's gift and Ártur knew it would be difficult to get the harp out of the boy's hands later. If he wanted to examine it, he had to do so now. Reluctantly, Kavan nodded, agreeing only because he wanted Ártur's honest appraisal. Ártur might not have followed his father into the family harp-making trade, but he had grown up around harps, had seen them in every stage of production, and thus would know more about this one's value then Kavan would.

"Cliáthan quarter-scale…unique wood and design, unlike anything I've ever seen in our shop. Likely commissioned for someone of wealth. A work of art to be treasured." He turned the instrument upside down and located the insignia on its base, the seal which all genuine Cliáthans bore. Each harp maker changed the seal a small amount to distinguish one craftsman from another, even within families. "Unless I am mistaken," he murmured in awe, "this was crafted by your great-grandfather."

Kavan knew enough of his family history to know that it meant this instrument was at least five hundred years old. For any instrument to have survived that long, in such pristine condition, meant that it had been well cared for, which made it even more of a mystery how a blind beggar in Rhidam could have possessed it.

"This is the one the beggar had," he murmured, taking it back and caressing the wood, "when Prince Owain and I..."

Intending to ask the King how he had come into possession of it, Ártur prepared for bed as Kavan silently tuned the strings. At least, the healer assumed that was what Kavan was doing as he touched each string without making a sound and then turned the screws that adjusted their tension. By the time the candles were extinguished and Ártur had settled in the bed, the boy was already playing simple melodies the way the family craftsmen did to test an instrument's quality.

Lying in the darkness, comfortable beside his cousin, Ártur mused over Kavan's many budding talents. There was no musical ability in their family beyond the basics that any man or woman could do, and Kavan had never received formal training. He had picked up a harp in the family workshop and began creating melodies when he was three years old, influenced, no doubt, by hearing his uncle and cousin tuning their creations before a sale. By the age of five, Kavan was performing worship songs at Gatherings and composing tunes far beyond the scope of most children his age. Ártur had been in Bhryell more often in those days to witness it, and he knew that he was not the only one to wonder what Kavan's skill would be like when he was grown, if he was allowed to continue this path. Some seemed to see such drive and talent in one so young as pretentious, especially in a boy as visibly different as Kavan was, and knowing this, Kavan insisted that no one understood him. He was already becoming jaded and increasingly reluctant to share his talents. Please, the healer prayed as he drifted into sleep, do not let them kill what is growing here, for like his faith, he knew Kavan's talent ran deep. Given the chance, it would not be long before the entire world knew of Kavan's gifts, and when that happened, few would find that talent amusing any longer.

Long after he heard the heavy breathing of his cousin's slumber, Kavan stopped playing, content that the instrument he held was not only in excellent condition but also superb in quality. He held the harp to his chest, rubbing his fingers over the insignia that linked him to the harp's maker. It was in need of a proper cleaning and could use new strings, but he could find no other faults with it. He could imagine his uncle's amazement, but Kavan would allow no one to take this treasure away from him. He would only give it up if he were able to return it to its rightful owner. This was of far better quality than any harp he had been allowed to play at home. And for now, it was his. Overjoyed, he placed it in its case and fell asleep with it tucked snugly under his arm.

To the relief of those who understood what was happening behind the façade of the royal family, the day of the coronation proved calm and uneventful. As Kavan watched from his seat near the front of the gathering, he knew that this was not the coronation he had glimpsed the night before. The angles of the imagery were wrong, and though similar in build, King Donal was not the man Kavan had envisioned.

Prince Bowen behaved in an unexpectedly civil fashion throughout the morning, mingling with the lords and ladies of the kingdom in a way that none were aware of the high tensions in the House of Lachlan. His appearance at the following banquet, however, was barely perfunctory and he slipped away as early as he could manage it. No one but Kavan appeared to notice, or if they did, it was not addressed. Though Prince Owain and Lady Ula attended the coronation, neither were at the banquet and only once did Kavan see the young prince's face peering dejectedly through a doorway before quickly disappearing. The day would end with a festival of dancing and music, but as one of only a few children in the keep, Kavan would not attend. His interests instead were finding the prince to bid him a proper farewell, and playing music of his own. The prince, however, could not be found, and that night, the music would not come. Kavan gave in to a restless night's sleep full of vaguely disturbing dream images that he could not recall upon waking.

Precisely at daybreak the following day, he was awakened by the sound of the portcullis opening and the clatter of wheels over stone as the coach containing Lady Ula and Prince Owain departed in the direction of her homeland of Neth. There was no fanfare, only the fading rumble of the wheels, and then the thud as the portcullis closed behind them, cutting them off from the royal family within the walls of the castle. No one had been there to see them off, to bid them farewell, not even Prince Bowen or the King.

And as he watched from his cousin's window until the coach could no longer be seen or heard, Kavan was overcome with the peculiar sense that someday he would be here again.

෨Chapter 6෨

As far as Ártur's healing gifts could determine, there was nothing wrong with Llyárá Cliáth's unborn first child. The rhythm of its heart was strong and Ártur detected a clear sense of self about the child, but thus far there had been no discernible movement. The healer could not offer the woman an explanation, but he visited her frequently and did his best to assure her that the child would be born healthy.

It was only her nephew's words that gave the woman peace. Conception was difficult for Elyri, and often pregnancies did not make it to term, and infants did not always live beyond their first year of life. If Ártur claimed the child was healthy, Llyárá chose to believe it. She did not believe he would lie to her about something this important.

She sat in the living room of her small home, sewing clothes for the child, awaiting the return of her husband from the village where he had traveled on horse to bring Ártur to them. With the birth imminent, the healer had promised to remain with them until the infant arrived. At times she wondered if such a promise revealed concern on his part for the health of the still child, but it was likely, she knew, nothing more than a normal worry from a healer and family member. There was always concern for the survival of the unborn, and the newborn. Surely Ártur's was nothing out of the ordinary.

There was the promise of rain in the cold tenth month's air, but it was warm before the hearth fire and she soon dozed, dreaming of the days and years ahead with this gift of a child she had been blessed with. A soft rapping on the door roused her from her dreams; with a groan, she lay aside the sewing that had partially slid from her lap and got wearily to her feet. It would not be either her husband or her nephew, as they would never have knocked. But the sound repeated, telling her it was not the sound of the wind knocking branches against the house either.

"Pardon the intrusion, dhábhyne," said the man on her porch. At least, the voice sounded masculine; she could tell nothing else about the figure wrapped in a hooded gray cloak that was soaked through with the rain that was pouring down at last. "I am separated from my company and have lost my way. Have you a room or a barn perhaps where I may wait out this storm?"

Having never been one to fear strangers, and sensing no evil about this visitor, she ushered him into her home. Violent crimes were practically unheard of in Elyriá; it never crossed her mind that he could be a threat. She took him at his word as she said, "Of course. Let me hang your cloak to dry. Have you eaten? Would you care for food or drink?"

The stranger lowered his dripping hood with gloved hands, revealing a face that looked much younger in the pale light of the oil lamps and fire then he sounded when he spoke. Even the deepness of his dark green eyes belied that youthfulness. As was typical of Elyri, his face bore no trace of beard and his weather-tousled hair was a deep sun-kissed copper color. She thought him handsome and managed an easy smile as he handed her the weather-beaten cloak. "Do not trouble yourself at this hour. Water will suffice…"

"Nonsense," she clucked. "If you are to be our guest, you must eat. The evening meal is already prepared and warm. Please, sit and comfort yourself while I fetch it."

He smiled and bowed his head. "As you wish," he murmured as he sat by the fire to warm his cold hands. With his gloves on his lap, he looked around while he waited, taking in the simple décor that suggested a mid-class family. No more than was needed to live comfortably, save for a few trinkets of art and family portraits that decorated the walls and mantle. Those small touches, common in the majority of homes in Elyriá, made him feel at ease and he relaxed until she returned with a tray of steaming barley soup, a chunk of thick bread, a slab of roast pork, and bit of cheese, along with a pitcher of water and small wooden cup.

"Thank you, Dhábhyne," he said. His sleeves fell back to reveal his hands and wrists for the first time as he took the tray from her. They were badly scarred as if burned, but his face showed no similar damage, causing her to wonder how he came by such an injury. It would be rude to ask, however; instead, she turned her gaze and attention to the large, silver, T- cross that hung around his neck on a silver chain, the sort of cross often called the Kílyn Cross or sometimes the Cross of Saint Kóráhm.

"Are you gdhededhá then?" she asked. While he did not bear the tonsure of a holy man of the Faith, that relic suggested otherwise. Perhaps he had not yet taken vows.

He shook his head. After swallowing what he had in his mouth he replied, "No, only a pilgrim to Hes Dhágdhuán in Clarys."

"Ah." Her home was far off the road to Clarys; he must have been lost from his companions for a long time, traveling from one of the smaller villages further up in the mountains. This might have made some suspicious, but it gave Llyárá no feeling of alarm. Pilgrims to Hes Dhágdhuán were a common occurrence throughout the year and there were many roads one could take to get there. Getting lost on the way, if one did not travel there frequently, was easy, particularly in the dark or in bad weather. It took her several moments to determine what occasion he might be attending at this time of year, and when she did, she smiled. It was the eve of the Feast of Saint Kóráhm, and Clarys was the only city in Elyriá that still honored that day. Judging by the relic he wore, he had good cause to be drawn there for the Feast.

She picked up her sewing and resumed it as he ate, not wanting to disturb him. It was a comfortable silence punctuated occasionally by the clink of his spoon against the soup bowl. So engrossed was she in her work that several moments of silence passed before she noticed him watching her. When she did notice, he nodded his head and asked, "Your child…it is due soon."

It was more of a statement than a question, but Llyárá nodded in response, thinking him a healer perhaps though he did not wear the healer yellow. He leaned forward, reaching with one hand, but stopped short of touching her swollen belly. "May I?"

There was nothing common in that question. No one other than a healer, a spouse, or one's children would have the right to touch a woman in that way. The question once again suggested to Llyárá that he was a healer, and she readily nodded in agreement. As his scarred hand made contact, she felt a jerking thump within that made her lurch back in surprise. The baby had moved. There was nothing else that sensation could have been. For the first time in her pregnancy, the child had moved. Her green eyes met the stranger's, wide with surprise, and were greeted with a warm smile.

"He will bring people much hope and joy but will know little of that happiness himself. Guard him carefully, Dhábhyne. For my sake."

"A boy?" she asked, feeling an ache begin within her heart at the thought of her child leading a less than happy life.

He nodded once. "Forgive me, Dhábhyne. It is given to me to know such things, but I may reveal no more than I know." He set the empty tray on a low table and got to his feet. "May I take my rest? I must continue my journey early and I am weary to my soul."

Llyárá stood. "Yes, certainly. Please forgive my inhospitality. Come with me." She led him out of the main room, up the stairs, and to a plain guest room containing a bed, dressing table, and a small stand with a washbasin and chamber pot of beaten copper. Most often her nephew slept here, but for this one night, she did not believe he would begrudge this traveler a dry room. "Do you require anything more?"

"No. This will suffice, thank you. No one can accuse you of inhospitality, Dhábhyne." He smiled again as he clasped her hands, and once again the baby within her moved.

"Rest then," she said in awe, "and I will have breakfast for you in the morn."

He bowed, and when she began to turn away, he caught her wrist. For a moment, neither of them moved; she stared at his hand on her arm and then up into his eyes, aware that his touch once more summoned movement inside of her. "I have waited long for this night, Dhábhyne; it is no small miracle that has brought me to you at this time, and I thank you for it."

Before she could speak to ask what he meant, he released her, stepped back, and closed the bedroom door between them. The child kicked again. Shakily she stood for several minutes, listening to the sounds within the room, enchanted by the feeling of life she carried and perplexed by the stranger's words. Only when the movement ceased did she realize that she had neither filled his wash basin nor gotten his name. She would ask him in the morning, she decided, and if he asked for wash water before she slept, she would fetch it then.

She intended to return to her sewing while awaiting her husband and nephew. The stranger's gloves lay on the bench beside where he had been sitting; she placed them on the table where he would be sure to see them at breakfast and then decided to clean away the remains of his meal.

There was another powerful kick, and a sudden squeezing stab that pulsed through her abdomen, followed shortly by wetness that seeped down her legs and through her layered clothing. Though this was her first child, she needed no healer to tell her what that meant. She hurried with her cleanup, set water to boil over the fire, and found every towel and cloth she could. She could not rely on her husband and nephew to arrive in time. Elyri children often came quickly once labor began; she knew there was no time to waste.

Fortunately, she did not have to wait long before her family came through the door. Rístyrd paced the living room or stood on the porch watching the falling rain, while Ártur, their nephew and one of the best healers they knew, remained at her side into the night. He encouraged her to walk, to drink the tea he prepared for her that would ease the worst of the pain, sang to her and held her hand when the final tearing began. A believer in the old ways, as most Elyri were, he squatted with her in front of the fire, breathing with her, using his gifts to lessen the pain and attempt to regulate her contractions. And in those moments before the warm fingers of dawn greeted the cold morning, the child came into the world, dropping into Ártur's waiting hands. Llyárá rocked back and collapsed onto the pile of blankets and pillows arranged on the floor around her as she watched her nephew sever the birthing cord that bound her to her son. The infant reflexively clutched the man's finger in his tiny fist and refused to release it.

"A boy," Ártur said, feeling those small green eyes boring into his face as he cleaned the afterbirth from the child's skin. "But he is not…typical…"

"I know…" At least she thought she did. The extent of his differences was not known until she took her son from the healer's hands. Only then did he release Ártur's finger. Only then did she see what her nephew meant. The babe's skin was as white as fresh clouds, his hair the pale silver of the receding moonlight. Those eyes that had ensnared the healer did the same to her, peeping out of his paleness like spring grass pushing through the snow. It was easy to see in that uniqueness how the stranger's words might be true. Whatever his future, the child would always be set apart. She stroked his cheek gently, marveling at the miracle of her son.

"Not even I knew…"

"There is a pilgrim put up in the guestroom…his gloves are on the table." She gestured in that direction with one hand. "He said the child would be a boy…would be special…would bring hope and joy to many but know little himself…he said I must guard him…and when he touched me, the babe moved. Truly moved, Ártur, for the first time."

Perplexed, and certain that she and the child would be safe by the fire, Ártur kissed the top of her head and stood. He went first to tell Rístyrd, who waited on the porch, that his wife and child were healthy, and then went upstairs to the guestroom. There was no response to his knock on the door, no sounds of any sort, and he cracked the door open far enough to peer inside. Though he expected to see someone asleep in the bed, the room was empty; the only indication that anyone had been there was a glint of silver on the dressing table. It was a symbol he recognized, but it made him more curious as he returned downstairs for the gloves on the table. Outside, the rain had stopped.

"I do not think your visitor was truly here," Ártur said quietly, knowing how incredible that must sound. But unless the man had gone out the upstairs window and made the long drop to the muddy ground in the rain, he would have had to pass the pair in the main room to depart…and he had not. No one else had been in or out of this room since Rístyrd had stepped outside save for Llyárá and Ártur. "The only proofs of his presence are these." He handed over first the gloves and then the silver brooch.

"The cross of málneag Kóráhm…he wore a pendant like that." She fingered the supple gray gloves and rubbed the velvety smoothness against the infant's cheek, causing him to coo happily. "His hands," she murmured with a note of wonder in her voice, "they were badly scarred as if he had been burned…but surely it could not be…Ártur? It did not occur to me before that he could be…do you think it was…?"

The healer sank into the nearest chair and rubbed his eyes. Rístyrd squatted beside his wife, touching her and the child, listening as they spoke. It was possible, Ártur supposed. Each year on the eve of his martyrdom there were reports and claims of seeing Saint Kóráhm, but Ártur had never given the claims serious thought. But he knew Llyárá would not lie about such a tale, and someone had clearly been in the house to leave those items behind. Who it was, however, the healer could not say.

"Kavan Kóráhm Cliáth," Llyárá whispered to the babe in her arms after a glance at her husband. The man beside her nodded in confirmation and agreement.

"You have named him?" It was considered bad luck to name a child soon after birth, as more often than not, Elyri children failed to live to their first birthday.

"If the Saint has blessed him, if he is to fulfill the Saint's words, of course, he will live. This way…he will always know who walks through life with him. He will always be protected." Rístyrd smiled, though it was one touched by melancholy as he, like his wife, wondered what lay in store for their son that warranted such a visitation on the night of his birth.

But neither would ever know. Shortly before Kavan's first birthday, fire consumed both their house and the harp makers' shop that was attached to it. Ártur had been there on one of his frequent visits; he, Llyárá, and the child had escaped but Rístyrd died in the blaze while attempting to save some of his work from destruction. The boy and his mother had afterward lived with Ártur's father, who was Rístyrd's half-brother. They took with them only the clothing they wore and the brooch and gloves that Kavan's first visitor had left behind. Not long after, the plague had swept through the Five Sovereignties, claiming both Llyárá and Ártur's older sister Hwíletá, and almost killing Ártur's father. Thus the orphaned child found himself in his aunt and uncle's care, with only Ártur knowing the reason the child bore the name of Elyriá's Heretic-Saint, and he guarded that secret, and his small cousin, with all of the care and love his parents could no longer give.

Escorting Kavan into the heart of Bhryell, Ártur wondered if the unusually early appearance of Elyri talent in his cousin was in some way connected to that stranger's visits and the prophetic words spoken that night. Kavan had learned to speak and read earlier than most, not only in the Elyri vernacular but in the old language and the Trade language of the Kingdoms. He exhibited great interest in knowledge of all sorts and showed a zeal and understanding of Faith that troubled most clergy who met him. Some thought Kavan precocious and pretentious, but Ártur knew better. There was no falsehood in Kavan. He was the most honest individual the healer knew.

All Elyri had some degree of natural talent, it, along with some physical differences, set them apart from the Teren, but it required several years of training to shape the energies properly and utilize that talent fully. Kavan seemed on his way towards mastery without any formal education. Training most often did not occur until a child was eight or nine years old, old enough to have some semblance of maturity and control of themselves and would continue until either the limit of one's natural gifts was reached or one chose to cease learning. Most Elyri opted for a shorter tenure; learning only the skills necessary to control their innate power was usually accomplished by the age of twelve or thirteen. Others sometimes chose not to begin training until they were much older, and a rare few received no training at all, but they were considered hwonághk: dangerous renegades, people who could not be trusted, a threat to themselves and others around them.

If Ártur's father had his way, Kavan would have been given the choice to train on his tenth birthday, as Ártur's brother and sister had been given. With Ártur, the choice had been different, because as with all healers, the traits that allowed them that path in life were present from birth. He had been trained accordingly, beginning as soon as he was able to walk and speak. Healers were common in Dháná's family and were widely accepted among the Elyri population, thus Tám had no misgivings about allowing Ártur that extended training, though he would rather have had his youngest son join him in the harp making trade.

There was little strong Elyri talent in Tám and Rístyrd's families. They were harp-makers several generations old. Llyárá's family had not displayed unusual talent either, at least in recent generations, and thus the fact that Kavan had shown such a strong display of Power at such a young age caused the elder MacLyr great consternation. When Ártur raised the issue of Kavan's training, his father tried to demand that the matter would wait, but when confronted with the news of Kavan's instinctive defensive attack on a bully in the castle, with Ártur tactfully leaving out the bully's identity, Tám was forced to admit that not to train Kavan promptly could mean embarrassment at the least, disaster at the worst. The last thing any Teren needed was an excuse to kill an Elyri. They had enough excuses as it was. There was no choice but to allow Ártur to take Kavan before the Bhryell lómesté to discuss early training. Ártur had strategically left out the mention of the handlight and the fact that Kavan had successfully navigated the Gate on their return from Rhidam. To Ártur's knowledge, no child, especially an untrained one as young as Kavan, had ever done that.

The lómesté met in a low wooden building, much of which was nestled into the earth so that it looked to be only half a building tall. There were steps dug downwards to the door and the clay tile roof was slanted towards the back of the building so that rain and snow did not easily accumulate in the doorway. Red brick disappeared into the ground, serving as the foundation for the oak walls above. It was one of the oldest buildings in Bhryell, older than the bhydáni who met there on a regular basis.

It was a building that Kavan had never dreamed he would enter. He knew Tam's opinion of those inside, of Elyri gifts in general; it had been logical to presume he would not see the inside of this building until he was much older. Today he was here, the focus of the seven bhydáni who greeted them and listened patiently to the healer's accounts of both Kavan's abilities and family history. This was the first time Kavan had heard the story of his birth, and while he felt a glow of pride, he did not fail to notice the disapproving expressions on many faces at the mention of Kóráhm's possible manifestation. Only a single man, one of the few in the room, with sparse patches of silky white hair and an almost skeletal thinness, nodded with a spark of approval in his intense gray eyes. He wore a look of a man with a purpose, a mission, a look that intensified until he eventually ushered Ártur out of the building. It was time for the lómesté to test the boy alone, without the interference or influence of his cousin.

The healer stood in the snow, staring at the sky; when he shivered it was not because of the cold. He had heard of llánec as it was prevalent in Elyri mythology, folklore, and history, but he had never known, or heard of, anyone alive who possessed it. Inevitably, those who did were reputed to have other unique, powerful talents. Most frequently they had been healers. But Kavan would not be a healer; nothing in him indicated that path of power. What then, Ártur wondered would his cousin's gift be?

The creak of the door disturbed his musings, drawing his gaze away from where the breeze lifted a fine mist of snow and pulled it through the boughs of a naked oak. It was the same bhydáni who had ushered him out of the building earlier. Ártur knew the man by reputation, almost everyone in Bhryell did. Tíbhyan was one of the oldest bhydáni in the land, and one of the few men to hold an office most often held by women. When the stooped figure motioned him closer, Ártur obeyed, bending down to hear him though he had never conversed with the man before.

"I have not seen another like this in all my years of teaching," the Elder said. "Perhaps not even before. We have not had the chance to discuss him amongst ourselves; the others are still speaking with him, but they will agree when I say he should begin training at once. There are many latent talents waiting to emerge, many which will likely show as a result of our testing. If he is to use them properly, he must be educated."

Was it common for gifts to awaken that way, Ártur wanted to ask, but he decided to get to the point. "Then I shall have him report to class?"

Tíbhyan shook his head so hard that his entire body swayed from side to side, making him appear as if he would topple over under the effort. "No. Not class. He shall require private instruction. With the extraordinary extent to which he carries the gifts and his intense natural accord with the power, class would not be appropriate. He is already far ahead of the youngest students. To place him in their midst may either inhibit him or produce hostility, inferiority, or fear in the others. There are none of his peers with whom he can train. Private instruction will allow him to proceed as he will." He put his hand on the healer's arm. "I would be honored to accept the responsibility of his instruction."

Stunned, the healer stared at him. "You are a man of high reputation and great talent. bhydhá is not pleased with Kavan's early show of talent; if he had his way Kavan would remain untrained for another four years. He has only agreed to this because it is necessary to avoid the social stigma of neglecting it. He would be unwilling to pay your usual stipend, even if he could." He sighed and looked at the closed door at the bottom of the steps. "But I too sense Kavan's potential and know he must be trained. It cannot wait. He wants it; I want it for him.

I can pay you for as long as I remain at Enesfel's court, if that is acceptable."

"Do you expect to be released?" What Tíbhyan knew of political matters outside of Elyriá came from reports that were often many weeks old by the time they arrived.

Ártur shook his head. "Not for many years…but after that, who can say? The tides of politics ebb and flow. Each royal death brings changes; what is accepted today may not be tomorrow."

The sage nodded knowingly. "Indeed. But it will do, ílMairós. If that time comes before his training is complete, we will make other arrangements, you and I. Many of my peers are intimidated by your cousin despite his young age, but I'm certain there will be some who will be as eager to train one such as him as I am. For that reason alone, I will accept half my normal fee, if you will agree to my offer. I want this student, ílMairós. I want to see him grow."

The offer of a reduced fee was even more unexpected than the offer of private tutelage. To be tutored privately by any of the bhydáni was the dream of many youngsters. To be taught by one of the top ten sages in all of Elyriá, to have been chosen by him rather than having sent a petition for education, was an honor that even Tám would have to acknowledge and be proud of. To reject this offer would be considered rude and would be one of the ultimate acts of foolishness an Elyri could commit. The healer lowered his head and bowed from the waist, pleased to have his father backed into this particular corner. "Your offer is generous, bhydáni. I accept your terms with gratitude."

The bhydáni smiled, tottered slowly back down the steps, and opened the door to beckon Kavan to join him outside, despite the looks of annoyance on the faces of others inside. The boy's face was blank except for a bemused sparkle in his eyes as the man's gnarled hand squeezed his shoulder with surprising strength in its gentleness. "I should be the one thanking you, ílMairós. You can be certain this is a responsibility I do not take lightly. You will have every resource and benefit I can provide. Good day to you…and to you, young Cliáth."

Once the ancient man disappeared back into the building with the door closed behind him, Kavan followed his cousin away without speaking. He cast Ártur a few sidelong glances but the healer appeared lost in thought and Kavan did not intrude on his private musings. Truthfully, he was afraid of what Ártur's pensive expression might mean. It was not until they had purchased Kavan's favorite fresh barley bread from the town's baker and sat together on the bench in the shade of the establishment's porch that Kavan finally worked up the nerve to speak.

"I am not good enough, am I?"

"Not…?" Ártur began to cough as the bit of bread he was chewing stuck in his throat. "What makes you think that?"

The boy's shoulders shrugged imperceptibly. "They asked me questions and read me as you have done before…then there were more questions before I was summoned outdoors and sent away. If I met their criteria they would have told me…wouldn't they?"

"The bhydáni do not always do things like everyone else. They are individuals of few words and unusual behaviors. When you have lived as long as they have, you do not need to say much and eccentricities are to be expected. Believe me, they were impressed enough that it has been suggested you begin training at once. bhydáni Tíbhyan is to be your private tutor."

At first, Kavan said nothing. His bread was placed on his lap and he stared absently into his open palm. A flame sprang up there, dancing to what seemed to Ártur to be a frustrated rhythm. Such easy mastery made Ártur's heart swell with pride.

As quickly as it had come to life, it was crushed as Kavan's hand curled into a small fist. "I do not want a private tutor. I want to learn with the other children."

The healer cocked his head. "Why? You do not play with them…"

Kavan threw a bit of crust to the raven at his feet. The bird caught it and flew to the safety of a tree branch to savor its treat. "I do not play with them because they ridicule and avoid me...and I do not understand their games. They think I am odd because I look different...because I enjoy different things. aene Dháná says to ignore what they say, but it is hard to do when it means I am always alone. Now the bhydáni say I am different too. If I do not receive training with the others, it will reinforce their opinions of me."

Ártur leaned against the wall, thinking of no way to refute that assertion. If he and some of the bhydáni felt dwarfed by the power the six-year-old boy possessed, untrained and unfocused though it was, how could the boy's peers feel any differently?

"Unfortunately, Kavan, you are different. I have never known any untrained child who could successfully manipulate the k'rylag on their first attempt. I have never known, or heard of, any your age mature enough in the power to attempt it, and most do not even care to try. I did not until I was twelve, and it took me many weeks to learn how. You cannot get much different than that."

The melancholy that touched the small face was almost tangible, and Ártur regretted what he had said. He sensed, however, that underneath that disappointment, Kavan appreciated his honesty. Many would have told him what they thought he wanted to hear or would have stressed the honor and privilege of private tutelage and pushed him to accept the honor for the family, whether he wished to or not. All Kavan wanted was the truth, the chance to see his choices and choose his own path.

"That does not mean I want to be different."

Ártur nodded and ruffled Kavan's hair. "I know. No one wants to be different. But think on this. There are no others your age receiving training. Postponing it for a year or two...to school you with them would not be wise. Next time you are cornered, you might seriously injure someone without intending to. If you are as gifted as bhydáni

Tíbhyan suggests, and I see no reason to think he is lying, to put you in a class with older children will either inhibit you or make the others resentful…"

Brushing crumbs from his lap, Kavan murmured, "I think they will be resentful regardless; either way I am alone."

The healer watched him cross the street and disappear into the copyist's shop. He had never considered that being gifted could isolate a person as much as it appeared to be doing to his cousin. Or maybe it would not be as bad as Kavan feared. He wondered how he would have fared in the boy's place, what he would have done to survive it. Knowing himself as he did, perhaps he would not have survived it at all.

He took his time with his meal, knowing that Kavan was safe in the shop and knowing the boy wanted to be alone. He was rising from the bench when Kavan appeared in the doorway, waving excitedly.

"Ártur! Come! Look!" he cried before dashing back inside. Kavan rarely exhibited such excitement, and so Ártur hurried to find him in a back corner amidst some large volumes that, from the layers of dust on and around them, had not been moved in some time. Leave it to Kavan, he mused with a wry smile, to find such a collection and be excited about it. Some of the stacks had been shifted and Kavan held a book towards him. Ártur took it, turned it to read the binding, and inhaled sharply in surprise. It was the Second Volume of the Articles of Kóráhm. It was a newer manuscript than the first volume he had bought for Kavan, with less wear on the cover and no yellowing to the pages, in spite of the thick, gray dust covering it. It too was written in the lyrical, poetic phrases of High Elyri, as the first volume had been, making it an equally rare find. Ártur peered around the shelves, eyeing the copyist, wondering if the man knew this was here. Only true collectors, and brave ones at that, would hold any of the banned volumes in their possession and keep them out in the open for others to find.

"May I have it Ártur? I have money; King Donal gave it to me."
In his outstretched palm were ten gold bhelts, a significant amount of
money by any standards, but the healer did not doubt Kavan's words.
Kavan was not a thief and King Donal was a generous man, especially
to those he was as fond of as he was of Kavan. "If it is more, I will
repay you. Please?"

"If it is more, I will be surprised," Ártur grunted. If the copyist
valued his job and his life, he would probably be grateful to get the
book out of sight. Since it seemed that Kavan had, at least temporarily,
set aside his despair, the healer found he could not refuse the request.

The copyist did indeed look as surprised to see the book as Ártur
had been, and as the healer expected, was so relieved to be rid of it
that he gave it to Kavan at no cost. Knowing he was respected in
Bhryell, both because of his family name and his healer status, Ártur
did not fear being reported to the Faith authorities over possession of
the banned book, particularly since the copyist would not want to be
associated with it. He did not think the gdhededhá would persecute a
boy for having them, and he knew that Kavan would protect them,
keep them safe and out of sight. His main concern was that word of
the 'purchase' might reach his father, but watching Kavan happily
clutch that book to his chest for the remainder of their walk home was
reason enough, in Ártur's eyes, for the transaction. It was only a book
after all. What harm could there be in words?

On the porch of their home, Kavan stopped with his hand on the
rail and a troubled look on his face as he stared at the door. Only now
did it occur to him the risk he was taking in bringing this book home,
in possessing it. He did not understand why the books had been
banned, or why Kóráhm was called both Heretic and Saint, but he
wanted to. Felt he needed to, especially after what he had heard earlier.
Much in his world had changed in the span of a single day; it overwhelmed him.

"Is it true, Ártur…that Saint Kóráhm came to my mother the night I was born?"

The healer's smile was bemused. "We never knew who he was. I did not see him, nor did your father, and your mother never told me more beyond his auburn hair and scarred hands. If it was not the Saint, then it was a messenger or follower. There was no doubt someone had been there…"

"And you still have the gloves he left? And the brooch?"

The hopeful light in those green eyes told Ártur what was coming next and he chuckled. "I planned to give them to you when you were old enough to appreciate them…older…but I can give them to you now if you wish." He did not think, given the course of the day, that there would ever be a better time. As much as Kavan treasured the Saint's writings, the healer knew he would likewise treasure the relics left to him.

Kavan looked down at the four-inch thick volume nestled against his chest. "I would like that," he murmured. "Though I shall need a bigger trunk…and a lock…"

Appreciating Kavan's understanding of the gravity of his treasures, Ártur replied, "I will find what you need if you agree to keep them out of his sight."

"I will," Kavan agreed, caressing the leather covering with one hand. "If the tale is true…if it was Saint Kóráhm…then maybe as he said, I am different for a reason. I will study with bhydáni Tíbhyan if aendhá permits. There seems to be no reasonable alternative…and perhaps it is what I am intended to do." For all of the certainty of his words, his tone of voice undercut them with fear; it was no surprise when he abruptly pressed his face into Ártur's stomach. The gesture brought an automatic tight embrace and a lump in the healer's throat.

"Promise me you will always come back to me, Ártur. I cannot…it will be lonely without you."

Smoothing the long white hair as he swallowed back tears, Ártur whispered, "I promise, Kavan. I have to come back. Elys…you…your music…you're the only things that keep me sane."

Seemingly relieved, or perhaps embarrassed by that moment of emotional weakness, Kavan pulled away and bounded into the house and up to his room without looking back. He would be engrossed in that book until someone pried him away from it. In Ártur's eyes, it was for the best. As far as he was concerned, there was no harm in books, and if this one gave Kavan solace and happiness, it was worth any price in the world he had to pay.

⧼Chapter 7⧽

I n the State Room, King Donal studied the map of the Enesfel-Hatu border that Guthrie had prepared. As with his father before him, King Donal was forced to direct most of his attention, energy, and country's resources to the ongoing hostilities with the southern-most of the Five Sovereignties. Hatu's internal instability, caused by too many immigrants from the south depleting the kingdom's relatively meager resources, had again caused the Hatu armies to turn their frustration into raids along Enesfel's bordering villages and farms. King Innis had won a temporary peace before his death, but it had only lasted fifteen months.

Diplomatic discussions between the countries had thus far failed to produce satisfactory results. King Perren Harcourt had more pressing issues to tend to within his own land, and hence repeatedly snubbed Enesfel's attempts at finding a peaceful settlement. He made it known that should Enesfel interfere in Hatu's politics, war would be waged, and while King Donal did not desire war, he could not sit idle and allow his subjects to be killed and his kingdom to be plundered by marauders. After several meetings with his advisors, the decision was made to send forces south to stop the raids, while preparing the larger bulk of Enesfel's army for the inevitable confrontation on the horizon. That had been three weeks ago, and while the attempts to divert the raids was meeting with a measure of success, the word had finally come that Hatu was amassing its forces, once again readying for war with its neighbor to the north.

"King Perren's men are gathering at these points," Guthrie indicated two areas along the river border that both men knew from battle-hardened experience were the shallowest areas of the river. "The only other place they could approach from would be the coast, but he knows he would be vulnerable there. There is still ice on the river, which might slow them, but if he intends to cross…if we allow it, he will do it with minimal injury."

The King grunted. "There has been no formal declaration of war…only the gathering of forces. As if they do not truly desire a fight…" He rubbed his bearded chin and moved around the table to study the map from a different angle.

"Yes, Your Majesty. They are waiting, doing little else. I estimate these units posted here to be perhaps a third of his total fighting power. The rest are likely employed elsewhere, dealing with whatever threat has roused Harcourt to arms this time. There could be more in route…"

"Or it could be bravado, an attempt to intimidate us into leaving them alone."

"Aye, that does seem their most expected choice, as it seems unlikely they would elect to wage war with so few men." Both knew Hatu's usual tactics and realized that stationing troops there for weeks, troops that could be deployed to fight elsewhere and who could not efficiently attack, or defend, against Enesfel's forces, only made sense if they were meant to be a decoy or deterrent.

King Donal stepped away from the table. "Then we strive to outwit them. Allow them to attend to their own problems, but continue to patrol the border for raiders. Instruct Captain McLeu to take his men to Jardin and await further orders. They will be near enough to intercept trouble yet far enough from the border that King Perren cannot honestly claim we are instigating war. You will keep the remainder of the forces here, ready to march if it becomes necessary. I put you in charge of this campaign, Lord General. Conduct it as you see fit and necessary."

The General nodded his head as he fingered the hilt of his dagger. He was not yet too old to lead Enesfel into battle, but he felt as though he were. There had been too much fighting in his lifetime, and though he was the finest general the kingdom had, it did not mean he savored war. He would, however, obey his King. Over the last year, King Donal had steadily gained the support of his kingdom, proving that he was not the apathetic, inattentive, inept ruler some had feared he might be. The prestige of this confrontation, should Guthrie win it for him, would fortify Donal's position as sovereign.

"Very well, Your Majesty. Is there anything more before I see to the details?" There was more he wanted to say on his own behalf, but he did not. Such things could wait until after the campaign. It was something to be dealt with in the future, not the present.

"No. Keep me abreast of the preparations, of the situation, but beyond that…you are dismissed."

The general bowed, murmured, "Yes, Your Majesty," and then left the room. He crossed the Grand Hall with purposeful steps and exited into the courtyard, his mind whirring with those details and plans the King had put into his hands. He stopped short, however, when he saw the Queen Mother seated on a stone bench watching the one-year-old twins play with a wooden ball, surrounded by a collection of nannies and ladies-in-waiting. The sight of her banished all thoughts of war from his mind. She was, as she always had been to him, the most beautiful and elegant woman in the world, and since King Innis' death, he had avoided her as though one of them carried the plague. He looked around the courtyard, hoping for some other path to where he wanted to go. The only way to reach the bunkhouse was to cross this stretch of courtyard, and she was directly in his path. To go around her would be rude. And should he continue forward, he would be forced to speak with her. They had talked often before her husband's death. Now, such friendliness troubled him.

His brain told him to move, not to stand there staring like a love-struck boy. It would only draw attention. But his feet refused to move. The prince spotted him first and scurried towards him with a yelp of excitement. Once he reached the general, he tugged on the man's pant leg and demanded to be picked up. It was a request Guthrie could not refuse and so he hoisted the boy onto his shoulders. He spent as much time as he could with the children, especially the prince, since their father's death, and was, he knew, the closest thing they would ever know to a father. And for Guthrie, Prince Arlan was the link to the late King that he desperately needed to keep from sliding down a darker path. Though Guthrie was loath to admit it, he and the prince needed each other.

Princess Deidre did not look up as they drew closer to her and her mother. Ártur had determined many months ago that, like others in the Lachlan bloodline, the little girl had been born deaf. When the time came, an Elyri tutor would be hired to teach her to read, write and communicate in a more appropriate fashion, but in the meantime, her handicap made her the darling of the royal court. She was beautiful, even-tempered, and friendly, easily showing affection to anyone who gave it. It was impossible for anyone, even Prince Bowen, not to pamper and love her.

The youngest prince, however, did not share that welcome. To many, he was just another prince in a long line of Lachlan princes. The King was the only one to pay the child any attention, frequently playing with him or carrying him around the castle when duties did not fill his time. Sometimes Guthrie wondered if the King was considering making Prince Arlan the heir to the throne since the King had no surviving children. Knowing that Prince Bowen, at least, would be furious about such a choice, the general chose not to mention the possibility of succession to the King. He would not be the one to place the young prince in the path of Bowen's wrath. The King would do what he believed best when the time came to do it. Guthrie trusted the monarch's choices.

Holding the boy in front of him as if he were a shield, the general reluctantly approached the woman with a forced smile. Her smile in return, however, while strained, was not forced. She appeared genuinely happy to see him and it made his stomach flutter giddily. When he bowed, she waved her hand.

"None of that, Lord McHador," she said lightly. "Good day to you."

He straightened as she wished after putting the prince down, and adjusted his clothes. "Good day to you, My Queen. How are the children this morning?"

Her smile was softened by a chuckle. With the weight of affairs of state having passed to Donal's wife, Cordelia was free to tend to her children and enjoy the simpler aspects of life. That, and having passed through mourning for her husband, had left her appearing younger, an effect Guthrie too frequently noticed. While King Innis had lived, keeping the fondness for the queen hidden had been a matter of respect and survival, and something Guthrie had found easy to do. Now that the man was gone, however, Guthrie stubbornly tried to cling to the honor of unrequited love, in spite of the increasing difficulty of doing so. He could not bring himself to ask anything more than the friendship they shared.

"I am queen no longer, Lord General. Please do not call me that." She gestured to the children. "As you can see, the children are healthy."

"Aye," he said quietly, watching the children play. Watching them meant he did not have to look directly at the woman beside him.

"You have been avoiding me, milord."

Guthrie swallowed hard, ashamed that she had noticed but unable to explain the why of it, particularly in the company of so many other women. Refusing to show his nervousness more than he felt was already obvious, he drew his shoulders back and said, "We may be at war soon."

The woman sighed; she had hoped that he would answer her indirect question but she was not surprised he did not. She wondered if he would have answered a direct one instead, but sensing his discomfort, she chose not to push the matter in this public place. "With Hatu?"

"The King is hoping to avoid it," he said, relieved to be talking about a non-personal subject, "but we both know it is inevitable. War with Hatu always is; they turn on us when they have other difficulties as if it will help them. If the Harcourts would pool their resources into a single venture, they might not have these continuing problems. It is a wonder their choices are tolerated. I have been given command..."

"As you should be," she said emphatically. "You know King Perren's strategies better than anyone, and you are the best military mind we have. Is that where you are off to? More preparations? Are you to leave soon?"

The general shook his head, feeling both the need to leave and the desire not to go to war again, not to leave her here. "Captain McLeu is being sent south. It should be me, but I believe the King still fears for his safety. Prince Bowen has been more unpredictable lately, spending most of his time away, or leering and brooding..."

Rather than voice her thoughts, Cordelia looked away and watched Deidre examine a nearby flower bush. Prince Bowen would be a thorn in Enesfel's side for as long as he was allowed to remain in Rhidam. There was little to be done about it. But it would not be enough to keep Guthrie out of an impending war. He would go, and she would worry about never seeing him again until the day he returned. She wished, as he shifted his weight, that they could speak frankly before those days came. Instead, all she could say was, "I will detain you no longer, milord...and I will look forward to speaking with you again."

By the look on the general's face, that was a prospect he both longed for and dreaded.

ᴈ◦*◦ᴈ

Kavan glanced across the wooden table at bhydáni Tíbhyan who leaned back in his chair, spidery arms folded across his barrel chest, apparently dozing. It was something the sage did often, causing Kavan to suspect that much of the time it was merely an act, a test to see how dedicated the boy was to his studies, to see if he would continue without supervision or if he would find some means of distracting himself. As Kavan would never dream of disappointing the old man or neglecting his work, being too eager to learn, he had never put his curious theories to the test. After the first few months together, time spent in the basics of psychic training that Kavan proved unusually adept at, it had been decided that the bhydáni would assume the role of teacher in every other discipline too. It made little sense to postpone other learning if Kavan was ready for it and already studying on his own.

Kavan had objected to the idea at first, but the objection had not lasted long. None of his peers could read or write at the level he did. Most were just beginning to learn. When they were frolicking in the streets or in their homes, Kavan was either reading books intended for mature readers or playing his harp. Gaining the exclusive attention of bhydáni Tíbhyan meant that Kavan could continue to pursue and enjoy his pastimes, and learning, without facing a constant barrage of ridicule or questions from the other children or their parents. No one had to know the details of that exclusive tutelage; that was between the sage, gdhededhá Bhílári, Kavan's guardians, and Kavan. Ultimately, it gained him and his family a measure of envy from others who wished their children had such exclusive mentoring, and this envy translated into an upward shift in social status for the MacLyrs that Tám was pleased about. It lessened his aggravation with Kavan; it was more important that the boy progressed sufficiently in his studies, to keep that exclusive arrangement in place, then it was to try to force him into the harp making business.

"Daydreaming?" asked the cracked voice, though the teacher never opened his eyes.

Kavan blinked and looked back from the open window. "I was thinking about Saint Kóráhm." He was not sure if that was considered daydreaming.

"You have many questions about him." The old man leaned forward, emerging from his stupor to engage in conversation. When he unfolded his arms from across his chest, Kavan was struck again by how thin they were.

"This mentions him," Kavan replied with a nod, indicating the faded manuscript he had been reading, "but without much detail. He is rarely anything more than a name rushed over in the books I have read. gdhededhá Bhílári will not discuss him when I ask. He was canonized...yet is called traitor and heretic...but why? What did he do?"

"It is not what he did," Tíbhyan explained, "though many then, as now, question the appropriateness of some of his actions. It is his writings that are considered offensive, particularly by the gdhededhá..."

Kavan cocked his head with a puzzled look on his face. "I have read nothing offensive in the first two volumes of his works...though there are discrepancies with the canonical teachings..."

"You have read the first two volumes of Kóráhm's articles?" the old man asked in disbelief.

Feeling as if he was shrinking inside, Kavan tried not to squirm in his chair. He had been warned to keep those books secret. He knew that merely owning them could be punishable by both the secular and religious authorities. But he was an honest boy at heart, with a deep desire to understand everything around him, and though he was tempted to deny it, he knew he could not. Particularly not with

Tíbhyan, whom he believed he could trust to keep his secret and who was most likely to provide him with answers.

"I have both," he admitted quietly.

That was almost more surprising to Tíbhyan than the thought of Kavan having read them. "In Elyri or Trade?" He, like most others, believed the books to have been destroyed.

"High Elyri," Kavan replied with a touch of pride, pleased that there seemed to be no judgment from the old man.

Tíbhyan was not only pleased to hear that the books were in their original language, he was also flabbergasted to hear that Kavan could not only read them but could, perhaps, comprehend their rigorous theological language. After what Ártur had revealed to the lómesté, the sage did not think it mere coincidence that the boy had come into possession of those ancient tomes. Tíbhyan believed in fate and in the hand of the divine. Hearing proof of such things made him more certain that his choice to take Kavan under his wing had been the right one. Anyone else learning of those books would likely have had them destroyed…and Kavan along with them.

"A treasure to be sure. Guard them carefully, Kavan. You know they may be the only copies remaining."

"I know…but why? Why are they deemed heretical?"

Tíbhyan shrugged. "Not the first two…nor his book of prayers…which may be why those you have survived. Anything that bore his name was supposed to have been destroyed, but some have felt as you do that those books possess no threatening words. It is the third volume that is considered the most dangerous; the k'gdhededhá have destroyed every copy they could find. I think some feared that reading the first two books would automatically lead one to make the same heretical conclusions Kóráhm presented in the third…or so I'm told…thus they were confiscated and destroyed too. I have never seen or read them, not even as a young man. If others have, I have not heard of it, but I do know that the gdhededhá will not discuss him with me either, not even as a matter of open secular debate. As you have noticed, there is said to have been differences between his theology and that of the k'gdhededhá. Towards the end of his life, they seemed to have disagreed on a great many issues."

That thought made Kavan frown. "I disagree with many things gdhededhá Bhílári teaches us, but I am not punished for it…"

The sage laughed, partially to hide the twinge of worry he felt for his young student. He knew Kavan to be headstrong in his quest for the truth, for knowledge, and that he was not easily swayed by arguments without proof. If Kavan spoke truthfully, if his young mind was already set on a path that deviated from the formal teachings of the Faith, he was destined for no easy life ahead. Even knowing this, however, Tíbhyan was not inclined to push a particular path of indoctrination. Whatever fates were at work in the boy's life, it was important for him to choose his own way. Tíbhyan was only there to teach and guide. The rest was up to Kavan.

"That is because you are a child," he replied, "and they expect you to outgrow silly notions as you are exposed to more of their doctrines. They do not expect one as young as you to grasp the finer details of theology, or to question what they are taught in any meaningful way, and they ignore what they do not want to bother with in the hopes of disavowing you of your beliefs."

"They must assume I understand enough to permit me Initiation…" Kavan muttered.

The old man smiled. "I do not comprehend the logic of the k'gdhededhá any more than you do, Kavan. I gave up trying long ago." He might, however, once again make the effort in order to best answer Kavan's questions. Kavan was inclined to formulate his own opinions in all areas of philosophy and learning; it was no surprise he would do the same in matters of religion and faith. The established religious order did not deal kindly with dissidents, with heretics, and if Kavan was to go down that path, the sage did not want him to travel it alone.

Kavan toyed with the edge of the ancient page he had been reading, considering carefully if he wanted to ask the next question or not. Some would consider such prying to be rude, a matter of curiosity only, but for Kavan, it was an important part of understanding the world in which he found himself. Finally, deciding that Tíbhyan would refuse to answer if he wished, Kavan asked, "Is that why you do not attend Gatherings?"

Tíbhyan felt no offense. Yes, he knew that the Gatherings were the highlight of many Elyri's lives and that it was expected of all to attend as often as they could. It was no secret that Tíbhyan no longer did, but no one in Bhryell was willing to call him to task for it, not even the gdhededhá. "I do not attend," he answered with a grin, "because it is too far to walk on these old legs and I tend to snore when I sleep."

Both were true enough and Kavan saw no reason to doubt those explanations. Tíbhyan's home was as far from the Gathering Hall as it could be while still being in town, and the ancient man's legs grew weaker all the time. Kavan sensed, however, that the reasons went deeper than that, but like his elders, he would not push the matter. The bhydáni's secrets were his own, and Kavan loved him too dearly to wish trouble upon him.

"Will you come to the next Gathering…for my Initiation?" It might be too much to ask, but without Ártur there, a given that Kavan expected, the boy hoped to have someone to support him. He might have brought the family unexpected prestige, but there would be little support from his uncle, and maybe not even from his aunt or cousin Sámel.

The old man patted his arm. "I would not miss it, Kavan. Fear not; I shall be there for you."

That reassurance was all that Kavan needed to relax, but his mind was still churning through their discussion, looking for answers to mysteries that no one seemed able, or willing, to solve. "If," he eventually asked, glancing down at the page and rubbing his finger across

Kóráhm's name as if to absorb it through his skin, "he was a heretic…if what he wrote was offensive…why was he canonized? Why is there a monastic order bearing his name? Why did my mother give me his name?"

Again, Tíbhyan chuckled as he found the boy's inquisitive mind to be refreshing compared to most others he regularly dealt with. He was unafraid to ask questions that other children, and most adults shied away from asking. "I can only speculate, Kavan. There must have been too much evidence to support canonization; the questionable aspects of his life were ignored, I suppose. As for the Order, most of the gdhededhá in it are not Elyri; perhaps their support of his teachings is what others find traitorous. If what your cousin said is true, a visitation by a saint would be reason enough to give you his name. I would have done the same thing if you were my child, and I am hardly a religious man."

That made Kavan smile. Most people frowned at him when they learned he bore the Heretic-Saint's name, and yet Tíbhyan embraced it. "As far as I'm concerned," the sage muttered with a twinkle in his eyes, "the whole canonization business is nonsense. A man's actions determine his sanctity, not the fickle whims of stodgy old men and women who consider themselves to be holy. But enough of that. If I learn anything about Kóráhm that may be of interest, I will tell you, but no more religious talk. How about music for an old man's ears?"

Kavan's smile widened, a smile that would have lit the room had it been dark the old man believed. Tíbhyan settled back into his chair, pleased that Kavan was satisfied with his explanations but knowing he would not stay that way for long.

᭺*᭺

The day of the weekly Gathering dawned cool and crisp, the spring thaw still many weeks away though close enough that a slight hint of warmth could be felt in the air. Daylight was painting the horizon when the bells called the villagers to worship. As was common practice for Initiations, the benches had been moved to the sides of the room to allow long wooden tables to be brought in. End to end, they ran the length of the room, from the doorway to the altar steps, and were worn from centuries of use for this same ritual. No one in Bhryell knew when they had first been made but they had been in use for this purpose for as long as the building had stood on this spot, and perhaps longer.

The townsfolk gathered around the table, two or three people deep in places; the attendance at an Initiation was always higher than normal, as bringing children into the Faith was viewed as an imperative duty by all of the faithful. Today there were seven children at the altar end of the table, the largest number since the plague had swept through Bhryell years before, and hence today's Initiation was more significant to the town. Children were a rare commodity, and so many being Initiated at once meant not only a continuation of the Faith but of their race as well.

Two of the seven looked uncomfortable, as if they would rather be anywhere else, elbowing each other, whispering, stopping briefly when they noticed their parents' chastising gazes, only to resume when they felt it was safe. Another four children stood properly silent and well-behaved in their finest attire, eyeing the tiny chalices on the end of the table expectantly. The Initiation was granted for most children at the ages of eight or nine years, and it was typically the first time they were allowed to partake of serbháló, the closest drink the Elyri had to wine.

The seventh child, the last in the row, dressed in the same white robe he always wore, kept his gaze downcast, his hands clasped reverently in front of him, and looked up only when it seemed appropriate. Somewhere further down the table were his aunt, uncle, and eldest cousin. The Gathering was the only time when his uncle seemed to have interest in what he did. Did Tám think him ready for this step, Kavan wondered. Was he proud of him? He could have touched the man's mind, sought answers to those questions in his thoughts, but he dared not. His uncle did not need another excuse to condemn him, and while Tám was not particularly sensitive to the Power, there was always a chance he could detect any attempt Kavan made to read him. Besides, Kavan was certain he would not like what he found there. It was better to leave his curiosity unsatisfied.

He swallowed his frustrated sigh as the first girl stepped up to the altar to begin the necessary recitations. The pair of altar attendants approached the table in the meantime with large loaves of bread and began passing them through the crowd. Each of the adults, or those children who had already been Initiated, would break off a piece, uniting in the consumption of the same meal, binding themselves together as a community in Faith. Kavan wished Ártur were there to share this with him, uniting himself with his family once more, but the healer had been unable to get away from court to attend. At least bhydáni Tíbhyan was there, making Kavan feel proud that the ancient man had made the effort for him.

One child after another took the vows, answered the questions, and recited the ancient formulas and prayers, many of which came directly from Kóráhm's writings although no one here would know that without having read the volumes. It felt to Kavan to be a great hypocrisy that the k'gdhededhá should use the writings of a man but call him rón. Yet Kavan had read enough of the man's works that he decided Kóráhm had best said many things that the leaders of the Faith wanted to say, and he doubted the gdhededhá had any idea where those words had originated.

"Kavan Cliáth."

He blinked, realizing his thoughts had been elsewhere rather than on the Initiation, but hopefully not long enough to make anyone question his behavior. gdhededhá Bhílári was smiling at him; it seemed he was safe as he stepped towards the altar. The loaves of bread had reached the last members of the congregation. One of the assisting gdhededhá brought the main chalice from the ambry and was waiting patiently to one side for his cue to offer it to the Faithful.

gdhededhá Bhílári put his hand on Kavan's head, both a symbolic gesture and one meant as a reading, to determine any falsehood in the Initiates as they gave their replies. Some children resisted the intrusion, others did not even know it was happening. Kavan knew and left himself open to the other man's probes. He had nothing to hide.

"Have you come here today of your own will, to join the Faithful in the service of k'Ádhá?"

There was that familiar comforting surge of static building around Kavan. Normally it gave him peace in a holy place when not much else did. Today, surrounded by the majority of Bhryell's population, he found no peace in it as he replied, "Yes, gdhededhá."

The man shifted his feet in agitation and glanced around him. Kavan could sense his disquiet but did not yet understand why. "Do you denounce the ways of wrongdoing and freely choose to follow the example laid down before us by Dhágdhuán the Intercessor, to aid others, obey k'Ádhá's law, and through this path find glory in a pure life?"

Kavan realized, as the gdhededhá spoke, that he was not the only one to hear the apprehension coloring the man's voice. A brief, guarded touch to Bhílári's thoughts revealed that the man was feeling the same static presence Kavan felt; it was the first time, to his knowledge, that anyone else had felt it with him. The gdhededhá's hand lifted from Kavan's head enough to break contact though not enough to be noticeable to his attendants, but it was obvious when Kavan met his gaze that the gdhededhá still felt whatever it was, for his nervousness did not dissipate.

He had to force the word, "Yes," out of his constricted throat, and from the back of the room, he heard his uncle's annoyed cough. No doubt, he thought Kavan was having a change of heart or had forgotten what he was supposed to do or say.

The older man's shaky voice continued, "What are the precepts upon which the Faith is founded?"

None of the other children had been asked that question, and it brought the attention of everyone in the room onto Kavan. He wondered if it was asked because he often questioned those precepts, or if there was some other purpose to the gdhededhá's inquest. Perhaps the man knew Kavan could recite them without fail and wanted to impress the congregation, or perhaps he hoped that engaging Kavan this way would cause that peculiar static sensation to cease.

Kavan cleared his throat, turned to face the congregation and began. "Dhágdhuán is first amongst the sons and daughters of k'Ádhá. A man of pure heart, pure thought, and pure deed, k'Ádhá took heed of the sacrifice Dhágdhuán made on behalf of all men and women. Because he was willing to accept death, even unto burning on the pyre to atone for the faults of his people, k'Ádhá took him into Ethenae and made him his son. So too shall all who live their lives pleasing to k'Ádhá's laws be brought across the great chasm, either as sons and daughters or as servants and záryph, each according to the life they have led."

Behind him, as he stared into the gathering, a pale glow had slowly grown to envelop the carved figure of Dhágdhuán on the pyre stake. The radiance grew with each word he spoke, although he could not see it and was unaware of what was transpiring. By the end of his recitation, the figure looked to radiate from within, the brightness of the light filled the entire náós; it was impossible not to notice. The assisting gdhededhá was sweating profusely, his hands trembling as he held the Chalice forth to Bhílári. The blessing was given and he began to pour serbháló into the seven smaller chalices on the table, a task which seemed to require greater than usual effort as he paused more than once to steady his hands. Kavan wanted to turn, to look at the figure on the wall and locate the light source himself, or else he wanted to search Tíbhyan's thoughts to confirm what his senses were telling him. But he did not, as he harbored the secret hope that, by not knowing, what was happening might cease to be real.

That everyone around him was growing more uneasy with each passing moment, however, told him it was very real.

gdhededhá Bhílári cast a chastising glance at the assistant for spilling tiny red droplets on the table and for nearly succumbing to the hysteria that was building around them. Perhaps if they continued with the ceremony without acknowledging the unusual, pretended that everything was normal, the congregation would find comfort and the abnormal events would cease. His efforts to do likewise, however, were nearly thwarted when he picked up the first miniature chalice. The metal was unusually warm to the touch as if it had been sitting too near a fire, causing him to nearly drop it. He succeeded in clinging to it instead and offered it to the first child.

One after another they gasped, whimpered or made small cries when they drank from their respective chalices and accepted the small token of bread into their hands. Never had Initiates reacted this way to the Gifts, which caused further unease to spread through the congregation. Bhílári was at a loss to calm them, but he continued with the ceremony, intending to see the Initiation through to the end no matter what it took.

Kavan's skin tingled beneath the growing strength of power around him. He thought he heard music, a simple melody of harp, pipe, and horn, coming from the choir loft above the main entrance door, but a quick side-glance told him what he already knew. No one was there. That glance did confirm, however, that he was not alone in what he felt and heard. Some in the room turned to find the source of the music, while others continued to stare in awe at the radiant figure of the Intercessor or watched the Initiates with concern.

When gdhededhá Bhílári stopped before Kavan, Kavan could feel the heat radiating from the chalice and suspected it was burning the man's hand. A warm, sweet smell rose from the cup, filling his nostrils, and he knew at once it was not the aroma of serbháló he was accustomed to. It was spiced, perhaps, with something he was unfamiliar with, although he had never heard of it being prepared that way for a Gathering. He met the man's gaze, wishing he could say something soothing, offer an explanation, or ask a question, but there was nothing he could do. He had no more explanation for what was happening around them then the gdhededhá did.

"bhair íth sílai phain Dhágdhuán. ebh ibh k'dhek thae k'gaeth; k'gaeth chóne ebh sun k'Ádhá," said the gdhededhá, holding the chalice to Kavan, thankful that after this one child, the ordeal would be over.

"kóh dást át árá. át bhekád sun átaelá raeyth," Kavan replied as he accepted the cup. It burned his hands, though not badly enough for him to drop it, and his lips stung where the metal touched, but he dutifully drank the steaming liquid, noting that it was thick, warm, and salty, not at all the way he expected it to taste. He bowed his head as he licked the remainder from his lips, feeling the chalice grow cooler within his hand. He did not want to know what he had consumed.

As he swallowed the last of it, there came a low, whispering, "sulás," from somewhere in the heights of the náós. Perhaps it was only the wind in the rafters that had suddenly come up, or his imagination, but no, the gasps throughout the room indicated that others had heard the sound too. The assisting gdhededhá spun, looking for the voice; the main chalice tipped, spilling the remaining liquid on the polished wood table. Flames sprang up as the thick red liquid made contact with the wood, but it burned only until Kavan absently, without thought, reached his hand across the table and smothered it beneath his palm.

Once the flame was extinguished, the wind, the music, the voice, the light around them, and the energy in the room he had felt, vanished.

There was stunned, awkward silence in Hes Índári as the congregation stared at one another, wanting someone to explain this phenomenon with some sort of rationale they could understand. gdhededhá Bhílári stared at the spot on the table where the flames had been. There should not have been fire; nothing in that chalice should have created it and the wood showed little evidence of the flames except for a small coin-sized scorch mark. He looked at Kavan's uninjured hand and then into the boy's face, reading the mixture of fright, embarrassment, fascination and excitement in the eyes of an otherwise neutral expression. Yes. The gdhededhá realized it as he connected each of this morning's events. Here was his answer. This child knew he had somehow been the center of this confusion, although he understood it even less then the gdhededhá did. Other than that moment of eye contact, Kavan kept his head down, staring at his unburned palm while the assisting gdhededhá gave the final blessing and benediction, and it remained down as the Initiates were ushered out of the náós to be joined by their families and be congratulated and welcomed into the Faith by the rest of the community. Once to the door, however, Kavan broke into a run and disappeared down the street, waiting for no one to approach him, not even bhydáni Tíbhyan.

Despite creeping doubts, despite how unusually gifted he knew the boy to be, Bhílári was certain that Kavan had not caused any of these events. He may have been the focus of it, the center, but he had not caused them. No one, Elyri or otherwise, could have caused all of that. Something divine had happened, and if asked, Bhílári would swear to that to any court.

But how did one deal with the boy?

ॐ*ॐ

Looking across the men scattered about him, General McHador settled before the campfire, bone-weary but satisfied with the day's progress. After decades of sporadic fighting with Hatu...the Casual War as King Innis had called it...Enesfel succeeded in forging peace with the southern kingdom. Not that King Perren had a choice. If Hatu, in its current state of upheaval, was to retain its sovereignty, it had to call an end to the hostilities before Enesfel crushed them. It had taken three days of continual deliberations, and several fits of anger, before a peace agreement between the kingdoms was hammered out. The terms were not perfect, but then again, they never were in any sort of political give and take situation. Guthrie felt certain, however, that King Donal would agree to the terms his General and the foreign King had come to. Enesfel's ruler would arrive within two days to sign the treaty himself. There would be peace.

Despite the initial chaos of raids and skirmishes, this had turned out to be the cleanest campaign the General had ever led. When King Perren learned of Enesfel's army gathering in Jardin, he withdrew his forces from other engagements and launched an attack against those he perceived as the larger threat. Guthrie held Enesfel's main force back as long as he could, hoping that King Perren would see the folly of such an action, but in the end, it had been necessary to bring his additional troops south, join with Captain McLeu's unit at Nelori, and meet Hatu head on in battle.

The King demanded no unnecessary actions against Hatu, with Enesfel's troops ordered not to ransack or destroy villages and not to harm non-combatants unless in self-defense. The General struggled to keep the fighting strictly between the armies. As his forces pushed further into Hatu, King Perren's army retreated, until they were forced back to their capital city, encountering the crumbling hulks of villages and farms as they went, further proof that Hatu was on the brink of destroying herself.

King Perren's other problem, the invaders along their southern border, did not cease simply because Hatu's army was otherwise engaged. Facing two sets of foes, as well as growing internal unrest, when Guthrie offered a cessation of hostilities in exchange for helping Hatu repel the southern horde, King Perren leapt at the opportunity. King Donal approved of that course of action; Guthrie and his troops spent an additional ten months in the field, helping Hatu secure her southern borders. That had proven to be a much bloodier undertaking than the war with Hatu had been, and many men on all sides were lost. In the end, however, the horde was driven back and a new Hatu-Enesfel alliance had been born.

Most of Enesfel's troops had begun the long march home under Captain McLeu's flag. Guthrie and a small battalion remained behind to draw up the treaty, to await the King's arrival, and to accompany the monarch back to Rhidam in triumph.

If the new treaty held, King Donal would forever be known as the forger of peace.

And out of the campaign, Guthrie intended to gain the one thing he had desired most since King Innis' death. He wanted to retire from active military service. He would recommend Captain McLeu be promoted to the office of Lord High General, as the man was suited to that position and sufficiently qualified for it. Though willing to train soldiers, and to remain in a position of Military Council to the King, Guthrie never again wanted to ride to war. The battlefield was no longer his place. War was for young men. Guthrie McHador felt old.

❧Chapter 8❧

Twisting awkwardly to the side, Kavan dropped the practice sword and stumbled backward against the nearest sturdy obstacle, which happened to be a tree. He winced at the unexpected burning in his shoulder, but though the pain felt real, there was no visible or tangible wound. Curled on the ground with his fingers probing the area, he lay with his eyes closed, trying to focus on the ache, seeking its source. For a moment, out of the haze of pain, the image of an arrow formed and then quickly dissipated. He felt the touch of hands on him, Ártur's touch he knew, and his eyes snapped open as he expected to see his cousin bending over him.

But Ártur was not there, only Phaedr, his kinsman and dueling partner, and Tíbhyan, both beside him with their mouths moving but not producing sound. Or at least, there was no sound Kavan could hear until the touch of his cousin's hands withdrew, taking the pain away with them.

"Kavan…what has happened?" asked the old man who leaned on the tall, red-haired youth for support as he touched the place on Kavan's shoulder the boy was nursing.

"I…do not know," Kavan admitted as he slowly sat up and rotated his shoulder to judge its wellness. The pain was gone. "I believe someone in Rhidam has been injured…"

"Your cousin?" The sage knew the psychic link between Kavan and the healer was strong enough that Kavan might have felt any injury the healer received.

"No. Someone else. Ártur healed them…but I do not know who it was." That made little sense but it was the only explanation he had.

"You may see if you wish."

The bhydáni placed his left hand on the boy's open palm. Each opportunity to touch that young, powerful mind was akin to smelling blooming flowers in his garden after a spring rain, but it was something he rarely did, and never without permission, finding the sensation all too addictive. Normally, Kavan was easily read when he wanted to be, but this time Tíbhyan could not identify what he sensed there. True, the eleven-year-old had mastered abilities far beyond his age, had learned skills known by the better-trained adults, and was beginning to master some that only the most talented Elyri knew. Some of the things Kavan could do existed only as rumors and stories in ancient Elyri texts, while other things Kavan had shown him Tíbhyan had never seen or heard of before. This instance was one of those.

How much will he master before he leaves me, the old man wondered as he broke contact? How long before he outgrows my usefulness and must teach the teacher?

Whatever this had been, Tíbhyan sensed that the pain had been real enough that, if felt in the right physical locations, at a great enough intensity, Kavan could have gone into shock and died from an injury not his own. That made this ability, whatever it was, a potentially deadly one for Kavan and caused Tíbhyan concern. Fortunately, Ártur had been on the other end to tend to the wounded. The bhydáni was interested in speaking to the healer, to hear what had happened in Rhidam. It was imperative for Kavan's well-being that they learn the truth.

"No more practice today," he said as he gestured to Phaedr to help him to his feet. As he straightened, Kavan rose from the ground, still fingering his shoulder in puzzlement. Kavan did not speak as he and Phaedr helped the old man climb the back steps into his home. Whatever had happened, he knew his teacher was troubled by it. He thought they would continue his daily lessons, as usual, but Tíbhyan shooed them both home, refusing to talk further. As the sage hobbled to his desk and a collection of ancient tomes piled there, Kavan went out the front door and stood on the porch for a long while, staring in the direction of home. He knew the sage's silence well enough to know that the bhydáni would not talk about what had happened because he was as baffled as Kavan.

❧*❧

The child prince lifted the tabby kitten from the cushion on which it slept and held it towards his sister, who took it tenderly to enable her brother to climb into the chair where he then pretended to sharpen the wooden sword Guthrie had given him. Their mother turned away to gaze out the window, watching the yellow disk sink below the horizon, pulling the last of daylight with it. Her heart was heavy tonight, so heavy that she found it difficult to allow the children to leave with their governess when Lady Johanna came to take them to bed. But she had no choice. They could not sleep in her room, not tonight. Her pacing would keep them awake and they needed rest. She had sent for General McHador as soon as the incident occurred but he had been in Levonne and had not yet returned to the castle.

She wondered if perhaps he would still avoid her. There had been no words between them since his return from Hatu. The glances they exchanged when they passed each other said all that needed to be said. She knew how he felt about her, and why he resisted her, and she chose not to push him. He visited the children when she was not with them, and she made a point to give him as much distance as he needed. After today, however, she knew she must see him. There was too much at stake to avoid each other any longer.

When a firm, familiar rapping pattern came at the door, her heart leapt into her throat, making it difficult to form words. "Enter," she called, her hands wringing in front of her.

The general stepped into the room, looking worn and tired, his dusty clothing and matted hair and beard suggesting that he had arrived at the palace and had come straight to her. Even though he stood at stiff attention and avoided looking her in the eye, it made her feel better, safer, to know he had taken her summons seriously and had chosen to come to her promptly rather than avoid her by taking the time to bathe and change.

"Thank k'Ádhá you came," she said, trying to keep her tremulous voice even. "I was afraid you would not…"

He swallowed the sick, nervous feeling in the back of his throat. He could sense that this was not the romantic summons he had feared, but something worse. "Your message sounded urgent; I came as quickly as I could. There are murmurings amongst the men…what has happened?"

Cordelia wrapped her arms around herself and turned away. "There have been rumblings for days…I'm surprised no one mentioned them to you…"

"What sort of rumblings?"

"There have been written threats…against my son…"

"Prince Arlan?" He could not imagine anyone threatening Prince Girvin. "My word!"

Removing the pins from her hair to allow it to tumble free to toy with the ends, a nervous habit Guthrie had seen before, the Queen Mother continued, "The King increased security around him, but none believed it would come to this…that the threats would mean anything…" Her resolve to be strong began to crumble and tears slid down her cheeks, but she refrained from throwing herself into his arms as she longed to do.

Unable to bear to see her cry, Guthrie closed the distance between them and hesitantly put his arms around her, the first time he had touched her in a personal way. "What has happened to…my…Cordelia?" Her name lodged in his throat but he managed to get it out at last. Titles in this place and moment made little sense. "Has something happened to the Prince?"

"This morning…someone meant to…Lord MacLyr…he could not…"

Unable to follow her words, fearing that something had happened to the healer and the prince, Guthrie assisted the woman into the nearest chair and knelt beside her. With her hands in his, he said, "Start at the beginning. Slowly."

In broken sentences punctuated by sobs and long pauses to squeeze his hands, she explained how the twins had been playing in the outer courtyard with Lady Johanna and four guards in attendance. The princess had begun to wander off, and Lady Johanna followed to retrieve her. The healer came into the courtyard then, on his way into the city, in time to hear the prince scream. A hooded figure with a small crossbow was seen disappearing over the castle wall, and three of the four guards ran to apprehend the perpetrator. Only a single volley had been fired; the bolt had hit the prince's shoulder. When Lady Johanna returned to find the healer removing the shaft and tending the wound, she screamed. While a thorough search was made, only a cloak was found in the cold river water of the moat. The culprit, whoever it had been, was not apprehended. The injury to the prince was not as bad as feared, but the Queen Mother, the healer, and the King, assumed it had been meant to be a fatal shot.

Guthrie did not know what to say. He was experienced in open combat, not subterfuge. He, and others, had suspected that this day might come. Many, including the Queen Mother, had feared it from the day the twins were born. There were too many princes, too many contenders for Enesfel's throne. None of them had expected an attempt to come this soon, however. Prince Arlan was not yet five years old.

"Ártur was not due back from Alberni until tomorrow," he mused. "He spoke of disturbing dreams that led him to return early."

The general scowled. "He should be careful who he says things like that too. There are people who will blame him for this."

Finding the notion a terrifying one, she exclaimed, "You do not think Healer MacLyr could be responsible?"

"No." He squeezed her hands to calm her. "I know a little about his training and the oaths healers must take to serve...and those King Innis made him take when he came here. Lord MacLyr would never knowingly harm anyone...particularly a child...and most especially a child of Innis'. I have yet to meet a dishonest Elyri, no matter what others might say of them. Besides, he could not have been on the wall, dropped the cloak, and tended to Prince Arlan at the same time. There were too many witnesses. And, he has no motive...unlike others..."

The woman's face paled. "Prince Bowen?"

The thought of it made Guthrie rub his temples. He did not like to admit it, but if she suspected it too, then his fears were likely justified. "As it stands, with Prince Owain gone, Prince Arlan is in line for the throne behind Prince Girvin. Everyone knows how unlikely it is that either he or Prince Farrell will father heirs...at least not legitimate ones."

Farrell had yet to marry, whereas Girvin had been through four wives, each of whom had died without producing children. Since his fourth wife's death of plague within months of their marriage, the prince, broken and devastated by the loss, had shown no interest in marrying again.

Guthrie continued. "And Prince Bowen does not seem prone to attract any woman other than Lady Ula. Bowen may be an old man before the throne comes within his reach, and I do not believe either he or Ula, have given up hope of Prince Owain reaching the throne in Bowen's stead. It cannot be proven, of course, just as one cannot prove without Elyri aid that Prince Bowen is Owain's father, but it is quite possible, even likely. The important thing is to protect your son."

"And Lord MacLyr." She was worried about her son, but her concern did not stop there. She did not want the healer to be a target as well.

"I suspect he can take care of himself, but I will remind him to be alert if he is not already." He patted her hands and pushed stiffly to his feet. "Where are the royal children now?"

"Asleep I should think. Lord MacLyr and Lady Johanna are staying with them tonight, and there are guards posted outside of their door."

"Good. They are in good hands. You must rest. I know sleep will be difficult, but you must try. I will think on this tonight and tomorrow we will discuss it further, perhaps devise a plan to keep Arlan from further harm."

He started for the door after a bow, prepared to take his leave of her though he had not been formally dismissed. Before he could open the door, however, she spoke again.

"Guthrie…" His hand stilled on the latch, clutching it tightly, knowing that if he relaxed his grip his hand would shake. "Do not leave me alone…please."

He could not turn. If he did, he knew he would be lost to his heart, and right now he needed to keep his wits if he was going to help the prince. "You will be safe, milady. There are guards posted outside. No harm will befall you."

"That is not why…"

Even though he heard her steps drawing nearer, he could not move, not even when her hand rested tenderly on his arm. His heart thundered in his chest, his throat went dry, and for a brief moment, his sight dimmed and he thought he would faint.

"Your Majesty...Cordelia..." he choked, "you are still the queen...at least in my eyes. I cannot...Innis would..."

"Innis is gone, milord, and he would have wanted me, wanted you, to be happy. You were his dearest friend. I am certain wherever he is, he would be happier knowing we had each other..."

His head shook from side to side but he felt trapped and unable to move away. "Do not...milady...please..."

Her fingers dug into his bicep more firmly. "Guthrie..."

That squeeze on his arm gave him the jolt he needed, allowing him to slide out the door and close it behind him. She did not follow and the guards at the door said nothing.

It was a long, difficult walk to his room on legs that threatened collapse at each step. He was grateful to encounter no one, for he would have been hard pressed to explain his state of disarray. Even once he was safe in his own room, alone at last, he found he could not shake the tension that weighed on him. On the table near his bed was his favorite flask, one he had not drunk from in a very long time. Without taking out a goblet or glass, he uncorked the flask and drank deeply of the old, bitter wine it contained. It did not ease his distress, but if someone should question his behavior and demeanor in the corridor, he could claim to have been drinking. A bath had been drawn upon his arrival from Levonne, but it had grown cold. Undaunted, he undressed and sank into the water, shivering, suspecting it was going to be a very long night.

A knock on his door woke him some time later. The sun shone through the window to his left and a quick look around told him that he had fallen asleep in the bath and was quite wrinkled. He grunted in annoyance as he climbed out of the cold water and grabbed the drying cloth that had been left for him. The knock was repeated, this time accompanied by the healer's voice, and Guthrie grunted again. He had forgotten about that first knock.

"Come in, Lord MacLyr," he called.

Ártur entered the room and bowed. If he noticed the man's nudity or his wrinkled appearance, he did not make mention of it. "Her Majesty asked me to look in on you when you did not respond to her breakfast summons. I believe she feared some harm had befallen you."

The general snorted, more annoyed with himself than with her for checking on him. "As you can see, it did not."

"Indeed." The amused sparkle in the healer's eyes belied his neutral statement.

"What time is it?" Guthrie strode to his trunk to find something to wear.

"Nearly noon."

The answer produced another grunt. "I arrived late last evening...and fell asleep while bathing."

"There is no need to explain yourself to me." Ártur smiled a little but it faded quickly. "You have heard about yesterday?"

"The Queen Mother told me. She sent for me when the threats began, but I was not near enough to arrive sooner." He stared at the healer. "She said you had dreams...?"

Ártur shook his head, looking for a seat but not taking one since he had not been given leave to sit. "Not a dream. My cousin had a premonition of someone coming over the outer wall. Knowing him as I do, I thought it prudent to return quickly, in case I was needed. I try to take Kavan's premonitions seriously, but I did not explain that to the Lady. She is an intelligent, compassionate woman, but she does not understand what we do...and my cousin's abilities are beyond my own comprehension."

Guthrie remembered the small pale boy that had struck him even then as somehow different from other Elyri he had met. But Elyri predicting the future? Seeing events before they happened? That was al-

most incomprehensible. "Whatever the case, I am thankful you returned when you did. You have saved Prince Arlan's life. But if I was
you, and I am glad I am not, I would be careful..."

The healer bowed his head. "I am, milord. His Majesty informed
me that already this morning there have been two separate accusations
made that I am responsible for this attack. It was bound to happen, me
being what I am, but fortunately, there were witnesses who saw everything."

"This is no time to pity yourself. If you were not Elyri, if your
cousin was anything else, this might have ended quite differently. We
must be a strong coalition, you, me, the Queen Mother, and the King,
if we are to protect the prince. I suspect, however, that he cannot stay
here if he is to remain safe. This is only the first attempt of what may
be several more...until one succeeds."

Ártur cocked his head. "You are not suggesting I take him to
Elyriá? With some already accusing me, were I to disappear with him,
it would look very bad for my people."

The general sat with another grunt and began putting on his boots
once his trousers were fastened. "No. That plan will never work. We
knew it when it was first suggested. I am trying to devise a satisfactory
solution, but thus far I have none." The only idea he had come up with
thus far would leave each person involved to fend for themselves, but
it might be the only way to protect Prince Arlan. Was such a drastic
measure warranted? Something in the general's gut said that it was.

Thoughts straying back to the previous night as he picked up his
shirt, he asked absently, "Can you heal emotional wounds as well as
physical ones, Lord Healer?"

Ártur leaned against the doorframe and asked, "What do you
mean? If there is something you wish to discuss, you can be assured
that what you say will go no further. It is part of my oath, to keep
confidence with my patients..."

"I do not speak as a patient, only as a man who has nowhere else to seek advice." He began to pace the length of the room and finally stopped beside the bed, aware that the healer was watching him toy with the flask on the bedside table, which had not been re-corked the night before. Both spoke volumes about his frame of mind, and it was the reason why he moved his hand away and instead went to the window. "Do you believe that the departed watch over us after they die? Do they see what we do, hear what we say?"

"I have no proof beyond my own faith, but I believe so, yes."

"Would they care about us? Our welfare?"

The healer watched the man's shoulders twitch and grow tense as he spoke. "The ones who knew us in life most certainly would."

"Would they object if their surviving spouse…if their best friend…" The general closed his eyes, unable to finish, and clutched the windowsill.

Ártur bowed his head to hide his understanding smile. "It would depend on the individual, I imagine. Some people, as you know, are jealous of their relationships and possessions in life…but those rarely have the close ties of which you speak. I think most would want those they leave to be happy, content, taken care of. If I were to die, I would want my fiancée to marry someone else if she chose, as long as she is happy and treated with respect. She deserves that. I think I would be unhappy, regardless of the joy of the afterlife, if I knew she was languishing because of me."

His words seemed to have little effect on the general; the man's stance, heart rate, and breathing did not relax. After a long pause to give the man time to reflect, Ártur started again.

"I did not know Lady Jezeel, but she told me the morning she died that she wanted you to be happy and was grieved because she could not give you that. You have lived in the shadow of her death too long, milord. As for…King Innis and I held similar views on some matters." That time the general's shoulder's twitched, at last giving a reaction that indicated he was listening. "He would not want Lady Cordelia to be alone and unhappy. You were his dearest friend; he would not have wished you unhappiness either. If your happiness was in each other, I would think he would be pleased, perhaps even relieved. He would know that together you would be stronger. Truthfully, I believe he knew of your fondness for her from her first day here."

The general's face grew pale and he was glad Ártur could not see it. He was not going to ask how the healer knew these things. Though the words should have been comforting, the thought that King Innis might have known how Guthrie felt for his wife made the general embarrassed and ashamed. "She is the queen…"

"Was the queen. She passed the title to Lady Meara when King Donal assumed the throne. She is simply the mother of royalty, the widow of the late King. She is no different from anyone else in regards to the needs of heart and body. A title does not change a person's fundamental nature. If she feels she has been alone long enough, then it is right for her to move forward. Do as your heart guides you, milord. King Innis is gone and you must not allow the past to cloud your future. But whatever path you choose, let her know why. She deserves that much."

He waited in silence for many minutes for Guthrie to say something, but the general did not speak. When it seemed that the matter was closed, or at least that Guthrie needed time to think about what had been said, the healer continued, "I must return to Prince Arlan, but before I go…I have been told that you have a niece near the twins in age."

The change in topic brought with it a relaxing of the general's shoulders as the man turned at last. "Brenna Weylin is near their age, yes. She is my sister's child."

Ártur nodded. "I recommended to the Lady that it is time to find a suitable companion for Princess Deidre, a handmaiden who cannot only assist her with the day to day matters of royalty but with communication too. A special confidante, as it were. She will gain an Elyri tutor come spring, but I think she would be happier and more confident with someone her own age to be with her…closer than the usual servants and ladies in waiting. There are none amongst the nobles whom I would trust for this if they had a daughter of similar age. If you think your niece would serve satisfactorily in this capacity, would you speak of it to your sister?"

"I shall." The general felt better already, lighter in spirit, even if his expression did not show it. "I shall think on what you have said, Lord MacLyr. Thank you. Knowing I can trust you is an invaluable gift I shall not easily forget."

Never before had he seen the healer look embarrassed. Ártur bowed with a murmured thank you and quickly backed out of the room. The general, clean and a little more at ease, set about the day's business. He would formulate his plan as his duties permitted, and once it was thoroughly thought through, he would take it to the queen. He did not want to meet with her again until he knew precisely what he would say.

When that time came, he waited at the window in her room, fingering the edge of his sleeve as she wiped tears from her face and turned her back to him. From the mantle, she picked up a small marble statuette of a mother holding a child and traced its contours with her fingertips. Innis had given it to her when he had learned she was to give him another child. She saw Arlan's face on that tiny infant every time she looked at it from the day he had been born. That impression was even stronger now.

"Is that the best you can do? Do you think that is the only way?" she asked in a tone of deep hurt.

Guthrie tried not to groan. "Perhaps not the only way, but it is the best I can provide on such short notice."

"Best for whom? For whom, Guthrie? He's my baby. I cannot simply give him up. What about you? Donal? What about me? How is this fair to any of us?"

There was tightening in his chest as he stared across the black rooftops of the sleeping city. Rhidam had been his home most of his life. Tonight it looked like something he was seeing for the first time and might never see again. The winter storms would begin soon; he could smell the change in the air and the chill of it cut down to his bones.

He sighed. "It is best the King never knows of this. We do not want to provide Prince Bowen anything he might be able to use against Donal. I know it is not fair to him, or to any of us, but it is the only way I can see to protect us all. I do not relish the idea of such a young child being without his mother. I know nothing of raising children, but I do know that as long as Prince Arlan is here, his life is in danger. You told us this the night of his birth and it seems to have come to pass. Ártur cannot take him to Elyriá without endangering every Elyri in the land. This life is all I've ever known, but there is no one else who can be trusted to do this. It must be me."

"Donal will be alone…I will be alone…we will all be alone." She paused for several minutes as she placed the figurine back on the mantle. "I do not want to be alone any longer, Guthrie." She glanced at him as he stared out the window and added, "Take me with you."

It felt as if a boulder had fallen from the sky and knocked the wind from him. He had expected her to make that request but actually hearing it proved unbearable. "I cannot. Not if we wish to protect your son. I can hide a child, but I could not hide both of you. If you were to go missing too, there would be a search unlike any other. It would be impossible to hide you. Besides, you have a daughter to think of…"

Cordelia wiped her eyes, knowing his words to be true and hating them because of it. She had envisioned taking the children to Elyriá, living there in peace with both of them, but she suspected as long as

Arlan was believed alive, someone would seek to take his life. She had to remain in Rhidam, with Deidre, as if her youngest son was lost to her forever, and pray for the best. "Where will you go?"

"I shan't say. If you do not know where I am, you cannot place yourself, or Arlan, in accidental danger. It is not that I do not trust you," he added, "but it is a risk we dare not take. I will only say that where I will go is no place for a woman of your station and breeding. If there comes a time when the King can no longer protect you and your daughter…if a day comes when you feel your lives are threatened, I will know and I will see to your safety. I swear that to you…"

"Healer MacLyr?"

Guthrie did not reply.

"I must know," she demanded. "How can I look to anyone for aid if I do not know who is to be trusted. At least give me that."

Stroking his beard, the general grunted. She had a point, as much as he hated to admit it. And clearly, they both knew the healer well enough to have considered him the liaison. "Yes…Lord MacLyr…but his part in this must never be mentioned outside of this room…never again. He will likely remain in Rhidam long after you and I are gone, provided the King's successors do not release him…or worse…his reputation must be left clean of this. He will know everything, every detail…and because of his relationship with the King, plus the fact that he is Elyri, will mean he is placing himself in grave danger."

The woman nodded, her expression grim. Anti-Elyri sentiment ebbed and flowed in the Five Sovereignties, and one never knew when it was likely to rear its head and strike, or where. Elyri had been safe during Innis' reign, and now Donal's, but who was to say what the future held. "Do you believe Arlan is in enough danger that you, the King, and the Lachlan Guard cannot protect him?" She knew the answer, even as she asked the question.

"I wish it could be, but the Lachlan Guard did not protect him this time, and it is foolish to believe such an attempt will not come again.

If someone wishes him dead, for whatever reason, they will undoubtedly continue to try until they succeed or are caught. Now that an attempt has been made, I do not think he will remain safe much longer, and I do not think we should be passive and hope for the best. We must act. If I thought I could provide adequate protection here, you know I would stay, Your Majesty." He paused for a long moment, looked at her, and added, "This is the only home I have known for decades."

She turned from him, trying to deny the truth of his words but failing to. She did not have to like the available options, but she had to weigh them carefully and do whatever it took to protect her son. Innis would have expected no less.

"When will you leave?" she finally asked in a small, defeated voice.

The fight was over, and while he should have felt relief, all Guthrie felt was resignation. Part of him had hoped she would provide some other course of action that might be as effective in protecting the prince, but Cordelia was not a tactician. "Two days hence. It will give me time to set my affairs in order, to do what must be done here while there is time. The prince will remain here until you and Ártur determine he will be safer elsewhere. I pray, for your sake and his, that your wishes are fulfilled, milady, and that the day never comes that the prince is in that much danger. Better that I live the remainder of my days in solitude then he be at risk. Ártur will know what to do…if it needs to be done."

He got up from the window seat at last and came to her, tilting her face upwards to look into her eyes. "I do not wish for you to be alone, but I do not see a choice. You and I can protect ourselves…can persevere through adversity. The prince cannot. He is only a child. You must play your part, milady, as we all must if he is to live."

She nodded tearfully and attempted to move away from him.

"Cordelia…"

His ragged voice, the use of her name, and the hand that caught hers made her stop, turn back, and collapse against his chest. He held her tightly and together they wept.

⋄Chapter 9⋄

Kavan lay beside the crystal clear stream, listening to the gurgle of the water as it rushed past into the fullness of the lake beyond. It was a warm day, one of the last he would enjoy with autumn fast approaching. He had implored Tíbhyan to release him from his studies today. The bhydáni had been reluctant, but since Kavan had already lost his morning hours to his first Gathering as altar attendant, and since he rarely asked for, or took, a day away from his studies, the sage had agreed. The boy deserved time to himself.

Kavan had not told anyone where he was going; he never did when he came here, for that would lead to questions about how he could travel such a great distance in such a short time. The less anyone knew about his gifts, the better. He found this place to be the most peaceful he had discovered, and the joy he experienced in the shapechanging that allowed him to come here was something he knew little of in most other pursuits. Today, both that calm and joy were things he felt deeply in need of.

He stared into the wispy white trails that drifted overhead in the mid-afternoon sky. This was his favorite place in the world, where this river met this small lake he had discovered the first time his wanderings brought him so deep into Enesfel. That had been nearly two years ago, and he had come here often since then, any chance he got. In this place, surrounded by nature, he could be alone with his music and his faith and strive to sort out what he was meant to do with his abilities and his life, ponder where he fit into the master plan of the universe. That many Elyri believed as the Teren did, that the capabilities of their race were tools of immorality, was deeply upsetting for him. He endeavored to live as virtuously as possible, but if he, with more Elyri talent than most, was inherently wicked, what good were his efforts? He did not believe that ignoring those gifts and not using them was enough. If having them made his kind evil, then nothing could be done to save them from oblivion and their spiritual pursuits were for naught. It did not ease his mind that the gdhededhá shied away from his questions every time he brought the topic up as if they too believed it to be true.

If Kavan was honest with himself, he honestly enjoyed the power he possessed. There was too much of it within him; to not use it made him restless and irritable. Even something as simple as a handlight gave him a sense of euphoric relief. But when the whispers circulated, talk about how different he was, every time he detected another murmured indictment, he wondered if the pale complexion that set him apart was a curse, cosmic vengeance for talents he had not asked for but must learn to harness lest he destroyed someone accidentally. The learning required using the power, and the using, in turn, brought him both a desire to do more and a deeper sense of confusion about who and what he was.

Such questions drove him to this place to spend hours in contemplation with his music, seeking answers that no one, not even the earth and sky, seemed to have.

Today he had a different purpose in coming here, however. Today it was an escape from the inevitable chastisement of his uncle. Dháná would have been unable to deflect it as she normally did, as she and Sámel had gone to visit her brother in the neighboring town of Turyn. Kavan was beginning to suspect, however, that even her matriarchal influence over Tám would not shield him for much longer.

There had been a burial that morning, of a distant relative of the MacLyr's named Phyóná Térari, who had died during childbirth. She had been young and apparently in perfect health, yet as sometimes happened with Elyri women, she had died despite everything the attending healer had done. Her child had not lived to be born. She was the first person Kavan had known personally who had died, the first Elyri burial he had ever attended, and as fate would have it, his first service as attendant to the gdhededhá, a task all Elyri performed at some time during their youth.

He stood at the gravesite holding the censer, the haze of strong incense growing thick around his head as he listened to gdhededhá Bhílári recite the ritualistic burial prayers. Kavan drifted into a dreamlike state where he could see and hear everything that was occurring but felt strangely distanced from it, as if he were no longer within his body. He could feel the familiar filling with power, although there seemed to be more power than he knew was normal, but he had no control over it. He never did. The energy pulsed and gathered like a living thing; if he had been alone, he would have welcomed the sensation, would have been eagerly curious about what was to come. As it was, he had known something was going to happen, there, in front of all of those gathered. He knew it, dreaded it, but there had been no way to prevent it since he had not felt able to move his feet.

From that removed view, he looked down upon the deceased's remains, her pale, exquisite form lying peaceful in its slumber. The incense smoke converged above her, slowly pulling itself into an image of the pyre stake. Murmurs ran through the gathered crowd. He saw his uncle's eyes narrow, glaring at the back of his nephew's head as the image twisted flat and sank lower until it rested directly upon the corpse. For a few moments, the body seemed to regain color and her blond hair fluttered in a directionless breeze.

The smoke shifted once more, wrapped itself around her, and he watched in awe as it appeared to be drawn into her body through her barely parted lips. Then it was gone, leaving a faint glow centered beneath the hands clasped between her breasts. The woman's husband called for a healer, believing this was a miracle meant to restore his wife to him, but by the time a healer was found and brought forth, the glow had faded, leaving only the coldness of dead flesh in its wake.

Her husband threw himself across her, clinging to her body; he had to be pulled away before she could be lowered into the ground. As soon as she touched the earth of her grave, Kavan felt a surge of power nearly knock him off his feet as he reconnected to his body and prepared himself for the stares and whispers that had followed the events at his Initiation. But only his uncle and gdhededhá Bhílári looked at him, the former in undisguised annoyance, and the latter with curious scrutiny. Kavan knew the gdhededhá connected him to this and knew that his uncle believed he had intentionally caused this disturbance out of disrespect. What neither man understood was that Kavan did not cause these things. They happened but he could not control them. He was a conduit, nothing more.

With the completion of the service, and after helping to return the holy trappings to the naós, Kavan retreated to his teacher's home, and then to the lake. He did not want to face questions, gossip, or accusations. He wanted only to be alone.

Sitting up, Kavan brushed the leaves from his hair and stared across the tranquil water. He suspected that if a healer had been readily available, the woman would have lived. Or perhaps it had been his duty to move forward and touch her, though at the time he had felt no compulsion to move, and having felt disconnected from his body, he doubted he could have moved if he had tried. Yet he was certain there had been a chance for renewed life there, a chance lost to the coldness of the earth that covered her, and he shivered at the thought. If that chance had been fulfilled, he would have been partially responsible for an incident that would definitely have been a miracle. He was grateful that it had not come to pass for that very reason, and then felt immediately ashamed of wishing to deny the woman life. With a groan, he hunched forward, arms wrapped around his knees, and closed his eyes.

A splash before him startled his thoughts. In the water near his feet, ripples spread outwards from where something had either fallen in or had come out of it and reentered. The water there was shallow, with no fish to be seen, and clear enough that once the ripples receded he could see something shimmery on the stony bottom. A quick glimpse around, and a fast but thorough reach outward with his senses revealed that he was alone except for birds in the nearby trees, but the object had to have come from somewhere…and not from the birds. It could not have materialized where it lay, where it had not been before.

He pulled up his sleeve and plucked the object out of the water, flinching with the shock of heat he received when he touched it. Heat in the icy water. It confirmed that this had not been there moments before.

What he brought out of the lake was a half circle pendant on a thick chain. Though silver in color, it was too brilliant and too heavy to be silver. There were symbols etched on it that he could not read, and as he stared at it, his mind's eye created the second half circle, one that would complete the script and make it legible perhaps. All he needed to do, he believed, was find the other half. Then he would have his answers. The image of a young boy's hand, clutching that other half, flashed through his mind.

Kavan knew.

This was a piece of that future he sought, a piece of what he needed, a piece of the path he was meant to follow if he were to fulfill whatever destiny was planned for him. The thought was frightening; he wanted answers, but this was not the sort of thing he had in mind. If anything, this pendant, what it meant and how he could have come into possession of it, only opened further questions.

The chain was fastened around his neck and he felt calmer for wearing it. Very well, he decided as he got to his feet. He would follow this unknown path wherever it led. But for the moment, it was time to return home. He was not looking forward to a confrontation with his uncle, but Dháná should be home by the time Kavan arrived. She, at least, would grow concerned at his absence; it was nearly dark and a long way home.

꘎*꘎

Prince Bowen perched on the edge of the table, swinging his legs, watching his brother and the Elyri healer with smug delight. He had come to the solar for an audience with the King, but the healer arrived shortly thereafter and had, as usual, received top priority. Even the attempt on Prince Arlan's life had not been enough to turn the King against the healer as Prince Bowen felt it should have.

"What do you mean he left? Where did he go? Why would he leave like this…without saying farewell?"

Ártur did his best to keep his face from revealing too much. "He did not say where he was going, My Liege. He confided in me last night that he was leaving your service. I presumed he had discussed it with you, had your permission, and did not attempt to dissuade him. I did not know he was acting without your knowledge, that he intended to leave so soon."

The King grunted and tapped impatiently on the table. "Does this have anything to do with his health? He told me recently he has not been feeling his best of late, that he feared his health is failing and thought it wise for me to seek a replacement. Has he discussed his health with you?"

The healer shook his head. "He has made no complaints of ill health to me, but it is a possible cause for his departure. He is a proud man, as you know. If he thought his usefulness was nearing an end…"

"Without saying farewell?"

"To avoid any fuss being made over his years of service…perhaps…"

The King shook his head, not believing what he was hearing. "He was my friend, damn it. I depend on him. After all that we accomplished together…how will I function without his advice?"

Ártur glanced at Prince Bowen, feeling the man hovering like a vulture waiting for weak prey to drop in order to move in for a feeding frenzy. It was something the healer knew he had to head off quickly. The King needed support and Ártur would give it. He cleared his throat. "You have been sovereign for nearly five years, Sire. I would think you shall be as effective as always. Lord McHador was good with advice; he was a wise man, but he knew little about the mechanics of ruling a kingdom. What you have done thus far has been by your own hand."

"Yes…yes…" The King paced, avoiding his brother's gaze but hearing in Ártur's words the same threat that the healer was detecting. He could not appear weak in front of his brother. He should have insisted that Bowen leave the room, but it was too late for that. How was he to know the nature of the news brought to him, even when the healer had tried to warn him? "Lady Cordelia?" he asked, changing the direction of conversation. "Have you spoken with her? How is she taking his departure? I know the two of them were close, both dear to my father…"

Glad that he was not speaking under oath, Ártur replied, "I suspect they may have been more than friends, My Liege." He looked at his hands. He had not anticipated this much difficulty. "She hinted that it could have been an argument they had last evening that caused him to depart. She feels she may be responsible…"

"Lady Cordelia and McHador?" Prince Bowen sneered. The vulture, it appeared, was ready to swoop. "How long has this been going on? Perhaps the twins are not roy…"

"Silence!" The King looked as if he would swing at his brother if the two had been but one step nearer one another. "Guthrie McHador would never dishonor our father. Unlike Owain, Prince Arlan looks every bit a Lachlan. The twins are our kin, our father's children, and I will not tolerate idle rumors. The next person I hear allude to such slander will be locked in the dungeon."

Ártur touched the King's arm, hoping to calm him before he did something he might later regret, although the notion of locking Prince Bowen away had merit. "There is nothing to fear, My Liege. From things both have said to me in confidence of late, this is a recent…"

"And why should we take the word of a lying Elyri back-stabber?" Prince Bowen hissed, angry about the threat made against him as well as Ártur's disruption. "How are we to know you did not kill him as you attempted to do with Prince Arlan? You should not be allowed to live to spread your vile…"

"Enough!" The King's fist struck home, knocking his brother backward off of the table. "Out of my sight! If you threaten Ártur or another Elyri again, I will have your head!"

The third Lachlan heir was as shocked by that blow as Ártur was, but he kept his temper as he rose to his feet, wiping blood from his mouth and nose. "Very well…brother…" he spat coolly. "But someday you will see this man and his kind for what they truly are. I only hope someone does not have to die to prove it." He stalked from the room, shoulders square, leaving a chill in his wake.

Ártur remained unmoving, slack-jawed, and unable to shake the shivers that spread through his body. He had heard such slanders against his people, but he had never been the target of them. He had believed his position as healer to the royal house would make his conduct above reproach. He had been wrong.

The King flexed his hand as he growled. "Do not allow Bowen to intimidate you, Ártur. He will never harm you, not while I live."

"You may not be able to prevent it, should he choose to come for me…and he may have a point," Ártur sighed reluctantly. "Perhaps I should separate myself from the Lachlan house before I bring destruction upon you."

"Nonsense…you will do no such thing. Everyone knows you had no part in the attack on Prince Arlan. There were witnesses after all, including the Prince himself."

Ártur was relieved to hear it, to know he had the King's support, but it did little to ease his mind.

The King collapsed at the end of the table with a heavy sigh. "Destruction will befall this house once I am gone, I am afraid, regardless of your presence or lack of it. Father knew it, which was why he insisted I take the throne and why I ask you to stay, to help me put off the inevitable as long as we can. I believe you may be the only thing keeping this House together. You must stay, Ártur."

The healer tried not to shuffle his feet. "Your Majesty, I…"

"Ártur, must I beg? With Guthrie gone, you are the only person, the only friend, I can rely upon. You have stood by me over the years, regardless of our disagreements, and have never steered me wrong. Help me keep the throne out of Farrell and Bowen's hands as long as possible. If not for me, do it for the Lady Cordelia, for Prince Arlan and Princess Deidre, for the people of Enesfel. Do it for the Elyri who are here. Do it for the peace of the Five Sovereignties. Do it for my father's memory."

The Elyri ran his hand through his short red hair and groaned. He had steered away from political affairs during his many years at the Enesfel court. Now he found himself waist deep in them, with the ground slipping out from under his feet as quickly as he tried to retreat. He had made a promise, however, taken this duty to heart. His role was set.

He bowed his head. "I will stay until your death, My Liege. Would that it be far off in coming."

Relieved, the King smiled. "Thank you, Ártur. I will give you anything I have to give in return; you have my word…"

"Just one thing. Permission to visit home briefly?" He felt the sudden need to talk to his cousin, to hear Kavan's music, to put his mind at ease.

"Granted." The King offered his hand. "Once you are certain that Lady Cordelia and the children have no need of you, of course you may have leave. It has been a long while since you have gone back. That is a fair request. But please…" There was desperation in his eyes that did not make it to his voice. He could not remember the last time Ártur had gone home. Had it been after his coronation, so long ago? "Do not stay long. Should something happen…I will feel more at ease having you here."

"Aye…I will do what I can, My Liege."

"And say hello to your cousin; invite him to Rhidam if he is free. I would like to see how he has grown."

The last place Ártur wanted Kavan to be was in Rhidam. The cold knot in his stomach told him it would not be safe for the boy here. It might not even be safe for Ártur much longer.

"I shall give him your request. These trying times will not be easy for any of us, perhaps you least of all, but I will do what I can to make them easier. I am afraid, however, that I may not be of much use to you, or anyone else, for very long."

The King nodded with a grim expression on his face and muttered, "I know, my friend."

☙*❧

The darkness enshrouding the náós was punctured by the feeble light of a lone candle that flickered on the altar and cast a soft white glow on the carved face of Dhágdhuán above. A solitary figure knelt in the dimness, soft strains of music coming from the instrument in his hands. His serene expression was marred by the unnatural energy in his piercing eyes. Around him gathered the unseen forces that defied explanation, above him the carved eyes bore into his soul, stripping him of his defenses. It did not frighten him to be defenseless in the face of this power. It had a cleansing effect he felt much in need of tonight.

Something was wrong. Not in the sense of mortal danger, but in a way that left him sad and uneasy, and he doubted it was connected to the pendant he wore. That incident had left him perplexed but nothing more. His brief visit with Tíbhyan afterward had given no cause for anxiety and he had done his best to put the burial events behind him. Nothing else had occurred in the past twenty-four hours that could account for this feeling, not even the icy silence that grew stronger between him and his uncle. Kavan had never felt close to Tám, and only his gratitude for Dháná's kindness kept him from leaving. If he had been older he would have acquired a home of his own. He had nowhere to go, however, at least nowhere that he would feel safe from his uncle. Nowhere except for Tíbhyan's house, and that was out of the question.

But that knowledge had never distressed him in the way he felt now; he let the ethereal notes of the brass harp strings soothe him, let himself find comfort in the ease of prayer. The feeling persisted in the back of his mind, however, like the lingering effects of a bad dream. Try as he would, it would not go away.

Then abruptly the energies around him vanished and the eyes above him clouded back into the sightlessness of the wood from which they had been carved. Thinking that perhaps he had done or thought something inappropriate, Kavan tried to pinpoint what his last musings had been, tried to reestablish the contact. A creak behind him, the sound of the Purification Chamber's door opening, told him there was someone else there, someone else had disrupted the power. It had been no fault of his. He breathed easier as someone stepped into the room and closed the chamber door behind them.

"Kavan?"

"Ártur?" It was an unexpected but welcome surprise. If anyone were to interrupt his meditation, he was glad it had been Ártur. "Welcome home." He stood as his cousin lowered the hood of his cloak and came closer. Fear, pain, uncertainty, and confusion radiated from the older Elyri, causing Kavan's heart to skip a beat. The source of his pain. He knew it. He had never seen his cousin in such a state. When Ártur reached him, he embraced Kavan hard, burying his face in the soft white hair to hide his tears but Kavan had already seen them. He held his cousin for a long while, and when the healer pulled away, the tears had been replaced by a tortured expression. Kavan took his hands and guided him towards the altar steps.

"Kneel with me. What is wrong? The King?"

Their hands remained clasped as they knelt, a new gesture that Ártur cherished. He refused to open his thoughts to be read, however, even though he could feel Kavan pressing against his shielded mind. "I do not know where to begin."

"You received my message about the figure on the wall?" The healer nodded. "I felt an arrow here..." Kavan touched his shoulder. "Someone did get hit by an arrow...and you healed them? Was it the King?"

Felt it? Dear lord, the healer thought, fear, and amazement in his eyes as he stared at his cousin. What did that mean? "It was not the King. Donal is doing well...physically."

Kavan waited for him to continue, but when he did not, he prompted, "Who then?"

The silence dragged out until at last Ártur replied, "Prince Arlan."

Swallowing the sensation of something sharp lodged in his throat, Kavan tried to push his anxiety away. What this meant would have to be examined later. "Why? He is not yet five. Who would wish to harm a little boy?"

"No one knows. The culprit has not been caught. But there are those who believe I had a part in the attack."

"They do not know you, do they?" Kavan scoffed.

"They know I am Elyri and that is enough. There is tension mounting in Enesfel. I may not be safe there much longer."

"Then you will stay here." There was hope in his voice, though Kavan knew Ártur would never come home to stay as long as he believed he was needed in Rhidam.

"If only things were that simple," the healer groaned. "I promised the King I would stay until his death, but I do not know if that will be possible. So many things have changed…General McHador has left court…"

"He did?" It had been Kavan's impression that the man would remain as part of the King's court until he died. "Was there a falling out? Where did he go?"

"There was no falling out…but I cannot say where he has gone. He is hoping his actions will save Prince Arlan's life…but I do not know how. It sounded like the right thing to do before, but I am no longer certain." He met Kavan's gaze for many minutes and then looked away in shame. "I had to lie to the King today. He has been my dearest friend for so many years…and for the first time I have had to lie to him. The general believes that if the King knew the truth it would damage his reputation and put his life and throne at risk. I am no politician…who am I to say if that is true? It would certainly not benefit Prince Arlan or anyone else if Donal were to lose the throne. But I have never knowingly lied to anyone. Was it wrong to lie to protect the lives of hundreds of people…or at least half a dozen or so?"

Kavan scowled as he pondered the question. "I have never thought about it…"

"I have," the healer mumbled, "and I cannot find an answer. Afterwards...Prince Bowen was there...he called me a liar. Not about that, but about something that honestly was the truth...but how could I refute his words? He was right. I am a liar."

"I do not believe that one or two lies make you a liar," Kavan said evenly. "It is not as if you have done it all of your life or were doing it for your own gain..."

"How do you know that? How do you know I did not agree to this charade because I stand to gain something out of it, be it my own life or the future of our people in Enesfel?"

Kavan scowled again. Yes, he realized it was possible that his cousin's position at court, the duty he loved, could have been his sole motivation, but he stubbornly refused to believe that to be true. "You did it to protect others. To protect a child. I believe that. If it had been a matter of only protecting yourself, or of personal gain, you would not have done it. Knowing the way you speak, you likely chose your words so that it was an omission rather than a lie. Am I right?"

When Ártur would not look at him, Kavan glanced up at the figure on the wall instead. He felt, rather than saw, the emotion in those wooden eyes, and it confirmed for him what he believed to be true. "Can you feel that, Ártur?"

"What?" Distracted by his own thoughts, the puzzled healer looked at his cousin.

"Him." He indicated the figure but did not look at the healer. "Even if lying to the King was wrong...k'Ádhá understands. He knows why, knows you regret it, knows there was little choice. You are forgiven."

Ártur knew about none of the manifestations Kavan experienced. Kavan had never written of them, nor had Dháná, and the boy doubted he would have heard about them from anyone else. The healer did know, however, that his cousin had an unusual relationship with the spiritual and divine, one that he often wished he had. If he had it, he might feel at peace with his decisions. He studied the Intercessor's form but saw only the carving on the wall.

"I do not know how you do that; of all of the things you do, that is the one I covet. Perhaps you should become gdhededhá…"

Kavan was grateful Ártur could not see his pained expression. His cousin had no inkling of what Kavan was capable of, nor did he know that Kavan would gladly give much of it away to be normal. "No," he said quietly. "I cannot. I have considered it…but I cannot."

Ártur snorted. "Do not start with the 'Elyri are not pure enough for His service' argument. I have heard it too often, and I do not believe it. Nor should you."

"I was not going to say that. I do not believe it either." He did not believe it, but sometimes doubt plagued him. He removed the medallion from beneath his robe; the metal flashed in the candlelight as he drew it over his head and handed it to Ártur. No one else had been allowed to touch it. "No, there is something else I must do…some other calling intended for me…"

The healer took it hesitantly, Kavan's words making him uneasy, and brought it closer to study. "By the Saints, Kavan…where did you get this?"

Kavan noted the amazement in his cousin's voice. "I found it in a lake…where I sometimes go. When I touched it, I understood that it is some part of whatever I am destined to do…but I do not know what it means yet."

"I have only seen this script on a few very ancient relics in Clarys," Ártur murmured as his thumb rubbed over the smooth surface. "It is said to be the writing of the phae k'kairá."

"The phae…" That was a possibility Kavan had not considered. No one knew who or what the phae were, but their writing and occasional artifacts surfaced throughout the Five Sovereignties, leaving little doubt of their existence. That those elusive, mythical beings might have left this item for him made it all the more significant. "Can you read it?"

The healer shook his head. "No one can. Does anyone know you have this?" What a clamor there would be, he thought, if they did.

Kavan took the pendant back and slipped it once more around his neck. "No. It did not seem appropriate to speak of it to anyone."

"That is probably for the best." It would spare Kavan public scrutiny and it was certainly wise not to interfere with the k'kairá. "If they are the ones who gave it to you, it may be wisest to await their instructions. I, for one, am quite curious what that will be."

"As am I," Kavan murmured.

Glancing at the harp on the step beside Kavan, he asked, "Did I interrupt something?"

"Nothing that cannot be resumed later. I suppose it is later than I should be out."

"No need to hurry home," the healer said with his hand on Kavan's. "I came to talk to you, to hear you play. I will explain your absence, though if I come home with you, bhyne will assume you knew I was returning and were waiting for me. Please...play. It will ease my burden."

Such a request from his cousin could not be denied, particularly when playing music was what Kavan loved to do most. He picked up the restored harp; its black wood glistened in the feeble candlelight as though wet, making Ártur whistle low in appreciation. With the instrument balanced on his thigh, Kavan had a sudden thought that might, he hoped, help his cousin find peace. "Try something with me?"

"Anything. What would you have me do?" He trusted Kavan and knew he would do anything asked of him, no matter how simple or far-fetched it might be.

"Place your hand on me. It may work best with your eyes closed, but if you wish to keep them open, watch Dhágdhuán's face. Clear your mind of thoughts. Do not think, only listen and feel." There was a chance the healer would feel nothing, but Kavan wanted to try.

Not knowing what to expect, Ártur did as instructed. He listened to the spell woven by the bell-chime sound of the brass strings. At first, he kept his eyes closed as Kavan asked and felt nothing for the longest time except the slowly melting turmoil of the past several days. As the song continued, however, an intricate tune that amazed the healer with its scope, time stopped and he began to feel something else. There was a gradually increasing energy building within Kavan, the likes of which the healer had never experienced. The strength of it made him uneasy and he opened his eyes in hopes of breaking the spell. His gaze settled immediately on the figure above them and he almost lost himself in awe.

Surely, it was his imagination. The figure of the Intercessor appeared alive, seeming to blink back tears in the suddenly smoky naós. Newborn flames flickered at his feet, and with the smoke came the distinctive smell of burning flesh. It was too real for Ártur, and thinking that he was seeing into Kavan's imagination, he drew his hand away in the hopes that it would stop.

The music did not falter as Ártur broke contact. The healer hesitated before daring to look up. Dumbfounded, he stared. It had not been his imagination or some product of Kavan's. And there was no way, he believed, that Kavan could be producing such a manifestation on his own. No man could do that. Compelled to act, he got to his feet, approached the figure, and reached with one hand to touch the bloodied feet through the flames. The heat of it made him tremble, as though it were a real fire, though his skin was not scorched, and what he touched was indeed flesh, hot and sooty, with smudges of singed skin rubbing off onto the healer's fingers. He almost lost what little his stomach held.

He stared at the blood on his hand, back into the tearful eyes of the animated figure and began to weep, feeling sick to his stomach again. The reality of burning a man alive had never struck him before. There were voices whispering in his head, and though he could not make out the words, he felt them to be promises of understanding and acceptance. Common sense told him he should deny what he was experiencing, but his senses, and his soul, knew this to be as real as he was.

He looked back at Kavan, who had stopped playing and was kneeling with his hands clasped in his lap, his eyes rimmed with unshed tears as the harp rested silent beside him. By his expression, Ártur knew that Kavan was not surprised by this but was waiting with apprehensive embarrassment for whatever his cousin would do. This, or something like it, had happened before? And Kavan had never written of it? Though partially surprised that the painfully honest boy would hide anything from him, Ártur knew he could find no fault in that choice. How much harder would it be to believe such things without seeing them with his own eyes?

Because he could not properly display how he felt, or describe it, the healer touched Kavan's mind. The boy's face broke into a grateful smile.

"See, Ártur. I told you, you are forgiven."

҂Chapter 10҃

dhededhá Bhílári wiped the primary chalice clean with a dry cloth, amazed and appalled at the substance staining the white fabric. The small, partially empty bottle on the table had been corked and sealed with wax; he wondered what should be done with it. He knew the mandates. Such events as he had witnessed today were to be reported to the ecclesiastical authorities in Clarys and relics like this, treasures of the Faith, were to be placed where everyone could see and venerate them. Those were ancient instructions, however, created at a time in Elyri history when such occurrences were, if not commonplace, at least more frequent than they were now. There had been no reports of miracles in over nine hundred and fifty years. Until today.

Would the gdhededhá in Clarys believe it? Bhílári was not sure he did, and he had seen it with his own eyes. But his congregation, or at least many of them, did believe. He heard it in their talk, saw it in the way they gazed at the young man whenever he passed. He heard it in the titles they bestowed on one of their own behind his back.

It was because of these things, and for the boy's sake, that Bhílári hesitated to do as protocol demanded. These events troubled the boy. This was his hometown. To display such evidence here in his home náós would cause people far and near to flock to Bhryell, to him. That would happen as soon as rumor spread to Clarys regardless. It would drive the boy from his home. Such relics might bring men to k'Ádhá, might bring pilgrims and donations to Bhryell, but it would harm Kavan, and Bhílári did not want to destroy one boy for the sake of the faith of others.

It had been a larger crowd at this Gathering than expected, but since the occurrence at Phyóná Térari's funeral two years ago, any Gathering at which Kavan Cliáth served had been marked by a dramatic increase in attendance. Bhílári suspected that, because today had been the young man's final mandatory service as altar attendant, the larger than usual number of people had come with the expectations of witnessing something spectacular. They had not, and had departed disillusioned that the boy, whom many called the Bhryell Saint, had failed to give them a sign.

Ah, but there had been a sign, the gdhededhá sighed, placing the red-stained cloth on the side table and replacing the chalice in the tabernacle. He then held the glass bottle up to the light, marveling again at the crimson liquid. A sign that only he and Kavan had witnessed. He did not know what it meant, did not know what any of these things meant, but it was a sign all the same. There had been none of the expected drama leading up to it. He prepared the serbháló prior to the service as he always did, but during the Gathering, at the time of Joining, when Kavan brought him the ceramic decanter, some change occurred because the substance inside had not been serbháló. It looked, and smelled, like freshly let blood.

There were legends of such changes in the Elements. The religious histories were full of such tales at the hands of the saints. But this was the only time in Bhílári's life that it had occurred. He had met Kavan's troubled gaze, nodded slightly, and set the chalice aside. Whatever it was, he could not allow the congregation to drink it. Maybe drinking it was what k'Ádhá intended; maybe if he had allowed it something more miraculous would have occurred, but Bhílári had not had the heart to follow through. He whispered to the gdhededhá beside him about the serbháló having uncouth debris in it, despite his usual care in straining it, and waited for the secondary decanter to be brought forth. The Gathering proceeded as usual with no one the wiser. But still, the event troubled him.

"gdhededhá?" called the androgynous voice that the man was familiar with. "You wish to speak with me?" Bhílári motioned him into the room towards the side bench. Kavan was not normally nervous in this chamber as many others seemed to be, but today he appeared anxious and skittish. The gdhededhá took his time putting his vestments away, hoping the delay would help the young man relax, and when he finished he sat as far away from Kavan on the bench as he could. It had become almost unbearable to be near this beautiful, almost fourteen-year-old young man, without touching him.

"You want to know about this morning? How I did it?"

The gdhededhá nodded, knowing he should have expected Kavan to know why he had been asked here. The young man's astuteness surprised him nonetheless. "I did not think you were responsible…but I would like to know how the transformation was accomplished…I have never seen such a thing…"

"Transformation?" Kavan looked at his hands, wondering what the gdhededhá meant while not sure that knowing would be a good thing. Finally, he said, "As we prepared for the Joining, my hands began to tingle. I knew something would happen…it always does when that feeling comes…but I had no idea what it would be. When I picked up the decanter, there was a shock…a jolt. The weight of the vessel changed, it grew warmer in my hands and the tingle was gone. But," he looked into the man's eyes, "I do not know what occurred."

Seeing that unease, Bhílári asked quietly, "Would you rather I not tell you?"

Kavan's eyes closed, his expression thoughtful, and when they opened again they were filled with resolution. "I would prefer honesty, gdhededhá."

With trembling hands, the man retrieved the cloth used to clean the chalice. He paused, glanced at the bottle on the table, and then brought it too. After another moment of indecision, he handed both objects to Kavan, who showed less hesitation in taking them. The cloth was studied first. Some of the red smeared on his fingers and he held them to his nose.

"It looks like…" Kavan studied the cloth a moment longer. "It is blood, isn't it?"

"I…believe so," the man said, watching Kavan turn the bottle around in his hands, holding it up to the light to study the liquid inside. The boy's expression remained carefully neutral.

"Will you…I presume you will follow the Mandates?"

"You know the Mandates?" Again, Bhílári was surprised. Very few lay people concerned themselves with the Mandates of the Faith's inner workings. That Kavan knew them made the gdhededhá uncomfortable. Perhaps he had learned them when these occurrences had begun, to prepare himself for a day such as this, but Bhílári still found it awkward.

"I know enough," Kavan replied. "I know you are required to report such things to k'gdhededhá Dórímyr…and that these…" his eyes left the bottle for the first time to look at the man beside him, "are to be displayed in the náós."

Bhílári's shoulders began to slump. "Would that trouble you?"

There was a change on Kavan's face at last as an anguished, tortured shadow settled there. The gdhededhá knew then that he had judged this young man correctly. "If such items were sent by k'Ádhá as symbols of His grace, mercy, compassion and power…then it is proper to display them, particularly if it will bring others to deliverance. But…"

At Kavan's hesitation, the older man dared to place one hand over the boy's. "Speak freely, Kavan. You have never censored yourself with me. Do not do so now. What is your objection?"

Kavan stared at the bottle. "To display them…no one here will look upon them as holy. Many have become…cynical. Few will look beyond them to find the divine. They will look and see only me. The things that have been done are not viewed as k'Ádhá's miracles…but as mine. These things will, I fear, lead people from the Faith, not to it. Saving a few souls by displaying these does not seem worth the hundreds of others it might damn."

Bhílári sighed and nodded his head. He had been thinking the same thing before Kavan's arrival. "You are wiser than many in the prelacy."

The corners of Kavan's eyes twitched. "I do not know about wiser, gdhededhá. My convictions are different, but that does not make me wiser." He resumed staring at the relics in his hands.

"What do your convictions suggest I do with these things?" Bhílári withdrew his hand.

Resting his elbows on his knees, Kavan looked from one item to the other and then asked, "May I keep them?"

The response was a puzzling one. The gdhededhá had expected a request to destroy them or to lock them away from public scrutiny. "Why do you want them?"

It took several minutes for Kavan to articulate a reply. "This is the first tangible evidence I have of these manifestations. I have often wondered if they were hallucinations, but this refutes that notion. I can no longer pretend these things have not…do not…happen. They do. This is proof. The only other options seem inappropriate. To destroy them would be blasphemy. To hide them in the bowels of the náós benefits no one. If you choose not to display them and not to send them to Clarys…they will at least benefit me as proof of the reality of my life."

Bhílári rubbed his eyes wearily. What must life be like for a child who experienced such things? "I cannot send them to Clarys. It would produce tenfold what we hope to avoid by not displaying them here…or else there will be a formal inquest into your life and I cannot see that benefitting anyone." It was difficult, in those moments, to view Kavan as a child. As he considered the issue, there seemed only one logical course to take. He made the decision then because he believed it was the right thing to do. "Keep them if you wish. I see no harm in that. If k'Ádhá sees fit to bless you with these things, it would be no sin for you to possess the fruit of your gifts."

Closing his eyes, Kavan's hands tightened around both objects. These events did not feel like gifts. He did not feel blessed. He felt confused and alone. "Thank you, gdhededhá." The cloth was carefully folded and pushed into the pocket of his white robe as he stood.

Unable to stop himself, Bhílári asked, "Do you know why these things happen?" even though he already knew the answer.

At the door, Kavan paused to look at the bottle cupped in his hand. Bhílári wished he could read the young man's face, knowing in his soul that this was the closest thing he would ever see to a living saint.

That was when Kavan spoke.

"I only know, gdhededhá, that I am not the Bhryell Saint."

Bhílári blanched. Kavan walked away.

☙*🙐

Severing the vine, Guthrie McHador pulled the strangled rabbit from the snare and secured it to his belt through a leather loop. His traps had not been profitable lately, and the approach of winter concerned him. He had never needed to rely on his own hunting prowess to feed himself for long, and though he was capable enough, he discovered he had not been as prepared as he had hoped for this new chapter of his life. It had not taken long, however, to master a few new tricks. Yesterday he had made one final trip into Chantel and had loaded his horse with as many supplies as the stocky beast could carry. He hoped it would be enough. His makeshift home in the forest of eastern Enesfel was safe from anyone who might hope to find him, as it was far removed from other inhabitation, but would it be an adequate shelter against the ravages of what looked to be a fiercer winter than last?

Having survived that first winter, however, he believed he would survive the second. Shoving his knife into its sheath, he started for home. The twisted shadows of the oaks told him it was nearing twilight, which made it easier for him to blend into his surroundings as he passed through the forest. What little wind there was blew from the south, carrying his scent behind him, and he moved with care, hoping to stumble across an unsuspecting deer. Instead, it was the sounds of men that came to him, men close enough that he could make out their words, and he crept cautiously closer to watch them and wait for them to be gone.

When he saw them, his heart caught in his throat. It was the King and a hunting party, out for a late autumn jaunt. There was a young boy with them, Prince Arlan he believed, though he never heard the child named and could not see his face through the overgrowth of brush behind which he hid. A pang of loneliness hit him, and Guthrie was torn between rushing to greet them and scurrying for his cabin. Quick movement would have given his position away, however, and facing them again would have undermined everything he was hoping to accomplish. No one in Rhidam had seen or heard from General McHador in over two years. For all anyone knew, the man was dead. How many times had he wanted to send a message to the King, telling him the truth, telling him he was alive? But every time he resisted, knowing he could never send such a letter, even if he were to write it. Better for things to remain as they were. As long as Prince Arlan remained safe, Guthrie would continue his solitary life, a safety valve for times of trouble if he was ever needed.

In the end, the hunting party began to move west, back towards Rhidam, taking the choice out of Guthrie's hands. He waited until they were far out of earshot, breathed a long, pained sigh of relief and regret, and with a heavy heart, pushed towards his home. Everything was as it had to be, but not necessarily as it should be.

֍*֍

Oppressive silence had settled over the MacLyr household, strangling Kavan with its tension as he waited alone for the inevitable storm. He wished for anything, the singing of birds, the chirp of crickets, or the sound of wind or rain against the windows and roof. But it was too cold for crickets and the birds had all gone to roost once the sun disappeared behind its hedge of mountains. He tried to push away the uneasiness, the tight, cold knot in his belly, as he meticulously folded his clothing and placed it into the leather satchel Ártur had given him. Better the silence, he decided, then the tirade he expected.

As it was, he was having difficulty shutting out his uncle's rampage from his thoughts, and the man was still in the center of town. When he could no longer tolerate the intensity of Tám's thoughts and words, Kavan placed his bag on the floor beside his locked trunk and his harp and settled cross-legged on the mattress. He funneled all of his energy into shutting out those hate-filled projections.

He needed to leave this house. He understood that. This day had been long in coming, yet he had barely turned fourteen and would not be considered an adult for another year. There was nowhere for him to run, except to bhydáni Tíbhyan's, and he was reluctant to involve the sage in his problems. Already most of Kavan's more personal and precious belongings had been stored in the bhydáni's home where Tám could never get them, but going there with all of his things, as a permanent resident, was another matter.

If he had thought he could make it safely to Ártur, Enesfel was the only other possible refuge. But his cousin knew less about the tensions in this house than the bhydáni did, as Kavan had never had the heart to reveal things to the healer that would only hurt and anger him. Kavan did not want to sow discord in the family, he only wanted peace. For those reasons, Kavan had stayed where he was for as long as he had been able. It saddened him to know that he had no home in the true sense of the word, but staying here was no longer possible.

Bhílári might not have spoken of the last miracle to his superiors in Clarys, but someone from Bhryell had. It was the only explanation Kavan could think of for the k'gdhededhá to have come to Bhryell when he never had before.

The thunder of his door slamming into the wall startled him, breaking his concentration. Tám's gaze traveled over his nephew to the heavy book that lay on the bed. Determined not to be intimidated, though he knew he should have hidden it from sight, Kavan picked up the book and clutched it to his chest with one hand. He swallowed hard, knowing it was too late to hide it.

"The Articles of Kóráhm." It was a serpent's hiss, not a question. "Not only do you dare to argue with the k'gdhededhá and his retinue about the heretic, you bring his writings under my roof?"

There was a sharp, heated pause. Kavan wondered if he were expected to confirm what his uncle had said. He could not deny either accusation nor did he want to, thus he decided it was wisest to stay silent.

"Give that to me."

Kavan did not speak. He did not move as Tám approached him.

"I will not allow those malicious, blasphemous words in my home. Give it to me."

Kavan shook his head and clutched it tighter. "I will not," he said firmly, his voice quiet and tense. His uncle had never read the Articles; how could he know what words it contained?

Tám's hand came up. "You will do as I say or…"

"Do not hit me."

He did not fear being struck as much as he feared that hot glow that had formed within him as Tám approached, just as it had done with Prince Owain many years ago. Kavan tried to harness it, hold it back while hoping his uncle would heed the plea. He had learned everything Tíbhyan could teach him, but he did not believe he could control this impulse if Tám lashed out at him, and that loss of control frightened him more than the threats did.

So many things happened next that Kavan would never be certain of the order of events. The hand came down, catching him across the face. Dháná cried out from the doorway, begging her husband to stop as years of pent up fury and fear were unleashed on the boy. Kavan did nothing to defend himself, only tried to shield his face and protect his book as he focused on holding back that ball of power. A final blow knocked him against the headboard with enough force that he nearly blacked out. The book slid from his hands to the floor when his concentration broke and the energy he had tried to harness burst forth. Dazed, he watched his uncle sprawl back against the wall, thrown by the unseen force that left the man stunned, his eyes glazed over and his jaw slack. Dháná stared, horror-stricken, not knowing what had happened or if Tám was alive.

Kavan forced himself to stand on shaky legs, feeling weak, drained, and frightened, afraid to know the results of that very same question. Murder in the land was rare; what punishment he might receive was horrifying to think about. The skin on his face burned. His shoulders ached from his uncle's bruising grasp. Dháná was sobbing, kneeling beside her husband as he began to moan, a sound that brought the boy relief even though he knew it ended his residency here.

At least he would not have to carry the man's death on his conscience.

He picked up his book, harp, and the satchel of clothing and paused beside his aunt, though out of range of his uncle's grasp, gracing her with the same tortured expression he had carried since early childhood.

"Get out."

"Tám…" the woman choked.

But he ignored her. His hard gaze was on the odd boy he had been reluctant to take in from the start, even if he was his brother's son. There had always been something unnerving about Kavan and Tám resented being afraid of a child. He was angry that Kavan brought unwanted attention, the wrong kind of attention, to a family whose name had been respected for all of its history. The honor of private tutelage with bhydáni Tíbhyan, and Kavan's accomplishments with him, did not balance the scales. Tám wanted to restore the honor he felt their name had lost and felt it could only be done by being rid of this unusual, irksome boy.

"I want him out of this house."

Kavan was not going to argue, as much as the frightened child within him wanted to beg for love and forgiveness from the only family he had. He wanted a home, wanted a family, but this house was not it. It had never been. Dhárá caught his arm as he started past her towards the stairs, steering clear of Tám, but her words were directed to her husband. "You cannot do this. He is only a boy…"

"Do not tell me what I cannot do, Dhárá." He looked as if he might strike her too, something unthinkable to most Elyri men. "If he is not…"

Kavan did not wait to hear the rest. Better that he leave and protect his aunt. She did not deserve to suffer on his behalf. He closed his mind against further intrusion, though Tám's thoughts continued to push at the edges, and left the only home he had known without looking back.

His eyes burned with unshed tears as he trudged blindly through the falling snow. By the time he stopped outside of the náós door to stare at the single stained glass window, he was beyond thinking, almost beyond feeling. There was only cold numbness and a weight on his chest and shoulders that felt as if it would never go away, that felt as if he might suffocate beneath it. Inside the building were voices, the choirmaster and some of the choir he realized, preparing for tomorrow's Gathering. He was supposed to play for that service but he was uncertain now if he would. He was uncertain of everything.

The voices eventually moved nearer the door. Not wanting to be seen, expecting recrimination, blame and ridicule rather than compassion, Kavan turned away. How long had he been standing there? He did not know. His mind was as disoriented as his body had become. His feet moved of their own accord but he was not surprised when he found himself before Tíbhyan's home. It was the only place he could go. The lamps inside still glowed, despite the late hour, and he knew the door would be unlocked. The sage rarely barred his door. Shuffling footsteps came and went as the old man's silhouette crossed the light. Reluctantly, knowing he could not stand in the cold all night, Kavan rapped on the door frame.

"Enter." Tíbhyan did not turn as the door opened, but he recognized the sound of his student's footfalls on the threshold. "Well, Kavan, what brings you out late in this weather?" It was not the first time Kavan had come to him late in the evening with some question or to show him some new trick he had mastered. But this time, Kavan did not reply, only stood in the doorway, barely blinking as his mind struggled to put words together. "Don't stand there with the door open," the old man continued when he received no reply.

Hearing nothing, he looked up from his cleaning; it was the first time Kavan had ever seen that look of alarm on the man's face, and he knew his appearance was worse than he imagined.

"Holy…child! What has happened to you? Move into the light that I may look at you…"

Kavan still did not move so Tíbhyan used one hand to steer him inside and the other to close the door against the snow. The touch on his arm broke through Kavan's daze enough for him to murmur, "I need a place to sleep tonight, bhydáni. I can no longer go home. I will find somewhere else tomorrow…"

"You know you are always welcome here as long as…" A shadow of fury settled on his wrinkled face. "He did not…" he growled as he made sense of Kavan's unspoken words and the red swelling on his face. "You are his blood kin…how could a man…there is no excuse for…come…I have a place for you to…I will…by all the saints and záphyr…"

The sage continued to fume as he prepared a pallet for Kavan in his study, his words coming in an incoherent stream as he railed about the injustice done to his student. Kavan was not listening; he knew the man's sentiments without hearing them and he found a small degree of comfort in knowing that Tíbhyan was on his side. Tíbhyan took his belongings, set them beside the pallet, and helped Kavan get comfortable before tucking the blankets around him. "Why? What could you have done to warrant such a monstrous thing?"

"I…" Kavan rubbed his eyes. He was exhausted and they burned. "I was involved in a debate with k'gdhededhá Dórímyr about Saint Kóráhm…"

"You…?" The sage began to laugh, softly at first, though the merry sound increased until he was clutching his sides. He forced himself to stop, however, when he realized that Kavan's broken expression had not changed. Clearing his throat, he patted the boy's hand. "I would have liked to be there to see it…Old Marble arguing with you about the Heretic-Saint…his least favorite topic and your favorite. Knowing the way you think, how persuasive and persistent you can be when motivated, I wager he completely lost his composure."

Not understanding his teacher's laughter, but knowing that Tíbhyan knew the k'gdhededhá better than Kavan, he nodded. "Yes, sir."

"And Tám was embarrassed, was he, that his own kin could match wits with, and out-smart, the leader of our Faith? gdhededhá do not know everything there is to know. Even I could teach Old Marble a thing or two if he were inclined to listen. They are men as we are, not special when it comes down to it. Anyone capable of taking on such a debate, brave enough to try, especially one your age, should be admired not punished."

Feeling an unexpected flicker of joy at being referred to as a man, Kavan added, "He found my book…the Articles. Either the book had to go…or I did. I would not relinquish it…and decided it was time to leave. I can care for myself, bhydáni." He did not yet know how, but he was determined to do so.

The old man studied his pupil closely. The bruises on Kavan's face continued to darken. A healer could do little for Kavan, and summoning one would lead to questions Kavan would not answer. Despite what Tám had done, Tíbhyan knew Kavan would never disgrace his family by making the incident public. And though he was upset, now that the numbness in his head was beginning to clear, his emotions were once again tightly controlled. Yes, the sage realized; Kavan might not be of legal age to be on his own, but he was more capable of caring for himself, better prepared for a life of responsibility, than many adults Tíbhyan had known.

Patting the boy's hand this time, bending down to kiss the top of Kavan's head, Tíbhyan said, "I will tend to this matter for you, Kavan. Do not fear." He began to dress to go into the snow.

There was a flash of panic in Kavan's eyes as he jolted upright. "Do not…I do not want to go back. I am not welcome there and it would be…awkward…"

"kyá…" the man laid a hand on Kavan's bruised shoulder. "You are welcome to remain here until more suitable arrangements can be made…however long that takes. I would never send you back to that life, you have my word. Do not trouble yourself about it further. You are safe here. Sleep; I will return as quickly as I can."

Though he did not think he would be able to sleep and knew that the sage would be gone a fair long while, Kavan whispered his thanks and fell asleep almost as soon as the door closed. Thankfully, he did not dream, and when he awoke later the next morning, there was bread, honey, and goat's milk on the table but the bhydáni was not home. A glance into the mirror told Kavan that he did not dare go out, not even to the náós where he was expected to play. It was too late for that, he realized. He had slept through the Gathering for the first time he could remember. After blessing himself, he ate a little, slept some more, and then awoke to seek solace in music once again.

It was late afternoon before Tíbhyan returned with a sealed scroll in his wrinkled hand. Without speaking, he beckoned Kavan to follow. Outside it was no longer snowing and the sunlight sparkled like stars on the blanket of white spread over the ground. The two of them passed the stone fountain at the center of town and went to an abandoned structure directly across the square. It was a building Kavan recognized, having passed it often as he went through the town center, a small brick affair with wood shutters, and an oaken door. It had been abandoned since before the time of the plague, empty all of Kavan's life. Though he knew nothing about it, it had always seemed to speak to him when he was near it. It was doing so now. The bhydáni pushed open the unlocked door and led the boy into the entrance hall.

There was a plainly dressed woman within, whom Kavan did not recognize, who looked to be preparing the place for occupancy. She did not look at them as they came in, making Kavan's attempt to hide his battered face an unnecessary one. He watched her wipe away dust as they passed, but did not ask his teacher why they were in this house. He would learn the truth soon enough.

Through the doorway to the left was the kitchen, a small room that consisted of a wood stove, a brick oven, and a stone-topped counter and washbasin. There were cupboards on the wall, empty except for dust. Another doorway at the rear of the entrance hall led into the well room and from there into an open rear yard. Tall snow-laden, untrimmed hedges and a small paddock and stable marked its perimeter.

To the right of the entrance hall was a single room that functioned as both dining area and main sitting room. Except for an expensive oak table and its six chairs at one end, and the fireplace at the other, the room held nothing. There was a fire on the hearth, whose warmth made this room one of welcome. It was easy to envision high-backed cushioned chairs within, a large harp in the corner, and candles lit everywhere as people gathered to hear him play. Kavan quickly dismissed the imagery however as too fanciful to become reality, and continued to follow Tíbhyan.

They slowly climbed the stairs from that room to the second floor where they found four small bedrooms and a water closet. One room was empty; two others held bureaus of the same design and wood as the table downstairs. These rooms smelled of wood polish, wax, and soap and were free of dust. The last bedroom, however, was furnished already with Kavan's own four-poster bed, the one he had slept in nearly every day of his life. The still locked cedar chest that Kavan had been unable to take with him the night before, which his uncle had thankfully not broken into, an oaken dresser like those in the other rooms, and an oak writing desk with two brass oil lamps and a high-backed chair filled the empty space. To the left of its tall, expensive colored glass window, there was a small, adjoining oratory, big enough for only an altar and three worship benches.

Trembling, his mind refusing to believe what his senses were suggesting, Kavan turned from the oratory to look into his teacher's blue eyes; only then did he notice the tapestry on the wall inside the door. It hung from ceiling to floor on a long iron pole and stretched from the doorway to the corner of the wall. Upon it was the image of a young shepherd in a dusty gray cloak, sitting with a harp on his knee, surrounded by a flock of serene sheep. The shepherd was looking upwards in awe at Dhágdhuán, who hovered before him with his scarred, bloody hands outstretched in welcome. There were záryph in the woven sky, their supple wings of black, silver, and gold surrounding the Intercessor like a halo against the backdrop of a twilight sky.

Kóráhm.

Kavan's shivering increased, he could not make it stop. Kóráhm's written account of this visitation stated that the záryph wings were the color of storm clouds heavy with rain illuminated by the brilliance of the sun, but Kavan had never successfully pictured that scene, and the artwork he had seen within manuscripts and scrolls had depicted the wings as the white most Faithful believed them to be, or even brown like an eagle's wings. But this? This Kavan knew to be accurate. He knew this story by heart, but seeing it vividly rendered made him queasy, as if he were standing within the scene and intruding on a private moment. The shepherd's auburn rimmed face was rapt with devotion, his lame foot twisted beneath him, and he bore none of the scars he would acquire later in his life. He was, Kavan was sure, the most beautiful man he had ever seen.

"What do you think?" asked Tíbhyan who had settled into the chair at the desk to watch Kavan fondly.

Voice catching and stuttering, Kavan replied, "I do not know what to think, bhydáni. I am not sure I understand what I see."

The sage chuckled affectionately. "I believe you understand already, Kavan. I can see it on your face. You have only to acknowledge what your eyes and heart tell you." He folded his thin arms across his chest. "This house once belonged to my daughter."

"I did not know you had a child…"

"Aye…I had a family once…a wife and daughter. She was my only child; she never had the chance to wed." He rubbed his fingers over the desk as if drawing memories out of the wood. "She died before you were born, before your cousin was born, and this, everything in it, belonged to her. There is no one to fill the walls, and I have no use for it. I am content where I am. I have been at a loss as to what to do with it. If you will accept it, it is yours."

"Mine?" Kavan whispered, circling the room again before coming to stop before the tapestry. Could he possibly accept such a grand gift?

"Yours," the old man repeated, as he waved the scroll he had been carrying. "The lómesté has drawn up all necessary documents. You may stay with me if you prefer, or you may make this your own at once. Either way, the house has been transferred into your name. It is yours." When Kavan did not take the scroll, Tíbhyan lowered his arm. "Until you are of legal age, your family must meet your needs for food and clothing; it is the least they can do…and your uncle does not want a scandal. I have rooms of furnishings that have gone unused for too long and there are some here, in the basement. You may have your pick of them. If nothing suits you, I will see that you are supplied with whatever else you require. You will be safe here, Kavan."

"But…" The boy's voice was a whisper as he traced Kóráhm's features on the softness of the tapestry. "Why would you do this? I am not…"

Tíbhyan smiled warmly. "You need somewhere to call home. I need someone to leave this place too or it will revert to the lómesté when I am no longer here to care for it. You cannot go back to that house…for good reason…and Rhidam would not be the place for you. Here, you may do as you please without interference from your uncle or a puttering old man." He chuckled. "You are as kin to me, Kavan, the nearest I have to family, and I want to see you are provided for. I believe it will suit us both. Will you accept my offer?"

Kavan pondered his teacher's words. It was true he had nowhere else to go. It was also true that, while he would be welcome in the sage's home, it would not be a practical long-term solution. The man had his own life, his own business to conduct, and Kavan knew he would feel awkward and ashamed imposing on the man's hospitality indefinitely. Here was this house, a house that had called to him from the time he was old enough to hear such whispers in the Power. He could stay here. Better him, he thought, than someone who had never known the sage.

Besides, the documents had already been drawn. The transfer of ownership made. If the house was already in his name, how could he not accept it? Why should he not live here?

He extended a trembling hand and took the scroll, his fingers brushing lightly over the older ones, transferring an expression of gratitude that he could never adequately express in words. As there were others present, however, and he did not want to seem ungrateful to them, he said aloud, "I am honored and humbled to accept. Thank you, bhydáni."

The old man pushed to his feet with a joyful expression. "You are welcome. Come. Let me help you make this your home."

❧White Pawn❧

୵Chapter 11୵

Huddling beneath the red woolen blanket that Elys had made for him years ago, Ártur stared into the fire, fighting the fever that had developed five days earlier. It happened to him nearly every spring, no matter what precautions he took, often causing him to wonder about his overall health and constitution. To keep the royal children healthy, he had not tended them during his ailment, leaving Mormer Nelsen, the Teren physician, to tend them in his stead. The healer knew the Teren doctor was delighted to have something to do that did not involve the surly Prince Bowen, Prince Girvin, or the palace staff.

With nothing to occupy his hours of sickness, Ártur found himself thinking more and more about Kavan. The healer had not been in Bhryell since his talk with Kavan three winters ago, and he felt immensely guilty because of it. He had made a promise to his cousin and knew he had broken it. He wondered often how Kavan was doing, how much the boy had changed. Correction, he thought, propping himself up on his pillows. Kavan was fifteen, a man by Elyri standards, though not mature enough physically to father children. Had he remained home or moved out on his own? Most Elyri did not set up their own homes until they married, and even then, many remained living with the family of one spouse or other, but Ártur could not imagine Kavan married. Maybe that was because he still thought of his cousin as a little boy. Was he supporting himself with music? If so, how was he faring? Ártur wished he knew.

A message had come from Tíbhyan before the turn of the year; Kavan's level of ability was such that the bhydáni was no longer his teacher. Payment was no longer required. This development surprised Ártur more than he cared to admit. Those Elyri who wished to push their talents to the limits sometimes spent decades under a bhydáni's instruction before becoming bhydáni themselves. The healer had assumed that, given Kavan's potential and passion, he would be under the sage's instruction for many more years. Yet, if Tíbhyan's words were true, Kavan had surpassed the sage's knowledge in the short span of eight years. That was, by any standard, remarkable. Though the two still visited frequently, the sage explained, tutelage was no longer part of those visits. What was Kavan like, the healer mused? How powerful was his young cousin?

That last letter had seemed strained and formal, leaving Ártur with an uncomfortable ache. Or maybe it was the knowledge of how much his cousin had changed and how little Ártur knew about him that made the healer feel that way. And maybe, he thought sourly, it was the fact that he was no longer required to send payment to the bhydáni, meaning that the only link that held him to Kavan was broken. Most likely, however, it was a combination of those things, combined with the fact that Kavan had not included a message for him yet again. How long had it been? Nearly a year? More? Ártur was not sure. Perhaps Kavan had concluded that, because Ártur had not written or come home, he no longer desired to hear from him. If that were true, Ártur could blame no one but himself. Whatever the cause, the healer felt abandoned and heavy-hearted. He could imagine how Kavan must feel.

There was no adequate excuse for not going back to Bhryell. The last three years in Rhidam had been blissfully uneventful. The twins were growing well and King Donal had solidified his popularity throughout the Sovereignties through wisdom, compassion, and justice. The healer had become more influential in the King's court after Guthrie's departure, a situation he did not enjoy as it kept him busier than ever although it afforded him prestige and a higher income. Yet no matter how busy he had been, he knew he had only to ask if he had decided to go home. The King would have granted the request, particularly if it meant Kavan might come back to Rhidam.

Ártur's new status, however had also created additional tension in the royal house, which he argued was the reason he had not gone home or brought Kavan to visit. Prince Bowen had grown angrier over the healer's increased influence, but other than attempting to sway Prince Farrell to his views, he had not caused trouble. Prince Farrell continued to show no interest in affairs of state; in spite of the King's efforts to school him. He came to Rhidam for festivals and feasts, or when some event required the royal family's attendance, otherwise he spent his time at the family's Kamin estate or hunting anywhere across the kingdom the winds called him. He did not actively avoid the Elyri healer because he was not in Rhidam enough to feel the need. Prince Girvin, on the other hand, would shrink from the healer, and leave any room Ártur was in if he could. Ártur was saddened that those he had served faithfully could suspect him of evil, and he did not want Kavan to see that. If he had gone to Bhryell, Kavan would have sensed the tension in him, and the healer did not want to talk about it. He did not want to hear from his mother and father the multitude of reasons why he should abandon his position in a potentially hostile land to return to the safety of Elyriá. His best friend was here, in Rhidam, and needed him. So did, he believed, Prince Arlan and Princess Deidre, and those were reasons enough for him to stay where he was.

His thoughts came back to the present, pushed out of his musings by his door bursting open with such fury that it startled him. Lady Johanna, the children's attendant, looked both pale and flushed as she cried breathlessly, "Lord Healer! Come quickly! Master Arlan!"

Not bothering with his outer robe, Ártur threw off his blanket and ran to the children's room where Mormer sat on the edge of the prince's bed, the lines on his face stretched tight as he tried to cool the child's forehead. The prince tossed feebly, as though movement took too much energy despite his body's need for it. The Teren doctor was wise enough to move aside now that Ártur had arrived. In immediate life and death instances, only an Elyri healer had the possibility of saving a life. Ártur took his place, cradled the boy's head in his lap, and placed his hands on the prince's chest.

Eyes closed, Ártur traced the weakening threads of life to the source of its battle. "A purgative, Mormer...water...blankets." But the Teren doctor, his expression shocked and grave at what those words implied, did not move. "Mormer..." Ártur demanded, and when there was still no response he said, "Lady Johanna...please..."

"Yes, milord." The woman wasted no time with a curtsey; she was already on her way out of the room before he began his request.

Ártur, meanwhile, did what he could to divert the poison from the child's organs, praying as he did so, feeling the small body swing between fire and ice beneath his hands. By the time Mormer shook off his shock and moved to assist, and Lady Johanna returned with the requested items, the healer was beginning to fear they would lose the child. Mormer did not need instructions to proceed; he wrapped the blankets tightly around the prince and administered the purgative while Ártur sank deeper into a healing trance.

It continued thus for over an hour as an audience gradually gathered in the doorway. The boy retched several times, and each time was given water and more purgatives to expel the toxins in his system. Not until the child slept at last and was out of danger did Ártur remove his trembling hands and sit in stillness, wheezing as his own ailment made breathing difficult. When he felt calm and strong enough to speak, he met first Mormer's gaze, and then the Queen Mother's, and lastly the King's, each lingering look saying something different.

"Poison. Fortunately, something relatively slow acting…and common I suspect. If Lord Nelsen and Lady Johanna had not been diligent in their care, if I had not been summoned, or if the agent had been more potent, we would have lost him. But he is out of danger…"

"Out of danger?" the King snapped, his relief transmuting into fury. "He will not be out of danger until we find this would-be child killer…"

Prince Bowen's voice pushed through the gathering from somewhere behind the King. "I think your murderer is in this room…"

The healer began to protest but the King was quicker. "I have warned you about speaking such slander against Ártur. He is…"

"Innocent?" The prince managed to shove his way to his brother's side where he could see and be seen, and also heard. His broad face was layered in shadows of hatred and anger. "That may be the case…but I was not referring to him."

Lord Nelsen's face turned gray as the prince's gaze fell on him. "It is true," he stuttered, "that I and Lady Johanna have been the only ones with the children today, but I have not…there is no cause for me to wish the children harm."

The King's gaze turned cold. "Ártur, read him."

The healer hesitated. He did not want to do it. Forcing his way into someone's thoughts was something he abhorred and almost never did. It was mostly the fact that the doctor, despite whatever fear he held of his colleague's abilities, reluctantly held his hands forward that allowed Ártur to continue. He placed his hands on Mormer's open palms and quickly did what he had been asked to do.

Ignoring Mormer's sickened expression, he said, "He is not the one, My Liege. He stayed with them while Lady Johanna retrieved the children's nightly milk, and she was present when he gave it to the prince. It was something the boy consumed…at dinner perhaps, or in the milk…"

Prince Bowen took a step forward but the King caught his arm and yanked him back. His eyes shot imaginary daggers at his brother as he growled, "Lady Johanna then? She was with the children the last time, and left in time to…"

The thin, stately woman's face flushed with indignation. "I have tended all of you in some capacity," she exclaimed. "I have no reason…I would never…"

"Ártur," the King ordered again.

Lady Johanna backed away. "Milord! There were witnesses. Do not let him touch me."

Interceding on her servant's behalf, Cordelia spoke sternly. "Must this be done? She has been a good and faithful servant and has no reason to…"

This time, when the words came, the King's voice was a low, black growl. "Ártur. Now." He rarely contradicted the Queen Mother, but he needed answers now.

The Elyri looked at the women sympathetically, while Prince Bowen impatiently tapped his foot, wanting to pull free of the King's bruising grasp but not daring to. Ártur knew the King and prince were hoping to find some indication of guilt from those present, but the servant woman submitted to the King's command without further protest, which to the healer proved her innocence.

"She is not the one, Sire." Ártur lowered his hands, wishing he could flee Prince Bowen's sharp gaze. "The pitcher of milk was waiting in the kitchen. She gives it to the children every night before bed. Many people know this and have access to the kitchen. Anyone could have…"

"Then why were neither Miss Weylin nor Princess Deidre affected?" the King snorted.

"They are given milk to help them sleep, Your Majesty," Lord Nelsen explained in a stammering voice. "The girls were asleep when it came. It seemed unnecessary to wake them for something as trivial as milk."

The King's grip relaxed enough that Bowen pulled free with a hiss. "It turned out not to be trivial." He glared at Ártur. "How do we know you are not lying about what you read in them, Elyri? How do we know that you are not in on this plot? I believe all of you are guilty of treason. And the two of you," he glanced at the Queen Mother and his brother, "are fools to allow this to continue. Why do you readily believe his words? They are sorcery. The taint of this man is spreading under our roof and you fail to see it!"

The King reached for his brother's throat but Bowen eluded his hands and slipped out of the room. Shaking with rage, the King growled to Cordelia. "The children and Lady Johanna are to stay with you tonight. I will place guards outside your chambers. Lord Nelsen, return to your room and remain there until morning. We will deal more with this then."

The Teren doctor bowed and departed as ordered, slinking past the Royal Family as if afraid of punishment. When he was gone, Ártur hesitantly asked, "My Liege…?"

"You are not well, Healer MacLyr, and should not be walking the drafty halls in your nightshirt. Return to bed. All of you."

To be sure he was obeyed, the King remained where he was until the last person left the room. Back in his own chambers, the King slouched on the edge of the bed, fingering the braided coronal he usually wore, studying the glow of its amber and crimson stones in the dying firelight. Meara, his wife, moved closer. She knew her husband did not want to talk; she put her arms around him, rested her head against his bare shoulder, and remained silent. If only she could have provided another heir, if either of their daughters had lived, these recent affairs would not be vital to the state of the kingdom. The bickering amongst Innis' Lachlan's sons would be for naught. And there would be no reason, not even a marginal one, for anyone to wish the youngest Lachlan prince dead. Not that she saw any reason for it, but some people, she sighed with regret as her husband turned to kiss her, needed very little reason to create mayhem.

꘏*꘎

The tallow candles had burned down long ago, leaving flickering stubs in the brass holders scattered about the young man's room. He slept fitfully, though not long before he had been feverish and retching, his body cold, damp, and limp. ílMairós Konsíl had stayed with him since early evening, using every technique and medicine he could think of to relieve the symptoms and make Kavan well. None of them had worked.

Finally, as Dháná debated the necessity of sending for gdhededhá Bhílári, Kavan convulsed a final time, curled into a ball, and drifted into a deep sleep. The healer waited until his patient's body temperature stabilized and he had settled into a more normal sleeping position before declaring Kavan out of danger. Dháná lingered in the doorway the entire time, afraid that if she looked away they would lose him. This was the first time in his fifteen years of life he had been sick, and the nature of this illness frightened her. She had lost children, relatives, and friends to the plague. She did not want to lose Kavan too.

"Lady Dháná, come away. Allow him his rest," said Healer Konsíl. He took her arm and she allowed him to lead her out of the room, though she freed herself from his grasp when they reached the staircase. Neither spoke as they descended into the sitting room where Tíbhyan waited near the fire in the chair Kavan had reserved for his visits. The old man had been in that same chair when Dháná had come with Kavan's weekly supplies late that afternoon. When Kavan had fallen suddenly ill, Tíbhyan remained with him while Dháná had gone for the healer, but he had not gone upstairs to witness the worst of the symptoms. His legs would not allow him to climb. The sage met her gaze; the dark circles under his eyes showing that he had not slept either.

"ílMairós? What was it? A plague?" She could think of no common illness that would have presented such symptoms.

The healer avoided the bhydáni's eyes as he replied. "I cannot say. The symptoms suggested poisoning…" Dháná's hand flew to her mouth. "But there was no trace of any substance in him. It was not the result of anything he has eaten as far as I could determine. It was not a seizure, not a sickness in any true sense of the word. Whatever it was, it came, and went, on its own. I had no hand in his recovery."

Tíbhyan closed his eyes. He recalled the injury that was not an injury; he remembered feeling certain that if a particular sort of harm touched Kavan in a very particular way, it could kill him. He had little doubt that this was the case now, but he was no closer to understanding how it could be. He had never had the opportunity to discuss it with Healer MacLyr as he had once hoped to do. He saw little use in speaking of something he could not prove or explain.

"Can we do anything for him?" the woman asked.

The healer shrugged. "Watch him for a day or two, see what he eats and drinks, where he goes…and let me know at once if this should happen again. I do not know how I can be of help, but a repeat of these symptoms will be worth noting." He opened the door and stepped out onto the porch. "Honestly speaking, however, this is likely as unique to him as all of his other features."

Dháná closed the door behind him without bidding him goodnight, disliking the ridicule in his tone and words. Even Tíbhyan's expression was uncharacteristically dark. Next time, if there was a next time, she prayed Ártur would be there. Surely, her son would know what to do.

And Tíbhyan, though not inclined to pray, prayed that if there was a next time, Ártur was wherever he needed to be to save the life at the other end of what seemed to be a power link. Anything less would cause Kavan to die.

"I shall sit with him," Dháná said. "He may need something."

"If it is not an imposition on your time and family…that would be wise. I will stay, of course, but I cannot go up…"

Knowing what he was implying about her family, feeling guilty that she had been unable to dissuade Tám from expelling Kavan from their home, Dháná returned to Kavan's room, blew out the candles and turned down the lone oil lamp to its lowest setting before settling at the bedside to watch over him.

❧*❧

Within an hour of daybreak, news of the second assassination attempt on Prince Arlan had spread throughout most of Rhidam. Rumors of responsibility were as plentiful and varied as the shops that lined the city streets, but the bulk of the accusations had shifted, without cause or justification, away from Ártur MacLyr and focused on Lord Mormer Nelsen. The healer pitied the man; regardless of the outcome of these events, and evidence to the contrary, Mormer's reputation stood to be ruined. No one in the Teren kingdoms would welcome the services of a man accused of harming royalty unless the King supported him, and while King Donal did not make accusations, and did not release him from service, Mormer's presence had begun to fill a room with a tension that had never existed before. He was as good as condemned.

Lady Johanna asked for personal leave to wait out the crisis and the Queen Mother granted it, eager to keep the woman she had known most of her adult life out of harm's way and free from further suspicion. She and Ártur could tend to the twins for the time being. Throughout the day, Prince Arlan steadily regained his strength and health, but privately his mother decided it was time to put the final phase of General McHador's plan into action. She did not believe she could wait any longer. The long lull between murder attempts had lured them into a sense of security, into believing the threat to Prince Arlan was past, but having almost lost her son twice, she did not want to risk his death in a third attempt. After speaking with Ártur, she tried to explain to her son what he needed to know, but the not yet eight-year-old prince did not understand. He did, however, understand that if he did not obey his mother's wishes, if he spoke of what she said to anyone, his would-be killer might be successful next time. He was a smart enough child to want to avoid that.

By the day's end, his condition improved enough that he was able to eat a small meal and then was encouraged to sleep again. The King lifted the guard outside of the Queen Mother's room, but the children still slept there, as it was deemed safer for them to be with their mother. It had been arranged that Ártur would come to her chambers when the rest of the palace slept. All she could do was wait, and the waiting, sitting beside the hearth with her thoughts churning through all of the possibilities in life, was driving her mad. She was there still, arms wrapped close around her body, when the healer finally arrived. Cordelia looked at him, her cheeks tear-stained and pale, and gave a defeated, heavy sigh.

"It is time?"

No happier about the situation than she was, Ártur nodded. "Yes, milady. The halls were clear when I came."

A tattered scroll was produced from her pocket and placed in his hands. "You should see this."

He read the message carefully and rolled it again with a sick feeling in his stomach. "We knew this would come. Whoever wishes the prince harm is serious. Next time it could be a poison I cannot stop. Or something worse. It is best that you chose to do this…for his sake."

"I know." She reached for the scroll. "I think it is best the King not know about this…in light of what we are about to do…"

"No. Let me keep it. It might be the best way to explain his absence tomorrow." A written threat was as good as admitting guilt…by someone at least, since the scroll was unsigned.

The queen sighed. "Where shall we put it?"

"I shall find somewhere later tonight. Do not concern yourself, milady. The less you know…"

"…the better." She grunted. "I am heartily weary of hearing that." Rising to her feet she continued, "I have put some things together. Do not look at me like that, Lord Healer. Arlan must have clothing, and I doubt Lord McHador will have anything appropriate for a boy his age."

Considering the short notice upon which they were acting, the healer knew that was likely true. He took the leather satchel from her and slung it over his shoulder.

"There is something in there from Innis too, something he said his youngest son was to have. He would not allow me to give it to Girvin, as if he knew there would be another…"

Ártur gathered the sleeping boy from his bedding and cradled him against his chest. "I think he did know, milady. He chose the name for a reason. He believed Prince Arlan will have a purpose to his life, which is why it is imperative to keep him safe."

Cordelia nodded and whispered, "There is no need to wake him. We have said our farewells." Not that it would make it any easier for the boy when he awoke in a strange place without his mother or sister. As long as he slept, he remained quiet, and not having to see his sad eyes or hear him cry would make it that much easier for his mother to let him go.

Patting the back of the boy's head, Ártur swallowed hard. "This is difficult, I know…but it is the best we can give him…"

"You know I will never see him again." She took a long look at her son's sleeping face, kissed his forehead, and tucked his blanket in around him. "I am resigned to that, but I wish I knew what he will look like when he is grown."

"Much like his father, I imagine." The prince already looked much like King Donal had when he had been younger, and Donal was certainly his father's son.

Cordelia managed to smile. "I think so as well."

Taking a step back, Ártur shifted his burdens to distribute the weight more evenly. "I must go, milady…he will be safe, and perhaps someday he will return, or one of his heirs, to correct whatever wrongs have yet to be done to Enesfel's people." With the King having no heirs of his own, the throne would fall to one of his brothers, and Ártur could not imagine any good coming of that exchange of power.

"I pray k'Ádhá hears your words, Lord Healer, or our actions are in vain." She watched them go through the door into the darkness of the empty corridor but did not follow. It was her part to pretend she knew nothing of her son's absence until morning. The door closed silently and she sank onto her bed to weep. Soon there would be no turning back.

Ártur encountered no one in the hall between the queen's chamber and the palace's upper oratory. He reached it without incident and entered the k'dhín bhólibh; it was the one Gate in the castle he knew he could access safely nearly any time he chose.

Moments later, he stood amidst the ruins of what had once been a great city. He sneezed, shivering in the chilled night air. The sound was enough to prompt movement, which alerted him to the presence of another, moments before Guthrie McHador emerged from the shadows. They exchanged no words as the ex-General took the child and pack from the healer. There was no time for words. This must be done swiftly, before the healer's absence was noted. As soon as the man disappeared into the darkness with his cargo, Ártur returned to the Rhidam keep in the same manner he had left. He made his way to the kitchen where he left the scroll tucked into a pantry where someone would eventually find it, and then made his way back to his room, once again encountering no one. Shivering, he climbed into bed with the feeling that the night's endeavors had been far too easy.

Morning brought commotion in the corridor outside of his room. Ártur sat up, listening, but decided against getting out of bed. His cold had worsened, as he had anticipated, and he nestled back into his blankets, pretending that last night had been nothing but a bad dream.

But he was not given the luxury of more sleep. There was a loud banging on his door, and when he did not answer, it flew open with a crash. Prince Bowen and two guards burst into the room, pulled him from the bed by his arms, and dragged him down the hall. He was not awake enough, or well enough, to struggle, and decided that three against one were not good odds. They stopped outside the King's private chambers where they allowed the healer to stand and make himself presentable. Apparently, he mused, they did not want the King to know they had manhandled him into being here. Ártur tried to ignore the spasm in his belly.

King Donal looked up from his breakfast, his weary face conveying doubt and disappointment. "You have some explaining to do, my friend."

"I do?" Ártur was not about to explain anything until he knew what was being asked.

"Prince Arlan is missing…"

Hoping his voice conveyed an appropriate amount of shock and concern, Ártur exclaimed, "Milord…!"

Before he could say more, however, the King cut him off with a wave of his hand. "The palace is being searched but he has not yet been found. Lady Cordelia believes he snuck off to play with the pups in the kennel…"

"Children do such things, my liege…"

His expression showed that the King was irritated by the interruptions, so Ártur snapped his mouth shut. "I know that…but there is no sign of him there, or anywhere else thus far. He could not have gotten past the closed gates…"

This time, the King paused as if waiting for the healer's thoughts, and Ártur dared to start again. "The prince is very good at hiding, and the keep is massive…"

The King did not cut him off, but Prince Bowen did, striking him across the face hard enough to silence him, and for once, the King did not intervene. Ártur felt the knot in his stomach sink lower, a sensation that had nothing to do with the physical blow. "You were seen last night leaving the Lady's chambers…" snarled the prince.

The King silenced his brother with a glance. "She said you were passing her room and that she asked you to check on Arlan because she thought he was breathing strangely. But you were seen leaving her room, carrying something…she says it was blankets." He paused and stroked his beard. "I want the truth."

"I…" Ártur knew he could not give the King the truth, and the pain of needing to lie was nearly unbearable. He hesitated only long enough to pull his nightshirt closer to his skin for warmth, giving himself a moment to phrase his words without seeming to be hiding anything. "The lady has no reason to lie to you, milord. You doubt her? How could I have taken the prince anywhere while in her presence without her knowing? You may not believe me…but I would think you would believe her." Given how long he and Donal had been friends, Ártur was surprised the King doubted him. He sneezed. "I could not sleep and decided to pray in the oratory. As I am unwell, I took blankets to stay warm. The Lady asked me to check on the prince, which I did, and then I went to the oratory…and from there back to my room…"

The King turned to his brother with an annoyed spark in his eyes. "Did Cocidius not follow him? He mentioned nothing of this?"

"Why should Cocidius follow him? It was late, and at the time there was no evidence of foul play," Prince Bowen retorted. "Why the oratory? No one goes there. Those rooms have not been used in decades."

Ártur straightened his shoulders. "The Faith is alive in Elyriá and I pray there often. Does it matter that I should choose to pray in a holy…?"

"There is nothing holy about you," the prince spat, preparing to strike again.

But the King rose to his feet and waved his hand. "Enough. Do not touch him, Bowen."

Not prepared to give up, the prince growled his challenge. "There should be enough dust collected that, if he has been there, footprints will remain. You should investigate his story before reaching hasty conclusions…brother."

King Donal's eyes narrowed at his brother as he removed his cloak and handed it to Ártur. "We shall. Wear this, Lord MacLyr. I do not want you to die of exposure."

Once in the oratory, it appeared as Ártur claimed. Footprints matching his were fresh in the dust and went to the front of the room and then into the k'dhín bhólibh, where the scuff marks on the floor could have been from knees and blankets. There was no way anyone but an Elyri could detect the presence of the Gate; to the Teren with him, this was a tiny room like any other. The healer could almost feel the King's blood pressure rising and he regretted being unable to confide in him.

"Bowen…"

The prince barked defensively, "This is not proof…"

"Nor is it proof that Lord MacLyr has harmed or done something with Prince Arlan. If he had brought him here, where could they have gone? No one was reported leaving the grounds last night…it is unwise to accuse a man thus, particularly one who is my friend, without evidence. He could not have taken Prince Arlan without the Lady's knowledge. I do not want to hear anything further on his guilt unless you have proof. Is that understood? Leave Lord MacLyr alone." To the two soldiers with them he said, "Continue searching the grounds and find anyone who may have gone out after the gates were opened. Perhaps someone came in, or left, early enough this morning that he did manage to sneak out...or was taken. We will scour all of Rhidam if necessary, all of Enesfel, and I will speak to the Lady again to be certain she heard or saw nothing. Question everyone who was on the grounds yesterday and allow no one to leave or enter until I give the word."

Once Prince Bowen and the guards were gone, the prince having left in a hasty huff, the King turned to Ártur with a sigh of regret. The Elyri's cheek was bruised and swelling where the prince had struck him, and he was shivering violently. "I asked them to bring you to me, but not like this. I am sorry, Ártur."

"No apology is necessary. You are the King, milord. You may do with me as you wish..." Especially, he thought sadly, because I am guilty of the very crime you are investigating.

The King's face was shaded with remorse. "You are my friend, have been my friend for many years. I should have believed in you...should never have doubted you. You are the most honorable man I know. I asked Bowen how this could be done without the Lady's knowledge...and I know you would never wish a child harm, yet you were the only suspect I had. I had to question you. I knew, I know...you are innocent...but I am afraid things may never be the same between us after this."

Ártur hung his head. Donal was the best friend he had ever had, despite the class and race differences between them; now it seemed their grip on their friendship was slipping. He wondered if they could hold on to it, particularly since he had the distinct impression that he was not the only one hiding something.

"I do not know, My Liege. That is up to you. I do not blame you for suspecting me; I would do likewise in your position. You cannot afford to show favoritism. If you feel it proper, dismiss me from court before further harm is done."

The King shook his head vigorously. "You have nothing to do with the collapse of the Lachlan dynasty and you know it. But it seems that someone is trying to stack evidence against you...and not just Bowen. Something is wrong, I fear, but I do not yet know what. For someone to put such effort into destroying you...me...our friendship...this is not coincidence. You know I cannot dismiss you; I need your advice and medical skills. Lord Nelsen is leaving service five days hence, and you are the only one I, or Lady Cordelia, can trust. However..." He sighed heavily and rubbed the back of his neck. "It might be wisest if you are not in the palace for a few days. You may be in as much danger as Prince Arlan, and I will not risk your life." The rubbing hand reached his eyes. "I will secure a room for you in the Eagle's Nest, where you will stay until I feel it is safe for you here. I pray no one finds, or fabricates, more evidence against you, Ártur, as I do not want to be forced to punish my best friend for a crime I know he did not commit. Ready your things. I will escort you to your temporary quarters in two hours."

The healer remained sitting on the front bench as the King left the oratory, fighting the strangling feeling of knowing that Guthrie had been right. Soon, no one would be able to trust anyone else. They would be forced to face this future alone. How much further would this go, he wondered, as he stared at the faded figure of Dhágdhuán and tried, unsuccessfully, to will himself into a sense of peace that he had not felt since Kavan had given it to him so many years before.

‿Chapter 12‿

For all of his adult life, Ártur MacLyr had been a healer. It was what he had trained to do from the day he took his first steps as a child. What he was born to do. To be unable to perform in that capacity on a full-time basis as he always had was pulling him into depression as he paced his rented room in the Eagle's Nest Inn. A social creature at heart, isolation was devouring him. He debated inviting Kavan to Rhidam, something that would not only give him solace and company but would have gained him access to the castle, and the King. But he would never risk his cousin's safety simply to satisfy his loneliness. Rhidam, in the healer's eyes, was no longer a safe place for anyone.

The five days of silence suggested that no one in Rhidam had found evidence against him. From his window, Ártur had watched enough traffic going in and out of the castle to know that a massive manhunt for Prince Arlan was under way. But the gossip gleaned from the inn's patrons told him no clues had been found, and that Lord Nelsen was still the primary suspect in the eyes of many save the King, although he was making no serious effort to show the Teren doctor support beyond keeping him in the Lachlan employment and refusing to arrest him. No doubt the search of Enesfel would last for many years unless the prince was found or the King called an end to it. The healer wondered how long Guthrie's hiding place could remain secure.

Rubbing his eyes, Ártur pondered returning to bed. There was little else to do. A fight in the streets below his room last night had carried the taunts of 'Elyri lover' and 'traitorous witch' pushing in through his closed window, rousing him from slumber. The Royal Guard had quickly broken up the squabble, but not before Ártur heard enough to chill his blood and instill new fear into him. It had been many hours before he had been able to sleep again, and when he awoke a second time, he still felt the urge to cower at each unpleasant, hostile noise from outside.

"Lord MacLyr!"

He did not recognize the voice on the other side of his door, and after last night, he hesitated opening it. But then the call came again, accompanied by much banging.

"Lord MacLyr! You are urgently needed in the palace. The queen!"

Those words pushed his fears aside to replace them with new ones. He grabbed his cloak and bag and ran into the hall. The young soldier there was out of breath and red-faced, but ran along with Ártur back to the castle. The healer expected to be taken to the King's chambers, to find Queen Meara in need of his skills, but instead, he was led to the Queen Mother's rooms and his blood ran cold. k'Ádhá, he thought, his throat constricting so that he could scarcely breathe. Not this queen!

The King was in the room with her, sitting at her bedside, holding the woman's hand. No one else was present, and Ártur thought she looked considerably frailer then she had five days earlier.

"I have done everything I could think of," the King said, moving aside to allow the healer to work, "but nothing has helped."

"What has happened? Where is Lord Nelsen?"

The anxious monarch rocked up and down on his heels. "She collapsed after breakfast. Lord Nelsen has already left, thus I sent for you."

The healer placed his hands on the woman's chest and closed his eyes. Her spirit was dimming, its color fading as life drained away. Destroyed by pain, loneliness, despair…and poison? "No. Not you," he groaned, shaking his head as though it would erase what he had seen and somehow stave off the inevitable. Her thoughts drew him closer and he tried to latch onto them. This had not been…someone else…she could not…

The thoughts were no longer coherent as they continued to bleed away; the only clear one he could detect was that she could no longer tolerate the pain. The pain of loss, he wondered, or of the poison? He fought for her as he had done for her son, but this time it was a losing effort, for she did not have the will to live. Take care of the children, she bid him.

Her light blinked to black.

"No." Ártur struggled to keep her from slipping away. "No. You cannot do this…"

The King watched as tears trickled down the Elyri's face. The healer's hands clasped the woman's shoulders, shaking her roughly, and then he pulled her limp form against his chest and sobbed. Donal could not recall ever seeing such emotion from Ártur, not even on the battlefield surrounded by death. After many minutes, the healer laid the woman back into her pillows as if to sleep; he wiped his face and stood, keeping his back to the King.

"Ártur?"

Hearing his friend say his name gave him a flicker of hope in his pain, but it was not enough to banish it. "I was too late. There was nothing to be done…I tried…the poison was not that strong…"

"Poison!" The King's whispered gasp trailed off into the thick air.

Ártur wiped his face on his sleeve. "She did not wish to live…willed herself to die. After losing Innis…Guthrie…Arlan…"

"Suicide? But she still has her daughter…and Prince Arlan might still be found. There is still hope." He could not believe that a woman of such endurance, who had shown such strength in supporting him, would take her own life, not with one child still dependent on her and another yet to be found.

Nor did Ártur, but he could not rule out the possibility. "I do not know…something she ate, perhaps…"

"Who…" After a long, pregnant pause, during which the King's fists clenched and unclenched, he growled, "Lord Nelsen."

The healer was noticeably shocked. "Surely not! He has no cause to do such a thing…"

But the King was not prepared to let the notion go. "He brought us breakfast, said it was the last thing he could do…Mr. Wyndham?" The tow-headed young soldier who had fetched Ártur appeared in the doorway. "I want Healer Nelsen found and brought to me. He should be on his way home."

The soldier clicked his heals and chirped, "Yes, My Liege," and disappeared.

But Ártur was still choking on the incredulousness of the King's suggestion. "Milord, you cannot believe this. What motive could he…?"

"That his services are no longer required and that you remain could be motive enough," the King growled.

The words made Ártur snort. "Hardly a motive. I do not remain in his place. He knows I am banned from…I would not consider my position to be one of prestige. If that was the affront, and he wished revenge on me, he would have come to me, not the Lady…"

The King grunted stubbornly. "He is the only suspect I have and I will have the truth."

"The poison was not the sole cause of her death, My Liege," Ártur continued, pressing for the other physician's innocence. "She died of despair. Lord Nelsen cannot be blamed for that. No one can…"

"You think not? What little you know of despair then, friend." The final word was spat out as though distasteful and Ártur stepped back, the color draining from his face. His legs hit the bed; he was trapped. If the King lost his temper and lashed out, there would be nowhere for the healer to go. "He will be questioned and you will determine the validity of his statement if you consider yourself loyal to me and this crown."

The healer sagged into the bedside chair as the King strode out of the room. The isolation was complete, as Guthrie had foretold. Oh, sínréc, he thought, his head in his hands, his fingers tugging through his hair. Why are you far away when I need you?

Tiny footsteps disturbed his grief. The two young girls looked at him with large, sad eyes. Princess Deidre stepped nearer, her attention on her mother's still figure. Ártur tried to grasp her arm but she eluded his hand and touched her mother's face. Slowly, deliberately, the tiny hand traced the woman's features, stroked her hair, and came back to her lips. The princess' companion, Brenna Weylin, hung back to watch. Finally, the princess turned away from her mother with a mournful expression and climbed onto the healer's lap. Brenna moved closer to stand beside them.

"Miss Weylin, tell her…"

"She knows, milord. The King told us. She wanted to be with you."

They cried then, the three of them together, their small arms around his neck and their child kisses on his cheeks and forehead, accepting his in return as they gave each other comfort. Sounds in the corridor interrupted them as the servants arrived to take the woman's body from the room and strip the bedding. Ártur watched in silence until he and the girls were alone again.

"Miss Weylin, do you remember what I asked of you once, concerning your uncle?" The girl nodded gravely. "The time is nearer. Soon I may be forced to leave here; when that happens, leave messages where I told you. I will come for them; as I promised. This is a grave responsibility for one so young…"

With a haughty tilt of her face up to his, she said, "I am almost nine, milord. Not such a child as you think. I will do as you ask and no one will know."

It still seemed foolish to bring such a young child into this nightmare, just as it had when he had asked for her aid, but Guthrie convinced him of the necessity of it, had sworn that his niece could be trusted. Seeing the determination in the girl's dark brown eyes, how much she was like her uncle in that respect, Ártur hoped that the choice was a wise one.

"You realize it could be dangerous…"

"I do not fear danger. If my uncle is still alive…and safe…I want to help him, and the princess, and Prince Arlan when he is found. And I want to help you," she reassured him.

He kissed her cheek and embraced them both one more time, not knowing if Deidre had understood any of what they had said. Perhaps someday they would be told that Prince Arlan lived, but this was not the time. "Thank you, Miss Weylin."

ॐ*ॐ

In the Grand Hall, the brothers assembled with a hasty gathering of the lords and advisors who happened to be in the castle this day. Even Prince Farrell was present, in Rhidam to gather supplies before setting off to hunt again. The news of Lady Cordelia's death, an apparent murder or perhaps suicide, had spread rapidly, and Prince Girvin looked as though the life had been drained from him. His eyes were glazed and red but he shed no tears. It appeared he did not quite believe the news. Everyone in the room cast concerned, curious, or accusing glances at the Elyri healer as he entered and then sat with his hands folded in his lap and head bowed, looking smaller and frailer than usual. The King entered and all stood. He called for Lord Nelsen to be brought before him after motioning for all to be seated. It was mid-afternoon.

The doctor looked confused, dazed, as though he had no idea what was happening. Perhaps he had not been told he was being arrested. The thought made Ártur feel cold.

"Lord Nelsen," the King started, his voice flat with only a hint of anger. The healer doubted anyone else could detect it. "Kneel before me." The man obeyed, though he cast wary glances around him. Ártur guessed he did not know of Lady Cordelia's death. "Today, at the tenth hour, Her Most Royal Lady, Cordelia Maser Lachlan died of poison…"

The only gasp in the room was Lord Nelsen's as he erupted to his feet with a cry. "Milord! If you brought me here to accuse me of treachery…"

The reaction alone convinced Ártur that the man was innocent, but the King was less easily swayed. "Kneel!" he bellowed, loudly enough that many in the room winced. Only after the Teren doctor knelt again did the King continue in a voice just above a whisper. "That is precisely why you have been brought before me. What say you?"

The doctor, trembling, replied in a shaky voice, "I knew nothing of her death, My Liege, until now…"

"Do you deny that you brought us breakfast this morning, a final duty to your King before you left our employment?"

"No, Sire, I do not deny it."

The King leaned forward. "Do you deny that you wished us well, specifically hoping that the Lady would be well?"

Again, Lord Nelsen shook his head. "No…but I meant no harm, I swear. I was coming to bid you farewell and encountered a servant in the hall with the meal. She asked if I would take it to you since I was going that way, because she…" His voice faltered and his head turned as though to look for the woman he spoke of. "She had been asked to bring Prince Farrell's breakfast to his chambers and she said she was late…"

Snickers ran through the gathering, though the King did not find it amusing that any servant would put duty to his brother over duty to the King. The Crown Prince shrugged casually. "She always brings me breakfast when I am here. Ask her."

The King glared at his brother. "Believe me, I shall." He had no doubt that breakfast was not all she brought to Farrell. Barely keeping back those tactless words, he turned his attention to Lord Nelsen. "You would still have had opportunity to…"

"Why would I wish her harm? If poisoning food had been my aim, why were you unaffected?" The words spoken, the doctor realized too late that his reply was too hasty when the King's eyes narrowed further.

"So…it was me you wanted in her place. She has never wished any man harm, it is true, and you had no cause to harm her. But I am the one releasing you from duty. I have been lax in showing my support during this time of tribulation. The only thing she ate that I did not was the honey. You know of my fondness for it…and you know that she did not, as a habit, consume it. That she chose today to eat it…and I chose not to…was a most unfortunate turn of events for you."

"I would never wish or cause you harm, Your Majesty," Lord Nelsen protested once more. "In all my years of service…"

The King cut him off with a wave of his hand. "Lord MacLyr, I want the truth from this man."

As the healer reluctantly rose to his feet, Mormer growled, "I will not let him touch me!"

Ártur did not look at him, or anyone else, as he spoke. "Not permitting this to be done is as good as admitting guilt…"

Lord Nelsen directed his response to the King with narrowed eyes, a challenge in his voice as he ignored the Elyri healer behind him.

"Then imprison or execute me if you think me guilty. I swear on my life I have never harmed the Royal Mother or any of her children and I would never attempt to harm you, My King. I am an innocent man." The healer sighed. "I believe you." He had known the Teren doctor for a long time and some things could be read in ways that any man could see if they looked hard enough. He prayed the King could see it.

Trying to keep his voice level, the King asked, "You refuse to be read?"

"I will never let him touch me," Lord Nelsen spat again, this time with obvious fear in his voice.

"Very well." There was defeat in the King's voice that Ártur felt no one else in the room would notice. "Until such a time as you choose to confess, Lord Nelsen, or submit to be read by Healer MacLyr, I declare you under arrest. You will remain in the custody of this..."

"Execute him!" cried Prince Bowen, shooting to his feet. "He has murdered royalty and must not be allowed to live. It will only encourage the rise of traitors to see such acts go unpunished!"

In a few short steps that the prince never anticipated, the King descended the platform, grabbing his brother by the front of the tunic and lifting him almost off his feet. "I will have no man executed until his guilt is proven. You are quick to accuse and seek execution, brother. Perhaps you wish to place blame where it may not belong in order to protect the one who is guilty. You, more than anyone here, believe you have the most to gain by my death."

A murmur swept through the room. The animosity between Prince Bowen and King Donal had been known by most of those present since the two men were quite young, and it was common knowledge that Prince Bowen wanted the throne. It was also widely speculated that he was not above taking it by any means possible if he saw an opening. But their reaction made it seem like this was news, or perhaps, Ártur realized as the murmuring died, the court was merely surprised that the King had finally voiced the fact that he knew it too.

With a shove, the prince was sent sprawling backward into Prince Farrell's lap and then slid to the floor. Farrell was startled but did nothing to assist his fallen brother. There was fury in Prince Bowen's eyes, anger at having been stripped of any pretenses before those advisors and lords he might one day have need of, but he did not speak or get up from the floor as the King focused once more on Lord Nelsen.

Face flushed, the King gritted his teeth. "Mr. Wyndham, take this man under arrest. I do not want to see you in my presence again, Lord Nelsen, until the truth is told." He turned his back on the man, and the audience, in a symbolic gesture and waited as the struggling doctor was hauled out of the room.

"May k'Ádhá have vengeance! I am an innocent man!"

The heavy oak double doors thudded closed behind him.

"Out. All of you," the King barked with his back still turned. Ártur stared at the monarch's clenched hands and noted their trembling. "I do not want to see anyone today. Girvin, prepare your mother's final rite."

"But…"

There was a growl that brought the prince scrambling to his feet. "If you want her to receive burial at all, do it." Girvin ran from the room.

One by one, or in pairs or small groups, the room emptied of its occupants, with Prince Bowen being the first to depart. Ártur remained, however, unable to bring himself to get up from the bench as he watched his friend's heaving shoulders. It was beginning to occur to him what the King was hiding; the thought made him shrivel inside.

Without looking back, the King said, "Be gone, Healer. I have no further words for you today."

Not surprised that the monarch knew he was there, Ártur murmured, "You are not well, My Liege."

Something in those words, or perhaps the realization that he no longer had a secret, made the King snap, "Why do you think I am working diligently to resolve these catastrophes?" He collapsed onto the throne, his body shaking, knowing that the outburst of anger was defensive as he did not want to acknowledge his failing health, not even to his best friend.

"You have not consulted me…" Surely, thought Ártur, nothing could be wrong with the King that the healer could not fix. The man appeared to be in perfect health.

"There is nothing you can do."

"Please…Donal…allow me to help you…"

Hearing the healer use his name produced another crack in the King's emotional armor, which he tried to patch by growling, "I do not want your help…leave me."

"What of the throne?" Had not King Donal wanted to reign as long as possible, to protect the royal family and the kingdom from what was likely to be chaotic days after his death?

"I am beyond your help. There is nothing you can do."

"At least allow me to try…to examine you…"

The honest pain and caring on Ártur's face, in his voice, and his persistence, were things the King had grown to expect. The healer had always known how to work Donal around to what needed to be done, but this time, the King knew it was futile. Ártur could not help him. Still, to honor the friendship they shared, he motioned the healer to approach and watched his friend close his eyes before placing one hand on the royal chest. It was the ultimate act of trust for them both. In his healing trance, Ártur would be vulnerable to any action the King might take against him, and the King knew that Ártur could easily kill him with that probing touch. Perhaps, they both realized fleetingly, their friendship was not in as much danger as they feared.

Ártur stepped away, his expression somber and his eyes creased with sadness. "It is as you say. Your heart is weakening." It was the sort of thing that no Elyri healing could solve. Damage could be repaired. Some illnesses and poisons could be cured. But the frailties of an aging body were beyond them. When that royal heart gave out, Ártur might be able to revive him a half dozen or more times. But it would leave the man weaker, open to failure again until that beating organ gave out completely.

"If you are satisfied with my condition, leave me," the King grunted with false gruffness.

Ártur shook his head. "I am not satisfied. That you are dying hurts me greatly, Donal."

"Why?" he snorted defensively. "Because it means Elyri may no longer be welcome in Enesfel?"

"No…because despite recent events, you are still my best friend," the healer admitted, refusing to be stung by the reflexive animosity in the King's tone.

The King stared across the room, using the vacancy and silence to calm his aching soul. "You are a healer," he said finally. "Death should not be a shock, particularly since you have always known you will outlive me."

Sighing, Ártur took a step backward to give the man space. He could not refute the King's statement. Only violence or disease could have caused him to die before Donal. He had been lucky enough to have encountered neither thus far. As there was nothing more to say on the matter, he changed the subject. "If it would please you, may I speak to Lord Nelsen in private? Perhaps I can persuade him to consent to be read, or to confess if he is guilty."

"You do not believe in his guilt?"

It was then that Ártur knew the King also trusted in the man's innocence, but as King, he could not afford to take such matters lightly. It would be a bad political risk to take.

Ártur shook his head. "He is not, My Liege, though for your sake, and that of the kingdom, I almost wish he were that this would be behind you."

"Do you think she took her own life?

"At first, I thought not. She has always been a strong woman and has a daughter who needs her. As you said, Prince Arlan will need her when he is found." Ártur swallowed back the lump of grief in his throat, knowing the truth would be harder on all of them if it were known. "However, she has been hurt greatly in recent years. Innis died, Lord McHador departed...Prince Girvin has not exactly been a model son...and then the attempts on Prince Arlan's life. Now the child is missing. Many would contemplate their own death to escape that grief. I do not know, My Liege. The contact in those final moments was not enough for me to determine if her death was accidental or intentional."

The King nodded once and Ártur took that as agreement. "Do you think speaking to him will be productive?"

"No...but what other chance does he have? He has to know I want to help him. Perhaps accepting a reading will be easier if it is not done before a room full of others."

"Do it. And Farrell and his chambermaid too. I will have them both with me when you return. If I thought Bowen wouldn't kill you for it, I would ask you to read him too. Go, quickly. Before I change my mind."

The castle dungeon was cold and damp, being built as it was below the ground in a region where the water table was high. Ártur had never come into this place; there had never been any reason for him to be here. Some of the areas were adequately lit, both by smoky torches and the occasional small windows built high on the walls though inches above the ground level on the outside of the castle. When the weather was good, they were open for circulation. When it was not, they were boarded closed, as they were today, increasing the feeling of foreboding. There were few housed here at any time as this dungeon was reserved only for those the King incarcerated, not for the common thieves and criminals of the kingdom. It made locating the Teren doctor easy. When the sentry unlocked the cell to allow Ártur to enter, Lord Nelsen looked up in disdain. The door closed with a heavy sound.

"I will not submit to your probes. I want nothing from you."

"Then you shall likely die here, Mormer," the healer said grimly.

"When the murderer is found, I will be released. I will not be held long."

The two men stared at one another for several minutes, measuring each other, until Ártur reluctantly asked, "How long have they been looking for the ones who tried to kill Prince Arlan. Has there been any success? It could be a very long while, Mormer…and the King is dying." The Teren doctor blinked in surprise, revealing that he had not known it either. "I have just learned of it myself. He has hidden it from all of us. If you are still here when he dies, I do not know what fate Prince Farrell will bestow upon you, if he considers your plight at all. But I do know that if Prince Bowen has any influence over him, your fate will not be good."

"Then you will have what you want, won't you?" the man sneered.

"Me?"

The doctor laughed, almost maniacally, a sound of fear to Ártur's ears. "You have much to gain from these events; I do not understand why the King cannot see you for what you are."

"The King is aware of what I am." Ártur was sincerely perplexed; he had never believed the other doctor thought ill of him.

"Then perhaps he is the murderer and you his tool in the crimes that have been committed. Once I am gone, you will have no competition; you will be the only physician in the keep."

Choosing to believe it was distress talking, Ártur tried to speak logically to him. "You do not believe the King is behind the death of the Queen Mother or the disappearance of Prince Arlan. And you know I am not permitted inside the palace except on official business. Once the King is gone, I will not be welcome here. No Elyri will be."

Lord Nelsen hissed, "You will have spun your web so completely that they will have no choice but to keep you here!"

He backed Ártur up against the door and the healer could hear the sentry outside fumbling through his keys. "You do not believe that…I am not that sort of man. Prince Bowen hates Elyri; nothing could make him keep me here. I know you are afraid, Mormer. Let me help you."

"I am afraid of nothing except your probes! Having you in here, planting suggestions, making me do things against my will." He tapped the side of his head. His eyes were wild. "Let them execute me. I shall never submit to you again, murderer."

Shock growing deeper every moment, Ártur protested, "You know that is not true. "I know you are innocent! You do not deserve to die!" The guard had the key in the lock.

"Yet you frame me to protect yourself. You will learn nothing from me! Nothing!"

Almost hysterical, his hands closed around Ártur's throat. Ártur could not free himself without force, and he was reluctant to use it because he felt in some ways that the doctor was right. Lord Nelsen's situation was covering Ártur's involvement in Guthrie McHador's plan and the truth of Prince Arlan's disappearance. But none of that had caused the Queen Mother's death and Lord Nelsen did not deserve death or imprisonment.

The cell door opened behind the Elyri and both physicians tumbled to the floor, Lord Nelsen on top of the barely struggling Ártur. The sentry pulled him off and shoved him back into the cell before helping the healer to his feet. As Ártur was escorted back to the stairs, the last words he heard from the man behind them were, "May your soul rot in hell, demon spawn. I would sooner die than submit to your sorcery!"

From Prince Farrell and the chambermaid, nothing of value was learned. Prince Farrell's desire for the throne was not great enough to drive him to actively seek it, and the girl had only gathered the tray from the kitchen, given it to Lord Nelsen when they passed in the corridor, and then scurried off to retrieve Prince Farrell's breakfast, eagerly looking forward to her rendezvous with the prince.

The cooks and kitchen staff were questioned next, the kitchen searched for clues, for poison. Other than the message the healer had hidden there, the threat against the prince's life that would now, unfortunately, bring suspicion and closer superverision of the kitchen staff, they were all found innocent. The only remaining likely suspects were Lord Nelsen and Prince Bowen, but the King chose not to force Ártur to probe the most volatile Lachlan prince. Though not pleased with Lord Nelsen's refusal to submit, the King insisted the doctor be well-treated in his prison and not harmed. The King accepted what medical advice Ártur could give, but both knew that he, and the kingdom, were running out of time.

The healer stood at the window of his rented room, staring at the stars, allowing himself to weep. King Donal was dying. It was Ártur's first close look at his lifespan compared to the relative shortness of the Teren he worked for and with. Men dying in battle, dying of disease or injury or old age were one thing. He and the King were a mere three years apart in age, yet Ártur looked no older than twenty. Unless he met some gruesome end, the healer knew he would likely live at least another one hundred and fifty years or more. It was maddening, frustrating, and enough to make him understand why many of his people who lived among Teren for any length of time eventually resorted to reclusive habits in their later years. A person could only lose so many friends, could only see so many generations of a family die, without going completely mad.

He was beginning to wish he had never chosen to come to Enesfel, that he had chosen a more mundane medical position such as town healer in Bhryell. Yet, he knew that sort of life was not for him. If he had not come here, how different would the world be? Would Prince

Arlan still be alive? Would Prince Bowen have killed the King? Could Ártur honestly say he would prefer to have given up his years as battle healer, and Donal's friendship, for the security of his hometown? The answer to the last question he knew to be no.

At least, he mused with a touch of warmth, Elys would be pleased to have him home when that time came. He had not seen her since he had last been to visit Kavan, but he had written to her faithfully every week. That there had been no reply in some time only marginally concerned him. Elys had never been one for writing letters, and Ártur had been too preoccupied lately to contemplate the matter.

King Donal. Dying. The man who had not wanted to be King, but who had become one of the most popular rulers in Enesfel's history, would soon leave the land to uncertainty. Prince Farrell might or might not rule wisely, depending on whom he allowed to influence him, but with Prince Bowen behind him, pushing him, the outlook did not seem promising. Ártur did not think Prince Farrell had the fortitude to stand up to his younger brother. The King was right to allow Enesfel to believe their peace would last, to hide his condition from the world. No one else needed to experience the sinking despair Ártur felt.

He would tell Guthrie and Prince Arlan the news when he felt stronger, perhaps tomorrow or after Lady Cordelia's final rite. He did not believe he could heal the pain of two others when he could barely contain his own. It would be hard enough to face them.

❧*❧

The full moon was a bright disc in the clear cloudless sky that night. Its reflection on the smooth surface of the lake was enough to illuminate the water's edge as though it were early dawn. There were no birds, no insects or frogs, only the sigh of the western wind blowing through the spruce trees. In the stillness, a rabbit looked up, startled by the emergence of another from the forest cover. Seeing only the second rabbit, the first resumed its feeding. A family of wild pigs rooted on the far side of the lake, and not far from them, a raccoon washed its dinner in the cold water. Many animals came here to drink, as it was peaceful and secluded, far away from the normal paths of men. More rustling, and though the animals showed no fear, they stopped their activity and parted, making way for the majestic creature that had come amongst them.

The white hart lowered its head and drank deeply. Its head stayed down for many minutes, studying its pale reflection in the water as it listened to the sounds of the night. Tonight its movements were slow, as if every twitch and stretch took painful effort, but there was no visible injury. Tonight it was a pain of the soul, an injury of uncertain origin, deep enough that only time could purge it. One silver hoof pawed the water's edge, sending wavelets across the lake. Then he looked up, took stock of the sights and smells around him one last time, and with a swing of his antlered head, stepped back into the shelter of the trees.

ॐ*๛

"And so the great dragon, once the scourge of the kingdom, breathed its last, and Geoffrey became the hero of…"

The boy looked up from the only book he owned and stared at the man who sat across the room carving arrow shafts. Guthrie McHador did not look as the child remembered him, but that memory was from long ago. The man's thick auburn hair was turning to gray, his beard was gone, and the creases around his mouth and eyes had grown deeper.

"Sir? What happened to dragons? Why are there none now?"

The ex-general stopped his work. The role of surrogate parent was coming a little easier than he had anticipated, perhaps because Prince Arlan was a well-mannered boy, but he was still uncomfortable and suspected that feeling would persist for a long time. He wondered continuously what Lady Cordelia or Lady Johanna would do in his place, only to quickly chastise himself. He would never be like them. He was not a woman and had never parented before. He was not a mother. He could only do his best and hope it served the Prince adequately.

"A dragon is a legendary creature, Arlan. A myth. If they ever did exist, they disappeared long before anyone I have ever known," he replied to the question. It felt awkward calling the boy by name, but if he was to function as a parent, it seemed the best thing to do.

"Why?"

"I do not know. Perhaps," he winked, "Geoffrey killed the last of them as the story says."

The prince giggled. "I should like to see a dragon," he boasted. "I would not be afraid."

"If you ever do see one, let me…"

A knock on the door interrupted him, startling them both. Prince Arlan scrambled into the other room of the two-roomed cabin, while Guthrie picked up his sword from the mantle. He was pleased that the boy was quick to obey that one basic rule. No one had knocked on that door since Guthrie had come here. No one knew he was here.

Except for one man.

"Good lord, Ártur," he exclaimed, helping the healer into the room and into the closest available chair before closing the door behind him. "You look like hell."

The healer coughed, trying to catch his breath. "I'm sorry to come like this…I had to leave Rhidam for a time…" The prince emerged from the other room, now that he recognized Ártur's voice and knew he was safe, and brought the healer a cup of water. "Thank you…"

"Has there been trouble?" the ex-general asked with concern.

"No, I…yes…I…" Ártur quickly drank the water, wondering how he was supposed to continue with such grim news on his shoulders. "I have not been allowed to stay in the palace since the Prince left.

They...Prince Bowen anyhow...tried to accuse me of kidnapping...which is technically true..."

Guthrie snorted. "You did as his mother requested, what was best..."

"Yes, I know. The King thought it best if I removed myself until tensions died down; I have been staying at the Eagle's Nest. Lord Nelsen was to leave court service...but he has been imprisoned..."

The prince knelt in front of Ártur and put his arms on the healer's knees. "Was he the one who tried to kill me?"

"No, my prince...never. He has done no man harm. It is all circumstantial. He is accused of poisoning..." His voice broke and he shook his head in sorrow. Closing his hands around the boy's, he looked at him, seeing Lady Cordelia, seeing King Innis, and almost sobbed. "I told the King that Lord Nelsen is innocent, but he is the only viable suspect and refuses to be read. Donal believes he may have been the intended victim, but I think..."

"Someone has died?" The healer's tortured expression was Guthrie's response. "Who?"

It took Ártur many minutes before his constricted throat allowed words to pass. "Your mother, my prince...she is...gone..."

Guthrie stumbled backward until his legs hit a chair, and though he tried to sit in it, he missed and landed on the floor. The prince got to his feet as if he would depart, but Ártur's grip on his hands kept him from leaving. The healer could not let go, wanting to offer comfort but not knowing how. Trapped, a sob escaped the boy as he hung his head.

"It should not have killed her. There was not enough in her system. I believe she died more of grief than anything. She missed you both, and your father...so much. I tried...but I could not save her. She...did not have the will to fight. I am sorry..."

The prince broke free then and retreated to the doorway of the other room, where he stopped and sagged against the doorframe. He wanted not to be touched, but he did not wish to be alone.

The healer continued, "She will be buried in the morning, but I could not stay…I had to let you know because…" His voice broke again and he scrubbed his face with his hands. "The King has given me leave to return home, but I will not do so yet. He is dying. His heart is weak. I suspect he will die within the year…two years at most. I have done as you asked, set up communication with your niece; we will know what is happening once I am unable to stay…but…I am deeply sorry I could not have done more…"

The prince's voice was barely audible. "Mother told me…I would probably never see her again…but I did not think she meant…"

Then he was gone and Guthrie put his head in his hands to weep. Ártur closed his eyes, sank back into the chair, and joined him.

❧Chapter 13✍

Laying his paintbrush on the lip of the easel, Ártur tried to decide if the image he had created of the Llaethlágárá was the best painting he had ever done or the most hideous he had ever seen. With his presence rarely required at court over the last seven months, he had indulged the desire to learn to paint that had dogged him since he was a little boy. He was not sure he had talent, but it was something to occupy his time, and since the inn's owner had purchased two of his paintings, and a few of the patrons had bought others, Ártur decided his efforts were at least passably pleasing.

For the fourth time in as many days, a squabble in the darkening street drew his attention away from painting to the window. The heat and humidity had made the Eagle's Nest patrons, indeed most of Rhidam, more quarrelsome of late. He again debated asking Kavan to visit him, but with the constant string of fights and brawls in and around the tavern, the healer decided it was simply too dangerous. Besides, he had not gone back to Bhryell, had not been in contact with his cousin for far too long. If the news of Prince Arlan's 'kidnapping' and the Queen Mother's death had reached Elyriá, Ártur had not delivered it. He was reluctant to let Kavan know the state of things in his life. Many nights he had lain in bed, feeling the peculiar mind touch of his cousin trying to contact him, but Ártur always clamped his thoughts closed and refused to allow communication. The attempts had become less frequent over the months apart and seemed to have stopped coming. Though he longed to talk to his cousin-brother, Ártur was not ready for that. Not until he returned home for good.

Stretching his neck from side to side, he stared at the castle through the window, wondering how Lord Nelsen was faring. The Teren doctor still refused to be read, refused to see his friends, and would not welcome an audience with any of his family. King Donal made certain the man was treated as kindly as possible, but would not discuss releasing the doctor until he had the truth. With Lord Nelsen unwilling to cooperate, it made Ártur wonder what the man could possibly be hiding.

The gossip that filtered into Ártur's life via soldiers who came to the Eagle's Nest for a drink suggested that the King was steadily isolating himself, driving away those he cared for and who cared for him in return. He had grown more impetuous, moody, more easily angered. If anyone other than Lord Nelsen or Ártur knew of his failing health, it was not public knowledge. Ártur had not spoken with Donal, had only seen him from a distance when he had been called to the keep to attend the princess or Miss Weylin, and he had no firsthand knowledge of how his friend was doing. He longed to see the man, to talk to him, to rekindle their friendship before it was too late. And after tedious days alone such as this one, the healer longed for anyone's company. Anyone at all.

"Lord MacLyr?"

Ártur turned, startled to see the young soldier, Mr. Wyndham, standing in his open doorway. Then he recalled he had left the door open to improve air circulation, and immediately chided himself for such foolishness. That sort of mistake could easily result in a blade in his back. "Yes?"

"The King has requested that you join him for dinner. Please come."

Dinner? The King had asked for him? It was a request Ártur could not deny, did not want to deny. If Donal wanted his company for any reason, the healer would happily oblige. But as he was escorted to the keep and led through the halls, he had to fight the sensation of sickness created by the gloomy atmosphere around him. None of the guards or servants spoke as they passed. He saw Princess Deidre through a doorway, but all the girl could do was smile and wave before her Elyri tutor pulled her back into the room. There looked to be fewer people around than usual, and not as many lit torches or lamps. The healer shuddered, trying not to think about the possible reasons for such changes.

His escort knocked on the door to the King's chamber and then led Ártur inside when they were summoned. The King turned from the mirror and the task of straightening his collar and motioned for the soldier to leave them. Ártur studied his friend without appearing to as Mr. Wyndham left the room. The King had grown paunchy in the middle and gaunt in the face since the healer had last spent time with him. While the changes seemed sudden, he had to admit that it had been too long since he had been in a position to notice such things.

"Sit, please, Lord Healer." The King sounded as tired and distracted as he looked. "Would you care for wine?" The Elyri shook his head no. With a shrug, the King poured himself a glass of the deep burgundy liquid, his movements slow and stiff to the perceptive eye of the healer. "Káliel's best. Let me know if you change your mind. There's plenty." He set the bottle on the table and gingerly placed himself into the chair across from Ártur. That movement set off alarms in the healer's head. King Donal was not a man to do things gingerly. "What have you been doing with yourself, Healer? I have not seen much of you recently."

Ártur looked at his hands, wondering if Donal was trying to goad him, make conversation, or had experienced a lapse in memory. The King knew Elyri avoided alcohol most of the time as their bodies found it highly toxic. He also knew why Ártur had not been seen much in several months. But the monarch deserved an answer, and so the healer replied, "Everyone has been blessed with good health," meaning he had little reason to come to the castle since Donal did not summon him. "I have been painting in my spare time."

The King appeared genuinely interested. "All these years…I did not know you could paint. Fancy that." How long had they known each other…and he was discovering the man he thought he knew was also a painter? "People? Architecture? Landscapes?"

"Landscapes so far…I just began. I don't have an eye for architecture, and I cannot yet capture people's spirits on canvas as I would like."

The King smiled. "I should like to see your work. You will bring some here and I will display it throughout the keep."

"Of course." The King might be smiling, but Ártur found the distracted tone disturbing.

"Come dine with me. The meal will grow cold if we wait. I had the staff prepare your favorites…pheasant, yams, wheat bread…" Their eyes met but the King quickly looked away, suppressing a cough. For a long while, they ate in silence, afraid to look at one another, eating only because it seemed polite, not because either of them was hungry. The King finally placed his napkin beside his plate and pushed it back. "You are wondering why I have asked you here tonight."

Ártur used cutting into the pheasant as an excuse not to look up. "The question had occurred to me, My Liege."

The King picked up his glass and drained it of wine before pouring more. "I have had a separate audience with each of my brothers and advisors today. General McLeu was here last. He drew up my final statement." The fork dropped from the healer's trembling hands. He had to clasp them in his lap, squeezing them together in an effort to fight against the overwhelming rush of horror and sadness. "Yes, I think my time is rapidly drawing to a close. I have been far too cold of late...and I am weary of fighting anymore. I had to see you again...to apologize for everything...set our friendship right. The thought of dying friendless has haunted me for many days."

He stood, paced aimlessly around the room gazing at artwork, out the window, the edges of the stonework. Anything to avoid looking at the healer. Eventually, he stopped at the mantle. With his back to the healer, Ártur could not see his face, but he sensed that the King was making every effort to control his emotions. "I have made provisions for you to be protected in Rhidam for as long as you wish to stay, once I am gone. Though it is my wish," he sighed, "I am afraid I will not be able to enforce it. You do understand...don't you?"

"Yes." How could he not? "The princess? The Queen?"

King Donal sighed again. "I have done my best to surround Princess Deidre with reliable and loyal staff...and I know Farrell adores her. She will be safe and well looked after. As for Meara..." His voice trailed off into a long silence. "She has known this was coming far longer than you, my friend...for which I apologize. She has readied her things and Mr. Wyndham will escort her to her brother's home in Wexel as soon as I am at rest. She will not remain here to endure Farrell's advances or to fall victim to Bowen's cruelties. She knows it is in her best interest to be away as quickly as she can be."

"She should be here when you...you expect that..." The healer could not bring himself to complete either thought. That the King did not respond to the half asked questions was confirmation enough. "I should bid her farewell," he said lamely.

"Not yet. There will be time enough for that later...after. First..." From the wall beside the fireplace, he removed a sword that had hung there for many years. It was lighter than most weapons its size, ornately carved, made of the finest alloys in the Five Sovereignties. As he returned to the table, its gold highlights sparkled in the candlelight. "I want you to have this."

"My Liege..."

"It was a gift to my father from the High Mother, you know. Your people. He gave it to me when I went into my first battle, but I have never used it. Nor did he. It has been a symbol of peace between our lands…and I do not want it to shed blood in Bowen's hands, as I am sure will happen once I'm gone…if Farrell doesn't sell it first. I think, therefore, it should return to the place from whence it came."

"I cannot accept this, milord. I know it has never…but I cannot willingly take a life…and to possess such a…"

"Then give it to Prince Arlan."

The sword clattered to the floor in Ártur's shock. The healer started to speak, but he was silenced both by a wave of the King's hand and by his own efforts not to choke.

"You know where he is. I know you do. You removed him from this place to spare his life…the only sensible thing to do since I could not protect him."

There was no accusation in the words, only acceptance of the inevitable. Still, Ártur could not find words as he retrieved the sword. What could he say? The King was staring at him as if intent on finding some answers on his face, but at last he shrugged and gave a faint smile.

"No one told me this, of course. You are the only one within these walls to know the truth. It was…a few days ago that the thought occurred to me. You protected a life, a child, as is your healer's duty. You did what you had to do…what I should have done. I pray it has been for the best, but I cannot fault you for it, particularly since I suspect you had Lady Cordelia's blessing, or at least her permission, if not her outright command to action." He reached across the table and put his hand on the healer's arm. "I have not spoken of my speculations with anyone. I should have known the truth all along, should never have doubted your integrity, but I was blind to everything except political duty, and for that, I was a fool. It has kept us apart when I have most needed your friendship, Ártur. You are a man of honor, a man who keeps his word regardless of the cost to himself, and for that, I treasure you. I know your choices, whatever they have been, have cost you dearly."

Those words lifted a great burden from the healer's shoulders, but they were not enough to free him of all of it. Not while the King's mortality was staring him in the eye. "What of Lord Nelsen?" he asked quietly.

"He has been released," the King assured him. "It is still unknown who was responsible for Cordelia's death, or the attempts on Prince Arlan's life, but I have never believed Lord Nelsen to be guilty and I have tried to assure him of that. Imprisoning him was as much for his own safety as my own. And I know it was not Farrell or Girvin to blame. Of all the suspects, Bowen is the only one I still have doubts about.

Ártur shook his head. "His protests have not been those of a man trying to divert blame. From my observations, I believe his accusations have been out of anger, hatred, and hostility; he sincerely believes Lord Nelsen, or I, am responsible for those crimes."

"Then he is a bigger fool than I am," the King snorted. He gestured towards the sword in Ártur's hands. "You will take it, Ártur? You will see that a proper Lachlan heir receives it?"

"If that is your wish, My Liege…"

"Stop calling me that, Ártur." The King returned to his chair, watching the healer turning the sword awkwardly in his hands. Ártur had no idea how to wield it. "Meara suggested more than once that I make Prince Arlan my heir…and I did consider it, but it never seemed prudent. He would not be of age for the throne, and regents would be too easily manipulated…by Bowen or anyone else. I have done my best, on top of our father's training, to be certain that Farrell is prepared to rule. He will not be a great King, I'm afraid, but I do not think he will be an abysmal one either. Underneath his rakishness, he is a smart man. As long as he rules long enough to keep the throne out of

Bowen's hands, does not give Bowen undue ear, perhaps even has a legitimate heir, the kingdom will survive my passing."

Ártur nodded but when he did not speak, the King tried to stave off the uncomfortable encroaching silence by speaking again. "I had a dream last night...the best I have had in years. A záryph came to my bedside, and placed his hands on my brow, on my face. They were warm...gentle...with such holiness as I have not experienced in a long time. I do not recall his words, as what he said came to me more as flashes of imagery and light then dialogue, but when I awoke this morning, I knew I had to see you...to apologize for what I have allowed to come between us...and to give you this."

He removed the Lachlan family ring from his right hand, a ring passed from a King to his heir, and held it across the table. "I have no son to give it to, and I will not leave it for my brothers. Farrell is likely to hock it in exchange for hunting supplies." He snorted and chuckled, trying to sound more lighthearted than he felt. "You...who are dearest to me in all the world, take it. Keep it."

The healer shook his head. "I should not possess part of the regalia. It is enough that I..."

"Then someday," said Donal sadly, "when a proper, decent Lachlan sits on the throne, give it to him. Or her. Will you promise me that? If your conscience will not allow you to accept what I bestow, then make it a symbol of approval..."

"It should not be my place to decide who the proper ruler of Enesfel is. I am not even a subject..."

"Despite my recent lapse, I trust your judgment. You will choose wisely and without personal bias. Will you give me your word, Ártur, or must I ask someone else to do what you will not?"

Ártur swallowed hard and extended his hand. He was not certain he should do this, but he knew that there was no one else the King could turn to for something like this. It was a burden, but one Ártur elected to accept. "I will do my best, My...Donal..."

The King pressed the ring into his palm and then clasped the man's closed fist between his. "That is all I have ever wanted of you, Ártur…and I regret having made you believe otherwise." He began to cough again, harder than before, and the healer got to his feet.

"You should rest. Preserve your strength." His hands on the King's shoulder stilled the cough but did little else to heal him.

"I no longer need my strength," Donal murmured. "I have done what I needed to do. I often wish…" his hand covered the one on his shoulder, "that you were Teren, or I was Elyri…I have never liked that one difference between us…"

"Donal…"

"More than the matters with Lady Cordelia, Prince Arlan, and Lord Nelsen…this is what drove us apart. I knew I was dying, resenting the fact that you will live long after I am gone. Perhaps it is for the best, as you will be able to carry my gifts to the rightful King…which is worth more than I can say. You are Elyri, and I am Teren, but we have been the best of friends. I do not resent your race, only that we must part too soon. In the end…are we really that different, you and I?"

Ártur did not reply. He had always been able to look past the prominent differences between Teren and Elyri. Tonight though, they glared at him like the light of a dozen bonfires, impossible to ignore.

"Help me to bed, Ártur. I am weary." As the healer assisted him, it seemed the monarch grew rapidly older with each step, as if Ártur could feel the life draining out of him. It frightened him, for though he suspected this could be the last time he spent in Donal's company, he had not considered that the end might come tonight. "Ártur? I have one more thing to ask of you…"

As he adjusted the pillows and blankets, Ártur replied, "What do you wish, milord?" If I can give it, you know I shall."

The King smiled. "When you return home, bid farewell to your cousin for me…and convey my regrets that I could not see him again.

And tell him…" He started to cough again, and after the healer stilled the cough with a touch, he gave the King a glass of water. "Tell him thank you."

"Thank you? For what?"

The King finished the water and gave the cup back to Ártur. He shook his head as if he would not answer, but then said, "His prayers. He promised after the coronation that I would always have his prayers…and I think they have done me well. Will you tell him?"

Though perplexed by the unusual request, Ártur nodded his head. "I will, Donal. He will regret not being here."

"I think," yawned Donal, "he is always here. Please fetch Mr. Wyndham." The soldier had remained in the corridor outside of the King's room and entered the chamber at the King's bidding. "Please…bring Lord McLeu and my wife. Healer MacLyr will stay with me until your return."

The soldier bowed and hurried to obey. Ártur sat on the edge of the bed, clutching the King's cold hand, willing him to live. He tried everything his training permitted, every means he had of healing, but by the time the general and queen arrived, Ártur knew his efforts were wasted. There was nothing more he, or anyone else, could do. The general stood at the foot of the bed while Meara climbed onto the mattress on the other side of her husband to stroke his thick, dark, barely graying hair with a nod of acknowledgment to the healer. She was calm, serene, and Ártur wished he possessed her strength. He was barely managing to keep himself composed. The King motioned to Mr. Wyndham, who closed the door but remained inside the room.

General McLeu bowed. "You sent for me, My King?"

"I have given Lord MacLyr the items I told you he was to have. See to it that no one questions his right to them. I want him to remain with me, but he cannot be alone here, else he will be blamed for my passing, accused of murder where there is none. You, Meara, and Mr. Wyndham will also stay to witness that my death is natural and not caused by his hands. When I am gone, please escort him from the palace and see that he is not harmed, Lord General. If he wishes to remain for the final rite, you are personally charged with his safety. Swear it to me."

The general nodded gravely. "I do so swear, My Liege. He will have my full protection."

"Mr. Wyndham?" The soldier took a step forward and watched the King touch his wife's cheek fondly. "Take good care of Meara. See that she is safe."

"On my honor, Your Majesty," he said as he bowed.

Only then, the words spoken and those he cherished protected as best he could provide, did the King settle into his pillows, feeling that everything he needed to say had been said and that the affairs of his life were in order. He closed his eyes, bone weary and aching into his core, but his hands reached for Ártur's and he clutched them as firmly as he ever had in life. His eyes opened long enough for him to murmur, "Guard well, my friend…live a long and bountiful life…and remember me always."

Ártur brought the cold hands to his lips and kissed them, blinking away tears that he did not try to hide as he held the King's gaze. "I could never forget," he promised. "Rest My King…my friend." Donal smiled, his tired eyes closed again, but their hands remained firmly clasped.

It was the second hour of midsummer's night, in the midst of a deep and peaceful sleep, that Donal Lachlan, Crown Prince, King of Enesfel, passed his soul into the hands of the awaiting záryph. The Elyri healer was there beside him, hands in his, to witness the crossing.

King Donal was dead. Long live the new King. Well might he reign.

☙*☙

"What are you saying, Elys? You cannot mean this." But the words could not have been clearer and some part of Ártur had known this was coming for a very long time.

The woman before him stood her ground, unaffected by his surprised, hurt expression. "I can and do mean it, Ártur. I like you...and yes, I loved you once...but I cannot marry a man who is not here for me."

Ártur wondered if it was simply chance that had caused Elys to be here, in front of the naós when he came home to Bhryell for the first time in many years. No one had known he was coming, he was sure, and yet she had been there, on the stoop, talking with another woman when he emerged into Bhryell's streets, and she had not seemed surprised to see him. That lack of surprise and joy should have been recognized as a bad omen. "I am here, aren't I? I am through at Rhidam. I am no longer wanted or required there..."

Elys sighed heavily. "But you want to be there. When they call you again, as they likely will one day, you will go back. Don't you see that? You are a healer above all else; it is the most important thing in your life. You have not had to say it; it is obvious in your actions, in the way you have lived. You have told me many times how you enjoy court life, and you are fond of the Teren, despite any faults, shortcomings, and prejudices they have..."

"No, you are wrong. You are the most important person in my life, Elys. The most important thing..." But he could feel her slipping away, in spite of his efforts to hold tightly to the strands that had once bound them, and he knew his words carried less truth then he wished.

The flaxen-haired woman turned her dun mare and studied closely the man she had planned to marry. He was still attractive to her, and she still admired him, but the years of solitary waiting had made her heart numb. "Are you saying that to convince me, Ártur, or yourself? Healing is your calling. Nothing is more important to you. I cannot honestly fault you for that because it was what drew us together in the beginning. I admired…admire still…your dedication to your calling. But if I were the most important person in your life, I would not have spent the last six years waiting to see you again. You wrote, and you hoped I would understand. I do, Ártur. I understand that I will never hold enough importance to keep you in Bhryell, and I cannot go with you to Enesfel. I will not struggle with anyone, not even Kavan, for that distinction anymore." Ártur looked as if he had been struck by her words, but she continued with the things she needed to say. "There is no future for us. I grew weary of waiting, of loving a man who seemed to have forgotten that he had a fiancée. I have needs for my life too. I shall always be your friend if you wish it, but I have agreed to marry someone else. I am sorry, Ártur. I truly am…and I wish you the best."

Her horse galloped away, taking her out of his life in a way that felt as final as death to him. For many minutes, he stared blindly at her, as if in a dream, something he could reach for but could never grasp. He did not know why he felt dumbfounded. Every word she had spoken was true. He had treated her badly; she was too good a woman to have endured the neglect he had heaped upon her. And he had no excuse for his actions and inactions, except that he had been selfishly absorbed in his own life and everything in Bhryell had seemed far away, another world and lifetime. Blinking did not clear his vision, but his feet started in the direction of home. He had not been there yet, and what he felt in need of most was Kavan.

That Kavan's welcome might be much the same as Elys' did not cross his mind. Kavan was family. Kavan always understood. Kavan's soul was pure, white as his skin, and he would never reject him…no matter how lax Ártur had been in his contact or in keeping his promises. Ártur needed him more than ever, needed a word, a touch, a song, a form of healing that he himself did not have but which Kavan had in abundance. He did not believe his cousin would abandon him, as he had done to Kavan. Ártur did not see those beliefs as selfish; he merely believed in a vision of Kavan he carried in his heart, accurate or not.

His father's home was empty when he arrived. There were no sounds of harp making in the shop and his mother was not in the kitchen as he expected. Ártur climbed the stairs, expecting that, even if Kavan were out for the day, his comforting presence would be in the bedroom they shared. But he stopped in the doorway and stared into the cold room, his hand gripping the latch hard enough his knuckles turned white. Where there had once been two beds, there was one. His own. Kavan's trunk, harp, his bed, all of his personal effects, were gone.

In a panic, Ártur dashed down the stairs and stopped at the front door, wondering where he should go. To Tíbhyan, he decided a moment later. Even if the bhydáni was no longer Kavan's teacher, he would surely know what had become of the boy. Ártur gave no further thought to Elys, other than to question fleetingly why she had failed to mention Kavan. Perhaps she thought he knew where Kavan was.

The bhydáni, however, was not home either, or if he was, he did not answer his door, which was locked for once, another clue that made the healer's chest seize in pain. He leaned against the door, his head on his arm and his back to the street, trying to breathe. Maybe, he desperately hoped, the two had traveled somewhere together. Surely, his cousin could not be dead. His family would have sent Ártur word of such a tragedy…wouldn't they?

He heard no one approach but was suddenly aware of a presence beside him as a light voice said, "Ártur?"

The healer spun and threw his arms around his cousin, recognizing that voice and presence in the same instant. "Praise be, you are well!" He did not want to ever let Kavan go.

"Of course I am…" Kavan pulled away, finding the intimacy disturbing, and kept his head bowed. "You have been home."

"Where are your things? What has happened?" he asked in a tight, animated voice as he reached for Kavan one more time.

But Kavan sidestepped the contact. His answer was succinct and to the point. "I moved out shortly after my fourteenth birthday." "Oh…I…" Ártur heaved a sigh of relief. He should have known. After all, Kavan was old enough to maintain his own residence, though not many Elyri his age struck out on their own. But when the words sank in, he paused and asked with alarm, "Your fourteenth…how…why?" Kavan had not told him about that move, but maybe, the healer was beginning to realize, that was more his fault than anyone else's.

Kavan hesitated before replying, uncomfortable speaking about such a personal topic. His cousin could never know about the events that had transpired that night. "I do not wish to talk about it. Tám and I disagreed, and since I could not comply with his wishes, I moved out. You will not confront him with this, Ártur. It is done and I like where I am. Come; see my home."

Too shaken by the shock and Kavan's avoidance, Ártur nodded. Tám was a difficult man for many to get along with, even within his own family. It was no surprise that Kavan had escaped as soon as he was able; it was only a surprise that Kavan had never spoken of it before.

Ártur followed his cousin to a small house nearest the stone fountain in the village square, one that the healer knew had belonged to Tíbhyan's family though he had never known the woman who had lived there. Kavan led him inside, into the high-ceilinged sitting room, where the healer settled into a cushioned chair near the fireplace. He stared dully at the claw foot legs of the chair across from him and only looked up when Kavan returned from the kitchen with a pitcher of cool red liquid that was poured into two matching copper goblets.

Seeing his cousin's hesitation, Kavan said, "It is not wine, k'tydhá." He wondered if the healer honestly believed he would serve him something potentially deadly.

Ártur took the cup, drank the sweet nectar in one effort, and then went to the window as Kavan sipped casually and watched him. Ártur could feel those eyes on him but he did not speak. He was used to being watched, but this was different. This he could feel and it made him uncomfortable. Rather than dwell on it, he tried to focus on the atmosphere of the room. It was silent here, and though the house was void of familial bustle, it felt warm and welcoming, as it should, for it was his cousin's home. Every nuance he could see and smell, the rose-wood oil in the furnishings, the books on the shelves, the Faith paintings and etchings on the walls, all of those things spoke of Kavan in comforting ways. Ártur rubbed his face and sighed. So many things had changed and he marveled at how foolish he had been to believe that even Bhryell, and Kavan, would be the same. Time had not stopped because Ártur had been preoccupied. Kavan had grown up without him. Behind him, he heard his cousin place his goblet on the mantle.

"Do you wish to talk?" Ártur shook his head. He had no words yet for what he was feeling, and now that he had come to a safe place to shed his burden, he was having difficulty being free of it. "Then I know what you do need. Come; we will take your mind off your troubles." The fifteen-year-old pulled him into the entrance hall.

"Where are we going?"

"Flying."

"Flying? Kavan I…" Surely, the younger man did not mean what Ártur thought he meant.

"…have done it before. You said it yourself."

"Yes, and I told you how I feel about it. Besides, I am not in the mood to try it."

Kavan dropped his hand. If anyone in the world would share something as special to him as flight, he had hoped it would be Ártur. "Elys spoke to you, didn't she?" The healer nodded with a defeated slump of his shoulders. Not only was that memory painful, he realized he had greatly disappointed his cousin yet again. "She begged me to tell you, but I refused. It was not my news to share. We discussed it several times. It was a painful decision for her, but it was the right thing for her to do if she is to live a fulfilled life."

"She knows you are here?"

"All of Bhryell knows." Kavan twisted and stretched his neck, his eyes closing as if in pain. "I wish they did not, but it is too late for that."

The healer considered the meaning of those words for a long moment before asking, "What of me? Does my happiness mean nothing?"

When Kavan's eyes opened, he stared into Ártur's with unnerving intensity. "Would you force her to marry you, knowing she would not be content? Would her unhappiness make you happy?" Kavan started for the back door without waiting for a reply, and Ártur followed, shaking his head. Kavan did not see the gesture but continued, "I did not think so. You have to admit you have not treated her with compassion. Love cannot thrive when it is ignored. If marrying her would have made you happy, you would have done it long ago. It was not meant to be, Ártur. It is time to let her go."

They stopped on the back step. Kavan stared into the gathering twilight as Ártur closed the door and took in the stable and the beautifully manicured roses. They were things he had known nothing about. If he had not been standing next to his cousin, hearing him speak and breathe, feeling his presence, he might not have believed this was the younger man's home. When he said nothing, Kavan asked without looking at him. "That is not all that is bothering you, is it?"

"That...and the fact that you scared me to death; I thought you had died."

There was no change on Kavan's face when he said, "I did not think it would matter," but Ártur hung his head, the words stinging mercilessly. Elys was not the only one he had abandoned and ignored and for some unexpected reason, the fact that Kavan had not shut him out of his life as she had done made the healer feel even guiltier. "I had given up hearing from you. Still…you would have been the first to know if that had been the case. Tíbhyan would have told you. I did not mention my move because it would have created needless worry and there was nothing you could have done. I knew you would find out whenever you came home. That had to be soon enough…"

"I…"

Kavan stopped him with a small hand gesture. "Why should you apologize? You are here. It is behind us."

Though his words were meant to dismiss the matter, Ártur heard and felt the pain in their depths. It seemed he was not the only one reluctant to delve into his innermost pain, discuss it, and why should Kavan? From what the healer was sensing, Kavan would have trusted no one else that way, and the one person he had trusted had turned his back on him. For that, Ártur felt he should apologize, but because Kavan had cut him off, the healer could not find an easy way to offer the apology again.

"There is more. What is it?"

Ártur grunted, mildly annoyed by his cousin's persistence because he knew it was required. Despite the years lost between them, Kavan understood him enough to know how much prodding and pushing were necessary to get him to reveal himself. With a voice that trembled and threatened to break, he choked, "King Donal died last night."

Kavan's voice was almost imperceptible when he whispered, "I know."

"How…?" The healer stared at him as the light of realization flickered within. "It was you! You went to Rhidam, went to him, didn't you? He thought he was dreaming of záryph, but there was no záryph. It was not a dream. It was you. How? Why?"

Kavan moved away, pacing like a trapped animal, and then sank heavily onto the stone bench amongst the flowers. He stared at his hands in his lap, not replying immediately to the questions. In the hollow of his cupped palms, a pale silver-blue light gathered and formed into a sparkling iridescent globe of shifting intensity. The healer watched in awe, having never seen anything like it.

"Why?" Kavan repeated softly. "I knew he was going to die…but what I Saw was an unhappy man left to die friendless and alone. Because it was in my power to change it, I could not allow that fate to come to pass. He was a good man; I liked him. I encouraged him to release the anger and regret that was isolating him and to let go of the past if he wanted to die with any of his friendships intact."

The healer sat beside him, but not too close to that unsettling globe of light. Stretching his legs out, he looked up at the sky rather than the light in his cousin's hands. "That explains it then. He asked me to say goodbye to you, to thank you…though he did not know what for."

"I…" Kavan brought the globe closer to his face, staring into it, the silver glow reflecting off his skin. He was visibly flustered. "I did not seek gratitude…I merely did what I had to do. I wanted him to have peace. Did he?"

"Yes…I was with him at the end. Whatever you said to him, he did find peace…and I suppose I should thank you for giving my friend back to me before I lost him forever."

Kavan shook his head. "You owe me nothing, sínréc, but I am grateful you are pleased."

The silence that followed was an awkward one as Ártur began to realize that Kavan had changed more than he had believed possible, more than he was comfortable with. There was tremendous power in his aura that sparked and prickled against the healer's skin despite his efforts to shield himself and the heaviness that rested on his young shoulders was the sort Ártur believed should not be there. In spite of that, there was soothing peace in Kavan's presence, a deep calm, but also a great sadness that was scored into the depths of his emerald eyes. That Ártur had forsaken him, had missed the transformation from boy to man, brought back the guilt and shame, yet Kavan seemed to have forgiven that transgression, else he would not have called his cousin sínréc. Ártur watched the ball of light in Kavan's hands shift subtly from pale blue, to faint pink, and then back to silver.

"How did you get to the King's room? Security is tighter than ever since Prince Arlan…"

Kavan accepted the change of subject without blinking. The healer had asked how before, and Kavan had known the question had not been forgotten. "There is a k'rylag in the royal suite."

Startled, Ártur jerked away and nearly slid off the bench in surprise. He assumed that Kavan had come through the oratory. He had not thought there any other practical way. "By the Saints, Kavan! You could have gotten yourself killed! They do not know about…"

Kavan showed no visible reaction to the outburst beyond a slight twitching at the corner of his eyes. "They do not know about any of them…and it was the most convenient for my purpose."

The healer's eyes narrowed. "It is dangerous there. Promise me you will not do it again."

Though he knew the answer, Kavan murmured, "Do what?"

"Go to Enesfel."

Shaking his head, the younger man sighed. "I cannot make that promise. If the situation warrants it, I will go back… as will you." He placed the ball of light in his cousin's hands. Ártur nearly dropped it. It was cool to the touch, almost calming, but he had not expected a sphere of light to be solid. Though he was curious about its composition, he refrained from asking, afraid that knowing might somehow make the magic even stranger. After a few moments, the glow dissipated and he was left empty-handed. He met Kavan's gaze as his cousin asked, "Prince Farrell is King then?"

"Unfortunately," the healer groaned, "yes."

"Farrell is not a bad man, Ártur, but his reign will not be as prosperous or popular as Donal's." He was quiet again as his eyes scanned the healer's face for something, an answer to unspoken questions, but there were no answers there. "That is still not what is troubling you. Talk to me, Ártur. What is wrong? I have tried often to contact you but you have shut me out. I wrote to you and you did not reply. You did not come home, not once in all those years, to see how I was. You will not fly with me, you chastise me for the things I have done, and you will not talk to me as you once did. Have I displeased you? Disappointed you?" His eyes darkened with pain but he did not look away. Ártur had not thought Kavan could look any sadder. He had been wrong. "Are we no longer sínréc?"

The healer covered the white hands with his. "You have done nothing wrong, k'tydhá. You could never displease or disappoint me. Any fault in this is mine. You are not at fault. We are sínréc forever if you will have me. I needed…time…space…" He gently squeezed Kavan's hands but then removed his as he wondered how much of his emotional state and thoughts the younger man could read in that contact. "With Prince Arlan no longer at the palace…Lady Cordelia dead…everything changed and I was drifting, lost in the strange predicament I found myself in with no direction. Donal is gone…and Elys has parted ways. I thought you were dead, that I had lost you, even though…and everything changed. I feel…alone. Lost."

"You have Dháná, Tám, Sámel. You have me. Most importantly, you have k'Ádhá…"

The healer snorted. "You do not understand…"

The bitter expression that flittered across Kavan's face sent violent chills up Ártur's spine, cut off his words, and made him look away. "I do understand. I am probably one of the few who can understand. You feel you have none of those you consider friends, allies, and comrades to turn to any longer. You have lost the station that gave your life meaning. At least you have had them…and you will have them again. I know you will. Being isolated is new to you and you find it difficult to bear. You could try being in my place."

He cut short any retort with a shake of his head. "There are four groups of people in Bhryell. There are those who consider me evil, vile beyond compare...people like Tám. Thankfully that number is small." He stood as though restless, perhaps to escape, but then reluctantly sat again. "There are those who think I am too...holy...for the mundane needs of friendship and companionship and treat me with nothing but reverence and awe. There are those who have heard me sing and play...and those who are stupefied by what I can do and feel humbled and inferior and avoid me unless they want something. Just because I can do things...because things happen around me. There are few I could call friend...except bhydáni Tíbhyan...I am not even welcome in the place I called home. Few treat me like a normal man, Ártur. I am not a saint. I am not phyróth. I am not lochi. I am merely a man like any other, despite my differences. If not for the presence of k'Ádhá and the steadfastness of the bhydáni, I do not know what would have become of me. Even you were not here for me as you promised." His eyes never left the man's face. "Would you like to be that alone, Ártur?"

The healer looked away, unable to bear those eyes any longer. He had never considered that Kavan's uniqueness might drive people away. He had assumed that others would feel the same pull towards Kavan that he did. That the young man had never mentioned being isolated before had kept Ártur from considering the possibility. Then again, Kavan had never mentioned any of the things he hinted at. He had not even told Ártur he had moved out of the family's house.

Kavan sighed. "Do not misunderstand me, Ártur. It is my lot, and I strive to accept it. Yet you should consider the trials of others before you wallow in pity."

"I know," the healer moaned. "Everything I worked for has ended...an end I knew would come someday, but I was unprepared for it. I have worked for the Lachlans since I became ílMairós...and I suppose I imagined I would remain in that position until I died. I am not welcome there. You say I will be…that I will go back…but I do not see it. I do not share your faith. I am beginning to understand why many discouraged me from taking that post. I have served two Lachlan Kings and have barely reached my prime. Their mortality scares me." He moved towards the corral fence; Kavan did not follow. "But it is more than that. On my way to the náós…to come home…" A shiver ran through him and he coughed on the bile in his throat. "Lord Nelsen had been accused of murdering Lady Cordelia, but was released as there was no proof against him and he was encouraged to be far away when King Donal's death came. For some reason, he lingered in Rhidam, and Prince Bowen convinced Prince Farrell that Lord Nelsen was a traitor…even without proof. He was executed…an innocent man. I had tried to help him, but he refused my aid, accused me of treachery. Kavan…they impaled him on a stake in front of the castle. It was the most appalling thing I have ever seen." He shuddered again and grimaced. "I did not know that they were going to do it, that he had been taken back into custody. I thought they were going to flog a common criminal on that stake…not impale a man. He was displayed there for all to see. I swear he looked alive still, his eyes following me as I passed…accusing me. I cannot believe anyone, even King Farrell, could do such a thing to another living being. It would never happen here in Elyriá." Eyes closed, clutching his stomach, he whispered, "I pray to k'Ádhá you never have to see anything like that."

Pushing his hair out of his eyes, Kavan got to his feet. "I already have." He ignored the shocked question in his cousin's eyes as the healer looked back at him. "It will only get worse before it gets better." He leaned on the fence beside Ártur and changed the subject. "When did you start carrying a sword?"

For those few minutes, the healer had forgotten about the weapon he had left inside. "It belonged to King Innis…Donal asked me to give it to Prince Arlan."

Kavan nodded but said nothing, as if he knew that the King had known Prince Arlan was alive. It made the healer wonder if the King's sudden certainty of the Prince's safety had come from Kavan.

"k'tydhá...play for me. Please?"

Again, Kavan revealed no surprise at either the change of topic or the request. "Gladly." Music would be a good escape for him; whenever words failed him, there was always music. "I need the practice."

"You? Need practice?" It had always sounded to him as though the music sprung from Kavan's fingertips fully formed and perfect.

"What do you think I do with my time?" the young man asked with a bemused, melancholy smirk. "I have registered for the musician's exhibition at the Festival of Candles." Though the revelation brought a sparkle to the healer's eyes, his weary, forlorn expression did not change. "Yes, I have decided to take my music outside of the náós walls...outside of Bhryell. It is time I put my gifts to good use."

"You will not regret it," Ártur said with a forced smile.

Kavan opened the door to the house and let Ártur pass first. Head bowed, he said in a sullen voice, "We shall see."

❧Chapter 14❧

Brenna Weylin, despite her dainty appearance and impish smile, had the heart of a lion. Or so Healer MacLyr told her every time he saw her. Not that those meetings were frequent. Usually she left written messages on the little window ledge that separated the two halves of the k'dhín bhólibh. She did not know how he retrieved them, only that when she returned in the morning, her letters were gone, and in their place would be instructions for when he would come again. Sometimes he was there to get them himself, but most of the time he was not. As far as she knew, no one else had discovered those messages. She had a ready explanation for the messages left for her, as one of the cooks' sons had willingly agreed to support her claims that the dates and times were for rendezvous' with him. She did not, however, have an explanation for the detailed descriptions she wrote of court life and events, and had to be especially careful when leaving them. She did not think the King, or anyone else, would believe they were pages of a journal.

Sometimes, however, like tonight, she was delayed by roaming guards and nosey servants, causing her to take indirect routes through the castle corridors to reach the oratory. Usually, at times like these, she would arrive to find the healer waiting, although she knew it was dangerous for him to be in Rhidam and had no idea how he came to be there unnoticed. This night she expected to find him waiting again since she had to avoid Prince Bowen and a woman who had stood talking in the hall not far from the oratory door for much longer than she liked. But the figure she eventually did find there this night, while familiar, was not the healer. Stopping in a panic with her hand on the door, Brenna took a deep breath and then a cautious step backward.

"No need to run away, Miss Weylin…or shall I call you Brenna?" King Farrell laid his arm across the back of the pew and beckoned her forward with a smile. She obliged with hesitant steps. The King did not frighten her the way Prince Bowen did, but he was the King and thus had the right to do anything he chose.

"Whichever you prefer, Your Majesty. Is there something I can do for you?" she asked with a curtsey.

"Not likely," he chuckled. "You are not old enough to be of any use to me." If he thought the innuendo was lost on her, he was mistaken, but to her credit, Brenna kept her expression neutral, save for the involuntary blush on her cheeks. The King was handsome enough that nearly all the women in the keep fancied him. Brenna was no exception. "Too bad though. I think you will be one of the most beautiful women Enesfel has ever seen. But you are like a little sister to me…just like Deidre. Do you object to that?"

Her blush deepened. "You may think as you wish, Your Majesty."

The King laughed and turned his attention to the gold ring on his middle finger. "You haven't, perchance, seen my father's amber ring?"

"No, milord. Should I have?" Such a strange question made her wary.

But the King, rather than becoming angry at her negative answer, only sighed. "I suppose not. Donal wore it all the time but did not have it when he died. Perhaps he lost it. Perhaps he gave it to Lady Meara. I was merely curious if you had seen it anywhere."

When he did not continue, Brenna shuffled her feet, fingering the letter within her night-robe's pocket, wondering if she should leave and worrying about what had become of Healer MacLyr. Not knowing if the King would welcome conversation, but curious about what he was doing here, she asked, "Do you come here often, milord?"

The King snorted with amusement. "Why would I? These rooms serve no function. But they do make a good place to be alone. I may come here more often, now that I have discovered it, especially if it keeps me away from my brother."

That would not be good, she mused, at least for her and the healer. She would have to find somewhere else to leave messages if that were the case. She did make note of his desire to put distance between himself and the brother she presumed was Prince Bowen. "You wish to be alone?"

"Alone? Me? I am never alone." He sighed heavily for the second time. Brenna decided that, as a man used to the freedom of a life of hunting and banquets, the new King was finding being confined to the castle and daily duty to be an unpleasant and stifling change. "I was passing and thought I heard noises, but there was no one here. I suppose I lost myself in the rare moment of solitude. You?"

"Me?" she squeaked.

"Why are you here, Miss Weylin?"

Fortunately, she had already devised a story in case she ever needed one and thus was able to answer promptly without seeming suspicious. "It is a good place to think and be alone, as you say. Healer MacLyr introduced me to it when he was at court. I like it here, especially when I cannot sleep."

"Ah…Healer MacLyr. You know…sometimes I miss having him here. I've known him my whole life…it seems strange for him to be gone." He scratched his arm absently. "Nothing more?"

With the mention of Ártur, Brenna wondered if the King knew about her letters, if perhaps he had been waiting for her. Perhaps the noises he had heard had been the healer, and he had arrested the Elyri and had since been waiting for her to arrive. "I…do I need milord's permission to come here?" she stammered, despite her effort to steady her voice.

He laughed again. "I have embarrassed you. A tryst perhaps? Maybe you are not as innocent as you seem." He stood and stretched and she felt a flash of relief. Better he think that of her than know the truth. "I shall leave you to it before your young man thinks you have traded him for the King. If he fails to arrive, come and find me, Miss Weylin. I am sure we can find some way to amuse ourselves on this sleepless night." Still laughing, he winked and left the náós, his fingers snapping happily at his side.

Brenna did not move for many minutes. Her heart was pounding so hard she could not think and could scarcely breathe. Did she dare leave the message for the healer, she wondered. She knew she would have to warn Ártur that their meeting place might be in jeopardy, but she could not do that now. King Farrell might be outside, watching, waiting for her beau to arrive. Deciding to follow through, that the message had to be left despite the risk, she left it where the healer would find it, lingered for another thirty minutes, and then raced back to the room she shared with Princess Deidre, glad that there was no sign of the King or anyone else in the corridor. In the bed, Deidre shifted in her sleep but did not wake. She did not even know her friend had been gone.

ॐ*ॐ

To some, the Festival of Candles was the holy week preceding the Feast of Saint Kóráhm. Villages, towns, and smaller cities sometimes held a simple Gathering ceremony marked with candles to commemorate the Feast, if they chose to acknowledge it at all. Not many did, given his conflicting image as both saint and heretic. But in the royal city of Clarys, where it was said Kóráhm had been born, the Feast was honored regardless of that debate with a weeklong pageant of candles and Gatherings. One day for each of the seven miracles he was said to have performed at the start of his ministry, thirty-five candles a day for each year he lived in the city before starting his work in Enesfel, and a single large green candle that would burn the entire week, representing the shepherd saint himself.

For most, however, the Festival of Candles had little to do with the Faith, with Gatherings, or with the Heretic-Saint. It had not been a fully religious holiday in centuries. Coming as it did at the end of autumn, it was the final chance for Clarys to draw in visitors before the snows blocked the mountain passes and the storms kept the seas in a perpetual state of upheaval. The carnival drew people from all over Elyriá and sometimes from other kingdoms, goods from every harvest and hunt, and the artists' showcase drew the finest creative talent in the land. Once it had presented musicians only, harpers in particular, venerating Kóráhm's harper status, but the festival had long ago given way to creative pursuits of any kind. Painters, sculptors, actors, writers, acrobats and jugglers, and musicians of all variety converged on Clarys during this week hoping to find patronage and success.

While the common folk enjoyed the display of art and the performances of music and theatrical productions, they could not afford patronage. They came mostly for the food, the wine, the goods for sale, and the atmosphere of merriment, with some of the most affluent townsfolk paying for private performances or artwork as their pockets allowed. In all of that, there was very little of Saint Kóráhm to be found.

The secularization of a saint. Kavan had been given the opportunity to attend before by well-meaning gdhededhá and by his own family who came every year in the hopes of acquiring new commissions. But the secularization had kept Kavan away, it seemed a defiling of his patron to wallow in such excesses when he should be in contemplation, and thus attending had been unthinkable. But this year, something had changed. When the idea to attend had come into his head during one of his late-night vigils on the altar steps, he had prayed on it, agonized over it, and had at last settled on it being a sign. It was time. Everyone had to begin their life somewhere, step outside of the comfortable and familiar and make a start in the world. Now that he was an adult, Clarys, the home of his patron, seemed the place to begin his. And the night of his birth, the night that Saint Kóráhm had appeared to his mother, the first night of the Festival of Candles, seemed a perfect time.

Ártur and Sámel traveled with him, Sámel on behalf of the family with the sole purpose of selling harps. There was too much tension in the family to have made the festival enjoyable if Tám and Dháná had come; thankfully, they were content with leaving the business in Sámel's hands.

There had been no confrontation on Ártur's first night home in Bhryell. He had gone to his childhood home and asked his mother what had happened between Tám and Kavan. His father had entered the room before his wife could speak, told Ártur sharply that the matter was not to be discussed under his roof, and then dropped it as he went upstairs. Dháná explained afterward in a whisper that the final straw had involved a debate between Kavan and k'gdhededhá Dórímyr, something she had not witnessed but had heard about later. On top of that, Tám had returned home to find Kavan's copy of Kóráhm's Articles. Ártur knew his father well enough to know how those things would have angered him. Tám was a proud man who despised scandal. It had been the necessity of avoiding dishonor that had kept him from turning Kavan and his books over to the gdhededhá. As long as both were out of his house, where Tám could pretend they did not exist, he was satisfied.

Ártur had announced over dinner that if Kavan was not allowed in that home, then he would not stay there either. Tám said nothing, but his expression said it for him. This was not the first time he had been disappointed in his youngest son, and Ártur suspected it would not be the last. Thus his return to Bhryell found him moving into Kavan's home, something that suited them both once they settled into a routine.

He resumed his practice as healer, but with the number of other healers available in the region, many of them distantly related to Dháná's family and thus to Ártur, he had little actual healing to do. He continued to paint as he had been doing in Rhidam, and as the plans for the trip to Clarys had come together, he chose to take some of his best works to the city in hopes that someone might be interested enough to buy them. The wagon was loaded with harps and paintings, hitched to Tám's sturdy horse, and with Sámel at the reins, the trio made the many days' journey to the royal city.

The lustrous white stone towers of the walled city and the golden domes and spires of both Chellé Udhan and Hes Dhágdhuán Náós could be seen as soon as the wagon approached the southern shore of Lake Eladhán. Rhidam's crumbling náós and Bhryell's humble smaller one seemed inconsequential compared to this splendor. The arched gateways of the city, constructed of both marble and quarried granite were taller than most homes or inns Kavan had seen. There was a thick crowd gathered there, as Kavan suspected there were at each of the city's other gates. People tried to push their way into Clarys at the expense of those around them, as if getting inside first was going to be an advantage in gaining room, board, or goods for sale. The selling stalls would not go up until morning, and those who had not arranged for lodging ahead of time were not likely to secure it now.

Finding the crowd, with its bumping and pushing and rude language, to be bothersome, Kavan closed his eyes and focused on the chaos around him. Very slowly, as he touched each tumultuous thought, he felt the shift. It appeared that the people nearest them began to step aside to allow them passage as they realized the wagon was there. Sámel did not think this unusual and was vocally grateful for the generosity of the people who moved. Kavan could feel Ártur's puzzlement, as the wagon lurched forward unhindered, and though the healer said nothing, Kavan imagined that, before the day's end, there would be questions to answer.

They traveled that way through the streets to the inn where Sámel had last year arranged for rooms. By the time they reached their destination, the healer was casting repeated odd glances at Kavan, as if he suspected that the parting of the crowds was somehow Kavan's doing, even though the younger man's eyes were open and he no longer appeared to be in deep concentration. Indeed, Kavan's attention appeared to be not on the crowd but on the architecture around them, the amalgam of centuries-old stone and lumber homes and shops scattered amongst those brick and mortar ones built within the last handful of decades.

When the wagon finally halted and they started to unload their wares, the great copper and tin bells stationed in the tower pinnacles began to peel, calling all faithful to the first Gathering of the Festival. By the time Ártur turned towards the sound, Kavan had already disappeared into the crowd. The healer gave his older brother an apologetic shrug and followed Kavan, as he was reluctant to leave him alone in a strange place for long. Kavan might be legally an adult, might have been managing his own home for over a year, but Ártur had missed much of his growing up and still saw Kavan as the little boy he had last known.

It did not take long to find his cousin, as Kavan had been brought to a halt outside the náós by the pressing crowd. He was staring at the sculpted záryph set into the building's façade as if memorizing their detail. As the crowd swept him forward again, Ártur had to grasp his arm and be pulled along with him or else remain outside the náós and lose sight of Kavan until the Gathering was over. Somehow the younger man was able to resist the flow of the throng to come to a stop inside the náós, with the faithful unable to budge him as they sought out whatever they considered to be the most advantageous seats.

Vaulted ceiling beams reached upwards as if clawing for the sky. Though lit by candles and the late afternoon sun that streamed through the western windows at the rear of the building, the upper reaches of the ceiling were obscured in shadows. Crimson carpet, flecked with dancing rays of light that came through the stained glass, ran the length of the náos, like a river of blood spreading down from the stairs before the ancient, gold encrusted altar. The pews and kneeling benches were likewise covered with luxurious crimson that showed little sign of the eternity of wear the benches had seen. Multicolored glass mosaics marked each station of Purification and filled the back wall of the clerestory above. Each station contained a carved marble statue of the saint the Faith taught best suited that personal virtue. Once, here in the city of Clarys, each station had contained a statue of Kóráhm, but after his fall to heretical status, most of those statues had been removed, sent to other náos, housed by collectors, or scavenged for other, smaller projects. Only one statue of Kóráhm remained, in the left rear station, and it was there that Kavan blessed himself and knelt in prayer.

Ártur found a place in one of the station seats; he would have preferred to sit in the main sanctuary, nearer the front with a full view of the pageantry, but much of that area was full already and he preferred not to lose sight of Kavan again.

The service passed as the sun set, with Kavan deep enough in prayer that he reacted to little of what went on around him. He did not participate in the chants, in the responsorials, or in the singing. He never sat or stood, but remained on his knees with a distant look in his eyes that Ártur mistook for prayer. Even when the congregation began to file back into the streets for the evening, Kavan did not move, and Ártur, not wanting to remain there all night and having no wish to leave his cousin there alone, stood and pulled Kavan to his feet and back to the inn where Sámel had already made arrangements for their evening meal. Instead of sitting to eat, however, Kavan stood at the window, staring at the spires of the náos that glowed golden against the fullness of the rising autumn moon. His expression had not changed. The healer and his brother looked at one another as they ate.

Sámel was far more use to such odd behavior from Kavan but he still found it disconcerting, and when the meal was cleared away and it was time to prepare for bed, Sámel took his leave to retreat to his own room and leave Kavan to his brother.

Kavan remained where he had been since coming into the room. Undressing, hanging his healer's tunic on a hook on the wall and his trousers over the back of a chair, Ártur asked, "Are you going to stand there until dawn?"

There was no immediate reply and the healer was not sure he had been heard. Part of him was beginning to feel as if he was being intentionally ignored for reasons he did not know. When he eventually opened his mouth to speak again, his frustration having reached its peak, Kavan cut him short without turning from the window, in a whisper of a voice. "I have to go back, Ártur. He was trying to tell me something."

Ártur shivered and scowled. "Who?"

"Dhágdhuán. k'Ádhá. Kóráhm. I do not know. But I feel it…just as I feel my breath coming back upon my face from the glass. I am certain of it. I must return to the náós."

Still annoyed, although now for reasons other than Kavan ignoring him, the healer grunted and climbed into bed. "You can go back tomorrow, Kavan. The night grows late and morning will come quickly…"

"Ártur, I must go."

There was a flare of intensity in Kavan's voice and in his eyes when their gazes met that made Ártur shiver more violently and bite his lip. He pulled the blankets up around his neck, wanting to look away from Kavan but finding he could not. Kavan was not going to release whatever hold he had on his cousin until he had an answer, permission. Ártur suspected that if he said nothing, or forbid it, Kavan would stay in the room the remainder of the night, but he would not leave that window, would not sleep, and would be unhappy. Ártur could not bear to be the cause of his cousin's discontent, and would never forgive himself if Kavan's debut tomorrow was ruined due to lack of rest.

"Go then," he sighed, rolling away from Kavan to look at the wall. "Get this out of your head so that you will be able to give your performance your full attention."

Kavan's smile of gratitude went unseen, but Ártur felt it in those few seconds of silence before the closing of the door indicated Kavan was gone. He closed his eyes to sleep, but he knew he would be unable to until Kavan returned safely to their room.

The young bard hurried from the inn into streets filled with revelers, both those on their way in for the night and those who were indulging in the carnal air that a festival night brought with it. Other than noticing they were there, however, Kavan paid them little attention. He was grateful they paid him no heed, nor prevented him from approaching the náós. Few of those out at this hour had any interest in religious matters and they had even less interest in someone who did.

There was no need to do this to play in the morning; Kavan was always ready to perform. He only needed to do this for peace of mind, to quiet the nagging in his soul that had kept him at that window, staring at the spires, throughout dinner. If not for Ártur speaking directly to him, breaking his trance, Kavan might be standing there still.

The tall wooden doors of the náós were unlocked; náós were considered havens, always open, always available to any who needed their sanctuary. Kavan pushed on the doors, their heaviness giving way to his hands, and he slid into the building as quietly as he could. The building might be open to the public at all hours of the day and night, but he neither wanted to disturb anyone who might be within nor announce his presence. He wanted to be alone.

Pausing in the near darkness, Kavan felt around him with all of his senses to see if anyone else was present. He could sense two in the thóres who had retired for the night; their auras were of peace and sleep. No one else was currently present. Shadows darkened the stained glass, taking away the colored light of the faded day, casting an uneasy pall over what had earlier been an uplifting display. The top of the vaulted ceiling was lost in darkness, the crimson of the carpet faded into the same blackness as if the colors had drained away like blood from a dried corpse. He shuddered at the thought and wondered why such an analogy had pushed into his head. It was certainly not the type of comparison one expected to make within a holy place.

Perhaps, he pondered, as he passed several of the statues on his way forward, it had something to do with the sense of mourning that seeped from the walls and sought to cling to his skin. He paused, feeling someone behind him, a hand on his arm, but when he turned abruptly to confront them, there was no one there. Whatever it had been, it was not the usual presence he felt inside of holy places. This presence had been bitter, filled with anger, linked to the great sadness he already felt. Skin crawling, Kavan took a deep breath, shook off the apprehension that tried to take root, and continued forward. This was a náós after all, he reasoned. Surely malicious forces did not reside within the confines of sacred ground.

He stopped, after a full circle of the room, in front of the statue of Saint Kóráhm. He lit a vigil candle and knelt to pray, but felt nothing akin to what he had experienced earlier, what he believed had drawn him to return. The source of negativity gnawed at the corners of his perceptions, clouding his concentration until he stood with a disheartened sigh. Whatever message had been intended, he had lost the chance to learn it. But he was not yet ready to return to the inn; he again wandered from station to station, admiring the art, the architecture, and the artisanship that had gone into everything he saw, lighting a vigil candle at each, and uttering an earnest plea to be given another chance to hear the message he had come for. Oddly enough, he realized, with each candle he lit, the negative presence he felt diminished until finally, he did not feel it at all.

His circle ended at the wrought iron banister that separated the majority of the congregation from the seats of the nobility and the altar itself. There was a single candle glowing on the altar, the consecrated green one that would remain burning until the Festival was over. Wisps of smoke from the ice blue flame left behind a trail of sweet incense, making him smile. He loved that smell and worked often to replicate the ingredients for his own use. With no one to hinder him, he pushed open the gate without its hinges making a sound, and then let it close after him when he was on the other side. In the softness of the candlelight, now that he was closer to the altar, he could study the magnificent splendor of its creation. As beautiful as it was, however, the longer he was in this place, the longer he studied the glorious objects and works around him, the more its grandeur began to wear thin. What would a truly benevolent deity who stressed compassion and generosity, care about such things as material adornment and wealth? Maybe, Kavan mused, the anger he had felt earlier came from a disappointment in the trappings of haughty mortality.

The stained glass image of Dhágdhuán, though dark with no light entering from behind it, beckoned Kavan forward. His knee touched the ground, his fingers touched his head, heart, and mouth, and he mounted the steps without taking his eyes from the window image until he stopped with his palms flat on the altar. The power that sizzled and jumped into him was like a shock, causing him to stumble back, wide-eyed, and drop to his knees. This time, he stayed that way. He had expected to feel power; he always did when he touched the altar in Bhryell. But in all of his relatively short years, he had never felt anything as powerful as this. The sound of swishing robes approached from his right, startling him, but though he looked towards the sound, he was still too stunned by the power to move.

The man who came towards the altar from a side door was Teren and looked to be about thirty years old. His right eye was covered with a black leather patch and his sandy hair was beginning to thin. His robes were pale gold, with light green at the hem, sleeves, and collar: the colors of the Order of Saint Kóráhm. Having never met anyone from the Order, Kavan reverently bowed his head.

Wondering if he should speak in Elyri, or Trade, Kavan settled on his native tongue and said, "Forgive me, gdhededhá. I did not mean to intrude." If the man had lived in Elyriá for any significant time, he likely knew the language.

The older man flashed a welcoming smile. "There is nothing to forgive, my son," he said easily in Elyri. "All are welcome in this place, though few would choose to come here at this hour." And, he thought with a quick glance around them, few would have the nerve or desire to breach the gate and approach the altar. "I have watched you lighting vigil candles. Is something troubling you?"

Not having sensed anyone with him, other than that dark presence, Kavan scowled. He should have known this man was there. As lying was against his nature, he replied, "When I was here earlier, during the Gathering, it felt as if someone was speaking to me…wanted to tell me something. I was not allowed to remain, but returned as soon as I was able…yet the feeling is gone. Whatever it was, I might never know." He glanced at the man's face for a moment and then looked down at his hands in his lap.

The gdhededhá settled on the step beside him so that they were at eye level. He had lived in Elyriá much of his life, but he could not recall ever seeing anyone, man or woman, as beautiful as this young man. It was not merely physical beauty, but also a beauty that radiated from the inside, a beauty that caused a longing to touch the boy's thick, silver-white hair, his face, his hands. But he did not. Nor could he recall ever being made uncomfortable by such a luscious androgynous timbre as the boy possessed. If the young man sensed his agitation, however, he did not acknowledge it, which allowed the gdhededhá to relax before speaking again. "If it was a message of importance, k'Ádhá will make it known to you, but you must allow it to come in His time, not when you will it to."

"Yes, gdhededhá," Kavan murmured contritely. He knew that, of course, but such reminders were sometimes needed.

The gdhededhá tore his gaze away from the boy's face and looked instead at the altar before them. "May I ask you a question?" Kavan, not looking at him to anticipate his thoughts, nodded. "When you touched the altar…why did you stumble away?"

Kavan closed his eyes. How could he explain to a man of Faith what he, a commoner, felt in the náós, in each worship altar? He had only tried to explain it a few times to Ártur, but his cousin could not grasp it. Kavan worried that anyone else would think him mad if he spoke of it. Finally, hoping he could change the subject, he murmured, "I know it is not proper for any other than gdhededhá to come to the altar…"

The man closed his hand over Kavan's and smiled again. "It is not my place to chastise or condemn you. You carry an air of great conviction, and k'Ádhá knows your heart's intentions. If you feel compelled to be here, that is where you should be…but to react so…?"

Kavan's hand trembled beneath the gdhededhá's. He rarely sought physical contact, for fear of being shunned, and when it was freely given, it had a powerful effect on him. In a small strained voice, he finally spoke. "It is difficult to explain, gdhededhá. There are times, if I lay my hands on the altar, any altar, I feel power. I believe its source lies in holiness, in the touch of k'Ádhá…but I cannot prove that. It is stronger here in this one than in others I have encountered before."

"Power, eh?" The gdhededhá removed his hand, feeling awkward, and stared at the stained glass image above. Though power was a common Elyri experience, part of their everyday lives, very few talked about it, and he felt sure that the sort of power the boy was referring to was not the same. "I believe there is always power in an altar. I have never felt it myself…nor has anyone else to my knowledge, but that does not mean it is not there. It must be. There are many things we are asked to believe without proof…I do not doubt your experiences. What is your name?"

Being believed without question was an uncommon enough experience for him that Kavan almost smiled. "Kavan."

"Are you a student of the Faith?" the gdhededhá asked. With the boy wearing a robe, albeit of a color the gdhededhá did not associate with any order he knew, it was a logical assumption to make.

Kavan shook his head. "No. I have not felt called to a religious vocation. I am a harper."

That made the man smile again. "Ah…come for the showcase tomorrow?" He smiled wider when Kavan relaxed further now that the conversation had moved away from the oddities of his faith and towards music. "Do you think you stand a chance of winning?"

As though confused by the question, Kavan cocked his head and replied, "I did not come to win. I decided it is time to play somewhere other than my village náós. Now that I am a man, I must make my own way. Music is the only tool I have with which to do that, and this is a good place to gain exposure."

If he was a man, that put Kavan at fifteen to sixteen years old, surely, the one-eyed man thought, no older. "Indeed. If one seeks employment and patronage, there is no better place in Elyriá than Clarys, especially during the Festival. Have you been playing long?"

"Since I was three. My family makes harps; they were always around me…"

The gdhededhá's face lit with an excited glow. "One of the Cliáth's perhaps?" There were other harp making families in the kingdom, some of them quite fine in workmanship, but none were as ancient as the Cliáths, and no harp in the land had ever surpassed the quality of sound and artisanship of a Cliáthan harp.

Kavan squirmed, wishing he could be seen as himself rather than as part of a highly respected family, but replied, "Yes, sir…I am." The gdhededhá got to his feet and held out his hand. "I have a harp in the choir loft; I play it during Gatherings sometimes, though I cannot say I am very good. Would you play for me?" "If you wish, gdhededhá." He would not deny a clergyman such a request. He followed to the back of the nave near the main door and up the steep granite stairs to the choir loft. Kavan stopped for a breathless moment to look into the náós interior from this new vantage point. From here, the ceiling was still lost to darkness, still seemed too far out of reach. What had seemed endless before appeared even more so.

"Come…please…" murmured the gdhededhá with an odd note in his voice as he tried to hide embarrassment. He could not believe his eagerness to keep this young man near him. Kavan shook himself with a slight shudder, as a bird might, to expel water from its feathers, and then came to where the one-eyed gdhededhá waited.

The harp on the pedestal was an ancient Cliáthan, one of the largest models his family had ever produced. The gdhededhá watched Kavan perch on the stool, and with his eyes closed touched each string. Though no sound was made, he assumed the young man was tuning the instrument somehow, by the tension of the strings perhaps, since he sometimes turned the tuning pegs and then touched a particular string again. It was a rare gift indeed, the gdhededhá thought, to be able to tune an instrument in such a fashion.

When the first notes filled the empty night, the blond man took a few dizzy steps backward, forced himself to sit lest he fall to his death, and closed his eyes. He did not know about the altar, but this man's music certainly contained power. He could feel it seeping into his pores, a sound richer, more beautiful, and purer than anything he had ever heard or imagined. The longer he listened, the more peculiar he felt, as the vibration beneath his skin seemed to lift him from his body to float on sounds this náós had not heard during his tenure here. It took great effort to reconnect himself to his body, but it was the sensation of being watched that finally made it possible. Yet there was no one with him except the boy, whose bright eyes were transfixed far away, an expression that suggested his mind was not focused on what his hands were doing.

Then the gdhededhá felt something else, a growing upsurge of static, a tingle of power surrounding him as the feeling of being watched grew stronger. Kavan may have been aware of that tingle, as his eyes fluttered closed and a smile tugged at the corners of his lips. For the gdhededhá, that response suggested that this was something the harpist was accustomed to, but while Kavan might not fear it, the gdhededhá found the unfamiliar to be unnerving. He wanted to speak, to ask the origin of this strange power, but he never had the chance.

Behind the harpist appeared a faint bluish outline of a robed figure with its hands resting on the young man's shoulders. The figure turned its head to look in the gdhededhá's direction, extended a hand towards him, and then ceased to move. The gdhededhá genuflected as he fell to his knees, not daring to take his eyes from the unexpected apparition. As abruptly as it had appeared, it was gone again, and the náós grew quiet. Realizing the music had stopped, the gdhededhá blinked several times before meeting Kavan's gaze.

Confused by the reverent expression on the man's face and the way he was kneeling, facing Kavan, Kavan looked from side to side, expecting to see someone there, but there was nothing. "gdhededhá?" he whispered, praying that the man was not worshipping him.

"Forgive me for staring…but surely…you are a man most favored…" He fumbled for words, feeling even more awkward in the presence of one so young, so talented, so beautiful, and so obviously blessed.

"Favored?" Kavan shivered, hating to hear that sort of talk.

The gdhededhá shook his head as excitement began to replace debilitating awe. "Did you not feel it? The hands on your shoulders? The individual standing behind you?"

"I…usually feel a presence when I play and meditate in a náós…but I have never…if someone was there…" He looked behind him once more and then slid from the stool to kneel with the gdhededhá on the floor. "Who was it, gdhededhá? Do you know? Was it Saint Kóráhm?"

"Saint Kór…why would you think that?" The Heretic- Saint would normally be the last individual anyone would believe had visited them.

"I bear his name," Kavan explained in a tense voice. "I was born on this night. It is said that he, or one of his followers, visited my mother on the night of my birth. Do you think it could have been him?"

"I…perhaps…" The gdhededhá rubbed his eyes. "I have been praying for a sign; my life has been in need of direction and I have been asking that he give it."

The corners of Kavan's eyes and lips twitched. "Then perhaps he did not have a message for me…but one for you, given through me. If he was here, if I was led here so that you might be given what you seek, then I hope I have been of benefit to you, gdhededhá." It was disappointing not to be the intended recipient of a divine message, but Kavan felt it was an equal honor to be touched and used in such a way.

The portly man scrambled shakily to his feet. "I must pray on this. Such a sign cannot be ignored. You may remain as long as you wish. I know you will do no harm." He almost touched the boy again but instead, he smiled and stumbled almost blindly down the stairs. Kavan followed.

"gdhededhá? May I ask your name?"

The gdhededhá turned back and paused as if seeing Kavan for the first time. "Jermyn Tythilius," he replied. "I hope we shall see each other again soon, young Kavan."

"I would like that," Kavan murmured earnestly as he watched the man go. So far, Ártur had been the only other person to experience what Kavan felt while creating music. That this paunchy Teren clergyman had experienced something, had seen someone, was significant. It had to be. Kavan shivered. Who had laid hands on him? A záryph? Kóráhm? Perhaps Dhágdhuán? Who…and why? With his thoughts spinning around the implications of this night's events, Kavan made his way back to the inn and up to the room he shared with his cousin, to find the healer still awake.

Kavan shook his head and tried not to express exasperation for being worried about like a child. "Waiting for me?" he asked as he closed and locked the door.

"I couldn't sleep," the healer shrugged as he adjusted the pillows behind his back to continue to sit comfortably against the headboard. "Did you find whatever it was you were seeking?"

"No…but I believe someone else did." He began to undress.

Ártur drew his knees towards his chest and studied Kavan for several moments. "I suppose you can't explain what you mean by that…?"

Once the lamp was extinguished, Kavan crawled into the empty side of the large bed. "There was a gdhededhá; his name was Jermyn Tythilius, of the Order of Saint Kóráhm. He asked me to play the harp in the choir loft for him after I revealed I am here for the showcase. He was…someone was there. He believes it might have been Saint Kóráhm who touched me. I felt nothing different than I normally do, but gdhededhá Jermyn saw him…behind me. He was praying for guidance and direction and believes what he saw to be his sign." Kavan's tone was excited and agitated. "Do you think it could have been, Ártur? Or a záryph? Or…Dhágdhuán? Could what I feel be because someone is there with me." He met Ártur's gaze at last. "Who or what am I that, whoever it is…Ártur? I am not important. I am no different than any other man. I am not special; I am only myself. Why do these things happen to me?"

Ártur watched Kavan, knowing how close his cousin was to weeping though he had never seen it before and there were no tears. During the months he had been home from Rhidam, he had heard the talk, heard the rumors, heard all of the stories that Kavan had never told him. Tales of such wonder that they birthed an awkward distance between the cousins, just as their relationship began to mend. Ártur believed in prophets and saints. To hear people speak of Kavan with those words, to learn of the deeds that only a prophet or saint should be able to perform, was unsettling for the healer...and as unsettling for Kavan it seemed.

There had been much soul searching as he had lain in bed awaiting Kavan's return. He was as guilty as anyone else, he knew, of holding Kavan apart because it was difficult to accept the differences between them. If Kavan was what others claimed, how could any normal person, even his cousin, be counted as a friend or companion? With all that Ártur had failed to do for his cousin, he could not be worthy. Kavan surely needed more than what a man such as Ártur could give him. But tonight, Ártur had begun to wonder if all saints and prophets had been treated the same, men and women whom society held apart...but who needed, perhaps more than others, the trappings of friendship, trust, and companionship.

Even Dhágdhuán was said to have had friends. Why not Kavan?

He finally murmured, "I do not know, Kavan. If it is true, who can say what k'Ádhá has in store for you..."

"You believe it too." There was pain in Kavan's normally passive, steady voice. The healer hung his head, stung by a stab of guilt. "Like everyone else, you believe I am something I am not."

Ártur shook his head, trying to think of some way to defend and redeem himself. "I do not know what you are, Kavan. I have not witnessed the things I have heard tell of. You will not even sing for me so that I might hear your voice. I find it difficult to believe that you are…but you are different from anyone I have ever known. You know that. You have more musical talent, more natural ability, more power than I have ever dreamed could exist in a single person. And I have met many holy, pious men in my travels, or men that have claimed to be such, but when I am with you, when you pray, I admit that I firmly believe you are the…" He stopped, words failing him, leaving him unable to finish.

Kavan continued to stare and demanded in a single word, "Yes?"

The healer lowered his eyes from his cousin's insistent gaze. "I have never met a man more filled with the love and grace of the divine. I do not know what you are, or what you are hoping to be. But you are special. There is no denying that. You may not be perfect, as no one can be, but you are as close as…"

"Why not?"

It took the healer a few moments to determine what his cousin was asking, until at last all of Kavan's prayers, fasting, and steadfastness of faith took on a whole new light. "Only k'Ádhá is perfect. Not even Kóráhm was. Dhágdhuán was the closest any man has ever come but…are you trying to be holier than him?"

"No!" Kavan looked distressed and ill at the suggestion. "I only want to be as k'Ádhá would have me be. If I am already different, if things are going to happen regardless of anything I do to prevent them, if people are going to shun me, whom else can I turn to? Why shouldn't I strive to be as He would have me be?"

Ártur shifted on the bed, lying on his side to face his cousin. "Do you know what that is? Has He revealed that to you? Do you know what is wanted of you? We all have different roles to perform in life, and you have already said that yours is not a vocation of Faith. What if yours is to be a harpist? What if he wants you to marry, raise a family, be like everyone else, except for being more devout, talented, and powerful?"

Kavan had never given the possibility consideration, and his expression proved it. But even as Ártur spoke the words, he was aware that they were his own pitiful attempt to pull Kavan down to the level of a normal man, something he had known Kavan would never be from the day the boy was born.

The reality of his life quickly won in Kavan's thoughts and his expression darkened. "If I was meant to be like everyone else, I would have been born like everyone else. I would look like everyone else, have the same capabilities as everyone else, not be what I am. The things that happen to me would never happen." The pain in his eyes as he indicated the fairness of his features in the mirror made Ártur look away and Kavan sighed. "Besides, no woman will wish to marry me," he finally groaned, lying down with his back to the healer. "Not when even you cannot see me as a normal man."

Ártur rubbed his face. It was pointless to tell Kavan that he was wrong, for Ártur knew that nearly everyone who met Kavan saw him in much the same way, something unapproachable, set apart. He had tried to convince women he met to visit his cousin; they either refused on Kavan's reputation alone or agreed only to leave soon after feeling as though they had come away from a gdhededhá. Ártur surrendered the discussion yet again. Maybe Kavan was right…but the healer prayed he was wrong.

It came as little surprise that gdhededhá Jermyn should be one of the showcase judges. Nor was the large number of other exceptional performers he would compete against a surprise. His fear that his work would be lost among the talent, however, proved unfounded. That he was the last living Cliáth gained him accolades enough. But he was also the only harper present this year, and the youngest in the showcase, both of which attracted their share of attention. Kyne Mórne, the matriarchal head of the k'lómesté and of all Elyriá came forth to present him with the second place prize personally and questioned him extensively on matters both musical and otherwise afterward. She gave private indication that, if not for some political maneuvering involving k'gdhededhá Dórímyr, Kavan likely would have won the competition. That she knew of his debate with the highest gdhededhá in the land embarrassed him, but learning that she found the tale to be amusing and stimulating eased his conscience. Her interest in him instilled a confidence in not only his abilities but also in himself that had nothing to do with Ártur's high regard, Tíbhyan's teaching, or the adulation of Bhryell's Faithful.

With Ártur showing his paintings and Sámel selling harps, Kavan had much of the week to himself. Although he had seen gdhededhá Jermyn long enough to exchange smiles after the showcase, Kavan did not have the chance to speak with the man again. A message had been left for the clergyman, asking to meet, but he learned that the gdhededhá had gone into seclusion and was not accepting visitors. Any hopes of discussing Kóráhm with someone knowledgeable were lost.

Left to his own devices, Kavan made it his mission to search every copyists and bookseller's shop in Clarys for any of Kóráhm's writings that could be found. The city's size made it the most likely place to find such rare treasures, although Clarys being the center of the Faith also meant that potentially heretical documents would be carefully hidden, if they existed at all. Careful questions asked brought him to a dilapidated copyist's shop on the outskirts of the city where he found the first two volumes translated from the High Elyri of their origin into the vernacular Elyri and the second volume translated into the Trade tongue. The copyist was not reluctant to part with them, but nor was he as eager to be rid of them as the copyist in Bhryell had been, despite the danger he could be in for having them. But Kavan had prize money to spend and haggled until he obtained them all, cherishing the softness of their leather covers, hoping to find the treasure that still eluded him, the Third Volume.

He did not find it.

Nothing more was said between the cousins regarding the conversation of their first night in Clarys. Ártur could think of nothing that might make Kavan feel more secure, and rather than risk an argument, he remained silent, watching Kavan engross himself in the search for books and knowledge. He knew Kavan was interpreting his silence as an affirmation that he was somehow too different, that Ártur too held him apart, but what could the healer say? What could he do?

On two separate occasions, Kavan was asked to play for others, once for a member of the k'lómesté at a dinner party and once for Kyne Mórne and a handful of clergy which thankfully did not include k'gdhededhá Dórímyr. Kavan obliged both requests and came away with a handsome purse for each performance that would support him for months to come, but the healer was not certain Kavan enjoyed the exposure. He remained pensive, sullen, and quiet, unable or unwilling to explain what he was feeling. By the end of the week, it seemed to Ártur that Kavan was mostly regretting his decision to come to Clarys.

The distance between them increased, and Kavan refused to address it. The healer grew more distressed by the increasing pain in his cousin's eyes. There had to be something he could do to make it right.

He could not lose the only person he had left to rely on.

❧Chapter 15❧

Vivid pennants of amber and burgundy hung from the lamp-posts and shops lining the narrow streets of Rhidam. Merchants from throughout the kingdom had set up tables and stalls surrounding the city square and along most of the larger avenues. Farmers and artisans journeyed from the surrounding countryside to participate in what promised to be a profitable three days of revelry. It was a time for the people, something many of them felt they deserved of their King after his recent series of lavish palace parties.

Enesfel had attracted more travelers and traders in the first five months of King Farrell's reign than it had in many years, due largely to the King's leniency in taxing them. The nobility and the merchants appreciated this boon. The peasants and working classes, however, were not as free with their praise. The taxation breaks had not trickled down to them; they continued to work as hard for little reward as they had all their lives. The King was spending money rapidly on projects that would, in theory, improve the royal city and the kingdom. Roads were upgraded, bridges built, decaying public structures repaired or replaced, but the lower classes could not see that these improvements benefited them in ways they needed most and knew that, eventually, more money would be required. They would be expected to produce it.

Still, they were thankful for the improvements and for these few days free of toil and concern. The King decreed that no one would be forced to work, save his own staff, and thus it was those out to sell their wares that would be working and they, by choice. Food, wine, contests, and various other attractions abounded. Minstrels wandered the overcrowded streets supporting the festival atmosphere with an undercurrent of constantly playing music. A trio of mimes performed on one street corner, and a slick, ferret of a man stood before a tavern performing slights of hand and robbing more than one passerby of his purse. Further along, there was a man performing feats with fire, while beside him a woman danced erotically with a massive, thick bladed sword. There was no shortage of ways to entertain one's self or to spend hard earned coin.

The first day of King Farrell's carnival was highlighted by a tournament, the second by a contest for musicians of all sorts. The new King had a weakness for good food, good wine, good music, and attractive people; his appetite for such things was insatiable. He was constantly seeking better, more attractive additions for his court and this time it was horses and musicians. He had invited performers from all of the Five Sovereignties, but no Elyri had agreed to participate. It was a disappointing turn since Elyri were generally superior musicians. He believed it would have been pleasant to have an Elyri musician in his court, but he knew that, upon his brother's death, Elyri felt less welcome and less safe in Enesfel, despite the King's efforts to prove otherwise. Prince Bowen, on the other hand, had made every effort to discourage the King from inviting them, but Farrell ignored him. The invitations had been sent. The King wanted the best, at any cost.

It was into this carnival atmosphere that the robed figure emerged, a carved wooden box tucked under his arm, his face hidden beneath the heavy folds of his hooded white robe. He glanced about, savoring the light tang of sea salt air that mingled with the aromas of food, animals, and unwashed bodies, before he began to walk, casually observing everything without interacting with it. It had been a long time since he had smelled such things, and he realized in the deepest corners of his soul that he had missed it.

He studied the wares with curiosity but little enthusiasm. He had no interest in food or slights of hand, and in general, the goods were not of the quality he could get at home. He had not come to Rhidam to shop. He did, however, purchase a crystal decanter of Káliel's finest Chablis; he had heard much praise regarding it, and because it was rarely available outside of the islands that produced it, this was his best opportunity to acquire it. The time for tasting it, however, would wait until he was in the privacy of home. With the decanter clutched to him, he passed the sword dancer who moved close, took his hand, and pulled it in the direction of her ample bosom. Appalled, he pulled free and hastened past, ignoring the chortles of a few drunken men.

Farther on, he found a silversmith and paused long enough to study the trinkets he sold. Amongst the rings and chains, pins and buckles, he discovered an ornately wrought T-shaped Kílyn Cross hanging from a chain of exquisite workmanship and value. Though the price was high, suggesting that this was not the work of this artisan's hands but rather something he had bartered for himself, the stranger bought it without haggling. He had been searching for such an item for many years and did not want to risk anyone else taking it while he negotiated price. It felt cold and heavy around his neck when he put it on, but it soon warmed and left a tingling sensation on his skin that made him smile.

Somewhere to his left, the sounds of the tournament rose up, a raucous cheer of bloodlust and excitement. He found his way there easily enough, guarding his possessions as he moved through the crowd. When he reached the arena, it was in time to watch the archers with their slender curved longbows aiming at targets that to him seemed ridiculously easy to hit. There seemed little challenge in their sport at first, but the targets became progressively more difficult until, in the end, only one man remained capable of hitting the mark every time. By then, the stranger, never having been much interested in sport, had grown weary of the contest and left the tournament to find entertainment elsewhere.

In the square directly before the castle moat, a wooden platform had been erected. It was currently occupied by a troupe of actors in faded and tattered clothing performing a pantomime. As this was more his idea of an afternoon's diversion, he found a spot as close to the stage as he could get while keeping a clear view of the performance and chose to watch. It was not a well-written or intellectual piece of entertainment, but it was light and humorous and pleased the audience. After observing the men and women around him, he concluded that most of this group would not have appreciated the type of intellectual pursuits he was used to enjoying. This sort of performance was ideal for those who wanted only to escape the drudgery and monotony of everyday existence.

As the sun began to sink in the west, the troupe left the stage to be replaced by a collection of six minstrels playing popular folk tunes from across the Sovereignties. Instead of dispersing, the gathering grew thicker as men and women came to dance beneath the smoky glare of torches and lanterns. Not wishing to be involved, particularly when the consumption of ale increased and the crowd began to grow loud and unruly, the stranger set off in search of an inn with a room, avoiding the hands of several maidens on the way who tried to draw him into the dancing. There were no rooms available, which did not surprise him. He knew of a safe haven, however, where no one would think to look for him or give him trouble, and he found his way there. There might be others at home seeking him, but none would ever guess he had come to Rhidam.

He repeated the same pattern the following day, although this time he spent most of his day at the platform, waiting for other musicians to arrive, observing the crowds. A crippled youth hobbled past on a pair of rickety, battered crutches, seeking donations; the stranger obligingly gave the boy the last of his remaining bhelts. It was a significant sum for anyone, and he wished he could see the boy's face when he counted his coins at the end of the day. It was nearly noon by then, and a group of workers arrived to erect a covered booth adorned with the amber and burgundy banners of the Lachlan House; he had no chance to follow the boy or talk with him. He was more interested in seeing which of the royal family chose to attend.

When their task was complete, the carpenters departed, and within the hour, a crowd began to assemble around the platform. It was a noisy rabble, as each strove to make themselves heard over the people around them, but with the eventual arrival of the King, his two brothers, and two young women, the crowd settled considerably. It would be impolite to show such disrespect to the King.

The blonde-haired woman would be the princess, he presumed. The other young woman was likely the niece of Guthrie McHador he had heard about, although he had never seen the girl before. The pair were giggling and discreetly pointing to the variety of musicians gathered along one side of the platform, no doubt admiring some and ridiculing others, while a man with a scroll and quill strode up and down the line making notes as he spoke to the performers. Kavan remained where he was, obscured by the crowd. The competition would last a couple of hours from the looks of it, and he had no desire to stand in that line beneath the scrutiny of the crowd for that amount of time. Such attention was unwanted. He would bide his time, spend it judging the other competitors and observing the Lachlans.

The King had changed little in the years since Kavan had seen him. His thick, dusty brown hair swirled around his face and shoulders in a swoop of curls. Unlike King Donal, Farrell did not sport the customary Lachlan beard. Despite his well-known excesses, the King was in excellent physical condition and knew it. He went to great lengths to dress and behave in ways that exhibited his physique and style to everyone. He had yet to marry and preferred to spread his affections to any beautiful woman who caught his eye, and it was rumored that he had sired several illegitimate children, rumors that he did not attempt to deny or address.

Stocky, blonde Prince Bowen had changed little either, although the lines around his scowling mouth and eyes were deeper. Prince Girvin, on the other hand, looked paler and had grown a beard in an effort to fill out his gaunt face. The princess had changed the most, having grown from a newborn infant to the cusp of womanhood. Anyone who had known the late queen could see that woman in Princess Deidre's features. It led Kavan to wonder what her twin had grown up to be, but if Ártur knew, he never spoke of it. In fact, he rarely spoke of his days in the Lachlan House any longer, as if he could forget that life had ever existed for him.

A few hours turned into several as performers from Hatu, Cordash, and Enesfel took turns on the stage, vying for the King's attention. There were a few individuals from the fringes of the Cíbhóló, and one whom, judging from his tightly laced crimson doublet and fur-lined boots was from Neth. Members of the audience came and went, seeking food or other entertainment as the afternoon waned. Prince Bowen and Prince Girvin did likewise, as neither particularly shared the interests of the King. Farrell never moved from his seat, smiled at any passing individual who caught his eye, listened to each musician with varying degrees of interest, and drank a great deal. It was the King the musicians were trying to impress, and it was his attention, or lack of it, that would determine how each entertainer fared. The performances ranged from drums, to mandolins and dulcimers, to flutes and pipes, to singers and dancers of every description. Some were good, some were bad, a few were excellent, but most were simply fair. Anyone who hoped they had a chance of obtaining royal favor and a life of luxury within the Lachlan castle, or who merely had the nerve to try despite a lack of talent, was in attendance. Life in Farrell Lachlan's court held a lot of promise, and it was always possible that a pretty face without talent might catch the King's eye as surely as a homely one with immeasurable talent.

As each performer completed their set of songs or dances, they left the platform and gathered on the opposite side. Meanwhile, the mousy man with the scroll recorded crowd response and the King's reaction, made brief notes before allowing the next performer on stage, and wiped his brow nervously throughout. When a handful of performers remained, Kavan moved from his vantage point and approached the scribe.

"Is it too late to be added to the list?"

The man did not look up but continued to write, though the young page beside him carrying the inkwell was staring at Kavan in barely disguised awe. "Not yet. Name?"

"Is it necessary?"

"It is if you want the King to select you."

Kavan considered it for a moment. The opportunity was tempting, particularly if it meant giving his cousin back the life the healer had lost. But Kavan did not belong in Rhidam; it was no safe place for his kind and he knew it. Reluctantly he replied, "I am only looking for the opportunity to play. I am not seeking employment."

Shrugging, the scribe continued to write. It was none of his concern if someone wanted to pass on a well-paying position of luxury. "Country of origin?" Kavan looked at the platform, debating if that was something he should reveal. "Country of origin?" the man repeated.

Since everyone would know what he was soon enough, Kavan replied, "Elyriá."

Only then did the scribe look up, surprise etched on his face. He quickly regained his composure enough to stop staring and made a few hasty remarks on his scroll. From the sound of the voice, the scroll keeper had expected to see a woman, and dressed as the individual was in a white robe with the hood up to hide his face the scribe believed it still might be. No Elyri had registered or been expected to participate. This individual whose face he could not see was either very courageous to travel in this land alone, or very foolish. Possibly both. "You will be last. The others were here before you."

"That is satisfactory." Kavan removed the harp from its wooden case to be sure she was in tune. He had taken to calling the instrument she lately, though not within anyone's earshot. The last three performers eyed him suspiciously as they passed on their way to the platform, each wondering who he was, where he was from, and why he was keeping his identity hidden. He knew it was better they did not know yet. It was safer, at least.

When the last scheduled performer completed his set, the scroll keeper motioned Kavan onto the stage. The sun was nearing the horizon; the sky was tinged with red and gold and lamps had been lit around the platform. Touching the newly acquired cross to his lips, he mounted the platform and balanced on the stool, aware that his attire was drawing stares. He gave in to the temptation and lowered the hood of his robe. There was a collective breath throughout the crowd, though whether it was because they recognized him as Elyri or because of his features he did not know. Harp cradled on his knee, he closed his eyes and began to play.

The King had turned away to converse with a handsome young man, but his attention snapped back to the stage as the song began. From where he watched, he could see the harper's hands clearly. They were white, slender, delicate in appearance, but they were definitely a young man's hands, even if his face was fairer than any woman the King had ever courted. He was marginally aware of the hush that fell over the audience, of the attentive interest of his sister and her lady in waiting. Mostly he was aware of the stirring of unfathomable sensations that swirled in his belly, in his heart, in his soul. He decided this was the musician he wanted. This man would be part of his court.

When his few songs were over, the harper rose to leave. He was satisfied with the crowd's response, a sort of awe and appreciation he did not find in Elyriá. This was a start to the musical future he envisioned for himself. But as he stood, the King did as well, speaking loudly enough that most in the crowd could hear him. "I wish to hear more."

"Sire?" Kavan had not anticipated that.

The King liked his voice, despite, or perhaps because of, its androgynous timbre. Perhaps this bard could sing. Would not that be worth hearing? "Those were common melodies. Play something original, of your own composition. Surely someone of your caliber has original works? If you can sing, do so. I want to hear you."

Audible excitement ran through the audience; the girl at the princess' side clapped her hands as the King watched expectantly. Kavan gauged it all, absorbed it into his soul, and after pushing the sudden surge of nervousness aside, sat once again. "As you wish, Sire," he murmured with his head bowed.

This would be the first time any of his compositions would be heard outside of his homeland, the first time his voice would be, and he wondered if he would be able to sing without the usual gawking and whispers he endured in Bhryell. He chose two numbers, and with great trepidation, sang. His voice was clear, pure, and sweet. It swept up into the heights of emotion, notes unrivaled by any other man, making the hair on Farrell's neck stand up as shivers raced up and down his spine. The King was shaking from head to foot and knew, from the quick glances he stole around him, that the audience shared his delight. He had to have this man.

But when the King stood to encourage him further, the harper had already gathered his instrument and case and disappeared into the crowd. The audience was too stunned to stop him. Kavan retrieved his decanter of wine and returned home. Let them wonder, he thought to himself with a smile. Someday these people would know who he was. His name would be known across the Kingdoms and it was a day he was beginning to look forward to with growing anticipation.

ও*ঙ

The bowstring released with a snap; the arrow found its center mark for the eighth time that day. Guthrie stood behind his ward, not speaking though he was pleased with the boy's progress. Before today, the prince had yet to hit his target's center. Eight times out of an afternoon of practice was promising progress. Prince Arlan was more comfortable and proficient with a sword in his hand but the ex-general insisted he practice with a range of weapons, reminding him that it would not do for a prince to be limited to a single form of defense, should he find himself in a precarious situation. Besides, as he repeatedly pointed out, hunting for dinner with a sword was not very productive.

"What do you think, Guthrie?"

The man appeared to look past the boy from many seconds until the growl in his stomach broke the silence. "I think it is getting dark. I think it is time for dinner." He picked up the quiver of arrows and turned in the direction of the cabin.

Hurrying to catch up with him, Prince Arlan grabbed the man's arm. "I mean, what do you think of my aim, sir?"

"I think you need a great deal more practice." That reply made the prince release the man's arm and lower his gaze. Guthrie chuckled and tousled his hair. "However, compared to yesterday, your aim is improving. Keep up the practice and you will be fetching dinner before long."

The prince smiled, a near identical duplicate of the one Guthrie remembered on Innis. A wistful longing crept into his gut but was quickly dispelled. He refused to allow the late King's memory to cause him pain any longer. He smiled back, the first one he had managed in the shadow of Innis' memory.

☙*❧

"By the Saints, Kavan! You could have gotten yourself killed!" Ártur watched him set down his belongings and remove his dusty cloak, resisting the urge to shake some sense into his younger cousin. He had spent the last few days sick with worry, and to find out that Kavan had been in Rhidam all that time only made the sick feeling more pronounced. "Have you lost your senses?"

Ignoring the accusing tone of the healer's voice, Kavan handed him the decanter of Chablis without meeting his gaze. "All of the Five Sovereignties were represented. Everyone else in Elyriá was afraid to try…"

"With good reason," Ártur snorted.

"The proclamation did state that the Crown would protect all foreigners, Elyri included. I have no reason to fear King Farrell. There is no evil in him, only apathy and narcissism…"

"Those aren't evils?"

Kavan shook his head. "You know what I mean. He wishes no harm to anyone; his thoughts are focused strictly on himself, but not to the point of being willing to harm others to get what he wants. Besides, until the end, no one knew I am Elyri. I told you. I was careful. I was in no danger."

Ártur put the decanter on the mantle with a frustrated groan. "The point is, you could have been. You would not have known it until it was too late. I don't know if you are merely stubborn or if you are trying to destroy yourself, but continue this path and you will not have to worry about what people think of you because you will be dead." Exasperated, he continued. "Or are you trying to become a martyr? Is that it? Spread yourself among those who would sooner kill you than listen to what you might have to say so that others can look back and say you were a saint?"

If Kavan's face had not already been milk white, it would have lost all color. "Please...do not say such things, Ártur...you know it is not true..."

The torment in his voice as the bard turned away and clutched the edge of the table he leaned against were enough to make the healer regret his bitter words. He bit his lip and drew blood. He knew it was not true, so how could he be so cruel to the one he loved so dearly?

"I am sorry..." he whispered.

"You know I am not a saint, will never be a saint, do not want to be a saint. I wanted to play. They liked me. King Farrell asked to hear some of my original works. I received more appreciation from Teren strangers than I have ever gotten in Elyriá. It was as much unlike playing here for a day's meal as night is from day. Farrell wanted me to stay, to be part of his court. Do you see? By doing this, I may be able to open the way for Elyri to be welcome in Rhidam again; maybe you can go back. Maybe this is what I am meant to do with my life, my destiny. If I do not try, Ártur, how will I ever know?"

The healer could not argue with that, nor, after having wounded Kavan, did he want to. Once, the first time he had taken Kavan to Rhidam, he had asked his mother the same question. Without taking risks, one never knew what pathway lay ahead. He sighed and muttered, "I hope you are not planning to join the Lachlan court."

"Of course not," Kavan assured him, his voice still colored with pain. "I do not believe my moral standards would sit well with the King." There was a touch of amusement then, in spite of the hurt. "And I have no interest in life at court, particularly with Prince Bowen there. He is the one to be feared...not just by Elyri, but by everyone. I only wanted to play, to know I could do it."

"I could have told you that, though you would not have believed me, would you? You only believe what you can prove to yourself." Kavan did not look at him or reply, but instead picked up his cloak and hung it on a hook by the door. Deciding that the topic had been dropped for the moment, Ártur gestured to the decanter and asked, "You brought this back for a reason?"

"You said it is the best, and I would not dare try it in Rhidam." If he had an adverse reaction to the wine, as Elyri were prone to do, he wanted to be somewhere where he could get help. Safe with his healer cousin nearby was the best place. "Consider it a gift for causing you worry. Would you share it with me?"

Ártur could not hide his wry smile as he nodded. Kavan seemed meek and gentle and cautious most of the time, and yet occasionally took such risks as this. The healer wondered if he would ever understand the workings of his cousin's mind.

Kavan stood before him with an honest glint in his eyes. "I promise to be careful in Enesfel, Ártur. I can take care of myself. If you could do it, I am certain I can."

The healer embraced his cousin hard, praying he was right.

❧Chapter 16❦

"And furthermore," declared King Farrell, standing before the assembly of nobles, royalty, and visiting dignitaries who had been invited to attend the latest of the King's 'events', "We, the Crown, do hereby make the declaration of our late King, Donal the First, invalid. From this day forward, our brother, Prince Owain Ustes Lachlan, lately returned from exile, is again eligible for the throne of Enesfel, and is entitled to the rights and privileges of this House. Owain Ustes, please come forward."

The blond prince, now eighteen and of impressive stature and condition, approached the throne with the confident air of a man coming home. He caught Bowen's eye and smiled as he knelt and placed his right hand on the sword blade the King extended towards him. Prince Bowen looked away.

"Do you, Owain Ustes Lachlan, swear to uphold the throne of Enesfel and the Lachlan name, to support and protect the people of our land who may one day fall into your care?"

In a voice as warm and smooth as velvet he replied, "Yes, My King."

King Farrell smiled, always finding that it pleased him to hear those words. "And do you swear fealty to us, the Royal Crown, that you will serve and obey at all cost to yourself and those you hold dear?"

"I do, Your Majesty."

"Rise." Prince Owain got to his feet and faced the crowd. The King took his right hand to raise it above their heads in triumph. "May I present to you, lords and ladies, Prince Owain Lachlan, restored to his rightful place within the Lachlan House and in our hearts," the King crowed.

There was applause, but it was not as joyous as the woman at the rear of the Grand Hall had hoped for. Even Prince Bowen's response was cooler and less enthusiastic than she wanted, less than she believed a father should show for his son. For many of the attendants, she knew this was merely another of the King's lavish productions; the reason for it meant little. They had come for the bounty more than to see Prince Owain welcomed back into the family. And though the King had wisely not spoken of where the prince had spent his years of exile, nearly everyone knew, knew and harbored doubts about all of those years spent in a hostile kingdom. But the time would come, she was certain, when her son would sit on the throne and be welcomed by the whole of Enesfel. She would see that he got his due.

Yet as the gathering of nobles rose and bowed as the King passed, she hurried from the room before anyone noticed her. Her son might be accepted here again, but she knew she was not. It would not be wise to allow herself to be seen. Too much was at stake. Once her son had what was his, what he was entitled to, she would be able to return to Rhidam with her head high. She looked forward to that day.

King Farrell led the procession into the banquet hall where a large meal was spread on long wooden tables. He had been sulky since his musician audition and was hoping that this celebration would put that mood to rest. It vexed him that no one knew the name of the harper he was smitten with. His scribe confirmed that the man had been Elyri, but that was all that was known, and all attempts to contact Kyne Mórne for information had either been snubbed with no reply or had gained a simple return message saying that no one had been sent to represent their kingdom. If the Elyri elite could identify the harper, it was clear they would not. The white-skinned bard was lost to Rhidam and King Farrell was extremely disappointed.

It would not, however, prevent him from enjoying his own party.

☙*❧

Tales of the White Hart of Enesfel had circulated throughout the Five Sovereignties for the last six years, although each telling aged its existence by decades until the stately animal was claimed to have existed since the dawn of time. The beast was most often seen at the base of the Llaethlágárá along the Elyriá-Enesfel border and occasionally in the southern-most forests of Neth. It was rumored to be a magnificent, magical creature, standing nearly as tall as a horse at the shoulder, with silver antlers that spread like tree branches, wider than a man's arm span. Each brief sighting of it spawned vast hunting parties as men quested for the animal. Some maintained it was an enchanted creature whose antlers and hide would bestow supernatural abilities on the one who possessed them. Others claimed that if it could be followed to its lair, one would find an abundance of wealth. Still others alleged that it was a manifestation of the phae k'kairá and to kill or wound it would bring their wrath and curses on the one to harm the sacred animal. Any sighting of it was considered an omen of good luck.

Thus far, no hunter had been able to pursue it long enough to find its lair or take a shot. A glimpse would send a flurry of men and dogs crashing through the forests, but they lost the trail almost as soon as it was found, as if the animal was a mist, more wraith than flesh. Those who set out in search of it were inevitably disappointed. It was those not looking for it that found it, as if the animal enjoyed the thrill of the spotting, the chase, almost as much as the hunters. It seemed to revel in the knowledge that no one could capture it, that it could outwit anyone it chose.

Today, this particular hunting party stopped at a stream to allow the leader to dismount and stretch his legs. His amber and burgundy cloak was slung over his shoulder as he squatted to examine tracks near the water's edge; the hounds beside him ignored them.

"These are days old," King Farrell muttered, "and I think too small for the animal we seek."

Prince Owain nodded in agreement. He liked these hunts with the King, and though there were plenty, he never grew tired of them. "I have never heard of him being spotted in the open like this. He's too crafty. If we want to find him, we will have to leave the horses and go deeper into the forest."

The King peered into the dense foliage for several moments before saying, "You are probably correct. Mr. Wyndham, stay with the horses. We shall return soon."

"Yes, Sire," said the single soldier in the group, watching the King, prince, and Master of the Hounds take the six dogs into the cover of the trees. The day was brisk and clear, the first autumn day of the season, and Farrell had been King for nearly two years. He was not as popular as his brother and father before him, but nor was he hated or feared. He just was, which suited him, as it gave him the opportunity to pursue the pleasures in life without undue pressure. He lived largely in his own little circle of the world and it was obvious he preferred it that way.

In the clearing, the white hart lifted its head, ears pricked towards the sounds of dogs and men. Its nostrils twitched as it stood and stepped gingerly into the underbrush. It saw its pursuers long before they could have seen him. Tail swishing, it watched. There were six dogs and three men, none heavily armed though burdened enough to make pursuit a challenge. Normally the hart would have faded away, avoiding those seeking it, but this was a different sort of hunting party, one that it could not resist toying with. Rather than disappear into the trees, it was instead content to wait. Turning his head to rustle his antlers in the brush, it watched as the hunters, alerted by the sound, inched cautiously closer. He had the wind to his advantage, which meant the dogs had not yet detected his scent. At the right instant, when he could wait no longer, he bounded out of the brush, dashing through their midst so swiftly that even the dogs were caught off guard. With a whoop of excitement, Prince Owain started after the hart, followed immediately by the others.

The pursuit lasted nearly an hour, through the thickest parts of the forest, back and forth across the streams and creeks that cut through its heart. King Farrell was certain this was the longest sighting and pursuit of the fabled beast to date. Having seen it for himself, the white hart was no longer a myth to him, and thus, to his predatory mind, it was considered attainable. What King Farrell wanted, he got. The hunting party could not get near enough, however, or be still enough to take a shot, and the dogs were having difficulty following the scent, but the joy of the chase would be reward enough for the King today. He would make a decree that no one was to hunt the beast but himself. He would chase down the hart with every breath in his body until it was his.

Hearing the sounds of field workers in the distance, he knew they were nearing the edge of the forest and it appeared their quarry would be lost. They could not chase it through a field of superstitious peasants, for though he desired to kill or capture the animal, he did not want the uproar it would create if he succeeded in a public place. He might have to call the hunt for the day, but he was not ready to give up yet.

The hart broke through the trees, also realizing it had run out of forest cover. Its pursuers blocked any attempt to double back, and it knew better than to charge across the field. Instead, he leapt onto an outcropping of rocks and had his efforts met by the heat of an arrow in his rear flank. Stumbling, he continued his course, seeking the dense thicket not far away. If he could make it there, he would be safe.

"I hit it!" the King exclaimed, dashing back into the trees in the direction the hart had taken. The dogs, on the scent of blood, howled and plunged in ahead of him.

In the field, the peasants saw the white hart stagger into the forest with an arrow protruding from its flesh. Three of them picked up the nearest tools, a thresher, a pitchfork, and a spade, and hurried after the hunting party hoping to save the mythical creature. They seemed not to recognize their King leading the hunting party.

"Antony! Take the dogs that way. Owain, go around there. We will corner him. He cannot get far on that leg. And remember…he's mine." The prince nodded and veered to the left while the Hounds Master went right. The King continued his course, following the prints in the damp earth. There was blood, a sure indication that he should find the animal soon. His heart thumped faster and harder within his chest as he sought further signs, but there were none beyond broken limbs that suggested the animal's passage. The amount of blood on the ground increased as if exertion was causing further hemorrhaging, but when he thought he should find the creature itself, he stopped in amazement.

On the leaves before him lay an arrow in a pool of blood. There was the scuffle of man-sized bare footprints mixed with those of the hart, and studying the arrow proved it was the King's. He had no doubt of it. The hart's prints stopped here, but the other, Teren prints continued on several more yards through the brush. The King could not tell where they had originated. They could have emerged from the undergrowth, which might have left no prints on the spongy earth, but where could the hart have gone? There was no way a single man could have carried an animal of that size, but nor could it have simply vanished. The King could not understand it, and that frustrated him.

There was a rustle of movement ahead. He crouched. Knocking an arrow, he inched forward, listening intently to the movement. His ears detected the twang of a bowstring. No! Owain cannot have him! He is mine! He straightened to get a better line of sight and felt fire erupt in his breast before crashing to the ground with a cry.

It was not quite a cave in which the man huddled, consisting as it did of intertwined branches, vines, and leaves, but it was hidden enough that the hunting party he could still hear would not discover him. Tearing the hem of his robe, he bound his bleeding thigh, ignoring the scratches across the rest of his body, and when he felt confident he was safe, left his shelter and slid down the embankment, cautiously approaching the sounds of dogs and men.

In the clearing ahead, lying on the ground, groaning in agony, one man of the hunting party bled profusely, an arrow protruding from his upper chest. One of the others, the one with the dogs, hurried towards the forest edge. The third man cradled the wounded one's head on his lap, but his back was to the observer and nothing more could be seen. After several minutes, the wounded man convulsed and lay still, and the observer, biting his lip, slid backward from his vantage point and disappeared into the trees.

"bhydáni?"

Tíbhyan looked up from his reading towards the man in the doorway. He was accustomed to interruptions. His home was open to visitors, and his reputation drew people from all over Elyriá. He had not been expecting this visitor, however. "How may I assist you, ílMairós MacLyr?"

The healer shuffled his feet awkwardly. Before Kavan, he had never been to this man's home, had never had reason to speak to him beyond passing pleasantries. And though he had provided payment for Kavan's education and shared communications with the bhydáni for many years, the ancient sage still intimidated him. "Pardon me for disturbing you…"

"Nonsense." The old man waved him inside. "It has been a long time since I saw you last. Sit. Tell me, how is Kavan?"

Ártur's jaw twitched. "You have not seen him?"

Tíbhyan shook his head. "Not for two weeks or more. He comes less frequently; I have little more to offer him as a teacher. He comes when he desires my company, or when he has discovered some new trick or technique or has a question that is troubling him."

"Does he do that often? Come to you with a new trick?" It was not the question he had come to ask, but if the sage had not seen Kavan recently, then it was answer enough.

The bhydáni chortled. "More often than I will admit to. It would not be prudent for one such as me to admit that a young student knows more than I do, would it? Why do you seek him? Has something occurred of which he should know? Has there been trouble?"

Running his hand through his short red hair, the healer shrugged. "I do not know. He has disappeared before…for days at a time. Once he went to Rhidam without telling me. He has been gone much longer this time than usual, and I fear something has happened to him."

Tíbhyan patted the healer's arm. "Have faith in your cousin, ílMairós. He's hardly a child. He is not foolish and has a tremendous resource of power at his disposal. I believe he is better equipped in many ways to go about in the world than you or me."

"He is barely an adult," Ártur grunted, even though he knew the man was right.

"He is adult enough to have maintained his home from the time he was fourteen. What more could you ask of him? Let him go, ílMairós. He has grown beyond childhood. Protection he does not want, only friendship, respect, and love. Give him those things and he will be content."

Ártur contemplated the bhydáni who had turned back to his manuscript. He started to speak, but Tíbhyan spoke first without looking up. "There is much in store for him that we will never understand; you alluded to that when you brought him before the lómesté. Let him live as he feels he must. It is the only thing we can do for him."

"I suppose," the healer sighed, "I do not have a choice, do I?"

"No, you do not," the sage replied with the barest hint of a mysterious grin on his face. "His choices are his own."

❧*❧

The stars' positions outside indicated the second hour of the new day, while in the darkness of the empty náós, Kavan knelt, eyes pleading with the carved statue on the wall, silver cross clutched in his left hand. Occasionally he raised it to his lips as his head bowed in supplication, only to lift again with deeper questions in his eyes. His leg ached, but not as deeply as his soul. He felt sick. He wanted to weep, but tears refused to come. Oppressive silence was the only answer to his prayers and even the presences that were his usual companions in this place were not with him tonight. Fortunately, gdhededhá Bhílári was not in the building. He would not have been able to explain to the clergyman what weighed upon him tonight.

The main door of the náós opened, allowing the cold night air to swirl around him, relieving him of his solitude. He shivered but did not turn. He knew who it was. He had come here, instead of going to his own refurbished private náós, to be alone, to escape his cousin's questions. But Ártur had sensed his return to Bhryell, sought him out, found him here. Kavan should have realized that there was no escaping his cousin.

The pale glow of lamplight grew closer. "Kavan?"

He did not speak. The healer caught sight of the white robes and knew Kavan was there without his needing to announce himself. Ártur closed the door and hastened to the náós steps. "Where on earth have you been? It has been nearly a week; everyone has been worried…"

"You mean you have been worried," Kavan murmured without looking up. "No one else noticed."

The healer set the lamp on the top step between them and sat beside Kavan. "Yes, I have been worried. Where have you been?"

"King Farrell is dead."

Ártur's face turned ashen. "Dead…? How do you…?" His eyes trailed down to where Kavan was casually trying to fold his robe to hide the blood stain there.

"I just know."

"What happened to your leg?" There was no reply, but at least Kavan stopped trying to hide the blood now that it had been seen. "Let me look at it. You are bleeding."

In a quiet voice, Kavan murmured, "I know. Leave it."

"Kavan…"

"Do not argue with me, Ártur. Leave me alone." Kavan crossed to the podium where he stood for several moments, favoring his injured leg, before hobbling back and kneeling again like a trapped, wounded animal. The unusually bitter tone of voice made Ártur flinch; Kavan had never been abrupt with him before.

Kavan, knowing that and regretting his harshness, sighed and decided to answer the questions. His cousin deserved that much for his worries. "It was a hunting accident. He took an arrow here," his hand covered a place over his right lung, "and died before a physician or help could arrive…before they could get him out of the forest."

Ártur listened. "How do you know this? llánec?"

"I was there."

"You were…?" Kavan's expression as he hunched forward stopped Ártur from continuing.

"Have you never wondered about the white hart? The legends? Am I so good at concealing myself, even from you?"

His voice was small. When he rose this time, he favored his wounded leg and moved closer to the altar where he paused to gaze up at Dhágdhuán. Ártur leaned back and stared at him, speechless. He had long known of Kavan's fondness for shapechanging, and despite his own feelings about it knew that his cousin continued to practice that ability. It had never occurred to him, however, that the white hart of the stories might be his white-skinned cousin. There had been no reason to connect the two, though now he felt it should have been obvious.

"The animal has never existed except in my imagination, and through me, in the forests of Neth, Elyriá, and Enesfel. It is me they all seek. King Farrell and Prince Owain...we had a good chase. The King was fortunate..." He looked at the bloodstain on his garment. "No one has ever wounded the hart before." There was a dark tone of irony in Kavan's voice that the healer found uncomfortable. "They thought they had me, but dogs always lose the scent once I change. I came behind them to find Prince Owain kneeling over the King. I followed them back to their camp, and then to Rhidam, where I examined the King myself. If the arrow's entry had not killed him, the removal of it would have; the damage to his lung was appalling."

There was too much information to sort all at once. "Prince Owain?" Ártur asked.

Kavan nodded without looking at him. "He has returned to Enesfel, and Farrell made him eligible for the throne." He closed his eyes, recalling that troublesome childhood memory, and added, "It has begun."

There was no compelling reason the healer could think of for King Farrell to bring Prince Owain back, although Farrell had been quite fond of Owain as a child and had probably kept in touch with him. He might have chosen to bring him home simply for his company. Perhaps, if Prince Bowen had provided the right incentive, he could have swayed the King to give him nearly anything. Anything except the throne. Perhaps Prince Bowen had arranged for Owain's return, but to what end? Ártur doubted Bowen would acknowledge the younger prince as his son; why should he want him back in Enesfel? To Ártur, it seemed to Bowen's advantage to keep Owain away.

"It has begun?" What has? The havoc that Bowen would most certainly wreak as King? But no, this was something else. Kavan's long ago admonition that sending Prince Owain to Neth would have dire consequences came to mind. He met Kavan's gaze with concern and the bard nodded. The healer felt his entire body grow cold from the inside out. "So…Farrell has died in a hunting accident…" Another King gone, another Lachlan he had known since the man was but a child.

Kavan sighed. "I have reservations about whether it was an accident or not…but I have no proof. Prince Bowen is to be crowned in two days, and I cannot help but feel this is foul play, like the assassination attempts on Prince Arlan. The blame is being placed on a trio of peasants who came to my aid…though none of them was equipped with a bow. Still, the Hound Master claims the King was killed because he injured me…there seems to be some belief that the hart is a divine, magical manifestation…"

There was an uncharacteristic note of disgust in his tone. "Bowen believes Farrell was assassinated because of taxation…but…Ártur…those peasants…the three accused and the rest in their village…all twenty-seven have been imprisoned in spite of their Duke's plea. They will be executed, one per day, until someone confesses to the murder of the King. None will confess because they are all innocent; none will claim responsibility to save the others. I do not believe, based on what I saw when I was there, that a confession would save the others anyhow, and I doubt they are even aware of the crime they have been asked to confess to. Bowen will kill them because he can…and I am responsible."

Ártur shook his head. "Even if you had not been there, if Prince Bowen or someone else was behind an assassination plot, or if it was simply an accident, the innocent would still have been blamed. That is the way some politics work; Neth is a prime example. And Prince Bowen, because of his relationship with Lady Ula, was tainted long ago, unfortunately. Bowen wants someone to blame. He wants an excuse to spill blood, I suspect. You are not responsible for his behavior, his actions, or his choices.

"Even the children, Ártur...eight of them. The youngest looks to be three. They will not be spared. Not...the children..." Kavan's words were laden with grief but there were no tears. "I have been praying for them, but this is not right. This is not justice. This is murder. Someone must help them."

The healer wanted to comfort him but Kavan was too far away. "You may not be able to help them," he soothed. "You did not see who fired the arrow, or who tried to remove it, and even if you had, or if you had read the arrow, the King would blame you and kill you and the peasants out of spite. All you can do is wait and pray k'Ádhá will avenge them."

"I have tried to warn the princess' tutor, but I do not think she took my warning to heart. So much...death..." He shivered in the dimly lit silence and waited for many moments before saying, "There is a k'rylag in the dungeon..."

"No, Kavan. Do not consider it." The thought of sneaking into the Rhidam castle while it was under Bowen Lachlan's control made the healer feel sick. "Whatever else he may be, Prince...King...Bowen is not stupid. If you could get past the guards and get each peasant out, or even the children, Elyriá would be the first likely place he would look for answers to vanishing prisoners. If he found no answers, I suspect the result would be war, or at least retaliation taken out on the Elyri in Enesfel, or Enesfel's entire population...and as you say, they may be in for a bleak enough time as it is."

Kavan whispered, "What of their immortal souls, Ártur? Am I not responsible…?"

The healer shook his head again and wished he had the right words to offer. "You cannot be responsible for the souls of all living things, Kavan, even if you would like to be. Each person's soul is their own. Do not hold yourself accountable for something you cannot influence or change, and that you did not cause." When Kavan's shoulders sagged, Ártur sighed. It seemed impossible to lighten Kavan's burden, but there was one thing he could do. "So…it is an arrow wound?"

"Yes."

"May I?"

Shrugging, Kavan came back to sit on a pew and parted the folds of his robe to allow his cousin to examine the wound. The arrowhead had been removed; the area was swollen and dark against the whiteness of his smooth skin, but the wound had not become infected. "It's not as bad as it looks; I've seen worse. You've tended it well." He pressed his fingers to the open flesh, closed his eyes, and in a matter of moments, the only trace of the injury remaining was the bruising and a bit of swelling. "It will be tender for a few days still, but you will be able to endure it. Come back to the house and sleep. You need to rest."

Kavan shook his head. "Later."

"Do not go to Rhidam, Kavan," Ártur warned, anticipating his cousin's intentions. "There is nothing you can do. You will not be safe there."

Avoiding the issue of Rhidam, Kavan murmured, "I will come back to the house. I want to finish my prayers."

Ártur nodded, choosing to believe that Kavan would heed his warning, despite Kavan not saying he would. He picked up the lamp, squeezed the other man's shoulder, and started down the aisle; part way he stopped to look at the back of Kavan's head. "How does it feel to be a legend?" He did not wait for a reply.

When he was certain he was alone, Ártur's presence having grown dimmer the further away the healer moved, Kavan stood, intending to return to the altar to kneel in prayer as he had indicated he would. But his heart called him in another direction, and instead of going home, he went to the k'dhín bhólibh. He knew what he had to do. Ártur was right in that he could not save all of the innocent peasants, but there was something Kavan could do. Perhaps he could not spare their lives, but he could attempt to ease his conscience. The mist quickly enveloped him and when it dissipated he was in the bunkroom of the Lachlan dungeon, a Gate long unused by any Elyri but one Kavan had discovered during the days after King Farrell's death. His thoughts stretched around him; there were two guards, one in the stairwell keeping unauthorized people from entering, and the other sleeping deeply in a corner with his hands across his lap.

It was to this one Kavan crept, staying in the shadows. Kneeling over him, he gently touched the man's eyelids, and with very little effort assured that the man would not awaken for several hours. As long as the sentry in the stairwell remained where he was and no one else came down the stairs, unlikely at this hour of the night, Kavan believed he would be safe. The door between the bunkroom and the dungeon was already partially open and a dim streak of flickering orange torchlight slid around it and spilled across the stone floor. Feeling confident that he was safe from discovery, he squeezed through the open doorway and into the passageway between cells.

It was a long and tiring process he used, but in the end, he had touched all twenty-seven peasants, reassuring them that their sacrifices would not be in vain, that they would be avenged. He hoped his efforts would give them peace as they faced execution. The three-year-old girl, however, he found difficult to face as she slept in her mother's arms, her tiny, round face streaked with dirt and tears. Touching the child's forehead, he wondered what future she should have had, and Saw the death that awaited her. He traced the sign of penance on her chest and forehead, praying that he could save her young soul. As he drew his hand away from her, watching her sleep, he decided he could not allow her to be tortured. She was far too young to understand why she and those she knew must die horribly, and too young to be guilty of any crime the Crown might accuse the adults and older children of committing. There was one way, however, that Kavan could spare her that, and though others might condemn him for it, he did not believe k'Ádhá would do the same. Not when he only meant to spare her horror and suffering.

He did not know if it could be done. It was not the sort of ability that was taught, not even to healers, as it would be far too dangerous in the wrong hands. But he saw no reason it should not be possible. He pressed his palm against her tiny body, closed his eyes, and focused on her life force. Pulling gently on her pliant consciousness, he drew her energy into himself little by little, and she came willingly, trusting him, instinctively accepting that his gentle spirit knew best. Soon he felt the tremor of her spirit passing from her body, through him, and into the light and the hands of the awaiting záryph. The rise and fall of her chest ceased and her head sagged against her chest. She was safe, at peace, free from what had awaited her at King Bowen's hands. For Kavan, however, there was no peace. That he had done the right thing for her he was certain, but it sickened him how easily he had been able to rob her of life. He doubted this was a skill he would reveal to Tíbhyan, or to anyone. He was not even certain he would be able to live with it. But it was done. He could not give her life back.

A kiss was brushed against her cheek before Kavan hurried from the cell to return to his own world, carrying the pinpoint weight of twenty-six souls within him. One a day would die, not at his hands. Twenty-six days he would spend in prayer and fasting until the last of those pinpoints was extinguished. Ethenae help the man responsible for their fate. If k'Ádhá did not punish Enesfel's King, Kavan knew he would.

ঐChapter 17ঐ

King Bowen was as vindictive and angry as a ruler as he was a person. He cared little for anyone or anything and seemed to find his only pleasure in perversely bending everyone to his capriciously changing rules. If someone would not bend, he was all too eager to break them. The tax increase King Farrell had initiated was doubled as a warning that matters would grow worse for anyone who chose to cross the new King. As promised, one of the accused peasants was executed daily, some hung, some beheaded, some drawn and quartered or tortured to death, all depending on King Bowen's mood of the day. Their calm acceptance of their fate gnawed at his already foul temper; by the time they were all dead he was more furious than ever. He took that fury out on the palace staff, cursing them, beating them, or dismissing them if they happened to annoy him sufficiently. Two were executed out of spite. Prince Girvin chose to spend less time in Rhidam and more at the family estate in Kamin to be out of the direct reach of his brother's ire. The King did not appear to notice he was gone.

The streets of Rhidam began to resemble a battlefield as the grisly reminders of the fate of wrongdoers increased. Heads and other body parts hung from lampposts or were staked to the facades of buildings. Animals and flies picked at the carrion and disease began to spread. The stench of death blanketed everything. Few people went out alone, and even fewer ventured out at night if they could avoid it. The flow of travelers through the city dwindled to a trickle. Taverns shut their doors at sundown and businesses closed or moved out of the city, into the outermost reaches of the kingdom, or into Cordash and Hatu. King Bowen saw these actions as weakness, failures of character in people who could not endure things designed to strengthen them. He accepted no blame for what was happening. The more people who moved away, the lower his income became, and taxes increased again.

He manipulated the ever-present, though sometimes dormant, fear of Elyri to his advantage. Princess Deidre's Elyri tutor chose to flee as Kavan had suggested, as soon as official word of King Farrell's death reached Rhidam, but her escape came too late. King Bowen declared her flight to be an admission of guilt and she was quickly apprehended by a group of rogues before she made it out of Rhidam. After a swift, inequitable trial, and several passionate pleas on the princess's part, the woman was burned at the stake for witchcraft. She was to be the first of many to die. Few Elyri dared enter the country, and few Teren dared sympathize for those who did, or those who died. Those men and women who did show compassion and offered aid, or those Elyri already in Enesfel who were not quick to escape, were arrested, tortured, and executed. The brutalized bodies were sometimes shipped back to their homeland, but most often, they were dumped wherever the soldiers found a place. If the dead were Elyri sympathizers, most often their bodies were displayed publically as a warning to everyone else.

Ártur continued to retrieve messages from Brenna during those dark days and thus Arlan knew of each horror visited upon the people of Enesfel. Many times, he discussed the situation in depth with Guthrie McHador, the two debating whether this was the time for Prince Arlan to make a bid for the throne. But he was not old enough, or mature enough, and both men knew that if such an endeavor was not conducted with the utmost planning and skill, the young prince would be dead before he saw Rhidam again.

But the healer never told Kavan of these nighttime forays into hostile territory. After the warnings he had given his cousin about venturing there, Ártur knew he could not. And as he had never discussed Prince Arlan's whereabouts with Kavan, or spoken of his continuing involvement with the prince, it seemed wiser to leave the matter alone.

Because of those trips, however, there was nothing of importance in Rhidam that Prince Arlan, approaching his twelfth birthday, did not know about. There was nothing he could do at his young age to stop the horror, except pray for Bowen's quick death and Girvin's long reign. As he had no fond memories of Bowen, barely remembered the man, the prince felt no disloyalty for wishing his half-brother dead. He could not say he knew Girvin any better, the only true brother he had, but the boy believed with all of his heart that Girvin would be a better King than Bowen was proving to be. Living deep in the forest with the ex-general as his tutor, mentor, surrogate parent and only friend made the prince feel distanced from those events as if they were happening somewhere far away and not in the kingdom around him. He often gave such things no thought at all, except when the messages came, or when he thought about the sister he dearly missed.

The most recent news received concerned a further falling out between the King and Prince Owain. Brenna was unable to provide details except to say that Owain wanted something the King had denied him more than once. The prince had departed the castle in a fit of rage and had not been seen in many days. There were security concerns being bandied about the keep, worry that there would be attempts on the King's life, but the princess and Brenna were pleased with his absence, as the princess had become the focused object of Prince Owain's affections. He pursued her, despite her efforts to express disinterest, and the princess was growing frustrated and afraid.

In their secluded corner of the world, Guthrie and his ward were safe from the King and eldest prince, however, and because the prince was more capable of defending himself, he was sometimes granted permission to spend time away from the cabin on his own. There were always conditions and rules, that he not speak to anyone, that he stay away from roads and trails, that he be diligent lest he encounter royal soldiers who might recognize him as King Innis' child. King Bowen had no need to know the youngest Lachlan heir lived. The time was not right for that.

Thus on this warm, late summer day, Prince Arlan secured freedom to do as he pleased as long as he did not stray far from the cabin. Under the cover of the spruce, pines, and oaks, he imagined he was hunting the great white hart he had heard about, the one that Farrell had been hunting at the time of his death. Bow and eight arrows slung over his back, knives strapped to his hip and his ankle, the prince followed the narrow river south. To the north lay Chantel and its farming communities. To the south lay more forest all the way to the sea and to the east the great mountains of Elyriá. Arlan did not think it likely he would be discovered if he followed the tributary away from inhabitation. It seemed safe to him.

The river grew narrower and deeper until it was little more than a foot across as it tumbled and churned over the rocks in wild, splashing spurts. It twisted beneath a patch of mossy brambles and then was lost from sight. If he was careful, as he always was, he could use the slippery rocks to cross the river in spite of the strong current. He knew this path. He came here as often as he could, and each time before making it to the lake that he knew to be beyond the bushes, brambles, and trees, he heard music. There were tales of strange magical beings said to live in such places as this, and of the phae k'kairá who would lead astray any who came too close to their secret dwelling places. Prince Arlan, young enough to take such tales to heart, believed that music had to be of unnatural origin since no one else was known to dwell in this stretch of forest. Though the curiosity was always there, he respectfully avoided the lakeshore.

Until today. There was no music coming from the lake today, and Prince Arlan was determined to make it there, to see if he could discover the secrets of that music in the safety of apparent solitude. Removing his boots to keep them dry, he slowly traversed the stones, the water frigidly numbing on his toes; when he made it to the other side of the stream he sat to rub warmth back into his feet. The underbrush was thinner here, enabling him to peer through; when he noticed that, he forgot his cold feet and crouched low to see what lay beyond the bushes. There appeared to be nothing unusual at first; he could see only the blue of the lake, interrupted by occasional ripples, and the forested shore on the other side. The prince pulled his boots back on, wondering if he dared get closer before shuffling sideways to a spot where he could part the branches for a better view and perhaps, he hoped, push through. But before he could get through the brush, something unexpected caught his eye and he froze.

Someone was in the water, either bathing or swimming, he could not tell which. Silver-white hair hung in damp waves against broad shoulders as white as the clouds in the sky. Prince Arlan waited, trembling, for a glimpse of the stranger's face, afraid that if he breathed or made any sound he would be discovered and scare the individual away. As it was, he was sure his thundering heart would betray him, but he could do nothing to calm it, and he could not pull himself away from the sight. He had to see more. The swimmer rose out of the water at last, not far from the prince's position, body glistening as the sun danced with the droplets on his pale skin. It was a man…or at least it was male. He stood for several moments with his back to the boy, head thrown back as if enjoying the sun, and then bent to pick up a white robe from the lakeshore and dressed. He sat on the bank, picked up a small harp, and began to play. From where he was hidden, Prince Arlan could not be sure what sort of man this was, but he knew he could not be Teren. He was too beautiful, to fine of form and feature, to be Teren.

Kavan had barely begun to play when his fingers faltered on the brass strings. He looked up but did not turn his head. Someone was watching him from the left; he could feel it as if it were fingers on his skin. There was something familiar in the presence, something he was certain he had touched long ago though he could not pinpoint when or where. There was no threat in the presence; indeed, whoever was there was more terrified and curious than they were threatening. Without moving, without ceasing the music, Kavan eventually called out, "I know you are here with me. You may show yourself if you wish. I will not harm you."

Prince Arlan began to tremble more. Did he dare do as the stranger asked? He had not moved, had barely breathed; how had the stranger known he was there, unless by the hammering of his heart? Or, he thought with a stab of anxiety, this person, not being Teren, had other means of detection, some form of dangerous magic. Which meant, he realized that stay, go forward, or flee, he was still found out, and he could be followed. He knew better than to lead anyone back to the cabin.

But whoever this man was, he was the source of the music the Prince had been hearing. Sweet, tender, lively, passionate, beautiful music. There was no threat in that, and the stranger had no weapons the prince could see, so he finally forced himself to emerge hesitantly from his cover. He could not lead this stranger to Guthrie until he knew if he was a threat, and he was not going to run away like a coward. He would stand and face this man and hope he came out of the encounter alive.

Kavan waited until the rustling of the brush ceased before looking up; when he did, his mouth fell open and he swallowed hard. He recognized the boy instantly. It was impossible not to. He looked enough like the paintings of King Innis, and even like King Donal, to be unmistakable. The harp was set aside on the dry grass and his head bowed reverently. He had never expected this.

The prince took several steps backward in alarm. Guthrie had been right. He was recognizable, even by someone who was not Teren. He thought he should run, but knew it was too late for that. He would never escape. Having come this far, he decided to face the consequences of his choices like the man Guthrie wanted him to be. Besides, the longer he stood there, the more he realized that something about this man made him want to stay. Running was less and less what he wanted to do. As the initial adrenaline waned, the prince realized he was not afraid.

Kavan held his hands out, palms up. "I am not armed, Your Majesty. I would never harm you, even if I were."

The prince tried to smile. Everything about those words and the man's gestures felt honest. "You are not Teren, are you?"

"Elyri, Your Majesty." He liked what he sensed in the prince. Strength, honesty, compassion, and curiosity. Integrity and courage. Whatever Prince Arlan's life had been like, he had grown up well.

There was an awkward silence as the prince studied the harper, who neither moved nor seemed bothered by the scrutiny. "I should have guessed...but after hearing you...I thought maybe you were phae..."

"No," Kavan smiled, "not phae. I wouldn't admit it if I were, would I?"

The prince chuckled. "No...I imagine you would not." Noticing the cross around the harper's neck, he asked, "Are you gdhededhá?" He had no exposure to religion, beyond what Guthrie could teach him.

"Some treat me like I am," Kavan sighed, "but I am not. I am merely a harper..."

"A very good one," the prince said enthusiastically, undermining Kavan's self-deprecation. "I have heard you play many times. I come here often, but never all the way to the lake…until now. I had no idea what manner of man or beast might be here and thought it best not to approach when I heard the music…although I always listened. If someone should recognize me…you did recognize me?"

"Yes, Prince Arlan. I have seen paintings of your father. Though I never had the opportunity to meet him, you do bear his countenance. My cousin told me many stories about him. He was a great King and an honorable man."

"So I have been told. I wish I had known him." He liked the stranger's soft, neutral voice. Its tone, the accent, its pitch and timbre took away the last traces of his discomfort."

"I wish you had too…but I sense that you are like him in many ways. You must be nearly twelve?"

"How do you know that…and how do you know so much about me?" He realized after saying it, that anyone might know his age, as it coincided with the deaths of his father and King Donal's ascension to the throne."

"I met you once…on the day you were born."

"Truly?" He sank down, genuinely interested in the stranger and comfortable enough to feel no fear when the harper shifted off his knees and sat beside him.

"I was seven," Kavan explained. "I had gone to court with my cousin…"

"Then you must have met my brothers! And my mother! And my sister!" But Arlan's excitement turned quickly into something else. Fear, though not for himself. "You have not been in Enesfel all of this time, have you? It is not safe for you here."

The bard smiled, a tender expression almost embarrassed in appearance. "I live in Bhryell, Elyriá. It is close enough that I come here frequently, but far enough that I am in no danger. Do not fear for my safety, My Prince. As for your family…I met them briefly, except for King Donal. He was a kind man. We were friends…if you can call the relationship between a young boy and a King friendship. Do you re-member Ártur MacLyr?"

The prince nodded. "Of course. He was our court healer. He brings us news from the castle…"

"What?" Kavan's abrupt turn sideways made the prince shy away. It took the harper several deep breaths to calm himself. This revelation did not truly surprise him; there had been many times that Ártur left the house at night when he believed Kavan asleep, and it was always at least an hour later before he returned. Kavan had known his cousin was up to something other than courting, but he had not expected it to involve the youngest Lachlan heir. Perhaps, given what he knew of Ártur's involvement in the boy's departure from the castle, he should have. Thinking about it, it was the only explanation for those absences that made sense.

"I am sorry, milord. I did not mean to startle you."

"Is it wrong for him to bring us messages from my sister and Brenna? Other than it being dangerous, I mean?" the prince asked.

"Only wrong because he continues to warn me of the dangers of coming to Enesfel while he continues going himself…to do something riskier than I have ever done. Do not fret; I would never cause him harm. He is my cousin…but I wish he had told me."

"So you came with him to the castle…when I was born." Prince Arlan picked up a stone from the ground and skipped it across the lake surface. "You will not reveal where I am to anyone, will you?"

"Never, My Prince. Your life is too precious; many people have gone to great effort to protect you. Your secrets are as safe with me as they are with Ártur."

"Good. Because I like you…and I want to trust you." He paused, trying not to stare at the glistening droplets on the skin of the man's throat. His gaze traveled downwards as he tried to look away, but it stopped when it fell on the crescent pendant on the man's breast. His brow furrowed and he gave a puzzled frown. "I have one like that…"

"Pardon?" Kavan's thoughts had been far away, on Ártur and the fact that he might not know his cousin as well as he believed; he had not noticed the trail of the boy's eyes.

A small hand hesitantly lifted the medallion as if afraid to touch the porcelain white skin. "This. Only mine goes the other way."

Kavan flinched as if burned and blinked at the boy in disbelief. So many things came together in his head at once that there was a stab of pain behind his eyes and a loud rush of air as he felt punched in the stomach. "Where…?" he started, his voice catching in a squeak, "where did you get it?"

Prince Arlan jerked his hand back, afraid he had hurt the man to cause such a reaction. "My father left it for me; mother sent it with me when I left Rhidam. There was a letter with it that said he wanted to give it to his youngest son, but if she knew where he had gotten it, she did not say. Where did you get yours?"

"Here…in this lake…right there." Kavan pointed into the shallow water not far from where they sat. "Many years ago."

Eyes sparkling with interest and excitement, the boy asked, "Do you think it is important that they are nearly the same?"

Taking the prince's hands in his, meeting his gaze, Kavan murmured in a shaky voice, "I am certain it must be. There cannot be many of these."

"What do you think it means?"

Kavan was already pondering that, but any explanations he could think of would only confuse and agitate the prince and each one made Kavan shiver with anxiety. Sensing the prince's growing restless eagerness, he finally replied, "I do not know, My Prince, but I think it connects us somehow. It is growing late and you should return to Lord McHador before it grows much darker. It would not be good to cause him to worry, and it is important that you remain safe."

"That's what he says," the prince nodded with a frown. "But I do not want…will I see you again?"

It was a question that had to be weighed carefully. Kavan suspected he was the first person Prince Arlan had met, or even seen, apart from Ártur and Guthrie, since his exile. The pendants bound them together, Kavan was sure of it. He believed the prince needed him, although whether that was an accurate perception, Kavan could not say. He could find no harm in granting the request, however, and it gave Kavan a sense of purpose that he had not yet felt, as if destiny was catching up to him. "I come here often, at least once a week. We can meet here if you would like, My Prince."

The boy smiled. "I would. But you do not need to call me your prince. You are not a subject of Enesfel, not my vassal, and I am not your superior. I want to be friends. Please, call me Arlan."

Kavan flushed and looked at his hands. He was not accustomed to such familiarity with strangers, especially with royalty, but for this one boy, he would make an exception. "Very well, Arlan. I will come the day after tomorrow if the weather is good." He placed his harp in its case. "Bring your medallion, if you can. I should like to see it."

"I will." Arlan stood up and bounced with excitement. "I will not tell Guthrie about you. He may be angry that I talked to you, told you about Ártur...although if Ártur is your cousin, and we have met before, then we are not strangers, are we? What is your name?"

Kavan realized he had not yet given it. "My apologies, Arlan...my name is Kavan."

Arlan offered his hand with a growing smile. "Goodbye, Kavan. I will see you in two days, with the medallion. I promise."

The prince scurried off into the woods in the direction from which he had come, and Kavan concentrated on his aura until the boy was out of range. With his head and heart full, Kavan returned to his own empty home where he put his harp in his room, combed out his hair, and changed into a fresh robe before retreating to the back garden to think in the solitude of twilight. He had planted a rose garden, the success of which impressed his aunt when she came on her bi-weekly visits. There was no secret to their thriving, as he had done nothing beyond the usual planting, weeding, watering, and pruning. And although he had chosen no specific bushes to plant, all of the roses bloomed white.

He was tending those roses in the settling darkness when the sound of a galloping horse approached. Ártur slowed the animal and dismounted within the confines of the small corral. The stable could house two animals, but there was only the one that Ártur frequently required for his medical rounds. The healer motioned for Kavan to join him and led the chestnut mare into the shelter to groom and feed her.

"You are home early. I did not expect you back until later tonight."

Ignoring the question behind his cousin's comment, Kavan said, "You have been riding."

Ártur chuckled. "I have to do something with my free time. I can only paint for so long before I have to get out of the house, find something to do. I suppose you have been to the lake."

"It is the only place I can have peace."

The healer laughed. "You have all the peace you want right here."

Kavan did not react to that. It was true that his home was peaceful and private, but it was never the same as being alone in the wilderness beside the lake. "You ought to come with me next time. I learn the most unusual things there."

Brushing the horse down as he spoke, Ártur asked, "What did you learn this time? Did you have a visitation from the k'kairá? Or Saint Kóráhm perhaps?"

Though the questions were in jest, it made Kavan uncomfortable knowing that either could happen when he least expected it. "I learned," he finally said, "that you have been to Enesfel, to Rhidam and the castle, many times since Donal's death."

Ártur's face lost color but he continued the currying and did not look up. And Kavan noticed. "Do not fear. I do not hold the deception against you; you were doing what needed to be done, and you are right to remind me of the dangers from time to time. You are, of course, allowed to be concerned for my welfare. I wish you would be a little more concerned for your own, however…and I wish you would have told me." The healer started to speak, but Kavan silenced him with a wave of his hand. "You likely felt you had good cause not to, but I would have hated to lose you, and have no way of knowing where you were…or what you were doing there. You should have trusted me."

The last words made the healer blush. "You did have a visitation," he muttered.

"Of a sort. I met Prince Arlan." The currycomb dropped to the stable floor; Ártur fumbled to retrieve it. "I did not look for him, did not know where to look. You kept his secret well. He found me. I knew who he was the moment I saw him. He looks very much like Donal…and his father."

From where he squatted on the floor, Ártur asked, "Does he know who you are?"

"That I am your cousin? Yes. We spoke only of his father and you before he asked to meet with me again." His voice lowered and he offered his hand to help his cousin up. "He is a very lonely boy, Ártur."

Ártur accepted the offered hand. "I hope you are not going to honor that request."

"Why shouldn't I?"

"I…it is not safe." It was a flimsy reason, but the only one the healer could think of. Kavan being involved in the subterfuge of Prince Arlan's life made Ártur uncomfortable.

"For him?" Kavan asked, "Or for me?"

"Both. Promise me you will not."

Kavan shook his head. Ártur had asked him not to go to Enesfel many years ago too. Kavan's answer had not changed. "I cannot promise you that. I must go back. I promised him I would. Besides," his hand rested on his chest where the medallion and cross lay against his skin, "he has the other half of this medallion."

Ártur gave a long, low whistle. "Are you certain they are the same?"

"He told me so. I see no reason to think he is lying, but I will know for sure when I see it, when we next meet."

"Saints and záryph…" the healer groaned, rubbing his face with one hand.

"You spoke once about the old woman's words…when I was an infant, remember? I did not die during my first trip to Enesfel, as she foretold might happen; I must have met my destiny. I met Prince Arlan. When he held my finger that first time, there was a static discharge…a tingle. Given the odd occurrences I was experiencing at the time, with the Power awakening, I did not think to question or mention it. Yet the arrow, the poison…things that have almost killed him, I have felt…"

The healer stared at him, aghast. He had not known that Kavan had felt those injuries, but maybe he should have. If he had not effectively shut Kavan out of his head during those years, he might have been able to detect his cousin's condition and distress.

"I told you a prince had been born to replace King Innis. I believe it may be Prince Arlan. I do not know what I can do for him, but I believe these medallions link us. Maybe I am to help restore him to the throne. Maybe I am to protect him. Maybe I am simply supposed to teach him and be his friend so that he will be properly prepared to rule one day. Whatever the case, there is no choice. I will follow my instincts." He watched his cousin lean against the wall, eyes closed as if he was trying not to faint. "But I must ask a favor of you if I am to do this."

Afraid of what he would hear, Ártur opened his eyes and met Kavan's gaze. "What?"

"I want you to promise me three things. One…that you will allow the prince to decide when it is time to tell Lord McHador about me."

The healer thought about the matter and replied, "There is no need to tell him. I know what I said, Kavan…but I know the prince will be safe while in your company. I will not speak to Guthrie." He did not know how Kavan would protect the prince, but he believed he would.

"Thank you." It meant a great deal to Kavan to be trusted. Not many people would give him that. "And please…do not hold this against me, or try to stop me. I do not want to fight with you…"

Those words made Ártur smirk. "I know. It is a foolish endeavor to try to talk you out of anything. And you know that I could never hold anything against you."

Kavan hung his head. "I know…but sometimes I wish you would."

After an uncomfortable silence punctuated by Ártur placing the currycomb on the shelf and wiping his teary eyes on his sleeves, the healer asked quietly, "What else do you want from me, sínréc?"

"If I get drawn into the politics of Enesfel, if I go to Rhidam…promise me you will come. I know nothing of politics and court life. You have been there. Come with me. Instruct me. I will need you. I believe the prince will need you as well."

Ártur suppressed the urge to hug his cousin. Of any man the healer knew, he suspected that Kavan would fit into court life with ease, more quickly than Ártur ever had. Kavan would not need him for that, or to teach him, despite how he might feel. But Kavan knew that Ártur wanted to return to Rhidam. He missed the atmosphere of court and he missed the Lachlans. He had never thought to have the opportunity to go back, and Kavan was offering it to him.

But could he do it?

Interpreting the silence as potential refusal, Kavan asked, "If nothing else, Ártur, grant me your moral support? Please?"

This time, the healer did embrace him, long and hard. "I will do what I can, Kavan. Better than I have done in the past. I pray, for all our sakes, that you are right about all of this."

Kavan awkwardly pulled from the embrace, whispering, "So do I."

୭*෨

Until the first winter snow, Kavan met Prince Arlan at the lake twice each week. He became the prince's second tutor, discussing books, music, art, philosophy, morality, and religion, things that Guthrie either knew little about or had not discussed at length with the prince. Once the snows came, it was agreed to stop meeting until spring. Neither of them wanted to risk the chance of someone following the boy's tracks in the snow. By the time they parted company, Kavan had established that the medallions were indeed a matched pair; he was unable to decipher the inscription but he had made a rubbing of them on a sheet of parchment to use in research during the winter months in the hopes of finding answers. Prince Arlan wore his medallion now as a symbol of their growing friendship.

As those months had passed and winter, in turn, crept by, Guthrie noticed the changes in his ward. Arlan grew calmer, wiser, and had not mentioned the mysterious lakeside music again. Where once he had shown distaste for reading, the prince spent much of the winter by the firelight doing that, devouring the pages of any books Guthrie could acquire. He had taken a renewed interest in discussing philosophy, politics, and military tactics, discussions that contained a deeper insight and focus than had been present before. A product of maturity, the older man decided, liking what he was seeing but beginning to wonder what he would do when the prince was man enough to want to leave this place, particularly if that day came before he decided to claim Enesfel's throne.

Prince Arlan growing into an adult had not been planned for.

There had been no new developments from Rhidam. As King Bowen's second year closed, the day-to-day routine in the kingdom rarely changed. People, Teren and Elyri alike, were tortured, burned, or executed in an array of horrible ways, and the kingdom's treasury decreased drastically and taxes had raised once again. The King ignored the treaty with Hatu, which called for trade and economic aid, thus causing an escalation of tensions on the southern border for the first time since Donal's hard-won peace. To the north, Neth had begun to direct small acts of aggression at Cordash, which occasionally spilled over into Enesfel's border towns. Halfway through his third year, winter brought nothing new to the land except that the greater than usual snowfall decreased the number of deaths by execution...and increased the number who died due to disease and starvation.

But as the snows melted and the rivers thawed with the birth of spring, something new had crept in, like a thorn festering beneath tender skin, drawing the angry pus of frustration to it which constantly sought an outlet. A poisoned seed germinated amongst the peasants and the lower classes in the capital city and once the weather made travel easier, that poison seeped outward to taint every village, every town in the whole of Enesfel. Once or twice it reared its head in the form of small revolts, only to have the King disarm it with brutal force, but such retaliation only served to drive the splinter of discontent deeper into the lives of those increasingly desperate to be rid of the pain.

Prince Owain knocked on the door to the King's bedchamber; Bowen looked up from his meal with annoyance, saw who his visitor was, and motioned for the younger man to enter and sit. He did not appreciate interruptions, but for Owain concessions were frequently made. The blonde prince, twenty-one and sporting a moustache, sat with a smile. "How's the meal?"

"Passable," the King burped. "Want some?"

The prince shook his head. "I have already eaten. I don't know why you don't dine with the rest of us. Your nobles expect it…"

The King grunted again. "Because I cannot stand the mindless chattering prattle of that pack of mongrels who call themselves lords and dignitaries." He ate a few more bites, and when Owain did not speak again, he glanced up and asked, "What do you want? You did not come here to watch me eat."

The prince leaned back in his chair and propped his booted feet on the edge of the table. Though it earned him a scowl, he did not lower them and the King did not demand he remove them. "I received a letter from mother. She says the atmosphere in Neth is too dangerous, due to the hostilities with Cordash. She wants to return to Rhidam."

Wiping his mouth on his serviette, the King shook his head. "Can't…I already told her why."

"You did it for me…"

"You're different. She is not one of us. She is not welcome here…"

The prince scowled. "By the people…or by you?"

Having nothing to hide, the King replied, "Both." Whatever he may have shared with Lady Ula de Corrmick in the past, it had disappeared long ago. He did not care if he ever saw her again.

"But she misses you…father…"

Bowen slammed his fist down onto the table and waved his dining knife in the prince's direction. "Not this again. I have told you not to call me that."

"Why? You have already admitted it to me. Why deny it to everyone else?" Prince Owain went to the fireplace, his shoulders square, and his voice level despite his annoyance.

"Because it would put me, you, my reign, and your future, in jeopardy. The people have great, fond memories of my father and will not forgive me, or you, for having deceived them…"

"Especially after the way you have been treating them," Owain snorted.

"You…"

The prince's narrowed eyes stared down at the still seated King as he interrupted him; he was likely the only person in the kingdom with the gall to do either. "They cannot blame me for something I did not do and knew nothing about until you became King. Yes, you can deny it, tell them I have known all along, but whom do you think they are going to believe? Besides, they hate you already; what difference will telling them make?" He eluded the hands that grasped for his throat as he was too far away for the King to reach him. "Most of the people who would remember Innis have passed. What should anyone else care? You brought me back to Rhidam for a reason…and it was not to entertain you. If you want me to see the throne one day, you will have to do it…"

"Farrell brought you back…not me. People may not remember his face, but they know the stories. Every bard in Enesfel has immortalized the man. There has always been speculation that you are not what you were claimed to be, rumors which were not helped by Donal sending you and your mother away. For me to confirm it would be bad for us both. They will kill you before you have the chance to think or save yourself. You will gain the throne if you have patience."

This time it was Owain who snorted. "You do not believe that any more than I do…"

"Girvin has no interest in another marriage and will likely never father children. He has never been in robust health. I doubt he will live beyond…"

Having always been fond of Girvin, as he had been of Farrell, Prince Owain growled, "What are you plotting against Girvin?"

The King ignored the question. "I plan to have no other children. I don't have the stomach for it. You are the only remaining Lachlan. Find a noblewoman, marry, ensure the bloodline. You will see the throne…"

"And if Prince Arlan returns?"

The King scoffed and settled back into the chair. "Prince Arlan is not coming back. He is…"

"Dead? How do you know…or did you kill him? Your own brother? The Elyri did not kill him. Lord Nelsen did not kill him. It would have had to be…"

"I did nothing of the sort," the King said in an icy tone.

"Then he may be out there. Somewhere. If he is not dead, then he is alive. I may be heir before him, but with the scandal of my history, as you say, the people would choose him over me…unless I am anointed by you to be the next King. Girvin would get over it. I do not believe he wants the crown anyhow. The only way to ensure my succession is to be legitimately acknowledged as your son."

The King had heard enough. "Out! This is the last time I will discuss this with you! I will not acknowledge you before the people. The charade has gone on too long for us to change it. Bring it up again and I will send you back to your mother and strip you of any chance of sitting on this throne more thoroughly than Donal did. If that does not put an end to your foolishness, your execution certainly will. Get out of my sight."

Prince Owain stalked as far as the door, looked back over his shoulder, and sneered. "You will regret that decision…father."

"Get out!"

The King's cry of fury filled the corridor behind Owain as the prince strode from the room and slammed the door. Beneath his anger, however, Owain felt a prickle of suspicion and apprehension as he wondered if there was more to the King's anger than there appeared to be. Was the King that disappointed in him that he would not acknowledge him as his son and heir? What could he possibly have done wrong?

The uprisings throughout Enesfel continued and King Bowen was obliged to spread his forces thinner to squelch them. By the following winter, death and desertions had stripped the royal military, leaving few qualified individuals to fight for the King. It was becoming more difficult to fill the diminishing ranks as fewer men volunteered for service, and the King felt it unwise to conscript men against their will who could later turn on him and use his own weapons and training against him. He knew he could not afford that. In an attempt to regain some level of stability and peace, he slashed the tax rate by two-thirds, which left the rate twice as high as it had been under both Kings Innis and Donal. It was not enough to change the opinion of his subjects, and King Bowen realized he was losing his grip on the reins of the kingdom.

Even within his own household, he was aware of the change. Servants did their tasks in silence, too promptly, too neatly, leaving him no one to snap at. A younger woman, Muriel, had replaced Lady Johanna as the princess's lady in waiting, and she, the princess, and Brenna Weylin were never in the same room as the monarch unless he demanded it. Prince Owain no longer stayed at court in Rhidam, and Prince Girvin continued to make his residence at Kamin. No longer was there a stream of petitioners to the court, as all feared the wrath of their King, and the lords and ladies of the realm stayed away unless specifically summoned.

When spring came once more, there was still no change, until the day word reached Rhidam that peasant forces near the city of Jardin had captured General McLeu. Though the reports could not be confirmed, they hinted that he had been executed. King Bowen knew the general held no love for him, but General McLeu had always been loyal to Enesfel and took his oath to protect the Lachlans seriously. The King was aware that the general was likely his only ally, thus he gathered what remained of his army, left Prince Girvin in charge in Rhidam, and rode to Jardin with the hopes of rescuing his general if the man was alive, or avenging his death if he was not.

Though heavily armed, the royal militia was no match for the several hundred peasants, merchants, and renegade soldiers awaiting them at the outskirts of Jardin. There was no sign of General McLeu among them. There was, however, the tall, foreboding presence of Prince Owain leading the opposition. This betrayal infuriated the King as nothing ever had before. He had never dreamed the Prince would resort to such extreme measures to obtain his goal of legitimacy. Because the King would not capitulate, the Prince made one new demand...for Bowen to step down from the throne and to appoint the prince as his heir, but the King refused this demand as well and battle was joined. By the day's end, almost half of his force lay dead or dying, another large percentage had fled or joined the opposition, until finally, Bowen's demoralized soldiers that were left lay down their weapons and refused to fight. The King was pulled from his horse into the midst of the waiting mob. He struggled, shouting empty threats of punishment for treason, calling to Prince Owain for mercy, for a compromise, but in the end, his cries were a wasted effort.

In Rhidam, Prince Girvin slouched on the throne, pondering his life, fingering the royal scepter. He was not comfortable here, in this place, in this chair, doing this job. He did not want to be there. Public life, decision making, leadership...the very thought of those things made him feel sick and full of panic. He had not kept abreast of the political climate or the state of the kingdom, did not know the condition of Enesfel's military or of the seething unrest of their subjects. Learning anything that might have meant crossing paths with his brother was avoided. He was not even sure where his brother had gone that had caused the King to leave him in charge. When a battered, bloody, dusty soldier stumbled through the Grand Hall doors and collapsed at his feet, telling him that the King had been killed in battle near Jardin, Prince Girvin's jaw fell slack and his face went white. He did the only thing he could.

He fainted.

➷*◈

"They pulled him from his horse, ran him through with a spear, and he was drawn and quartered!" Prince Arlan's face was flushed with excitement, although there was a note of fear and near disgust in his voice. "The people actually did that!"

Kavan walked silently beside him, listening to the prince yet not hearing him. He was thinking of the twenty-six helpless, innocent peasants that King Bowen had executed for spite and sport. The deed was done. Those peasants were avenged. Somehow, though, Kavan did not feel the satisfaction he had expected at Bowen's death, but he did feel relief that this particular Lachlan King could no longer terrorize Enesfel.

"People will go to great lengths to rid themselves of a tyrant," the bard said, although he knew that it had not truly been the people who had done this. It had been Prince Owain, acting behind and through the people, and that cold fact concerned him.

The prince did not notice his friend's agitation but continued to speak. "Now Girvin is King. I hope he will rule for many years; at least he will be kind to the people…a good King."

The Elyri stopped mid-step, seeing a familiar face in his mind's eye, contorted in horror though obviously dead. He closed his eyes with a shiver and tried to will away the nausea that always accompanied the Sight. He knew what such a sudden vision meant, though not how it might come to pass. In a stern yet gentle voice, not wanting to alarm Arlan, he said, "My prince, you must hear me. Girvin will not rule as long as you might hope. Do not ask how I know this, but believe what I say to be true. The time has come for you to prepare yourself to take the throne."

Prince Arlan laughed. "I do not desire to be King, Kavan. It used to be what I wanted; it was all Guthrie encouraged me to want. But I would rather remain here, in the forest, learning from you."

Having never considered himself a teacher in any true sense, when he was little older than the prince, Kavan would have been flattered by those words if the situation before them was not so grave. "That is not realistic, Arlan, as much as we both desire it. I have limited wisdom and knowledge to impart. After that, what would we do? You will grow bored of this soon enough. When Owain becomes King, you are the only hope Enesfel will have of regaining its path. He must not be allowed to..."

"He is my brother. He is first in line..."

Kavan shook his head. "He is not Innis' son, My Prince, and his reign will not be good for anyone. He is not meant to sit on Enesfel's throne. He must not be killed, but he must be brought down when he comes to power."

"For Elyriá?" the prince asked with a frustrated huff.

"For Enesfel. Elyriá is safe. Nothing Owain can do will harm us. But he can harm himself, Enesfel, and possibly Cordash, Neth, and Hatu if he is not stopped. It is your destiny, Arlan. I have known that since you were born."

The boy turned to look at him with an expression of confusion and skepticism. "Known what since I was born?"

It felt to be a risky question to answer because the boy was clearly annoyed, but Kavan knew he must. "That you would be King..."

Prince Arlan snorted, shook his head, and began walking again. Kavan followed. "I do not want to lose you. If I become King...I will...the way I lose everybody."

Watching the soft cushion of moss and leaves pass beneath his feet, unaccustomed to that sort of sentiment, Kavan took a long time before replying. "I will come with you if it is your wish..." He had suspected that possibility would arise, but now that it had, the very real chance of it made him feel cold inside.

"It is too dangerous in Enesfel for you," the prince protested. "You cannot live here..."

"You can change that. You can change anything that suits you. When you are King, you can make Enesfel safe for everyone, restore the kingdom to its former eminence. You have the knowledge, the wisdom, and the skills to make such decisions. Lord McHador and I have given you..."

"Is that all this has been to you?" Prince Arlan backed away, his eyes flashing and his cheeks burning crimson. "You did not come here to be my friend...you did it to get me on the throne. You do not care what I want...no one does. Go home and stop meddling in my affairs, Elyri. This is not your land. Leave us...leave me...alone. I do not want to be King and I do not want to see you ever again."

Kavan reached to stop him as the boy ran in the direction of the cabin, but he decided to let the prince go and allowed his arm to fall short of catching him. The prince needed time to think this through. Torn between his affection for Arlan that encouraged him to abandon responsibility, and between the duties he felt to a crown that was not his own, Kavan wondered why he could not have both. Why could he not be friends with the prince while Arlan sought the throne? But he could not force the prince to speak with him, nor could he force him to accept his responsibilities as a Lachlan heir. Prince Arlan would be fourteen by winter's end, legal age to claim the throne. Perhaps by then he would have changed his mind, would have come to an understanding and acceptance that some things in life were greater than an individual's own desire. If he did not, the Sovereignties might have lost their best hope for peace and prosperity. Feeling responsible for the prince's reaction and choices, Kavan did not intend to let it come to that.

⊱Chapter 18⊰

King Girvin's sunken, pallid face was grayer than usual as he paced the Morning Room, following a well-worn path in the symmetrical patterns of the Hatu wool rug. The last seven months as king had not been kind to him. He had lost an unhealthy amount of weight from his already lean frame, developed a nervous twitch in his right eye, and began to stutter when he felt stressed. His light brown hair had thinned and he moved about slowly, as though a man twice his age.

But as a monarch, he had performed diligently and admirably. He had done what he could to restore order to a kingdom he did not view as his. He could not shake the feeling that he was a temporary custodian, sitting on the throne until Bowen returned or until the rightful ruler, whoever that was, arrived. Wishful thinking, his advisers reminded him, but Girvin did not want to be reminded. He preferred the fantasy instead of the reality that he was King no matter what he wished. Taxes were not reduced below what Bowen had slashed them to, but the new king put the money, and the excess Bowen had secreted away, to use restoring buildings that had been destroyed during the various uprisings or that had fallen into ruin in recent years. This included both shops and private homes. He lent vast amounts to individuals and merchants in the hopes of creating a renewed surge of business and travel. But as the kingdom failed to respond to his gestures in any significant way, the King grew more certain that his subjects felt it too, that they knew he would not be in power long enough to see his measures bear fruit. Someone else would take his place and undo every good thing he was striving for. No one was willing to extend their hopes too far.

Across the room, General Ferghus McLeu sat rigidly, his sun-browned face pinched in an unhappy frown as it had been since he had received the news of King Bowen's death. He had not been in Jardin at the time of the uprising; he had not even been in Enesfel. He had traveled to Cordash to discuss the situation with Neth with King Laird. He wondered why King Bowen had forgotten that. Though relieved that the man was no longer in the world to torment people, the general was miserable about the way his name and steadfast reputation had been used against the monarch of Enesfel.

The new king spoke at last, his expression dour and weary. "I have said it before, Lord General. The people will not be punished. There were too many of them; if we try to punish them, we might as well punish the entire kingdom. Bowen did that beforehand; I think they have endured enough."

"What of Prince Owain?"

The King rubbed his temples and groaned. Yes, he thought miserably, what of Owain? The prince returned to the royal house in Rhidam within two months of Bowen's death as if nothing had happened. He had not denied his part in the revolt; it was public knowledge after all. What was not clear was how much of a hand he had in the King's actual death. To many of the people of the kingdom, however, Prince Owain was a hero, and Girvin could not bring himself to punish the man. From everything the new king had learned since assuming the throne, Prince Owain had rid the kingdom of a horrifying tyrant. The King had no heir, was not anticipating having one, thus someone would have to rule after him, and while the people might not object to a female ruler, Deidre's inability to hear made her unsuitable for the throne. No, King Girvin did not think he could punish his brother.

"I do not mean to speak ill of him, Sire," the general said, squirming awkwardly, "but he could be very dangerous. He has clearly been influenced by his years in Neth. His way of dealing with discontent is to kill the offender, even his own father…"

"Bowen was no better…"

"That is not the way to solve problems, or to deal with kinsmen. You could be his next target. You would be wise to punish him, show him that you will not tolerate such behavior…"

"He is royalty, the heir to the throne, and he did the realm a favor." The King wiped sweat from his brow with his hand. "He means me no harm."

The general was not prepared to back down. "At least a brief prison term, milord…something to show the people that you hold him responsible but not something harsh enough to turn the people against you…"

The King poured himself a goblet of wine; whether he was thinking about the issue or merely avoiding it, the general could not tell. At last, after drinking the entire glass, Girvin sighed and said, "House arrest for six months…but he will be taken care of as his station demands. He must agree to that…"

Prince Owain did agree. He remained guarded in his room and was allowed one hour of escorted outdoor walks every day. He did not object, except to bemoan the hunting opportunities he was missing. In fact, he seemed to enjoy his captivity save for the lack of hunting, which was not what General McLeu had intended or hoped for. He debated with the King on lengthening the sentence or placing harsher restrictions on the prince, out of principle, but the King could not see any value in such action. He could barely justify to himself the idea of keeping his brother under house arrest. Lengthening the sentence or changing the terms was out of the question. At the end of six months, Owain was released back into the full life of a Lachlan prince.

Not long after, the threats began. Pranks at first, anonymous threats to put salt in General McLeu's tea if the King did not give a certain Lord a tax break, threats to give the princess' wardrobe to the poor if flowers were not displayed throughout the city, insistence on a holiday commemorating the King's birth or else dung would be burned before the castle gates. The King found humor in these games and went along with them at first, until the day their tone changed from harmless pranks to menacing threats. Threats to kill Prince Owain's hunting dogs, steal the King's horses, or damage royal property. Most of the threats were directed at the King, but there were others directed at the general, at Prince Owain, and even at the princess. The King did not think he could afford to ignore them. Night after night, as the threats worsened, the King had nightmares of the past and the deaths he had seen in his family. It felt to him as if the dead were returning to torment him. Often he dreamed of himself meeting Bowen's same grisly fate.

In an attempt to stop the threats, the King went to great lengths to make his subjects like him. He established a number of holidays and lowered the taxes below the threshold that his father had held. He created five new lords and gave each royal funds to build their estates. Yet it seemed that, the more he did, the more frequent and intimidating the threats became. Soon enough, they became threats of death.

It reached a point where the King would not sleep in his room alone, and eventually, even the presence of General McLeu sitting at his bedside was not enough to give him peace. He looked behind him constantly, bolted at the slightest noises, refused to eat for fear his food was poisoned, and would not go outside the castle lest someone shoot at him from the walls as had once been done to Prince Arlan. He kept guards with him wherever he went. He took to having the general prepare his meals in his bedchamber, where he could watch its preparation, but as time passed, even that became suspect. What if the ingredients had been poisoned before the general brought it in to prepare? Everyone in the castle watched their King slowly go mad.

The attention that Prince Owain had once shown the princess had grown more fervent since King Bowen's death, making life unbearable for her until she finally made complaint to the King. Angered that Owain should behave in such an unseemly way when his primary concern should be castle security and the King's life, and angered that he showed no respect for Girvin's favorite sibling, the King forbade the prince to go near their sister until the threats ceased. He posted guards outside of her door and allowed the princess to go nowhere without Brenna, her attendant Muriel, and at least two soldiers. Sullen and offended, Prince Owain submitted to voluntary self-exile in his rooms, as if he were once again under house arrest, but this time he gave himself no daily outdoor walks.

For the King, it was one less matter to think about, and so he put it out of his addled mind.

Only ten of the palace servants were retained by this time, individuals who had been with the Lachlan family since Girvin had been a small boy. Everyone else was dismissed indefinitely until the perpetrator of the threats was apprehended. The general remained with the King day and night. The castle became filthy, disorganized, cold, and deserted. The King did not mind. The fewer people there were to watch, the fewer people there were to harm either him or his household.

On the anniversary of King Innis' death, terrified shrieking filled the halls of the House of Lachlan. The King's bedroom was open; he was found, hands clutched to his throat, eyes wide and staring but unseeing. A search was made through the castle grounds but no one could be found who should not have been present. Each person was questioned extensively. A physician was brought in to examine the monarch's body, but there were no physical injuries and no trace of illness or poison. King Girvin had apparently died of self-induced terror. No one had been in the room with him that night. He had insisted that he be left alone for the first time in months, and General McLeu had been drinking and playing dice with his fellow soldiers at the time.

Owain Ustes Lachlan was the King of Enesfel.

ᭅ*᭥

If Kavan was nervous, Ártur saw no indications of it as the younger man mounted the altar steps with the náós choir. In the light of the Udhár candles, this year's choir looked particularly small. Its numbers were certainly fewer, four boys and four men other than Kavan. Most years there were at least four times that number, and usually there were women and girls as well, but illness and travel had kept its usual members away this year. Or, thought the healer, hearing the whispers and feeling the excited tension around him as Kavan took his place, it was the stubbornness of Bhryell's people at work, the only means of coaxing Kavan to sing.

This perplexed Ártur further. He knew Kavan could sing. Obviously, all of Bhryell knew. Kavan had served in the choir as a child, performed whole Gatherings set to music alone, and had written of those events with an excitement reserved only for his harp and his studies. Tíbhyan's letters had indicated that Kavan was as exceptional as a singer as he was with everything else. But Ártur had never been home on those occasions to hear him, and Kavan had not sung publicly in the years the healer had been back in Bhryell.

He could have asked anyone what had happened, what kept Kavan from singing, but he knew he would not believe the answers. Each would be too embellished to glean the truth. And asking Tíbhyan only gained the healer one of the old man's curious smiles. Since Kavan would not explain, Ártur had tried to content himself with not know-ing. When gdhededhá Bhílári came to Kavan, begging him to sing this year because the choir had too few members for the Udhár Eve Gath-ering and their usual soloist was confined to bed due to illness, it had been Ártur's pleading that broke Kavan's resistance.

"Just once," the healer begged. "Let me hear you, and I shall never ask again. I want to know what I have missed. I want to share it with you. Nothing can be as bad as you insinuate with your silence and resistance."

Kavan had looked at him with an expression that, although Ártur could not name it, made every fiber of his being, every corner of his soul, hurt. The younger man had gone out the door and Ártur did not see him for several days. He believed Kavan had refused. When Kavan returned, the matter was not brought up again.

That had been three weeks ago. It was with considerable surprise that the healer saw Kavan go forward tonight in one of the red and black velvet choir robes. He stood in the back row of singers, two men on both sides and the four boys in front. Ártur knew all of them to varying degrees; he had grown up with two of the men. As the choir began their opening hymn, accompanied by the instrumental trio of two lutes and a recorder, he heard no reason why this Gathering should be eagerly anticipated by the congregation or dreaded by his cousin.

It was not until he stood for the Prayer of Union that he learned the truth. Eyes closed, he waited for gdhededhá Bhílári to begin the prayer. Instead, one of the lutes sounded a single note. The prayer would be sung. Not customary, but not unusual either. There were a few moments of silence, during which Ártur held his breath and prayed it would be Kavan's voice he heard.

When the first note started, low and sweet, a sigh escaped him. The singer was one of the boys. The song built, twisted, and dipped in ways that caused his skin to tingle beneath the vocal caress until it crescendoed into heights the healer could never imagine hearing from a child. Nor could he believe that any of these four boys, all of whom he knew, possessed such a mastery of breath control, tone, emotion, and enunciation. No child possessed such strength and range. Tears pooled in the corners of his eyes, his breath came in short gasps, and he knew his face was flushed in an unseemly fashion. The need to know the truth caused him to raise his head and look up. His heart felt as if it stopped within his chest.

Kavan.

The other choir members had stepped aside, leaving Kavan to stand alone. There was such innocence on that beloved face, raw emotion in his eyes as he sang. Such a register belonged to a boy or a woman, but no one else was singing. Though logic said it could not be, it clearly was. A shudder of ecstasy pulsed up and down Ártur's spine and he fought to remain standing. Though some part of him understood Kavan's reluctance to sing, Ártur could not imagine anything more beautiful, more musically perfect, except perhaps a harp in Kavan's hands.

Kavan met his gaze; his voice did not waver but his eyes betrayed the fear he felt. The healer reached reassuringly with his thoughts as the prayer song drew to a close, thrusting as much love, support, and admiration through the link as he could. Though Kavan's expression did not change, there was, to Ártur's ear, a transformation in those final notes, a self-assurance that had not been there before.

The healer felt complete, as if a part of him had been lost but was now replaced, a part he had not realized was missing. As difficult as it would prove to be, now that he had heard such perfection, he was determined to keep his promise. He could listen to that voice for an eternity and would let his cousin know it, but he would never again insist on hearing it. If the bard ever sang for him again, it would be because he wanted to.

The final note faded into an echo at the back of the building as the congregation knelt to receive the final blessing, all clearly as affected by the song as Ártur had been. Kavan rejoined the choir; his expression conveyed relief and something more.

Peace.

Ártur wondered if he was the only one to see it, the only one to understand.

🙵*🙵

If nothing else, King Owain's first year as King proved that he was an astute politician. Though he consulted no advisors, his actions were carefully thought out, planned and executed, and proved to be highly popular. He raised the tax rate to slightly higher than it had been during King Innis' reign and set about restoring the structural, cultural, and political damage the kingdom had sustained after many years of upheaval. A call was made for an all-volunteer military; not surprisingly, after his success against Bowen, he accumulated a thousand-man force within the first three months of rule. Many were not paid in wages but were housed, clothed, fed and trained, giving them better living conditions than most had ever had.

Many of those individuals imprisoned by King Bowen's whims were given their freedom. Others were allowed to petition the Crown if they believed they had been accused unjustly. Most of the laws Bowen had initiated were repealed, and of the five new lords Girvin created, two were allowed to keep their titles and land due to their success and prosperity. Thus, King Owain's popularity was solidified, but there were some less trusting, some who remembered that this man had killed one brother, possibly more, to get where he was. Such a man could never be fully trusted.

❧Chapter 19❧

Sixteen-year-old Deidre Lachlan was in every way her mother's child. Everyone in the kingdom adored her as they had the late Lady Cordelia Lachlan. Princess Deidre shared the same golden curls, petite figure, blue eyes, and snub nose as her mother, but the curve of her mouth and chin were her father's. Her beauty, kindness, and gentility made her popular with nobles and commoners alike, despite her handicap. She did not consciously care about such things as popularity, but this life was the only one she had ever known and she could not imagine things otherwise.

She glanced across the sewing table to where her raven-haired companion and confidante also embroidered kerchiefs. It was a quiet day, one without duties or parties, or the need to be outdoors in the cold. On such days, the two of them, usually accompanied by Lady Muriel, would retreat to the princess's ante-chamber to sew. For the most part, it would mean the women were undisturbed, and today, Lady Muriel was not with them either. It left the two friends alone together, which was how they preferred it.

Their solitude was short-lived, however, as the door opened and the King entered. He closed it behind him with a heavy thud. His face was flushed, his hands clenched at his sides, his eyes narrow and red-rimmed as if he had been either drinking or crying. The girls glanced at each other, wondering what had angered him today, knowing from experience that it could have been something as insignificant as a rat crossing his path. He was less irritable than King Bowen had been, but lately, he was too easily annoyed, too quick to anger, and that concerned both girls.

Brenna lay down her sewing. The King had persisted over the past year to persuade the princess to marry him, but she continued to refuse as she had done when Girvin had been King. Owain was her brother, after all; such a marriage would be wrong. Nor did she want to marry someone she did not love unless he forced her to. None of her other brothers had thought to arrange a marriage for her; each had been too caught up in their own affairs to give her much thought. Unlike most women her age, the princess was still unmarried. The King could, if he chose, arrange one. Both knew he would never choose anyone else for her, and he apparently wanted her to marry him of her own free will. Unless he changed his mind and forced the issue, the princess concluded she was destined not to marry. The last time the King approached her, however, he threatened retaliation if she did not accept him. Brenna sent word to her uncle, asking for help or advice, but there had been no reply yet and Healer MacLyr was not due to return for another two days.

"What do you wish, Your Majesty?" Brenna asked with a curtsey. It was her duty to stand between him and her lady, to relay his wishes to her on paper when necessary, and despite the King's demeanor, Brenna did not believe he would hurt either of them.

"You know what I want," the King grunted, looking past her towards the princess. "Ask if she has changed her mind."

Brenna obeyed, even though she knew the Princess already knew what the King wanted, and both women already knew the answer. The princess shook her head. The King, ill-pleased with the response, took a step forward, paused, and asked again. Torn between fetching assistance and protecting her friend, Brenna repeated the proposal, losing her belief in their safety. For some reason, the question held more significance for the King; today he did not seem likely to take no for an answer. Stubbornly, Deidre shook her head harder. The King reached for her arm, intending to pull her to her feet. Without thinking about her actions or the consequences, Brenna was between them and slapped away the man's outstretched arm, something she regretted as soon as it was done.

King Owain flung her aside and snatched at Deidre with a violent snarl. Again, Brenna lashed out, kicking him in the back of the knee and motioning frantically for the princess to leave. She knew that her service to the royal house was at an end. If she was not executed for this brazen attack on the King, she would, at the very least, be dismissed. The princess understood her signaling and tried to scurry around the King, but Owain again grasped for her arms, and again Brenna struck, drawing blood as her nails raked across his cheek. He spun, grabbed her by both shoulders, threw her to the floor, and was astride her before she could scramble to her feet. Deidre watched in horror from the doorway, the door not yet open, as he tore her friend's skirts away.

Not thinking of anything more than the princess's safety, Brenna continued to fight, trying to encourage the other girl to flee while struggling to free herself. Both knew that going for assistance was no longer an option. Brenna had been defiant and disrespectful; she had attacked the King and drawn blood. He could punish her as he saw fit. When he finally rose to his feet, he did not even look down at the girl he had raped.

"Tell her," he snorted, glaring at Princess Deidre as he closed his trousers and straightened his clothes. "I am tired of being patient. If she will not accept my generosity, I can force her to marry me, and I will if I must. Next time, if she continues to deny me, it will be her turn…and then she will have to marry me, for no one else worth marrying will have her."

He strode from the room, his shoulders set, as if nothing had happened, and barely acknowledged the princess as he pushed past her.

Crying hysterically, Deidre knelt beside her friend, signing frantically, wondering what to do about the blood and Brenna's torn clothing. The dark-haired girl's expression was dazed and blank, her eyes bearing the coloring of shattered faith and trust.

"I am…no…I am not fine," she signed back eventually, wiping away tears and swallowing sobs. "It hurts. No, you will do no such thing. A man like that does not deserve a wife. He is trying to frighten you. I do not believe he would do it to you…he does not want to hurt you. He is an angry, spoiled child, use to having his way. He is living as Neth taught him…"

The room was quiet then as the princess fetched one of her own gowns for her friend and brought the washbasin for Brenna to clean herself. As Brenna dressed, Deidre disposed of the torn dress in the fire and cleaned the blood from the stone floor as best she could. It would not do for Lady Muriel, or anyone else, to ask questions. When she turned her attention back to her friend, Brenna was curled up asleep on the divan, a pillow beneath her head stained with tears. The princess barred the doors, closed the shutters, and waited in the darkness, considering the options for her future and Brenna's.

By the time the dark-haired girl awoke, it was nearly nightfall. She jerked up in a panic but only the princess was with her, sitting alone by the fire, watching her with large, sad eyes. She came to the bed and signed when she saw that her friend was awake.

"I cannot leave you, milady," Brenna replied. "I am supposed to be your servant. He could execute me…yes…I suppose I could be." She had not considered that possibility. "You are right; he cannot be given an heir…though he might not recognize an illegitimate child as his. He would blame someone else. No child deserves such a father. Where can I…? Arlan…" It was the only possible answer that might allow her to save herself.

Deidre looked at her with wide eyes.

"Yes…he is still alive. I do not know where he is…but he is alive. He knows what is happening here…he will come for you, milady. He will not let the King hurt you." She had to believe that, and more importantly, the princess had to believe it. "I could go to Chantel while I wait for him; I have an aunt near there. Perhaps she will know…if I go before the gate closes…yes…" She moved slowly, her whole body aching and stiff. "In the Purification Chamber…in the oratory. Leave messages there…he will get them, I promise. Tell him where I have gone…we will find each other and will come for you."

They did not gather any of Brenna's belongings. She took what she wore, one other dress from the princess' closet, a cloak, boots, and gloves as protection from the cold. Deidre pressed a coin pouch into her hands.

"Are you sure I should leave you, milady? I will stay if you think I…yes…very well. Take care, my friend. May k'Ádhá bless you…"

She hugged the princess tight but the blonde-haired woman pushed her away and into the corridor. The longer Brenna tarried, the less chance she had to get away. The King would eventually look for her, either to punish her or to apologize; it was hard to guess which. Deidre watched her go, noticing the awkward way Brenna moved. This had to be the right thing to do. Brenna could not stay, and if she were right that the King meant Deidre no harm, the princess would be in no more danger with Brenna safely away then she was with her here. She was a woman. She must prove she could fend for herself. Even against the King.

☙*❧

The white, silver-tailed kestrel circled the figure that lay face down in the fresh blanket of early first-month snow. He could not tell how long she had been there, but there was a light dusting of snow on her back so he knew she had been there long enough for the last snow to leave its print. It had stopped snowing over thirty minutes ago. She had to have been there at least that long. After a final circle, the bird swooped into the shelter of the trees; Kavan emerged in his true form moments later and approached the woman cautiously, looking around for anyone who could either assist or harm them that he had not spotted from the air.

He felt for her pulse. She was still alive but desperately in need of shelter and warmth. The nearest Gate he knew of was several hours away; that was an impractical solution, but where else could he take her? Removing his cloak, he brushed the snow from her hair and skin and wrapped her snuggly. He removed his gloves and melted snow in his hands using the power within himself, and then poured some through her cracked lips, trying to make her drink. There were no visible injuries beyond the effect of prolonged exposure to the cold, but when he first touched the skin of her face, he recoiled in revulsion. Her pain flooded him, engulfing him in its horror. Forcing himself to touch her again to make her drink, he sought the source of her distress while doing his best to block that fear and pain.

How could any man do such a thing to an innocent girl, he wondered? He held her to his chest, wanting to protect her from what had already happened, to take her pain away. He had heard of such things, but in his sheltered world, he had never encountered it. Such violent crimes as rape were extremely rare in Elyriá. She had come from the palace five days earlier, had ridden part of the way on a wagon and then had walked the rest. As he studied her face, wondering what she was doing here, the image of Guthrie McHador formed within his head and then faded.

Yes. That was why he recognized her. He could take her to the former general. The man's cabin was not far; it was her best hope of survival. Leaving his cloak wrapped around her, he lifted her with ease and trudged through the snow towards the desired haven.

He had not seen Prince Arlan since Bowen's death had left Girvin King of Enesfel two years earlier. Kavan continued to go to the lake as he always had, hoping the prince would come, would find him there, would change his mind about never wanting to see the harper again, but Prince Arlan had not come. Many times Kavan had approached the shelter the prince called home, but he never asked for entry. He had been unable to bring himself to intrude where he was not wanted. Now, however, he felt he had no choice. This young woman needed them. But as he stood in front of the cabin, looking at the door with trepidation, he had to force himself to knock, had to suppress the urge to leave before anyone found him there.

Prince Arlan did not respond to the knocking, though he did slide his chair a bit further from the door. Since Guthrie was not there, and the prince did not want to risk being recognized, he ignored the sound and refused to open the door. It was not Ártur's usual signal; therefore, it must be a stranger. When the knock became a bang, as if someone was kicking the door, the prince leapt from his seat, grabbed Guthrie's sword, and prepared for a fight if someone should burst into the room.

"Prince Arlan. Open the door. Please."

The prince's heart caught in his throat and he coughed as he choked and fought for air. How he had longed to hear that beautiful voice during the past two years. But along with that longing returned the anger and the sense of betrayal he had felt on the last day that they had seen each other. Not his friend, he told himself again, though the mere knowledge of the bard's proximity beyond the door took more edge off that irritation than he expected. He realized he was not as angry anymore, and shook away the shiver. Kavan would not force entry into the house to see him. The prince was sure of that. Thus he forced himself to return to eating, trying to ignore the man even when the knock came again. Then again.

"Go away!" the prince finally shouted in tearful frustration. "I do not want to talk to you."

Kavan sighed, swallowing his own despair and pain to do what needed to be done. "My Prince...I would not trouble you...but I have a lady with me, come from the palace. I found her in the snow not far from here. If you do not let me bring her inside, she may die from exposure. Please open the door. For her sake."

The prince's hesitation was brief. There were not many women in the palace likely to come in this direction except Lady Weylin, and perhaps his sister. If either of them had come, it had to be too important to wait for Ártur to deliver a message. Despite his annoyance with the bard, he knew the Elyri would not lie to him to see him, else he would have done it long before.

Cautiously he opened the door. Kavan's paleness against the backdrop of darkness and falling snow was eerie. And though he had not seen her in many years, he knew the young woman in Kavan's arms had to be Lady Weylin.

"What happened? Where did you find her?"

"No questions yet," Kavan replied as he stepped into the warmth and light of the cabin. "She must be made warm and will need food and water. Is there a bed where I may put her? Extra blankets?"

The prince nodded and hurried to provide the things that Kavan requested, all past animosity forgotten for the moment. Taking care of Brenna was more important than that disagreement, and the truth was, seeing Kavan again had stripped the last of the animosity away. Arlan was relieved to see him, although he was not yet inclined to admit it.

Guthrie saw the footprints that led to the cabin, with only his own leading away from it, and frowned. Whomever these fresh one's belonged to, it was not Prince Arlan's. They were too small and narrow. With his hand on his dagger, he carefully approached the door, listening to the sounds of the night, smelling the air for any trace of something that should not be there. Smoke curled from the chimney and from the outside there looked to be nothing amiss. When he pushed open the creaky door, he noticed nothing unusual within either, only the prince's meal abandoned on the table. Arlan's voice drifted from the back room and a softer, unknown voice replied. Perhaps it was Ártur, but the instincts that had kept Guthrie alive through innumerable battles told him this was not the healer in his home. Irritated and concerned that the prince had disobeyed him and allowed someone into the cabin, he closed the door loudly enough that the sound brought the prince to him.

"How many times…"

He was unable to finish as the prince interrupted, "Brenna's been hurt, Guthrie. Kavan brought her to us."

The older man heard only his niece's name before pushing past to see for himself that she was here. He did not recognize the stranger in the room as anything other than Elyri. "Brenna…" he groaned, sinking onto the edge of the bed and clasping her cold hands. "What has happened?"

Kavan stepped back to not interfere. "She is…I cannot speak for her physical condition, for I am not a healer. She has spent many hours in the cold and seems not to have eaten in several days. She has been…she may be with child…" It was difficult to say those words. There was no doubt in Kavan's mind that she was, but he saw no reason to confirm it until she was aware of it herself.

"She is not that sort of lady, sir…" Guthrie protested with a growl.

"Indeed. It was not…she was…" Uncomfortable with the admission, he finished, "King Owain is responsible," as if that was answer enough.

Guthrie clutched the smaller hands tight, letting the words sink in, ignoring the man who had spoken them. There was no mercy for anyone, he thought bitterly. She had been their link to the castle and the princess's brightest hope for survival, and most importantly, she was Guthrie's blood kin. He had put her into that place. His only desire was to care for her and exact revenge from Owain, but how did one do that from a King without an army behind him?

When Kavan left the bedroom to give the man privacy, the prince, who had been standing in the doorway, followed him, though Kavan wished he had not. He did not think Prince Arlan had put the past behind them, and Kavan was not quick to forget the pain of rejection either. He picked up the cloak he had wrapped around Brenna, and as he placed it around his shoulders and clasped it in place he said, "I will go, My Prince, and inform Ártur of what has happened. He will come as quickly as he can to be certain the lady is well."

"You will do no such thing," the prince snorted, moving to block Kavan's path to the door. "It is too cold and the storm is growing worse. You will end up like her."

Surprised by the gesture, Kavan's steps faltered, as did his resolve to leave. "I will not be harmed. I will be home before the storm is a threat. Do not be troubled for my well-being. It is not your concern."

Though the bard tried to keep his voice even, the prince heard the sad quaver nonetheless. Or at least, he believed he did, perhaps because he wanted to hear it. He looked away in embarrassment and relaxed his stance. He had not realized how deeply his behavior, his avoidance, might have hurt the other man. He had been too busy believing Kavan did not care. Not for the first time, he considered that Kavan had not been the one responsible for the extended distance between them.

In a low voice, he replied, "It is my concern. I will have no friend of mine killing himself in this weather. You may have your cloak, but that will be little protection from the worst of the elements." Kavan glanced at his hands, knowing those words were not quite true, though he knew the prince had no reason to think otherwise. "I have been a fool..."

The bard shook his head. "No, you have not, My Prince..."

"Yes, I have. Do not argue with me; I am a prince, as you say…though not your prince…" He tried to grin but the attempt at levity fell flat. "You did not consent to teach me simply to make me King. I have known that for the last two years but was too much a stubborn fool to admit it, especially to myself. You spent time with me because I was your friend, as you were mine…isn't that so?"

"I…"

The prince began to pace, not waiting for Kavan to finish. "You know it is. I have been to the lake many times, listened to your music…but was unable to face you. My pride kept me from it. That, and I thought you would hate me for behaving like a selfish child."

"You are a prince; you have the right to do with me as you see fit…" Kavan started, even though that knowledge did not take the pain away.

The prince snorted again. "My social status does not give me the right to mistreat a foreigner without just cause. It does not give me the right to throw a tantrum because I did not like what you had to say. Nor does it give me the right to abuse my friends. You are still my friend…aren't you?" He stopped in front of the fire and stared at it for several long quiet minutes as Kavan remained where he was, not moving, only staring at his hands. The prince was hoping for an answer from the bard but did not really expect one. He believed the answer was yes, even if Kavan could not put voice to it. "Kavan…why…?"

Relieved with what he hoped was a change of topic, that he did not have to answer the previous question, Kavan looked up and asked, "Why what, My Prince?"

"Why everything? Why did you wait for me? Why was I stubborn and foolish? Why have all of these evils befallen Enesfel? Why did Owain…rape her?"

Not certain that his answers would suffice, Kavan sighed. "I do not know why King Owain did what he did. From what I have heard he is…unstable. His years in Neth have likely colored his outlook and warped his behavior. You will have to ask the lady what happened, and she may not want to talk about it for a long time. She may not even know why he acted this way. He might not have had a reason. And the things that have happened to Enesfel…each man has free will, Arlan. Some choose the path of harm, or selfishness, or apathy, not realizing that when they are men of power, their choices affect everyone in the land." He shifted his weight and clenched his hands nervously. "As for your…you are strong-willed. I think it is an inherent family trait, as your brothers and your father exhibited it too. It is not necessarily a bad thing; it may save your life someday, or guide you down a just and honest path…but if left unchecked, it could also destroy you the way it did Bowen."

Prince Arlan nodded. "Yes…Guthrie has said it as well." He waited for Kavan to continue, and when he did not, the prince prodded, "What about the other?"

Kavan did not look at him. He did not want to answer, but knew he would be hounded if he did not. "I frequently go to the lake to practice and compose. You know this; I have been going there since I was a boy."

"You were waiting for me. I felt it. I know it. I've known it all along. There must be a reason…"

"Must there? Not everything has a…"

"So…" Guthrie sounded weak and tired as he came back into the main room, cutting Kavan off, bringing an abrupt but welcome end to the conversation about his feelings.

"Is she asleep?" Kavan asked, keeping his gaze averted from the prince's disappointed face.

The ex-general nodded once. "Yes. How do you know the King violated her? Did she tell you?"

"I found her in the snow, about a mile from here. When I rolled her over to see if she lived, when I touched her face, I felt her pain…saw his face as she had seen it. This was the only place I could think of that was near enough for her, if she were to live. Knowing she is your niece, I deduced she was likely seeking you; it seemed wisest to bring her here."

Guthrie took a chair near the fire and leaned forward with his elbows on his knees. "How do you know who she is? Who I am? How did you find us here?"

"He is Ártur's cousin, Guthrie," the prince answered before Kavan had the chance.

Enesfel's former highest-ranking general stared long at Kavan, searching for something familiar, and then nodded when the recollection came to mind. Yes, the face was familiar now that Guthrie knew something about him. The last time he had seen Kavan, the Elyri had been a small boy, but there was no forgetting the white skin, the pale hair, and the emerald of his eyes. His gaze turned from Kavan onto Prince Arlan. "I suppose he is what took you away from the cabin for hours on end? Why did you stop?"

The prince shuffled his feet, embarrassed that his mentor had noticed, and wondered what he should say. This time Kavan spared him the need to speak. "Ártur never spoke to me of your location, milord, if that is what you fear. I spend a great deal of time at a nearby lake and that is where the prince found me. He was in no danger. I made certain of that."

Hoping to redirect any potential wrath and not wanting to explain his foolishness, the prince interrupted, "Kavan has been a wise teacher and a good friend…though I have treated him abysmally for his kindness," he ended with a sigh. "Are you angry with me?" The question was directed at both men, although he looked only at Guthrie as he spoke.

"Angry? Guthrie shook his head at the strangeness of this turn of events. Judging by the way the prince had grown under this man's tutelage, it seemed it had been in the prince's benefit. "No…I cannot say I am angry…but this is most peculiar…"

Kavan stiffened and his head snapped towards the fire in the middle of Guthrie's words, making the other two stare with concern. "Kavan?" asked the prince, but the Elyri did not respond. What he was seeing in his mind's eye was not in the room with them, but it would be very soon.

"Riders…approaching from the west…from Rhidam. Six of them. They are searching for her…following her trail…the storm delays them but they draw nearer…and they will come here." He blinked, ignoring the throbbing in his head, and looked at Guthrie as he came out of the trance with his vision clear. "Do you have horses?"

"One," Guthrie replied, already on his feet. He had spent enough years in Ártur's acquaintance to know not to take an Elyri's premonitions lightly. Besides, was not this the same cousin who had given Ártur the warning that had caused the healer to return to Rhidam in time to spare the prince's life after the first assassination attempt?

One horse would have to do. "Is there anywhere else you can go? Somewhere defensible. If you are here when they arrive, you will both be in grave danger. Caves? Anything?" Leaving would create tracks in the snow, but with enough of a head start, they might be able to remain safe.

"The only thing near are the ruins of a village where Ártur meets me…" Guthrie gathered belongings into a sack as he spoke.

"Maybe that will mean a route of escape. We will have to take that chance. You must lead, Lord McHador, as I have not been there. It will be slow in the storm, but it may be our best chance." He briefly considered staying behind, a decoy to throw the soldiers off, but if his hunch was right, staying with them would afford them more protection and have less chance of their capture or harm.

To no one in particular, Guthrie muttered, "They will follow our tracks in the snow…unless we are fortunate enough to have the snow fill them…"

"We can hope. Lord McHador, if you will take the lady on horse-back, I will bring Prince Arlan…"

The prince, left out of the preparations and planning as the older men took charge of the situation, crossed his arms, and shook his head. "I'm not going anywhere until someone tells me what is happening." "This is not the time to be stubborn, Arlan," Guthrie chastised gruffly. "Do as he says. Get the things we must have, things that would identify us if left behind. I have a feeling…" he looked at Kavan, "we may not be back. Kavan, if you will tend my niece, I will get the horse, and if you can…let me know what is happening with our uninvited visitors."

Fifteen minutes later the horse was ready and everything Arlan could carry had been gathered together. Blankets, food, and water, since it seemed they were to undertake a long journey, and what few personal belongings they had. Kavan wrapped Brenna in the bed linens and carried her outside to where the ex-general waited on the horse. He lifted her for the man to take and helped them get adjusted. "Go. We shall follow."

Guthrie started to speak, but after having told the prince not to argue or question Kavan's instructions, he chose not to. He chose instead to trust the stranger to keep them safe. He spurred his horse into action and started to the southeast through the trees.

"We will never keep up with them," the prince grumbled as he watched the horse disappear. When Kavan did not respond as expected, he turned to see that in Kavan's place stood a tall, snowy white hart, the size of which Prince Arlan had never seen. The animal nudged his hand with its warm nose and came to its knees so that its back was at an easy level for the young man to climb on. Its eyes were the greenest Arlan had ever seen in an animal…as green as Kavan's eyes. And the bard was not there. The prince's courage faltered. Could this be Kavan? The animal nudged him again. In spite of his fear, the prince hesitantly climbed onto the animal's back, clutching the belongings he carried. When he was settled, the hart rose to its feet and bounded in the direction the horse had gone, circled back to the cabin once, and then followed the horse again, with the prince clinging to his neck for fear of falling off.

The six horsemen stopped before the cabin. Horse and deer tracks led away from the structure, the largest deer tracks any of them could imagine. After arguing over who would search the cabin and who would follow the tracks of what must be the legendary white hart, three riders followed the trail and three took to investigating the small dwelling. It was deserted, but the logs still smoldered from a doused fire and a half-eaten bowl of lukewarm stew remained on the table. Everything of importance or value appeared to be missing, or perhaps the inhabitants owned nothing of interest. As far as any could determine, it was a hunter's or woodsman's cabin, but the military insignia pin one of the three produced from the back room indicated that no simple hunter lived here. No simple hunter owned an insignia like this. Very few in Enesfel's military had ever held this rank. If this was who each man thought it might be, it was worth waiting for the occupant's return. There might be a large bounty for this man, or at least they might gain favor for finding him, even if they failed to find the girl they had been sent to bring back to Rhidam.

The snow was coming down in furious flurries when the hart stopped near the ruins, out of sight of Guthrie to reduce time-wasting questions. Once the prince slid off and landed in a heap in the snow, the hart reverted to its natural form and Kavan offered a hand to the younger man. Prince Arlan refused to take it, got to his feet on his own, and followed Kavan through the trees. He might not have followed, but he was more afraid of what was behind them then what could be in front of them, or even of the man he followed. The bard he had thought he knew, this night's events, and what his future held, were all matters the prince would have to contemplate later. Nearly twenty minutes had passed; they did not know how long they had before they were caught.

"Here," Guthrie called when he saw them emerge from the trees nearby. If seeking safety was not immediately imperative, he would have asked his own questions of the Elyri. "This is where Ártur meets me."

Extending his senses around him, Kavan followed the static prickle in the air until he located what he had hoped to find. He wondered how Ártur had known this was here. "Praise, k'Ádhá," he murmured breathlessly, stooping to brush the snow from the patch of ground where the sensation emanated the strongest. There were symbols carved into the stone beneath his hands, unfamiliar and strange, but the energy signature indicated a Gate. Touching the power source gave him a jolt, causing him to jerk his hands away, but the jolt was not unpleasant and served as a boost to his own stores of energy.

"What?" The prince was shivering from cold, shock, and apprehension. He had known all of his life that Elyri were different; stories about them were plentiful and varied and nearly always fantastical, but this night was proving how little he knew. He had considered the bard a man, nothing more. He knew he was wrong. There was nothing to be seen in these ruins except crumbling stone walls, the shadows of trees on the white earth, and snow. Perhaps, he worried, Kavan was mad.

"It is a k'rylag…a Gate. There is no time to explain. The longer we tarry, the more likely we will be caught. I have never taken a Teren through, but I can do it. It will have to be one of you at a time." Kavan thought he could take more than one through, but these lives were too important to risk experimentation.

Guthrie did not see a gate of any sort he was familiar with, but still he said, "Whatever it is, take Arlan first. I have done nothing wrong; they have no reason to harm me. And I can defend Brenna. But Arlan must be kept safe. Whatever you are going to do, do it quickly." Again, he was putting his trust in this stranger, only now he was praying that he was not making a mistake.

Kavan pulled the prince towards him, placed the boy's hands palms up, and placed his own on top, palms to palms. "Trust me, My Prince. I will not harm you. Clear your mind of everything. Relax. Think of music, or sunshine, or something peaceful...and nothing else..."

The prince felt a warm mist swirl around him, warmth where there had been cold, and he tensed, too terrified by the disassociation he felt between mind and body to form actual thought. Despite that tension, Kavan was able to make the connection to where he wanted to be, and when the mist cleared around them to be replaced by the night's chill once again, they were no longer amidst the ruins but in a small, cramped room. Kavan motioned for silence, listened to the night for several moments, and then led him out. The prince guessed, judging from the pyre icon on the wall, that the humble building they were in was a náós, but he could not imagine how they had gotten there.

"Stay here. Do not move or speak to anyone. I will return as quickly as I can."

The process was repeated with Brenna, as Guthrie watched and wondered what was happening. This had to be how Ártur came to him, from wherever he lived, but where had Kavan taken the prince? To Ártur? How could a man vanish into the air and reappear within moments?

Horses whinnied in the distance and his prayers for safety intensified. He was not a particularly religious man, but if there was any power in the universe that might be interested in his well-being and the future of the kingdom, perhaps that power might listen to him. Kavan's sudden reappearance startled him; the bard could hear the sounds of men and horses drawing nearer as he materialized. Judging from the proximity of the sound, there was no time to initiate the Gate and be gone before their pursuers arrived. A diversion was needed.

With a lunge, the Elyri transformed before Guthrie's eyes into a massive, silvery wolf. Guthrie backed hastily away from the beast with a sinking sensation. This had been a trap. This man was not an ally but had harmed the prince. He tried to draw his sword but stumbled into a snowdrift and watched as the wolf charged the horse he had ridden. The animal reared and pounded off, herded in the direction of the approaching riders, through the previously made tracks, marring their precision making it impossible to tell who or what had passed.

The three riders pulled their mounts to a stop as they saw the terrified horse plunging towards them, followed by a large wolf. The canine stopped to look at the riders, out of range of any weapons they might have, and then loped back towards the ruins, leaving the party to regroup, and one man to remount after the crazed, unmanned horse plowed through their ranks and knocked him into the snow.

"Come." Kavan returned to Guthrie and pulled him out of the snow where he had fallen. "You heard the instructions I gave Prince Arlan. Relax. If you do not…if you fight me…please, Lord McHador…"

But Guthrie would not relax and instead struggled within the grasp of slender arms of incredible strength. Kavan had no choice. If he did not act, there would be no chance of escape. Through their bodily contact, he reached into the ex-general's psyche, touched a small corner of his mind, and the man's weight quickly slumped against Kavan. "I apologize for this, sir," he murmured as the transporting mist gathered around them.

By the time the three riders entered the scatter of brick and stone, only footprints, equine, canine, and some Teren were all that remained. The trail had ended.

Ártur awoke from his dreams with a start. It was snowing heavily outside and the room was bitterly cold as if he had forgotten to close the window. He did not want to leave the warmth of his bed, but the need to check the window nagged at him until he reluctantly got up. The window was not open, however, yet still the chill would not leave him, and as he stood with his hand on the window latch, he thought he heard Kavan calling to him. Such a summons warranted investigation, but after going to his cousin's room, the oratory, the sitting room, and finally the back garden, Ártur could see that Kavan was not home. It was late, too late for him to be out unless something was troubling him and he had gone to the náós.

Náós. That was it. The healer dressed and left the house, grumbling about the cold as he trudged across town. This had better be important, he thought to himself, knowing that it had to be even as the thought came forth. Kavan's mind had not reached out to his in such a way in a very long time, not since he was a boy when Ártur was employed in Rhidam. As he opened the náós door and saw the gathering in front of the altar, he knew at once why he had been summoned and how important the situation was. Brenna lay in her blankets, and beside her, Guthrie appeared to be asleep. Prince Arlan was the only one standing, his expression dazed but he seemed unharmed.

"Ártur," Kavan said without turning to face him. He knelt beside Guthrie, his hand on the man's forehead.

"May I ask...?"

The bard interrupted him. "I found Lady Weylin in the snow near their cabin; she has been badly mistreated by the King. The cabin was the closest place to take her to get her out of the cold, but there were soldiers following from Rhidam. Lord McHador led me to the ruins you use; I brought them here to keep them safe. There was nowhere else to go. Lord McHador fought my attempts to bring him through..."

Kneeling between the two prone figures, the healer examined Guthrie and knew he was well, only sleeping as Kavan indicated. He cast a look of awe at his cousin, as such a feat was something not many other than healers could do. Instead of asking questions, he turned his attention to Brenna and scowled. "I will take her to the house. It is too cold here, and it will raise questions for others to find them here like this. Lord McHador is too awkward to carry, so if you will stay with him until he wakes…"

Kavan nodded but did not speak. He retreated to his favorite kneeling spot, bowed his head, and clasped the Kílyn Cross pendant in his hand. He wanted to help, had done what he believed best, taken the only available options he could see, but awareness of the way the prince's eyes bore into him as Ártur went out with Brenna made Kavan wonder if he had, perhaps, been wrong.

"What are you doing?"

"Praying."

"For what?"

Surprised that Prince Arlan was speaking to him, Kavan squeezed his eyes shut and replied, "Guidance. Strength. Understanding."

Footsteps broke the silence as the prince approached and sat beside him. "You are right. I do not understand. Where are we? How did we get here? How did Ártur know we were here? What will happen to us?"

Kavan exhaled slowly. "We are in Hes Índári Náós, in Bhryell."

"Elyriá?" the prince asked in a whisper.

Seeing that his prayers would be postponed until the prince had his answers, Kavan shifted off of his knees and lifted his head. "Yes. There are Gates, ways of traveling great distances in a very short amount of time. They were built long ago, either by my people or by those who came before. Most of them are not used any longer; my people do not even know where most of them are, and most of us do not know how to use them. Never before, to my knowledge, have Teren been told about them, except perhaps for a rare few who live in

Elyriá. You should not know about them, but there was no other choice if I was to keep you safe. Your welfare was my first priority."

Embarrassed, the prince lowered his gaze. "Are there Gates in the castle? Is that how Ártur took me to Guthrie? I was asleep in my bed, with my mother nearby, and when I awoke, I was no longer in Rhidam."

Kavan sighed, thinking about the Rhidam castle for the first time in a long time. "Yes, there are Gates there, but I do not know for certain that Ártur used one."

The prince seemed to accept that answer because he nodded his head and looked around him for several quiet minutes. "I apologize…for being…I have always known Elyri are different. Everyone has said it. But I never knew how different…"

"I am more different then you realize, My Prince, unlike any other you will likely meet…you are afraid of me." Kavan hoped that honest statement did not convey the fullness of sorrow behind it.

Prince Arlan began to deny it and then shrugged his shoulders. "I think I have cause to be. I have seen Ártur work, but I have never seen anything like what you have done tonight. If you were me, if you had never heard of such things, wouldn't you be intimidated the first time you encountered it? It is not that I do not trust you; you have gone to great lengths to prove yourself. You have been my friend, respected my foolish demand for distance, and saved Brenna's life. Mine too. Next time, however, try to tell me ahead of time what you plan to do. That way, I shall be better prepared."

"Next time?" It had not occurred to Kavan that there could be a next time.

"If Brenna is here, my sister is alone. After what has happened to Brenna, I do not think my sister is safe in Rhidam. We cannot take her out of there the way I was taken out, as much as I wish it, for that is likely to start a war. Owain may not have any knowledge of what you can do, but after his time in Neth, he might be inclined to blame anything inexplicable on your people, or he might retaliate against Enesfel the way Bowen did. I don't want to be responsible for either outcome." He looked at Guthrie as the man shifted in his slumber. "If I am to help my sister, I am going to need your help. I cannot overthrow Owain; he is in line before me, regardless of who our fathers were. He is already King. I can challenge him, gain the backing of the people perhaps, but a coup seems unlikely to accomplish anything. I think the best I can hope for is convincing Owain to accept me as the next heir to the throne…with you, Guthrie, and Ártur there to help keep me safe, I'll be in a better position to protect Deidre. I will discuss it at length with Guthrie and see what plan we can devise. If I am to step into a vipers' nest, I want people with me I can trust. Guthrie, Brenna, Ártur, and you. Especially you. Say you will aide me, Kavan. I cannot do this without you. Please."

There was no doubt in Kavan's mind as he listened to those words. The time had come to face destiny head on. There was a sick feeling in his stomach as he realized fate was catching up to him. Did he want to go to Enesfel? Did he want to do what needed to be done? Could he do it? Did he have a choice?

"If that is what My Prince wants…"

The prince took his hands and held them fast. "I am not your prince. I am Enesfel's prince…as you said. You are not of Enesfel…but you are my friend. It is what your friend asks of you, nothing more."

Kavan looked into the carved eyes of Dhágdhuán on the wall above him, unable to sustain the prince's gaze for fear of weeping. A friend. "As you wish, Arlan. If I may be of service to you…I will be."

ॐ*ॐ

King Owain was not having a good day. Breakfast had left him feeling ill that morning and he had dismissed the cook out of spite. His confrontation with Deidre had not improved his mood either. With Lady Weylin gone, having no one to defend her, the princess was exhibiting a surge of independence, stubbornness, and determination that she had never shown before. When she refused to see him and again turned down his request for marriage, he had, in a fit of rage, thrown her into the dungeon. The household guard had taken her there reluctantly, particularly when they saw the strength and pride the beautiful girl showed in the face of the King's fury. Enough time had passed that Owain regretted his actions, but stubbornness kept him from releasing her. She had to be shown who was in control. He had to show her he was king. He could not let her think of him as weak and easily swayed.

As his six scouts returned from their quest seemingly empty-handed, he knew his day was only going to get worse.

"Report."

One of the six stepped forward. "We followed Lady Weylin towards Chantel, as you bid, but none in the town had seen her, not even her kin. We searched for her. As we were leaving, we met a trapper who claimed to have seen a young woman walking alone; he offered her aid but she refused. We followed his instructions, and footprints in the snow, to a cabin, but no one was there. We did, however, find this." The insignia he carried was placed into the King's hand.

King Owain knew the rank of that pin. Lord General McLeu wore his daily. If it had belonged to a previous Lord General, such an heirloom would have been kept within his family. While there was no proof of which individual this might belong to, the cold pit in the King's stomach nagged at him, reminding him that it likely belonged to Lord General Guthrie McHador. He was the last man to hold that rank, the only other likely to still be living. Owain had not known the man well, but his reputation made the name worth fearing.

"So," he coughed, "he is still alive." The soldiers looked at one another, puzzled. "Lady Weylin is his niece…or so I was told…going to him would be logical…but I thought he would be dead by now. I heard he left the court due to ill health." He clutched the pin in one hand and rubbed the back of his neck with the other. "She had to know that the Weylin estates would be the first places I would look…but no one would think to look for a man thought dead. No one was there, you say?"

Another one of the six shook his head and replied, "There was evidence of a fire on the hearth; whoever was there left not long before we arrived. Perhaps she knew she was being followed and they fled together. We tracked them as far as the ruins of Clebhest, but though there was a horse there, there was no sign of anyone."

The King refused to pace, despite the sick, nervous feeling that clawed at him. There was nothing Lady Weylin could do to harm him, except give birth to an heir she could use against him someday. That fact had made him more eager than ever for marriage, but it seemed his behavior had cemented Princess Deidre's dislike. He could only hope that, in time, she would give in to his request to be free of the dungeon.

He told himself he did not fear McHador. The general could do little to him. The man was old, surely, and lacked resources that could threaten a king. But in the back of his mind, there was a nagging alarm that refused to be silenced; he ordered a reward posted for McHador's arrest and decided not to tell the princess of these developments. It might strengthen her convictions that she could get out of this marriage. The King was more determined now that she would be his, McHador be damned.

৯চChapter 20৯৯

S haking out his damp cloak, Kavan rested near the fire of an empty, dilapidated tavern in the Enesfel town of Tarsee near the Neth border. Despite the proximity to Neth, the residents of Tarsee and other settlements in Northern Enesfel were mostly untainted by the Elyri hatred of their northern neighbor, or by the fluctuating beliefs of the crown in Rhidam. The necessity of trade with Elyriá had made these towns more sympathetic than others. It was in these cities and villages bordering Elyriá that Kavan had decided to start his role in the venture Prince Arlan had chosen to undertake.

Brenna's child would be born soon, the bard realized as he removed his new boots. She had not been particularly strong throughout the pregnancy and had spent a great deal of her time bed-ridden. As soon as she was up to it afterward, however, assuming she lived, she and the prince were to be wed. This would give the child a father, protect Brenna and the infant from King Owain, and give Prince Arlan a much-needed consort and heir, things that would be to his benefit because they were things Enesfel's King did not have. That the two had decided to marry surprised and relieved Guthrie, but Kavan was not surprised at all. He had known it would happen from the moment that the two, now grown, had seen each other for the first time since childhood.

"Good evening, sir." A dowdy woman, her flaming red hair pulled into a high, tight bun on the back of her angular head, appeared in the doorway to his left. "Is there something I can get for you?"

"Water, if you please, and bread if you have it."

She stepped behind the counter. Such a pretty face, she mused, though she refrained from speaking her opinion aloud. Elyri, as a rule, were beautiful people, but this one was exceptional. Perhaps it was his paleness or the green of his eyes. "You have a travel-weary look about you, sir; rather cold out to be walking, don't you think?" Kavan nodded. "Also dangerous for one of your persuasion, but I suppose you know that. What brings you to Tarsee?"

The bit of small talk with a stranger made him smile. Small talk with passersby was something he experienced very little of in Bhryell. "I am a harper, milady. I am looking for places to play." She came to the table with a mug, half a loaf of bread, a slab of cheese, and a tin pitcher of water. Those were set on the table before him and she glanced at the case containing his harp. "Do you know of anyone who could use my services for an evening or two?"

Her returned smile was heartwarming. "I think we could use you right here. We haven't had any excitement in a good long while, at least none of a pleasant variety. Can't afford to pay you, but I can offer room and board if you keep yourself out of trouble."

"I intend no harm to anyone. Your offer is most generous. Thank you." Coin would be helpful during his travel, but he was content living off of the generosity of his hosts. Food and shelter were all he truly needed.

The woman liked his smile and his voice and decided that this night might be more promising than usual with him here. After showing him to a vacant room, she had a bath drawn for him, something normally provided to only the wealthiest guests, brought his meal to his room to allow him to finish eating in private, and later called him down to the tavern as the evening patrons began to trickle in. She bustled about in anticipation, having made the establishment cleaner and more festive than it had been in many years. This attractive young man should bring in much business for however long he stayed. She did not have to hear him play to know this. The fact that he was an Elyri bard was enough.

She was right. On his first night alone, her small establishment had more customers than she could count. Not since King Donal's death had an Elyri musician wandered Enesfel. It had been even longer since one of this man's talents had traveled here. His repertoire was a blend of popular tunes and original compositions, all sublimely executed. Though he sang little, his voice was divinely clear and exquisite. Why some wealthy family did not employ such a musician, his audience could only guess, for they saw his talent, wisdom, and humility as something far greater than they had witnessed in their lifetimes. Long after the tavern closed for the night, the townsfolk lingered outside talking to the stranger. To the innkeeper, he seemed all too eager to entertain them.

He was. In Elyriá, a musician, no matter how talented, ran the risk of being just another musician. Kavan had gained national honors more than once, had won the showcase two years in a row before choosing not to attend again, and he was frequently invited to the sprawling capital of his country to perform for both the High Mother and the hierarchy of the Faith. He usually declined such offers from all but the High Mother, feeling that the majority of politicians, religious leaders, and wealthy nobility did not appreciate or understand him. The pay was substantial and allowed him the sparse, simple life he led for a very long time between performances, and had allowed him to accumulate a savings he had never expected to have.

Here in this foreign land, among strangers who did not know his name or his face, he felt he could use his gifts to their fullest and know that he was appreciated, perhaps even needed, simply by gauging his audience's response. That these people were interested enough to set aside prejudices and take the time to speak with him made him feel light-hearted for the first time in his life.

He used this freedom of expression to accomplish two objectives. The first was on behalf of Prince Arlan. Kavan was to plant the seed of hope in these people that a savior would come, a prince who would rightfully lay claim to the throne and purge the taint of treason and despair from a weary, burdened land. Kavan mentioned no names, gave no details; he worded his tales and songs carefully enough that he could legitimately claim to be amusing and entertaining the crowd without malicious intent. As he traveled from town to town, he gradually felt the ideas germinating within his audience, the rebirth of hope and passion in their lives.

His second, more personal, objective was to reawaken the Faith in these people who had once carried it but had long ago forgotten what faith was. Neth had driven religion out of the land when they had ruled over much of the Five Sovereignties, but the roots of it still existed deep in the everyday lives of Enesfel's people. The stories were there, the morals and rules of life. Those things merely needed to be cultivated to bring Faith forth again. Rather than use coercion and preaching, things Kavan either did not believe in or felt he was unqualified to use, he relied on subtlety and the belief in leading by example. He was deeply pleased when he sensed that at least a few members of his audiences were taking these messages of faith home with them after every performance.

As his time in Enesfel passed, each new day proved as emotionally rich and intense for Kavan as had been his first in this new land. More and more often he found himself the center of attention wherever he went. Peasants and merchants alike came to him for advice, brought their children to him for blessing, and asked him to share his music. His reputation preceded him from town to town, each time producing ever-growing crowds. Before long, he began to realize that he was also gathering an unanticipated, and unwanted, following. He did not object to those who followed out of appreciation of his musical talent, and he appreciated the hospitality of his admirers. But there was something beneath that, something deeper that frightened him. Many had latched on to his reverence and spirituality and, in his eyes, were misinterpreting who and what he was. Nowhere did he feel free of the looks, the thoughts, the idea that he was somehow more holy than a mortal man should be, as many in Elyriá had grown to see him. The realization that he might never escape those sorts of rumors made Kavan scared and sad. He wanted only to be a man, not some sort of saint.

At the eastern edge of the vast torrid expanse of endless dull yellow sand on the west side of the Derkun Ridge, Ártur was having moderate success in his efforts to bring support to Prince Arlan's cause. There were few physicians among the Cíbhóló nomads, only shamans and elders trained in the medicine practices of the desert; in exchange for the healer's aid, Ártur gained a following of fifty-seven men and boys willing to assist the prince in any way they could. He was not surprised to not find more. Nomadic tribes were scattered throughout the vast wasteland and were difficult to reach. Word might spread in time, drawing others to the cause, but Ártur could only draw volunteers from the few tribes he came into contact with during his stay. Also, the Enesfel kings had done nothing to the nomads directly which might cause animosity, as the nomads did not fall under Enesfel's rule and normally kept to themselves. For the most part, the rulers of the Five Sovereignties ignored their existence. But there had once been extensive trade between the nomads and Elyriá, and with Elyri unable to pass safely through Enesfel, trade had almost ceased. For those men who offered Prince Arlan their services, anything that held the promise of increased trade and aid to their tribes would be welcome.

Ártur hoped it would draw others to their cause as well.

When nightfall made him cease work each day, as he lay down to sleep, Ártur often felt the touch of his cousin's mind, like he used to many years ago. Rather than shut him out as he had once done, however, each contact was now welcome. He was aware that Kavan's mood was growing more distracted, confused, and distressed but the healer did not possess the ability to respond over such a great distance. He could only set his thoughts to sympathy and hope Kavan derived comfort from it, and worry each day about what sort of trouble Kavan was facing. After several years of sharing a home, the healer missed his cousin desperately and wished with all of his heart that he could be there to help.

When it seemed he would find no further supporters amongst the Cíbhóló without waiting for other tribes to come to him, Ártur returned to Bhryell in the eighth month of Eltail, arriving before Brenna's baby was due. He found seventeen-year-old Arlan now sporting the start of a beard and learned that he and Brenna had chosen to marry as soon as she was healthy enough after the child's birth. Brenna almost welcomed the babe now, and had spent the passing months preparing not only clothing for it, but also those things that would someday become the prince's royal standard, the banners, cloak, clothing and other things he would need when it came time for the arduous expedition from Bhryell to Enesfel's crown seat. The prince had helped when he could, but most of his focus was spent studying military tactics, strategy and weapon use with the best minds Bhryell had to offer. The healer was satisfied with the young prince's initiative and diligence and prayed it would pay off.

Meanwhile, Guthrie acted as emissary to Hatu and Cordash. He could not travel freely in Enesfel for fear of recognition; he did not yet know there was a price on his head, but if he was seen, there would be questions, and it would only be a matter of time before the King came after him. Yet he refused to stay in Elyriá doing nothing more than keeping the prince company. He knew the rulers of both Hatu and Cordash, knew their court members, their politics, their customs, and he knew their ways of thinking. If anyone could sway them to back the prince, it was Guthrie.

Hatu proved ripe with volunteers and supporters for Prince Arlan when Guthrie sailed across the Bay of Phállá and landed on its shore. It was as expected. His reputation remained unblemished among those he had fought against. They knew him to be a man of honor, one who kept his word. Since King Donal's death, the tension between Enesfel and Hatu had gradually built, though had not yet come to a head. If what Guthrie claimed was true, if there was a Lachlan prince available willing to end the strife and restore good relations…even if that heir was one of King Farrell's bastards…then Perren's heir, King Geir, was a willing supporter. He could not yet amass an army to send north; King Owain would interpret such an action as one of aggression and would send his troops for a fight that Hatu could not afford or win. King Geir did, however, agree to lend support to the would-be usurper, whoever he was, and would be ready to send support troops when and if they were needed.

The ex-general did not have as much success in Cordash, however. It took him two months to gain an audience with King Ahern Valdis, but it was time he did not squander in idleness. He gathered rumors of King Owain's rule from members of the Cordashian court and the servants and staff who supported them. There were newly imposed taxes, a rise in executions of petty criminals, the stripping of lordly titles from all but five lords, and the repossession or apparent stealing of lands to consolidate and increase the royal holdings. If allowed to continue, it seemed likely that most of Enesfel would become Crown territory. Yet the King was doing all of this in a way that, from one angle, appeared legal and just. He clearly had more political savvy than his recent predecessors, even Kings Innis and Donal. While disapproving of his actions, Guthrie was forced to admire the way

Enesfel's King got things done. But the people of the land were growing unhappier; the wounds King Bowen had inflicted were still too
fresh for them to look dispassionately on their King.

There were also rumors that King Owain had imprisoned the princess, which would explain the lack of messages left for the healer. Despite Brenna's instruction for those messages, there had been none
there the few times the healer went to Rhidam, and eventually he had
given up trying to avoid the risk of being caught. Those who told Guthrie this rumor did not believe it was true, however. It had the air of
gossip, and Guthrie suspected that the original tale had involved the
princess's handmaiden, his niece Brenna. He had no doubts that the
King would have imprisoned Brenna, or worse, if she had not fled
Rhidam. But if she had not been imprisoned, why were no messages
left for them? Why had all communication with the palace ceased?

While many Cordashian compatriots were sympathetic to the need
for soldiers and supporters for the unidentified prince and most agreed
that Enesfel's King should not be allowed to continue pillaging the
kingdom unchecked, Cordash had problems of her own. Neth was becoming more aggressive and King Ahern was pooling his resources
into defense against them. He and Guthrie agreed that a mutual defense pact would be beneficial, but until the prince was identified and
established in Rhidam, the Cordashian King was not willing to risk
sending troops. In time, Guthrie might be willing to reveal the prince's
identity, but this early in their undertaking, he would not risk the news
getting into Owain's hands. King Ahern understood that precaution,
the dangers inherent in premature revelation, but he would not be
swayed. He did, however, promise refuge for the prince and his followers, should the need arise.

Guthrie came away from Cordash with a retired military captain
and eight young, untrained men who were looking for adventure outside their homeland. He was thankful that Hatu had pledged their

support and glad that Ártur had secured men who were even now making the pilgrimage from the desert into Enesfel to await the arrival of the one they were to serve. He hoped that, with whatever support they might glean in Enesfel, it would be enough to stand up to Enesfel's military machine.

❧*❧

Kavan awoke in terror, not knowing what had jolted him out of his slumber. He had not been dreaming, and he could sense nothing around him that should have caused alarm. The loft in which he slept was empty except for a field mouse building its nest in the fresh hay on which Kavan slept. It was dark, though approaching dawn, as he climbed from the loft and stopped to listen to the sound of cattle and horses wheezing and snuffling in the cold air. Fortunately, there had been no rain recently; it had made traveling easier. The elderly couple he encountered on the road had offered him food and shelter in exchange for entertainment and assistance repairing the fence around their cattle yard, a turn of events far better for Kavan then sleeping out beneath the stars in the cold would have been.

Outside the barn, he closed his eyes and turned his senses and body in the direction of the powerful, negative emotions he was feeling. The direction of home. The images formed and faded quickly, telling him what he wanted to know. The terror had come from Prince Arlan. Sighing, he looked into the graying sky to the east. He had hoped to be there for the birth of the child, but that would not be the case. By the time the sun topped the horizon, there would be a new Lachlan prince. For a brief moment, he Saw a glimpse of a battlefield, but he recognized none of the faces of the soldiers. Was it the child's future or some event currently transpiring, he wondered, doubting he would ever know?

"A boy, My Liege," Ártur said, coming from upstairs where Brenna's cries had ceased several minutes before to be replaced by the wailing of an infant. Now there was silence. He found Guthrie and the prince anxiously perched before the fire in the sitting room, the prince looking pale as if he would faint or be sick. None of his upbringing had prepared him for what he had been hearing. Arlan could not imagine anything good resulting from such an ordeal. Had his mother endured such trauma to bring him and his sister into the world? Despite Guthrie's assurances that Brenna would be well, the prince spent the entire time feeling horrified and sick. Brenna had been in such poor health during the pregnancy and seemed weak and frail to him. How could she possibly survive so much pain? Seeing Ártur's face, at last, the Prince was relieved it was over. Standing on legs that threatened collapse, he cast a quick, uneasy glance at Guthrie before asking, "How is she? Can I see her?"

Ártur clasped his shoulder. "She is tired but healthy…and she would appreciate it if you did."

The dark haired girl appeared exhausted and pale but smiled when the prince entered and held the baby towards him. He hesitated, having never dealt with a child before, but noting Brenna's eager expression, he wanted to please her; he took a deep breath and took the child from her. The infant, small and wrinkled and endlessly squirming, was quite pink, its full head of wet curls quite blonde. Deidre and Cordelia had been blonde, but he believed that anyone looking at Muir Innis Lachlan would know that Prince Arlan was not his father. He had prayed that the child would be blessed with Brenna's dark hair. That such was not the case disappointed him. Managing a weak smile, he gave the baby back to its mother, kissed her mouth as he stroked her hair, and then walked out of the room, down the stairs, past Guthrie and Ártur, to the front porch and the cold morning air.

He pulled his cloak closer and watched his breath form a misty trail. Where was Kavan? He dared not discuss his fears with Guthrie.

The man viewed this baby as a grandchild of sorts and did not consider hair color to be an issue. Nor did the prince feel comfortable discussing those feelings with the healer, and he knew bringing up the matter with Brenna would only upset her. Especially now after everything she had suffered. They had discussed this possibility before. No, Prince Arlan felt that if he wanted an unbiased discussion he would have to wait for Kavan's return.

That nothing had been heard from the bard, except his brief psychic contacts with Ártur…if they were even real…worried the prince. Kavan had not said he would contact anyone, had not said he would report back to them, but Prince Arlan felt that he would have, especially since Kavan had said he would like to be present when the child was born. Certainly, he would have known that Brenna's time was due and would have come home if he could have. Did that mean Kavan was in trouble? Ártur tried to console the prince with the knowledge that Kavan often did what he felt best without consulting others; if he was in trouble, the healer swore he would know. Not knowing the nature of Elyri gifts and abilities, the prince could only presume that the healer was telling the truth, but it did little to ease his troubled mind. He wanted Kavan beside him. Now.

But as the sun climbed higher in Elyriá, Kavan was miles away from the loft in which he had spent the night. He had eaten breakfast with his hosts before dawn and then set off towards his next destination. Early fall had arrived; if he hoped to cover the remainder of Enesfel before the snows came, he could not dally nor take the time to return to Bhryell. There was too much work to be done on Prince Arlan's behalf. The longer Kavan was in Enesfel, the more uncomfortable he became with what he saw of the King's methods and with the ever growing belief amongst the people that this pale bard must be more than a harper, that he might be a saint.

☙Chapter 21❧

A s the last leaves of crimson and yellow drifted from sturdy branches to the ground and the first snows came early to Enesfel, a large company of supporters and the curious surrounded Kavan wherever he went. People had begun to follow him from one town to another, and every cluster of inhabitation now had great crowds awaiting his arrival. He heard the murmurs in the streets, the increasing talk of someone who would come and free Enesfel from oppression. There were tales of a man so pious and righteous that he must be a great saint, a prophet of a new age of prosperity, peace, and enlightenment. Each time Kavan heard these things, his stomach lurched, his mouth went dry, and he automatically reached for the cross that hung around his neck as if it would ground him and keep him from being swept up in the tide of growing religious fervor. He had stopped the covert preaching long ago but to no avail. Word spread on its own. To those he met, he was as divine as the deity of whom he spoke.

Rhidam was his final stop before returning to Bhryell to wait out the worst of the winter. Tension within the royal city was palpable; he felt it in the watchful eyes of every person he passed. Perhaps it was the color of his skin that drew their attention. Perhaps it was because some remembered him as the only Elyri to play in Rhidam during King Farrell's reign. Or perhaps it had to do with the unwanted religious epitaphs heaped on him. The rumors planted elsewhere were more pronounced here than anticipated which gave explanation to the increased security around the castle and the presence of soldiers that thumped through the cobble and mud streets night and day. It might also explain why a stranger, particularly one as visible as Kavan, would be watched with wary eyes. Caution was his only hope for survival; he decided against telling tales of a savior prince here. There was no need to stir a pot which was already poised to boil over. Instead, Kavan spent his first day and evening in Rhidam gleaning whatever information about the King and the princess there was to be had. Some of it proved to be information he wished he had never heard.

Three men had taken the stories of a savior prince to heart and had organized a group of followers for an upcoming rebellion. They had been arrested and hung after being interrogated about the one who was to lead them. Hearing this, Kavan's heart sank. The men did not know who their savior prince would be, could not say where he might come from or when he would arrive, but the story he heard most frequently was that most believed the prince would be one of King Farrell's bastard children. People firmly believed in this prince's arrival and these three continued to proclaim it until the moment of their deaths. Now, several weeks after their execution, they had become martyrs for this new, uncertain cause and the dissidence was growing as King Owain began to scour the kingdom for any children known or suspected to be Farrell's. Such a search was impossible, given that there was no way of knowing how many women the late King had bedded, but King Owain did not want to take chances. He would find this upstart and put him down if he could.

This news encouraged Kavan to shorten his stay in Rhidam even more than planned. He would stay only long enough to determine the well-being of the princess before escaping to Bhryell. There was no word of her on the street; no one had seen her in many months. One elderly man claimed she had left the kingdom. Some believed she had gone to the Lachlan estate in Kamin. Still, others believed she had been secretly wed or had taken ill and died, although there had been no official proclamation of her marriage or passing. There was nothing else helpful to be learned without entering the palace. Kavan's hope of returning home with news for the prince about his sister seemed likely to be unfulfilled.

ॐ*ॐ

Guthrie bounced three-month-old Muir on his lap, cooing softly, oblivious to the healer across the room reading in the candlelight. He was quite fond of the child, despite its parentage, or perhaps, he sometimes admitted, because of it. Brenna was his kin, after all, and though he despised the method of the child's conception, it was not Muir's fault. Muir was a happy, friendly child, easy to like. It was fortunate for him that he had the support of the ex-general and the healer because he had little, if any, from his surrogate father, who passed by the room, glanced quickly and with barely disguised darkness, at the child on Guthrie's lap. Smoothing down the unruly blond curls, Guthrie wondered if Arlan would ever find love in his heart for Muir.

ॐ*ॐ

The first month of the new year dawned in Rhidam beneath freezing rain that fell steadily for days from the steel gray sky as Kavan performed for his third and final time. It was time to give up the futile search for the princess and return home. It did not bother him to play beneath the shelter of a porch roof; it was no more damp or cold there then it was indoors, and he had performed in worse conditions. With nothing more to accomplish in Rhidam, he was eager to be gone. The worst of the winter storms had yet to begin but already the streets oozed with dark mud as torrents of rainwater poured from the sloped rooftops.

Few people were out this evening, only a few on important errands and those who had gathered to hear him play. Though not as large of an audience as he would like, it was larger than he had expected in this miserable weather. Amongst the crowd, he counted at first five palace guards towards the rear, and then eight, men who watched the performance dispassionately but who seemed intent on staying. Eventually, most of those soldiers moved away, but Kavan was grateful that the core of his audience chose to stay longer than usual when three of the soldiers continued to loiter after the music ended. It proved to the bard that they were not there to listen to his music. Pushing the damp strands of silver hair from his face, he groaned softly as the last of his audience became aware of the lingering soldiers and scattered nervously towards their homes, leaving Kavan to face the soldiers alone. He packed his harp and donned his cloak and gloves, pretending that there was nothing amiss and that they did not trouble him, but soon enough he heard the sound of their heavy boots slosh closer through the puddles of rain and mud.

"Elyri, you are to come with us."

He could feel the dismayed glances of those people who lingered in the doorways and shadows around him, felt their pity, and in his stomach, a hard knot formed. The harshness of the command suggested that he should have cut his performance short while there had been a crowd to act as a buffer. Now he was alone. "Are my services required somewhere?" he asked casually.

"Not your services. You. His Majesty wishes to speak to you."

The knot in his center tightened into something born of anxiety and apprehension. "Who am I to deny a King?" he asked. "Lead the way."

The soldiers cast curious glances at one another as they hesitated. Though the bard was obviously Elyri, and Elyri were known for pacifistic beliefs and behaviors, the soldiers had not expected easy compliance. Didn't he realize he might be taken to his death? Was there something about this unusual looking man that they should fear?

Kavan managed to smile at their hesitation and started in the direction of the castle gates, harp tucked under his arm as if this sort of request was made of him every day. When his escorts did not immediately follow, he paused to wait for them, glancing over his shoulder with another smile. Because this did not appear to be an arrest, with Kavan going willingly and the soldiers not binding or manhandling him, the city folk watching eased their worry, as Kavan had hoped they would. He could not risk a public incident this close to the King.

The soldiers followed cautiously with their hands on their swords, keeping a vigilant, or perhaps respectable, distance between themselves and the harper. None of them moved to his side until they reached the bridge, when one flanked him on either side and one came behind. The youngest of the group took a firm hold of Kavan's arm above the elbow, but a slight tilt of the bard's head and expression that seemed both blank and dangerous was enough to cause the man to release his hold. None of the three attempted to grasp him again, though they did remain near enough to apprehend him should he try to run or fight.

The palace had accumulated an unhealthy air of silence and tension in the years since Kavan had last been there. Few of the passages on the way to the King's antechamber were illuminated. He found himself holding his breath in an effort to shut out the musty smell of decay, dampness, and death, as well as the tendrils of anger and depression that seeped from the cracks in the stone. The floor was cold and slippery, making movement slow. He did not notice any servants or any visiting dignitaries, which struck him as odd and caused him concern. Soon enough, he could hear arguing ahead of them; the largest of his escorts entered the room they eventually stopped before, and when he returned a few moments later he led the bard inside.

The King of Enesfel, older now than when Kavan had last seen him, looked up from the desk and then stood abruptly as they entered. "You!" His now animated face was weary and white with shock. The man beside the King, a military officer it appeared, glanced from the King to the bard but did not speak. It appeared the King had forgotten his presence. "I never thought to see you again. What are you doing here?"

Kavan refused to be intimidated by angry words, particularly when he could feel the surge of fear behind them. He might have been afraid of Prince Owain as a child, but he was no longer. "I am a harper, My Liege. Nothing more."

"A harper?" The King remembered that short-lived friendship, that evening spent in the kitchen and courtyard, the blind man with the harp that, in his eyes, had been the initiator of the fight between prince and Elyri. He snorted. "Of course you are. I suppose that you are the man responsible for inciting my subjects to revolt?" His eyes narrowed and lips pursed together as though he had eaten something distasteful as he moved from around the desk to approach the bard.

"I have not spoken of revolt…"

There was a second angry snort, like a bull eager to charge. "My sources keep me apprised of such things…it seems you have been telling everyone that someone is to overthrow me." He was now face to face with Kavan, looking down at him with distaste, though his body language spoke of a man ready to flee.

Kavan did not move except to tilt his head up to look the King in the eye. "For a bard to be popular, he must play to an audience, give them what they wish to hear. I have made no reference to any monarch by name, or to any kingdom. It is not my desire to become involved in Enesfel's affairs. I aim only to amuse and entertain." It was the closest he had ever come to lying, and he hated the way it made him feel.

Though taller and stockier than the Elyri, King Owain suddenly felt as if he was not the one looming and intimidating. Something in those green eyes made him feel small and vulnerable and caused him to take a step back. To disguise that action, to hide its potential weakness, he hardened his expression and began to pace. What Kavan said was true…to an extent. He had seen it often enough in Neth. People would believe anything they heard, particularly if they felt it would better their condition, and for a performer of any sort to be popular, they had to give the audience what they wanted. Commoners often twisted songs and tales to suit their desires, while paranoid ones twisted those same words into threats against them. It was not Kavan's fault if the people wanted to hear of their King being dethroned…or if they turned his words to suit them, any more than it was Kavan's fault if lords and ladies, and even the King, found threats in those same words. It was on his audience's heads, not the bard's.

But the King did not appreciate what that said about his subjects, or himself; he did not want to look into the mirror at his life too closely. He had made mistakes, yes, but he was trying, with his own vision of Enesfel's future, to be a good King.

"Whether it was intended or not, I have had to execute seven men for treason this morning because of these stories," he snarled.

The bard's gaze wavered and dropped. He had not heard about these new executions; that more had died because of the seeds he had planted upset him, even though he knew that, before this undertaking was over, many more would die. "I meant no harm to anyone, milord. If the people have taken the songs and tales to heart, I shall return home and not…"

"No." The word was spoken harshly but Kavan thought he detected something else behind it than the mere desire to stop him from inciting the kingdom further. Or perhaps it was wishful thinking on his part, he admitted reluctantly as the King continued, "I do not trust you to keep your word. None of your kind can be trusted." King Owain smelled a weakness, something he could exploit and use to his advantage if he could only figure out how.

Seeking to understand the King's words, Kavan asked, "Have I done anything to be mis…?"

"Your memory is poor if you do not recall our last encounter."

The bard straightened his shoulders. "Our last encounter was before the coronation of King Donal. You gave me a wooden ball. I, in turn, left it with Lady Cordelia to give to the twins when they were old enough to play with it. I apologized, in case I had any part of you being sent away from Rhidam. I know now that I had nothing to do with King Donal's choice. I was untrained, a novice, but I meant you no harm then, and I mean you none now."

King Owain swallowed hard, the sound easily heard by the other men in the room. This man's memory was better than his own. Owain had forgotten about the ball, and about his own fleeting sense of being taken away from a potential friend, despite the rocky start their acquaintance had experienced. That surge of remembrance, the fleeting tails of childhood loneliness, added difficulty to the decision of what to do with this man. The bard seemed to be an honest and fair man, but the King could not shake the suspicion that Kavan was hiding something, that the harper's return into his life would be a bad portent as it had been all those years ago. Their last meeting had seen Owain banished to Neth. What would this meeting bring?

He donned an air of gruffness and bitterness that he no longer felt. "I think you know more than you are telling me, Elyri, and I want the truth. All of it. You will remain here until you tell me what I want to know, until I finish with you. For now, however, I do not wish to see you anymore." He motioned to the guards. "Take him to the dungeon…and see that he is in a more informative mood when I call for him again."

The soldiers did not need to use force; Kavan kept his shoulders square as he was led from the room, walking on his own, and the King made note of it. Wondering if the bard suspected the reason that underpinned his choice to keep Kavan close, Owain ground his teeth and drowned his frustration in a glass of wine. Now that the soldiers and the prisoner were gone, the King again became aware of the man he had been arguing with previously, saw the man's questioning expression, and snapped, "You have a question, General?" His tone suggested he was in no mood to be trifled with.

"You know that man?" General McLeu asked.

"MacLyr's cousin."

The general blinked and coughed. "Ártur MacLyr? The healer?"

Pouring another glass of wine, the King muttered, "Who else?"

"Then surely…"

"What? Do you expect the healer to retaliate for keeping him here? He would have to break his oaths to do that, and I do not believe he would break them, even for his kin…"

"Family is everything to them…"

The King growled, not wanting to discuss the meaning of family with the general. "We do not know if Healer MacLyr is alive. Or where he is. Or if they are on speaking terms. Besides, he is only being detained for questioning. Once I learn what I need to know, he will be released."

Ferghus very much doubted that. "Is torture necessary?"

"Who said anything about torture?" the King replied defensively with a dismissive wave. "I only instructed them to convince him to talk."

"You know how that will be interpreted, milord. And what if it succeeds but you do not like what you learn?"

The King left the room without replying, feeling a twinge of guilt at the notion of torturing the pale man. If he was honest with himself, he had no idea what he would do if he did not like what the bard told him. Something within believed he could not afford to let the Elyri go, and for once, the King was inclined to listen, no matter how he accomplished it.

Kavan walked silently before the guards, disturbed that his part in Prince Arlan's plans had already led to the deaths of innocent men, disappointed in Enesfel's King, and unhappy that his first encounter with Owain had embittered the man against Elyri. There was good in that man, Kavan could feel it, even though it was buried beneath layers of conditioning from his years in the north. The bard shivered and held his harp closer, wishing again that King Donal had listened to him and not sent the child prince to Neth. Things might be different now.

Once they reached the dungeon, one of the guards pulled the harp case from Kavan's arms and tossed it callously into the first cell they passed. They meant to keep him here, in isolation. Kavan bit back the words he wanted to say as the case hit the wall and popped open, dumping its precious contents, harp and a collection of parchment pages, onto the dirty stone floor. There was an abrupt plinking sound as a brass string snapped. The second of the two guards spun him roughly around and shackled his hands to the wall near the bunk room with his face pressed against the ancient stone, while the first fetched a thin wooden pole, and returned with it slapping against his hand. Kavan tensed and felt profoundly afraid for the first time in his life. He had not anticipated this. The King had said nothing about a beating…or had he and Kavan had missed it? He belatedly realized that perhaps he should have escaped when he had the chance.

"Maybe a little coercion will convince you to talk when the King summons you. He always gets what he wants, one way or another. You have the face and voice of a woman; let us see the rest of you." He tore down the back of Kavan's robe, exposing him to the waist. "White as a virgin." Both men laughed. Kavan flinched, hurt by the words more than by the frightening actions.

He held his breath and closed his eyes, trembling, waiting for the first blow to fall. It did. He clenched his jaw to stifle the cries that threatened to escape; any sign of weakness would likely lengthen the abuse, he believed, and that he did not want. Beyond the arrow in his thigh, and the blows his uncle and Prince Owain had given, Kavan had never known such physical abuse, and he had never imagined anything like the searing sting of wood against his flesh. Ribs cracked, skin bruised and bled, and he wondered if he could escape this. But he could not focus enough power to stop them, and could not think clearly enough to devise any sort of escape plan. That familiar ball of energy grew in his center, but because he did not want to kill his captors, only make them stop, he had to struggle to concentrate on containing that power that threatened to erupt.

It was the only thing that kept his mind off the agony.

Why, he kept asking himself? What have I done? It was nearly incomprehensible that he, an innocent man, should be subjected to torture to gain information.

Blows continued, drawing forth welts and more blood, until his knees buckled and he hung limply by his shackled wrists. The threatening ball of power dribbled away with the remainder of his strength. The words of a hymn formed in his mind, replacing the unanswerable questions, but he did not have the strength or concentration to dwell on them. When the beating finally ceased, the shackles were unlocked and he was shoved roughly into the cell beside his harp. Hitting the stone floor with such force sent barbs of fire lancing through every corner of his body, and the words of the hymn broke free from his lips.

"ithé donaiibh, ergothé ebh zenár;
monás donaiibh, aimairós ebh zenár
aitaethó donaiibh,
zólágk k'gaethaelá aidóbhae."

Enduring grief, we are given strength; enduring pain, we are given healing; enduring suffering reveals His compassion.

The soldiers could not understand him, having never heard the Elyri language before, thus they assumed him to be delirious. They closed the barred iron door, snickering between them, leaving him in a crumpled, trembling heap. His thoughts grasped fleetingly at images of Ártur, of Prince Arlan, and at snatches of prayers as he repeated his rough song until his voice cracked and gave out. As darkness pooled around his thoughts, pulling his vision with it, he whispered, "Kó-ráhm…"

In a nearby cell, a female face, peering through the grate in her door, watched the entire proceeding, weeping for the blood he shed. She wondered what this meek, humble man had done to obtain the King's wrath, though she knew he might have done nothing at all. From appearances, he was likely as innocent of wrongdoing as she was.

That he refused to give in to the pain, that he remained standing in the face of torture, gave her a renewed sense of conviction and hope. She could not go to him to soothe his pain or cleanse his wounds, but she wished him well. Her hand reached through the grate but he had not seen her as he was shoved into a cell. In that moment, she knew she had seen him before.

But she did not see him again that night, and it was several hours later before she turned away from the door and lay down on her pallet with no intention of sleep.

❧Chapter 22❧

"It is not the finest wedding attire for a prince, but it will suffice," Guthrie said, straightening Prince Arlan's velvet amber and burgundy cape. "You are as regal and handsome as any prince can be." Noting that he again received no response, and the prince continued to stare at a spot on the wall, he continued, "You have been very gloomy today. You could pretend to be happy. Brenna will think…"

At the mention of his bride-to-be, the prince's head snapped around; he glared at the man and tried not to verbalize the snarl in the back of his throat. "I know what she thinks. My mood has nothing to do with her and she knows it. You know it too. We've discussed this. It is what we both want; she knows I am delighted about this union. She knows I love her more than my own life. But Kavan swore he would be back before my birthday and not miss the wedding…even before I knew there would be a wedding. We have postponed the ceremony almost two months but there is still no word from him. Even Ártur has heard nothing…"

Guthrie barely resisted rolling his eyes. "What is it about Kavan that drives you to such distraction? He is only a bard…"

"He is not 'only' anything," the prince snorted, crossing his arms with a huff. "He is different from everyone…special…even Brenna believes it. I do not think I am being unreasonable. If something has happened to him on my behalf, doing what I asked of him, then I have an obligation to protect and help…"

"You cannot protect a man who works without orders, who gives no indications of his plans or intentions or whereabouts, who obeys his own mandates. I've known a few of them in my years of service. They are frequently invaluable; they do the greatest service; they have the brightest, but usually shortest, careers. You cannot spend your life worrying about them. If he is that type of man, there is nothing you can do except appreciate what he does for you, and pray that he comes to his senses and stays safe. He will return to us when he is able."

"And if he does not?"

Reading the desperation in the prince's eyes, Guthrie sighed. He understood that Kavan was the prince's friend, and he knew what it was like to lose a friend, but he did not think his words of wisdom were what Arlan wanted to hear. Still, he said, "Then you must let him go. But have faith. He will come back to us." He did not know why he was certain of it, but he was.

The prince groaned. He was not prepared to let his first, and best, personal friend go. "I wish I had your faith."

Making one last adjusting tug at the prince's collar, the ex-general pointed towards the door. "Come. They are waiting for us." He wished the prince had his faith too.

In the frosty gloom of Rhidam's dungeon, the man they spoke of lay battered, bruised, bleeding, and barely aware of his surroundings. He had eaten little during his captivity, though his captors had offered him food, and when he was conscious enough to pull the straw around him, it did little to keep out the damp chill of winter. He did not have the strength to keep himself warm. The King's determination to gain what knowledge he believed Kavan held had led to further beatings, none of which had proven successful. But the two men, bard and King, had not faced each other again. Today's abuse had been the worst, and from what Kavan could recall he was scheduled for execution within a day or two, weather permitting, unless the King changed his mind or Kavan talked. And talk Kavan would never do. His only recourse was escape, but concentration through his pain had proven too difficult thus far and he had failed in all of his previous attempts. He believed that, if he failed tonight, he might not have another opportunity. Lying prone, face down in the dirt and straw, Kavan attempted to force his mind clear. The exertion did nothing except bring blood pounding into his ears. He groaned and reluctantly relaxed. Perhaps he should resign himself to death, he mused; perhaps he had fulfilled his life's purpose and this death was to be his destiny. Yet, there was some part of his soul that urged him to try again, some part of him that refused to give up. Until the actual moment of execution, he still had opportunity to escape, thus giving up was not truly an option he was prepared to face. If escape was possible, if there was a chance the King would set him free, k'Ádhá would not deny Kavan his life. He only needed to keep trying, to discover the method he had not yet found or try previous means again.

When his pulse had slowed and his breathing came easier, he pulled his legs under him and sat with difficulty. Without turning his head, his swollen eyes scanned the cell until at last his gaze fell on the harp that lay against the wall. It looked small, dull, and abandoned in this place, lifeless in a fashion it had never seemed before. He had not played, had not touched the instrument, since he had been locked in this place. How long had that been? He was not certain. With slow, aching determination, he crawled across the small space, his bare knees scraping over the rough stone as they dragged behind him, until at last he was able to reach the harp, to pick it up and rub his stiff hands over the wood to remove dust and dirt and inspect it for damage. It was amazingly unscathed after the abusive treatment it too had endured, a single broken string the only damage it had sustained. It was still in tune. There was life in it yet, life that gave Kavan hope.

He had long ago learned how to play around the misfortune of broken strings. It had never hindered his playing before. The miracle of the harp's survival fueled the desire for his own; he closed his eyes, put his bruised fingers to the brass strings, and opened his heart and mind to music and prayer. It took several minutes for his hands to move satisfactorily, but soon a song poured forth from his soul in waves of agony and despair, calling, crying, and searching for assistance and comfort. Outside the cell, the attending guards, two different men than those who usually kept this watch or performed the beatings, paid no heed to the music, as if it were an expected or common occurrence. The cross around Kavan's neck grew warm, causing his skin to tingle as the familiar energies formed and gathered around him. Such reassuring familiarity brought him peace for the first time since his incarceration.

Whether it was his weakened condition or something more, Kavan believed that this time the energies he typically felt around him were stronger. There were voices, little more than the sound of the wind to most listeners, but he knew they were voices, bidding him cling to his faith and offering consolation for the torment he had endured. He could feel the brush of soft, invisible robes against his bare arms and back. His hair, matted and clinging to his skull and neck, ruffled as the sensation caressed his face. He sighed and bowed his head.

Then he became aware of something else, something different in the air that he did not recognize. He knew that someone stood with him in the cell, though the door had not opened, someone bidding him lift his head and look. Opening his eyes, Kavan beheld a dim, bluish figure before him; it had no face, no discernible features, but it was vaguely man-shaped, and as he watched, it extended one arm-like limb towards him. His breath caught as a hand rested on his head with a touch that filled him with security and serenity. "You came," he whispered, not at all sure who he was thanking.

As quickly as the sensations had come, they were gone and he was alone in the cell with the harp silent in his hands. His breath was exhaled in one slow, shaky hiss. He felt empty now that the presences were gone, but the previous fogginess in his head had been replaced with a focused reserve of energy. He could escape. He knew he could.

Extending his senses, he discovered that his two jailers were slumbering, a product of the visitation he presumed since he had done nothing to cause them to sleep. The image of a mouse formed in his mind; the familiar prickle of power at the back of his neck spread through his body, and in a blink, the mouse shape became his, the harp in his lap merging into his newly acquired body. He delighted in the experience, aware that the transformation had not been as easy as it normally would have been, but he had succeeded in changing shape and that was all that mattered.

Slipping between the bars of his cell, through the gap that allowed drafts in and trays of food to be left, the mouse moved quickly along the wall towards the bunkroom where he knew the Gate to be. No one would have thought anything of a mouse scurrying across the floor; there were rodents aplenty here. Only when inside the bunkroom, sitting in the place where the Gate was because he was too weary to stand, did he resume his own form. The double transformation made his whole body ache and he felt weak and disoriented from the loss of blood, lack of food, and continual cold. What strength he had received from his ghostly visitor was largely depleted already, and he could only pray that there was enough to operate the Gate, to take him home. With great effort, the harp clutched to his chest like a shield, he sought the point of connection between where he was and where he desired to be. Though dizzy and disoriented, he willed himself to stand, to concentrate long enough for the reassuring mist to envelop him. It did not last long, however, and as it dissipated, his body collapsed, without Kavan knowing if he had succeeded or failed.

Ártur remained behind after the prince's wedding to assist in readying the náós for tomorrow's Gathering. The task, involving removing the candles the Prince had insisted on using and the bouquets of flowers placed around the altar, as well as cleaning the floor of mud and snow, had been completed quickly, but he had not yet returned home. He dusted benches, polished bits of metal with the sleeves of his shirt, anything that kept him there and required little thought to do. By now, the festivities at the house would be over and everyone would likely have retired for the night. He was sorry to have missed them, but he had not been in the mood to celebrate.

He now knelt alone in the place where he often found Kavan, reaching out with all of the energy he could pull from within and around him, hoping to touch his cousin's mind. There was nothing. To a degree, that did not surprise him. Ártur did not possess that ability to the extent Kavan did, and Kavan kept his mind so shielded that reaching him without permission was rare. Yet the lack of contact between them was disheartening. The last several weeks without it had been torture, in more ways than one. The healer awoke every night in agony, his mind and body aching, stiff, and groggy as if he had spent too much time riding, or rather too much time falling from his mount, and feasting too much on heavy foods. He sought an explanation for it, but there was none, and his healing techniques failed to ease the discomfort. The pain was always gone in the morning, but Ártur had begun to dread each coming night, especially once he decided that these reoccurring episodes and the lack of contact with Kavan had to be connected.

Tonight he was berating himself because he had yet to reconcile the differences between him and Kavan that arose that night at the Festival of Candles many years ago. He had managed to keep conveniently busy, and Kavan would not broach the matter himself. The rift between them had grown wider, and though they were still close, the special closeness they had shared when Kavan was a boy, that Ártur had tried to rebuild after King Donal's death, was gone. Ártur could no longer lie to himself and view Kavan as simply a favored younger cousin; the bard had changed too much in ways that were impossible to ignore. And most recently, Ártur had become aware that Prince Arlan had, perhaps, replaced him in Kavan's affections, and though he did not want to admit it, he felt some degree of jealousy and resentment towards the prince for stealing Kavan from him…when he knew that the true fault was his own. As he wiped tears from the corners of his eyes, Ártur wondered how he would have felt if Arlan was a woman.

The sound of something falling against the door of the k'dhín bhólibh startled him. There was nothing inside the chamber that could have fallen, and nothing outside that would have hit the door if it had. Rising, he crept cautiously closer, listening as he approached, but he could hear nothing. After a pause outside the door, he slowly opened it to peek inside and stepped back in alarm as the limp, bloody body of his cousin tumbled out at his feet. He knelt and placed his hands on the white chest dark with bruises and blood, every healing sense he possessed working feverishly to survey Kavan's condition. He could learn nothing about how this had happened; even unconscious, Kavan kept his mind tightly closed against intrusion, but he was alive, and had, as far as Ártur could tell, returned to Bhryell of his own volition.

Not daring to move him lest he cause more damage or pain, Ártur settled on the floor, removed the few tattered remains of cloth that hung from one shoulder, and set about the task of healing every injury he could find. For the first time, it struck him how physically perfect his cousin was in both shape and proportion. He swallowed hard, weeping as he worked, determined to leave no scars or trace of this abuse. He wanted to know who had done this and why. There was no reason he could think of for anyone to desire to harm Kavan, except, perhaps, because he was Elyri.

Several hours passed that way before Ártur relaxed, stretching his back to ease the stiffness his position had created. The visible damage, save for the bruises, was healed, and the fractured bones and abused organs mended as much as he was able to mend them, but there would still be many days of pain ahead from the abuse Kavan's body had endured. There was little Ártur could do about that, and what he could do to ease it would have to wait until he regained his own strength. He retrieved a choir robe, clothed Kavan in it, and carried him and the harp into the thóres. Fortunately, gdhededhá Bhílári was not in tonight. Odd, the healer realized, none of the gdhededhá ever seemed to be here when Kavan had need of the solace of this place. Taking Kavan home tonight would raise unwanted questions from the others, who might hear them when they arrived, and Ártur neither wanted to, nor could, answer them. Besides, he did not want to ruin the couple's first night of marriage or deny them the chance to spend time together. Instead, the healer placed Kavan on the gdhededhá's bed and settled in a nearby chair, attuning himself to any indication of Kavan's revival as he closed his eyes to rest.

Kavan awoke before dawn, head throbbing mercilessly, body aching, though not as much as he thought it should. That he was in a proper bed was the only thing of which he was certain. His swollen eyes would not focus; he tried to sit but the motion made him dizzy and nauseous and he groaned. Ártur was awake instantly at the sound.

"Kavan! Praise k'Ádhá you're alive!"

"Ártur?" His voice was thin and hoarse; Ártur almost could not understand him. The healer poured a cup of water from a pitcher at the bedside and held it to him, and though Kavan could sense the movement, he could not see it. "Where…my sight…" The cup was placed in his hands and then the healer sat on the bed beside him. As Kavan drank, he held the younger man's head between his hands; when they dropped into his lap, Kavan's sight was clear. The bard closed his eyes with a grateful moan, afraid to look at his cousin. "Thank you. I made it home?"

"You are in Bhryell, yes." Ártur watched him, more worried than he was letting on. "By the saints…what happened? You looked frightful when I found you. Who did this?"

Kavan's injured expression stopped him from speaking further, but it was many minutes of Kavan nursing the cup of water before he answered. "Owain has not forgiven me for the headache I gave him," he finally murmured. The empty cup was returned to the healer's hands. "Thank you."

"Owain did this to you? You did not go to…" Ártur did not think his cousin foolish enough to intentionally cross paths with Enesfel's King.

"I had to," he replied, cutting the healer off. "I went everywhere, the length of Enesfel. I do not think there is a single village I missed. Prince Arlan has many awaiting his arrival, more than he and the general can imagine."

Exasperated, Ártur cried, "But why the castle? You said yourself it would be dangerous in Rhidam…"

Kavan rubbed his forehead. "I did not intend to go to the castle…but I had to travel to Rhidam, to judge the atmosphere for myself and seek news of the princess. The whole of Enesfel is smothering in tension, but I knew Rhidam would be the most accurate indicator of the state of things." He shifted on the cot, seeking comfort he knew he could not find by adjusting his posture. "At least ten people have taken the stories as truth; I do not know what they did, but I know they were executed for treason. King Owain blamed me for their dissidence and arrested me. When I did not tell him anything he hoped to hear, he…" His voice faltered under the weight of those memories and he shrugged,

The healer growled. "I will kill him."

Kavan grasped his cousin's arm tightly with a shake of his head. "No. You will not break your vows on my account. I am well enough. Despite what he allowed to be done, he does not deserve to die. For others, he deserves punishment, perhaps; but his cruelty is not like…he is not inherently bad, Ártur. There is good in him…"

"Not…how can you say this after what he has done?"

"I just know. He does not belong on Enesfel's throne, but he does not deserve to die." He waved off further discussion of King Owain by rubbing his temples. Recognizing that his cousin was in pain, Ártur put his hands to Kavan's head, found the source of discomfort, and removed it quickly. The thanks he received was a small smile.

He was unable to fathom his cousin's compassion or the rules of morality by which Kavan judged men. Accepting the unspoken desire to change the subject despite his need to understand, Ártur asked, "How long?"

The bard eased back against the headboard and tried to remember. "About eight weeks…I think. I lost track. There was food…but I could eat only a little. It was always dark…and cold. I saw no sunlight save for a little that fell in the passage between cells. I tried to escape several times but could not…until last night. Someone came…I managed to gather the strength…I might have been executed if I had not…"

The stilted, flat speech revealed much, but Ártur doubted he would ever get the full story. He started to ask for more details, to protest the notion of Kavan's execution, but again the bard changed the subject. "I learned nothing of the princess. No one has seen her outside the castle in several months and no one knows why. I am certain she is still alive…it was something I sensed when I was there…but perhaps she has taken ill." He paused for a long while, eyes closed to avoid looking at his cousin, before adding, "Those ten men were executed because of me."

Not this again, the healer thought with a shake of his head. "Kavan…they died for Prince Arlan and his cause…not for you. Not because of you. Like it or not, many more will die before this is over." There was an uncomfortable silence between them as Kavan weighed those words. "If it were only that…I could accept it. But this is more. You do not know. It is not merely a savior prince they are seeking…expecting." His voice dropped to a raspy whisper. "They believe me a saint, Ártur. Here, Enesfel…everywhere. No one said it directly, but everywhere I went, they wanted me to play for them, tell them stories…touch them as if I could bestow healing or blessing. At first, I thought it was the music, the novelty of my face and voice…but I realized quickly that it was…I overheard talking, felt it when they looked at me. They believe my every word as if it were gospel, and would die if I asked them to. I cannot go back, Ártur. They think I am more important than…"

The healer pulled Kavan into his embrace as the younger man broke into tearless sobs for the first time Ártur had ever seen. Seeing it now made Ártur feel obliged, and blessed, to be trusted enough to share this and to comfort him. "Let the people believe what they will, Kavan…it is not who you are," the healer murmured.

Kavan choked on his words. "I cannot allow them to believe a lie."

"How do you propose to change their minds? You do not…you are not responsible for what they think, and even force will not change it. Think of Bhernal, or Mátán, or even Kóráhm. They lived their lives as they felt called to do. That people followed them, listened to their teachings, died…as long as you build up their faith instead of tearing it down, it does not matter what they think of you. That is between them and k'Ádhá. Lead them in faith if you think you can, but do not feel that you have ultimate control over their souls. You know the truth of who and what you are. As long as you retain your faith and humility, k'Ádhá will know your intentions. Do not blame yourself for things you can neither prevent nor control, sínréc. It is not healthy."

Only Kavan's tearless lament broke the silence. His head knew the truth of Ártur's words, but his heart could not grasp it. He had been wrestling with this burden for months; it was not going to leave him overnight. When he finally began to calm, uncomfortable in that embrace despite how much it meant to him, he drew away from his cousin and rubbed his eyes.

Unable to stand the silence any longer, feeling empty and alone now that Kavan had withdrawn, the healer spoke again. "I want to offer my apologies, sínréc…"

Without looking at him, Kavan whispered, "You have done nothing that warrants an apology."

"You think not?" Ártur slid back, putting more distance between them before continuing. What he had to say was difficult enough for him without compounding it with his cousin's nearness. "I am as guilty as anyone…perhaps more so. You are not a saint; I know this. Only the gdhededhá can make a saint, and if someday they choose to make you one…" he cleared his throat to cover how awkward that thought made him feel, "That is between them and k'Ádhá. Now you are merely a man. An Elyri. My own blood kin. That you happen to be the holiest, most powerful man I have ever known should not be cause for me to hold this distance between us…"

He stood and paced aimlessly about the room as he continued. "Elys was right. She told me once that no one would ever be more important to me than you are. I tried to deny it, but I find that I must acknowledge it to you, as well as myself, if I am to heal this rift. I have been envious of Prince Arlan and the place he holds in your heart, but I am beginning to see that your following, like it or not, may be much larger than the prince and myself." He returned to Kavan's side and knelt beside the cot. "Take me back into your confidence. Teach me, sínréc. I want to know what it is that makes you who you are. I want some measure of your faith and peace. I want to be as we once were, before my selfishness drove us apart."

It was not easy for him to say words that he had not thought out beforehand, and Kavan could hear it in his voice. The bard stared silently at the healer for a long time, knowing that speaking those words had been as awkward for Ártur as hearing them had been for him. Nothing he could say seemed appropriate, but when he realized that Ártur was growing uncomfortable beneath his gaze, uncomfortable with the silence that might be deemed rejection, he said softly, "Ártur, there is nothing to forgive. I am not bhydáni, not ílDaeni. I have no profound thoughts or wisdom to depart to anyone, particularly to you. I only have that which I know and believe, and the music…"

Ártur's eyes shone with fervent love and zeal. "Then I shall listen to all of it, and perhaps see something that you do not. Allow me to try. I need what we had before, Kavan. You are all I have."

"You have a mother, a father, a brother…things I will never…"

"They are not…" Ártur stopped abruptly and stood up, going to the window as he trembled beneath the weight of what he had almost said. Had he meant that or was it something thought in the passion of persuading Kavan to accept him into his good graces? Clenching his fists, he closed his eyes and suppressed the urge to scream. He felt stupid. He had not tried this hard to win back Elys.

Sighing, Kavan resisted the urge to go to him. Whatever the healer had been going to say, Kavan was certain it was better left unsaid. He knew what the words would have been and he did not want to hear them. Instead, he said, "I have never shunned you. I need you as much now as when I first asked you to help in this political dance we have undertaken, as much as when, as a child, I asked you not to forget me when you were in Enesfel. That has never changed. I have grown up, that is all. Prince Arlan and you are not interchangeable. You are different people. I need you in different ways. Only promise that you will never call me savior or saint, and that shall suffice, Ártur."

Ártur released a deep, relieved breath. "I promise, sínréc." He found a brush and comb in the nearby dresser and proceeded to untangle Kavan's hair; it was an awkward gesture of devotion, but the only one he could think of to show his sincerity. At first, Kavan felt uncomfortable with the dramatic display, but because he knew his cousin needed the outlet, needed to do something for him, he forced himself to accept the attention. Neither spoke again until Kavan's hair was smooth and soft once more, although it was still in need of cleaning.

"We have all worried about you, particularly Arlan. He will be much relieved at your return. He has changed a great deal during the last several months; he and Brenna were wed last night…"

Eyes downcast, Kavan replied, "I did not expect them to wait for me. I could not come sooner."

The healer rubbed Kavan's shoulder, heedful of the sore muscles beneath his hand. "They waited because they wanted to, even Brenna. However, Guthrie pointed out that it would be futile for Arlan to continue to wait if he wished to be ready to leave when the time comes. He and Brenna have gone to the Cáner's cabin for the week; they would have left at dawn. I can keep Guthrie from troubling you if you desire rest and solitude. You will not have to face anyone, or talk about any of this until you are ready."

"The prince will want to know why I was not here for him. I cannot lie to him. I will not."

"Nor can you tell him that Owain almost killed you…intended to kill you. Do that, and he's likely to ride for Rhidam right now to avenge you, as I would have if you had not stopped me. As it is, he and Guthrie have tentatively planned to act as soon as the weather permits, traveling around the borders first, gathering men as they go, to end in Rhidam and confront the King. A much sounder plan, I daresay, then going to Rhidam alone to seek revenge on your behalf."

"I was, perhaps, too efficient," Kavan admitted sheepishly. "The King is expecting trouble…although it appears he believes the usurper may be one of Farrell's bastard children."

"There are plenty of those to keep him hunting for years I imagine," the healer said gravely, worried now for the safety of an untold number of innocent children.

"I pray he does not find them," whispered Kavan.

Ártur nodded in agreement. "Come…I will tell Guthrie what you have told me and allow him to decide what is best. You should eat and rest. The náós will be filling soon; I do not think you want to be here to answer questions when Bhílári returns…"

Kavan nodded wearily, inclined to agree, and took the hand that offered to steady him. The healer picked up the harp as he helped Kavan to stand, and then bore most of the bard's slight weight for the slow trip through the sleeping town.

❧White Pawn❧

࿁Chapter 23࿁

The sandy-haired man turned, his long robes of pale gold and green swishing the floor around his feet as the King entered the room. He smiled to himself as he bowed; the King was of imposing stature and physique, which, the gdhededhá presumed, accounted for much of the man's purported arrogance. Still, he had never feared authority and did not see this monarch as an insurmountable obstacle on the path he followed.

"Thank you for agreeing to see me, Your Eminence. I hope all is well with you."

King Owain grunted and scowled, not certain why he had agreed to an audience with this one-eyed holy man. He did, however, approve of the man's choice of epitaphs. "What do you want, gdhededhá? I do not have time for socializing, and if you have come to preach to me, I will not hear you."

"I have come for neither, milord," he replied, though he believed the man was likely in need of both preaching and socializing. "I have received word that you hold within your dungeon, a devout man…"

"I hold no gdhededhá," the King hastily retorted.

Despite his upbringing in Neth, and the Neth nobility's notorious hatred of the Faith, this monarch, at least, appeared to respect the clergy.

"Not a gdhededhá," the visitor assured him, "merely a pious man who has the support and admiration of your subjects. If you would be benevolent and release him…"

"Who is this man you believe I hold?" He knew of only three prisoners, though it was possible the guards had arrested someone recently without the King's knowledge. None of those three seemed likely to be the man the gdhededhá sought.

"His name is Kavan Cliáth, Your Highness…"

The King came up off the throne as if he had been stabbed. "He is not a holy man!"

The gdhededhá almost smiled. That the King knew who Kavan was, was a start. "He is! Ask your subjects. They will tell you that he is a holy man who has restored happiness to the souls of your kingdom. The people think very highly of him. There have been miracles. We have raised two thousand crowns to secure his release."

After swallowing back his outrage and astonishment, the King sat and motioned one of his attendants to approach. There were a few moments of hushed dialogue and then the attendant left the room. Owain had not heard of this part of the bard's activities, only about those deemed treasonous by his spies. While not a religious man himself, the King could see where allowing such a thing among his subjects could be to his benefit. A return to the old religion might mean peace. He had seen firsthand what driving the Faith out of people had done for Neth. It had left shallow, empty people with little hope or happiness. He did not want that for his kingdom. Leaning forward, he asked, "Where did peasants get two thousand crowns?"

The gdhededhá shook his head. "Not only peasants, milord. Many merchants and nobles support him, if only because of the miracles…"

"Elyri do not perform miracles."

"The people believe he does. He is not a healer, but many have claimed to be healed…"

Despite his curiosity, the King's eyes narrowed stubbornly. "The people are wrong."

"They are demanding his release…"

Half standing again, his hands gripping white around the arms of the throne, the King asked, "Who are these people to demand anything from me. I am their sovereign. I do what is necessary for the strength of the kingdom. He has incited revolts…"

Bowing, having expected a retort, the gdhededhá murmured, "My humblest apologies for misspeaking, milord. Peasant fancies. Surely, you know peasants will believe anything, even children's tales if they think it will better their lot. Can a bard be faulted for what the masses take literally?" For once, he was grateful that he was good at thinking on his feet.

The attendant returned and spoke quietly to the King. Jermyn could not hear the words, but he could see both men's faces. The King's expression twisted with anger and annoyance, but he did not yet speak. His soldiers asleep? The Elyri bard vanished through two locked doors without a trace? How could that be? The King could not reveal this, nor could he claim to have executed the bard. If the people's opinions of Kavan were truly so high, either story would produce unwanted results. There was no way to search for his former prisoner and take him back into custody without creating an unwanted scandal. Though he wanted the money the gdhededhá offered, this time the King knew he could not get it without force. Such an action was not worth taking.

"You are too late, gdhededhá. He was released at dawn and is likely on his way home."

The gdhededhá's round face brightened. "Then I shall catch up to him. He cannot have traveled far. Your benevolence is appreciated, milord. Your subjects will praise you for what you have done this day."

When the King dismissed him with an angry grunt and wave, Jermyn left the throne room without looking back. He was not certain the monarch was telling the truth, but he did believe that Kavan was no longer a prisoner. Perhaps he had constructed a Gate. Perhaps k'Ádhá had rescued him. Or perhaps the King had already executed him. Whatever the case, the gdhededhá knew where he had to go next. Mounting the horse he had been given by a sympathetic merchant, he rode hard to the northeast, hoping to find the man he sought.

ॐ*∾

That Kavan did not emerge from his room during the next three weeks did not trouble Ártur. That he ate little and refused to speak with anyone, including Prince Arlan and bhydáni Tíbhyan, did. The bhydáni came only once, the day of Kavan's return, as if he had known his student was back in Bhryell. Though Kavan would not see him, he asked Ártur to assure the sage that he would come to speak with him soon. The old man accepted the assurance without question and left behind an expensively bound copy of the Prayers of Saint Kóráhm, written in High Elyri, that he had found during Kavan's absence.

Prince Arlan, however, was not as forgiving. On return from the week spent with his bride in the Cáner's cabin, the prince was relieved to find that his friend had rejoined them. But as more days passed with Kavan keeping to himself, the more resentful and bitter the prince became, assuming that he was being ignored and avoided. The healer tried to explain that Kavan had been through a terrible ordeal and needed time to rest and heal, but the prince either did not believe him or else his desire to see Kavan overrode any sense of courtesy and compassion. He paced before Kavan's door much of the time, stopping only to eat, sleep, or spend a few moments alone with his wife and the child.

At last, on the twenty-first day after his return home, Kavan felt strong enough to face the world. He was tired of the same walls, tired of being indoors, and tired of being alone. He needed a change. It was time. Darkness still hung in the sky as he went to the porch, careful not to disturb the sleeping household. There, he breathed deeply of the scents of late winter, heavy wet earth, icy crisp air, and from somewhere far off, the aromas of baking bread. He stared at the peaceful town before him, knowing how much he had missed it while he had been gone, even if the village and the people in it had not missed him. Though the air was cold, he could feel that spring was rapidly approaching and he longed for warmth again. He had been cold too long. It was good to be home. There had been many nights lying in Rhidam's dungeon when he believed he might never see any of this again. Might not enjoy the distant sounds of households coming awake, the náós bell tolling on the other side of town, the call of birds one could only hear in a quiet little village like Bhryell. He had not meant to be selfish on his return, but he had needed the painless sleep and the time to meditate in his own bed and private prayer room more than anything else. He needed to assimilate everything that had happened, the adoration of the people, the brutality of a King, in order that these things did not gnaw at his soul and prevent him from the duty that lay head. Now that he was rested and at peace with himself and the world once again, he felt ready to face the inevitable questions this day would bring.

Harp in hand, he perched on the porch rail and began to play a quiet hymn dedicated to his freedom. To the east, the first light of morning crept like ivy vines over the mountains beyond the town's outer limits. It warmed the air enough to remove the chill and made him smile for the first time in many weeks. It was rare for him to feel truly at home. For once, in that moment, he did.

But the feeling did not last long. "You have risen from the dead." The voice that shattered his moment of bliss belonged to Prince Arlan, but the tone was unlike any Kavan had heard him use. The bard looked at him long enough to recognize that, with the beard, the prince looked even more like King Innis' son than ever. Then he looked away wearily with a long, deep, sigh.

"I needed time alone, My Prince."

Prince Arlan wanted to grab his shoulders and spin him around to face each other, but he had never gotten over his fear of touching the man. Instead, he grunted and said, "Because you could not face me after promising to be here for Muir's birth and the wedding?"

Kavan looked at his hands on the harp strings. He had been wrong to think he was emotionally strong enough to deal with the tirade he felt swirling behind the prince's words. The lack of understanding and respect hurt more than he had anticipated. "I wish I could have been…but I made no promises. I said I would try to be back if I could be. The child was born, and your original wedding date set before I finished the mission you gave me. And it is difficult to attend a wedding when one is a prisoner."

"Prisoner?" The prince climbed onto the railing beside him, noticing finally how gaunt the man's normally narrow face was, how sunken and dark his eyes were. Perhaps Ártur had been telling the truth.

"Ártur did not tell you?"

Prince Arlan looked away, ashamed to admit the truth, but finding he could not lie to the man, he said quietly, "He said something terrible had happened, that you needed rest and solitude. I did not believe him. I thought you were avoiding me…ignoring me." The tone was no longer angry or sullen, but rather that of an insecure boy. "Was it terrible, Kavan? What happened?"

The silence before Kavan spoke was one of the most uncomfortable the prince had ever experienced, and long enough that he almost retracted the question. When the answer did come, the pain in the whispered words made his skin crawl and his hair stand on end. "I traveled to every village, every town, every city I could throughout Enesfel. You have many people awaiting your arrival…though they do not know it is you they are waiting for as we agreed. At least ten men have been executed for treason for rallying to your cause…and the people have, I suspect, made them martyrs. I went to Rhidam to learn what I could of your sister, but before I could learn anything useful, I was arrested for inciting revolts…"

Prince Arlan thought about all the things a ruler could do to a man accused of such a treasonous act and shuddered. "Did Owain beat you?" The Elyri did not reply. "Damn it, Kavan…did he?"

It took several minutes before Kavan could lift his head. It was going to be one of the top questions on each person's mind, and he knew he would have to answer it again, but knowing it did not make the doing easier. "His soldiers did. I was scheduled for execution…but managed to escape…I am sorry I missed your wedding, My Prince. I would have given anything to be here."

Angry now, with himself as well as the King, Prince Arlan slid off the railing and began to pace, as much to avoid the pain he felt radiating off of Kavan as it was out of his own feelings of restlessness. "He will pay for what he has done. I will take his…"

"Do nothing hasty. I disrupted his kingdom. He had the right to…"

Prince Arlan stopped mid-step and stared at the bard in disbelief. "He did not have a right to call for your execution! You are as innocent as…"

"As?" The two men stared at each other until the prince swallowed and looked away. When he did not answer the question, Kavan continued. "I am free and safe. The body has healed. What was done was done. It is over. I know you are angry, but do not punish him on my account. He does not deserve it." Seeing the bearded boy about to protest again, Kavan quickly added, "Please…may we discuss something else?"

After several gulping breaths and a battle within himself, Prince Arlan leaned against the rail, staring into the brightening sky, and reluctantly gave in to the request. "No word of my sister?"

Leaving the harp on the porch, Kavan came down from the rail and the two men walked. The prince talked about what he had been learning and doing in their months apart, asking questions he had pondered, knowing the Elyri would give him some insight he had overlooked. He felt selfish, pouring his questions and problems onto Kavan when the bard surely had his own, but he also felt justified. If they were to move into Enesfel soon, he felt he needed many of his answers now, and Kavan, at least, seemed reluctant to discuss his own difficulties. But the prince did realize something important as he listened to the gentle voice now tinged with disillusioned pain. Kavan was no longer the man the prince had known, would never be the same man again. Something irreplaceable had been taken from him and nothing the prince could do or say would fix it.

Hoofbeats sounded ahead of them; Kavan heard them before the horse could be seen. He and Arlan had made several circles through town but had passed the house once again when the horse could be heard. Kavan looked back at his porch, feeling the need to withdraw, but it was too far away to retreat casually, thus he stopped moving and watched the horse and rider draw closer. When the gray nag was some twenty paces from them, it stopped and its rider hastily dismounted and ran towards Kavan. At this distance, the bard recognized the robes the man wore, and when he saw the eye-patch, he almost smiled in delight until the gdhededhá threw himself at Kavan's feet, took the white hands in his, and kissed them reverently. Prince Arlan stared.

"Praise k'Ádhá and Kóráhm you are alive, milord," the gdhededhá panted. "I have ridden long to find you and was beginning to despair that you were dead."

Embarrassed by the attention, Kavan helped the man to his feet. "As you can see, I am not, gdhededhá. Please…stand. How have you been faring? Did you get my message after we last met?"

The blonde man shook his head. "I did, but not until long after you had left Clarys, I'm afraid. I had gone into seclusion, to meditate on what I had seen with my own eyes."

Kavan had never forgotten that night and now awkwardly stepped back. "Did you find the answers you sought?" He supposed the gdhededhá must have by now.

"I did...and those answers have led me back to you." He smiled and wiped his brow on his sleeve. "I have traveled as a missionary through Cordash, Hatu, the Cíbhóló, and Enesfel. During my travels, I heard tales of a devout man, a holy man, and from the description they gave, I knew it had to be you. I had hoped to join you, travel together, but then I heard that you had been arrested."

The horse had edged closer to them and the gdhededhá patted the saddlebags on the animal's sides. "Two thousand crowns, milord. It was given to secure your release, but when I went before King Owain, you were no longer there."

Kavan stared at the saddlebags filled with coins as if they were deadly vipers. It was both flattering and frightening to think that people would go to such lengths on his behalf. He did not know what to say.

The gdhededhá gestured again, still smiling. "Please, accept it, milord. It is yours."

"I have done nothing to earn this..." His stomach was knotted to the point of sickness.

Jermyn smiled and shook his head. "It is a gift, not earnings, milord. The people raised it for your benefit. They will be disappointed if you reject their sacrifice."

"They need not know what has become of it..."

But the gdhededhá held firm to his convictions and could see that nothing short of forceful persuasion was going to change Kavan's mind. "If you will not take it, milord, donate it to a worthy cause. It is

yours to do with as you please. I have no need of it and would find it
wrong to give it to the k'gdhededhá without your instruction."

The bard bowed his head. He had not expected any devotion or
this sort of generosity from strangers, though perhaps he should have.
"Prince Arlan. It is yours." The prince looked at Kavan, at the stranger,
at the bags of coins, and then back at Kavan.

"Arlan?" the gdhededhá puffed, moving nearer to inspect the
young man's face closely. "Prince Arlan Lachlan?" His tone was like
a prayer as he fell to his knees again, this time clasping the prince's
hands instead of Kavan's. "Then it is true, all of what you said. Praise
be! I had hoped they were more than tales meant to give the people
hope." To the prince, he said, "If Lord Cliáth will not accept this, then
it is good you should put it to use liberating the people who gave it to
me." He glanced at Kavan with adoration. "Is that your wish, milord?"

What Kavan wished for was that this whole matter would disappear, but since that would not happen, he nodded. The prince would
need money for this venture, after all; perhaps this was meant to be.
The prince hoisted the saddlebags from the horse, amazed at their
weight.

"Please," Kavan said, feeling the need to offer something to the
man in return for the delivery of that offering. "Join us for breakfast,
gdhededhá. It would be the least I can give in return for what you have
given." The gdhededhá agreed though he denied he deserved repay-
ment, but there was silence among them as they led the horse to Kavan's home.

The household was beginning to stir as they entered. Brenna was
in the main room nursing the child Muir. Ártur was cooking in the
kitchen and Guthrie could be heard singing loudly, and mostly off-key,
from upstairs. Kavan greeted each of them and held Muir while the
others talked or went about their morning tasks. The infant clung to
him with all of his strength, his wide gray eyes demanding Kavan's
attention. The child's acceptance made him smile wistfully in a way

he had not done in many long weeks. He could see Owain in those gray eyes, and something else—a strong desire to leave home. Sighing, wondering what those premonitions meant, he cradled the baby against him and murmured a soft lullaby as the others bustled about. Muir snuggled close and drifted to sleep.

At the table over the morning meal, gdhededhá Jermyn tried to turn the conversation to the night he met Kavan, to that first visitation and what it had led him to discover. He felt a need to tell everyone the tale as he had been doing for months, but Kavan continually steered him away from any talk about himself. No one else present except Ártur knew about that night's events, and Kavan had no wish for them to know. It was bad enough they must have heard rumors about him during their months in Bhryell. Thwarted at each turn, gdhededhá settled into small talk with the others until the meal was over and then the men moved nearer to the fire while Brenna cleared the table.

"Since we're all here, we should get to the business at hand," Guthrie started, sitting on the window bench beside Prince Arlan, watching as the others got settled. The gdhededhá sat on a stool opposite him, as rigid as if he were a soldier rather than a man of the cloth. A smile tugged at Guthrie's lips at the thought of gaining the backing of the largest religious organization in the Five Sovereignties, but it faded when his eyes turned to Kavan sagging in the corner against the wall watching Muir crawl across the floor. The bard's expression was haunted, his posture weak, his speech and manner more hesitant that it had once been. He was the portrait of a man beaten and broken.

But there was intensity in his green eyes that belied that impression. There was an internal strength to this man, the tenacity to survive in the face of impossible odds, something that Guthrie saw in few men. Even when his mind and body were pushed to the brink of defeat, this man had a soul that refused to give up. Guthrie did not know what ordeal the Elyri harper had been through on Prince Arlan's behalf as he had not felt it right to ask, but he was beginning to understand how important this man would be to them in the months ahead.

"Kavan, Ártur tells me you have prepared quite a welcome for us in Enesfel…"

It was the gdhededhá who spoke, interrupting Guthrie before Kavan had the chance to reply. "If only you could see it. All over Enesfel, people are talking about a prince who will save them from destruction and bring them into a new age. They believe it as fervently as if the prince himself had spoken it. They will do whatever is required when the time comes, especially when they learn that a true Lachlan heir, and not a bastard child of King Farrell's, lives and will fight for them."

Guthrie nodded, not sure what to make of this one-eyed holy man but appreciating the information. "They will know soon enough. One look at Prince Arlan and I suspect many will know him to be a Lachlan. It doesn't matter if they think he's Farrell's son or not…at least not for now." The prince swung his feet, his wide-eyed expression unchanging.

"Lord McHador," Kavan started. "I too believe there will be adequate support for the prince. Ten men have already died at the King's command, accused of treason for…"

"More than ten have died," interjected Jermyn, seemingly not noticing the varying expressions of shock and dismay on the faces around him. "In the outer cities and villages, I have seen whole families butchered for their refusal to follow the King's decrees. They believe their savior prince is coming soon and are willing to defy the King to the death in support of that belief."

Prince Arlan groaned. "It would seem best then if we move as soon as possible…"

"The snows are not finished; it would be best to wait for their end. Traveling will be extremely difficult…"

"We should use that to our advantage, Guthrie, should we not? Owain will not be expecting any half-sane resistance movement in the midst of winter. If we begin to gather forces now, we might have the advantage of surprise; weather may slow down news to the castle. It will take many months to make a full circuit of the kingdom. Even the money you brought us, gdhededhá, will not be enough to hire or bribe troops; we should have a sufficient force to..."

"Money?" asked the ex-general in a perplexed tone.

Kavan spoke without looking at anyone. "A long story...suffice to say the gdhededhá has brought a sizable donation for our cause. I hope it can be put to good use on the prince's behalf."

Turning back to the prince with a bemused expression, Guthrie continued. "Anything will help. This is not going to be an easy task, nor an inexpensive one. We may obtain donations and support along the way, but having financial backing would be to our benefit. As for travel...our biggest obstacle will be the passes; there is no way to cross the Llaethlágárá at this time of year. Foul weather would trap us..."

"There are Gates." Seeing Ártur's shock at the suggestion, Kavan shrugged and continued, "I documented those I could find. The papers have been lost in Rhidam's dungeon I fear, but I know where they are. I could take us anywhere in Enesfel you desire to go..."

"Now King Owain has a list of...?" the healer croaked in alarm.

Kavan looked at him with dismay. Did his cousin have so little faith in him? "No Teren can read what I wrote. Nor can most Elyri. If he manages to find a translator, it will be a list of cities and villages; that won't tell him anything."

The healer looked away, embarrassed, as Jermyn clasped and kissed the harper's hands. Guthrie glanced around and saw that he was the only one in the room who did not know what Kavan and Ártur were talking about, which annoyed him but not enough to prompt him to interrupt.

"I knew he had not been truthful," the gdhededhá gushed. "He told me you had been released, but I did not believe him. I have not told anyone you are no longer a prisoner, for I did not know it to be true.

Most of Enesfel believes you are either still a captive or have been executed, and the King's reputation has suffered for both."

Seeing the pain that flickered across Kavan's face, Ártur decided to speak, hoping to make up for his own hasty, inaccurate judgment by deflecting focus away from his cousin. "It appears that, between those willing to back the prince, and Kavan's following, we could be a force to be reckoned with."

The bard changed the subject by asking questions of topics that did not address his involvement. "What of Hatu? Cordash? The nomads?"

Guthrie cleared his throat and rubbed his neck, relieved to be getting back to business. "There are nine men from Cordash who will be waiting for us in Rhidam, and about fifty nomads who are planning to do the same. Not a large number, but that many Cíbhóló fighting men will be like a small army in itself. Cordash could not spare any military personnel due to their ongoing conflict with Neth, but King Geir promised to mobilize Hatu's forces and send them as soon as the word is given."

"That would be a good distraction," Prince Arlan said enthusiastically. "An army amassing on Hatu's border might be enough to divert Owain's attention from us…"

The ex-general shook his head. "The Harcourts cannot afford to draw Enesfel's army into a war. Hatu would be destroyed, and I, for one, do not want that on my conscience. We can start that piece moving when we are closer to our final objective, or when the odds against us are so high that we have no other choice." Running his hand through his beard, Guthrie looked from Ártur to Kavan. "Rather than ride to Enesfel from here, I think we should use those Gates…if we can…and if it is acceptable to you both. We could then depart as soon as can be arranged."

Brenna had come into the room for Muir; she nodded at her uncle, agreeing with his assessment of the situation though she was far from pleased about being separated from her husband for what could be a very long time. When no one gave any objections, Guthrie stood. "Very well. Arlan, Ártur, you know what you must do to be ready to travel. There is nothing you need concern yourself with, Kavan, except resting and gathering whatever personal effects you require for such an arduous journey. That is…if you are coming with us."

Kavan nodded without looking at him. "It is my duty. I have no choice." The certainty with which the bard spoke, his choice of words, made Guthrie uneasy. At the same time, however, it was also oddly reassuring to hear. "You will be welcome. We need as many supporters as we can get. We shall depart in two days if your health permits."

"I will be ready."

gdhededhá Jermyn leaned forward on his stool. "May I join your ranks, Prince Arlan? I would be honored to serve you in whatever capacity I can, be it scribe or servant." The blonde man looked like an excited boy about to venture from home for the first time, enthusiastic and wary all at the same time.

Kavan spoke before Prince Arlan could. It was not that he disliked the gdhededhá, but he had to think about the prince's future…and his own capacity to travel for months with a man who practically worshiped him. In time, age might temper Jermyn's adoration, but they had neither time nor age right now. "gdhededhá, you are not well known in Enesfel, are you?" His questions brought curious stares.

"As well-known as a humble gdhededhá of a discarded religion can be in a foreign land. Some may recognize me, remember me from my visits, but I think those will be few. I am not very charismatic, I'm afraid, and even with this," he rubbed his eye patch, "many will not likely remember me. What do you have in mind?"

Kavan looked at the prince, indicating that, though the idea was his, the final decision would be Arlan's. "It may be better if you travel separately from us…"

"Separately?" The sandy-haired man was visibly disappointed. Though he often shied away from physical gestures, Kavan touched the man's arm, knowing it would soothe the gdhededhá's agitation better than any words he could say. "It is not what you desire, but it may benefit the prince more. You could gather people to come to Rhidam under the pretext of going to witness a miracle…"

The touch on his arm had the desired effect. Jermyn smiled and chuckled. "You would be better suited to that…"

"No," Prince Arlan said emphatically. He did not know what Kavan was thinking or intending, but he knew that sending Kavan on such an errand would be dangerous to the Elyri's welfare after what had happened to him previously. "If he was arrested once, he would likely be arrested again, and I doubt the King would hesitate to execute him this time. Doing this for me, gdhededhá, could increase our supporters, but I will not command you. Such an undertaking is not without risks, as you know, and you are not my subject."

The portly man leaned back once more, smile fading from his face at the sobering reminders. "I am a subject of righteousness, and your cause is righteous. It is worth the risk and I do not fear danger. Do you believe I shall be more useful serving you in this manner?"

Prince Arlan gave the question a moment's consideration. "Yes, I do."

Jermyn folded his arms across his chest and glanced at Kavan before allowing determination to settle on his features. "I shall do this, then, and meet you in Rhidam. I certainly do not want further harm to come to you, Lord Cliáth. This whole thing, if you succeed, will definitely qualify as a miracle. There would be nothing dishonest in such a claim and if we fail…" he paused and chuckled, "I would not be the first prophet to find his prophecy unfulfilled. How shall I proceed?"

Without consulting Guthrie for an answer, the prince replied, "It does not matter, as long as it is legal and you keep your story consistent. Use your imagination. I will trust your judgment, gdhededhá, because I know Kavan does." He glanced at the bard and smiled, "You will play for us tonight, won't you, Kavan?"

With a heavy sound that suggested he would rather not, Kavan murmured, "If you wish."

Not detecting that reluctance, or perhaps choosing not to acknowledge it, Prince Arlan grinned and squeezed the bard's shoulder before bounding up the stairs, followed by Brenna who carried Muir on her hip. Despite his budding maturity and the beard, in many ways, the prince was still a boy. Kavan hoped he would not lose that quality in the struggle to come. Ártur patted his arm reassuringly and went to begin his own preparations, which would require visits to his patients to let them know he would be unavailable for the foreseeable future. The general likewise gave the bard a glance as he left the room, appreciating what seemed to be a man with a good head on his shoulders. Kavan hoped the gdhededhá would likewise leave him, but since he had no packing to do, only a horse to tend to, Jermyn was in no hurry to move. He waited until they were alone, looking long and hard at Kavan, before asking, "They do not know, do they?"

"Do not know what?" Kavan believed he knew what the gdhededhá was asking, but he hoped that feigned ignorance would cause the man to drop the subject.

"About your gift, the visitation…?"

Kavan groaned; luck was not with him today. "I am not sure I would call it a gift, gdhededhá. It is just something that happens…"

The man's eyes grew wide. "It has happened more than once?"

Regretting his choice of words, Kavan replied, "It happens frequently, though I have seen someone with me only one time. Ártur knows of these things, but he is not the only one to…"

"There have been others?"

He nodded reluctantly. "Most of Bhryell has seen things."

There was an excited reverence about the gdhededhá that Kavan found ever more unnerving. This conversation was going deeper into territory the bard would rather not discuss. "There have been many across Enesfel. People claim to have seen and heard záryph when they are near you. Some have claimed healing. I know peasants can be a superstitious lot, prone to fancy, but I do not think they are stupid. And it has not been merely peasants telling me these things…"

The bard groaned louder. His eyes hurt. His head hurt. But most of all, there was pain in his chest as his lungs fought for air past a throat constricted with anxiety. "Stop, gdhededhá. I do not want to hear this."

"Why? Because you believe if you ignore it, it will cease to be true? I do not know if it is true or not, since I was not there to witness the events…and I admit I find some of the stories farfetched…but I do know what I saw and felt the first time I met you…"

"Enough." Kavan stood up to leave the room, but dizziness at the sudden movement made him pause. "You have put me in the same ecclesiastical boat with the saints. I am nothing other than myself, gdhededhá. You should know better than to put such titles on men. How do you know it was not some evil spirit you saw, that the others see? How do you know it is not some Elyri trick meant to deceive you? You do not know k'Ádhá's heart…"

"Nor do you," the gdhededhá snapped, his face flushed with embarrassment. It took great effort for him to regain his composure. Kavan stopped in the doorway, stunned into stillness by the gdhededhá's words, words he had never fully considered before. "You do not know what is wanted of you, nor do you know if the people see and experience as they claim. I do not know what it was I saw, but I know what it was not. I believe it was not an act of deception on your part, as I do not believe it is in you to deceive others. That visitation led to much personal growth, led to numerous conversions, and led me back to you and to Prince Arlan. That is certainly not something spirits of evil intent would encourage. If these things we see are evil, I believe you would know. That you tolerate it, even welcome it, speaks more of their nature than the events themselves. Stop denying what you do not know and accept what you do know. I am only gdhededhá, it is true, and I have no right to call you something you may not be..."

The logic and rightness of the argument vaporized with Jermyn's last words and Kavan glared over his shoulder with narrowed eyes. "And what would you have me be, gdhededhá? Would you have me believe I am the holy man everyone thinks, be their leader, use them the way some have in the past for my own agenda? I do not want followers; I do not want..."

"Then you will need to become a recluse. You may not be a saint, and I am not saying you are, but you are the closest any of us living will see. We are drawn to you like moths to candles because you are the only light we have in a life of darkness. You are honest, decent, benevolent, and talented. The people of Enesfel have had little hope for many years, and certainly no hope for anything eternal. You have offered them a path to both. You are special to them because you have given them hope. Accept that. I have been trying to do the same since I met you. I wandered the Sovereignties trying to give faith and hope, and while I have had some success, it was nothing like the success you have had. You are one of them, one of the people. I look like a gdhededhá, sound like a gdhededhá, act like a gdhededhá. If you really want to help them, do what you do best. They will follow and they will believe. We can do much together, you and I; I have the authority to build naós and appoint gdhededhá, but I lack the ability to fill them. You do not."

Kavan left the house, no longer able to bear listening to the weight of those words. In his soul, he knew Jermyn was right. He had always known those things, but having someone else see it, express it to him, was startling. This was his burden in life, to be a light to people around him, but he did not have to welcome it. He only had to live with it. Right now, however, he had a prince to attend to, a prince to make into a King if he could. That had to be his focus. If, while doing what he

must to secure the Lachlan dynasty, he could give the people something more, did he have the right to refuse?

He stopped on the porch and looked across the town square. There
was nothing he could do inside beyond pack a few articles of clothing,
and he was not in the mood for further conversation with anyone regarding his time in Enesfel. Instead, he chose to roam the cobblestone
streets of Bhryell, shutting out the thoughts of everyone he passed. It
was early enough that the streets were not yet filled with people, only
a few individuals out on early morning errands. Thus, he was alone to
wander without interruption. He did not have to dwell on gdhededhá
Jermyn's words, or King Owain's torture, or of the adoration of the
masses that made him ill at ease. He could focus on the buildings
around him, many of which had been abandoned during the plague
and had yet to be re-inhabited. As slowly as the Elyri population grew,
he knew it would be many centuries before they were filled again, and
pondering that emptiness gave him a welcome feeling of solace.

His wandering brought him back to the fountain in the center of
town that had been erected in honor of the village's founders. His own
ancestors. He had never studied it before, never considered himself
part of a continuing tradition. He was the last Cliáth. What would his
parents say if they could see him? Would they regret that he had not
continued in the harp making tradition as his name suggested he
should? Would they embrace him as their own, applaud his skills and
talents, or would they have shunned him and turned him away as his
uncle had done? His father he could not recall, except as a voice crying
out from the flames that filled his infrequent nightmares. His mother's
memory was also faint, but if he tried, he could call up the sound of
her voice singing a lullaby. Voices without faces. They were the only
recollections of family he had.

He turned around to look at the place he called home. He had never
expected to have a home of his own, although he had always known
he could not live with his kin as many Elyri did. He felt a twisting pull

at his stomach and heart. He felt like weeping without knowing why. The realization that formed within him refused to leave. Though he had no proof, he suspected that it was an accurate perception.

"You will be leaving Bhryell soon."

Kavan did not look at his teacher who had appeared silently beside him. He had felt Tíbhyan's approach before the man reached him, though it puzzled him why a man who rarely left his home was out at this early hour. "Yes."

"Does it trouble you to be leaving Bhryell for what could be a very long time?"

Kavan closed his eyes and did not speak for many minutes. When he did, his voice was small. "What troubles me is that I may never be back. This may be my final farewell."

The sage shifted his weight from one weak leg to the other. "Do you honestly believe this is goodbye?"

Kavan pushed his hair from his face before opening his eyes. "I only know that I do not belong here. I am not like the others; they do not understand me. Sometimes I do not understand myself. Though Guthrie and the others claim differently, Prince Arlan will have to fight for the throne of Enesfel and has asked me to be his confidant and house bard if he succeeds. I will go with him because I must. It is my destiny. After his death," he paused with a shudder, "I do not know what will transpire when that time comes, but I suspect something will keep me in Enesfel for many years to come. I may never see you again."

Tíbhyan smiled and patted Kavan's arm. "You have grown much since I agreed to teach you, Kavan, not just from a boy into a man. You long ago outgrew my knowledge; I have nothing left to give but friendship. True friendship knows no distance. There comes a time for everyone when they must move into the world, to learn what it has to teach. You have proven yourself to everyone except yourself. As I told your cousin, I have never met another better equipped to venture into the world than you are."

Kavan met the older man's gaze. "Do you sincerely believe that?"

"I believe in you, that you can do whatever you set out to do. Do not allow fear to hamper you, Kavan. You are ready for this. Do what you must. Live your life."

The bard's expression softened but his sadness did not dissipate.

"I will miss you, bhydáni. Thank you for the book."

Tíbhyan smiled. "You are welcome. I knew you would appreciate it. But I am no longer your bhydáni. I am Tíbhyan. We are as equal as two men of our ages can be. I will miss you, Kavan. If I do not see you again, I pray that peace goes with you all of your days."

"I pray I shall see you again."

"I pray likewise."

"I…"

Shaking his head, melancholy crept into his smile. Tíbhyan interrupted and patted Kavan's arm one more time before stepping away. "Enough. It is time."

Kavan remained where he was, staring at the frozen water in the fountain as the sage hobbled in the direction of home. Tears broke free and slid down his white cheeks. He made no effort to wipe them away.

☙Chapter 24☙

The sun sank over Alberni's skyline, bathing Kavan in its pale crimson glow as he watched the sky from the second floor of the town's most respectable inn. There were few street lamps to mar his vision from this corner of town, and Kavan found it peaceful and serene here. He preferred this stillness to the bustle of people and activity he had endured earlier in the day. Though he could not see the town square, he could hear the gathering of people loitering there. From his vantage point, all he could see were the shingle roofs of the surrounding buildings and on the hillside to the south, he could make out the lights of the small manor that overlooked the town.

Had anyone asked, he would have admitted that, of all of Enesfel, he liked Alberni best. The town was set back from the edge of the sea, allowing them access to a port on the river, and it was small, lush, and best of all, tranquil. The architecture had changed little since the original Elyri settlement, though the hill manor was of slightly newer construction. If not for the obligations that had occupied him all day, he would have gone to the manor and petitioned the owners for a glimpse of the inside. As it was owned by Brenna's brother, Guthrie's nephew, Kavan had little doubt he could have gained permission. But he would not get to see it any time soon. Duty came first.

He and Ártur brought the others in their party through the Gate early that morning: Prince Arlan, Guthrie, twenty-nine-year-old twin brothers Bhríd and Phaedr Cáner—distant cousins of the MacLyr's who had befriended the prince during his months in Bhryell—and their sister Syl, a petite woman of twenty-five who was also a healer. The brothers were excited by the prospect of adventure outside of Elyriá, and their sister would not allow them to confront dangerous armies without her healing hands to assist them. Though Guthrie fretted about having a woman in the ranks, he discovered he could not be rid of her, and reluctantly admitted that they would need as many healers as they could procure. With some trepidation, he agreed that she could travel with them.

Afterward, Kavan took gdhededhá Jermyn to the city of Jardin where he had elected to begin his mission. It seemed prudent to each of them for the wandering force and the proselytizing gdhededhá to begin in different regions to limit the likelihood of anyone suspecting they were working towards the same goal. The bard lingered long enough to see that the one-eyed gdhededhá made it safely out of the abandoned náós, and then he joined the rest of his companions in Alberni.

With everyone where they should be, Brenna and Muir safe in Bhryell with the Cáner's parents, a large community room in the inn was secured. Guthrie chose not to endanger his nephew by seeking to lodge in the Weylin manor. Hanford Weylin would be in enough danger as it was, for he had provided the fledgling rebellion with weapons, horses, and had arranged for several of his personal household guards to accompany the prince on his travels. The Duke had also insisted on being the financier for their undertaking, a dangerous but welcome patronage. As a new relative to the royal Lachlan dynasty, Duke Weylin was eager to assist his sister's husband and support his Uncle's mission. Should King Owain learn of it, however, the duke's life would be in grave danger.

Prince Arlan supplied Kavan with a beautiful, well-crafted sword, though the bard vehemently opposed accepting it. Since he could not ease the prince's mind by telling him how he would defend himself without it, should the need arise, Kavan was forced to accept the blade. Unlike Ártur, whose oaths precluded such deadly weapons, Kavan was trained and proficient with it; but he never intended to use it. He had no use of such things. Kavan felt his gifts were dangerous enough without the need for a blade in his hands.

The requisition of supplies and outfitting of horses and men had taken most of the day. Now it was late evening, the sun had finished its descent over the western horizon, and Kavan was alone in the room except for Phaedr and Syl who had already turned in for the night. The company would leave before dawn thus he suspected the others would be arriving soon enough. Now, however, they were speaking to the gathering of townsfolk in the city square.

Kavan shivered. On his arrival that morning, people had swarmed around him, wanting him to touch them, play for them, and visit their homes. They were overjoyed that he was no longer a royal prisoner and seemed to want nothing more than his attention; they showed little interest in either Guthrie or Prince Arlan. Despite having been fore-warned, Ártur was shocked at their reaction to his cousin and was unable to blame Kavan when the bard admonished the townsfolk to listen to Guthrie and then stole away in search of solitude. Kavan had not left their room in the inn since then. If not for Duke Weylin's persistence, they might have been following Kavan still.

Sensing a presence behind him, Kavan turned to see Guthrie's broad silhouette in the doorway of the room. The general paused, wondering if Kavan had heard his footsteps, and then motioned. Kavan followed. "I need to speak with you," was all the older man said as they left the building and went into the darkness. The gathering had finally disbanded; the streets were silent and many of the street lamps had been extinguished. Kavan found the night soothing, but he could feel Guthrie's unease as they passed each shadowy alley. They did not stop until they reached the empty commons, but even there Guthrie did not let his guard down.

"Where are the others?"

"Bhríd is checking on the horses and supplies once more before turning in. Arlan and Ártur were speaking with Hanford when I left; they're likely on their way to the inn now. I told them I was going to turn in, but I wished to speak with you first."

Wondering why, Kavan asked, "Were you successful?"

"Once we got their attention, they were willing to listen. I could not believe…" He shook his head. "Only the older folks recognize Innis in Arlan, but most agree he is a Lachlan. A mixed blessing. Without revealing his identity, only that he is the rightful heir to the throne, it might keep the King off balance for now. At least that is my hope. Let them think he is one of Farrell's bastards. That is good enough…better actually. Everyone was enraptured by what Arlan had to say; he has the makings of an excellent diplomat. A credit to you, no doubt, as oratory is not one of my skills. With word of mouth at work, we should have quite a following by morning. We do not need fanatics, but if people feel compelled to protect you, we will accept them into our company."

"I did not mean for this to happen, Lord McHador…"

"Call me Guthrie. Everyone does…and it will be a long journey if you call me Lord the whole time." He smiled to reassure the bard of his sincerity. "I know it was not your plan. Even uneducated people know a leader when they see one." He shook his head as Kavan started to speak. "Not everyone born to lead wants to. I have seen many men who did not want to lead become the best leaders in their field. Donal Lachlan was one of those. You've made a promising start in that direction, however unintentional. The people see it in Arlan too. Together, I think the two of you will provide us what we need to succeed. Having the duke on our side will be a blessing too; it will make it a little easier to sway others and provide us with much-needed funding."

"Will it be enough?"

Guthrie shrugged. "I do not know. We will only know by swaying one duke…or ex-duke, at a time. What did you mean this afternoon about having the means to scout ahead of us as we travel?"

Kavan stared at the sky. The offer had been made, but at the time, it seemed no one had heard him. "It is a skill rarely used by my people; most cannot do it. Though Ártur does not fully approve of my use of it, he does agree that in this instance, it might be in everyone's best interest if I do."

"Will you be in danger?"

"No more than I would be riding beside Prince Arlan, where he wishes me to be," the bard replied.

There were several minutes of silence as Guthrie pondered the matter. He did not know how it would be done, but he did think it sounded like a good idea. Any advance warning they could get of trouble would be in Prince Arlan's best interest. "I say do it. The locals claim the King has spies and soldiers everywhere; we have gathered some twenty-four men, with more to follow I believe, but the last thing we need is to be ambushed this early in the campaign. We need time to establish a strong following. If you can provide us with that time, and with some safety, do it. I will answer to the prince."

"Very well." He waited to see if the general would say more, and when he did not, Kavan said, "Something more is troubling you."

Guthrie's shoulders and the corners of his mouth twitched. "I do not know why that surprises me. Ártur does it all the time. Yes, something is…I know who is in command of the King's army, and I do not like the thought of potential combat against him. I trained Ferghus, taught him most of what he knows. A battle between he and I is death for everyone. I must talk to him. I do not know how he feels about the King; he knows Owain is not Innis' son, and he is likely uncomfortable with Owain's methods of leadership, but when he took his oaths, he swore to protect the Lachlan family. He takes his oaths and words literally and will protect the King, because he is a Lachlan, no matter what. He did the same for Bowen. If I could prove to him there is another Lachlan, or at least plant the suspicion that there might be, while he might not side with us he would not likely fight against us either."

"He would have to choose, and it would seem likely he would choose the King to avoid execution for treason."

"Ferghus is crafty," the general smirked. "He would devise some way to avoid breaking his oath. He has done it before. He got out of doing much of Bowen's dirty work by finding diplomatic reasons to be in Cordash as much as possible."

"Why are you telling me this?"

"I want you to take me to him."

The request came as a surprise. "Me? Not Ártur? You know him better than you know me…"

Guthrie chuckled. "Indeed. I know that he would refuse immediately. I did not even consider asking him. While he has been in the political arena for many years, I do not think he always comprehends the intricacies of diplomacy. Despite your lack of experience, I think you do. It does not necessarily take years of familiarity to know when you can trust someone, when someone is right for a given task."

The bard accepted the compliments without any indication of approval. "Does General McLeu lodge in the guardhouse or the castle?"

Guthrie thought about the question. "Likely in the guardhouse; after I first left court, he refused to move into my room and he is, as a whole, fairly resistant to change."

The billows of clouds above them parted to reveal the half moon. Though the air felt heavy with rain, Kavan felt confident that this storm would pass. Finally, he spoke. "I will not take you."

"But…"

The bard shook his head. "I understand what you say, and agree that if he cannot be persuaded to join us, he must at least be persuaded not to be against us. However, it will be difficult, and dangerous, to get you into the castle grounds. I think we should give careful consideration to how, when, and where to approach the general. Think on it more, and if you have not changed your mind by the time we reach Chantel, I will arrange for the two of you to meet."

"Temperance. You are worse than…" The man grunted in annoyance, though he understood and agreed with Kavan's assessment. "Very well. I will wait. But I will not change my mind. It needs to be done."

"I do not expect you to change it. I merely ask that you give it more time before approaching him."

Guthrie nodded. "I will. Goodnight, Kavan. You should rest. We ride before dawn."

Kavan did not move as Guthrie started back towards the inn. When the man was no longer in sight, the bard went to the náós, wondering why most Gates had been constructed within the confines of holy ground.

Guthrie wanted to meet with General McLeu. So be it.

He found it surprisingly simple to get from Rhidam castle's third-floor oratory to the room that had once been Guthrie's. There were few sentries posted, except for those outside the King's chamber, from whence could be heard loud arguing. The sentries were looking away from Kavan and thus did not see him enter, and they could not hear him over the sounds of the argument. As Guthrie had indicated, this room had been unused for many years, but Kavan had thought it best to rule it out.

Opening the wooden shutters, he looked across the courtyard in the direction of the guardhouse. One light burned there, but there were too many men patrolling between the castle and the guardhouse to make approach easy. For Kavan, however, it would not be difficult. He took a deep, calming breath, closed his lids, and pictured the raven in his mind's eye. His skin prickled as if he was sleeping bare-skinned on straw, a sensation that caused him a moment of trembling before the air around him shifted. He spread his new white wings and took to the sky. Men in the courtyard below cried out in amazement as he circled higher; he had forgotten that to see a raven in Rhidam this early in the year was often viewed as an omen of bad luck. He flew out of sight of the men to find a place to land where he could approach the guardhouse unseen, amused at his own unexpected choice. Let them believe in the bad luck curse. For some, this time the omen might prove accurate.

The raven perched on the windowsill when he found the room he wanted, watching the man within who sat at a rough-hewn desk trace circles on a sheet of parchment with his pheasant quill pen. Every few minutes he would look up towards the fire, distracted by thoughts that would not allow him to sleep. He could not shake the feelings of apprehension that plagued him, and added to that now was the feeling of being observed. When he finally noticed the rustling sound at the window, he looked to see a small white raven ruffling its feathers, watching him steadily. Once eye contact was made with the bird, it left its perch and settled on the desk in front of him, never looking away.

Ferghus slid his chair back but did not otherwise move as cold sweat formed on his forehead and the back of his neck. He was not a superstitious man by nature, but he did not think this could be a fortuitous sign. A raven in winter. A white raven at that. The bird cocked its head. Images flashed through Ferghus' mind, not clear enough to decipher, but still a message he believed he was going to need time to sort out. The door to the room opened and the young soldier there stopped at the sight of the peculiar bird on the general's desk. Ferghus motioned for him to leave but the soldier was rooted in place.

The action did not startle the bird into leaving. It remained as it was for a few more moments, tilting its head this way and that as though trying to communicate, and then, with a throaty caw, it ruffled its feathers again and flew out the open window. The soldier hurried away without speaking, forgetting whatever he had come for, leaving the door open behind him. Ferghus stood on shaky legs, closed the door and window, and quickly readied for bed as if he could hide beneath the blankets from what had happened. Many hours passed, however, before he found anything akin to restful sleep.

Sunrise found Prince Arlan's followers on the road to the town of Chantel. One hundred and six men, mostly peasant youths, and vagabonds, had joined Duke Weylin's twenty-five personal guards overnight, but the sheer number of bodies bolstered the prince's spirits so that he sang most of the morning and kept looking behind him as if expecting them to be gone when he looked. Only the empty bay gelding beside him, with sword and wooden harp case strapped to its sides, troubled him. He had chosen the horse and sword for his friend, and now they were little more than a pack animal and extra weapon. Guthrie explained that he had given Kavan a special duty to perform, but as the prince had requested the bard's company while they rode, he found it difficult to accept that Kavan would take Guthrie's command over his entreaty.

Yet there was no sign of Kavan as they traveled. Even when they stopped for the midday meal he did not appear. Prince Arlan ate quietly, watching a snowy kestrel devour some small animal in a nearby tree. Morning's enthusiasm waned as sore muscles became a growing reality. As he remounted, after making certain Kavan's harp and sword were still in place, the prince wished for the bard's presence ever more fervently. And he wished that all of this were over already.

General Ferghus paced the King's study as he awaited an audience. He had never felt nervous approaching the King before, but then, he realized, he had never come to ask for anything personal. Even when there had been deaths in his family, he had not asked for leave, had never asked for compensation for personal losses. He considered himself a servant of the Crown and believed that a servant did not ask for such things from their master. If he were not here to protect the King, who would be? After all, King Bowen's death, when Ferghus had been out of the kingdom, was a perfect example of what could happen. He had never again asked for anything that would take him away from his all-important duty.

But this time, things were different. Had not the raven appeared to him, bid him make a journey to Chantel, a city he had never been to and where he knew no one? How could he explain this need to the King, when he did not know why he felt called to be there, or what he was supposed to do when he arrived. Stopping at the window, he leaned his elbows on the sill and watched the livery brush down a trio of horses. The tall, stocky, pied stallion, the King's usual mount, pulled stubbornly at his harness, hoping to break free of its caretakers as it frequently did. That meant that the King had returned. It was brisk outside and felt like snow; it was the King's favorite kind of weather.

The monarch entered the room then, disheveled and muddy from the morning's hunt, but smiling widely. "Well, Ferghus, the hart continues to elude me but you should see the one I did get."

"Congratulations, milord. I shall go see it indeed. Am I to take it there shall be venison for dinner?"

"Tomorrow. It is too late in the day now," he replied as he slid off his boots and sank into a chair. "Robret told me you wanted to see me? What about? The princess?"

The general shook his head. "No change, milord. She eats but refuses to acknowledge anyone except Lady Muriel. She is unwell, and Lady Muriel claims she is getting worse daily. Unfortunately, I do not think she will change her mind about…" Deciding the final words were best left unsaid, to avoid angering the King, he said instead, "She did, however, inquire as to your health."

King Owain shrugged, ignoring the subtle suggestion that he should give up on his quest to marry Deidre. "I hope Lady Muriel told her I am well. Have a physician tend her, please, and tell him to report her condition to me at once."

"Yes, milord; I will see to it."

When the general said nothing more, the King looked at him expectantly. "What is it then? Trouble with Hatu? More revolts?"

"None that I am aware of, and Hatu was silent at last report. However…" He swallowed hard and watched the King pour himself a glass of pale red wine from the liquor cabinet.

"Speak freely, General. If something is worthy of your concern, you should feel free to share it with me."

It was hard not to shuffle his feet, but the general kept still and bowed his head. "Yes, milord. There may be…trouble…but I am uncertain of its nature or origin. Last night I saw a raven…"

The King laughed merrily. "Superstition!"

Pretending not to be embarrassed, Ferghus nodded. "Normally I would think so, for I am not a superstitious man. But this raven was white; it came into the guardhouse and landed on my desk. It looked me full in the face and showed no fear of my movements. It seemed to be trying to tell me something, but of course, ravens cannot speak. When it departed, I fell into a daze filled with strange, disturbing dreams of war. I do not know their meaning, or why I should see such things, but I believe the raven brought these things to me and has summoned me to Chantel to ward off this disaster…whatever it is…"

"What on earth is in Chantel? Do you have family there?"

The general had not expected the King to believe him, for he barely believed himself, but the perceived ridicule still stung. "I have no living family, save my son and his wife in Tarsee, and the only person I have known from that region is long dead I am sure. I can think of no rational reason for this, but I am certain I must go. I have never asked for anything from the Crown, not even when my wife died did I ask for leave. You must think me crazed, but believe me, milord, this is no fever. Allow me three weeks to attend to this matter and I shall return as soon as I am able."

The King studied the general silently. What the man said was true. In all of his years of service to the Lachlan family, he had never, to Owain's knowledge, taken any personal leave of absence nor taken time off except for the gravest of illnesses. Every Lachlan since King Innis had employed him, and every one since King Donal had retained Ferghus as Enesfel's top general. There was no logical reason to deny the man the chance to pursue ghosts, regardless of how silly it seemed.

"Very well, General. Three weeks and no more. I do not care what you find, or if you find it, but I want you back here in three weeks."

"Do you wish to know…?"

"Only if you think it is a matter of security, something I need to know for the sake of the kingdom. Otherwise, keep this to yourself. The men do not need to be haunted by rumors of ravens, ghosts, and superstitions."

The general bowed and departed, both relieved that the King was allowing him to pursue this and embarrassed that it took superstition to draw him away from his obligations. But he believed this to be duty too, a matter of importance to the welfare of Enesfel, else he would not be going.

Shaking his head, the King did not watch the general depart. Perhaps, he mused, it was time to consider looking for a new general. But Ferghus was the best he had, and until he was certain the peasant revolts were behind him, he wanted Ferghus there to fight for him. Let the old man chase a few dreams. It could not hurt to let him get it out of his system.

☙*❧

"It is about time you joined us," Prince Arlan barked, causing those nearest to him to look up. The sun had set many hours ago and some among them already slept. The camp was impressive to the young, inexperienced prince, with many small fires scattered in a rough circle around him. He had never seen this many men gathered in one place. "Who gives the orders? Guthrie or me?"

Kavan resisted the temptation to look at the ex-general. Instead, he took out his harp and began to tune it. Though he had not yet eaten, he did not feel particularly hungry. Only after circling the encampment several times to make certain there were no threats did he rejoin the unit. He was weary to the core; he had never used his power this extensively, had never retained another shape this long, but he had discovered, though it came as no surprise, that he enjoyed the experience. He felt both depleted of energy and elated, but he did not feel up to arguing with the prince.

"My Prince, you know I am at your service…"

"Then why did you not ride with me as I asked?"

"I am in your service, but my priority is to keep you safe. I am of little use to you with a sword I will not use; what would my riding at your side gain you? I know you desire my company. I, too, desire the company of those I trust. However, if such comforts must be set aside to accomplish the task at hand, that is what I shall do. Such burdens should not be placed on one so young, but you are mature enough to know the risks of your choice. You accepted this responsibility freely and must endure the hardships that come with it."

The Prince looked away, his cheeks scarlet beneath his beard. "Does being a king mean one must forever endure loneliness and hardship?"

"I know nothing of kingship, Arlan, but the hardship and loneliness have begun for all of us…your men included. Such things will pass in time. Endure."

Kavan allowed the harp strings to speak for him then, first a series of jigs to accompany the men as they finished eating, then, as more turned to sleep, he switched to more soothing melodies. From across the fire, he felt Ártur's eyes on him. The healer had smiled more since this trip had begun. Having first served King Innis as a field doctor, Ártur was back in his element amongst a group of soldiers…however ragtag that group might be. Though Kavan did not return the smile, he did touch his cousin's mind reassuringly.

"Sing for us," the healer said with a yawn. "Once before you put it away."

Kavan finished the piece he was playing and then paused for several minutes. He had not yet sung for the prince. Though Arlan approved of his harp playing, would he view Kavan's unusual voice in a similarly favorable light? The healer had not asked Kavan to sing since that Solstice Gathering, though Kavan had known he wished to. Tonight, for some reason, perhaps because they were far from home and in a precarious undertaking, the healer wanted to hear him sing again.

In the end, it was his willingness to please Ártur that gave him the courage he needed. The words were High Elyri, and though only the two healers understood them, the sound of deep sleep quickly filled the camp. Syl wiped tears from her eyes and snuggled into her blanket, knees pressing against Ártur's back. The healer sighed, smiling, and closed his eyes.

Song complete, Kavan returned his harp to its case and stared into the fire.

"Kavan?"

He did not need to look at the prince or read the young man's thoughts to know what the coming question would be. "My Prince?"

"Are you…your voice…?"

The bard felt Ártur's tension as the healer realized what he had done by making his request. "What is it, Arlan?"

Fidgeting, the prince started again. "It is…you sing with the voice of a child or…"

"A woman?" Embarrassed, Arlan did not respond. "It is the way it is, my natural voice. I cannot explain why it is this way. If you find it displeasing, I shall never sing in your…"

"Oh no! I did not mean to imply that!" the prince exclaimed in earnest. "You have the most beautiful voice I have ever heard, whether singing or speaking. I am surprised, that is all. Are there others…?"

"Not naturally; at least none I have ever heard of." Kavan relaxed, hearing no dishonesty in the prince's voice. Eventually, Ártur relaxed too.

After an awkward silence, the prince spoke again. "What did you sing?"

"A prayer."

"What language is that?"

"High Elyri. Few of us speak it anymore."

The prince huffed. He knew the language of Enesfel, he knew Trade, and during his time in Elyriá, he had begun to learn some of that language too. High Elyri, however, was unfamiliar. "That is unfortunate. It is beautiful. I am glad you speak it…it suits you."

Kavan bowed his head to hide his embarrassment. "Thank you."

After another pause, the prince asked, "What did the prayer say?"

Kavan rolled his head from side to side to ease the stiffness in his neck before replying. "Bless us in this we do, k'Ádhá. For we are servants and know not what we should. To endure is hardship. From pain comes all things blessed. We shall see justice. Your righteousness shall we know."

"You say that with great conviction, sínréc," Ártur said without opening his eyes. Kavan did not acknowledge the remark.

"Did you write that?" Arlan asked when the bard did not say anything more.

"No. I do not consider myself much of a poet. I set it to music. It is a prayer of Saint Kóráhm, written when he went amongst Teren to share with them the words of Dhágdhuán. This occurred early during the first great persecution of Elyri; he was afraid."

"Are…are you afraid?"

He briefly considered denying it, but could not bring himself to lie. The prince deserved the truth. "My fears are…yes…" he finally said, "I am."

Prince Arlan stared at the fire for some time; Kavan watched him from the corner of his eye, seeing the thoughts and emotions flicker randomly across the prince's young face. Voice very low, he finally said, "I think I am afraid too. Is it allowed for a King, or a prince, to be afraid?"

"Fear alone is not harmful, but for the sake of your men, you must never show them your fear or they may turn on you and abandon you. Unfortunately, you must always appear strong, even when you do not feel that you are."

With a grunt, the prince settled into his bedding. "So Guthrie says too. I will be watching for the kestrel tomorrow. At least I will know you are safe."

The young man forced a smile and fell into an exhausted sleep. Kavan studied the fire until it was nearly spent, thankful for those silent moments of solitary peace. After rekindling it, he too lay down and allowed sleep to overcome him.

❧Chapter 25❦

By the time they sheltered near Chantel, another eighty-two farmers, woodsmen, fishermen, and peasants had joined Prince Arlan's ever-growing ranks. With them were fifteen women who came to provide cooking, sewing, and whatever other services were required by the burgeoning ranks of men and boys. Chantel could not house them all thus camp was set on the north side of the village, where locals brought them food and drink and gathered to hear what Guthrie McHador had to say. Word had apparently traveled fast before them. Two days were spent gathering supplies, a few more horses, and whatever men wished to join them, and at dawn they were to be on their way. Guthrie had not brought up meeting with General McLeu again, choosing to believe that Kavan would arrange such a meeting as he had promised when he deemed the time to be right.

His concern now, though he saw no way to avoid it, was the effect this diversion of labor was going to have on Enesfel's economy in years to come. He had not anticipated this many followers so early in the campaign. Prince Arlan needed the support if he was to prevail, but there would undoubtedly be lean times ahead if this number of men was any indication of the number they would gather along the way. How would the kingdom feel if the prince succeeded, knowing that he had been instrumental to their hunger?

Outside of the village shops, Ártur and Syl tended to the medical needs of the community, with Kavan beside them playing tunes to keep the unruly crowd at ease. Knowing that the visitors would be gone soon, the gathering was thick with those wanting help for minor aches and pains and injuries, and those wanting to get close to the bard with the hopes of touching him. A sudden shifting and parting of the crowd drew Kavan's attention and he spied, at the rear of the gathering, a large gray horse with a perplexed rider astride it. He recognized the man that studied the gathering curiously, and pulled the hood of his cloak over his face. Both healers looked at him, startled, when he laid one hand on each of them. Without speaking, Ártur chose to continue his work while Syl went in search of Guthrie as Kavan bid.

Kavan slipped through the press of the crowd until he reached where the man had dismounted and was tethering his horse. He had not been certain the general would come. "General McLeu?" The man stared at the cloaked figure, hand on his sword in its scabbard as he turned to face the speaker. "Please, put away your weapon. I mean no harm. Will you please accompany me?"

"Who are you? What do you want?" The general relaxed his sword arm but not his guard; he could not see the face inside the hood and that worried him.

"I sent for you; that is why you are here. Please. Come with me."

The general did as the man asked, although he was not sure why he dared believe this stranger meant no harm. No one had sent for him, only the compulsion of dreams given by that mysterious raven had compelled him to make this journey. Unless this man controlled the beasts of the air, there was no reason to think the two things were connected.

He was taken to a windowless room in the city's abandoned náós. His escort bid him sit, and then a young Elyri woman entered before the general could question him further. Both went out, leaving him alone.

He recalled those white hands, and now that he had a moment to think, he recognized the voice. This had to be MacLyr's cousin. He supposed it had been this same man who had won King Farrell's admiration many years ago. How had he escaped the dungeon, and what did this Elyri want with him? Was he an emissary for the High Mother? Or did his being summoned here have to do with the imprisonment this bard had endured under the King's hand? The door creaked open, but it was neither the bard nor Healer MacLyr that entered the room.

"Guthrie?" He stood to greet his mentor, but the other man's stern demeanor stopped him from approaching. "Thank goodness you are still alive and safe."

"Why? So that you may arrest me for treason?"

Ferghus looked genuinely perplexed. "Treason? Whatever for?"

"Kidnapping my niece?" Guthrie replied with a smirk.

"Everyone believes you are dead. Those charges are…"

"Still in effect until there is either proof of my death or King Owain pulls them from the record. You know that."

"Is that why you brought me here? To have the charges dropped?"

Not a cruel man at heart, Guthrie took no pleasure in the other man's discomfort. "I did not bring you here; a friend arranged for us to meet at my request. I planned to go to you, but he saved me the trouble by summoning you. As for the charges, I care nothing for them. I did not kidnap Brenna; she came to me of her own volition. She and her baby are safe and out of harm's way. Did you know the King fathered her child?"

"I…" Ferghus turned, though not with his back to his mentor. Pieces of the overall picture were falling into place. He had known something had happened between the King, the princess, and Lady Weylin. Her departure from court had been abrupt and unexpected and the King had been too eager to find her. "No, I knew nothing about that. After she left…well, we were not sure she was alive. Of course, you being a relative, she would go to you for protection, much safer than if she had gone to Alberni or her kin here in Chantel. I am amazed she could find you."

"We kept in touch."

Ferghus wondered how. "Then why do you seek me? Does it have something to do with the Elyri bard? I told His Majesty that torture was unnecessary, that MacLyr would get revenge somehow. Is that it? Did MacLyr track you down and demand retribution?"

Guthrie kept his disgust and outrage from his face. He had deduced that the King had held Kavan prisoner, but had known nothing else and chose not to ask Kavan for details. This revelation cleared the mystery surrounding the changes in Kavan's demeanor. "If Ártur wanted retribution, I suspect he could do it alone. As could Kavan. But Kavan has insisted we spare Owain; if he had not, I might have killed your King already. What he did was senseless and stupid, but you know that, don't you?"

The general nodded solemnly, wanting to turn away completely but not daring to. When Guthrie saw that he was going to get no further comment, he continued, "I wish to discuss a very important matter, one that will affect the future of Enesfel and the Five Sovereignties. But before I continue, I must have your oath that you will do nothing until I have said what I need to say, and that regardless of what conclusions you reach, I will be allowed to leave Chantel without harassment."

"You have my word, Guthrie, though I do not understand…"

"North of here, I have troops assembled who have but one objective and purpose…"

"To overthrow the King? I know you never liked Owain…"

Guthrie scowled. He had made no secret of his disapproval of the current King's background, but that had largely been because of the lies it had heaped upon Innis' legacy. Owain had been a child when Guthrie had last seen him; he had never disliked the boy. "I have nothing against him personally…except that he does not seem to know how to rule a kingdom wisely. But he is not Innis' son. Ask him, he will not deny it."

"He is a Lachlan…"

"His name and right to rule are not in question. We do not wish to overthrow him, though it may be for the best if we did. We want something far more peaceful, something that does not require bloodshed."

"What is it you want? Gold? Your position back? The price off your head? To have your niece's child recognized as the legitimate heir? I think, if you but ask, King Owain will do anything to keep the throne."

"That is what concerns me." Staring steadily into Ferghus' eyes, he said, "We wish to restore Prince Arlan to the family and have him recognized as the heir to the throne of Enesfel, regardless of whether Owain fathers further children or not."

Ferghus choked. "Ar…he's not ali…?"

"He has been in my care since he disappeared from Rhidam. It was Lady Cordelia's choice to remove him from the threats on his life, to keep him safe. He is alive, strong, wise, and fit to lead Enesfel."

Ferghus weighed the what-ifs, sorting the jumble of questions that crowded into his mind. Finally, he asked, "Can you prove his identity?"

"I raised him; I have nothing to prove. If you think over the past, you will know it too. As for others, one look at him and anyone who remembers King Innis or has seen the portraits will know. He can tell you things about his childhood that no one except Princess Deidre could confirm…though I suspect she is unavailable to…"

Not realizing Guthrie was fishing for information, Ferghus declared, "The princess is alive and safe, I swear it. Or at least, she was when I left Rhidam to come here, and I know the King wishes her no harm." He paused. "What stakes do the Elyri have in this?"

"None. This expedition is not Elyri backed if that is what you ask. There are five Elyri among us, two healers, two merchants, and a bard. The Kyne did not send them and is unaware of our efforts or intents."

"Is Ártur MacLyr with you?"

"Does it matter?"

Ferghus sighed. No, it did not matter, but knowing one of those two healers might have made him feel better. He had respected the healer during the years they served Kings Innis and Donal together. "It would be difficult…but I believe I could persuade the King to give Prince Arlan position in the family, accept him into Rhidam if he is who you claim. But the man has his pride and will not likely be willing to make him heir over any sons he produces. He would be more willing, I think, to make your niece's child his heir…"

"It is both or nothing, and we will fight to secure both."

"It will be my duty to stop you, Guthrie…"

"Would you? You swore to protect the family and the throne. Would you harm one Lachlan to protect another?"

The faintest ironic expression touched Ferghus' face as he stopped what he intended to say. "You know me well, Guthrie."

"I trained you."

"War between Lachlans, led by you and me, would destroy the kingdom…"

"It might. I have no wish for it to come to that, Ferghus, nor does Prince Arlan. Nor do I have any desire to pit my battle strategy against yours. No one will win."

"Let me see the prince."

"Faith, Ferghus. You believe me, or you do not. You must decide on faith. To reveal the prince to you will give you the proof to hold to the King, and we are not ready for him to know the truth yet. You know the events of the past; you know me. You know I would not lie about this."

"This is too important to base solely on…"

"Faith."

"You force my hand. To choose to believe you…if you are correct and truthful, I…and if you are lying, I will look like a traitor and a fool. If I do not choose, or choose to disbelieve you, there will be war." He paused and muttered curses beneath his breath before continuing. "There will be war regardless, won't there. No matter what I say or decide, there will be war."

Guthrie did not reply.

"You know what you want, but you also know what the people want. You always have. They will push to depose the King if there is another suitable Lachlan to replace him…even a bastard of Farrell's. Even if you try to keep your demands simple, the people will insist that you do what should be done, and you will do it because there is no choice. Any true Lachlan would want to right the wrongs done, not compound them. You brought me here to warn me…and because of my oath…"

Guthrie saw no need to deny it. "Yes."

"By not letting me see this proof for myself, you place me in danger, keep me in doubt…"

"I am not keeping you in doubt. You know enough to make a choice. And if you choose to doubt…as long as the doubt is there, you will not act against us. Whether you saw the prince or not, you would be in no less danger. It is less of a risk for us if he is kept secure…"

"Risk…" Ferghus scoffed.

"You can tell the King you believe Prince Arlan is alive, but you cannot give him proof. The King is less likely to believe without proof, just as you are now."

Shoulders sagging, the general said, "This is hardly fair, Guthrie."

"Things in life rarely are. As you say, there will likely be war. As much as I do not like it, and as much as the prince believes otherwise, I am afraid that the King must be overthrown before we can get into Rhidam and instate him as the Crown Prince. No amount of proof, or coercion, or bribery will convince King Owain otherwise. He has spent too many years in Neth to make this an easy transition."

"What choice do I have…?"

"You could join us."

The men stared at one another. "You know I cannot. I cannot fight against the King. And if Prince Arlan lives, I cannot fight with the King either. My hands are tied. Why are you doing this to me, Guthrie?"

"I do what I must for Enesfel. It was a promise to Lady Cordelia, and it is what King Innis would have wanted. The kingdom has been astray too long; it must be restored to its proper course. I do not ask for your choice now, but you will need to make it soon. I thought it best for you to know before it is too late. I must go. You will remain here until we are gone in the morning, at which time you may do as you think best."

He left quickly, leaving Ferghus in stunned silence. There was a click at the door. The general was locked in. "Guthrie!" he cried, banging his fists on the door. "I gave you my word!"

Ꜯ*∾

They would reach Tarsee in two days, but since leaving Chantel, Kavan had spent little time in the camp. He came long enough to retrieve his harp, or return it, and always while the others slept. Apprehension had dogged him since seeing General McLeu, although he did not think the general was the cause of it. From his conversation with Guthrie, he knew Owain's general was now in a quandary and would not hinder their progress, but something was amiss and Kavan could not pinpoint what it was.

Tonight, the camp was set at the edge of the forest that separated Enesfel from Elyriá. Kavan was familiar with this territory as he had spent many hours roaming these forests in the guise of the white hart.

The agitation he felt was worse tonight, and as he rested on a fallen tree northwest of camp, he strained his senses in every direction, searching for any sign of a disturbance or source of danger. Behind him, the camp was quiet. He felt Ártur's mind touch, but he shut it out without acknowledging it. He sighed in annoyance and then sighed again for being annoyed at his cousin's concern. With the night drawing tight around him, his frustration with the unknown was making him unnecessarily irritable.

He rose and walked further into the forest. He knew he could not go far enough tonight to ease the feeling of captivity, but each step took him that much further from the press of the hundreds of men camped with Prince Arlan. An owl screeched in the treetops, but other than that, the night was blissfully quiet. There was freedom in silence, in being alone, freedom he needed. The foliage grew thicker and his progress slowed, but as he did not have a destination, that did not bother him. He wanted to be away from camp.

A sudden prickle shot up his spine as the apprehension he carried blossomed into a clear sense of imminent danger. Only then did he become aware of the sounds of men and the crackle of a campfire somewhere ahead of him. He inched closer, sniffing the air, stalking quietly through the brush to get a better view.

Royal militia. Seven men. Not enough to be a threat to the prince's large company. There seemed to be no need to confront them; he could avoid them, warn the company, and they could move on. But as he turned to go back, a wave of nausea hit him. The image of the prince and ex-general sprawled face down beneath an ambush of arrows flashed in his mind's eye. Blood was everywhere, as were sounds of chaos, and he was certain that both men were dead.

He felt terror. He felt sick. He felt cold and shocked. Though not thinking of how he would accomplish it, he knew he had to change those events. Here. Now. Without conscious thought, he bounded forward into the midst of the gathering, taking the wolf shape he often used when threatened, an angry growl rising in his throat.

The seven men scattered with yelps and shouts. Each scrambled for their weapons, hoping to chase off the unexpected attacker.

The silver-white wolf slashed its fangs across the chest of one, causing the man to spin sideways and fall on the short sword he had picked up. The wolf's leap ended with its fangs clamping around the throat of the second man. There was the crunch of bone, a gush of blood, and the body fell to the ground with its head twisted awkwardly to one side. A third man swung a mace, aiming for the beast's head. Barely avoiding the blow, the wolf locked on to the man's weapon arm and the mace dropped. The soldier pulled his now mangled arm free, shouting in agony as he hopped about in search of something to stop the bleeding. Of the remaining four, one watched, dazed, from beneath a nearby tree, while the other three approached the animal, trying to determine how best to deal with it.

It did not take long for the three to back the wolf against a thick cluster of brush. Too late, Kavan realized he was outnumbered. Two swords and a spear faced him, and if the man beneath the tree regained his composure, there would be a bow to contend with.

It was in that moment that he also realized he had killed two men and maimed a third, quickly, easily, without conscious intent. He felt sicker than he had before, but there was no time to lament. He had to protect Prince Arlan. Pulling all of the energy he could gather without jeopardizing his shapechange, he caused a faint blue glow to gather behind his three foes. The soldier beneath the tree yelped, astonished, causing his companions to turn. The brief distraction was all Kavan needed to melt from the lupine form into the more familiar kestrel one and lift into the night sky. The glow faded. The soldiers turned their attention back to the threat, only to find the wolf was gone. Gone, when it should have attacked them when their backs were turned.

Taking possession of his own form, Kavan watched from the shelter of a high tree limb as the soldiers regrouped, searched the perimeter for the mad animal that had attacked them and tended to their wounded and dead. He was shaken to the core. He had never thought himself capable of killing. Yet he had, in a manner many would consider more heinous than if he had been wielding a sword. The tang of sweat and blood lingered in his mouth. He felt demoralized as well as sick. Could he have done anything differently? Was there any other way he could have protected the prince from this menace without killing?

The answer that presented itself was simple and would have required no bloodshed if he had thought of it sooner. That he had not, that he had reacted on some baser level of instinct he had not known he had, increased his self-loathing. Blood had been spilled, there was no way to undo that, but he could use this ruse to divert the remaining five away from the prince. In kestrel form, he came down from the tree, and resumed his own shape, beyond the firelight's range. Reaching with his thoughts to touch the minds of the soldiers, he took a step forward.

"Do not stay here."

The already unsettled men jumped at the voice. Again, weapons were raised but a graceful wave of a ghostly white hand caused the soldiers to either drop or sheath them. The misty, almost glowing visage seemed to hover at the tree line but came no closer.

"This is no place for you," he said, energy directed into bending and shaping their wills to match his own. He could do it with one man, but could he do it with more than one? "Others will come. Danger. Do not stay. Take your dead or you will join them. Be gone. Do not make me come again."

He melted back into the forest leaving the soldiers unsure whether anyone had actually been there. They looked at each other as though they did not know why they had been staring into the forest. Kavan listened as they calmly agreed to return to Rhidam with their fallen comrades. No mention was made of the blue glow or the ghost in the trees, though one of the five did comment that if one harsh winter caused a wolf to become rabid, they should be hunted and destroyed. The others grunted. They mounted their horses and started away, not giving the hour of the night any thought.

It was several hours later, only after he was certain the soldiers were truly on their way to Rhidam, before Kavan returned to the camp. The men on watch paid him no heed. They rarely did, other than to stare at him with expressions of awe or curiosity. From the stars' positions, he knew camp would break soon; rather than sleep, Kavan waited with his back against a tree and watched the sky. A hand rested on his shoulder, startling him. He looked into Ártur's face.

"Want to talk?" the healer asked.

"No. What's done is done. I do not want to think about it ever again." He swore then that no one would ever know about the lives he had just taken. He would take that horrific secret to his grave.

❦*❧

King Owain smiled at the woman on his left and then at the one on his right who looked away in an effort to hide her teary eyes. It had been a difficult winter for the princess; she was gaunt, pallid, and according to the physician who attended her, not at all well. Her lungs were weak, he had said, and if the King forced her to remain in the damp dungeon any longer, she would surely die. Hearing that, the King had ordered her immediate release. He might have wanted to punish her, bully her into accepting his proposal, but he did not want her to die. That would only be punishing himself. Upon her release, he made certain she had the finest food and care provided, an entirely new wardrobe, and even refrained from visiting her, lest he upset her while she recovered.

Tonight, feeling that enough recuperation time had passed, he had required her attendance at a banquet. During the course of the meal, he announced that, on her nineteenth birthday, Princess Deidre would become his wife. Enesfel would have a queen and, with any luck, an heir the following year. He seemed not to notice the scornful glances cast at him; how could the man marry his own sister? But none would voice those thoughts, as they knew what fate would be theirs if they did. They could only pity the princess who was, they could see, powerless to resist. She did not know Owain had released her because of her health, and she feared she would be returned to the dungeon if she dared to contradict him. Despite her previous resolve, illness and solitude had worn her determination thin. Perhaps it was best to do as he wanted. After all, if Brenna had found Arlan, surely her brother would have come to her aid by now.

"Owain," said the august woman to his left, "we need music. It would be proper for you to dance with your betrothed."

"Quite right, mother. Minstrels, a song for the lady."

The musicians conversed amongst themselves then began a spirited tune. The King bowed before Deidre and extended his hand. She glanced timidly around the room, unsure what was transpiring. She could only guess that, with the musicians playing, he was asking to dance. Gently, he coaxed her to her feet, but it was many more moments before he got her to take a few hesitant steps towards the center of the room. Then she stopped and stared at him with frightened eyes and refused to move any further.

A man at the far end of the room lurched up from the table and exclaimed in a slurred voice, "I think she needs a few lessons." He staggered into the midst of the dancers, shoved his way between the King and the princess, and grabbed her arms. Owain pulled her away from his clerk with fury in his eyes.

"Get out! Your service here is terminated!" Inebriated or not, such behavior would never be tolerated.

"Perhaps," Lady Ula spoke quickly, hoping to avoid an altercation, "she would prefer something slower."

"What difference will that make?" The clerk glared at the King, drunkenly trying to remain on his feet, either not realizing his error or his precarious position or feeling some misguided need to intervene on the princess' behalf. "How can she dance to something she cannot hear?"

The King whirled about, prepared to knock the man to the floor with one balled fist. The clerk staggered backward to avoid what was coming and fell without being hit. Deidre flinched, expecting to be struck. The only thing that aborted the tirade was the opening of the Hall doors.

"General McLeu! What a welcome surprise." The King, as relieved with the interruption as everyone else was, managed a forced, tense smile. "You are back early. Did you find what you sought?"

Seeing the clerk on the floor at the King's feet, Ferghus knew he had walked into something unpleasant. He bowed, noting the princess was there, but he was afraid to ask what any of this meant. "I did not find…as for…pardon the interruption, Your Majesty; I merely wished to announce my return."

The King gestured to the place where the clerk had been seated. The drunken man had gotten to his hands and knees only to be dragged from the room by two guards. "Please join us, General. We are celebrating Princess Deidre's decision to marry me on her next birthday."

The timid girl beside the King wiped tears from her cheeks. Ferghus knew she could not hear Owain, but he found himself doubting the accuracy of the King's proclamation. This was not her decision; this was the King's. Though he had not seen her in many years, he recognized the thin, regal Ula de Corrmick seated at the table. Her presence made him uneasy. The general was torn between what he wanted to say, what he should say, what he must say, and wanting to say nothing at all. He coughed uneasily.

"Congratulations, milord. I wish you many happy years together. I must decline the invitation, however. I have ridden hard today and have not been feeling well."

"Shall I send a physician to see you?" the King asked. The rare honest touch of concern in his voice did not go unnoticed.

"No. I think I merely need to sleep in a decent bed in front of a good fire."

"Then, by all means, rest. You will give your report tomorrow. As for the rest of you, get out." He waved one arm about the room. "You too, mother."

"Yes, Your Majesty," Ferghus said with a bow. He quickly retreated to avoid speaking to anyone and to avoid the King changing his mind.

The King put his arm around Deidre and led her from the Hall into the library. Once the door was closed and they were alone, no longer caring whether his guests left or stayed and ate the rest of the meal, he escorted her to a chair and bid her sit. She looked afraid of him, and that made him frown with regret. He took a sheet of parchment from a desk drawer, along with a vial of ink and a quill and began to write.

"I am sorry about this incident," he wrote. "In my haste to please my mother, I forgot that you cannot dance because you cannot hear the music. I often do not think before I act. You shall never have to dance again. I will not force you." He held the parchment for her to read, but her cornered rabbit expression did not change.

He took the parchment back and continued writing. "I am also sorry about Lady Weylin. And the dungeon. I should have done neither, but again, I did not stop to think about the consequences of my actions. My pride got in the way of reason…and Neth has influenced me badly, I admit. I would apologize to Lady Weylin, but we have failed to find her. But I can apologize to you. I truly mean you no harm. I must marry you, Deidre. I love you."

This time, when he was through writing, she took the pen and parchment. "You are my brother," she wrote. "It is not proper."

"More precisely," he wrote back, elated that she was, at last, communicating with him. "I am your nephew, though I am older than you. My mother says Bowen was my father. I suppose it sounded better to claim Innis as my father. Does this make a difference? I cannot marry another while you live, nor can I stand to see you marry someone else. Please, Deidre."

She read his words but her expression did not change. Then, slowly, she wrote, "I will consider your offer." There was no choice since he had already announced their marriage, but for the first time, she felt like he might listen to her if she refused.

With an excited smile, he took the quill. "I will make it up to you, all of the bad things I have done. You will be safe with me and you will have everything you desire. No more threats. I will find Lady Weylin and bring her back to you if I can and she will be safe here too. Truce?"

Coming around the table, she stood behind him for a few moments. He did not move, wondering what she would do. Perhaps she would kill him with the quill she carried. He closed his eyes, waiting for whatever was to come. If he had to die, he could think of few better ways than at the hands of the woman he adored. Instead, to his surprise, she kissed the top of his head timidly and dashed from the room.

Dazed, the King stared after her, his hand resting on the place her lips had touched. Clutching the paper, he gave a squeal of delight and spun around the room, knocking the table and chairs aside before falling dizzily onto the divan, listening to the thump of his heart in his ears, and feeling the warmth of wine, and love, in his veins.

ᚨChapter 26ᚨ

Travel was again uneventful after departing Tarsee. Though the weather was warming, the change in altitude and the fact that they were moving northwards kept the spring warmth from reaching the prince's band of mercenaries. As the ranks grew to over three hundred men, Guthrie worried more that the King would send the militia to rout them, but thus far there had been no signs of danger. The inner circle of the prince's court had determined the truth about the ever-present kestrel and Phaedr eagerly volunteered to do as Kavan was doing, doubling the scouting range. Still, there was no sign of Enesfel's army.

As they neared the town of Bryn, the forest grew thicker, making travel for such a large group cumbersome. Guthrie took one-third of the forces, Bhríd, Phaedr, and Syl, and continued towards Bryn, while Prince Arlan led the remainder into the city of Erleta. They would re-group in Durham. Erleta proved unfriendly to the mass of men and their reputed prince. Duke Loring Gottfrid was one of the nobles King Girvin had created whom King Owain allowed to retain his title, thus he felt some degree of loyalty to the King. Once convinced of Arlan's identity, however, he made a pact with the prince. Rather than donate men and supplies or offer shelter in Erleta, he would remain silent on their activities. There was little choice but to trust him, as Prince Arlan did not want to resort to force and violence to assure the man's cooperation. After a single night in Erleta, the company pulled up camp with a gain of not quite fifty men.

❧*❧

Guthrie reigned in his horse, causing the others behind him to pull up short. The horses snorted their annoyance at the abruptness of the action. There was smoke in the air; he could smell it but could not yet see it. The horses fidgeted at the smell. Several minutes of searching the sky told him that the source of the smoke lay ahead of them.

"What is it, sir?" Bhríd asked. "Forest fire?"

"I think not. The forest is still. Phaedr, will you take a look and tell me what you see?"

The red-haired man slid off his mount. "I'd be glad to," he said with a grin before disappearing into the trees at the side of the road.

Guthrie was about to speak when he first noted movement in the brush approximately one hundred feet ahead of them. It could not be Phaedr. "Send word back to be on alert. Possible ambush. We keep moving, but be ready."

Whatever he had seen in the trees continued to move ahead of them as they resumed their advance. The screech of a hawk startled the general as the now familiar red hawk landed on Bhríd's arm. The bird screeched again and took once more to the sky. Understanding his brother's message, Bhríd nodded his head at Guthrie. There was trouble. Guthrie wondered what Phaedr had seen.

Fifteen minutes passed before the sounds of clashing weapons and screaming met their ears. Spurring his horse to full speed, Guthrie drew his sword and rode over the rise into the valley that housed the chaos of the now smoldering town of Bryn. With an angry shout, he led the charge and his one hundred followers rushed in behind them. He only partially heard the cry of voices greeting them as royal militia;

his focus was on the horsemen that were setting fire to existing buildings and cutting down all in their paths.

One stocky rider, his head covered with a heavy fur hat, did not have a chance to react as Guthrie growled, swung, and neatly decapitated him, sending the body sprawling into the bloodied mud of the street. Bhríd let out a whoop and charged in beside Guthrie. It had been a long time since he had been in battle, the ex-general realized, feeling his arm tire after taking down five more riders. Fortunately, the men behind him had done an admirable job; the attacking force was defeated with only a handful of men escaping to flee north. Guthrie slid from his charger and kicked aside the body lying on the ground at his feet.

"Milord, how did you know we were…General McHador?" The man who spoke emerged from the rubble of a nearby building holding a small, weeping child. Both were dirty and frightened looking, but the man, at least, lost the fear on his face as he recognized Guthrie. "I don't think the King sent you…" He was trying to calm the little girl as he spoke."

"Luc McDermott?"

He clasped Guthrie's hand. "Aye, sir. Most of us thought you were dead. What are you doing in these parts…with all of these men…?"

Guthrie had served with the man, considered him a good soldier and fine individual, but he was not prepared to give away too much until he could better assess the situation. "I could ask the same of you."

There was amusement in the other man's eyes but it did not push out the effects of the raid they had endured. "I had to go somewhere when I left service. After you left…well, you didn't think I would stay on until Bowen became King, did you?"

"I would have been surprised if you had." That he had not, reassured Guthrie more than most things would have. "Neth raiders? What are they doing here?"

Setting the child down and taking her hand now that she had stopped the worst of her crying, the wiry man replied, "Don't really know, sir. Why does Neth do anything? They came with no warning, attacked during the morning meal and carried off some of the women and children. Most of our able-bodied men rode after them…and then these men arrived. We were defenseless…and the others have yet to return. Those of us who live are very much in your debt."

Guthrie scowled as he tried to make sense of Neth's actions. They were raiders by tradition, but this seemed odd even for them. "Gather survivors and take count. I want to know what damage has been done and how many are dead or missing. The prince will want to hear of this."

"Prince, sir? His Majesty has no heirs…"

"King Owain might be inclined to sympathize with his mother's people, but Prince Arlan most certainly will not."

"Prince Arlan…is alive? Then it is as the harper foretold? Bless you, sir!" The man scurried off to spread the word and to do Guthrie's bidding, leaving the child in the care of an elderly woman.

Guthrie was left to assess his own losses as he continued to ponder Neth's motives for this raid. Thirty of his one hundred men had been killed, peasants and boys who had not had the skills required for battle. He did as he had always done after a fight, learning the names and hometowns of the dead, and after writing an appropriate eulogy for them, sent two men back to tell the families they had left behind. All of the dead were buried.

These deaths hung particularly heavy on him. They were the first battle martyrs for the prince's cause, though fighting Neth raiders had never been part of the bargain. He wished he had more appropriate words to say to their families…and wished he knew what he would say to Arlan when they met again.

❧*☙

Rain pounded Durham relentlessly for the sixth consecutive day. Prince Arlan had intended to drill his green troops whilst they waited for Guthrie, but the spring storm only allowed that for the first two days. Then it had worsened enough to make any period longer than five minutes outdoors unbearable. The náós had been offered as a haven for the drenched men, but when that proved too small to house them all, many townspeople opened their homes. The city of Durham had been very generous, offering food, supplies, and weapons. One merchant offered the prince several horses. But the men with him were most grateful for the lodging that kept them out of the rain.

Despite the generous gifts and donations, the prince remained moody and anxious for the return of Guthrie and the others. If the King's army found them here, the prince did not feel confident enough in his own military knowledge and leadership skills to combat them. By his calculations, Guthrie should have arrived several days ago, even if the rain had slowed them. Kavan volunteered to search for them, should the downpour ease, but thus far that had not happened. The prince had to be content with the náós and the company of the other one hundred and sixty-one individuals squeezed into the drafty building.

Tonight, the prince was pacing, stopping now and then to listen to Kavan's harp playing or his prayers. He found he was not able to sleep until the bard lay down each night. There was something in the darkness here, when everyone but he and Kavan slept, something in the atmosphere as he listened to the breathing of those who had pledged their lives to his cause, something unsettling. Kavan had never hidden his religious self from the prince or anyone else, but watching him kneel before the long unused altar to pray night after night, watching him clean the altar and polish its mahogany surface and then anoint it with water and oil, struck an uncomfortable chord in the prince. That still rapture, something he could not understand, disturbed him.

The last man had bedded down before Kavan took up his harp and settled on the altar steps once again. Beside Prince Arlan, Ártur dozed, listening to the music in a half-conscious state. Only the soft glow of the candles Kavan had placed on the altar lit the sanctuary. The prince got up and picked his way between the sleeping men until he reached Kavan's side. The bard did not seem to notice, his eyes brighter than usual as they remained transfixed on the image of Dhágdhuán burning on the pyre. The prince stared too. It was featureless compared to the one in Hes Índári, but that seemed to make little difference to Kavan. He was looking beyond the figure rather than at it, to something that the prince could not see no matter how long he stared. Many minutes later, he became aware of the silence, that the music had stopped, and that Kavan was studying him curiously.

"Is something troubling you, My Prince?"

Arlan did not look at him. "I wish you would not do that."

"Do what?"

"Play. Like that. At this time of night."

Kavan scowled, his brows furrowed. "I was not aware my playing disturbed you, milord." No one else had ever suggested such a thing.

"It is not your playing…"

The puzzled expression deepened. "You said…"

"Forget it, Kavan." The prince stood and went to the altar. "Forget I said anything. I do not know what I meant."

Laying the harp aside in deference to the prince's wishes, he motioned for Arlan to sit with him. "Lord McHador will rejoin us soon. If the storm has hampered them as it has us, they likely sought shelter. Once the storm has passed, they will arrive as soon as they are able."

"I wish I had your faith…"

"You must simply decide to believe, Arlan."

The prince did not think that to be true, but he knew better than to argue such things with Kavan. He was not in the mood for a philosophical debate tonight. When he spoke again, he asked, "Why did they do that to him?"

Kavan blinked and cocked his head. "Do what to whom, milord?"

Arlan motioned to the image of Dhágdhuán. "That. To him. All I ever hear is how righteous he was. But they did that anyhow. Why?" To his way of thinking, the man must have done something to deserve such a fate at the hands of the peace-loving Elyri.

"Fear, milord. The people feared he would bring the establishment down on them with his words and teachings, feared he would be the cause of their deaths if they did not stop him. They could not allow him to upset the way of things. People tend to destroy what they fear…if they can."

"But to torture him first…surely such humiliation was unnecessary. And they could have stopped there; they did not need to kill him."

"For one such as Dhágdhuán…torture and humiliation would not have silenced him. It would have strengthened his need to speak against their corruptions. In their eyes…he had to be killed. They needed him to be an example…"

"Is that why Owain wanted to kill you? Because he feared you? Because he wanted you to be an example?"

Kavan seemed to back away without actually moving. His eyes were wide with what looked to the prince like horror. "There is no similarity between what happened to Dhágdhuán and my imprisonment. I do not know if the King fears me…and I do not think I was to be an example to anyone. I was merely being punished as a wrongdoer…"

"You did nothing wrong…and you are not a citizen of Enesfel. He should have no jurisdiction over you. Can a man, a foreigner, be punished for the things he says?"

"Owain can, unfortunately, do as he wishes. He is the King and I was in his kingdom."

"Kings are appointed by k'Ádhá...or so Guthrie says...as did my mother. Does this mean k'Ádhá approves of the things Owain does?"

"What do you think?" The prince did not need to answer. Kavan already knew what he would say. "Monarchs are not necessarily appointed by divinity. They become rulers by the order of their birth, or by might. The first Lachlan King won the crown through war against Neth. The rest have been born to the throne. k'Ádhá may have had a hand in the initial triumph...who can say...but I do not think he condones the sort of ruler Bowen was...or the rulers of Neth..."

The bard looked at his harp and caressed its wood with his fingers, giving the prince time to ponder his words before speaking again. "Why does my playing cause you annoyance? No one has ever spoken thus about my music...you have never said anything before." From the tone of his voice, he doubted his talent now, wondering if the people who had praised him all along had lied to him out of pity.

"No, Kavan...it is not your playing; it is not your music, and it is not an annoyance. Your music is exquisite. When it is late like this...when everyone is asleep and you play in this place...it feels as if someone else is here. Someone other than the men...someone who should not be here. I never noticed it until we came here. I feel as if I am being watched, and it...I can explain it no better. It centers on you...whatever it is...and it does not seem to like me."

Kavan hung his head to hide the relieved smile that tugged at the corners of his mouth. "It is a good omen, I think, that you feel it too."

"A good omen?" Good was the last word the prince would have chosen to describe the sensations.

"When I play in a holy place," Kavan explained, "there is a presence. Someone is with me; perhaps there are more than one. I do not know who they are, or why they are there...but they bring tremendous energy...and peace. It has happened to me for as many years as you have lived. I once thought my mind was deceiving my senses, but others have experienced them with me. I think that it must be important if you feel them too."

"Is it záphyr? The phae k'kairá?"

"I do not know. Maybe neither. Maybe both. I do not believe they mean you harm. If they disliked you, I doubt you would feel them. I think what you sense is that they are wary of you because you do not believe or accept what you feel when they are present. That they have made themselves known to you is significant."

The prince snorted. "If it meant something, I would know," he said sullenly. "I think it has something to do with you, that's all. I do not like to feel I am being watched by someone who will not show themselves."

"Would you rather I not play within your company when we are in a holy place?" It was not the choice Kavan would make on his own, but he was willing to make concessions to Arlan.

"Wait until I am asleep, then you can play all you desire."

The bard bowed his head. "Very well. But think on this. There will come a time when you must make a choice in this, or you will lose their contact. If that day comes, nothing I can do will bring them back. You must do as you feel called. Goodnight, milord." He picked up the instrument and retreated to where his blanket lay behind the altar in the shadow of the pyre stake.

"Kavan?" Prince Arlan stopped, eyes turned to the figure above him. He tilted his head to the side, certain he was hearing voices, but perhaps it was only Kavan beginning his prayers since the bard did not reply. The prince sank to the floor, back against the altar, staring at the shadows cast by the shrinking candles, lost in thought.

❧*❦

General Ferghus turned towards the window with a groan. It had begun. Nothing was happening the way he had thought it would, however. For many days, he had been receiving reports of a large group of people traveling through the northern reaches of the kingdom, but no one could supply him with numbers or other details. The force he knew must be Guthrie's had not yet caused trouble. Since his meeting with McHador, the peasant unrest had ceased except in the southernmost reaches of the kingdom. He believed it to be the calm before the storm.

"You could have heard the rest of his tale," the other man spoke, gesturing after the boy that had left the room. "Shall we inform the King?"

Ferghus looked squarely at Ternce Wyndham. The blonde soldier had matured nicely in the years since King Donal's death and now the King had appointed him as Ferghus' second in command. The general suspected that one day Ternce would replace him. He did not like the idea as he saw no flexibility to the younger man's thinking. Such rigidness, he believed, would be restrictive in battle and leave no room for weighing moral issues against legal ones.

"His Majesty informed us not to disturb him at any cost short of war…"

Ternce Wyndham objected. "This is not war? Neth has initiated open hostilities…"

"Raiding parties. Such occurrences are not uncommon in that region, and the raiders have been dealt with…" Ferghus said, hoping to soothe the other man's temper.

"Perhaps not uncommon, but surely this is serious enough to…"

"There is no proof…"

The younger man stood his ground. "What the boy described is nothing short of the total destruction of Bryn! A raiding party does not typically destroy an entire town. It is not normal behavior for Neth. And what of that band of men that came to Bryn's defense? Is there no significance to that? Could it be the same force we have received reports…?"

Ferghus did not like the angry, judgmental tone and cut Ternce short. "We do not know. They have caused no harm, and from the sounds of it may have spared Bryn from annihilation."

"What if they are in league with Neth and trying to instigate war? He admitted he had not stayed long enough to learn what happened…"

"The King's mother is from Neth, in case you have forgotten. It is not likely Neth would war against a kingdom they have interest in, and would not likely initiate war with someone they cannot defeat. Besides, if both sides were in league with each other, they would not have fought against one another. You do not kill those on your side. However," he sighed as he paused to drink from the wine cup on the table, "I will prepare a report to give to the King when he returns. Take twenty-five men with you and find out whatever you can. Report back to me promptly…"

"Twenty-five…they numbered at least three times that…"

"I said investigate the incident in Bryn…not do battle," Ferghus growled. "Only the King can declare war. Besides, if it comes to a skirmish with either a peasant rabble or a Nethite raiding party, do you not think our forces are competent enough to defeat them?"

Ternce stopped in the doorway on his way out. "And what if, as the rumors claim, Guthrie McHador is leading that rabble."

Their eyes met. "Then pray you escape with your life." For Ferghus had no doubt Guthrie would do whatever he had to, to protect this prince in his care.

The two soldiers standing watch outside of General Ferghus' quarters looked at each other as Ternce stalked past them. The crash of glass erupted within the room. The story of the white raven on the general's desk had spread rapidly throughout the military ranks; since that time, those closest to the general had begun to notice his odd, sometimes confused behavior, and they wondered if the incident had driven the man mad. Now, with the rumors of an unknown force roaming the land, possibly led by a man said to be dead, a new rumor had begun to circulate.

Perhaps the raven had not been an omen meant only for the general.

Perhaps it had been a warning for all of Enesfel.

ॐ*ॐ

At last, they were leaving Durham. It had been the morning of the eleventh day before the rain stopped, allowing the prince to drill his men in the cold mud, and it was that evening before Guthrie and his men arrived with news about the skirmish with Neth raiders and the decimation of Bryn. Thirty men had been lost in that tussle, but they had gained two hundred and forty-six more, mostly men who had been displaced by the raiders or peasants they gathered along the way. They also brought with them several Nethite horses and Luc McDermott, who was to be placed in charge of a regiment of the prince's followers. There had been two more days of drilling and restocking, and then last night Guthrie decided it was time to continue. They had stayed too long in one place, leaving them open to attack should royal troops catch up with them.

Kavan sighed wearily, alone within the náos at last. It would be another hour before their daybreak departure, but the others were already preparing for travel. With the soldiers gone, gathered at the southeastern edge of town, there was silence in the building at last.

The prince fled its confines and Kavan's company the first chance he got and had slept in the outdoor camp with the men while Kavan remained behind. The bard had not spoken to him since. When they came within sight of each other, the prince looked away and Kavan's stomach knotted uncomfortably. The ache within, the feeling of abandonment, was something he had not felt in years and had hoped to never feel again.

Every memory of his youth came back, his first service as altar attendant, the funeral, the blood in the chalice, and the debate with k'gdhededhá Dórímyr that had been the last straw on his uncle's patience. Though no one had said it to his face, and he had never actually overheard the conversations, he knew of them. Bhryell Prophet. Bhryell Saint. The fear and confusion in Prince Arlan's eyes were the same as Kavan had seen in Bhryell's townsfolk, the avoidance no different from that of Kavan's elders, peers, and Bhryell's children. He knew that, even if the prince managed to get past his feelings now, there would be other events more extraordinary than this one. How long would it be, how many so-called miracles would it take, to drive Prince Arlan away for good?

"Are you ready to go, Lord Cliáth?"

Why Bhríd Cáner, his cousin, insisted on calling Kavan lord, the way many Teren did, he did not know. The stockier than average Elyri called everyone except his own siblings by a title. He stood now in the doorway, his unusual black curls pulled away from his face with a black cord, his smooth blue breeches and brocaded jerkin showing no hints of the morning's preparations. Kavan suspected Bhríd had already changed clothing. No one else had brought as much clothing as Bhríd Cáner; his desire to be clean and affluent in appearance was surpassed only by his personal formality. He was a perfect candidate for life in a royal court, and Kavan knew that if Prince Arlan gave Bhríd the chance, he would stay in Enesfel.

"Is everything else ready?"

"Everyone is mounted and your horse is ready, though I know you will not be riding. Phaedr is already scouting ahead. If you will give me your harp, I will see that it is secured and we can be on our way."

"Of course." He handed the harp into his cousin's care. There was no need to admonish Bhríd to be careful; the man was careful in everything he did. Casting a final glimpse at the carved figure on the pyre stake, Kavan murmured, "Let us be gone from here."

He followed his cousin without looking back.

☙*❧

Ternce Wyndham mounted his horse and looked back on the rubble that had once been the town of Bryn. So much destruction. Timbers charred and broken, stone scorched and cracked. Thatched roofing turned to gray ash and metal tarnished and blackened with soot. Few structures had escaped complete destruction, and fewer still had remained unmarred. He wished there was something he could do to assist those townsfolk remaining. There were few here, and those who remained had nothing but praise for the renegade force that had come to them in their hour of need. They could not, or would not, confirm McHador's involvement, which was the most important bit of information Ternce had hoped to glean in coming here.

Kicking callously through the rubble of what had once been his parents' home, he hoped for signs of life. There was none to be found, not even a rat or a stray dog. He glanced into the mountains separating Enesfel from Neth and turned his horse north. He had sent most of his men back to Rhidam; if he was to cross the border into hostile territory, it was best he not travel with a small army in his wake. Two other men riding with him would be enough.

Someone had to pay for what had been done here. He swore to find the ones responsible, to find his family. Despite his loyalty to the crown of Enesfel, Captain Wyndham's primary loyalty was to his family and his home. That, he suspected, was something General McLeu would never fully comprehend.

☙*❧

"I do not want excuses, mother; I want answers."

The King did not rise from the throne but sat poised with the contained intensity of a cat preparing to pounce on its prey. He had been on one of his frequent hunting expeditions when the news of Bryn's near destruction had come, and arrived home this morning to find General Ferghus waiting with the grim tale.

"I want to know why Neth authorized this attack on my subjects, and I suspect you know."

"Must I know everything my brother does?" Lady Ula asked coolly. Though fashionably adorned, the years had taken their toll. She had grown too thin in recent years, like a skeleton covered over with perfumed parchment skin, and only his relationship to her kept Owain from shying away in distaste. He watched her smooth the sleeves of her gown, a nervous habit he was used to, though she was not aware of doing it. If not for that clothing and her jewels, he thought she would be quite plain and homely, and once again, he wondered what his father had seen in her.

"I believe you know, else you would not be coy. If you do not tell me what you know, I will have you executed for treason"

She laughed. "Treason? You are a fine one to talk of treason. I am not a citizen of Enesfel. Treason would not apply, and my execution would result in war. Oh, I will admit that he sent troops at my supplication, but I did not ask him to do that."

That brought the King to his feet. "You requested this?"

"Someone had to do something about the band of marauders roaming the countryside," she replied with a haughty tilt of her chin. "I heard they were traveling towards Bryn, and since you were not here to attend to the matter, I took the liberty of requesting assistance from Ander. That his men took it a bit too far…"

"A bit too far? They attacked one of my cities. They destroyed it and carried away my subjects. From what I was told, those who did survive joined this band of wanderers, the target your brother missed completely."

"So? What do you want? What's done is done."

It was not the first time the King realized how different his ideals were from his mother's. She had no regard for anyone or anything except herself, despite her claims of doing everything she did for her son. He circled her several times, growling viciously, before stopping before her to stare into her face. His hand beneath her chin kept her head up. "You think I care little for the people I rule? I want every person they abducted returned. I demand reimbursement for every person they killed, every farm and business they destroyed, and for the loss of revenue those people, and the Crown, have sustained because of this. I want the head of the man who gave the order to do what has been done. I demand restitution. If that person turns out to be Ander, or he refuses to compensate me, there will be war as you have never seen it and you will rot in a prison cell. And if, dearest mother, I do not get what I want from him, it will be your head on a platter. Is that understood?"

Lady Ula bowed stiffly after lurching her chin from his touch. "It is, milord, but be warned. I have more influence with my brother than I do with you. You may not be as safe as you believe."

"Is that a threat?" His eyes narrowed and his fist bunched at his sides.

"Not a threat, son," she replied with the deadly hiss of a snake. "A reminder."

⚬Chapter 27⚬

Bhríd circled his hefty roan back to where Prince Arlan, Ártur, and Kavan kept the other horses in tight rein. Throwing back the hood of his dark brown cloak, he wiped the spray of the river from his eyes. "Nothing downstream as far as I can tell; it gets wider until it reaches the sea I imagine. Our only choices are to continue and hope we find a bridge that has not been destroyed, or backtrack until we find a place where the horses can cross safely."

"That means extra days of travel," the prince complained. "I don't like this. If Owain burned these bridges, he could be waiting for us anywhere. What hope do the four of us have against an army?"

"The bridges might have been washed out…" Bhríd suggested.

"They would likely mistake us for horse traders…unless they recognized you…or me…or Kavan," Ártur said, looking back up the river for some way to cross.

Ignoring him, the prince continued to grumble. "What happened to Guthrie and the troops? Did they make it to Dorshur or did they get ambushed?"

Kavan did not look at the prince but stared into the swirling white water in front of them as he replied, "I do not know, milord, but I could scout further for a crossing if you allow…"

"No. That is final, Kavan."

Groaning at the prince's lack of decisiveness, the healer turned his horse. "Well then, we had better get started if we want to make any further progress by sunset."

"Ártur…" started the prince.

Kavan's tone lowered as he struggled to mask his annoyance. It was not like the prince to be unable to make a simple decision, but since learning of the battle with the Neth raiding party, and being struck with the reality of the possibility of death all around them, Prince Arlan's faith had been shaken. The bard did not know how to assist in restoring it. "Do you propose we camp here for the rest of the day then, My Prince?"

Stung by the bard's tone, the prince snapped the tether to his string of horses and started back down the road they had come. It was infuriating that Kavan spoke to him as if he were a child, especially when he realized he had been behaving like one. He dared not admit how frightened and unsure he was, despite the nagging voice in his head that told him Kavan understood. Since he did not feel he could speak, his fears were coming out as indecisive frustration, and he regretted it at once.

They did not find a suitable place to cross the river that day, nor the morning of the next. The spring thaw had reached the mountains that separated Enesfel from the great desert and Cordash, and the run-off from those heights was now filling every river in the west. It was possible, the Prince reluctantly admitted, that the bridges had been washed out instead of maliciously destroyed to hinder them, but he was afraid to believe that. By the time Bhríd found a suitable crossing and led the horses to the southern side, the sun was low in the sky. They continued until they could no longer see the sunlight through the thickening growth of forest; when they found the first appropriate campsite, they took it.

Ártur, who Kavan noticed had been having difficulty sleeping of late, took the first watch. But Kavan could not sleep either this night and instead stared past the campfire into the trees with his harp in his hands while the other two slept. The bard appeared to be listening to something, but the healer heard nothing out of the ordinary. Perhaps Kavan was only listening to the stillness as he often did. The healer watched his face without his cousin seeming to notice. They had not spoken privately since undertaking this venture, as being surrounded by men in constant need of a healer for minor injuries or discomforts left little time in the healer's day for socializing. Every chance he had, however, Ártur stayed near to Kavan, listening to everything he said, craving each moment with him as if it were a life-saving tonic. The more time he spent with him, the more he desired. He wondered if there was some reason for the ever-growing compulsion but decided he would rather not know what that reason was.

"Would you like to talk about it?"

Kavan looked at him as if he had not understood the question, but asked, "About what?"

"About whatever has been troubling you since we left Durham. You have spoken little, and the whole time we were in Theron you were not to be found. I know it has something to do with Prince Arlan..." The pained expression on his cousin's face confirmed the healer's suspicions. "Do you intend to keep it to yourself or let me help you?"

From the way the bard shrugged his shoulders, it appeared as if he was not going to answer. When he finally did speak, his tone was flat and nearly emotionless. "He feels it too; in the náós in Durham he felt it. The power...the presence. It frightens him. I frighten him. How can I blame him for that when I sometimes frighten myself?"

After many silent moments, Ártur sighed. "He's young, Kavan..."

"Age has nothing to do with it. You know it. The people in Bhryell...the stories...you have heard them. He thinks of me no differently than they do."

The healer shook his head. "You are wrong. He knew you before he knew any of that, and I think Bhríd and I sheltered him from most of the talk in Bhryell…"

"Perhaps you shouldn't have."

"He loves you. It is a shock, perhaps…it certainly was for me…"

Kavan looked at him then with a gaze that left the healer feeling naked and exposed. "And things are not the same between you and me as they once were, are they?"

It took effort for Ártur to resist looking away. Swallowing hard he murmured, "Not yet…but they are getting better. Wouldn't you agree?"

It was Kavan's turn to pause, to think, and to realize that perhaps time was all that was needed. "Yes, they are, and I am grateful for that, sínréc."

The healer smiled with relief. "So am I. The prince will come around. Give him time." He took a long drink from his water skin, allowing Kavan time to think further before changing the subject. "Do you think Lord McDermott crossed the border successfully?"

"He had less than ten miles to travel. King Ahern promised sanctuary should we need it. Lord McDermott took the sealed document of promise with him. As long as the King does not go back on his word, there should be no difficulties."

Ártur tossed a twig into the fire and grunted as it ignited with a popping sound. "I don't like it. The more men we have, the better we will be able to defend ourselves, but Guthrie has sent practically the entire force into Cordash…"

"Traveling with such a large, untrained group would be expensive, difficult to maintain, and would arouse King Owain to action sooner than we wish. As long as our numbers remain small, he will feel less threatened and we should have a better chance at success. In Cordash, they will have the opportunity to train and drill. Maybe they will succeed in recruiting more Cordashian aid. I think it is a wise choice."

Ártur's head shook in bemusement. "Perhaps you should have taken more study in military strategy. At least you understand it."

"I understand the need to protect as many lives as possible and to keep King Owain off guard as long as we can. That is what Lord McHador is trying to do. I do not think that is strategy; I think it is common sense."

"Are you saying I lack common sense?" laughed the healer.

With a small smile, Kavan replied, "Not at all, cousin, only that you sometimes do not look at the whole picture."

"It is hard to look at the whole picture when you are in the middle of it. You are more adept at seeing beyond the normal boundaries than I am." There was no shame or embarrassment in admitting that. He stretched and yawned. "Are you going to sit with that thing all night or are you going to play it?"

Kavan's fingers traced absently over the strings and the dark wood frame. "I cannot."

"Cannot? I have not heard those words from you in a long time. What has come over you that you can no longer play?"

"It is not that I am unable, but…" he hesitated. "Can you not hear that?"

Though Ártur strained his ears, he heard nothing unusual and shook his head. "I hear nothing except horses, crickets, the wind in the trees…Bhríd snoring…your voice. Is there something more?"

"A sound…like a drum…coming from the west?"

Ártur frowned. Drums could not be good. "I hear nothing. Are you certain?"

He could have been insulted about not being believed, but because Kavan had asked for his cousin's input, he took the question at face value. "I am. It is faint…but it is there." He got up after putting his harp back into its case. "I should investigate. If it is the King's troops, we are in no position to take on an army. I shall distract them if necessary…"

"How…? Do you want me or Bhríd to go with you?"

"I think it wisest if you both stay to protect the Prince." He did not address, as he walked into the forest, how he might distract an army if necessary, which worried Ártur. Though logic and fear demanded he follow or stop Kavan, he did not. A knot formed in his stomach as he again realized that there were things he could not do for Kavan, and that knot became a cold hard pit when he admitted that he was but a small part of a world in which his cousin was much more attuned.

Now was such a time.

The white hart moved through the forest as if on wings, its silver hooves barely touching the carpet of new spring grass, listening to the pulse growing louder and more insistent as he drew closer to it. It had been a long time since he had taken this form, but tonight it would offer quicker movement and more concealment should he have need of it while putting him nearer the ground than the kestrel form would have. The freedom to roam the forest because he wanted to was a pleasure he had not enjoyed for longer than he cared to think about. Yet he knew he was not free to do as he wished tonight. He had a mission and a duty.

Unsure of what he was seeking, other than what sounded to him like a drum, he paused to drink from a stream. The sound was now mixed with the tinkling of bells; he lifted his head to look in the direction of the sounds, both of which seemed suddenly closer to him. He took a few cautious steps forward and leapt onto the high bank on the other side of the stream. Ahead of him was the dark form of a crumbling, moss-covered wall; behind it was a soft glowing light. As he drew nearer, he recognized the chime of a harp, so faint that even when he stood at the wall and peered beyond it, he could barely discern the tune.

The nearly twenty shadowy figures twisting and swaying around a globe of pink light were dressed in white. They appeared to be of the same age, young and vigorous, in the prime of health, radiating an overpowering aura of vitality and wellness. All except one of them had dark curly locks. That one's hair shone pink in the glow of the light source, though it was likely pale blonde or white. He was the harper. Each dancer wore dark ribbons of silver bells on their wrists and ankles. One had a wooden drum that beat to the rhythm Kavan had followed. The air was warmer and heavier here, fragrant with the scents of flowers, fire, sweet wine, and roasting meat though there was no visible food or wine or fire. The only flowers Kavan could see were entwined in the dancers' hair.

Unaware of his actions, Kavan made his way around the wall and came abruptly face to face with the harper, who had stopped playing and appeared before him without seeming to move. The music, the drumbeat, and the dancing all stopped. All of those present were now facing Kavan, staring at him with wide, childlike eyes.

"Do not be frightened, innocents. Lord Cliáth means us no harm."

The man's voice was as warm as the air, his violet eyes friendly and welcoming. There was power here, stronger than any Kavan had ever felt before. It overpowered his senses. He took a few hasty steps backward and realized he was in possession of his own form though he could not remember having changed. He fought against panic and focused on the image of the hart in his head but nothing happened. Kestrel. Again nothing. Failure. This had never happened to him before. He was psychically paralyzed. That these people seemed to know who he was, and that he was defenseless, frightened him. He wanted to back away further but was now pressed to the mossy wall, trapped.

"Lord Cliáth, you have no reason to fear us; you never have before. You will discover that, when in the presence of us or ours, your abilities will not function, at least not without our approval or excruciating effort on your part. You have experienced this already. Even Lord MacLyr's healing would be useless here. We bear you no ill. Have we, or I, ever caused you harm?"

Kavan fought to find his voice and choked, "In truth, I cannot answer that, for I do not know you."

The stranger smiled. "Yes, you do, but your eyes were not trained to recognize what you saw. Your power was untrained and hid us from you. Now it is balanced, intense, well-controlled, and you see us as we are for the first time. Does it unsettle you so much?"

The words meant nothing to Kavan and did not explain how he could know this man or any of these people. There was a vague feeling of having been in their company before, but surely he would recall such a powerful man if he had.

The harper smiled. "Come. Play for us. News of your talent has reached us; it is rare that we have one such as yourself to entertain us at the Feast of Llyr. Please...play for us."

"Surely my talent is small compared to yours..." The others drew closer, pulling him into their circle, until he stood beside the blonde harper, ringed by dark-haired ghosts. The wall that had been behind him was no longer there, although he could see it from the corner of his eyes some ten feet away.

"So humble. Let us be the judge of that, friend. We wish to hear what you have made of the gift we gave you."

Kavan did not have the chance to reply or ask what the stranger meant before his host's large harp was thrust into his hands. He gasped as though burned. The instrument was an ornate Cliáthan, the likes of which he had only seen in paintings of the old Elyri High Royalty. None like this had been built by his family in at least fifteen hundred years.

The harper motioned. Bowing his head, Kavan humbly began to play. The circle started to sway in an orgy of movement, the bells ringing in time, the pulse of the drum throbbing in his head and through every nerve in his body. The harper rested one hand on Kavan's shoulder and Kavan found bits of music pouring from his fingers, songs he did not know, had never heard. Perhaps he was composing them. Perhaps the tunes were coming from the touch on his shoulder. The figures became a blur of movement in his unfocused eyes, the floral scent thicker in his nostrils like the richest of incense. Fear left him. Thought left him. All he knew was music.

ᡐ*ᡤ

Sunlight roused Ártur from his slumber. He had been dreaming, a sensual dream that would have embarrassed him if the object of that dream had been nearby. Fortunately, she was not. Nor was Kavan, he noticed. He yawned, stretched, and got up, brushing the dirt from his clothing. Bhríd dozed, slumped against the tree where he had decided to wait out his watch. Both had kept longer watches than planned since they decided it was best not to wake the prince and have to explain Kavan's absence. There were no signs around camp that Kavan had returned. The healer touched Kavan's thoughts with his own; the bard was sleeping peacefully wherever he was, a sleep Ártur knew he did not often get in camp. He woke Bhríd to tell him that he was going to seek out their kinsman and then began walking in the direction the bard had gone last night.

He was relieved that no harm had come to his cousin as far as he could tell and that whatever Kavan had been pursuing had turned out not to be a threat. Still, he wondered why his cousin had not returned to camp. Not that it mattered; Kavan had stayed away often enough in the past that this time should be no different. But last night his absence had affected both Ártur and Bhríd and could have been very dangerous for all of them. The healer felt his cousin owed him an explanation.

After nearly an hour of trekking through damp underbrush, he crossed a stream, climbed the steep embankment on the other side, and entered a secluded grove. There, Kavan slept, curled into a tight ball, his hair and robe moist with the night's dew. Something about this place made Ártur feel as if he were intruding on holy ground although he saw nothing unusual about it. More than likely, Kavan had sensed it, which explained why he remained here rather than returning to camp.

"Kavan?" He touched his cousin's shoulder, wanting to wake him and be gone from this place. Perhaps Kavan felt comfortable here, but Ártur felt as if he did not belong. The bard stirred, stretched, and when he opened his eyes, it was to a moment of panic until he recognized Ártur. "Are you alright?"

Looking around him, Kavan shrugged. He recognized none of his surroundings, and with the confusing heaviness inside of him, as if he were wrapped in layers of wool, he was not sure if he was well or not. "Where am I?"

"In the forest. Did you find the drums you heard?"

"Drums…?" Perplexed, his brow furrowed until his gaze came to rest on a charred spot about three feet away from him, a circle approximately the size of the pink globe of ethereal light. "Yes!" he exclaimed, animated now by the memories. "There was a drum…and a harp…a Cliáthan…centuries old. A man with violet eyes…and an accent I did not recognize. It was a feast…the Feast of Llyr he said. They asked me to play. There was a wall there…" he pointed in the direction Ártur had come from where there was no wall to be seen. "I was the hart…and then myself…" Rubbing his eyes, he murmured, "I don't know…it sounds impossible, Ártur…my memory is hazy, like a dream, but it was no dream. They were here…"

Ártur helped him to his feet, noticing the charred grass, evidence that supported Kavan's claim. "I am sure they were…whoever they were. There is something unusual here…as if it is sacred…I don't like it…"

"Yes…sacred…that's it." The faraway look in his cousin's eyes sent a shudder down the healer's spine.

"We should return. Prince Arlan will be upset if we're gone longer. We are about an hour's distance; I suspect that will be too long as it is."

"Then perhaps we should not walk," Kavan challenged with sparkling eyes.

"Kavan…"

"You do agree that flying would be faster than walking?"

The healer rolled his eyes. "Yes, of course, but…oh…never mind. I see I will not win this time. But tell me something. Why do these things only happen to you? Why don't I, or anyone else, see or hear or feel…?"

A small whimpering sound caught in Kavan's throat and he looked at the ground as if trapped in misbehavior and awaiting chastisement for it. "I do not know, Ártur. They said something about my power…but I do not know. They knew your name…they know you are a healer…" He did not want to discuss it further. He had no answers to questions he often asked himself. "This place will not allow changes to come easily…if at all. We shall have to move away…"

He led Ártur down the embankment and across the stream, away from the power that conflicted with his senses. When he felt safe, he quickly took on the familiar kestrel shape and Ártur had to struggle to change and keep up with him as Kavan climbed higher into the sky in ever broadening circles. Realizing his cousin was toying with him, Ártur stopped pursuing and headed instead towards where the horses were tethered and their companions camped. Kavan reluctantly followed. They both came to ground out of view of both men and horses and walked back into camp, Kavan with an uncommon look of joy on his face.

The sight made Bhríd smile. It felt good to see his kinsman happy. "You have found our merry wanderer."

Kavan bowed to his dark-haired cousin. "It is a beautiful morning, certain inspiration for music." He assumed Bhríd knew how long he had been gone.

Prince Arlan, however, might not have known, but he was not happy to have awakened to both Kavan and Ártur's absence. "Then I expect you to have something new to share with us tonight," the prince muttered, his gaze hard as if he knew they were hiding something from him."

"Very well, My Prince," Kavan readily agreed, in no mood for an argument and willing to comply with the request.

"Have you eaten?" Bhríd indicated the cheese and bread he had readied for them. The healer accepted the offering but Kavan did not, turning his attention instead to readying the horses for travel. It would be best to stay busy and avoid the prince's wrath, and he was ready to continue on.

⮞*⮜

The two riders approached the city's edge, followed by the four others who kept a watchful eye on them but were careful not to ride too close or intrude. King Owain smiled as he pointed out various points of interest to his companion. It was the first time his bride-to-be had been out of Rhidam and the morning ride on the beach of Kamin seemed to favor her. She had never looked happier, or lovelier, and the King was pleased with his decision to bring her here. Now, as they arrived at the Lachlan manor house, a soldier on horseback approached; he looked to have been waiting at the gate for their return, which immediately set the King's nerves on edge. The soldier saluted and the King gestured in response.

"Milord, I must speak with you."

The King held up his hand to silence the man and then helped Deidre from her horse. He kissed both of her cheeks, and then her hand, and waited until she was almost inside the manor house walls before taking his eyes from her and turning his attention to the waiting soldier.

"Captain Cornell, how are things in Rhidam?"

"Satisfactory, I suppose, though your mother is of the opinion she rules in your absence," the man replied, hesitating to speak ill of the King's mother though both knew the words were true.

The King grunted. Wiping a gloved hand across his damp brow, he grimaced. "Typical. Accursed woman. Has she done anything rash?"

"Not to my knowledge, sir. She stays in her rooms much of the time. I do not see her often."

"It is best you do not. She is even more of a bother when you must deal with her daily. How are General McLeu and Captain Wyndham?"

"Captain Wyndham has not yet returned from Bryn; your mother says not to be concerned, that King Ander will not harm them."

The King uttered a gruff sound of disbelief, secretly hoping Ternce slaughtered any Nethite he found in Enesfel and sent the bodies to King Ander as a gift. He motioned for the Captain to continue speaking.

"General McLeu's health is still tenuous. He cannot keep food down much of the time and has frequent fainting spells. The doctors have been unable to determine the cause but are working diligently to restore him to good health. It is the opinion of some that he be forced into retirement, milord."

Expression grave, the King asked, "You have known him longer than most. Is that your opinion as well?"

"No, sir. He is still capable of leadership, though I do not think he would live long in the field. The other officers are in agreement with me."

"Then his mind is not failing?"

"No, he is as sharp as he always was."

That brought the King relief. "Then I see no reason to ask him to resign yet. We are not in a state of war, and even if we were, his is the best military mind we have. There is no reason he cannot perform the duties he is still capable of while someone else leads the troops in battle...should it become necessary. As for Captain Wyndham, if he has not returned by the time I return to Rhidam, we will take action on his behalf. But..." he looked the soldier over critically, "you did not come here to discuss any of that, did you?"

The soldier shuffled awkwardly. Try as he might, his face had always been too easily read. "No, My Liege. There are reports of a gdhededhá in Kilmacud preaching that a miracle is to occur in the greatest city in the Five Sovereignties. He seems to have originated in Jardin. He was detained and questioned by the authorities when his followers became so numerous that they had to congregate in the town square. He insists that he does not know what the miracle will be, or in which city it will occur. He did indicate he believes it will be in either Clarys or Rhidam. Because of this, we have begun seeing an influx of pilgrims into Rhidam. There has been some speculation that this may be connected to the rebels..."

"They are not rebels, Lord Cornell...at least not yet. Was this gdhededhá Teren or Elyri?"

The captain shook his head and shrugged. "I was not told that, Sire. I did not think it important enough to ask..."

"Find out. It could be very important. And what about this band of wanderers in the north? Any news?"

"The last report claims that their numbers have diminished drastically. Though the bridges along the upper Tegid have been destroyed as per your orders, the remaining bunch of them arrived in Dorshur without horses. There have been several more sightings of a man fitting the description of Guthrie McHador and there have been unconfirmed reports that the Elyri bard you imprisoned last year has returned."

The King stared across the horizon, lost in thought. His mother had drilled action into him during their exile in Neth. She had also tried to teach him to read the enemy's actions and use it to his advantage. But this motley band did not yet fit any description of enemy he knew, and he saw no point in playing a cat and mouse game with them when their actions might be a ruse for something more detrimental to the kingdom. Neth or Hatu could be behind it, or even Cordash or Elyriá, and he did not want to risk war until he knew whom he was battling. If it was simply a collection of peasants trying to rise against him as many had in the past, his army could deal with them without any great loss of life, time, or resources, should it come to a fight. Thus far, that did not appear necessary.

"We will not move against them yet. They have caused no trouble and I will not act on rumor alone. If they are gathering to stage a protest, I will hear them. If it is McHador leading them, he may be looking to get the price off of his head…or looking for his niece. Let them be for now, but keep watch on them and find out what caused the drastic reduction in their numbers. Determine where they are going and why, what they want. Investigate any possible connection between them and this miracle-predicting gdhededhá, and do what you can to confirm reports of the Elyri bard. I do not want that business to come up again. He was a threat once; he could be again." Kavan had been far less a threat to the kingdom than he had been to the King's peace of mind, and Owain did not want to travel that path again.

"Currently the situation with Neth is more critical, and with Hatu beginning military drills, they are a force to be watched closely. It is usually an indication of something gone wrong for their monarchy, which means we can anticipate border skirmishes. When General McLeu is up to seeing you, tell him to send men south, just in case. But I repeat, until you have more solid information about McHador, or whoever is behind this band of peasants, I want nothing more done than investigation."

"But…"

"Peasants are no match for a well-trained, well-armed military…"

"That is what King Bowen thought," the captain said quietly, hoping that the King would not consider him insubordinate for voicing that opinion.

Countenance darkening, the King did not look at the soldier. Bowen, in his eyes, had been a fool and had not had the resources Owain did. He had barely any military at all, and he had not had Owain on his side. The King was determined not to make the same mistakes his father had.

᠙*᠙

Captain Wyndham opened his eyes but did not recognize the dank, dark, putrid smelling hole he was in. The skin on his back was tight and stung with every move he made and the pain was enough to bring vague recollections to the surface of his memory. He had been ambushed, beaten, and passed out without telling his captors anything of value…as far as he could recall. He wondered who his captors were. Certainly not McHador this deep inside of Neth. Probably bandits seeking a ransom, he groaned, trying to shift into a more comfortable position but barely able to move his abused limbs.

Though not certain of his location, he could tell it was now morning. He could hear movement outside of his cell, and there was light coming through the open window, bringing with it the crowing of a cock. There was the sound of a key in the lock and he forced himself to sit. The style of the fur boots was recognizable, but the paunchy man wearing them, or the two men behind him, were not. The first man tilted his head and his companions retreated, closing the door on the way. He leaned against the doorframe, crossed his arms, and looked down at the captain smugly.

"If you plan to kill me, do it," Captain Wyndham hissed. "You will get nothing from me."

"Temper, temper. I have no plans to kill you. I need you alive. You do not know me?"

"Should I?" A cocky smirk was the man's reply. Captain Wyndham narrowed his eyes. "Should I?"

"Ander de Corrmick."

"The man I wanted to see." Now that he had the man's name, his swollen eyes could make out the slight resemblance he bore to his sister. The only thing remotely intimidating about this fleshy, boy-faced King was the sword that hung at his side, but he doubted the man was fast enough to best him in a fight even in his beaten condition.

"How fortunate. Then we can both accomplish our business without further delays. Please. I insist. You first."

Choking back his initial choice of words, the captain tried to straighten as he spoke. "I come on behalf of King Owain. He demands to know the purpose of the raid on the town of Bryn, what you have done with the abducted people, and who was responsible for the order."

Though he did not laugh, the Nethite King still appeared amused. "My sincerest apologies for that. It was not meant to be a raid. We intended to intercept the band of ruffians roaming your lands. The general leading the campaign got carried away, but be assured he has been reprimanded accordingly."

"King Owain will want proof of that…"

"Will the man's head be enough?" King Ander smiled, rubbing the stubble on the rolls of his chin. "I will send it with you when you go, if you believe it necessary, though by now it is surely creating quite a stench. Your subjects have already been sent on their way. If you stop in Bryn on your return, you should encounter them there, unless they decide not to rebuild and move elsewhere."

Ternce growled. There was no way of knowing, of course, if any head King Ander produced belonged to his general, or even to the man responsible for the raid…or if the man would be a hapless victim innocent of any crime. Likewise, if the citizens of Bryn were not in the town when he returned, the captain would have no way of knowing whether they had been released from Neth or had moved elsewhere. He knew this was a futile mission.

"The King will be displeased with the way you treat emissaries…"

"Unfortunate, yes, but I am sure we can work out an arrangement, Lord Wyndham. Yes, I know who you are. I apologize for the treatment you received previously, but we cannot be too cautious. How were my men to know you were an emissary and not a spy?"

"They could have asked…"

"And you could have lied to them. There is no way of ever knowing anything about a man for certain. Now, I wish to do business with you."

Ternce grunted again, feeling as though he had gained nothing of what he had been sent here to accomplish, but asked, "What sort of business?" The King was not going to release him until he heard him out.

"Your General McLeu and my nephew do not seem eager to be rid of the menace stalking your kingdom. I have heard rumors that McHador has been stirring up revolts and that he has Elyri backing."

Finding that hard to believe, Ternce challenged, "General McLeu's health is poor; the only thing he is eager to do is recover. And so far, we have received no evidence that McHador, or the Elyri, are involved in this…"

"I can hear in your voice that you believe he is…"

"What I believe is irrelevant. McHador has never been a threat to Enesfel. Whatever his intentions might be…"

"He is working for the Elyri. I have had several sources confirm this…"

"I'm not sure I would trust your sources any more than you trust me, Your Highness. There is no way of ever knowing anything for certain, remember?" The captain watched a flicker of confusion play across King Ander's face and wondered whether Ander was ruling the country or if his advisors, or even his sister, were. "Besides, what could the Elyri hope to gain? They have everything they need; there is nothing in Enesfel to interest them."

"Do not deceive yourself with that lie. This land, all of it, was once theirs. Any student of history knows that. They want it back, have always wanted it back..."

"Then maybe..."

"There will be no peace until they have it all or the last of them have been butchered. They know, however, that to come out from behind those mountains will be their end, thus they have enlisted McHador to assist them..."

"One Teren..."

"Can make a difference if he knows how to gain popular backing."

"And McHador knows how to do this?" Ternce asked skeptically.

"You have seen the results for yourself," was all the Neth King said.

"What is his cut in this? If they want all of us destroyed, he is surely wise enough to know they'd kill him too. What would cause him to betray his own kind, his own country, his life? And what are you expecting me to do?"

"Every man has his price, Lord Wyndham. All I want of you is to persuade your King to act, to stamp out this menace before irreparable damage is done. I offer my assistance in any way possible of course..."

"Of course," Ternce said, managing not to sneer. "What will you gain?"

"That the Elyri are stopped will be enough..."

The captain snorted and rubbed the back of his neck. "I do not believe they have anything to do with this, milord. I have not heard a word of their involvement. Besides, from what I know of them, from what I know Neth doctrine teaches about Elyri powers, if they truly desired to drive us away or kill us all, they could have done it easily, and without physical violence, long ago. I do agree, however, that something must be done about McHador…if it is him. I will continue to strive to change the King's mind, to spur him to action, not because you ask it but because I believe it is necessary. I will also inform him of your offered assistance. You know as I do, however, that he is a very willful man…"

King Ander laughed. "He is of de Corrmick blood. Of course, he is. That is why I am seeking your help. My sister has failed to provide satisfactory results. You and your general are the only people he listens to. You must succeed or the Five Sovereignties will fall."

Ternce did not believe that, but said, "I will do my best." He was not certain, however, that his best would be enough.

❧Chapter 28❦

K avan leaned his elbows on the sun-bleached wooden balcony, watching Guthrie drill the troops in the early morning sun. They had arrived in the town of Dorshur to find an armed force of two hundred men awaiting them. There was panic at first as it appeared they were royal militia, but the men turned out to be a collection of older soldiers who had previously served under King Donal and had long ago retired from the Lachlan employ. Under the leadership of the grizzled Lord Oberon Cervasian, the men had gathered together to learn if the rumors of McHador's return were true. Guthrie recognized many of the faces though he had not seen them in over a decade. Duke Affrid Niall, his family, retainers, and friends, had also united in support of the former general. They and a cluster of fifty-two Dorshur men were welcomed into the swelling ranks. To have former militia on their side made many in their company more confident, and went a long way towards improving the prince's outlook and mood.

Tomorrow they were set to leave for the city of Talladegah. Lord Oberon would take a second five-hundred-man regiment into the Derkun Mountains to train and await the signal to regroup. The prince had covered half of Enesfel now and had been hindered only by inclement weather and destroyed bridges. Traveling had been peaceful, despite increasingly frequent rumors of military activity as they moved south, and Prince Arlan was beginning to believe that King Owain was no threat. What the prince needed, Kavan thought with a sigh, finding Arlan amidst the soldiers training below, was something to jolt him out of his complacency. Phaedr rode beside the prince, carrying the flag that was to represent the royal standard, and shouted up to his kinsman on the balcony.

For a dizzying moment, the unit of training soldiers appeared to be in actual combat. The flag Phaedr carried was green and black; its bearer swung and knocked the prince from his horse. A flurry of activity gathered around the fallen rider, and in the turmoil Kavan caught a glimpse of the Lachlan standard trampled beneath the rush of horses' hooves and booted feet. A rider in a green surcoat approached, stopped before him, and waved his fist in the air with a triumphant shout.

"Kavan, come down and join us!"

Kavan blinked and shook his head to clear his vision before focusing on Prince Arlan below the balcony. The green and black worn and carried by the riders was gone and there was no blood to be seen. He shivered and shook his head. "My place is not in combat, My Prince."

"You might find it stimulating, Lord Harper," the prince laughed before galloping back to join the others.

Shaken, Kavan sank onto the edge of the bed. He knew bloodshed. There was nothing stimulating about it. And the training drills Guthrie put the new recruits through were nothing like the chaos of battle.

What had he seen? A future battle? Prince Arlan's ultimate fate? No. He shook his head. He did not believe that. He had seen the prince's coronation long ago, thus he had to believe they were on the right path. The Sight rarely contradicted itself, and so he clung to the belief that they would succeed. He closed his eyes and lay back with his hands behind his head, trying to puzzle out what he had been shown and what, if anything, he was supposed to do.

He looked up only when the door opened behind him. Ártur and Syl entered the room, arm in arm, laughing between them. After Ártur gave her hand a squeeze, she went out again, looking back over her shoulder as the healer watched her go. Only then did he turn to Kavan and his bright face instantly creased with a frown. "You look troubled. Is something wrong?"

Kavan shrugged. "I do not know yet…I pray not."

"Want to talk about it?"

"Not particularly." There was no need to create panic until he deciphered what his vision meant.

"Then why don't you join Syl and me? We are going to ride…"

"You've not had enough riding?"

The healer chuckled. "On the contrary; I have had so much riding that this waiting with nothing to do is beginning to annoy me. Are you coming?"

"I would be a distraction."

Ártur stared at him with an odd expression. "What do you mean? That is why I came up here, to ask you to join us. You have been alone in this room for the last two days; you need to get out. Besides, your horse hardly knows you."

The bard decided not to argue. He was not in the mood for it. "Very well; I will join you. But I am doing this under protest, Ártur. I would prefer to be left alone."

Ártur smiled playfully and almost pushed him out of the room. To Kavan's annoyance, Syl was waiting outside the inn with the three horses, his unsaddled as he preferred when he rode. They had either presumed he would ride before asking, or else Ártur had intended to make certain he would. Kavan took the reins of his horse with a scolding look at his cousin. But when he put a hand on the animal's neck to steady it, his nostrils filled with the pungent smoke of hearth fire, and he froze.

He was in a room filled with thick, choking haze. He could not see the way out but he could make out the shape of a cloak hanging on the bedpost. Reaching for it, he realized that the hand he was seeing was not his own. Nor was the cloak. Both belonged to the prince; he was seeing the blaze through Arlan's eyes.

Kavan sagged forward and came to rest against the side of his horse. The animal skittered at the abrupt, unexpected weight, but did not move away. Gasping for air, Kavan waited for his sight to clear; he could sense Syl and Ártur's concern but could not speak to address it. Beyond them, a figure in a dusty gray cloak caught his attention. The figure was looking directly at Kavan, though he could not see a face within the hood of the cloak. Kavan tilted his head; the stranger seemed to nod. The reins fell from his hands and he sank to his knees, staring in the stranger's direction.

"Kavan?"

He made no response, so Ártur shook him gently. Still, there was nothing. He could read no indication of illness or psychic activity that might indicate a trance-like state. In fact, Ártur read nothing at all, which concerned him more. He started to lift his cousin, help him to his feet, but Kavan looked at him abruptly with narrow, almost feral eyes. The healer backed away.

"Is he well?"

Ártur shrugged. "I do not know. I have never seen him like this. Perhaps we should stable the horses…I dare not leave him alone…"

Though Syl's face revealed her disappointment, she began to gather the reins to lead the animals away. Ártur looked in the direction Kavan was staring but saw only someone in a gray cloak now moving out of sight. It was peculiar and noteworthy that as soon as the figure was gone, Kavan looked at his cousin with clear but confused eyes.

"Kavan?"

Syl hesitated mid-step, hoping for the chance to ride after all.

"Ártur? Where am…where are you taking the horses?"

"Back to the stable. It didn't look like we would be riding today. What happened? llánec? What did you see?"

Kavan surged to his feet and gripped his cousin by the shoulders. "Yes…no…I…Ártur, we must leave Dorshur at once. We can stay here no longer."

"At once? Kavan, it's midday…"

"If we do not, we may all perish. There are troops approaching who will stop at nothing to see Lord McHador dead."

"Troops? Who…?"

Frustrated, Kavan released him and brushed the dust from his robe. "There is no time to explain…"

"I cannot go to Guthrie and say we must leave immediately. He will ask the same questions. Without good reason, he is not likely to start out at this late hour…"

"Then we will be destroyed," the bard moaned, deciding to speak with the ex-general himself.

"Not if you talk to me. Did you see destruction?"

"A fire, in the inn. Prince Arlan will perish in that fire if we remain here. If we wait until evening to depart, the armed force will be upon us, the city will be destroyed in the fighting, and the prince will die. Only if we depart now will Dorshur, and the prince, be spared, and we will gain the element of surprise over our enemy. Victory will be ours, but only if we act quickly."

The healer did not like what he heard, but he squared his shoulders. "Very well. Syl, get my things, please, I will speak to Guthrie."

Guthrie readily agreed to depart the city as quickly as they were able. He had been given no cause thus far to doubt Kavan's words, and if it seemed likely that lives were at risk, he was not going to take the chance of finding out the hard way. Better to do as Kavan directed than risk the alternative. Within two hours they were southbound, men weary from the morning's drills marching in annoyance at the change of plans. Yet there was also an undercurrent of excitement and fear. Perhaps they were riding into battle, or perhaps the King was on his way to stop them. Fortunately, the terrain in this region of Enesfel was clear and open, allowing for easier and faster traveling. With that benefit came one drawback; there was only the occasional hill and the forest three miles to the west, to provide cover. They were exposed and every man knew it. It was less likely they could be ambushed here yet there was nowhere to hide if they were.

Phaedr scouted ahead and to the west, while Kavan scouted behind and to the east. He was troubled to find no trace of enemy troops. Perhaps they were approaching from some other direction. Or perhaps, he admitted grimly, his rabid need to place some meaning on the two visions he had received had led him to fabricate stories in order to force them to make sense. But no. The stranger had been there, had told him what must be done. That message had not been the Sight. The danger had to be real.

Even when Guthrie insisted the men stop for the night because they could no longer travel without the aid of lanterns and torches, the night being cloudy and moonless, Kavan refused to give up his search. The enemy had to be there. Somewhere. He needed to find them. To return to camp without locating the threat would make him the target of much annoyance, anger, and ridicule, and that he did not desire to face.

Prince Arlan was hunched beside the fire, watching Guthrie repair a spear that had lost its head in the morning's drills. No one had told the prince the reason for their hasty departure from Dorshur. None of the men knew. It seemed, only Guthrie and Ártur and Syl knew the truth. The ex-general claimed that he had changed his mind about remaining in Dorshur, deciding instead to move again without further delay, but the prince could sense that something was wrong. The fact that Kavan had not rejoined them, and the fact that Ártur lay watching the sky for several hours after everyone else retired, seemingly looking for his cousin, heightened the prince's anxiety.

"Ártur?"

The healer looked at him across the spark and sputter of the fire's glow. "You should be sleeping..."

"I can't. Where is Kavan?"

The healer groaned. "I do not know. I wish I did. We would all sleep much sounder, I think, if we knew where he was."

"Do you think something has happened to him?" That the bard might be dead, that this undertaking could result in his mentor's death, had not occurred to him before, and now it worried him more than he admitted.

"If you mean has he been injured or killed...no. I sense that he is anxious and disturbed but he has not been harmed."

Gathering up his bedding, the prince moved closer to the healer. "How can you know?"

Ártur rolled onto his side to face the prince. "Elyri...or at least some Elyri...are capable of projecting their physical condition, emotional state, and even complete thoughts sometimes. Usually, in order to receive such a projection, the receiver must have a strong bond with the sender. Kavan is very adept at projecting to me. Sometimes he does it without trying."

"Could he project to me?"

"I do not know. We shield our minds from Teren; if we did not, it might give us away to those we would rather hide from. It is already too simple to tell Teren from Elyri; we do not need to do more to expose ourselves and compound the problem. I'm not sure that projecting to Teren has ever been tried, but I suspect, if anyone can do it, Kavan can."

"How close does he have to be for you to hear...or sense...what he sends?"

Keeping his voice low, the healer explained, "It varies from one individual to the next. For most, I would say no further than ten miles on average. Some of us can do more; some of us cannot do it at all.

Kavan can project himself to me at least as far as the distance from Bhryell to Rhidam, possibly further."

"That was how he…how you knew…" Eyes wide, he started, "Kavan must be…" but he stopped, unable to find the words he wanted.

"Powerful?" The prince nodded in response to the question, and Ártur continued, "More than any man or woman I have ever known."

"Does that mean…he could be miles away from us right now?"

The healer sighed. "Yes."

After another long silence, the prince asked, "Does his absence have anything to do with our abrupt departure from Dorshur?"

"I am not at liberty…"

The prince crossed his arms and huffed. "I am a prince, the rightful heir of Enesfel, and in theory, the leader of this venture. I see no reason for such things to be hidden from me. If we are riding into something, or rather away from something, it is fair for me to know what it is."

Ártur closed his eyes, wondering what he should say. The prince had a point. This was not something that should be kept from him; he was no longer a child to be shielded from the truth. If asked, Kavan would have been honest; the healer decided to be likewise.

"We left Dorshur because Kavan Saw that, if we did not leave when we did, you would have died tonight in a fire…or in battle…"

"Died? Me? We put the company through a forced march to save my life?"

The healer chuckled. "You are the reason they are here, My Liege. Some have already died for you. To have you killed in a fire now, when it could be avoided, would have been a terrible waste of time, resources, and men. As well as a loss of their hope. It was the only thing we could do. To some of us, you are more than the prince of Enesfel; you are also our friend. Kavan did not tell you before because he felt that you would not respect his gift of Sight, and it would have hurt him to experience that disbelief first hand."

"I do not…" Prince Arlan stopped midsentence again, knowing that he did still doubt Kavan's abilities and that he would have argued against traveling regardless of such a possible risk. Instead, he changed the subject. "The hart…that Farrell…that was Kavan, wasn't it?"

"Yes."

The prince swallowed back the uneasy quiver in his throat. He had believed that since the night he, Guthrie, and Brenna had been forced to flee the cabin he had called home. "He is…do the things he sees…like this fire…do they always happen?"

"As far as I know, yes…unless steps are taken to prevent them. Or so others with the Sight have said throughout our history. He might not ever witness the events he is Shown, however…and he rarely speaks to me of what he Sees. He does not feel that I fully respect his gifts either."

That surprised the prince; he had thought Ártur never doubted his cousin. They always seemed close to him, but perhaps that was only an illusion. He was beginning to think that Kavan never got close to anyone. "If you can…will you tell him to return to us safely…and soon?"

"I will try." Ártur stretched and lay back. "Sleep, Arlan. Morning will come sooner than you think." And if Kavan's instincts held true, it might come even sooner than they expected.

❧*❧

Captain Wyndham looked through his tiny window, waiting. The problem was, he did not know what he was waiting for. He had visited Bryn and confirmed that some of those abducted citizens had returned. That much of King Ander's words seemed to hold true. The captain's mother was reported dead, his father unaccounted for. The numbers were few, however, mostly women and children, and he had no way of knowing if those who were missing had moved elsewhere, had died in battle chasing the Nethite raiders away, had been killed in the raid…or had joined the wandering band that had aided Bryn. Perhaps they were still in Nethite prisons. His impression of King Ander was that the man would tell him whatever he wanted to hear, whether it was true or not.

Upon his return to Rhidam, he made his report first to General Ferghus and then to the King. King Owain was furious over the way King Ander had treated his captain, but he had at least been partially satisfied to learn that some of the kidnapped citizens were sent home and the general claimed to be responsible for the raid was dead. King Ander had also sent the requested compensation for the destruction caused and for the future income lost. However, the King showed little concern for those still missing, believing as Ferghus did that those people had moved on rather than returning to rebuild the destroyed town. When Ternce broached the subject of possible Elyri involvement in the plot, the King laughed.

Though King Owain had heard the captain out, he did not take to heart the warnings and dismissed Ternce with the admonition to keep his suspicions to himself until he had proof to support his claims. Since he had none and could think of no way to get it, Ternce returned to his quarters and spent the better part of two days in sullen withdrawal. He finally decided that such behavior was unbecoming of a man of his station. He would return to his duties in the morning and continue searching for the proof that would convince his King that he was right.

ॐ*ॐ

It was still dark when Guthrie was shaken awake. It took a few sleepy moments before he recognized the face bent close above him, but the intruder on his sleep did not wait for recognition before speaking.

"Guthrie...to our rear and east...less than an hour's ride. The green and black flag...I have found them." Kavan was breathless as he spoke, panting and gasping for air.

Having never seen the bard in such a state, Guthrie sat hastily and reached for his boots without bothering to rub the sleep out of his eyes. "How many?" He had no doubt Kavan spoke the truth.

"Between fifty and one hundred...I could not get an accurate count. They were setting camp when I found them..."

"What time is it?"

"There are about four hours before dawn."

With a grimace, Guthrie allowed Kavan to help him to his feet. Any force pushing through the darkness late into the night had clearly been desperate to reach a specific goal; it was likely only exhaustion that had forced them to stop so near to what they sought without catching them. That exhaustion, however, could be used to the benefit of Prince Arlan's troops. Rather than flee, this was the best opportunity they might have to put down at least one troublesome force. "Help me wake the healers...and Bhríd and Phaedr. Let Arlan sleep. There is nothing he can do at the moment...and then we gather the troops..."

Within an hour, Guthrie had gathered an experienced cavalry force of one hundred men and had them riding to rout the enemy. He did not think he would require more men than this, particularly if their pursuers were freshly camped. They rode in the darkness, each close enough to see the man in front of him, using the cover of night to their advantage. The general listened to everything, watched for any slight movement around them, his senses heightened further by Bhríd's excited presence beside him. As they crested each hill, his sense of anticipation grew; each time he expected to find the camp at the top of the next rise. Instead, as they rode over another gentle ridgeline, he spotted the camp in the shallow hollow of the valley. He kept his men back to stay hidden by the hill and then crept forward on foot to inspect the opposition.

ᐁ *505* ᐁ

Whoever they were, they were not camped in tents and exhibited no particular pattern to their sleeping arrangement. Only a few fires continued to burn; most had been extinguished or had died for lack of burnable fuel. On the perimeters, he could see two sentries on each square side. Everyone else appeared to be asleep.

He returned to his troops, mounted his horse, and motioned to Bhríd. The signal went back, and with a nod, he led the charge. Behind him, Bhríd let out a whooping war cry and led the faster horsemen careening past their general, maces, axes, spears, and swords raised and ready.

The shouts of Prince Arlan's men were joined by cries of confusion as the enemy soldiers, jarred from their slumber, scrambled to react to what was happening. By the time they determined they were under attack, the cavalry was upon them. Guthrie swung and took down the first person he encountered, a sentry wearing a green and black surcoat with a wolf on it. The standard of Ander de Corrmick. Guthrie growled. What the hell were Nethite soldiers doing this deep within Enesfel? Teeth grinding, he ripped his way through several more people before turning his focus to a sweep of the perimeter, intending to keep anyone from escaping. They did not want any man to report to King Ander. Over the clamor, he could hear Bhríd's war cry rise up a second time, a chilling sound that made the ex-general thankful that the young Elyri was on Prince Arlan's side.

In the chaos, he saw a thick gathering around one horse, its rider swinging his sword expertly before sliding off his mount. There was no time to consider that soldier's fate as a heavy pole struck Guthrie's horse. The animal reared and slid sideways and then came crashing down across the general's legs. The attacker thrust a spear into the horse's middle; the animal screamed, thrashed, and then did not move again. The blade pierced through the horse into Guthrie's leg. Unable to defend himself or flee, Guthrie did the only thing he could think of. He bit his lip hard enough to draw blood and allowed it to trickle from the corner of his mouth. He hoped that, with his eyes mostly closed in the dark and heat of battle, he would be mistaken for dead.

"Sir!?"

He heard Bhríd's voice and the clash of weapons overhead. He peered up in time to see the Elyri spin sideways and decapitate the man who had felled Guthrie's horse. A second soldier approached but lurched forward when someone behind him tumbled backward against him. Bhríd's broadsword thrust clean through both men's abdomens and with one heave, he lifted both off the ground, the blade biting deep into the sternum of the first and shattering ribs in the second. He kicked them from his sword as another man rushed him from his blindside. His heightened Elyri senses allowed him to detect his attacker's approach. He raised his shield to impact the studded front into the man's face. The force was enough to throw the fellow backward to the ground; he did not move again. Bhríd straightened, shield and sword raised above his head, and let out a bellowing roar, waiting for the next person who dared challenge him. None did. By now, the valley was littered with bodies; the only conflict was at the northern edge of the encampment where the last remnants of soldiers were being captured as they tried to flee.

With no one left to fight, Bhríd knelt beside Guthrie, silhouetted by the rising sun, and felt for his breathing.

"I'm alive," Guthrie groaned.

"Praise be. I would have hated to tell the prince we lost you our first time out. With the blood and all…"

The general chuckled. "A trick I learned in Hatu. What better form of protection than to feign death…although it doesn't always work."

"I shall remember that, sir. Are you injured?"

"That spear there…it's in my leg I think. With the weight of the horse, I've lost feeling…"

"Should not bring horses into battle anyway, sir. A waste of a perfectly good animal. I will get someone to help me move it."

"Check our troops first. Look for those more wounded than I am. Send someone back for the physicians and the healers if necessary. Take a count of the losses. I will be well enough in the meantime."

"Are you certain, sir?"

"Go. There are probably men dying out there, and I am not one of them." At least he was not dying yet.

It was some time later when Guthrie was roused from sleep by the sensation of the spear being pulled from his leg. There was little pain at first until the weight of the horse was lifted away. The sudden rush of blood to his legs took some moments to register, but when it did, he had to struggle to keep the nausea from overwhelming him.

"Sorry, sir." It was Bhríd again. "As you said, there were men dying, and there aren't enough healers to spare. I couldn't carry you and the horse…"

"You could have been a little gentler," he barked, knowing that nothing except an Elyri healer would suppress the agony of sensation returning to his legs.

"We have a pallet for you; we are ready to start back to camp." He bound Guthrie's wounded leg with cloth strips as he spoke.

"I will not be carried into camp."

"With all due respect, sir, you cannot walk…"

"I will ride back; get me another horse. There are horses, aren't there?" He forced himself to sit, ignoring the pain as much as he could.

"There are. We lost seven but captured sixteen."

"And men? What are our losses?"

"We have four dead, twenty-two-wounded. Lord MacLyr says three of those will not live until evening, and another five are uncertain. One of those five…" his voice dropped to a whisper, "is Phaedr."

"My…" He looked around, watching his men moving about having no idea what they were doing. Looting for supplies, food, and weapons most likely. He detested battlefield scavenging, but sometimes it was necessary, and when a unit was as sparsely supplied as

Prince Arlan's followers were, this was one of those times. When he looked once more at Bhríd's face, he could see the young man's concern for his brother, but as soon as the Elyri realized he was being watched, his expression went blank.

Guthrie waved Bhríd off to find him a horse and waited for enough feeling to return to his legs to be able to stand shakily. He was weak from loss of blood, but not so weak that he would allow others to carry him back to camp. When Bhríd returned with a horse, he and another soldier aided Guthrie in mounting.

"Are you certain you can ride, sir?"

"I've done it before. Tie me on so that I will not fall." Bhríd looked skeptical but obeyed while the ex-general surveyed the valley. "Where is the enemy?"

"Already buried, sir. We suspect that a few escaped despite our efforts, but we did take three prisoners."

"Good…maybe they can answer a few questions."

Prince Arlan helplessly paced the camp as the first of the wounded were carried back. The sound of hurried and chaotic movement woke him an hour earlier to discover Syl arranging the nearly deserted camp in preparation for the casualties to come. The prince was relieved to find Kavan asleep under a tree, but his relief dissipated quickly as his confusion over what was happening grew. Now, however, as wounded began to arrive, he knew what had happened, and though he was angry about not being included in their first battle, he decided to do what he would expect a King to do. He moved among the returning soldiers, offering praise, comfort, and consolation. At the first sight of serious injury, a soldier with three ribs exposed, he had to turn away, barely stifling the impulse to vomit. He had seen dead and wounded animals before but never another Teren. Determined to be undaunted by the sight, he forced himself to continue. These men needed him, and he needed their information.

No one had the time, or ability, to answer his questions, however. Syl directed the mildest cases in one direction where the women among them could tend them, while the most severe injuries were sent another way, where other more experienced physicians addressed their needs. Arlan assumed that, since he could not see Ártur, the healer had gone to wherever the fighting had occurred. Unable to assist the medical staff, and feeling as if he was in the way, the prince retreated to where Kavan slept through the din and watched for Guthrie's return.

Near midday, a tent was hastily erected and within half an hour Ártur arrived and disappear into it with someone on a pallet. Someone important, the prince presumed; fearing it was Guthrie, he got to his feet, but by then the ex-general's slouched figure rode into view with Bhríd riding beside him, leading the man's horse by the reins. A quick glance at Kavan showed that the bard still slept; Prince Arlan picked his way through the forest of moaning men towards the horses, hoping for news.

"Lord General," he said with concern, "you do not look well…"

"I fared better than some, Arlan. I am not as much an old man as some might like to think." He slid from the horse as Bhríd unbound the ties that secured him in place, and though the prince tried to catch him, the two of them landed in a heap on the ground.

"Your leg…tend to it at once…"

"The physicians are busy," Guthrie scoffed. "The wound is not that serious; I wish to report…"

The prince crossed his arms and glared. "Tend that wound and then give your report. I assume the battle went in our favor, else fewer would have returned…"

"There are…"

"The report can wait. Do as I say. Bhríd, take him to Syl and stay with him until he has been tended."

After one glance towards the tent, which the prince noticed but did not question, Bhríd murmured, "Yes, milord."

As he watched the pair shuffle in the direction where Syl worked, the prince breathed more easily, grateful that they were both alive. He was aware that, despite the man's protests, it was the first time Guthrie had deferred to the prince's demands, suggesting that some shift in their relationship had occurred this day. It also suggested that the ex-general was acknowledging him as his lord now, rather than his charge.

"My Liege...we have three prisoners...should you wish to interrogate them..."

The unfamiliar, unexpected voice startled him and he stared at the bright-eyed youth eyeing him expectantly. Interrogation? No one had taught him how to do that. What was he supposed to do? Or ask? He glanced over the young man's shoulder to where three shackled men were being tied to some small close-growing trees. The prince swallowed back the discomfort he felt over the request and said, "I believe Lord McHador will want to have a word with them...but I suppose...it will be interesting to hear what they have to say."

He followed the young man, a red-head who was a few inches shorter than him and of wirier build, across the short distance between them and the prisoners, but the care with which they had to pass the weary, aching soldiers slowed down their progress. One of the three captives, an older gentleman with thinning hair, looked up as they arrived and muttered in surprise, "A Lachlan?"

Rather than give anything away, the prince snorted, "Who were you expecting?"

"We were not told this was a civil war between Lachlans," said the youngest of the three. "Our only orders were to find and kill Guthrie McHador."

"Who sent you? Who gave those orders?" There was no response. The prince cleared his throat, hoping it sounded more menacing than it felt. "You can cooperate or we can find other ways of extracting the information we seek."

"Torture is nearly useless against them, Your Highness," one of the attending guards remarked. "Nethite soldiers are trained to tolerate high degrees of pain."

"Neth?" Prince Arlan felt both shock and fright though he fought not to show it. Nethite soldiers? In Enesfel? Looking for Guthrie? Would Owain be desperate enough to send foreign soldiers to do his work for him? Why? And if Neth and Owain were united against him, the prince's chance for success decreased. But he was smart enough to know he could not show those concerns to the enemy and made every effort to sound more certain as he grunted and said, "You may be capable of tolerating great pain, but I do not need to inflict any to learn what I want to know. The Elyri will take the information whether you talk or not." He turned to his escort. "Soldier, what is your name?"

"Caol Dugan, Sire."

"Mr. Dugan, please ask one of the Elyri to come here at once…"

"No!" cried the youngest prisoner, before the soldier Dugan could move. "They will destroy our minds. We were only told to find McHador…"

"Whose orders?" the prince barked again. The three looked amongst themselves, and when no answer was forthcoming, he said, "Mr. Dugan…"

"The orders came from our King," the young prisoner replied quietly, wincing as he spoke, afraid of his comrades and his King, but even more afraid of Elyri interference.

"Did King Owain have anything to do with this order? Did he summon you here?"

"King Ander does not take orders from anyone," snorted the oldest of the prisoners, "his bastard nephew included. However…" He looked beyond the prince at something, his expression growing concerned, "he might be inclined to act on behalf of his sister."

"Lady Ula?" The prince could not remember her, but he knew her name. But if she had manipulated her brother to action, had it been her own doing or at her son's request? "That is helpful...thank you." To the soldiers guarding the three, he said, "Keep these men here. As soon as an Elyri is available, and General McHador is free, I will return." He smirked to himself at the expressions of panic on the three faces, and then turned away, motioning for his escort to come with him.

"Mr. Dugan, how old are you?"

The young man with the flaming red hair did not look away when spoken to, but his voice quavered on the edge of nervousness as he replied, "Seventeen, Sire."

The prince started to ask if perhaps the boy was too young to be riding into battle, but he quickly realized that only a year separated them in age. He wondered why he felt older than eighteen. "Did you have a hand in the capture of these prisoners?"

"I did." There was no modesty or discomfort in that reply.

The prince smiled. "I will see to it that you are given double rations tonight. And remind me of this once we reach Rhidam."

Beaming, the young man was almost dancing in place. It was an honor to be praised by the prince. "I only acted on your behalf, Your Majesty. King Owain's forces executed my father...and I believe you will right that wrong. To see you crowned King will be reward enough."

"I am not going to..." In the young man's face, Prince Arlan saw something he had not before. Open, unabashed adoration and respect. The fellow trusted him and looked up to him as one did to a father or older brother, though they were only a year apart in age and were likely as different in upbringing as any two men could be. And clearly, the prince realized for the first time, there were expectations on him that he had not anticipated. He had planned to win his place in the family, within the castle, in line for the throne, but he had not seriously considered becoming King, at least not in this fashion. If Caol Dugan expected it, others likely did too. Could he do it? "I will see that King

Owain answers for his crimes," he heard himself saying with the feeling that he was listening to someone else speaking. "In one way or another, he will pay for them."

"Thank you, Sire. In return, I will serve you until my death," said the young man with a proud smile.

"Let us pray it does not come to that, Mr. Dugan. Go and rest. It has been a very long day."

Troubled by these realizations regarding his future, and proud of himself for having gotten a small scrap of information from the captives, the prince returned to where Kavan was now sitting against the tree, his knees drawn up to his chest, his harp lying beside him. The dark circles under the bard's eyes and the haunted, blank expression hinted at continuing exhaustion, but he was awake when Prince Arlan joined him. It was surprising he had slept through the chaos so long.

"You found our enemy. I am grateful."

"It was my…"

"Duty? That is what everyone says to me…as though nothing is ever done just because you like me." He smiled. "Duty or not, you saved my life again and kept us from being caught unaware. I am grateful to have you on my side…as my friend…"

Kavan quickly looked away to hide his embarrassment from the prince. "Wounded?"

The prince stared across the quietly mulling camp. "I do not know how many. Guthrie was one of them, and I ordered him to tend to his injury before giving his report. It seems like so many…but I know they are in the best care…"

"Yes…they are…" The harper let his head rest on his knees.

"I did not realize this scouting is tiring for you…" He did not like the way the bard was acting. It distressed him and made him feel guilty for having felt the task of scouting was taken only because it was fun and to keep him away from the prince.

"We are not meant to retain another form for long. It is a great strain on both mind and body…"

"But you enjoy it? The strain of it?"

Kavan did not need to think about the answer, but there was a sudden reluctance to admit the truth. He could not think of another Elyri who enjoyed pushing their personal limits that way, which proved again how different he was. "Yes…I do."

Prince Arlan tried to smile. "That is what is important. I know you do not require my permission to continue doing it…but I want you to know I will never again try to stop you. You have proven its value, and I would be a fool to ignore that. But please…" He put his hand on Kavan's arm and squeezed gently, "Do not kill yourself with exhaustion in the process of protecting me." He intended to say more, but approaching footsteps pulled his attention towards his other mentor and a few other men who had come to join them. "Guthrie…please, sit."

Kavan raised his head as the ex-general gingerly lowered himself to the ground, favoring his right leg. The wound was gone, thanks to Syl's adept hands, but there looked to be lingering pain and stiffness which sometimes could not be helped.

The prince moved closer to Guthrie, which drew him away from Kavan. "How went the battle?" he asked with excited nervousness.

"They were camped about an hour northeast of our position. Given the state of their camp, they were not expecting confrontation. We lost four in battle, another died during treatment. There are two men Ártur feels we will lose tonight. The remaining nineteen are being treated now…and one of those is Phaedr."

The Prince's face lost color. Phaedr was his friend, had trained with him and taught him during the long months in Bhryell. He had never had a friend close to death before and it chilled his soul. A quick glance at Kavan revealed nothing except the bard's eyes closing. "Is he well? Will he live?"

Guthrie shrugged. "I do not know. Ártur is still with him, in the tent. From what Bhríd told me, it was some sort of head injury. Most men do not live through that sort of thing, but it is possible. I'm surprised he lived long enough to make it back to camp for treatment. Until Ártur comes out...tells us...we have no way of knowing."

"He will be well," the prince murmured. He had to be. The potential loss of a friend was difficult to bear. "Did we defeat them?"

The older man patted the prince's arm in reassurance. "Most. I cannot say all; some may have escaped into the darkness, but we killed the majority of them and took three prisoners."

"From Neth, I know. I spoke to them briefly. King Ander sent them after you, Guthrie..."

"How did you...?"

Grinning with a touch of pride, despite the gloom of worrying about Phaedr, the prince replied, "The threat of Elyri involvement to extract information proved useful. He glanced in Kavan's direction, but the bard's head was on his arms and he did not see it. "It seems Lady Ula...they indicated this was her request...although they may have said that to protect their King. From the sounds of it, Owain doesn't know they're here."

Guthrie grunted. "Ula has been the driving force behind Owain since his conception. If she feels I am a threat to him, she would stop at nothing to remove me from the picture. It is probably a fair assessment that the King knows nothing of this...he would not likely tolerate foreign soldiers doing his work for him unless his military strength is suffering. What I've heard about Enesfel's militia gives me no reason to think he is lacking for troops...but Lady Ula...She cannot command the armies and would have to resort to the only military she has available to her, going behind Owain's back. Once he learns of this, I suspect he will be busy dealing with his mother; it should distract attention from us temporarily."

"Neth? Is that the green and black…?" Kavan started to ask without looking up.

"King Ander of Neth, specifically…de Corrmick militia. I should have realized that sooner, rather than in the midst of battle."

So should I, Kavan mused to himself. He had studied such things growing up, but royal and noble crests changed over time, and more than one family claimed those colors for their standards. For Kavan, however, that was a poor excuse for not recognizing the enemy sooner.

Guthrie shifted his weight and continued. "That means that Neth, at least…and Ula, suspects I'm involved…which means that King Owain will know soon, if he does not think it already. We will have to be more cautious against spies. I will give our prisoners time to contemplate more unpleasant methods of coercion, and will then speak to them myself." He did not doubt the prince's words or the information that had been gained already. Having more experience in the arena of interrogation, however, he hoped he might be able to learn yet more from them.

"When will we move?"

"I don't know, milord," the ex-general sighed. "We should move soon, lest any who escaped bring reinforcements…but we cannot travel until the healers give word. Some wounds you simply cannot move."

"We'll run out of supplies if we stay here too long…"

Raising his head at last, Kavan interjected, "Perhaps you should send most of the force ahead to Talladegah…leaving enough here to assist in attending the wounded and defending them if necessary? Perhaps thirty men? They can rejoin the main force when the worst cases have recovered enough to be moved."

The prince looked skeptical but the general scratched his chin thoughtfully. "If reinforcements do come looking for me, the thirty men they would find here would be at best a brief distraction…and at worst it would be a slaughter. We could lose our healers…"

"Would it reassure you if I said I can protect all of those who remain here…if it is necessary?"

He felt the prince's eyes boring into him with amazement and curiosity, but Kavan did not look at him. Instead, he held Guthrie's gaze; the man did not balk, did not even blink at Kavan's suggestion, as though such a thing was the most expected, logical choice in the world. Guthrie had questions, but he refused to ask them. After what he had witnessed thus far, from what he knew of the bard's character, if anyone could fulfill such a claim, it was Kavan. "Yes…I think you could do it. I believe you. Thirty men will suffice if you will stay with them."

"I will if the prince approves…" He did not have to capitulate to the prince's wishes. He could have chosen to do it on his own. But he wanted the prince to be an integral part of the campaign now that it had taken this military turn; it was important to give the young man the chances to make such decisions and live with their results. He expected a barrage of doubts and questions, however.

Instead, though the doubt was clearly muddying the prince's blue eyes, the prince chose to keep any questions to himself. If Guthrie trusted Kavan with this, after what the bard had done for them, then Prince Arlan knew he should too, even if the idea sounded ludicrous. "Agreed, Lord Harper. Guthrie, it is too late to begin today, but if you can ride on that leg, you and I will start the men south in the morning. Kavan, you are to stay with Syl and Ártur, help them if you can, and get some rest."

"It's settled then." Guthrie got to his feet on shaky legs, grateful that the tree was there to offer support. "I will determine which men to leave and inform the others we ride at dawn."

The prince rose with him and offered his shoulder for support. "I will assist you. It will go faster, and Lord Harper needs to rest. Go back to sleep, Kavan. If you are needed, someone will let you know."

Nodding stiffly, Kavan watched them go before lying on the ground once more. He glanced at the harp case beside him, as if considering playing, but when he closed his eyes, he was asleep almost instantly.

Ártur rubbed his stiff hands together and then ran one of them through his hair as he took one last look at his patient. He sighed wearily and left the tent for the first time in several hours.

"How is he?" asked Bhríd, as Syl asked, "Will he live?"

The healer held his hands up in a gesture of surrender and sighed with a shrug. "That's going to be up to him now. I don't know how he lived this long to begin with…that he's held on must count for something. I've healed everything that can be healed…but it may be several days before we know if there will be any remaining damage."

"What sort of damage?" the dark haired Elyri asked as he put a protective arm around his sister.

"He might be blind…" Ártur did his best to ignore Syl's gasp. "He might have lost all or partial use of his limbs. He might be unable to feel or manipulate the power any longer. The losses, if there are any, could be temporary…or permanent. We will not know until he can tell us himself and until time passes. He is sleeping now, but I want one of us to stay with him. Should he wake and find himself crippled in some way, he will require immediate reassurance and attention."

Bhríd nodded with a grim expression. "I will stay. With the patients taken care of, you should both rest. You have worked harder than any of us soldiers today." He stopped his sister's protests with a loving squeeze. "That is an order, taene. I will let you know at once if he should wake."

Grateful for the reprieve, Ártur put his arm around Syl where Bhríd's had been and steered her away from the tent, using a little more force than he wanted to get her to move. "He's right, Syl…we will be useless to Phaedr if we are both exhausted. A few hours of sleep will help." She was shivering beneath his arm. Until today, though she had performed admirably, she had never practiced her healing craft in a battle setting, had never seen such blood and mutilation, or had to face such a loss as her brother was now facing. It was no wonder she was afraid. Ártur completely understood.

"He should live, Syl. I've given him that much at least. If we can persuade him to accept whatever damage may have been done…"

"I know…" she whispered, "but I am afraid for him."

Kissing her hair tenderly, he murmured, "We can only pray for him, Syl."

The sun was setting as he tried to sleep with Syl crying softly in his arms. He was hungry but in no mood to eat. He listened to the discussions around him. Guthrie and the prince would depart with most of the troops in the morning. All but six of the wounded would be going with them, and one of those six Ártur did not expect to live through the night.

And Phaedr. He had done all he could, surprised that he had been able to keep his kinsman alive, but the effects of the lack of blood to the brain, or too much, were things he could not undo. Nor could he predict what effects the injury might have. Such things were beyond an Elyri's healing skill; this was not the first time Ártur had wished for the skill to heal every injury he encountered.

Kavan settled beside him then, appearing as if from nowhere with his harp in his hand and concern on his face. Not speaking not wanting to further upset Syl, Ártur shook his head. Kavan nodded in reply, understanding his cousin's unspoken words, and began to play a soothing melody, singing a High Elyri hymn meant for their ears alone. Syl lifted her head a little to watch him.

Very soon, Guthrie, Prince Arlan, and Caol Dugan joined them. The prince appeared to have taken a liking to the fiery-haired youth. Kavan was both saddened and grateful by this. Despite his deep affection for the prince, Kavan had learned over the course of the past few weeks that he could never be the type of friend Prince Arlan would need by his side at all times…a Teren friend. There were too many differences between them, too big of a gap that no amount of genuine love could bridge.

He stopped playing when all but the ex-general and prince slept. They were talking battle strategy and tactics and Kavan did not want to participate. There had been enough bloodshed for one day. He did not want to discuss more of it. They did no more than look at him when he stood, and quickly resumed their conversation as he walked to the hospital tent, harp in hand.

"Good evening, Lord Harper." Bhríd sat on a stool, leaning against a trunk with his feet propped on his brother's cot. When Kavan pushed open the tent flap and entered, he straightened as if he had been caught neglecting his duties.

"How is he? Ártur did not tell me, but I assume, from his and Syl's moods, that the outlook is not good?"

"We're confident he will live." Bhríd was confident, even if his sister was not. "But Lord MacLyr feels there could be damage within his head that will leave him impaired. We will not know his condition until he wakes, and even then it may be several days before we can determine how bad the damage is."

As grim as the diagnosis sounded, the uncertainty of its outcome also meant that there was a chance that Phaedr could awaken to normalcy, and that was the hope Kavan chose to cling to. "Sleep, Bhríd. Today's victory was well fought; it is time for you to rest. I slept most of the day. Allow me to watch over him for a while."

"Thank you…but I prefer not to leave him…"

Kavan smiled reassuringly. "Then sleep here. I will play for you both; music often helps those in need…perhaps it will help him…"

"Yours more so than most, Lord Harper." Too tired to fight with his cousin, he lay down near the tent entrance to sleep where he would also be able to intercept any enemy that might try to enter. Kavan touched the harp strings, creating a hypnotic effect that brought Bhríd sleep almost at once. Kavan played for Phaedr, and for the other wounded within the tent, all of whom slept in varying degrees of discomfort. The music wove its spell, and soon their breathing turned to sighs of relief as their bodies and souls found the rest that had eluded them.

Eventually, Kavan laid the harp on the trunk beside him and rested his elbows on the bed to stare at Phaedr's face. Whatever damage had been suffered, there was now blankness where the familiar thought patterns should have been. Perhaps it was the effect of unconsciousness, Kavan thought, having never witnessed such a thing before. What he was sure of was that something was not right. Even Teren projected thought patterns he could detect and probe when asleep, but from Phaedr there was nothing. Kavan studied that blankness for many minutes, and when he learned nothing, he picked up the harp to play again.

Someone called his name. He was sure of it, even though there was no one else in the tent that could have called to him as they were all asleep, injured and uninjured alike. A surge of energy pulsed within him and spilled outwards to fill the tent like a shockwave. He nearly dropped the harp under the onslaught of power that rolled about him like boiling water. The sensation grew stronger and then, as suddenly as it had come, was sucked out of the room to settle into his trembling hands. Afraid of the feeling, and for his harp's care, he set it aside again and he focused on his hands, trying to understand what had happened and why the tingling would not pass. Outside of the tent, a faint white glow appeared, drawing him off of the stool to investigate. He was afraid to touch the tent flap, but reluctantly pulled it back to see who was outside.

There was no one there.

"Kavan?" Phaedr was sitting, reaching his hands in the bard's direction. "I heard music. Kavan…is it you? I cannot see you…I cannot…"

The commotion of his brother's increasing panic brought Bhríd awake and to Phaedr's side, to catch his arms as the man began to panic. "Yes, Kavan is here. Please…do not fight me…" Bhríd tried to soothe him, but his efforts had no effect. The struggle lasted but a moment before the two healers burst into the room, both having felt that panic in the same instant. They pushed past Kavan, barely seeing him. The wounded man was trembling and convulsing and then abruptly, as his body surrendered to being pinned, fell limp.

"I cannot see…I cannot see…"

"It is as I feared…" Ártur started.

"No!"

"Bhríd, take her outside. Please. I cannot work with her like this. I will do what I can…"

Kavan, however, remained where he was, feeling compelled to do something but not knowing what he could do. Ártur straddled his patient on that cot, took Phaedr's head in his hands, and closed his eyes. As the necessary contact with the pathways of his mind and body were made, Phaedr began to convulse again but he did not fight to be free. "It is…no use…" the healer muttered. "I cannot…"

Kavan looked from his cousin's tense hands to his own that still tingled, burned, and trembled in a most unusual way. As a cold knot of realization formed in him, he swallowed hard, inhaled sharply, and whispered, "May I assist…?"

"There is nothing you can do, sínréc…"

Ártur did not notice Kavan approach and lay his hands on Phaedr's head, but he felt the jolt of power that flooded his patient, pulsed brightly for the span of a single heartbeat, and then steadily began to fade. As the heated sensation receded, the healer felt something else, something he had not expected, the distinctive mental print that was Phaedr's which, until this moment, had been missing. It floated unfocused between the power in Kavan's hands, a force that intimidated Ártur with its strength. Little by little, it grew stronger, its tendrils reaching out to reestablish connections within Phaedr, until at last everything was as it should be. Kavan removed his hands first, and when Ártur did likewise, he met his cousin's tortured expression.

"How in the name of…you did that! It was not me…it was you! You restored him…but how?"

Kavan fought to find his voice. He recalled past situations when those peculiar feelings had come to him, how he had not acted, or even felt compelled to act, and yet had been convinced afterward that something miraculous would have happened if he had. What had happened this time confirmed those suspicions, and left him with a muddle of confusion, anxiety, guilt, and awe. "I do not know. Truly I do not…I felt the impulse to touch him…and it was done…"

The healer's breath escaped in a whistle. "A miracle…"

"Do not call it that…please…" He felt as if he was going to be sick, and hearing that word attributed to the event made the feeling worse, even though miracle was the only word for it. It had certainly not been Kavan's power, but some external force working through him, that had allowed this healing to come to pass.

"What else should I call it? You are not a healer, and even if you were, no healer could have done what you have done for him. If it was not a miracle, then you have some unheard of healing gift…"

"I do not know what it was, Ártur…" He turned away, put his trembling hands on the crate he had previously been leaning against, and hung his head. "If word of this gets out…"

It would. There was no doubt in Kavan's mind. Others in the hospital tent had been awakened by the commotion and had heard and witnessed what had happened, had heard the healer's words. Ártur checked his patient's pulse and respiration, and then straightened his coverings; he was not thinking about such possibilities when he said, "I cannot take credit for this, Kavan. Even if I wanted to, I could not. Syl knows there was nothing I could do. It was k'Ádhá's miracle; he simply used your hands to do it. You cannot deny that."

Kavan was tempted to try, but such would be blasphemy and he knew he could not. "What will they say…?"

Wiping his hands on his trousers, Ártur asked, "Does it matter?"

Kavan lifted his head to meet his cousin's gaze, his long hair hanging in front of his eyes as if to shield him from the inevitable truth. "To me, yes. It matters very much."

"Place the credit where it belongs…"

"I can do so…but can they?" He indicated the others in the tent with a sweeping gesture of his arm.

"That is between them and k'Ádhá. You shouldn't worry." He went to the tent door and looked back. "Are you coming?"

"You go. I will…stay with him…a little longer."

The healer paused before leaving, the realization of what had happened sinking in more with each passing minute. What must it be like for Kavan to live with such things? He wanted to embrace his younger cousin, reassure him, but Kavan had physically distanced himself from Ártur as much as the tent would allow, which indicated his wish to be left alone. Ártur offered a grateful, worried, smile, and went out.

Outside, he met Syl's eyes first because it would be she who would find the truth hardest to believe. It was difficult to find his voice. "He is sleeping."

"And?" she asked.

"There was nothing I could do. He will, in all likelihood, be blind for the rest of his life. However…" he swallowed and looked away from her eyes long enough to steady himself, "his gifts have been restored…"

"That is not…you said…we cannot do such things, Ártur. No healer can."

He nodded and opened his arms to her. "You are right. We cannot. But Kavan…"

Bhríd gasped and asked, "Lord Harper…?"

"k'Ádhá saw fit to restore Phaedr…and used Kavan to do it."

"Another miracle…?" Syl whispered, hardly believing it to be true.

Unaware of others, assuming she referred to some of those events that had occurred in Kavan's childhood, Ártur sighed. "Do not say that to him, please…you know how sensitive he is about such things. He will not call it a miracle, but what else can it be? I think it best we let this discussion go no further…for his sake…and accept what has been done…"

Bhríd nodded, letting his disheveled dark hair fall before his eyes only to push it away again. "May we see Phaedr?"

"In the morning. He is sleeping, and Kavan would rather be alone. Let us get our own rest…and offer thanks for this blessing…"

Inside the tent, however, Phaedr was not sleeping. He was listening apprehensively to Kavan's restless pacing. He knew what had been, knew what was, and knew what had to have occurred in order for the change to have taken place. What he did not know was how he had gotten here.

"Lord Harper? Where are you? I cannot see you."

With a heavy sigh, Kavan paused, turned, and settled on the bedside to touch the other man's face. "I know."

"What happened? I recall sliding from my horse, being hit in the head…"

"The blow robbed you of your sight…"

"…and nearly robbed me of everything else…my life included I imagine. I am thankful for what Ártur has done…and I thank you for…but perhaps it was a waste of your energy and k'Ádhá's…"

"Such a thing is never a waste of…"

Phaedr gripped Kavan's wrist. "Of what use am I? I cannot fly to scout. I cannot fight. I am useless to the prince; to return home blind and inadequate and..."

The bard silenced him with a finger to his lips. "You are not useless. You are a bright man and I am certain you can continue to be of use to the prince."

Phaedr shook his head. "I do not want to advise. I want to fight."

"To fight in battle may no longer be possible, but we were taught as children to fight and defend ourselves without our eyes..."

"That was against a single or double opponent...and we were children." He smirked. "You always bested me. In battle, I could not..."

"Use your skill to train others..."

Phaedr's voice dropped and he said roughly, "I cannot..."

"You could if you try."

There was a long pause, during which Phaedr wrapped his hand around Kavan's and held it tightly. It was one of those rare occasions where Kavan felt no discomfort or awkwardness over the contact. "You believe so?"

"I do," Kavan assured him. "Think on it. Do not abandon hope while there are alternatives. You have been spared for a reason; there is purpose yet to your life. Trust and seek it out before you give up hope."

Phaedr tried to smile. "You have gifts unlike any I have heard of or seen. If you say there is a purpose, then there must be. But...I...if I run out of alternatives...I beseech you to allow me to leave life gracefully, of my own accord."

Kavan knew what the man meant and it pulled that cold knot in his belly together once again. "That should not be in my hands, Phaedr. I am not your immediate family."

"But you are family. Sometimes those closest to us are particularly selfish about another's needs and welfare. They may prevent me...but I do not think you would. Promise me..."

The bard sighed. "If you promise not to give up until every alternative is tried…until there are no other options…I will do as you ask. I will pray on this and help you find your solution. Have faith and sleep."

There was another, fainter smile and his unseeing eyes closed. "You will stay?"

"I will remain until you wake," was the gentle, reassuring reply.

By the time Ártur returned to check on his patient, Prince Arlan and the troops had already departed, leaving behind twenty-nine men under Bhríd's command. After a night's rest, the Elyri healers could tend to the other five patients more fully, meaning that three of them would likely be fit to travel the following day and would depart with ten of those twenty-nine soldiers. The other would take longer to recover from his injuries, and Phaedr would remain until both were deemed fit to move.

One of the prisoners, the youngest, had died during the night. There were no injuries, no indication of poison or foul play that Ártur could find. His death appeared to be natural although quite strange. To Guthrie, it did not matter. They had learned all he felt they were going to, and the remaining Nethites would be left in the Talladegah prison.

For the next four days, each of his kin worked with Phaedr, helping him relearn the basics of dressing, feeding himself, and moving around the tent by using Elyri power to guide him. At first, progress was slow, as Phaedr was certain it was futile and would give in to fits of temper at the slightest failure. At those times, Kavan's harp became the source of encouragement, and Phaedr would soon be willing to try again.

At the end of the four days, it was decided they should travel south. The six days of riding it took to catch up to the main force brought Phaedr the ability to navigate his horse around obstacles almost as adeptly as he could have done with the use of his eyes. They rejoined Prince Arlan's company, now grown by another one hundred and twenty men, and remained in Talladegah long enough to restock supplies for the stragglers.

Their next destination, Seres.

☙Chapter 29❧

Lady Ula's pinched face was ashen as she sat unmoving, awaiting the arrival of her only child. She had done what she had always done, what was needed to protect him, his position, and his future. That she had failed him again, as she had done innumerable times, meant little to her at that moment. Her only concern was her fate. She questioned why the two soldiers from her brother's forces had come to report their failure here, not only to her but to her son, when Owain was not meant to know about any of this. Perhaps Ander thought her son knew of the plan. Or perhaps her brother had betrayed her.

Then there was the matter of another prince, or at least the rumor of one. She had never believed Prince Arlan to be dead, any more than she had believed McHador to be dead, and Farrell had likely fathered innumerable children. But she had not anticipated that this gathering of men was led not only by a man she had strong conflicting emotions about, but also by some prince who would now be of legal age to claim the throne. If this prince was in league with McHador, the odds were high it was Prince Arlan. She did not know if that information had been shared with her son; the soldiers said they had not, but as with everything else involving her brother, she doubted she could trust them to tell her the truth.

The door behind her opened; she did not rise or cower as the large shadow crossed the room and came to loom over her.

"Leave us, general." The King's voice was remarkably steady, although cold, something that made her proud. Perhaps she had not failed her son as thoroughly as it sometimes seemed. The door closed but he did not move. "You should at least rise in my presence, Lady. I am your lord and master…"

"No man is my lord and master," she snorted, trying to sound as neutral as he did.

"In this kingdom and in this House, it is I who give the commands. I warned you about involving yourself in affairs of state behind my back, and about interfering in the way I run this…"

She spun to face him without rising. "The way you flee from your kingdom like a fawn from a wolf? Instead of ridding your kingdom of McHador and his…you take holiday with that…it is disgraceful…"

"That I am marrying her against your advisement, or that I do not obey you as I did as a child? I did not know any better then, mother, but I do now. Do you have proof that it is indeed Guthrie McHador leading this so-called band of mercenaries and that they mean me harm?"

"I have my sources."

The King snorted. "I am sure you do, though they are not under my employment, nor do they share their knowledge with me…"

"They tell me, and I tell you. Can you not trust your own mother?"

"The woman who lied about my father? The woman who disobeys me and brings foreign forces into this kingdom when I have not…"

"I did not bring them here," she insisted. "I suggested to Ander that something should be done, and encouraged him to help us if he knew of a way…"

"That may have been what you said, but I suspect that is not what you meant, and your brother knew perfectly well what you were asking. He will apparently risk war with me to appease his harlot sister…"

Lady Ula stood at last, the color returning to her cheeks. "How dare you speak to me in that manner? I put you where you are…"

"…by treachery and murder…"

"…and I can as easily take you down…"

"You cannot do so from prison, mother," he sneered, crossing his arms over his puffed out chest.

"Prison?" Her face lost color again.

"Exile is too convenient. The only place I could send you would leave you free to manipulate your brother into causing me further aggravation, and I plan to make sure you can never do that again. McHador or no, I will deal with him on my own terms. Not yours. General McLeu!" The general, having waited outside of the room as instructed, entered with a wary expression. "Escort this woman to the cell Deidre occupied. I believe it is still furnished with the few luxuries she was allowed. The lady is to have no visitors without my permission and I will see to it that you, or Captain Wyndham, deliver her meals. You," he glared at his mother, "will no longer be able to manipulate me, or anyone else, or be able to interfere where your input is not welcome."

He walked to the window without a glance at his mother. She glowered at him, but then followed the general with a defiant toss of her head. He would not keep her there for long. He needed her.

Exhaling after they were gone, the King reached for the crystal decanter on the table beside him and hurled it after them. It struck the door and shattered into hundreds of tiny points of light. In the corridor, Lady Ula jumped, started, and for fleeting moment thought that perhaps she had pushed her son too far.

His spies had shared the rumors of another prince in Enesfel, one who was said to be working to undermine the King's position with his subjects. Owain knew Ander had one son; though he did not think Prince Loris was bright enough to carry out such a venture on his own, with the right backing and coaching, he was certainly a likely culprit. It was not the Halu prince, as he had recently been crowned King of the southern-most sovereignty. Was this prince one of the three heirs to the Cordashian throne, or was it a ruse meant to throw the King off the scent of whatever McHador really wanted? Because despite the lack of concrete evidence, King Owain believed the former general of Enesfel's army was involved.

But the bard…there had been rumors of a prince to overthrow a king early last year too, rumors Owain thought had been subverted. Had the bard returned to revive the rumors? Had he failed to locate one of Farrell's children during his sweep of the kingdom? Or was there perhaps an Elyri prince, or its equivalent, seeking the throne of Enesfel?

Or, he pondered with an uneasy shiver, was Prince Arlan still alive? He would have had the proof if his mother had ceased meddling in his affairs. Damn her for ruining his trap. He perched himself on the edge of the table, staring out the window, rethinking his strategy yet again.

❧Chapter 30❧

Prince Arlan beckoned his comrades closer around the hearth fire and waited with his elbows on the table. Bhríd, Phaedr, Guthrie, Ártur, Caol Dugan, and Kavan gathered around him, and all but Kavan leaned forward to hear what the prince had to say. After a tedious sojourn that felt longer between stops than before, it felt good to be sitting at a proper table, eating a kitchen cooked meal with good wine once again. The prince felt awkward about not sharing such luxuries with the rest of his men, but there was no room for them all here, and he had needed a well-lit locale with a table and privacy to discuss and map out their next strategic phase. Perhaps he had eaten here, but he would sleep in the field with his troops.

In Seres, they had been joined by three hundred men of noble or merchant birth under the leadership of the duke's youngest son, a man named Hewett Colson. Hewett had risen to the rank of captain under King Farrell's rule and had been released by King Bowen for no known reason as soon as the man had gained the throne. On hearing the rumors of Guthrie McHador's return, Hewett had gathered this group of seasoned soldiers who, in times of war, were supposed to fight for the King on behalf of the Duke of Seres. They were restless men, with great respect for the former general of Enesfel's army, but they gathered without the Duke's knowledge or permission. The youngest Colson knew his actions put his father at risk, but in good conscience, he needed to know if the stories of Guthrie's return were true.

Some of these men, however, did not believe there would be fighting and merely wanted to come for the thrill of anticipation and possible prestige if the prince did gain the throne. Hewett shared no such delusions and professed as much to Guthrie and Arlan. He was being given a regiment of five hundred men in the morning and sent west into the forest along the mountainous border of the Cíbhóló desert. Prince Arlan would be leaving Seres with fifteen hundred men strung out behind him.

"Guthrie, you will take five men, no less, and travel to Hatu to secure their aid. I do not care what you have to do, what you have to promise, to gain it, but you will gain it and get them safely to Rhidam. You will not have a healer with you, only a physician; I want you to be cautious. I know you do not want to take anyone with you, but I will not allow you to travel alone. Someone has to make it to Hatu, someone they will trust and respect, and someone has to be with you to bring word back of your success. You either take the five, or you take an entire squadron."

"I'll take five," the designated general of Prince Arlan's army muttered. While not pleased by either prospect, he was willing to concede to the prince's demand of five men to accompany him. "I get to select them."

"By all means," Arlan agreed. "Bhríd and I will take the remaining troops south, traveling with you initially. When we separate, he and I and the rest of the men will also go west into the forest and hills, where we will await your signal to regroup in Kilmacud. Gather supporters in Wexel, Jardin, and Nelori. Do not, however, take any chances with Duke Bottrili. If he makes Nelori too dangerous for you, bypass it. I do not want him to get word to Owain of our actions."

"Of course," the general agreed.

"Kavan?"

The bard looked up from the fire, surprised to be included in this conversation since he was not a fighting participant. It surprised him further to think he was being given some errand to perform. His only functions to date had been to protect the prince, provide entertainment, and to scout ahead for trouble; the prince preferred to keep him as close as possible. Kavan wondered what he had in mind. "Milord?"

"How likely is it that Káliel will give us aid?"

Looks passed around the table. No one had seriously considered the isolationist islands of Káliel as a viable source of recruitment or support.

Guthrie cleared his throat. "They are unlikely to allow anyone close enough to discuss the matter…I think they are unlikely to help us."

Grinning, the prince leaned a little closer and asked, "Would they be more likely to listen, or aid us, if I sent an Elyri ambassador?"

Heads bobbed. "Yes," Kavan replied, proud of the prince's thinking, even if the odds were still against them, "they would be."

Fingering the edge of the table, the prince was quiet for many moments as he looked around the table from one Elyri to the next. Finally, he focused on Kavan. "I cannot spare Ártur or Syl. You and Bhríd are my best candidates for the task, and I would prefer to keep Bhríd with the troops to train any who might benefit from it…and fight if need be. That leaves you, Kavan…"

"Milord," he started to protest, "That is not wise…"

"Why on earth not? You are the most qualified…"

"Have you forgotten what I have told you?"

The blank expression on the prince's face answered the question. Kavan looked towards the fire, his shoulders sagging. It was Ártur who answered the question. "Your life…"

"You should listen to him, Arlan," Guthrie grunted. "He has not been wrong yet."

The prince scowled and crossed his arms over his chest. "Would you rather we tuck our tails between our legs and flee back to Elyriá? It is right that I fight for this cause; it is mine more than anyone else's. Nothing Kavan can do is going to protect me…unless he plans to ride into battle." He stared at Kavan. "Are you going to do that, Lord Harper?"

Knowing he could not, Kavan replied, "No," without looking up.

"You are the best qualified to go to Káliel…in every way I can think of…and I am going to do this. Anyone who insists on preventing me is inviting my wrath. Besides, Kavan…you told me that returning to Rhidam is my destiny. If that is true, I am not likely to die…"

Thumping his mug of ale onto the table, Guthrie grumbled, "Unless you take foolish chances and refuse to heed warnings…"

In a milder tone, understanding their concerns while simultaneously disliking the smothered feeling it sometimes gave him, the prince said, "I will be careful. You have all taught me well…I can do this. Have faith in me. And I need you to do this for me, Kavan. No one else is suited for it. You will travel with Guthrie to Hatu and go to Káliel from there. Do what you can to gain their cooperation. I realize it is unlikely, but if anyone can convince them, it will be you. Do not spare much time there, as I want you with us when we reach Rhidam…but do what you can."

Still refusing to look at anyone, his posture one of defeat, Kavan closed his eyes and murmured, "Very well, milord."

"Good." The prince smiled. "Thank you. Phaedr, you and three others will remain in Seres to be my eyes and ears should any news of Owain's activities come this way. When we are ready to move south, we will send for you."

Smiling, greatly pleased to be entrusted with any sort of duty, Phaedr bowed his head. "I am honored, milord."

Then the prince turned to the last man at the table. "Mr. Dugan…I have a special assignment for you."

The young man's face lit up. "You do?"

"It could be dangerous…"

"I live for danger," he smirked. "I will do anything."

The prince chuckled at his new friend's cockiness but his expression remained serious. "I believe you would. I need someone to go to Rhidam, someone who does not look like a soldier that the King will not recognize. While you are there, I want you to contact a one-eyed dedhá named Jermyn Tythilius…if he's made it there…learn if he has done what I've asked. If he has, you should find people who believe they are in Rhidam to witness a miracle. If he has not been successful, or has not yet reached Rhidam, I want you to start rumors to that effect…that something miraculous is about to happen. Also, there should be men from Cordash and the Cíbhóló there. Contact them and let them know we will arrive soon. Perhaps you can devise some distractions for the King…nothing that will get you killed but something that could occupy him and divert his attention away from us for a while longer. I know it is a great deal to ask, many duties to perform, but I trust you to do this…if you can."

Many would have been overwhelmed by the nature and number of the responsibilities placed at their feet, but Caol neither blinked nor balked. They knew little about him, of his talents or skills, but he was eager, resourceful, and the prince liked him. To his credit, he nodded and said, "That should be easy, Sire. What kind of trouble would you like?"

"You will have to decide what fits the political climate when you get there. But do not," he emphasized, "jeopardize our plans. None of us can afford mistakes…including me." The prince turned to his general. "Does this sound feasible to you?"

Guthrie thought it over, looking for obvious loopholes. He did not see any, did not foresee any problems so long as they were cautious and attentive, but that did not mean there would be none. "Provided the King is not already ahead of us, yes."

Bhríd grunted with a nod. "The reports of militia activity have quieted since that last incident. Perhaps he has his hands full with Neth…"

"And his mother," Caol giggled.

"He will come after you," Kavan said softly, watching the flames lick at the pine logs in the fireplace. Without thinking about it, a small flame sparked to life in his palm; he snuffed it out before anyone noticed. His power had been too long confined to one use.

"Of course he will," Guthrie agreed. "He would be a fool not to."

"I mean he will come soon…sooner than we expect…there will be many deaths…long before we near Rhidam."

The healer touched his cousin's arm. "How soon?"

"I cannot say…but it will be before I rejoin you." He stood abruptly and went outside into the warm night air to escape those at the table. Prince Arlan tried to take Kavan's visions seriously but still found it hard to do. Twice in Talladegah, Kavan had seen the same gray-cloaked figure he had seen in Dorshur; both times, he had Seen the same battle. The prince falling from his horse, the royal standard trampled under the feet of sweltering horses. Something would happen to the prince. He knew it. He could try once more to persuade the prince not to fight, but Prince Arlan believed it was time to prove himself, both to himself and to those following him. Knowing what happened when the prince was injured in the past, that Arlan was not the only one who would suffer, Kavan thought grimly, 'You will…but at what cost?'

"You are troubled, kyá."

Kavan did not know the voice, but in the dimness of the smoky porch lamp, he recognized the stranger's gray cloak and robe. He could not see the face within the folds of the hood, and the man's hands were hidden within flowing sleeves. But there was nothing frightening about this man. His presence had become familiar and comforting.

"Do I know you, milord?"

He did not need to see the man's face to know the stranger was smiling as he replied, "Do you? That is not for me to say. You must decide that yourself. Come. Walk with me. Tell me what troubles you." Kavan took a single step forward but hesitated. The stranger sighed.

"Your hesitancy is understandable, given your penchant for distrusting yourself, but I do wish you would trust me after all of this time. Yes, I know much about you, my friend. What is on your mind? Your prince?"

For some reason, Kavan did not find this man's insight into his personality to be surprising. After having seen him many times recently, Kavan felt sure this man knew a great deal more about him.

"Harm will befall him. I know it. Yet he refuses to heed my warnings. He insists that if I stay with him instead of doing as he asks, I must go into battle…"

"To what? Protect him? You know there is nothing you can do. The same will befall him whether you stay or go…and if you ride into battle beside him, you will both die." He nodded in response to Kavan's morose expression. "You suspected that, didn't you?"

"I had hoped my interpretations of what I have Seen were wrong," the bard admitted.

"He must do this on his own. As he says, it is his time. He must stand alone, without you or Guthrie to bolster him. You know he will succeed if you let him go. And you must go where he bids. What awaits you there may bring long-sought answers, but only if you heed the signs." He chuckled. "You are wise, kyá, but you must learn to trust your instincts, as your prince must learn to trust his. They will not fail you. They never have before. k'Ádhá be with you, átaelás mai."

The stranger leaned forward. Kavan closed his eyes as the warmth of the man's lips brushed his forehead. He opened them again when the stranger touched his hand. He had barely enough time to look from the Kílyn cross that slid from beneath the man's robe to the touch of auburn that slipped free of the hood of his cloak, to the man's hand on Kavan's. Then the stranger turned and disappeared into the shadowy streets, leaving him a single word. "Káliel."

Kavan took one dizzy step after him, stumbled from the porch, and fell to the dusty street. He wanted to speak, to call the man back, but he found he could not. His voice refused to respond to his brain. Kneeling, he raised one hand towards the sky in supplication and opened his mouth, but could do nothing more than release a soft moan before his hand dropped into his lap.

"sínréc?" Kavan's only response was to wrap his arms around himself and rock slowly as the shock of revelation boiled within him. The healer knelt and put an arm around him, aware that the people who passed were eyeing them strangely. Kavan sagged against his shoulder for a few moments before sitting upright. "Are you alright?"

"I…think so. Ártur…promise me something…" He grasped the other man's arms fervently.

"You know I will do anything for you."

"Sometime after Kilmacud, Prince Arlan will be wounded in battle. No one can prevent this…it has been foretold…it must come to pass. Do not let him die, Ártur, or everything we have done will be in vain."

Deeply concerned, Ártur said, "Perhaps you should tell him again."

"I have done so, many times, but you know he does not take my warnings seriously."

"You suspect that…"

"Not suspect…it has been confirmed. This is his fate, a lesson he must learn, something he must face on his own…but please help him…and urge him to be careful."

"I will. Whatever you have Seen…must have been distressing to have shaken you thus. Do you know what will happen? What kind of injuries he will sustain?"

"Only that he will fall from his horse and the flag will be trampled. I know nothing more specific. But that is not what has…it was…the gray cloak…in Dorshur. Do you remember?"

"The man you saw in Dorshur and Talladegah?" The healer had seen the retreating cloak only once but knew of the other sighting.

"I saw him. He was here. He spoke to me…kissed my forehead…touched my hand…it was him…"

"Who, Kavan?"

"He wore a Kílyn cross…he touched me and his hand…as it is told…here…" He indicated his wrist joint. "Deep scars of ropes…and here…" he pointed further up his wrist, "two punctures…like nails…burnt…horribly scarred…but even without seeing his face, I know…it had to be…"

"Kóráhm."

It was not a question. Ártur knew the description, knew the story of the saint's miraculous escape from the burning T cross during the final attempt on his life. It was said that the flames had marred his entire body except for his face. Once the ropes had burned away from his hands, feet, and waist, he pulled from the double nails that held him and had walked from the fire into the waiting arms of a nameless woman who had led him away into the annals of history. The healer grasped Kavan's hands and kissed them. What could he say? His cousin had seen the Heretic-Saint whose name he bore. Not many could claim that.

"Yes…he was…flesh and blood…"

"Like your mother saw…"

"My…mother…" The snatch of lullaby came back to him and he shivered.

The healer smiled, the effort strained but sincere. "The málneag appears to have great interest in you, kyá sínréc." Once again, he felt that great gulf that separated his world from that in which Kavan existed, but he felt happy for him nonetheless. "Let us go inside."

He helped his cousin to his feet, up the steps and then waited in the doorway as Kavan looked back in the direction the stranger had gone. He stared wistfully at Kavan's expression and then smiled again as they entered the inn.

❧*❧

Princess Deidre fingered the burgundy lace train of one of the possible wedding gowns the King had chosen for her. Of the six she had viewed this morning, this was the most exquisite, lace and satin and pearls. Not that the others had been shabby; Owain had shown he had excellent taste in fashion and knew what she might like. He was behind her now, speaking to the dressmaker, though Deidre had no idea what he was saying. She only knew his demeanor by the way his hands moved as he spoke, though what he had to be irritated about she could only guess. Perhaps there were not enough dresses to choose from.

At least he was too busy to notice her trembling hands or misty eyes. All of the discussion of dresses, banquets, and guests made her sad. The only thing that kept her from falling into despair was the hope that Brenna had found her uncle, had found help that might spare her this fate. There had been no opportunity to leave messages as Brenna had instructed her before she had been thrown into the dungeon, and by the time of her release, she suspected no one would come for them, even if she chose to leave them. As the months dragged past, that hope dimmed. Brenna must have failed. Deidre had been forgotten. Taking her handkerchief from her pocket, the princess dabbed her eyes. There was no choice but to accept the inevitable. What sort of life would she have if she did not?

She jumped as the King's hands rested on her waist. His touch was amazingly tender. He indicated the dress hanging before her and looked at her in question. Nodding her head, the smile she flashed masked her tears, though she doubted he noticed them. As he resumed his discussion with the dressmaker, she slipped from the room, not even sure he knew she was gone.

ॐ*ॐ

Clutching the sides of the metal pail, General Ferghus closed his eyes as his stomach rejected the last of its contents. He no longer liked this game. He did not enjoy spending the majority of his time pretending to be ill when he was perfectly healthy. Crazy, perhaps, but healthy. He took the damp cloth from the chair beside his bed, and wiped his forehead and face, fighting the tremors that always seized him after a bout of nausea. It was worse immediately after taking a draught of his homemade elixir, which was why he waited until late at night to take it.

Hurry, Guthrie. I hope you arrive soon if that is your plan. I cannot continue this forever.

Forcing himself to his feet, he pulled his blanket after him and wrapped it around his shoulders as he trudged to the wall mirror. The gaunt, skeletal visage with sunken eyes and blotchy skin was a face he barely recognized. Very much more of this and he would honestly be ill. He touched his unshaven cheeks gingerly, rubbing his fingers across the entire line of his jaw. Who are you, he thought. Why are you here? What do you want from me?

His stomach tightened and lurched again and he fought his way back to the bed and his pail.

ॐ*ॐ

"Kóráhm," Kavan whispered, leaning on the sill, staring at the moonless sky. Saint Kóráhm had come to him. Not as a visitation should be, however. He had heard stories of the saints appearing to people in some ethereal state. Kóráhm had been flesh, as warm and alive as any man. But the time quoted for the man's death was over twenty-seven hundred years ago. Elyri were long lived, but surely not that long-lived.

Still, the presiding k'gdhededhá had assigned a date of death to the man, but there had never been any proof that he had died. It was assumed that the attempted burning had killed him, for it was unlikely anyone could live after being burnt so badly, even with the help of an Elyri healer. When the reports of his sightings began nearly twenty-five years later, they were always the same. Gray cloak, badly scarred except for his face, nail and rope scars on his wrists and ankles. The k'gdhededhá had ratified his death, canonized him after much debate, and closed the matter.

A scrawny dog padded loosely through Kavan's field of vision, stopping to drink from a puddle in the road before continuing. In the room behind him, he could hear Ártur mumble something about Syl in his sleep. It was not the first time it had happened, and Kavan wondered what sort of dreams his cousin was having. The healer rolled away and his breathing grew softer.

It was vaguely irritating that the prince insisted on procuring a room for Kavan every time they entered a town or a village. Instead of declining the offer, which did no good, Kavan allowed Ártur or anyone else who wanted it to sleep in the comfort of a bed. Kavan rarely stayed in the rooms. He was here tonight, however, because he dared not be alone. He did not trust what he might do.

Kóráhm was correct in that. Kavan rarely trusted himself. But right now, if he were to trust his instincts, he would have to admit that, somehow, the man that had touched him had truly been Kóráhm, talking, breathing alive. How that could be possible, he could only guess. He only believed it was true.

And it made no sense to him at all.

ᏔᎧ Chapter 31 ᏔᎧ

The youth looked cautiously up and down the street, took one last look at the tattered and stained clothing he wore, and stepped from the alley into the bustle of Rhidam's busiest quarter. He touched the pouch of coins hidden within his shirt to be sure it was still there. He had not wanted to sell the horse, but he could not keep it and play the street urchin too. He could not risk being caught. Even now, if anyone found him with this pouch of coins, he would never pass for a beggar. A thief, yes. A beggar, no. At least the horse he had ridden here and been forced to give up had been one of the poorer animals in the prince's care, one of those confiscated from Neth's militia. Its sale had given him enough to live on for most of his expected stay in Rhidam if he managed his spending wisely.

Pausing at a street vendor, he purchased a sweet cake and settled under an awning to watch the passersby. He did not know quite where to start now that he was here, but often he found that people watching was a good place to begin any endeavor. It was late afternoon, and he decided his first priority should be to find a place to bed for the night while there was still light to see by. He finished his meal and began to lick his fingers before noticing a cluster of people approaching from his left, heading, it seemed, towards the castle. Most bore the appearance and mannerisms of retainers and armed escort, but it was the central figure that caught his attention. He dusted off the seat of his worn wool breeches and moved closer, hoping to get a better look.

The woman in the midst of the cluster was the most beautiful he had ever seen. Her thick blonde hair hung in loose curls around her neck and shoulders, held away from her face by combs of gold and onyx. From her elegant saffron gown of what he guessed to be Káliel linen, he judged her to be of the aristocracy until he caught sight of the black eagle pendant she wore on a braided gold chain. He had seen that symbol on the standards of Prince Arlan's troops and concluded this was the Lachlan princess, not missing as many had come to believe. He waved frantically, shouting and jumping up and down to attract her attention, but she did not see him amongst the fawning crowds until her escort reached the spot in the road near where he was and motioned him aside. Her gaze met his; she blushed and looked away.

He quickly fished in his pocket for the one item he had brought at Ártur MacLyr's insistence and tried to move near enough to give it to her. A servant pushed him away, as another guard took him by the arm to move him forcibly, but the princess motioned for whatever was in his hand. If he had risked himself to give her a gift, no matter how small or insignificant, she would take it. Besides, she found his red hair stunning and was as curious about him as he was about her. He looked at her open palm for a moment, knelt, and kissed her fingers as he pressed what he carried into her hand. Then he stepped back to allow the party to pass without further hindrance. He was surprised to see her look back and wave; excited, he waved in return.

Delighted with his luck, knowing the prince would be happy to learn his sister was safe, he waited until the entourage was out of sight before resuming his mission. His mind was full of her loveliness and thoughts of how Prince Arlan might thank him for this news. It took effort to shake his head clear and focus, but the sounds of deep-toned bells helped and drew him in the direction of the náós spires that lifted high above the city. The healer had assured him that at least that place should be safe for him.

There was a large gathering around the náós, people with blankets and bedrolls, crude sacks and large squares of dirty cloth. An unkempt, unshaven man sat on one side of the steps, plunking randomly on a battered mandolin, singing with a small group gathered around him although the noise he played could not be called a tune. A merchant had set up a cart nearby and was providing nourishment to those in the gathering who had money to pay for it. Under a willow, not far from the musician, a man in time-stained gold and green clerical robes, with a black patch over one eye, watched the ever-growing crowd without any particular interest in any of them.

The one-eyed gdhededhá. It had to be him. Caol doubted anyone else would fit the description better.

As he approached, he spoke with people he passed but learned very little. Most had come from as far away as Jardin to witness a miracle that was to take place before the close of the year. There was some doubt amongst them about whether the miracle would be here, Clarys, or on the island of Káliel, but under the influence of Jermyn of Alberni, most believed that Rhidam would be the site and had followed him here. They had come riding the tails of his belief, or to be able to laugh at him when the miracle failed to come to pass. And yes, as he suspected, the man beneath the tree was gdhededhá Jermyn.

The gdhededhá watched the red-haired youth approach, and when he was near enough, asked, "Are you in need, son? Do you require shelter? Food perhaps?"

Caol had not thought the man was paying attention to him and wondered if the fellow was usually this trusting and benevolent, but he did not show his surprise or questions on his face. "I was told this place could provide sanctuary should I need it."

The man's head bobbed. "That is its purpose. Are you a pilgrim?"

"Of sorts, dedhá, though not in the sense these people are. I suspect, however, we are waiting for the same thing. You are the one called Jermyn of Alberni?"

"I am."

Caol squatted before him to speak in a quieter voice. "I come to prepare the way for Enesfel's true prince and to bring you regards from the white bard."

The older man's face lit with joy. "Boy, you are doubly welcome if you come in the name of that blessed man, as well as on behalf of Enesfel's hope. Pray tell, how fares everyone?"

"All are well, though Phaedr Cáner has lost the use of his eyes. Pray for him, dedhá. He asked that of you. Lord Harper should be in Hatu with the general now, to procure outside assistance. The time is nigh."

"What is your name, boy?"

Caol shook his head with a scowl. "That is best not spoken. I have errands to tend to, and the princess knows I am here…although she does not know who I am or what my business is. For now, until my duties are complete, it is best no one knows anything about me. Safer for both of us. I will be in your company only to sleep if that is permitted."

"If you are looking for our brothers, I have heard that the desert children are camped northwest of Rhidam and have been trading profitably. Our northern allies are staying in the inn nearest the keep.

As he began to speak, Caol noted an approaching guardsman and made a gesture of piety, hoping he got it right since he had never been a religious man. "I will remember your teachings, dedhá, and live as you bid. Thank you for your blessing." The passing soldier gave them a dour look, watching the gdhededhá lay his hands on the young man's head, but was past and gone about his way by the time Caol stood and returned to his own business.

After weaving through the crowd and skirting at least three more soldiers, Caol found his way towards the castle, only to find that there were two inns there instead of one. Being from Durham, near the Cordashian border, he knew Cordash custom and dress; finding those he sought should be easy. He entered the first inn he came to and sat at a corner table, watching for anyone familiar. The innkeeper, however, took one look at the apparently scruffy, penniless urchin and promptly expelled him from the premises. Annoyed at such rude treatment, Caol brushed himself off after rising from the dusty street and then decided to try the other inn, which turned out to be appropriately named the Eagle's Nest. He entered, looked around the nearly empty room, and approached the barkeep who looked him over with a look of disdain.

"We do not serve your type here…"

"Please, sir. I am but a peasant. Milord sent me to find some gentlemen from Cordash. He has business with them…but they did not tell him where they were staying. Do you have such gentlemen here?"

"I do not make it my business to know the country of origin of my patrons…"

"But surely you'd recognize them for…"

A gravelly voice interrupted the budding argument. "You seek us?"

When he turned, Caol recognized the closely tailored to the body attire the speaker wore and bowed stiffly with his hands at his side as the men from Cordash usually did when greeting strangers or superiors. "I believe so, sir. May we go somewhere to speak?"

The man looked him over skeptically but nodded. "Ale for myself," he said to the barkeep, "and your finest wine for my friend." He beckoned Caol to a corner table and remained standing until his guest was seated. "It is true I have been doing tasks to pay my way while I am in town, but I have no business with peasants. What is it you seek?"

"Are you here for business or pleasure?"

He scowled. "Depends on who wants to know. Business can be pleasurable if one is working for the right lord and right cause."

"A cause then." No sooner had Caol spoken the words than he realized the Cordashian's guard had gone up. The barkeeper brought their drinks and slowly retreated. "I do not work for the bastard King if that is your fear. I come on behalf of General Broken Eagle."

The use of the agreed upon password caused the man to relax. "I hope Broken Eagle is being restored to his former health."

"That is why I am here, to make certain everything has been prepared for his arrival. Milord will not be pleased to arrive and find his estate in disarray."

"Everything is ready, though we grow bored of waiting." He drank deeply from his ale.

Caol had not touched his wine yet but decided to drink it out of respect. "The wait shall not be much longer, I should think. I was told to bring you word that our progress is going well."

"Good. We look forward to his arrival. I have made contact with those trading from the desert; they are prepared and eager. And I have more laborers coming from home to complete the work we've begun.

That was unexpected and good news, which made Caol smile. "How many? Any number would be welcome, but I will admit he is hoping for many more laborers."

The Cordashian shrugged. "Unknown." Seeing the suspicious look on the barkeep's face as he passed, the man scowled again. "It is difficult to find good help these days, but you may tell your lord that I have prepared his way as he requested."

Caol nodded as he glared at the back of the barkeep's head as the fellow disappeared through a back door. "Are the flies always this thick here?"

With a laugh, the other replied, "It is summer boy, and the heat does strange things to everyone…even flies. No one can relax in this weather. I must join my comrades for the evening meal. Will you join us upstairs and tell us more of your lord's work?"

"It is better I do not." He thought he saw the door pop open enough for someone to peer through and then close again. "Suspicions do not need to be roused further, and I have much to do while here."

"Agreed. I understand. Can you tell me how soon your master will arrive?" They stood as they talked, returned their glasses to the bar, and made their way towards the front door.

"That will depend on continuing favorable weather and other events beyond our control. But it should not be long; I suspect you will hear from him before the summer is past. I will tell him of your good work; perhaps he will have other tasks for you while you wait."

"If the payment is respectable," the man grinned, "we would be honored to work with him further. Please, convey my sincerest wishes for his safety on his journey and for a hasty arrival."

"I shall."

They touched palms in the ritual parting of Cordashian men, and Caol left the inn under the watchful eye of the barkeep who had come back into the room. It was growing darker outside and Caol had the feeling something was amiss. Wary of being followed, he ducked into the shadows of the nearest alley and sprinted in the direction of the náós. Footsteps came behind him, approaching faster than he could run. He slipped into an open doorway, backed flat against the wall, and waited, trying to calm his gasping breath. They came closer and stopped. Caol drew the dagger he always carried in his belt and held his breath.

A hand reached around the corner and caught his arm. Caol spun out of his hiding place and drove the dagger deep into his attacker's bicep. The man, who was not much bigger or older than Caol, screamed and grabbed for the blade. A kick to his abdomen caused the man to double over and stagger backward. As he fell, the blade came free into Caol's hands and he leapt; in a single move he had one arm tight around the fellow's neck and the blade buried deep into his back. The attacker coughed in surprise and collapsed. Only after making sure he was dead and that there were no witnesses did Caol flee the scene.

The one-eyed gdhededhá saw Caol returning at a run and scrambled to his feet. What trouble could the boy have gotten into already? It did not appear that anyone was following the young man; when Caol was close enough, Jermyn caught his arm and pulled him down beside him to share the fire he and the musician had built.

"Is something wrong?" At least if he was seated with the pilgrims, he might be overlooked by anyone pursuing him.

Realizing from the direction of the man's stare that there was blood on his shirt, Caol removed it with a shrug. "Most of what I sought, I found. There are still things to do before I return to the fold. As for trouble…" He glanced in the direction from which he had come and tossed his soiled tunic into the fire. "It was nothing I couldn't handle."

Jermyn frowned. "I hope you will stay out of further trouble. We need all the supporters we can get. If you desire…absolution…let me know. Would you care for lamb stew?"

"I would, thank you." He smiled as he stretched his legs towards the fire. "I haven't eaten a decent meal in days. Then, if it will not offend you, I think I will sleep. I might take you up on absolution later…when I have more to atone for." He smirked and dug into the bowl of stew.

Not sure if he should find the young man's impishness refreshing or worrisome, Jermyn nodded. "Eat and rest, my son."

⮞*⮜

Seated alone at one of the small arched windows in what had once been her mother's room, Princess Deidre watched the last of the golden glow of day leave the sky. She did not feel comfortable sleeping in this room with the King on the other side of the door she kept locked at all times, but she accepted it as she accepted everything else…because there seemed no other choice. She stared, she mused, she sighed, until it grew too dark to see anything except the glow of evening lamps in distant windows, and then she closed her window against the drafts and went to the library to read, smiling at a passing servant but encountering no one else in the corridors.

The King would be with Captain Wyndham. The two were alike enough in interests that the princess often thought they seemed like brothers. They frequently met after the evening meal, leaving her to her own pursuits...which she much preferred over the King's company.

It had been a good day overall. Her morning ride with the King had been pleasant since he made every effort to be kind and dote on her every need. She had lunch with the wives of three of his advisors, an uncomfortable affair, but at least not a boring one. Her shopping excursion had been an enjoyable stroll through town that provided the cloth for two more gowns. The King frowned upon her making her own dresses, though he always gave high praise to the finished projects. Some work, he said, was not meant for the hands of royalty. But the princess enjoyed sewing because it kept her hands busy and her mind off of things she preferred not to dwell on.

She thought fondly of the handsome red-haired beggar she had met on her way home and looked at the ring he had given her. The amber stone was large and warm. Why would a poor man give her something that was likely the only item of wealth he had? Had he stolen it and wanted to get rid of it before he was caught? It was too large for her small fingers, a man's ring, she decided, and so she had strung it on a braided ribbon and wore it around her neck. The King had asked about it and she had explained that it was a gift from a townsman. Because she was frequently given gifts by the adoring subjects who loved her, the King had smiled at her and allowed the matter to drop.

In the library, she lit the reading lamp but was distracted from books by the long wall of family portraits. There was room for seven kings on that wall, but only six hung there now. The seventh slot was reserved for King Owain's portrait once it was complete. She studied each one as if seeing them for the first time when in truth she looked at them often. Kings Girvin, Bowen, and Farrell. She stopped at King Donal's and compared his portrait to King Innis as a young man. Odd that she felt more like Donal's daughter than Innis'. In the portraits, Donal looked older, but she could see the similarities in their features. And not one of those Lachlans on that wall bore any similarity to Owain.

She noticed something else in the portraits that she had never noticed before. Donal, Innis, and Innis' grandfather each wore a large amber stone ring. None of the others did. Perplexed by its familiarity, she reached for the ring she wore about her neck to compare it to the one in the portraits.

It was the same.

Where had the beggar gotten part of the regalia? He could not have taken it from King Donal, as he looked no older than she was. He would have been too young to have stolen it. Had someone else stolen it and he was returning it? Was he perhaps one of the many rumored bastard children of King Farrell's, given this ring as proof of his nobility? If not, when, and where, had the ring been lost? How could he have gotten it? And why should it reappear now after all of these years?

She was determined to find out. Removing the necklace and pocketing the ring, she blew out the lamp and returned to her room with the chosen book of poetry. She could not risk the ring being recognized. The King must not know of this until she could determine what it meant. He had not recognized it before, but when he did, he would demand to have it and the beggar who had given it to her could be in terrible danger. She planned to learn the truth before letting anyone else see it again.

❧Chapter 32❧

Thin robe billowing in the crisp salty breeze, Kavan watched Guthrie's figure grow smaller as the fishing boat left Natrona's port, bound for the island of Káliel. Their journey into Hatu had been uneventful except for a minor skirmish outside of the town of Wexel with a group of bandits that was quickly dispatched. They lost one of the five soldiers Prince Arlan had sent with them in that skirmish. Another soldier was sent to rejoin the prince with the volunteers they gathered in Wexel. Guthrie sent a third back with those recruits gleaned from around Nelori, and the fourth soldier and physician had traveled into Jardin to gather supporters there, with orders to regroup with Arlan's main force on completion of their task. That left Guthrie, Kavan, and one other man to complete the journey into Hatu, which was what Guthrie had wanted to begin with. Three would go unnoticed and untroubled better than seven. There was no difficulty crossing Hatu's border and they easily found an escort in Kílyn to accompany them to King Geir in the capital port city of Natrona.

The Hatu King was true to his word. With the general's arrival, King Geir called his soldiers to arms, keeping them away from Enesfel's borders. Hatu's four hundred cavalrymen would travel with Guthrie by land, while Hatu's infantry would sail across the Bay of Phállá to the mouth of the Tegid River. Depending on the size of the ships available, the infantry would either disembark in Levonne and march into Rhidam, or else they would sail up the Tegid and disembark much closer to their objective. While Guthrie worked in Natrona with King Geir to secure merchant ships for this purpose and to train and outfit the cavalry for the upcoming venture, Kavan was traveling to Káliel to discuss with the Prime Magistrate the possibility of the ships docking in the island's harbor for supplies. It would lessen the number of ships required if they could restock supplies along the way.

Kavan walked to the bow of the ship once Guthrie was too small to be seen. The chance of gaining harbor long enough to restock food and drink from Káliel was slim. The island's inhabitants were known to be isolationists; only the infrequent wine, silk, and linen traders journeyed away from the cluster of five islands that made up the realm of Káliel. Few ships were allowed to approach, and those that were allowed were part of treaties or contracts that had existed for centuries, mainly with Elyriá. Kavan could think of no reason for the Prime Magistrate to grant Prince Arlan's request, nor any reason for them to allow Kavan onto the island. Still, Kóráhm had sent him there, as surely as Prince Arlan had, and Kavan was resolved to go. Now he watched the water pushing past the side of the ship, feeling none too comfortable with this journey.

"G'day yere l'rdsh'p." The captain of the vessel, a dark, squat, stocky fellow with gnarled hands and thin gray hair, leaned on the railing beside Kavan. "I'ill take us nigh unto six days t'reach the islan', e'en at our bes' speed. I 'ope tis 'right wit' ye."

Though the man's speech was difficult to understand, Kavan had an ear for languages and deciphered his words with ease. "Six days is the best time I heard from anyone, which is why I chartered your vessel. Speed is a necessity. As I have never been to sea before, I look forward to a fascinating experience. I do have one question, however…"

"Ask. I knows all's t'know 'bout these wa'ers."

Kavan stared across the waves towards the islands they sought but saw nothing but miles of endless water capped by white rifts as the surface broke beneath the wind. "Is such sickness common?" The captain laughed heartily and hooked one stumpy arm around Kavan's. "Mos' ever' one ge's it firs' time ou', e'en I did. 'as t'do wit the rockin' of the waves an' such. Some folks fin' bein' up 'ere on deck watchin' the wa'er eases they pains; others 'fer t'go b'low deck. Some chew on plants, drink brews an' the like t'get by. Ye'll li'ly ge' o'er it, though there're some who ne'er do. If I'ill 'elp, ye can use me quar'ers. I's the o'ly one wit a hamm'ck…bes' way to sleep a' sea."

"I shall be fine," Kavan replied stubbornly, though with no great certainty behind the words.

The captain nodded, but his eyes showed he knew better. "Jus' don' make a mess'a me ship. Room's yere's fer the takin'. I'd 'vite ye fer a bit t'eat, but tha's no' wise in yere state. If ye be needin' anythin', jus' fin' me."

The bard nodded but did not watch him go. Instead, he continued to stare at the azure depths, trying to will away the increasing discomfort in his stomach. When he finally had to admit that staring at the sea was not helping, he reluctantly accepted that perhaps going below deck where he could not see the constantly teetering horizon would be the best thing to do. He found the steps into the bowels of the boat and saw the captain nod his head. Kavan tried to smile back. Likely, these sea folk thought his predicament amusing, but the captain, at least, had the respect and politeness to treat him with sympathy. He reached the man's quarters, a small niche in the wall large enough for a desk and chair and narrow hammock. Kavan climbed into the scratchy rope bed, pulled the blanket hanging over one end up over his body to ward off chills, and closed his eyes. Having looked forward to this first trip at sea, he was disappointed to be forced to bed and prayed the sickness would pass.

ᚲ*ᚲ

"What do you want with me?" Caol protested as the armored man at his side pulled him roughly along by the arm towards the castle.

He had risen at dawn, eaten a simple meal with the pilgrims and the one-eyed gdhededhá, and then sought the camp of the Cíbhóló nomads. They were terse and not overly friendly, but they assured him they were prepared for whatever lay ahead and were eager to be done with the waiting. Assuming they were brusque because of his age, as he hardly seemed old enough to be an emissary for the prince, or because they had interpreted his discomfort at being dwarfed by their stature as hostility, Caol chose not to take offense. He could not afford that now.

He spent the remainder of the morning contacting what beggars and city poor he could find, suggesting to them that their lot could improve and encouraging them to stand up for their rights. One vagabond, whom he suspected was neither lame nor blind as he posed to be, relayed to him that there was already an underground movement of dissidents who would, at the signal, create any diversion needed to overthrow the King. Caol could think of no need for such a move, but knowing he had allies, a source of help if needed, gave him more confidence in what he was doing. He had been eating an apple, reveling in a morning's worth of successes, when this burly, cocky soldier found him.

"I am one of several sent to find you, to bring you to the castle."

To the castle? Caol's heart jumped into his throat and kept him from breathing normally for several seconds. "Why? I haven't done anything! You've no right…"

Grip tightening on the struggling man's arm, the soldier grunted, "I have a duty. I can't answer your questions."

By the time they crossed the bridge, Caol stared at the massive grey towers on each side and felt very small, insignificant, and vulnerable. It was his first time viewing it up close, and he did not recall ever seeing anything of such size before except mountains. Had his cover been blown by his morning's zealous activities? Had he not been careful enough? Had someone linked the death last night to him? Had he, on his first mission, failed in his overwhelming desire to please the prince, and somehow jeopardized the cause? Knowing he would rather die than tell anyone anything that could prove fatal to Prince Arlan, he thrust his shoulders back and tried to remain calm as he followed his escort towards his fate.

That fate happened to be an empty room which appeared to be a library, not the sort of place he imagined someone under arrest would be taken. He opened his mouth to ask questions, and then snapped it shut as the soldier spoke again. "Remain here and do not touch anything. Their Majesties will not take kindly to either theft or you wandering in places you should not be. You will be joined shortly."

Now the situation seemed even odder to Caol. He was a stranger, seemingly a peasant, and yet he had been left alone in this room…in Rhidam's castle. He imagined there were guards outside, imagined he would be searched when he left, if he was allowed to leave, and decided he was being tested. The thought did little to reassure him about his fate. The strangeness of the situation only made things worse.

He sat, and then stood, and then sat again, only to get to his feet once more to pace. He had never seen this many books in one place, and the tapestries and artwork that he had seen had been those passing through his father's merchant business when Caol was much younger. There were paintings too, portraits of past kings done by the finest Teren artists in the kingdom. Few Lachlan kings had ever had an Elyri artist available to paint them, and even fewer would have permitted it.

Caol had been born during King Donal's reign and thus he did not recall much about those days, except that his family's situation had declined tremendously after that King's death. Since then, death had touched every corner of Caol's world. If he could end his family's suffering, then he would have accomplished something in life, and that desire had brought him into Prince Arlan's circle.

He counted backward from King Girvin's portrait, looking for familiarity in each face, and stopped when he reached King Innis. Although much younger than the man in the portrait, Prince Arlan was undoubtedly King Innis' son.

The click and creak of the door made him spin around as if he was guilty of something. The sight of the beautiful Lachlan princess smiling at him with parchment, stylus, and inkwell in hand was the last thing a young man of his station expected to see. She was dressed in a plain style gown, the color of honey, and her hair was plated high on her head today. With a wave of her hand, she sent away the servant who followed her, closed the door, and indicated the small wrought-iron table near the bookshelves. She sat, staring at him, and waited for him to join her.

Caol did not move. He felt cold, and his instinct was to seek escape. Not that he felt threatened by the princess, she seemed innocent and friendly, but it was one more oddity in this visit and he felt sure her being here was some trap set by the King. Caol did not like feeling cornered, and that was how he felt now. She removed something from a velvet pouch at her waist and held it to him. When he did not take it, she began to write on the parchment and he recalled then that she could not hear. After more hesitation, and against his better judgment, he took a seat across from her at the table, making sure to keep a respectable distance between them as he watched the door out of the corner of his eye.

"The ring you gave me," she wrote, "is part of the regalia. It has been missing for many years. How did you come to have it?" Her face showed no accusation as she slid the parchment to him. After all, perhaps King Donal had merely lost it.

"I did not steal it if that is what you think," he wrote back, glad for the first time that his father had insisted he learn to read and write, despite Caol's resistance.

She smiled. "I did not think you had."

"I shouldn't…if I tell you…the information might reach the King…"

"Why should I tell him anything you say? I have opinions of my own and my own thoughts."

"But he is the King. He could…"

She took the paper before he could finish. "I will tell him nothing. I swear to you. Tell me where you got it."

"Telling you might place too many people in danger…" He stopped again as she touched his hand, a soft, gentle touch that made him shiver. She took the stylus once more.

"I know something is happening in Enesfel. I have seen the crowds gathered before the náós, I have heard the rumors of war. Owain will not tell me what is happening, but I know something is. There is some belief that because I cannot hear, I must be ignorant or at least protected from the truth." Caol shook his head to indicate he did not think that was true. She smiled gratefully and continued. "But with that belief comes a certain amount of freedom. I can pretend to know less than I do and he does not question me. You are no beggar; you can read and write and do not wear the bearing of the poor. Who are you?"

"A merchant's son, from Durham. That is all I can say. Does the King," he scratched the last three words off and started again. "Are you treated well? Are you happy?"

"I am treated very well now. For a time, he…" Her hand trembled as she hesitated, then she finished, "We are to be wed on my birthday."

Caol's shocked expressions startled her as he roughly yanked the stylus from her hand. "No," he wrote. "Do not do that. Do not bind yourself to this tyrant. Milord will be sorely grieved."

She stared at the handsome lines of his young face and guessed, from the twitch at the corner of his eyes and mouth, that his lord would not be the only one who would be grieved. She tried a disarming smile, hoping to soothe him, but it only caused his expression to darken further. Sighing, she started writing. "Why do you say such things? Why should you concern yourself with my happiness? Who is your lord to be grieved over my impending marriage?"

Caol rose and escaped to the nearest window, tugging one hand through his hair in frustration. Knowing that the prince would be devastated to learn of this, he had to find a way to stop her, but did he dare tell her the truth?

"Do you love him?" he finally wrote when he returned to the table, his shoulders slumped.

"Does it matter?"

"It could matter a great deal. As you say, there is something very important happening in Enesfel. Your answer could make a difference."

Princess Deidre watched him write, wondering how and why her marriage to the King could have such an effect on the kingdom. It had never before occurred to her that her actions could be important to anyone else. "I am marrying him because I must. He insists on it. He is kind to me and has expressed a great desire for us to be wed. I will never marry otherwise, as he will allow me to wed no one else."

"You do not love him."

"I do not know."

Her expression told Caol that she sincerely did not know how she felt about either her impending marriage or the man to whom she was promised. Caol took up the pen. "I received the ring from the Elyri healer, Lord Ártur MacLyr; King Donal gave it to him before he died."

He was caught off guard when she threw her arms around him, embraced him tightly, and then began to pace the room. She was smiling, occasionally wiping her eyes, and he wondered what she was thinking. "You have spoken to Brenna Weylin? And Guthrie McHador? Is he your lord?" She knew that General McHador had connections to Healer MacLyr, thus it was a logical assumption to assume these people were connected to the young man before her.

"If I speak, you must never reveal what I tell you to the King or to anyone…"

"Never. Your secrets die with me; I swear on my life."

"Not your life, milady…never that." Maybe he was a fool to trust her, he argued with himself, but he did. This was the prince's twin, after all, and she would certainly not want her brother to be harmed. He did not know she thought him to be dead.

"General McHador is well, as is Lord MacLyr. I have not met Lady Weylin, but I am told she and her child are safe in Elyriá." Her expression grew dark but she motioned for him to continue. "Your brother has sent me to Rhidam to…"

"My brother? Arlan…?" Her trembling legs failed to support her and she slumped to the floor; Caol caught her before she landed and held her quaking body in his arms. She looked at him with pleading blue eyes.

Knowing she would not hear any explanation, he helped her to her chair at the table and began to write. "He is alive, milady, and has been in General McHador's care as I understand it. He is well, married to Lady Weylin, and is on his way to Rhidam…"

Wondering if the child was her brother's or the King's, the princess felt hatred for Owain for the first time since her release from the dungeon. "Arlan will depose Owain."

Not sure if she meant that as a question or whether she already believed it to be true, he replied, "He has not said that is his intent, but that is what many of us want."

She bit her lip. "I think, perhaps, it is my wish as well." A far-off bell peeled through the corridors and she lifted her head. "I will see you to the bridge."

Assuming the conversation was over, he got up; instead of doing likewise, the princess continued to write. "Are you going to him now? To my brother?"

He shook his head and bent over the table to write, "I have things to do in Rhidam before I go back."

"But you will return to him?"

"I intend to, yes."

She smiled, relieved to hear it, and wrote, "Good. I shall see that the King never learns of his existence or plans from me. You and my brother and the rest will be safe. I beseech you to be careful, however, for I do not know if I can protect you if he learns the truth from someone else."

Caol nodded, understanding what she meant though not expecting her to be his protector. She crumpled the parchment on which they had been writing and tossed it into the fireplace where a dwindling fire burned. The details of their discussion were reduced to ashes, smoke, and memory, where nothing short of torture was likely to find them. She smiled and motioned for him to follow her.

At the bridge, she took his hands and kissed his palms. Embarrassed by a gesture he did not understand from someone royal, regal, and beautiful, he bowed and kissed her ringed hand in return as was expected. When she pulled him to his feet and embraced him, again unexpectedly, with a kiss on his cheek, it was all he could do not to faint. He knew he was blushing as he backed away and ran across the bridge. He did not notice the King as he past, nor did the King pay him any heed. The King's confused, disapproving gaze was fixed on Deidre, who waved and hoped that, over the distance between them, the King would believe her smile to be sincere and that the wave a greeting was for him.

ॐ * ॐ

There was nothing threatening in the stranger's aura as Phaedr felt him approach through the crowded streets. He turned his face towards the fellow, holding his wooden bowl up for whatever coins the man felt obligated to deposit in it. During his days here, he had developed an unfailing accuracy for reading people in the streets who approached him. If he had been begging for his own existence, he would have felt shame and self-loathing. But his efforts were for Prince Arlan, a gathering of both funds and information for a growing army, and Phaedr had no regrets.

The visitor coughed, hesitated, and squatted down before him, putting Phaedr on alert. "Are you the one called Medhyr?"

The Elyri's shoulders did not relax. He still felt no threat from the man, but he knew he could be wrong. "I have recently come by that name, good sir."

"You have been blessed by the white hands of k'Ádhá?"

Good. An ally with a message. His body relaxed. "His servant touched me and gave sight that is not sight," he agreed, listening as the man fumbled for something within a sack or pouch.

"No spare change today, fellow, but I have bread and fruit." The words were spoken loudly enough that passersby would think nothing of his visit. Then his voice dropped to a whisper. "I bring this from Gray Eagle. I was told I would find you here. See to it that Broken Eagle and the Fledgling get this." He pressed an apple and a large chunk of bread into Phaedr's outstretched hand. Phaedr's fingers found where the message had been pressed into the bread to hide it.

"Thank you, kind sir. A gracious gift. May you be granted many safe returns."

"The thanks will be ours when your work is complete."

His footsteps moved away, leaving Phaedr to nibble on the bread that he had broken apart in search of the scroll he knew the loaf held. Confident that no one was paying him any mind, he thrust the message inside of his shirt, wondering what news Lord Cervasian had sent for the general and the prince. He would not know for many more days. The prince would send someone for information, and then, perhaps, he would be read the contents of the message. Phaedr continued to eat and occasionally stretched out his bowl as more people passed. He heard the clink of metal within. Funds for the opposition, he thought with a smile, as he called thanks and blessings after his benefactors.

ॐChapter 33-ॐ

This's far's we c'n go, yere, l'rds'p," the captain called as Kavan came above deck in response to the summons. The bard had spent the six-day journey confined to the hammock; sailing did not agree with him and he now had to dread the voyage back to Natrona and the upcoming voyage from Levonne with the foot soldiers King Geir would send in Arlan's support. Despite the captain's claims to the contrary, the hammock had not helped Kavan. Weak, dizzy, disoriented, and shaky, he squinted beneath the glare of sunlight he had not seen in days and shielded his eyes to get his first look at the islands.

Káliel's main harbor was filling with local passenger sloops and fishing boats coming to moor for the night, the smaller boats skirting around Kavan's transport with experienced ease. The smell of fish, of sea salt and exotic spices wafted across the water, and though he normally would have relished those scents, today they made him more nauseous. He stopped beside the captain, clutched the railing to remain standing, and swallowed back the bile in his throat.

"W'll 'ave t'get one o' the loc'ls' 'tention if ye wanna go t'land; they won' le' me come nigh clos'r."

There was no need to attract attention, however, as a small rowboat was already cutting through the water towards them. On its bow, a slender, bare-chested young man in brown, lightweight breeches that clung to his body from the surf's spray, was watching them cautiously as he approached. Wielding a small crossbow in one hand while his companion stopped the boat a safe distance away, he called out to them, "You have no place in our harbor. State your intentions or leave."

"We ain' in yer 'arb'r," the captain called back, then under his breath with a smirk in Kavan's direction he muttered, "A'leas' na yet."

"State your business before I shoot…"

Hoping to avoid a counterproductive altercation, Kavan held up his hand and said in a strained, rough voice, "I have business with the Prime Magistrate. This ship is not coming into the harbor; only I have need of passage. The rest will go about their way."

"Is Lord Dilyn expecting you?"

Switching to his native tongue, since his accent was lost to the effect of the wind and his poor physical state, Kavan continued, "No, but if you tell him Kyne Mórne sends her regards, he will be pleased."

The words did the trick, as the crossbow lowered. "Elyri, eh. That makes a difference. You are the only one in your party?"

"Yes, I am."

The man looked skeptical but eventually said, "Good, then you may come ashore. Allow me to pull alongside and I'll take you myself."

The smaller vessel moved as close to the larger one as it was able and the crew slung a rope ladder down over its hull. After setting aside his bow, the shirtless man caught the ladder and held it taut. Kavan thanked the captain for his hospitality, said a silent prayer to ease his fears, and then clumsily began his descent with his pack of belongings slung over his shoulder. Seasickness made keeping hold of the slick, wet rope difficult as the boat swayed in rhythm with the waves. Kavan was thankful when he made it into the smaller boat, but that sense of gratitude lasted only long enough to realize how small the craft was. His stomach lurched as he settled into the center, fearful of getting too near the edge despite his skill at swimming. His host, however, nudged him to one side to sit beside him. The man who had been rowing used one oar to push the tiny boat away from the larger one, and soon they were skimming towards shore.

"I hope your business here is important, something more than wanting a few bottles of wine or a few bolts of cloth. Lord Dilyn will not treat you, or me, kindly, if that is all you want."

Eyes closed, Kavan nodded. "I do not generally drink wine and have no need of cloth. My business is more...political in nature."

"Elyriá want a new treaty?"

They were closer to the shore now, and the ship Kavan had come in was moving away from the island; Kavan felt it unlikely they would try to expel him from this boat or the islands for telling the truth. "I do not come on behalf of Elyriá."

His host scowled. "You said..."

"The Kyne always wishes Káliel and its people well. Our relations with your islands are valuable and vital. I did not say anything untrue."

The shirtless man swore under his breath and pushed his dark, damp hair from his face. "Whom do you speak for then?"

"That," Kavan replied as he slid towards the center of the boat as another small craft passed by, "is a rather complicated matter that I can only discuss with Lord Dilyn. Once I have completed my business, I will depart. There will be no trouble, you have my word."

The other man grunted but did not argue, and the rest of the trip to land was silent. His host was undoubtedly having second thoughts about bringing Kavan to shore, and though Kavan regretted the way it had been done, it was imperative that he speak to the Prime Magistrate in person. Whatever annoyance the man felt, however, was not enough to prevent him from offering a hand to shore when the boat was tied off to a mooring post and pulled up onto the sand. Kavan's tremendous relief at reaching solid ground was short-lived, as he discovered how difficult standing and walking was after six days spent at sea.

"First time to sea?" his escort chuckled. Kavan grasped the offered arm and nodded. "Sea legs; you'll get used to land again soon enough. Lean on me; move slowly. By the time we reach the villa you should be better off. Come; I will take you there."

Crossbow slung over his back, he helped the Elyri through streets lined with petite, whitewashed shops and dwellings towards the inland edge of town. Everywhere Kavan looked was a garden of exotic flowers, clinging grapevines heavy with the last grapes of the year, hanging ferns in earthenware pots, and lush green bushes and trees such as he had not beheld in months. He breathed deeply of the intoxicating and invigorating scents, knowing he could easily grow to like this place if it did not require traveling by sea to get to it.

When at last they reached the vast, pink-stoned villa sprawling amidst its jungle-like setting, the man with him spoke to one of the four attending sentries, a large bear-like man who stared at Kavan with unabashed curiosity, before he and Kavan were allowed to pass through the black wrought iron gate and up the winding limestone pathway to the villa door. The escort pulled a stout blue cord that hung beside the door; it produced the faint chime of a low-pitched bell within the house. A few moments later, a woman dressed in gray, wiping her hands on a red linen apron she wore, answered the door and escorted them inside without a word. It seemed she was familiar with Kavan's escort since the two shared a smile and a nod before she bustled down a corridor to their right. When she returned shortly thereafter, she pointed at the archer and said, "He wants to speak with you."

Left to lean weakly against the banister, Kavan turned his attention to the room where he stood and away from his shakiness. The walls bore the same pinkish hue as the building's exterior, suggesting a quality in the stone rather than any surface treatment as he had first believed. A curved staircase of pale green mottled marble led up to a balconied hall that disappeared to his left. In the banister itself were carved delicate záryph, modeled after any number of old Elyri artistic designs, each inlaid with some sort of metal which sparkled gold beneath the yellow glow of candlelight. He slid one finger over them, admiring the detail of each tiny figure, his thoughts blissfully empty until footfalls at the top of the stairs caused him to lift his head. His heart and breathing stopped.

The brown eyes that locked onto his fluttered playfully as their owner flowed down the staircase with an ethereal grace. The young woman was dressed in beige breeches, a full white blouse cinched tight at the waist, and brown suede boots. She held matching suede gloves in one hand while the other followed the banister down. Never before had he seen a woman in man's attire, nor imagined it. Her chestnut auburn hair hung loose, falling midway down her back but pulled away from her face by a delicate blue lace ribbon. When she smiled, a look that matched the playful glint in her eyes, Kavan took one awkward step away from her, feeling threatened without understanding why.

"Welcome to Káliel, Elyri. Are you here to see Lord Dilyn?" Her lilting voice was rich and earthy, a pleasant blanket of a sound that made his hands tremble.

When he replied, it was with a squeak. "I am."

She continued to smile. "Does he know you are here?"

Kavan's head bobbed up and down slowly without his letting her out of his sight. "I…am sure he must; he is speaking with my escort."

She smiled wider and continued down the stairs. Her hand on the railing brushed against his and he jerked away as if stung. "Then I am sure my father will see you shortly. I would stay and attend you, but I have an engagement to keep. Perhaps I will see you at dinner."

The look she gave him, coy and playful, left him speechless; as she left the house, escorted by a bulky man in armor who met her at the door, there was nothing Kavan could say. He collapsed onto a nearby dais, shaking badly, an effect he stubbornly chose to attribute to lingering seasickness rather than to the woman he had just met. He barely had the opportunity to calm his rapid, shallow breathing before the servant returned to the room with his archer escort behind her.

"Sir," the younger man said, "I will take leave of you. Lord Dilyn is waiting to speak with you; Delia will take you to him."

"Thank you," he managed to say after swallowing hard. The archer made his exit after a proper bow and handshake, then Kavan followed the woman across the entrance foyer, around a corner, and through the first door in the corridor they reached. A portly, bearded man wearing a doublet of coral pink silk pinned at the throat with a golden brooch…a coral serpent rising from the sea depicted on it…got up from behind the desk and held forth his pudgy hand in greeting.

"Welcome to Káliel. I'm Ulstar Dilyn. Gratz tells me you have business here, though I find it odd that I knew nothing of your coming. I do not normally receive unannounced, uninvited callers, but you are here, and I endeavor to maintain a good relationship with Elyriá. Please, sit. Would you care for refreshment? Something to eat perhaps?"

His actions and cordial demeanor were hardly those of a people who snubbed outsiders. Kavan might have thought him being merely polite if not for the sincere friendliness on the fellow's round face and in his small, merry brown eyes. Surprised that he, like the others he had met here thus far spoke to him in Trade, Kavan gratefully accepted the offered seat as the servant left them alone, and replied, "No, thank you, sir. I appreciate the offer…and this audience."

The Magistrate sat. "What is your business? What is so pressing that it brings you to me without formal request…that leads you to mislead my harbor patrol?"

Expression darkening with embarrassment, Kavan lowered his gaze. "My apologies for that." He had not lied to the man, had spoken in honest earnestness, but he had not been open about his purpose. "It was vital I speak with you…and I was led to believe that you would not have granted me audience any other way."

Magistrate Dilyn smirked. "Maybe…or maybe not. You resort to honest trickery. Impressive. I would never have thought your people capable of that." Not that he had met many Elyri, and those he had met had been either merchants or diplomats, hardly a sampling of the general population of Elyriá. "What is it you seek? How can I help you?"

Deciding that directness was his best approach, particularly after the methods he had used to be here, Kavan asked, "How much to you know about Enesfel's current state of affairs?"

The man took a sip from the wine glass on the desk before him and dabbed at his lips with a stained cloth. "Elyriá is involving itself in the affairs of outsiders?"

"Not all of Elyriá, no. Only myself and a handful of others…"

Lord Dilyn smiled, a small gesture that was nearly devoured by the fleshiness of his face. This peculiar Elyri had gall; he had to admit that. "I have heard that this latest King is not the most popular of rulers and that there is general discontent among the population…although that seems to be a common state of affairs wherever you go. No one is ever satisfied. But I have heard nothing more of interest. Should I have?"

"You knew King Innis, did you not?"

Removing a handkerchief from his pocket, Lord Dilyn wiped his nose. "We met twice. He was a good, wise man. I was grieved to learn of his death, but his reign was long and good. No man can live forever."

"Then you know that his queen bore twins the night of his death?"

"Yes, so I heard," the portly man nodded, "though if memory serves me, one is a deaf-mute and the other died during King Donal's reign."

"That child, Prince Arlan, did not die," Kavan corrected. "There had been attempts on him and his mother arranged to remove him from the castle to protect his life. He has been in General McHador's care for the past ten years and is now moving to Rhidam with the intent of being restored into the family. Lord McHador suspects that King Owain will not accept him and that, along with the people's desire to overthrow their King, will lead to civil war. We do not want war, but the King may leave us no choice. Prince Arlan has a substantial following and has received the backing of both Cordash and Hatu…"

"If you came seeking troops…" Ulstar Dilyn's red face frowned.

"No, that is not what we wish. The prince is aware that Káliel does not involve itself in the affairs of others; it is a policy Elyriá admires and largely adheres to itself. If not for my cousin's involvement in Prince Arlan's disappearance from court, and my own friendship with the prince, I would not now be involved. Prince Arlan has no desire to impose on your people." Kavan paused as the Magistrate poured himself more wine without looking at the glass. "I am aware of King Owain's style of ruling, what he is doing to his kingdom, his people…and I support the prince's desire to rectify the wrongs of previous kings. I do not, however, support any action that would lead to King Owain's death."

Lord Dilyn arched one brow, drank from his glass, and motioned for Kavan to continue.

"I was sent here not to request military backing; King Geir of Hatu is sending soldiers to assist Prince Arlan if they are needed, and both he and Lord McHador believe it will be faster and more prudent to send them to Enesfel by sea. I have come to request allowance for those ships to stop here, not necessarily in your harbor, to restock food and water. King Geir has set aside funds to pay for whatever you can provide."

The Magistrate sniffed and crossed his arms. "I cannot respond to this request. Unlike your kings, I cannot make decisions for the people I represent. It will be necessary to bring this up before the Council and let them decide. They will convene for usual business the day after tomorrow; I can bring your request before them at that time if you wish. However, I can save you the trouble of waiting and tell you that this request will, in all likelihood, be denied. Supporting a mercenary army that is partaking in a civil war in another country is not something the Council will approve of. Perhaps there is justification for the actions you are taking, but we could not assist you any more than we could assist King Owain if he were making the same request."

Kavan tried not to show disappointment or regret and rather clung to hope as he nodded gravely. "I understand, sir, but I am compelled to await the Council's ruling on the issue in order to take official word to the prince…that is if you will allow me to remain on your island. There is always a chance that the council may vote in the prince's favor, and I would be remiss if I did not try."

Smiling, the Magistrate nodded. "Of course; that is a wise choice, even if a futile one. My house is open to you…though I apologize…I have not yet learned your name."

Odd, Kavan realized, that such a formality had slipped by both of them. "Kavan Cliáth, milord."

The Magistrate's reaction was typical of those learning his name for the first time. "The harp-makers?"

"I do not make them," Kavan replied. "I discovered quite young that I have no talent or desire in that trade. That is my uncle and cousin's calling. I am a musician."

"All the better," sniffed Lord Dilyn. "Craftsmen can be so tedious. It is an honor to have a member of such an august family on our islands. You are more than welcome in my home."

Having not expected such hospitality, Kavan got to his feet as the Magistrate did. "I do not wish to be an imposition."

"Nonsense. It will be no imposition. As you realize, we rarely have foreign guests, and I am sure my daughter will be delighted to have company. If you would play for my household after our evening meal, I will consider it an even exchange for room and board."

Kavan sighed as he bowed his head. "I would gladly, but I have not brought my harp; I feared losing it at sea."

The other man waved his hand. "If it was one of your family's harps, I do not blame you for that, but there is a harp on the premises. I will ask Delia to find it and have it brought to the dining room."

"Then I shall play as you request," Kavan said with a bow. Gladly, too, for it had been too long since he had been able to make music, and playing for a meal and a bed was a life he was accustomed to.

"Splendid. I look forward to hearing you." There was another blue cord in the corner of this room that, when pulled, brought the servant woman back. "Delia, please give Lord Cliáth a room. He will be staying with us for a few days. I want you to see that he has everything he needs. And see if you can, find that old harp and move it to the dining room."

She curtseyed with a smile. "Yes, milord. Come this way, sir. I will show you to a room."

Taking leave of his host with a bow, as the man drained the last of the wine from his glass and poured yet another, Kavan followed the woman up the marble staircase and into the left corridor. At the top, he paused when he heard the front door open. Lord Dilyn's daughter entered, her face and clothing stained and soiled with dirt and leaves and long strands of hair pulled free from its ribbon. She looked up at him and smiled, and when he realized that he found her appearance more alluring in its disheveled state, he gasped, shuddered, and turned towards the servant woman calling him from further down the hall. Delia motioned him into an open room and he escaped inside gladly. He could not, however, escape the odd twinge and tightening within his stomach.

"I hope this will suffice. The meal shall be served shortly, but there is time for you to refresh yourself after your journey. Shall a bath be drawn?"

The luxury of a bath sounded like exactly what he needed, so Kavan bowed and replied, "If you would be so kind, yes."

Delia curtseyed and went out, only to return quickly, as Kavan was unpacking his single small bag of belongings, with four pages bearing steaming pails of water for the tub. She waited as they each made two more trips and then asked, "Will that be all, sir?"

"If you will summon me once dinner is served then yes. Thank you" He was not sure he would be able to eat, but he was hopeful that a long soak in the hot water would restore him to his usual self.

"There is a cord there," she pointed to the corner nearest the bed, "if you require anything."

He bowed his head, murmured his thanks again, and waited until the door was closed before removing his robe and boots and immersing himself in the steaming water. The sting of it brought a sharp breath of discomfort, but his aching muscles relished the soothing heat and he quickly relaxed. It was gratifying to rid himself of the sticky feel and scent of sea salt, if only for a few days, and he looked forward to meals that consisted of something other than pickled fish, hard bread, and water. He closed his eyes, reached along the threads of power within his head, and sought Ártur's presence. Though the healer could not project any specific thoughts to him, he could assure his cousin that everyone around him was well, knowledge that put Kavan more at ease.

With his head dropped back against the thick edge of the wooden tub, and his eyes closed to outside stimuli, seeking relaxation in that place of solitary peace, Kavan did not hear the gentle tapping on the door. He jerked to awareness and almost stood in surprise when it opened and the young woman he had encountered on the stairs entered with a tray of steaming food. Fortunately, he suppressed the impulse in time to avoid embarrassment, but he continued to stare at her in shock.

"Father has been called to the docks to mediate a dispute; he will not be able to join us for dinner and instructed us to dine without him. I detest eating alone in the dining room and thought that perhaps after your journey, you would prefer to dine here. Thus I have brought dinner to you." She placed the tray on the dresser, positioned it not to fall, and smiled at Kavan once more. "I am Gabrielle Dilyn."

"Kavan Cliáth." He did not want to speak with her, not now, not while sitting in the bath, but he knew he could not be rude to the daughter of the man whose favor he was here to gain. He squirmed uncomfortably beneath the water, but try as he might, he could not take his eyes off of her. A modest blue smock and clean face had replaced the dirt and confusion of earlier, and her hair was free of its ribbon and the accompanying leaves, but nothing else about her had changed. She was the loveliest woman he had ever seen, and that realization unsettled him.

Gabrielle plopped herself on the furthest corner of the bed, scooped up Kavan's soiled robe, held it to her face and breathed deeply. This time he did look away with shame and embarrassment over actions he did not comprehend. "I adore the fragrances of the sea; I find it invigorating," she explained. "I often wish I had been born a sailor's child rather than a politician's…and a boy rather than a girl so that I could be a sailor. Would you like this cleaned?"

"Yes," he replied hastily, hoping she would leave and take it with her. The aroma of roast fowl whetted his appetite but he saw no way of getting to his dinner in his current state of undress. Nor did he dare ask her to bring it to him and risk her seeing his nudity. He groaned silently and watched her smile as she laid the robe on the bed beside her, apparently with no intention of leaving.

"I know who you are, harper." She lay across the red velvet draped bed on her stomach, her chin propped on her hands, bare feet in the air as the folds of her dress fell away to reveal long, smooth calves.

Kavan realized then, as he tore his eyes away from a sight he had never seen before, that she was enjoying his discomfort. Perhaps, he decided, if he appeared not to be affected by her beauty and behavior, she would give up her game and leave him in peace.

"You do?"

"I heard you play at the Festival of Candles in Clarys, the year King Donal of Enesfel died. I did not recall your name, but I remember your music and your voice vividly…and your face."

The purr in her voice crept under his skin. Despite his resolve to remain unaffected, or at least appear unaffected, he flushed and became flustered all over again. "I…for your people not leaving the islands, that is a long journey for you to make."

Chewing on her little finger, she smiled coyly and replied, "Not as long as you might think."

"Your father approved of you traveling?"

"My father," she said with a giggle, "did not know I was gone."

Kavan's brow shot up. "During the time it took you to travel from here to Clarys and back, he never knew you were gone?"

"I like to travel and consider fooling my father to be a worthy challenge." She sounded almost bored with that revelation as if the challenge was no longer something she enjoyed. "I knew I recognized you in the hall; it took time to remember why but your face is not easily forgotten…nor is your music. Do you still play?"

Her compliments, though he had heard such words from others before, made his skin grow warm. He looked away before replying. "I do."

"I thought that was why Delia had great-grandfather's harp placed in the dining hall. It has not been played since he died. It is not in the best condition and is probably horribly out of tune, but I imagine that will not hamper you much. I remember that you were quite good. I hope to hear you play while you are here."

"I have been asked to…though apparently not tonight."

"Probably not…with my father away…although you could play for me…" She studied the lines of his finely sculpted face as he squirmed again, still not looking at her, and asked, "Why are you here, on Káliel?"

Kavan groaned. He was not sure he should tell her and he was getting frustrated with the meal being near enough to smell but being unable to reach it or eat it. "Milady, I do not wish to be disrespectful, but I should like to complete my bath and eat, if I may. If you would allow me to do both, I will gladly answer your questions as best I can afterward."

"Oh, of course. I am sorry." Her tone and expression were sincere, but she did not move for many moments, but rather maintained eye contact with him. When he did not move, her eyes eventually widened and her pink lips formed a silent O. "You wish me to leave…for privacy. Why didn't you say so, milord? Please, forgive me." She stood, stretched casually as though she was in no hurry to depart, gathered up his soiled clothing and then went to the door. Part of the way out of the room, with the door mostly closed behind her, she looked back at him with another warm, playful smile. Relieved as soon as the door was closed, Kavan reached for the towel, stepped out of the tub, and had barely wrapped it around his lean waist when the door burst open and Gabrielle's head popped inside. She laughed with delight at his horrified expression as he stumbled backward to the floor, then she closed the door and skipped down the stairs.

The serving woman met her at the foot of the stairs, her expression scolding Gabrielle for whatever mischief she had caused. "Does his lordship approve of the meal?" she asked.

"I think so. He did not say. Delia, do you think him handsome?"

The woman waved her hand and started up the stairs. "When you get to be my age, child, nearly all young men are handsome."

"No…honestly. Is he?"

"He is certainly unique."

"Unique," Gabrielle whispered, swinging around the banister with a hum. "See to it this is cleaned." She tossed Kavan's robe to the woman. "I suppose I shall be in the dining hall or back terrace if he asks for me." He had said he would answer her questions. She assumed he meant tonight. Delia rolled her eyes and continued about her duties.

❧*☙

Ártur's amused smile looked out of place as he listened to Bhríd and Prince Arlan discuss the condition of one of the horses that had spooked earlier in the day during training drills. After a chase through the trees, the animal had tumbled into a shallow ravine. There appeared to be no broken bones or major injuries; other than abrasions the healer had easily tended, the horse appeared unharmed, but it had behaved erratically the remainder of the day and Bhríd was concerned about its condition.

"What is so amusing, Lord Healer?" the prince asked with a scowl.

Trying to wipe the grin from his face, the healer shook his head. "Nothing that concerns you, my prince…"

But the smile could not be contained, and he was not going to reveal what he knew to anyone; he excused himself and walked apart from the camp where no one would see or hear him. When he was certain no one would disturb him, he opened himself up to further contact with his cousin and allowed Kavan's chaotic state to fill him. The bard was perplexed by the behavior of a woman he had met and he did not know how to deal with her. From what Ártur could ascertain, she appeared to be flirting with his cousin, and that Kavan could not comprehend it was, to Ártur, highly amusing. Unable to give advice, all the healer could do was to offer reassurance. Kavan, annoyed with the lack of helpful answers, responded with a snort and broke contact.

Ártur looked into the late summer sky and laughed.

❧*☙

The pied gelding stamped its hooves and pulled at the reins; King Owain barely noticed since the horse did that every time he mounted.

❧ 583 ☙

In general, the animal was nothing but trouble. He was disposed to biting those who tended him, he kicked when he felt slighted, and he only allowed the King to ride him. He did not even make a good stud animal since he drove off any other horse that came near. Not even gelding him had helped his demeanor. But the King had developed a fondness for this stubborn, cocky animal, perhaps because it was one of the closest friends he had.

It was too warm to make good hunting weather, but riding was a passion the King would not give up. The four attendants with him squirmed uncomfortably within the sticky heaviness of their armor, but they did not voice their complaints. Just once, the King thought, I would like to hear them complain like normal men. But he knew they would not. They knew, or thought they knew, how complaints were dealt with in Neth, and assumed therefore that their King, having been raised in that environment, would deal with complaints in the same fashion. In truth, the King did not know how he would deal with such things; he wanted men to be men and not live in fear of him.

He tugged the reins and directed his horse into the city streets; his retainers followed. None of them looked back as he waved at the princess who watched them leave from the third-floor window of her room.

Today was market day, the King assumed, as the rabble that filled the streets, buying produce and other items from the street vendors, parted to allow him and his entourage through. He knew little about such things; his mother had shielded him from the drab duties of everyday existence; he often needed to remind himself that food and other commodities did not simply appear by magic in his possession. It was another reason to hate her, one of so many recently that Owain had lost count of them.

There were beggars among the sellers and a few whores. He watched the crowds, hoping to catch a glimpse of the boy the princess had invited into the palace. Her gesture did not trouble him, as he knew her to be a generous and trusting soul, but her distracted gaze since that day did. She explained that she had not been sleeping well, that she had been suffering from disturbing dreams of her brothers Farrell, Bowen, and Girvin, all of whom had suffered violent deaths during her short life. Enough to frighten anyone, the King had to admit, as dreams about those men sometimes plagued him as well, and thus perhaps her explanation was true. Then again, perhaps it was not.

So many people…subjects whose faces he never saw from within the palace, all beholden to him. He contemplated the still peculiar turn of events that had made him king and his amazement that there were more people here then he knew, as he turned a corner into the heaviest business district in Rhidam. Less than a third of them bowed or gave some other gesture of deference. The others either moved out of his way with a look of annoyance or showed no recognition. He did not travel with the typical royal retinue, after all, nor did he carry the standard or wear royal emblems. He wanted to mingle and be anonymous. One of his attendants prepared to smite a fellow who appeared particularly disrespectful, but the King raised his hand and prevented it. Such force was unnecessary. He had long ago given up trying to obtain the reverence of Enesfel's people. He was accustomed to being ignored, but he longed for even a single sincere gesture of recognition and respect for himself and his station that was not obtained at the end of a sword.

Approaching the crumbling, ancient náós, he saw for himself the gathering of men and women congregated in the hopes of witnessing a miracle. As long as the population of Rhidam did not complain about their presence, the King saw no need to dispel them. If some sort of miracle was to occur, no matter what form it took or how insignificant it proved to be, he preferred to have people nearby who could tell him what was happening. Other than leeching off the city's resources, which had yet to affect the royal purse, these people had done no harm, had created no riots or incidents, and the King was content to let them be.

An unexpected stinging sharpness ripped through his back, toppling him from his horse into the street. Owain landed face down in the dust, and to his surprise, after skittering sideways in response to the abrupt shift in weight, the piebald moved to stand over the fallen King. Chaos erupted around them. There was shouting, screaming, and some crying. For me, the King wondered with amazement. He could not see much as the pain was too great for him to dare lift his head. The commotion of two of his attendants and some passersby wrestling someone to the ground about six feet away was all the King could see to one side; to the other, he caught a glimpse of swishing green and gold robes as they pushed through the crowd in the fallen monarch's direction. He should recognize those colors, he thought, but the wet agony spreading along his shoulder and the throb of heat radiating from its center refused to allow him to concentrate. A cough rose up in his chest; he tried to suppress it and in doing so lost his hold on consciousness.

≈*≈

"Good morning, Lord Cliáth," Gabrielle said with an enchanting smile as Kavan descended the stairs. "I wondered what had become of you when you did not come down last night." She was seated on a hall bench, suede gloves in her hands, dressed in her breeches once more; it seemed as if she had been waiting for him.

Kavan bowed as he fought the impulse to escape. To be honest, he had not felt capable of facing her and had instead opted for much-needed sleep in a bed that, to his senses, still seemed to be rocking upon the waves. "I lay down to rest after my meal and fell asleep. I slept little on my journey here." He glanced awkwardly at his hands. "It seems that sea travel does not agree with me."

Her bright smile turned sympathetic. "I am sorry to hear that. If it is a comfort, it happens to the best. My father can barely stand the sight of a boat without getting ill, much less a journey at sea. I feared that I may have offended you and you did not wish my company. Were dinner and breakfast to your satisfaction?"

The honest worry in her voice made Kavan feel guilty for having avoided her without an explanation. He wondered if avoiding her the way he had marked him as a coward. "It was, milady; thank you."

"Good. Now then, would you care to go riding with me? Father will be involved in business most of the day; the politest thing I can do to make up for my impetuousness would be to entertain his guest."

That feeling of panic experienced last night came over him again and he shook his head. "Do not go out of your way on my account. I did not come here to interrupt anyone's routine..." It was the only polite way he could think of to decline the offer without lying to her. He might feel guilty about avoiding her last night, but he did not feel comfortable with the idea of spending an entire day with her.

Not sensing anything peculiar, Gabrielle smiled and came closer. "Believe me, you are a welcome interruption, Lord Cliáth. I can show you the island and you can tell me your purpose for being here..."

"I..."

The servant Delia bustled into the hall then, her face red and moist as she wiped her hands on her apron. "Lady Gabrielle, Lord Drantz is here for you. He is at the side entrance."

"Oh! Bl...I forgot about...Delia, will you tell him I am ill or..."

The matronly woman shook her head. "That is not proper behavior towards one's suitors, milady," she said sternly.

"Surely there must be etiquette to deal with unexpected guests?" Seeing in Delia's face that, even if there were such etiquette rules, she did not intend to let the Magistrate's daughter out of her obligations, or have her disappointing her suitor, Gabrielle groaned and shrugged her shoulders. "Oh, very well. We will have to postpone our ride and tour until later today, milord. I seem to have forgotten a previously arranged engagement. Will you excuse me?"

"Of course." It was difficult for Kavan to disguise his relief; Gabrielle did not notice as she flounced out of the room, but Delia did.

"Please forgive the lady, milord. She has an unladylike interest in political affairs and enjoys interrogating her father's guests."

Of course, the woman did not know the full extent of Gabrielle's interest in Kavan, or what form her interrogations had taken, but Kavan chose not to correct her. "There is nothing unladylike about affairs of state, particularly if she might succeed her father as Magistrate. It would be wise of her to understand how things work. But I do appreciate your intervention. I am not up to riding and was unsure how to decline her invitation politely...as she was rather adamant about me joining her."

"She is adamant about all of her pursuits," Delia chuckled.

Tucking that tidbit of information into the corners of his mind, Kavan asked, "Would it be permitted for me to go into the city? I would like to see the island while I am here."

"Certainly. I will leave word for the sentries to allow you to come and go as you please."

Grateful for the freedom to wander, Kavan strolled casually through the house gardens, examining the flora and fauna with great curiosity, unhindered by the Káliel guardsman who roamed the grounds. In his younger years, he had spent time in the forests alone, seeking solace from the confusing life amongst other people; Kavan had grown up with a great respect and awareness of all aspects of nature. A gentle mist was falling as he left the villa grounds, dusting everything with a light sheen of moisture though the sky was mostly clear of clouds. By the first hour's end, the precipitation had ceased and everything around him, from the buildings to the smallest leaf and bud shimmered with sparkling droplets. It was tempting to fly, to see this dazzling spectacle from above, but he did not feel he had the strength for that after the long sea voyage, so he settled for spending his time going in and out of the small, but bountiful shops, talking with anyone who chose to approach him, and basking in the beauty of Káliel. To his delight, he happened upon a bookkeeper's shop and on the dusty back shelves, he uncovered Kóráhm's first volume in the Trade tongue. The storekeeper was not eager to part with it, but after much haggling, he gave it over to Kavan for a substantial fee. The money meant nothing to Kavan. He would have given the fellow everything he had for that book. Clutching it, he strolled along the dock, found a shady place to rest that was not overly damp, and relaxed to read, comparing this translation to those he already knew intimately.

It was several hours later when he realized that the sun was sinking into the sea before him. He had not intended to be out all day, but he had not anticipated finding this book either. Reluctantly he marked his page with a long blade of grass and returned to the Prime Magistrate's villa. The guards at the gate let him pass without question, although the large bearded man he had seen before eyed him with continued curiosity. Kavan was relieved to find that Gabrielle was not home, as she had accompanied her father to Jaffe, a neighboring island under Káliel's rule. Neither would return until the following evening, but Lord Dilyn had relayed Prince Arlan's request to two trusted Council members and the Council would discuss the issue if the Magistrate was unable to attend.

Alone in the villa except for the servants…Delia, her husband, and the four pages…Kavan continued to read by the light of the candles in his room. He felt distracted and restless, however, and soon lay his treasure aside and went to the dining hall where the harp waited. As Lord Dilyn had indicated, it was not a Cliáthan harp and was badly weathered and worn, strung with gut rather than brass. Still, it was an expensive instrument, and after tuning it to his satisfaction, he closed his eyes to play. The notes stirred something within him; as an unfamiliar melody began to piece itself together, his stomach and throat constricted uncomfortably. Gabrielle's image formed and dissipated in his mind, causing his fingers to freeze over the harp strings. His eyes flew open and he found her standing on the other side of the room, in the open doorway.

"That was beautiful, milord. I was correct in thinking you would not squander your talent; in fact, you have improved where I had not thought improvement possible. You have restored life to that harp; perhaps I can persuade Father to give it to you. It is of no use to anyone here."

Kavan cleared his throat, but the words that came out were little more than a squeak. "I thought you were on Jaffe with your father?"

She glided across the room and sat close to him. Kavan immediately slid away. "I was…and I should be…but I needed to speak with you. My aunt lives on Jaffe; she is dying. When Father comes home tomorrow, I will be expected to stay with her until she passes. I may not see you again, and I must know why you wish to see my father…what business you have put before the Council."

As she spoke, she inched gradually nearer, and Kavan continued to retreat away from her until he reached the end of the bench and found nowhere to go. "Why this consuming desire to know my business?"

"You blush prettily, milord," she murmured stopping her pursuit now that he was trapped. "I have had dreams of late, vast ships sitting near our harbor, armies looking out from them. I fear we may be under attack."

"You suspect that I have come either to offer assistance or as a prelude to war?"

She nodded. "I doubt you carry a threat, or my father would not welcome you, but if the risk of war still looms, I must know."

"You may be assured Káliel is safe, milady. I have come to secure supplies for possibly eight ships that will sail from Hatu to Enesfel."

"Warships?"

"Yes," he replied reluctantly.

Gabrielle leaned against the wall behind her and stared into the dimness of the room. "Is Hatu going to war with Enesfel? With Elyriá's help? This time by sea?"

"Hatu is not going to war with Enesfel, nor is Elyriá involved. The night King Innis died, his youngest two children were born. After attempts on one of the twins' lives, he was removed from Rhidam to protect him. He now wishes to return to Rhidam and to be accepted as a rightful member of the Lachlan house. However, we believe that King Owain's resistance to the idea will result in civil unrest, possibly war. Fortunately, Prince Arlan has a substantial following; Hatu has agreed to send men in support of the prince, in case he has need of them."

"Hence the ships."

For several minutes, Gabrielle said nothing, though Kavan could tell without looking at her that she was deep in thought. Eventually, she said, "I have not heard much that is positive about King Owain, though we do not get much news…only rumors. He is handsome…but handsome is not enough to rule a kingdom. I met him once when I was in Rhidam, though I doubt he would remember. He knows the rules of etiquette and diplomacy and is courteous, but he does not seem secure, is ruled by anger. I can't imagine he has endured an easy time of it. I suppose Father has put the matter to Council vote?"

"They vote tomorrow."

Gabrielle sighed. "It will fail. They will never approve such a thing, though k'Ádhá knows they should stand up for something…"

"You support us?" That surprised him, and he was curious to learn why.

"I see no substantial reason for King Owain to deny position and privilege to a member of his family, but you are wise to prepare for the possibility. I believe Káliel should open our doors to supply your ships…or any passing ships. It would be good for our economy. Isolationism is good as far as it goes, but some day an outside force will confront Káliel and no one will come to our aid because we failed to assist everyone else. We are not big enough to defend ourselves in a fight. We will be destroyed if that happens. We need to reach out to other kingdoms. We need to make treaties…make alliances. Helping passing ships would be a start."

On her feet and pacing now, she paused long enough to ask, "Will you kill him?"

It was refreshing to discover that beneath that coy, playful, giggly girlish exterior, Gabrielle held a sharp mind and clear, precise, thoughts of her own. Kavan wondered how she would fare as Prime Magistrate. Her path would not be an easy one.

"I pray not. I do not want to see it come to that, nor does Lord McHador, but I fear Prince Arlan and many of Enesfel's subjects may wish it. I will continue to work to persuade the prince towards leniency, but it will be his choice to make."

"Why are you concerned with the King's safety after all he has supposedly done?" In her experience, that sort of altruism was rare.

"He does not rule justly, and is not a child of King Innis, but I do not believe he is a bad man."

Gabrielle smiled. "Mercy and compassion. I like that in people…and see it too infrequently. It is better than brutality and anger. Perhaps you should be king."

The bard vehemently shook his head. "I have no inclination towards a political calling, milady. I fear I would be a much worse ruler than King Owain could ever be."

"I doubt that," she laughed. "I believe you would be very good at it, and I wager many would support you if you were to make a bid for the throne, even though you are neither a Lachlan nor a citizen of Enesfel, nor Teren. Did you know King Owain intends to marry?"

The odd segue caught him by surprise. "No...I have not heard that." It was not good news. "Do you know who his bride is to be? When he is due to be married?"

"No, I've not heard any more than that. I believe it is intended to be before year's end. Speculation suggests it will be King Ander's fifteen-year-old daughter, but there are many noblewomen he could choose from. I thought you should be aware of his intentions in case a marriage produces an heir before you and your prince are in a position to act."

It was a good thing to know, Kavan had to agree. Odds were, unless this was another victim of rape, there would be no heir before Prince Arlan and his company reached Rhidam, but a conceived child could be a threat. "Prince Arlan will be grateful for the information. Thank you."

"You are welcome," she said with a smile. "I must get back; I have been gone too long. I will see what I can do to help, but I can't make promises."

Kavan got to his feet, intending to be polite as she took leave of him. "If you are on Jaffe, how will I...?"

She smiled into his eyes, their faces inches apart. "I will try to see you before you go...never fear..." she said with a chuckle. "And if not, I will leave a message for you."

Kavan's heart was pounding in his throat. His mouth opened, possibly to speak although no words came to mind. Then she was gone, sliding into the darkness of the hall before he could stop her. Feeling both the threat and promise of her words, Kavan started to follow, but by the time he got to the door, he could not see her. He stared bewildered into the blackness of the passage for a long time.

Not far from the smoky billowing ashes of the evening fire, gdhededhá Jermyn twisted his sleeve absently. There had been mixed reactions to his gesture of kindness towards the fallen King, much of it partially, or totally, hostile. The young man the prince had sent to Rhidam had been particularly angered, but Jermyn knew he would have done nothing different without direct, divine interference. Owain was the King, after all, and despite his shortcomings, he did not deserve assassination, especially if the gdhededhá could prevent and save him. He was relieved to have done his part to spare the man's life.

Royal retainers had pushed him away before he could do much, however, thus he had no idea if the monarch had lived or died. There had been no word from the palace either way. King Owain's death would mean a quick end to the game Prince Arlan was engaged in, but there was no way of knowing who would rule in the interim; it could be the princess or it could be someone who could make matters much worse for all of them. Jermyn preferred order to uncertainty and prayed fervently for the King's health. His fate now was in the hands of k'Ádhá.

☞Chapter 34☜

The rabble gathered before the palace gatehouse consisted mostly of Rhidam's outcasts. The beggars, cripples, the blind, and homeless, all of those who knew they had little to lose by standing up to the perceived source of their misfortunes. There were also a large number of petty criminals in the crowd, though today they were not out to make a living. They were gathered for a cause. Even some of Rhidam's townsfolk, and a portion of those gathered in the hopes of a miracle came to participate, some out of curiosity, some out of anger at the Crown, some out of boredom. All began arriving during the night and by daybreak, it was not possible for anyone to leave or enter the castle. They were quiet and posed no threat thus far, but King Owain continued to watch them from the tower window, perturbed that he was unable to take his morning ride.

His upper back still ached where the arrow had sunk its barbs into his flesh, and the pain did little to lighten his mood. Fortunately, there had been no serious damage. Princess Deidre had tended him until he was strong enough to get out of bed; she had been the one to tell him that, if not for the aid of a gdhededhá near the náós, he might not have survived. The King supposed he should be grateful, but all he felt was bitterness and annoyance.

"What do they want?" he asked General McLeu and Captain Wyndham who entered behind him. The general looked pallid and emaciated; he sometimes lapsed into bouts of incoherent muttering and rambling and had occasional fainting spells, but the King continued to leave him in command of the army. Owain's respect for the man's knowledge and the loyalty he had shown the Crown for many years had kept Ferghus employed, though both knew that arrangement might not last much longer.

"They are waiting for their leader to arrive," the general muttered.

"Can we move them?"

Ferghus shook his head. "Any attempt to do so may result in a riot." He was in no frame of mind, or health, to combat a riot, and from the size of the gathered crowd, he could see no good coming from such a confrontation.

"Then we may have to have a riot," the King growled. "I want that mob gone by noon."

Captain Wyndham, disliking the general's defeatist attitude clicked his heels in salute and said, "It will be done."

But efforts to open the gates, to get a single man across the bridge, failed, and by noon, the throng was still there. None in the crowd had made effort to stand on or cross the bridge. From the King's vantage point, the crowd appeared to have grown larger. He spotted clubs, threshing forks, spears, poles, and other large tools among them, leading him to believe the crowd's intent was less than peaceful. Maybe they did not plan an attack, but they were at least prepared for one should the King threaten violence. He knew, as General McLeu had indicated, that the forty soldiers currently within the keep would not suffice to dispel such a mob. They needed reinforcements they could not get because they could not get a message out. Shortly before dusk, as torches began to flicker in the midst of the crowd, a message came at last. The mob's leader had arrived and wished to speak with the princess.

All of this to allow another beggar or peasant to visit Deidre? It might have been laughable if being held hostage in his own home was not so infuriating. The story of the boy Deidre had invited into the palace must have spread widely and now every unfortunate in the kingdom would want to meet her. There was little harm in allowing her to interface with his subjects; the King was smart enough to know that such interactions would work in his favor, show his benevolence. And though he did not fear for her safety, as he knew she was well-loved and well received by everyone, he could not allow this sort of fiasco every time someone wished to see her. Something else had to be done.

He sent a message back demanding that the crowd disperse before he would consider allowing such a meeting. The mob leader replied that he would not send the crowd away for fear that the King would harm him without their backing. He would have the crowd draw back, however, and meet her at the end of the bridge, accompanied by guards if the King wished it.

Though still annoyed, the King was also amused that a peasant, for that was surely what he was, would flatter himself in this fashion. Because he wanted the crowd gone before morning in order that he could ride, he agreed to the request, selected ten soldiers and retainers to accompany his bride-to-be, and sent word to the princess that her presence was requested on the bridge.

At the castle gate, the crowd drew back as agreed, forming a semi-circle around their chosen leader, about fifteen feet away from him. He waited at the lip of the bridge, keeping a watchful eye on the towers for any sign of impending attack. His lean frame might have indicated hunger, and the patch over one eye and a dirty rag tied around his head made him appear older and frailer than he was. Beside him, the young-ster he had recruited for his ability to communicate through hand ges-tures stood wide-eyed and shaking. This was the closest the child had ever been to the castle, and he had never dreamed of meeting a princess. He was as excited as he was wary of the same threats his employer feared. They waited for the princess's arrival, the older man hoping she would agree to what he had in mind. It was a long shot, one that could get him killed, and he knew how dangerous this could be for those behind him. They knew it too. If all went as he hoped, though lives could be lost, something far more crucial could be gained. Precious time for Prince Arlan and his growing army of supporters.

The gate eventually groaned open, metal and wood scraping through well-worn tracks over the stones, and the princess, after pausing to look at the great mob of people before her, hesitantly crossed the moat with the ten armed guards behind her. The man and child moved forward to greet her, and as they moved, the mob moved too, maintaining their fifteen-foot perimeter. After another glance at both watchtowers, he lifted the child onto his hip and began whispering his words to the boy who signed them to the deaf princess in return.

The sudden flurry of attention she had received over the last few days both fascinated and flattered the young woman. She often received gifts from nobles and dignitaries throughout the Teren kingdoms, usually attached to hopes that a marriage could be arranged that would put them in good stead with the King, but it had never been like this. Yesterday it had been three bouquets of flowers, a silver tray of pastries, and a small music box with poems inside. Today it was this mob with its half-blind leader. She smiled at him, flushed at his initial compliments, and began the awkward conversation.

There was small talk at first, inquiries of health, happiness, and fortune. He addressed the plight of the mass behind him, the suffering of the poor, and she offered to assist them in any way she could. She had access to money and influence with lords and merchants, all of which could be used in favor and support of the suffering poor. She paused as she digested his next, more surprising question, and regretfully shook her head. "No…I cannot marry you…I am already betrothed," she signed back, wondering why that admittance made her feel sadder than usual. "Still, I thank you for your offer, sir…"

The child relayed the reply as he was set back on the ground and the mob leader raised his right hand to his head as if in some sort of salute. From his high vantage point, the King could not tell what he was doing, but something suddenly felt amiss. He had been focused on watching the princess, on making sure the stranger did not harm her, and like the guards around her, did not immediately notice the encroaching nearness of the mob. King Owain realized what was happening and gave a shout to the men on the bridge, as the mob leader's hand snapped down. People from within the crowd swarmed in, grabbing the Princess, their leader, and the child, and pulled them into their midst as the ten guards began to fight and arrows rained down from the gate towers and walls. Those shots were cautious, however, as none wanted to accidentally harm Deidre, and the ten soldiers on the bridge were ineffective against such a mob. The rabble stormed forward, pressing towards the inner entry, forcing their way into the outer towers with whatever crude weapons they possessed. The mob leader was swept along by the throng with the child in his arms; when he was a safe distance from the castle and the chaos created there, he set the child down, took up the sword and shield someone thrust into his hands, and charged back into the fray.

More guards began to pour from within the castle, but the gate towers had now been taken, and those who knew how to use the captured bows were shooting at the King's men with no real accuracy, keeping them from crossing the moat, confining them to the castle. A horn sounded and the soldiers retreated as the inner gates were closed and barred. The King and castle were safe, but the moat and gate towers belonged to Rhidam's poor. For the next several hours, until late into the night, the crowd continued to hurl rocks, flaming torches, and rotten food across the moat at the ancient stone fortress of their King.

Having seen it all from the second story window, the King was even more furious when Captain Wyndham arrived to report Deidre's capture. There had never been a reason to believe the beloved princess would be at risk, and though the captain tried to assure him that there was no cause yet to believe she was being harmed, Owain continued to berate himself for being duped, for having dared to put his trust in the people he ruled.

"We are doing what we can to drive them off," the captain was trying to calmly assure him, "but until we can get word out…"

"Then get word out!" the King roared. "I don't care how! Find her, bring her to me, and bring me the head of the man who dared defy me. If you have to kill the entire mob, then do it!"

୭ * ଓ

Deidre looked up with fright as a shadowy figure entered the room. Other than bruises on her arms from those who had jostled her out of the melee and dragged her here, no one had harmed her or even spoken to her. Still, as she huddled alone in the dark, cluttered room that smelled of dust and rot, she was afraid. More afraid than she had ever been of the King, though this place reminded her very much of a dungeon. Her fear intensified as the stranger moved about the room, lighting lamps. It was the one-eyed mob leader. He carried with him a paper, stylus, and ink, and when he sat across from her, he removed both the eye-patch and the rag that had covered his carrot-red hair. To her amazement, it was the same youth who had given her the royal ring, the man connected to her brother. That news might have comforted her if not for her surroundings and the circumstances that had brought her here.

"I am Caol Dugan. Please, do not be afraid. I am sorry to have frightened you, but I did not know any other way to do this. The more I thought about you marrying the King, the worse I felt. When he

learns of Prince Arlan's plans, he may insist on marrying you immediately. I cannot allow that, both for your sake and the prince's."

They stared at each other for many quiet minutes. The princess did
not doubt his words, though she did not understand what significance
her marriage plans might possibly have on either Caol or her brother.

"You have placed yourself in great danger."

"I don't care. If I can postpone your marriage...or prevent it...it
will be worth any price. Your brother asked me to stir up trouble, provide the King with distractions to keep his attention away from the
prince...and this seemed the ideal way to do that. Hopefully, he will
be too busy trying to locate you; he will concentrate his efforts here in
Rhidam and not on what your brother and his army are doing."

Her posture and features relaxed as she read his words. "Where is
Arlan finding an army?"

"All over Enesfel. Peasants, townsmen...anyone who wants to
join us. There are some from Cordash and the Cíbhóló, and if Lord
McHador is successful, Hatu will send men too. The King will have
to accept Prince Arlan as a Lachlan and the heir to the throne or there
will be war."

Princess Deidre shook her head with a sigh and wrote, "Owain
will not want to do that."

Though it pained her to admit that, and Caol could see it, he could
not keep from grinning. "That is what I hope for." His grin faltered,
however, when she stared at him grimly, obviously not approving of
his thirst for war and blood.

"What do you want from me?"

Chastised by her gaze, he took the quill and replied, "I would ask
your aid...for myself and your brother. I can release you now if you
wish...I only ask that you protect me from the King. Or, you could
remain here with me as my prisoner for a short time. It is not noble
accommodations, but it is the best I can offer under the circumstances.
You are safe, and I will see that someone is always here to give you

everything you need. As long as the King is looking for you, his focus will be away from your brother…that is all I need. Once I think this game has played long enough, you will be escorted safely back to the castle."

She read his words as he wrote them, understanding what he intended without further explanation. This dark, dank room was frightening, but not nearly as much so now as the dungeon had been. She could endure this, especially if it meant seeing her brother again.

"Will you be in danger?"

Caol shook his head. "Don't worry about me. I can take care of myself. I'm doing this for your brother…and for Enesfel. Will you help us?"

Her fingers traced over the back of his hand as if memorizing their shape before she took the quill from him. "I will stay. Allow me to write a letter to Owain, telling him that I am unharmed…for now…I can give him your demands."

At first, Caol thought to object. He had not kidnapped her for a ransom. However, when he met her gaze and read the twinkle there, it made him grin. Not only was she willing to stay, he realized, she was offering to be an accomplice. After all, the King would be expecting a ransom demand. It was a logical choice. "Yes…that would be fun…and to our advantage. Here…let's see what we can do."

☙*❧

King Owain smoothed the parchment over his knee to counteract the document's natural curl, and muttered as he read the pristine, elegant handwriting he was so familiar with. The contents of the missive, the demands it contained, infuriated him, but his mood was tempered by the knowledge that Deidre was safe, and, if the steadiness of her handwriting was any indication, not overly frightened or threatened by her situation. It filled his heart with pride to see how strong she had become and to know he was responsible, although when he thought about how she had gained that strength, because of his cruelty and temper, he also felt shame. The combination of conflicting emotions brought sporadic twitching to the corner of one eye and to the muscles along his jaw.

"One hundred thousand crowns…" he grunted, "twenty of my finest horses…one must be white…twenty swords…unhindered passage to the desert…one thousand gemstones…permission to marry Deidre despite her refusal?" The more he read, the tenser his body grew, until he stood up in a huff, allowing the parchment to fall to the floor. "Since when do peasants resort to blackmailing their King?"

General Ferghus stooped to retrieve the letter as the King stalked away and read the message himself. "You are certain this is the Lady's hand?" he asked, although he already knew the answer.

"Of course I am certain! Writing is the only way I can communicate with her, after all. What is it this fellow really wants, Ferghus?"

"I don't know, My Liege…I think his motives speak for themselves." Judging by the page held between his fingers, the fellow's demands looked obvious, but it seemed that the King believed there was more to it than what was written.

"This is preposterous! He must know she would refuse such a proposal from a penniless peasant. There is something more…"

Watching the King pace, the general started again, "Perhaps if we wait for another message…"

"And risk her life? No. That won't do. She seems to be safe…but for how long? Free passage to the desert I can grant, twenty swords is a simple thing…and though it would pain me to part with the horses, those could be replaced. But one hundred thousand crowns? One thousand gemstones? That is ridiculous!"

"Perhaps he would be willing to negotiate. If he is in some sort of desperate predicament that has driven him to action…tell him what you can offer and see if he will accept your terms."

Owain grunted again and yanked the parchment from the older man's hand with a "Humph." He gestured towards the State Room and stormed in that direction without looking back. "Find the chancellor and chamberlain and sit with me. We must decide what we can realistically offer. I must get her back, General. Whatever the cost."

&Chapter 35&

I t had been decided. After two days of intensive deliberation, despite every means Kavan had to persuade them, the Káliel Council almost unanimously denied Prince Arlan's request for harbor and supplies for the warships from Hatu. On their second day of deliberation, Kavan appeared before the collection of fifteen men, most of who were bearded, elderly, and dressed in silks and velvets that put them above the station of common people. He knew before he began, from the mostly haughty or detached expressions on many of the faces in that chamber, that his mission was doomed to failure, but he had been determined to try. Lord Dilyn expressed his regrets and apologies and publically chastised the Council for their cool and ungracious welcome, yet when he offered to extend Kavan's visit for as long as the bard cared to remain on the islands, Kavan declined. His decision had nothing to do with any lack of welcome or lack of success of his mission. The main reason was that the prince's cause could wait no longer. Kavan needed to return to Arlan.

The other reason was more personal, and one Kavan would never speak of to the Prime Magistrate. He could never admit discomfort around the man's daughter. Thankfully she had been kept away by her aunt's poor health, but the constant apprehension of expecting her return was eating at Kavan's stomach so that he could barely keep food down. Blaming Gabrielle for his departure would be impolite and foster discord. It was enough to say that it was time to rejoin Prince Arlan. The fishing boat he had chartered would sail in the morning.

With his bundle of belongings ready for departure, Kavan looked at the harp in the dusky lamplight of the dining hall. Lord Dilyn had offered it to him, at Gabrielle's insistence, he was certain, but Kavan respectfully refused the gift. There was no practical way to transport an instrument of this size during the weeks that lay ahead. Besides, even if no one in the family could play it, such an heirloom should remain with the family, a testament to some part of their history. Still, it was a beautiful instrument, and without his own harp to ease his spirits, this one would do; he sat, adjusted his position, and played a few simple melodies, quietly to avoid waking those who had already turned in for the night. The thought of sailing, however, made Kavan restless and unable to sleep, and so the music became his solace. When there came a quiet knocking at the door, unexpected in the near empty villa, he lifted his head, let his hands still on the strings, and called softly, "Come."

The door cautiously slid open as if to avoid making a sound, and a slim figure in a sheer linen gown slipped into the room. "Gabri…" he choked, more startled by her filmy attire than by her actual presence. She raised her fingers to her lips for silence and then closed the door behind her.

"Quiet," she whispered. "Father must not know I am here. I did not know if you would still be here until I heard the harp." She smiled as she approached, but the look in her eyes was serious. "What of the vote?"

"We will not be stopping at Káliel for supplies." He barely managed to speak and had to keep his eyes averted as she drew nearer.

"As I anticipated. Those old men are fools." She had reached him now but kept distance between them. "When will you leave?"

"The boat is in the harbor; I will leave before dawn."

"Then it is good I came tonight. I told you, you would see me again." She smiled, ignoring the fact that the look made him squirm.

"Your aunt?"

"Was asleep when I left. I bid one of the servants to sit with her while I came…I told her a suitor was leaving the islands and I wanted to say farewell…" There was a twinkle in her eye as Kavan inched away in embarrassment. He did not consider himself a suitor, but he had surmised that she viewed him as such. "Would you prefer to avoid the trip at sea?"

Thankful for the change of subject, he nodded. "I would prefer any method of travel over boats."

She offered her hand. "Then come with me and bring your things." She was not surprised that he stood without taking her hand, and made sure to put his pack of belongings in the hand between them so that she could not take his. His defensive caution made her smile wider as she again motioned for silence, opened the door, and led him towards her father's office. The full moon shown through the windows, light filtering through the waving tree boughs danced on the floor as they entered. The window was open, allowing a fragrant breeze to swirl around them, thick with the perfume of blooming night flora. When the office door was closed, Gabrielle pointed at another door to their right.

"There," she whispered.

He stared at her. "A closet?"

"You doubt me?" she giggled. "How else do you think I come and go without my father's knowledge?"

Curious despite his skepticism, he opened the door and peered inside but saw nothing unusual save for its large size. Its shelves held books and scrolls, as well as a few wicker baskets and small wooden chests, and one wall was lined with a row of pegs for hanging cloaks. There was only one way, he realized, this could be to his benefit, and he cast outward with his senses until he found a familiar prickle of power he had not expected and thus had not looked for.

"A Gate? How…?"

Gabrielle's smile was now one of a girl pleased with herself. "You have not tried to read me."

"I believe in a person's privacy." He knew he would never trust himself, or her, to touch her for a reading.

"Particularly your own." She giggled again. "Yes, I have tried…but I quickly gave up. You shield your thoughts, milord, too well for me at least. My mother was Elyri…though Father apparently did not know it. I do not know how he could not have known; there are some differences you cannot hide." She laughed when his expression indicated he did not know what differences she referred to, but she did not elaborate.

"When it began to be obvious that she was not aging as he was, she could not bear the thought of seeing him wither and die, and she feared telling him the truth…and feared the Council, I suspect, and thus she staged her death. I know it was staged, but she never told me what she would do after…where she would go. If she lives, I do not know where she is or how to find her. She was not very gifted…or so she claimed…but when she realized I carried some of the talents, she taught me to use a few of them. Unfortunately, my Teren blood is proving to be a problem."

Intrigued by her story, Kavan set aside the uneasiness he felt in her company and sat beside her on the door-side bench. "How so?" She smelled clean and warm, and he could see the gentle rise and fall of her chest as she breathed; the effect of both was hypnotic, holding him there as she shrugged and shifted to face him with her knee pressed lightly against his. For once, he did not attempt to move away.

"I've never been very gifted, but I can read people…project basic images and emotions…and operate the Gates. Over the last few years, however, it seems the more I use the Gates, the harder it gets to do. It's like…" Her face scrunched in thought. "Like the ability is fading. I thought it should be the other way, that it would be easier the more I did it. I have not heard of any other Elyri-Teren children; I have nothing to compare myself to. I suspect that eventually I will not be able to operate them. It takes nearly a minute now to achieve the proper results. While I still can, however, I want to use it to help you and your prince."

"Help us?"

"By leading you to this Gate to start with. I can at least spare you seasickness." She giggled again. "There is a Gate in the náós in Natrona; do you think you can make that connection, or shall I show you?"

The sudden thought of her hands touching his made him shake his head. "No…I can do it."

"Good." If she was disappointed, she did not show it. "I also pledge you the supplies you need, if you still desire them."

"You…how…?"

She patted his knee, and only then did he move his leg away from hers. "Let me worry about how. Sail your ships to the east side of the island. There is a sheltered cove there that fishermen sometimes use. I will arrange to have two boats waiting for you with the things you require. I hope it will be enough. Any more than two will look suspicious. My father will not know about this, nor will the Council…if they did, they certainly won't approve. You will need to sail into the cove at night, with no lights. If I fail…there will be no boats there and you are to sail on."

The bard bowed his head at this unexpected generous turn. "You are most kind and daring, milady; I do not know why you risk yourself in this manner…but I thank you on Prince Arlan's behalf."

"I do it because I like you…and because I think your cause is just," she quickly added, deciding to spare him further embarrassment. "I will send a message and payment to your fishing boat and tell them you have no need of their services. I can deal with my father if he discovers me here; being the only child has its advantages, particularly when you are the only daughter of a powerful, doting man." She grinned and stood. "Do not worry about me. You must go because I should return to Jaffe and I have much to accomplish here before I do. Take these." She gave him a cloth sack containing two heavy wine jugs. "A parting gift since you will not take the harp. I shall have it to remember you by. I will probably never see you again, milord, but if you are successful in your endeavors, I bid you send word to let me know."

Flustered, nearly speechless, Kavan bowed his head and replied, "I shall, milady, I swear it."

After some hesitation, warring between wanting to remain with her when he knew he should not, and needing to do his duty to Prince Arlan, Kavan rose from the bench, lifted both of his sacks over his shoulder, and turned towards the closet. Gabrielle caught his arm, pulled him around, pressed herself against him, and kissed him soundly on the mouth. Stunned, Kavan's free hand moved impulsively to the curve of her waist, where the flesh beneath sheer fabric was warm and soft. The moment could not last, however; alarmed by the fire that welled up within and spread throughout his body, Kavan pushed her away with a gasp and fled to the safety of the Gate. The closet door swung shut behind him with a crack. Shaken and dazed, it took several attempts to establish a link with the Gate in Natrona's náós. He was tremendously relieved to find himself within the comfort of holy walls, but for many terrifying minutes, he remained unmoving, half fearing, half anticipating that Gabrielle would materialize behind him to assault his senses again.

She did not.

He stumbled into the sanctuary, avoiding the dusty eyes of the carved figure of Dhágdhuán that hung on the wall behind the altar, and found his way to the thóres. There was no way he could bring himself to face Guthrie or anyone else tonight, thus he sought refuge where he was. The building had been unused for centuries; there were no furnishings, no lights save the moonlight that pierced through cracks in the ceiling and cut the darkness. There was little danger of being discovered here. Kavan curled into a corner, arms wrapped around him, his cloak pulled tight for warmth, and lay staring numb and dazed into the night. It was a long while before he slept.

❧*❧

Restless, Guthrie sighed and stopped pacing long enough to open the window and gaze across the now familiar field behind Hatu's royal house. He had spent nearly every waking minute of the last seventeen days on that field, drilling Hatu's cavalry, schooling them in some of the finer points of mounted warfare, a feat Hatu's military had never been good at. If Enesfel ever went to war against Hatu again, their forces would be more evenly matched, provided these men retained and continued to teach what Guthrie shared with them. But both he and Prince Arlan agreed that such a risk was necessary as insurance against King Owain and Enesfel's army. Besides, the prince intended to maintain peaceful relations with King Geir and his successors once he was welcomed into Rhidam.

Hatu's cavalry had been slow to understand at first, being so entrenched in their own military training that they found it difficult to grasp the advantages of what the general was trying to teach them. With encouragement, however, they gradually began to master the few points he showed them, and now Guthrie felt more confident of their chances against King Owain's military if it came to a fight. They would drill again today, but Guthrie was eager to depart Hatu. There had been no news from Enesfel, not even rumors, to stir him, but Kavan's prediction that something disastrous would befall their prince nagged at the general until he had difficulty sleeping most nights.

The fishing boat Kavan intended to use docked in Hatu's harbor with word that he had found other transport, but thus far, the bard had not been seen. Had Kavan been successful with his plea and remained on the island to make arrangements, Guthrie wondered, or had he remained to continue to persuade the reclusive islanders to change their minds? Guthrie wished he knew so that he and King Geir could plan accordingly.

There was a knock on the doorframe behind him, the hollow sound of knuckles on plaster that the general was still not used to. His room here, indeed the entire keep, was starker, more inauspicious than Rhidam's castle, made of earthen brick and lumber instead of stone and mortar. The outer walls were strong enough, the general knew that from experience, but the interior walls seemed to him barely able to withstand battle, should the castle be put to siege. It caused him to wonder how much more Enesfel might have to offer Hatu, should this relationship of cooperation continue. There was nothing lavish about Hatu, but after months of traveling, it was comfortable, and in an odd way, Guthrie would be sorry to leave the palace and its comforts.

The squire was flushed and breathless as he stepped into the room. "Lord McHador, the King requests your presence in the State Room."

Good, the general thought. Something to occupy his time. As long as it was not bad news, he was looking forward to whatever the King wanted. To the squire, he nodded and said, "I will be there. Thank you."

ॐ*॰

Camp had been quiet since the unit set up here days ago; despite their inactivity and the lack of information they received about the movements of King Owain's forces, there had been few complaints in the ranks other than the occasional shortage of some commodity or other, or the usual brawls and skirmishes that idle men were sometimes prone to. The stream that ran through the nearby ravine offered them abundant water, and there were enough capable hunters and woodsmen among them that there was little danger of starvation. The occasional messengers sent back and forth to Seres brought supplies too. Still, on nights such as this when the men were quiet, many asleep, others talking and drinking around the fires, Prince Arlan wished to be anywhere other than where he was.

Ártur claimed that it was the prince's willingness to endure the same hardships as his men that accounted for the low number of complaints. It was a rare member of any royal house who would set aside comforts and luxuries to be on the same footing as the men he was asking to fight and die for him. King Donal had been the only other man the healer had known able to lower himself and his station that way. Not even King Innis had done it. When Donal Lachlan had gone into the field, it had been as a soldier, never as a prince. Of course, that had been before he had become King. After that, it had changed, largely due to his success at ending the war with Hatu. Arlan often wondered if he would be able to do the same if he became King one day and was forced into war.

Become King. That thought still made him either want to laugh hysterically or else run back to Elyriá to the safety of Brenna and the baby. He was confident he could rule; Guthrie and Kavan had instilled that confidence in him and taught him well. After hearing the reports and rumors about the way King Owain ruled, the prince believed he could do no worse than the current monarch. Still, he clung to the desire he had voiced to Kavan long ago, to stay in the tranquility of the forest, raising a family, oblivious to the rest of the world. Such a life was the one he claimed to long for. But deep down, he also desired to follow his calling, live up to the legacy of the royal name and blood he carried, to accomplish the things he knew his father and mother had expected of him. The two diametrically opposed life goals could not be had simultaneously. He had chosen this responsibility, and would now have to live with that choice. There was no turning back. None of those men around him who had placed their faith in him would ever be able to accuse him of abandoning them or his heritage. He could not allow their faith, and the sacrifices being made for him, to be unrewarded.

ॐ*ॐ

Caol paced the small room, reading the King's message aloud though he knew Deidre could not hear him. Saying them out loud, hearing both the King's words and his own thoughts, helped him to problem solve more effectively, although it was often a luxury he could not allow. Some thoughts were better left unspoken.

"He'll give us the swords and ten horses and allow me passage to the desert...right. He'll waylay me on the road somewhere to take them back and leave me for dead, a victim of bandits. I know how that works. But no gems? No crowns? What sort of fool does he take me for?"

Frustrated, he plopped down at the table across from his willing hostage and began drafting a response as he continued to talk to himself. "Fifteen horses and the swords are to be brought to the gate towers, where one of my men will take them. If they are there tomorrow, and my agent is not harassed, I will release control of the towers. Any attempt to search the city afterward, and any deaths resulting from such a search, will mean that he will never see you again. However..." He lifted his head and smiled mischievously. "To gain your release, he will have to supply one hundred gems and fifty thousand crowns. That should be more to his liking...more suited to his coffers."

The princess watched him write, though she could not read it from where she sat, and though she did not know what he was saying, she could read his excitement and found it contagious. His smile made her shiver, for once not out of fear but out of anticipation. His small, nimble hands deftly rolled the parchment and tied it with a dirty string before he got to his feet, still talking.

"You will not get off easily, my King." Those words, as he looked straight at her, were understood, as was his smirk. "And even if he does, it will take a little more time and negotiation. I am not ready to relinquish my prize yet."

He lifted her hand, pressed his lips to her knuckles in a way that made her fingers curl and tighten around his, and with another, gentler smile, he left in search of his messenger.

❧*☙

Cold, gray morning sunlight stretched its fingers through the windows, warming the chill of the library, but it did little to improve Guthrie's first impressions of the pale man who sat near one window staring across the horizon. The bard did not look well; his eyes were dark and haunted and his face and hands seemed gaunter than usual. The ex-general settled his large frame into a chair as close to the Elyri as he dared, knowing the man had difficulty with people invading his personal space, and rested his chin on his hands before speaking.

"When the boat returned without you, I'll admit I was concerned, Kavan. You found another I take it?"

"I discovered a Gate," Kavan replied quietly, still staring out the window. "Sea travel does not agree with me."

The general frowned but understood. He did not enjoy travel by sea either. "Neither did Káliel from the looks of it. How did it go? You weren't imprisoned and beaten again, were you?" Such a notion would not be in keeping with what he knew about the islands and their relationship with Elyriá, but he found it hard to believe that the bard's condition was solely due to seasickness.

"No. I was very well-treated, actually. Lord Dilyn..." He sighed. "The Council denied our request for aid." He did not wait for Guthrie to react before continuing. "Lord Dilyn's daughter, however, has promised to have one or two fishing vessels waiting for us in a cove on the east side of the island. She will see that our ships are supplied, against the wishes of her father and the Council."

The breath Guthrie had not realized he held gave way in a relieved rush. "Praise be...I have been having nightmares about what would happen if Káliel failed us. I can have the cavalry ready to depart by sunset; we can leave first thing tomorrow. By my calculations, it should take thirty-five days to reach Levonne...unless we encounter trouble."

Kavan's head nodded once. "You will."

With a grunt, Guthrie leaned back in his chair. "I expect so. Owain will not knowingly allow Hatu's cavalry to ride through his kingdom, even if we were to send an envoy ahead assuring him we are on a diplomatic mission. The nine ships King Geir has set aside are not the best, but they are seaworthy and should make it to Levonne in fourteen days, fifteen if you permit time to stop to resupply."

"Fifteen..." Kavan groaned as he rubbed his face. The very thought of another extended trip at sea made his stomach lurch and roll.

"Would you rather I go with the ships and you lead the land expedition?" It was an impractical suggestion, but a concession Guthrie felt compelled to make. Hopefully, Kavan would not take him up on it.

The bard shook his head. "No. I am not proficient in warfare; I could never effectively lead the cavalry in the event of battle...and the prince needs you with him. Lady Dilyn may expect me to be with the ships when they restock; it makes sense that I stay with them."

Feeling genuine pity for the man, as well as deep respect for what the bard was willing to endure on the prince's behalf, Guthrie clasped his shoulder with a nod of his head. "I will ask King Geir to supply something for your seasickness; his physicians must have something available. I have seen many infantrymen suffer at sea; you can bet you will not be the only one. The King will provide for his men."

The thought that he would not be the only one suffering was less reassuring than it should be. Preferring not to dwell on the sea or the sickness, he changed the subject. "Have you heard from Arlan?" Guthrie's hand dropped back into his lap. "No. I have not heard anything from Rhidam either, but news from there could take weeks to reach Hatu. I don't like not knowing what is happening." It was why he was eager to be on his way now that Kavan had returned.

Eyes turned to the window, towards the sea and Káliel, Kavan murmured, "I did hear one piece of possibly useful information. King Owain is due to marry before the end of this year. Speculation suggests he may marry King Ander's daughter, although with Nethite troops being in Enesfel without his knowledge, I am not sure I put stock in that rumor."

"On the other hand, if it is true, it would give King Ander every reason to send his forces…to secure his daughter's safety and try to secure favor with King Owain." Guthrie scowled. "I will get word of this to Arlan, and pray we arrive in Rhidam in time to stop it. Making an enemy of King Ander by harming his daughter is the last thing we need. Are there any other messages you would like to relay?"

Kavan shook his head. "Give them my regards…and tell them they are in my prayers. I intend to see everyone in Levonne."

"Very good." Standing with a stretch, eager to get about the day's business of travel preparations, he added, "I have to ready my things and see to the troops. Do you still want me to take your harp?"

As much as he longed to hold it, make music again, the bard nodded his head. "Yes. Please. I do not want to chance losing it at sea." Of course, there was a risk of it being damaged in a fight too, but at least there would be no sticky salty-sea air to cause damage. "Take these." From the pack at his feet, he produced the two bottles of wine. "I will not use them; perhaps you and the prince will appreciate them."

Guthrie smiled at the offering, the first Kavan had seen on the man since coming into the room. "We shall save them for our victory celebration," he proclaimed, clasping them to his chest. "If I do not see you again before morning, Kavan, k'Ádhá be with you and keep you safe."

"And you, milord. See to the prince's welfare...do not allow harm to befall him."

The smile faltered. Guthrie remembered Kavan's dire warning. If the prince had not already been harmed, there was still the possibility of that ahead of him whilst Kavan was away. "I will do my utmost." The ex-general intended to protect the prince with his own life.

๛*๛

Frustrated, and growing sicker and angrier with continual worry, the King growled at the two men with him. "So we have the bridge and the towers back. I've lost fifteen of my finest horses and enough swords to arm a small army! Have you no idea where he is keeping Deidre?"

Captain Wyndham shook his head. The gates had only just been opened; how the King could expect results immediately, the captain did not know. "None thus far, milord. This is the first time we have been able to leave the keep to look. We lost the child sent with his message, and those we have spoken with do not seem to know his whereabouts. The beggars and vagrants will not knowingly betray one of their own without us offering them something in return. I can have some interrogated...bribed...if you wish? We have begun questioning the pilgrims too, but thus far to no avail."

"I suspect," Ferghus McLeu said between coughs, "they are hiding outside of the city. The men who took the horses went northwest, to the other side of the river. The animals are reportedly under heavy guard by several Cíbhóló nomads…"

"Nomads?" The King's distress, as he stood to face his advisors, was undeniable. The dark-skinned nomads rarely came deep into Enesfel or any other Sovereignty except as traders. Being known as ruthless, fearless fighters, nearly every ruler in every kingdom tried to recruit nomads into their forces. None had, as far as King Owain knew, succeeded. These men could be traders, as such groups did occasionally come to Rhidam from the desert, but from the look on Ferghus' face, even a trading group was something to be watched, especially if they were guarding the ransom spoils. There were too many pieces on the playing board now, and the King had no idea whose side any of them were on anymore. "What…how long have…oh…never mind. Someone find out what they're doing here…what they want." He rubbed his red face. "There are no further demands?"

General McLeu nodded. "None since your last reply. Perhaps he has left…"

"Without sending Deidre back? Oh…" The King was about to burst in a fury of worry when a knock on the door interrupted. "What?" Owain barked. A young soldier entered, bowed, and stood trembling before him. Ferghus got the immediate impression that this was the bearer of bad news, although perhaps the man's fear had to do with the King's current red-faced mood.

"Pardon the intrusion, Your Majesty. I have arrived from Nelori with distressing news; there has been a mass movement of troops within Hatu."

"Not drills?" asked Ternce as he straightened in his chair. Across from them, the King's tension spiked. In times past, Hatu had often been known to drill troops near the Enesfel border to remind their northern neighbor not to trifle with them. None in the room believed this man had ridden all of this way merely to announce drills, however.

"No...Sire. That was what we thought, at first, but our sources indicate that their infantry has converged in Natrona, and their cavalry was last seen moving into Kílyn with many days of provisions."

"What are their numbers?" asked the King, already calculating what his odds and advantages were. Hatu was not known for having an extensive or well-trained military. What the kingdom was known for was tenaciousness and stubbornness.

"There was no count when I left, Sire. They were moving about in small units, still arriving when I was dispatched...I don't believe anyone had gotten near enough to make an accurate assessment..."

General Ferghus bobbed his head, almost as if he was falling asleep while the soldier gave his report. "Not their usual tactics, Sire...but they have never had much of a cavalry; perhaps they are trying new training exercises...their horses are not well-suited for battle, and as you know, they have never been successfully deployed in mounted warfare. If they intend war, routing their cavalry should be a relatively simple matter."

"Simple, perhaps," agreed the King with a snort, "But we cannot afford to send many troops. More than a third of our forces are monitoring the Neth border."

"They will have to be recalled, Sire." Ternce shifted in his chair, uncomfortable with giving such ultimatums to his monarch. "Hatu may be unskilled at warfare, but they are persistent. If it is what they are planning, they will not easily surrender..."

The King sighed and rubbed his eyes. He knew his captain was right, but he also knew he could not leave the northern border open to his uncle's whims. "General Ferghus, take half of the available troops..."

Ternce bristled and a shadow crept over his face. "With all respect, Sire, the general's health is not good; he should not be in the field."

"He is the expert on Hatu's tactics..."

The old general shrugged his shoulders. "Send Lord Wyndham…or Captain Cornell." He tried to look and sound disappointed at his inability to lead the troops. There was no reason to connect Hatu's upheaval to Guthrie McHador, and Ferghus felt compelled to protect his King, but the Captain was right. He was in no condition to go to war. He was relieved but disappointed with the captain's intercession to keep him off the battlefield. "I have taught them both all I know about Hatu, and Captain Cornell fought against them during King Donal's reign. There is no reason either of them should be unable to carry out this mission without me."

The King got up from the table to pace as he pondered the idea, weighing the pros and cons of what his closest advisors were suggesting. He knew the man of whom Ferghus spoke, had been the one to promote him to captain, and knew him to be strong and capable. But was sending him out in command in this instance the wisest choice?

It seemed to be the only one that made sense. "Tell Captain Cornell he will lead our forces against Hatu, if necessary. Lord Wyndham, I want you to gather our forces from the northern border, bring them here, and have them ready in case Captain Cornell needs reinforcements. Lord General, you will find and retrieve the princess. Deal with these matters quickly, gentlemen. I do not have time for this nonsense." Almost as an afterthought, as he prepared to dismiss them, he asked the question that had been one of the main reasons for this meeting. "Has there been any further word about the roving band supposedly led by McHador?"

His advisors exchanged a glance and Ternce shook his head, his expression dour. "They were last seen south of Seres several weeks ago, a small group said to have crossed into the mountains into the desert."

The desert meant more nomads, but perhaps that had been the target all along, since other splinter groups had been reported as having crossed into the desert. It took them far out of the King's reach, and thus were one less thing to worry about. "Good…it appears they are out of our way. Get to work, gentlemen. Oh…and General Ferghus, check on my mother. She may have knowledge that will shed light on some of these events, and I want to know her condition."

"Yes, My Liege."

The two advisors stepped into the corridor, as did the messenger, though he went in a separate direction. When they were out of the King's range of hearing, Ternce cleared his throat. "Do you believe Captain Cornell can effectively handle Hatu's military?"

Ferghus looked at the other man skeptically. "I see no reason why he cannot. He is bright, energetic, and a natural leader. The men like him, you know that. He knows everything I, and Guthrie McHador, were able to teach him…and he has experience fighting Hatu. You do not…and as you say, I shouldn't be out there in battle…not this time. You know he will do well. Have faith."

The younger officer side-eyed the general as they walked. There was something about the man's behavior and demeanor that troubled him but he could not pinpoint what it was. There was a method to his madness, or at least his ailment, perhaps. Concerned about how this perception might affect the kingdom, both due to Ferghus' peculiarities or his own distrust and perhaps over-wariness, Ternce was determined to get to the bottom of the situation. In order to investigate, however, he was going to have to avoid arousing anyone's suspicions. "I have to go to the cellar for supplies to travel. I can check on the Lady whilst I am there; you can concentrate on finding her royal majesty…and instructing Captain Cornell of course."

It was the General's turn to be suspicious, but he shrugged the concern away. If Ternce chose to do something stupid like play liaison between the King's mother and King Ander, bringing Neth further into conflict with the King, Owain would never allow the man to serve again. The captain would be lucky to escape without accusations of treason and execution. It would not upset Ferghus to have Ternce

Wyndham removed from the ranks. In spite of his capabilities, the captain rubbed the general the wrong way and he would rather not have to deal with him.

"Very well. Have a safe journey, Captain…and return quickly. If for any reason, I am wrong in my assessment of Captain Cornell, you may be needed sooner than expected."

He did not see the puzzled, concern expression that crossed Captain Wyndham's face as they parted, but he did not need to see it to know it was there. His face would have looked much the same way if someone had issued such a warning to him.

❧Chapter 36❧

G uthrie had not felt right about his men's unimpeded progress for several days. He had plotted their route so that his four hundred horsemen, sixty or so grooms and servants, five field surgeons, two captains, and one sergeant could avoid major centers of inhabitation as they pushed into Enesfel's heartland. He had chosen this route in order to avoid confrontation while continuing to expect it. But even now, as they camped a half day's ride west of the city of Kilmacud, there was no sign of the opposition he anticipated and he was uncertain if this was a matter of good fortune or one of foreboding.

Prince Arlan and the main body of men were due to join them within eight days. Once that happened, Guthrie felt confident they could hold off the bulk of Owain's army when confrontation came, or at least be able to avoid all out slaughter. Right now, without Kavan's uncanny foresight and comforting presence, Guthrie felt vulnerable. He kept a quarter of his forces awake and alert at all times as they waited. Though the terrain here was flat and open, with few trees or hills to shield them, he did not want to risk a surprise attack. The men slept without tents and lit no fires once night fell. There was no singing, no merry-making, and no commotion that might carry over great distances in the night. Instead, they kept as near to silent as they could manage.

The diligent watch paid off. Shortly after dawn on the sixth day, the posted sentries spotted the large mounted force riding towards them in the distance from the north. The first two hundred men were mounted and away swiftly, while the remainder were roused and prepared to join what would likely be an ugly skirmish.

When they came within sight of the other cavalry force, the flag-bearer carried the Lachlan standard, telling Guthrie that King Owain had been pushed to arms. Prince Arlan's last chance to turn back was behind them. He did not recognize the crest on the lead horseman's shield, however. It was not the King's crest, and it was not Ferghus McLeu's. Both sides brought their followers to a halt, each assessing the other for weaknesses; Guthrie rode forward to meet the leader alone.

"Your men bear the flag of Hatu," said the other man whose approach was more hesitant than Guthrie's. "But your bearing on your horse is not. Who are you? What is your purpose in Enesfel?"

Guthrie could have lied. It would have been easy, with the majority of his forces still far back out of sight, to claim to be on a diplomatic mission to see the King and thus tried to win over the opposition. But as he tried to place the familiar voice, he chose not to lie. This was no time for subterfuge. This was time to put their fortitude to the test. "Do I know you, soldier?"

The other man was having the same sense of déjà vu. He was supposed to proceed to the border, prepared to confront Hatu's troops there. No one had anticipated Hatu's soldiers pushing into Enesfel. They never had before. And the speaker's voice was familiar, although he could not immediately place it. Against his better judgment, feeling that his opponent deserved a respectful answer though he could not explain why, he replied, "Minos of Theron, sir."

Within his helmet, Guthrie smiled. "Ah...Duke Cornell...I re-member you. You have advanced far in the ranks of the Bastard King..."

"A child of King Innis is no bastard," Duke Cornell exclaimed indignantly.

"King Owain is not a child of King Innis. Ask him. He will not deny it." Such a claim was a gamble, but Guthrie believed it to be true. Spoken with assured convictions, he hoped the Duke would take his words on faith. "As advisor and truest friend to King Innis, I swear to you that which sits on Enesfel's throne is no son or heir to what was his." As he finished, Guthrie removed the helmet in order to fix his gaze on the other man.

He did not need to remove the helmet, however, for the Duke to know who he was. Words crashed together with the familiarity of his voice to paint a vivid picture in the Duke's mind, revealing who he was toe to toe with this day. "Lord General McHador!" Despite the fact that Guthrie no longer held that title, it was the one most had known him by, and it rolled off the Duke's tongue without prompting. It came out in a surprised gasp and began to spread like fire behind him, but Captain Cornell quickly collected his wits. He had to or else there would be chaos in the ranks as others realized who stood before them. "The King will be pleased to know it is you...instead of Hatu's..."

"Pleased?" Guthrie laughed. "No, I do not think so. I think he will find the news disturbing. Particularly when you do not return from battle this day. I have no intention of allowing you escape. Be-sides...do you truly pay such homage to your King? Do you approve of his methods, of the way he treats his subjects? Surely you have no desire to see the slaughter of innocents, the stripping of Enesfel's lands and wealth to fill the royal treasury?" Noises behind him, and the nerv-ous shifting of the Duke on his horse, told Guthrie that the second third of his men had joined him, doubling the cavalry's size. "I can assure you a pardon from Prince Arlan if you choose to side with us now, Captain."

"Prince Ar…" The Duke's composure slipped again, and those men nearest him began to murmur amongst themselves. "Lord General," he continued, trying not to stammer, "I am but a soldier. My lot is to obey, to follow commands, not to question…"

"I thought I trained you better than that, Captain." Guthrie shook his head and replaced his helmet and adjusted his shield. They were small gestures, but ones that served as a prelude to combat, and the Duke reacted accordingly.

"I serve who I have sworn to serve," he growled. "You…"

"Have never sworn to serve King Owain, nor shall I. My loyalties lie with Prince Arlan as they did with his father before him, and with the people of Enesfel. If you consider it, I'm sure you will conclude you are in the wrong…"

"It is you who are wrong, bringing foreign forces to bear in our kingdom."

"They have only come to protect and serve. They did not come in search of war, only to see that Prince Arlan is welcomed back into the royal family as is his due."

Captain Cornell sighed. "I cannot grant you that, and while you lead foreign troops, I cannot allow you to pass, Lord General."

He might have said more, for surely they could send a messenger to the King with the request and settle the matter peacefully, but Guthrie was not about to take chances with the prince's life. "Then we shall have to force passage," he said. "Do not doubt I shall war with you, Duke Cornell. I have a duty to uphold as you do. I can still ride and wield this sword, and I shall. Do you care to test me?"

Perturbed that there seemed no chance of peaceful negotiations, the Duke spun his horse and started back to rejoin his troops. With a flick of his hand, Guthrie's cavalry, now numbered the full four hundred, lunged forward, a move that caught the captain unprepared. He swore, shouted to his men, and rode to meet the charge. He had not thought McHador would attack in this manner, not while his back was turned, against overwhelming odds. McHador had always espoused honor and caution in battle, had drilled it into his soldiers; Minos Cornell had been one of them. It was that training the ex-general would employ against the men he had once led into battle, and the captain realized too late that McHador had the experience to be able to fight outside of his training.

Horses and weapons crashed together in a wave of calculated chaos. McHador's troops were outnumbered nearly three to one, but being able to use Enesfel's training against them gave Guthrie and his cavalry an advantage. And as the opposing force became aware of whom they were fighting, both leaders felt the hesitation building in Enesfel's one thousand men. Captain Cornell realized quickly that under McHador's direction, Hatu's cavalry was more potent than the King or General Ferghus had anticipated. Who would have known that McHador and Hatu were in league together?

Torn between his duty to the crown, fighting a man he had always respected and almost feared, and the nagging feeling that if Prince Arlan was alive, McHador might be justified in his loyalties, the duke did not fight as effectively as he normally would have. He had heard the rumors of King Owain's true parentage; to hear McHador confess the same troubled him. Finally, out of frustration and uncertainty, he motioned to his standard-bearer.

The flag was dropped; his troops scattered.

Some one hundred or more men fled towards Rhidam. Seventy-five others lay battered and trampled beneath them. The fighting continued as more of Enesfel's soldiers spun in confusion, watching Captain Cornell fight first the enemy, and then his own men. Several sided with Guthrie McHador openly as soon as they realized who he was. Those who hesitated were cut down. The duke spurred his horse to the edge of the battlefield, hoping to regroup, but Guthrie followed, cutting through those who tried to hinder him.

In the end, the victory belonged to Guthrie and the Hatu cavalry. Those nearly eight hundred Enesfel cavalrymen who remained alive swore an oath to serve Prince Arlan and his general; they trusted McHador's honor and leadership and they did not want to return to Rhidam knowing what fate would likely await them there for their failure.

To Prince Arlan's benefit, Duke Minos Cornell also swore allegiance to his former mentor.

⍆*⍥

The princess read the words Caol had written and looked up at him with sadness. The King had relented to his demands; he would leave two thousand crowns at the bridge crossing at the edge of Rhidam; if it was there by sunset, as promised, Caol would be leaving Rhidam tonight.

"What will happen to me?" she wrote with a trembling hand and quivering lip.

Wondering at her reaction, if she was afraid he would not release her or was sad that he was leaving, Caol replied, "You will be escorted to the castle at dawn by ten children. No one will harm you…I swear it on my life. I will have enough people looking out for you along the way that I personally guarantee your safety."

"What if he insists on marriage…in the hopes of keeping me safe now…?"

That was something that Caol tried harder and harder not to think about. When it did spring into his mind, it filled him with sickness and rage. "Try to stall him. You said you could do it. I will ride to meet with Prince Arlan, who should be on his way to Rhidam now. Pretend you are ill, pretend this ordeal has been too distressing, anything that will put him off. We should be here soon, and I suspect with Hatu now on the march, the King will have more important things on his mind than marriage...but we cannot take chances. You will have to be strong, milady...I know you can do this."

Her fingers caressed his cheek. "Will you be safe?"

The gentleness of her touch and the gesture seemed to answer the questions about her intentions. He nodded, his expression embarrassed. "You don't need to worry about me." Unless I am double-crossed, he thought bitterly, choosing not to voice that concern. "I have protection on the way out of Rhidam. Hopefully, the prince is not far away." He covered her hand with his and then added, "I must go."

Her gaze lowered, her cheeks flushed at his touch, and then she wrote, "I will remember your people for what they have done for the kingdom. Please be careful. I will miss you."

Despite her affectionate gestures and her very real sadness, her words were a surprise. He brushed away the tears which formed at the corners of her eyes. He had never expected to fall in love with the princess. A man of his station...and royalty? He could not imagine a bigger mistake. Still, when she kissed his palm, he impulsively pulled her against him, his mouth meeting hers for the first time in a hungry, if hesitant, kiss. She allowed it until the strength of unfamiliar emotion frightened her, and she backed away, unable to stop her tears. He bowed stiffly and left the room without looking back. This could never work.

He did not see her blown kiss.

She did not see his tears.

❧*❧

Kavan stared beseechingly at the marble figure of Dhágdhuán in Natrona's ancient, decaying náós but received no response to his prayers. He had not left this building, had not moved from the altar unless it was necessary. His heart was heavy, his spirit empty, his mind dull. The energies did not come to him and he had no harp to beckon them. He considered making a pilgrimage to Kílyn, to the site of the martyrdom of Saint Kóráhm, hoping that might ease his conscience and appease k'Ádhá, but King Geir requested that he remain in Natrona in case the ships had to depart ahead of schedule. Nothing he had done could assuage the feelings of pain and guilt. He felt it was slowly killing him.

'k'Ádhá help me,' he thought, and then raised his eyes once more to the figure on the pyre. One hand firmly around the silver pendant at his throat, the other clenched into a tight fist on his lap, he moaned, "Gabrielle…why are you doing this to me?"

ॐ*ॐ

"She appears to be unharmed, My Liege, but she is complaining of stomach and head pains, and general weakness. That is understandable, considering her previous condition and what she has endured," explained the doctor as he put his tools back in his bag. "I recommend she be allowed to rest and recover."

The King was visibly relieved that she was not injured or abused in any way. He had endured constant nightmares during her abduction, his imagination conjuring all manner of suffering she could be facing. When he saw her coming across the bridge, he wept tears of joy and relief, and when she collapsed against him, he carried her here, swearing to himself that he would never again let her out of his sight.

"Did she say anything about who he was? What he did to her? Where he might be found?"

The doctor made a clucking sound and shook his head. "She knows very little, My Liege. She was kept in a dark room, thus could not provide an accurate description of anyone. He probably did not confide in her. Perhaps when she has had a chance to rest and regain her strength, her memory will improve."

"I pray so. I will have his head for this. May I see her?"

The doctor could see few reasons to deny the request, other than the King's well-known violent temper. Knowing better than to mention that, or to refuse him, he nodded. "Do not stay long; she needs to rest. And do not pressure her for details of her ordeal; it may drive them further from her recollections or drive her to madness." The King nodded in eager agreement though he was looking past the doctor, hoping for a glimpse of Deidre in that darkened room.

The physician left and General Ferghus remained in the King's chamber while the monarch entered the princess's room alone. She lay on her bed, curled into a tight ball, but when she saw him, she willingly accepted his embrace. He held her as she wept, pleased that she finally needed him for something.

The general, meanwhile, paced the King's chamber. Thus far, the mixture of fish oil and basil he was allergic to had enabled him to appear sufficiently ill to the doctors, and his feigned lapses of memory and incoherency had convinced the King that he could not serve efficiently on the battlefield. But for how much longer, he mused, now that they were certain that Guthrie McHador was alive?

Though the King had, rightfully, been furious with the defection of Captain Cornell and a large portion of Enesfel's cavalry, the general felt a grudging sense of admiration for the man. The Captain had not hesitated to act, even though it placed him at odds with the King. Captain Cornell had believed whatever Guthrie had told him, had joined the opposition, as had many other men. That many were willing to take the risk and follow McHador told Ferghus one thing. The ex-general must be telling the truth. Why, then, did he still find it hard to believe?

A message had been sent to Captain Wyndham to hasten the man's return from the northern border. Ferghus was torn between allowing Tymm Revaugn to ride with only fifteen hundred men, and warning the man that somewhere McHador likely had forces other than Hatu's cavalry and Captain Cornell's regiment to back him. The general wondered where those forces were, those so-called splinter factions that had gone into the desert, and he wondered how long it would be before King Owain insisted that, illness or not, Ferghus should lead Enesfel's troops against his mentor. He desperately hoped it would never come to that.

ॐ*⬧

Holding his right hand towards the kneeling man, Prince Arlan cleared his throat before speaking. "Welcome, Captain Cornell. Guthrie speaks highly of you. You are a welcome and valued addition to my ranks. I hope the Lord General has not been too harsh on you."

Captain Cornell, unable to believe his eyes, shook his head. This young man before him had to be a Lachlan; he was the precise image of King Innis in his youth and looked a great deal like King Donal. Any doubts he may have harbored were gone. "No more than I expected, Your Highness," he said with a bowed head. "That you are alive and here answers many of Enesfel's questions, and I am honored to be among those who have chosen to serve you."

"The honor is mine, Captain. You will have to tell me what I have missed in Rhidam once we are fit to travel. I know I have spent eight days in the saddle but I do not want to remain camped any longer than necessary. Our destiny is in sight. We must act if we are to seize it; we cannot risk the King hindering us."

Guthrie was relieved to hear the enthusiasm in the prince's voice. In the weeks they had spent apart, to his eyes Prince Arlan appeared to have grown older, stronger. If his words were any indicator, he had found more focus of purpose. "There were seventeen casualties, and one man lost his shield hand…there was nothing we could do for him without an Elyri healer. He will live and may be able to fight again, but until he recovers and retrains, he will be of no use to us. We can leave him and the other injured under a doctor's care in Kilmacud when we ride in for supplies in the morning, and we can be off the following day."

"Very good, Guthrie," said the prince with a smile. "I have placed five hundred men under Lord Niall; they are a day's ride behind us. He will travel towards Rhidam by the most direct route and will claim to be going to offer military support to the King if he is intercepted. We have had time to practice our combat skills; I think we are ready for whatever lies ahead. Captain Cornell, attend your men; I am sure they have questions. I need to speak with Lord General." Minos bowed and departed, relieved to have been easily accepted. When he was sure they had privacy, the prince turned his attention to Guthrie. "Only seventeen dead and one major injury? I am impressed."

Guthrie shook his head. "Don't be. It was luck. If it had not been Duke Cornell leading the cavalry, and his men had not been turned to our cause, the results would have been much different."

Chastised, the prince started to frown, but he stifled the reaction and said, "I know…but I am thankful that fate favored us. This gives us a less of Enesfel's troops to contend with and more of our own. There are over three thousand men here, Guthrie. Including those with Lords McDermott, Cervasian, Niall, and Colson, and the Hatu infantry, we have nearly eight thousand men."

"So many?" Guthrie had lost track during his weeks in Hatu. Their army was the size of Enesfel's standing force now, and many of those who served Prince Arlan should have served the King. By gathering men from around Enesfel, the King had been left with few available men to draft or recruit. That would, the general and prince hoped, work in their favor.

"He will have difficulty creating a force to match us…"

"The size of the force is not always the deciding factor, remember that. Over two-thirds of our forces are peasants and farmers with no battle experience. Many are barely more than children. Drills are one thing; our first battle, when it comes, will tell us more about whether we can stand against the King. And to potentially lose many of Enesfel's workforce will take its toll on the kingdom in coming years, whether we win or lose."

The prince sighed and crossed his arms. "I have to think positively, Guthrie. If I do not, the desperation of this quest will drive me mad."

Guthrie clapped him on the shoulder. "I know. Keep the reality in mind and your judgment and decisions will continue to be sound."

Such praise from Guthrie was always welcome; it made the prince smile and relax again. "How did it go in Hatu? How is Kavan? I suppose he had good reason to remain behind?"

"Yes. King Geir is sending his ground force by sea to join us in Levonne. Kavan will be with them. He was well enough when I left him, but sea travel does not agree with him. I imagine by the time he reaches Levonne, he will be quite ill."

The prince scowled. "I hope not. I need him. I will see that Ártur is ready for his arrival. First, however, we have to get to Levonne."

⮞*⮜

Captain Wyndham crumpled the message in one hand and tossed it into the fire pit. Lady Ula and King Ander had been right, or at least partially right. Guthrie McHador was on the move and had now become a threat to the stability of Enesfel. He was grateful that he had consulted with the Lady and had gone to her brother for support. While the Nethite King could not send many men, he could at least send enough to replace those lost along with Captain Cornell. The traitor.

Despite the Captain's respect for the man who had schooled him in warfare, however, there was no reason in Captain Wyndham's eyes for the man, for any man, to turn on their King and their country. Captain Cornell had always been loyal to Enesfel, if not necessarily to King Owain. What had changed?

The captain surveyed the men who would be riding to Rhidam with him as his thoughts wandered. Exactly what ace was McHador holding that would turn Captain Cornell and hundreds of cavalrymen from their oaths to the King? Ternce expected he would soon find out first hand. In the meantime, McHador was the enemy and would be treated as such, his previous service to the crown and kingdom be damned. Ternce Wyndham was determined not to betray his King, regardless of how enticing the incentive might be.

❧Chapter 37❧

The lone rider with his string of fourteen expensive well-bred horses traveled swiftly over the largely flat countryside, aware that somewhere behind him, royal forces had set camp for the night. He did not know if they were pursuing him or were intending to meet Hatu's forces further south, but it made no difference. They would dispose of him if they caught him. He had heard the report from his Cordashian contacts; the cavalry was Hatu's, but their leader was General McHador. That meant that Prince Arlan would not be far behind and they might already have combined forces. He prayed that was true. He would feel much safer finding himself in their midst instead of being out here alone with the fruits of his ransom demands.

Because Captain Wyndham had not yet returned to Rhidam, and General McLeu had lapsed into his most severe bout of illness yet, another young officer, one whom Guthrie had neither known nor trained, had been given command of the royal forces and instructed that, under no circumstances was he to allow General McHador to live. The returning soldiers had incorrectly estimated Hatu's losses to be fifty or more men and horses, though the number he had gained through defections would still have placed McHador's military strength at over twelve hundred horsemen. King Owain had sent the entirety of his remaining cavalry, some fifteen hundred men.

Of course, the rider smiled, what the pursuing Commander Revaugn did not know was that, if Prince Arlan had joined forces with Guthrie and Hatu, that fifteen-hundred-man unit might not stand a chance.

He stopped at a narrow, shallow stream and allowed the horses to drink as he scanned the horizon. He could see no one. Once the horses had their fill, he started south again, his pace slower in the twilight. As darkness fell, he debated stopping for the night, but he feared being taken unaware in the open and decided to sleep in the saddle. Falling off the horse was safer than an ambush by King Owain's men.

Eventually, the sounds of men and horses wafted towards him on the warm night air and as he continued south, the tiny pinpoints of light on the horizon grew to be the familiar glow of campfires. Whoever was there, they did not seem to be aware of him; he hoped to catch a glimpse of someone or something, a flag or crest, to tell him whom he was dealing with. Surely not the King's men. They could not have gotten around him, and he knew he had not doubled back on himself. By the time he spotted a pair of sentries on duty, they had also spotted him.

"Halt!" He froze as the sentries approached, their swords drawn. "Dismount."

Caol obeyed. He recognized neither man, but the piecemeal armor reinforced his belief that these were not part of Enesfel's official forces. Hopefully, that meant only one thing.

"State your name and business."

"I..." He always hesitated giving his name to anyone he did not know. That precaution had been drilled into him by his father at a very young age. Finally, he replied, "Does it matter? I am seeking General Broken Eagle."

That carefully guarded code name for Guthrie McHador was enough to put the sentries at ease, although they insisted on accompanying him into camp without speaking. A wise precaution, Caol was sure, but it irritated him to be treated as a potential enemy after every-thing he had done to prove his loyalty and worth. They led him and the horses to a circle of men and women near the center of camp. One of the sentries pushed him forward a little too roughly as the other bent to speak with the prince; Caol caught himself to keep from falling across someone's lap or into the fire, his patience at an end.

"Prince Arlan! Lord Healer! Lord McHador! It's me! Caol Dugan!"

The prince was swiftly on his feet, as were several others around the fire and he pulled Caol into a friendly embrace. That welcome sat-isfied Caol; no one had forgotten him during his time away. "We were not expecting you! Welcome! Is anything wrong? How was Rhidam?"

Grinning in that embrace, although he now wondered if he had been expected to remain in Rhidam until the prince's arrival, he re-plied, "On the contrary, My Prince. Things went remarkably well."

They separated and Arlan indicated the collection of horses clus-tered at the fringe of their circle. "What is this?"

"Tribute...of sorts," he grinned as he shook the other offered hands. "Wait...there's more..." He unloaded the horse he had used for a pack animal, beaming with accomplishment as he handed the bags over.

The prince and others sorted through the goods, whistling and ex-claiming their surprise at each new discovery. "Horses, swords, crowns...what did you do? Ransack the castle?" asked Bhríd.

"I might as well have," Caol laughed. "The white horse is yours, My Prince. I was lucky to get him. Mythical princes always claim vic-tory on a white steed...I thought it fitting you should have one too. Please, might I have something to eat while I tell you what happened?"

He was pulled down to sit beside the prince as someone thrust a plate of food into his hands. "dedhá Jermyn? Did you find him? Is everything ready?" The prince was bouncing and squirming like an excited child who could not wait until the end of the story.

Nodding, Caol spoke as he stuffed bread into his mouth. "The dedhá and his followers are camped in front of the naós, praying, singing, and generally loitering…staying out of the way of the King's soldiers as much as possible. Someone tried to kill him while I was there…"

"Kill dedhá Jermyn?" asked Guthrie with concern.

"No…King Owain." Faces and murmurings around the campfire reflected their surprise. "The assassin was unsuccessful…I think he was hung. The fellows from the desert have a cozy trading camp set up this side of the Tegid, and the Cordash segment is staying in the inn nearest the keep. I spoke to one fellow who claimed to have reinforcements coming from Cordash; our allies are awaiting your arrival, My Prince."

"Where did you get all of this?" Ártur asked, sweeping his hand in the air over the collection of goods and money as he shifted position to hear better. Beside him, Syl already slept and had not stirred with Caol's arrival.

The young redhead grinned sheepishly. "You asked me to stir up trouble…to keep the King occupied. I hope I kept them out of the way long enough."

"We have only had one encounter thus far," Guthrie started.

"With Duke Cornell. I heard. He was sent as a precaution against Hatu…they weren't expecting you. There is another mounted force on my heels…camped for the night…commanded by someone named Revaugn. There are about fifteen hundred men I heard…nearly all mounted. We'll probably meet them tomorrow."

Guthrie folded his arms across his chest and stared thoughtfully into the fire. "Thank you for the warning. We will be ready. Did you by chance hear any news about the King marrying?"

Caol winced. "Where did you hear that?" He did not think that many knew that detail, though doubtless many expected it. He supposed the news had come from someone amongst Captain Cornell's men, perhaps from the Captain himself.

"Kavan heard the news on Káliel. Is it King Ander's daughter…?" Snorting, Caol finished his first plate of food. "I wish it were…but hopefully, I have put an end to his wedding plans. On my first day in Rhidam, I encountered your sister, My Liege…walking through the city under escort…"

The prince's eyes sparkled in a way they had not in a long time; even the healer smiled with relief. "How is she? Is she safe? Owain has not harmed her?"

"No, he has not. She is quite well." And beautiful, he thought with a soft dreamy sigh of remembrance. "I was able to give her the ring you sent, Lord Healer. She recognized it and brought me into the castle to speak to me. We talked for a time; she was in high spirits until I mentioned Lady Lachlan and the child…then she offered to assist us if she could. With the aid of the city's less…privileged…I was able to kidnap her and capture the gate towers and bridge for a time. King Owain was desperate to win her freedom, and after a little haggling, he gave me all of this to get her back." He waved at the plunder he had collected.

Guthrie gave a low whistle. "You arranged, and carried out, a kidnapping and siege?" The general had not realized Caol Dugan had such resourcefulness and now looked at the prince's friend in a new light.

"I did," Caol grinned.

He would have said more, but the prince interrupted him. "My sister? What became of Deidre?"

"She returned to the castle…"

The prince frowned. "You should have brought her with you."

"Believe me, Prince Arlan, there is nothing I desired to do more. I think she would have come if I had asked. But had I done so, I doubt I could have gotten out of Rhidam alive. She did agree to aid us from inside the keep if she can. It is the safest place for her right now, I think."

"Mr. Dugan is right. It would not be safe for her with us; she would be too vulnerable. Besides, these accommodations are not suitable for a princess." Guthrie put his hand on Prince Arlan's knee, hoping to calm him. It would have been a difficult choice to make, had he been in Caol's position, but Caol's decision had been the right one.

"But he will kill her if he learns that she…"

"No…he won't…at least…I doubt it." Caol glanced at his empty meal tin and set it on the ground at his feet. "She assured me she has become very good at hiding things from him…she's had to be good at it…and she swears he honestly has no interest in harming her…"

"How can she be certain…?"

"Because," Caol said weakly, "they are to be married on her birthday."

"No!" It took both Bhríd and Guthrie to hold the prince down. "She would never marry him! Brenna told me how much she despises him. He must be forcing…"

"Forcing, no…but coercing. He kept her prisoner until she agreed to his proposition. She believes he loves her…and I think she does feel some genuine attachment to him. It probably grew out of necessity…" He found it as painful as the prince did to think about, but for entirely different reasons. "But her devotion to you is equally strong, despite how long you've been apart…and she does hold some bitterness against him over something he has done. She will help us…but I am not sure she will outright betray him."

Prince Arlan tore at his hair in frustration. How could his sister marry the monster who had raped her best friend? It made no sense. He wanted to shake the strong hands that contained him and ride into

Rhidam, to challenge the King to any form of duel the monarch might choose. He believed he would win out of sheer rage and determination. Sensing this need for rash, impulsive action, Bhríd made eye contact with Ártur, hoping the healer could do something to help. "Tomorrow we will confront the King's army; conserve your fury until then," the dark haired Elyri suggested. "It will serve you well during battle."

"But…" the prince started through clenched teeth, paying no attention to the healer who had gotten to his feet and now stood behind him.

"They are expecting only the horsemen they left behind," said Caol, "and Hatu's. King Owain sent the entire remainder of his cavalry…save for a couple of hundred he is pulling from the northern border. My sources said around fifteen hundred soldiers…"

"Then they will drown in our masses." Prince Arlan snarled as Guthrie released him, started to rise, but promptly slumped into Bhríd's arms as the healer caught each side of his head between his hands.

Ártur backed away. "He should sleep until dawn. We couldn't risk him dashing off in the middle of the night to start a war while we sleep."

Guthrie, his head full of everything Caol had told them, and the possibilities it presented, grunted. "No, we could not. The King's donations will prove useful, and he will be displeased to learn they are being used against him. With Arlan asleep, we won't have to be concerned about his ruining our strategies. Well done, Mr. Dugan. Now, we should rest. Tomorrow promises to be a very long day. I doubt Enesfel will be easily routed this time."

❧Chapter 38❧

The frigid water at the southern reaches of the Bay of Phállá lapped lazily at the bare feet that stood, unmoving, on the pale red sand of Natrona's beach. The sea was too calm, and there was no sign of wind. All authorities on the matter said that the winter storms should have begun by now. Instead, a stiff, unyielding lull had fallen over the water, preventing the nine ships from leaving port. The normally swift current was still. The ships should have departed six days ago. There had been hope that the lull would pass quickly; it showed no sign of doing so however and they all knew that if the ships were to reach Levonne on schedule, they could not delay much longer.

Kavan squatted and scooped a handful of moist sand, not caring that his robe was dragging in the gentle surf. He had gradually begun to eat again, but the dark circles under his eyes proved he had slept little. The sanctuary of the náós had been abandoned as he felt certain k'Ádhá had forsaken him. Once the ships prepared to sail, Kavan spent all of his time on this beach, seeking acceptance in nature that he could find nowhere else. But that had not helped either and there seemed nothing left to live for. Only Prince Arlan and the cause, which was, even now, denied him as he prayed despondently for the wind they needed to sail.

Standing, he barely resisted the urge to submerge himself forever in the sea. No one would notice. It was nearly dark; there was no one about to be his witness. But not yet. Not until Prince Arlan was successfully reinstated into the Lachlan family in Rhidam. Besides, Kavan was not sure he had the courage to end his own life.

Unexpectedly, not hearing anyone approach, he was struck by a powerful blow and sent spinning backward into the water. He was pulled up as though by his hair, but sharp pains shot through both legs and his lower back, causing him to fall flat again. A heated, cutting sensation slashed across his left cheek. With his vision suddenly swimming in redness, he lost consciousness and collapsed face down in the surf.

◈*◈

Bhríd wiped his blood stained hands on his even bloodier trousers as he sank to the ground beside Guthrie. The general had a gash over his right eye and looked exhausted and disoriented, but he appeared otherwise sound. The dark-haired Elyri's upper right arm was bandaged and he moved with a limp, but he too was otherwise well. The camp was dark, filled with the muttering and moaning of wounded, aching, dying men. Very few had bothered to build fires this night. It took more energy than most of them had.

"That's the last of them. Mr. Dugan's seeing to the burials. They'll be out there all night digging a chasm big enough to…" Bhríd stopped as the other man raised his hand. "Sorry."

"Is Phaedr…?"

A dull throbbing began in his temples and the corner of his mouth twitched, but Bhríd forced himself to speak. "We lost him. He did not live long enough to get him back to a healer."

Guthrie closed his eyes with a groan. "I'm sorry, Bhríd…I wish there was more I could say or do…" That Phaedr had found his way into the midst of battle to Prince Arlan's side was a tragedy none could foresee.

"No need. There is nothing…and I know your wishes are sincere." He inclined his head towards the tent flap. "How is the prince?"

The general shrugged. "Ártur has not come out since I brought him in…but he did not look good."

"That much damage?"

"Legs crushed under warring horses…spear through his back…open facial wound…and that's just what I could see. k'Ádhá knows if he lives, he may never stand again."

Bhríd touched the general's arm. "He will pull through this. He has the best healer in the…"

"I should not have let him go," came the snorted reply. "Kavan warned us…"

"You know we could not have stopped him; this fight is his. He had the right to be there. Only binding him in chains would have kept him away. The important thing is that he lives…"

"But at what price? Will Enesfel prefer a cripple to a tyrant?" Seeing the Elyri's expression, Guthrie sighed again and scrubbed his face with both hands. "I am sorry…I should not take it out on you."

"You are right to blame me, sir. I was to protect him…I failed."

"You could not have prevented this. The best plans quickly become worthless in the heat of battle. You did everything you could. Now we must hope that Ártur does likewise…and pray Arlan lives."

❧*❧

The first sound to sift into Kavan's ears as he pushed towards consciousness was a stranger's grating, gravelly voice saying, "There are no injuries to suggest an attack, no damage or wounds I can find. It must be some sort of seizure…"

"Can you treat him?" That voice, low and almost monotone, belonged to King Geir.

"I do not know what to give an Elyri, milord…especially when I don't know what's wrong. They're not like us, you know."

"But enough like us that you can call it a seizure. Physicians. You are all useless. Leave. I will tend to him myself."

Kavan forced his eyes open and willed them to focus enough that he could see the bowing form of the willowy physician and then the blurry, yet recognizable face of Hatu's King loomed into view. "See! His eyes are open already. I just had to get you out of the room. Lord Cliáth? Can you hear me? It's Geir…"

When he tried to speak, only a rasping sound came out, followed by coughing as his throat and mouth fought against the effects of too much ingested sea water.

"Drink?" The tall, wiry King placed a cup in the white hands after helping Kavan sit, and then helped direct it to his mouth. "Is that better? What happened? A couple of fishermen found you lying face down in the surf last night. We feared you had drowned. Did someone…?"

The bard shook his head. "I was not attacked." His vision was slowly beginning to clear, though the King was still fuzzy around the edges. "I do not know exactly what could have…" Realization dawned and he dropped his face into his hands. "Arlan…"

Geir sat on the bed beside him. "What about Prince Arlan? Has there been news?"

Kavan felt he could trust this man, but should he? Not many, Teren or Elyri, understood his differences and revealing such things was a risk any Elyri took. There was no other way to explain it, however, and he felt that the monarch deserved an explanation. "I have been blessed with…or perhaps cursed with…some sort of connection to the prince; any wounds he receives, I feel in kind. It is likely that he has been wounded…and that I have experienced that attack."

The King might not understand how such a thing could be true but he did not debate the explanation's validity. "Is he dead then?"

The bard searched within himself for an answer to that question. "I do not believe so…but I do not know." If the prince was dead, Kavan believed he would be too, but he had no way of knowing that.

King Geir straightened. "Then we act on your belief that he lives. There are storm clouds out to sea and the winds blow at last. I sent word yesterday afternoon to Lady Dilyn. The ships are awaiting your word to sail. I should keep you in bed until you are recovered, but we must take advantage of the wind while we have it. Can you travel?"

The bard nodded and slowly turned his legs to the edge of the bed. "I shall have to. We must get to Levonne."

"Good lad," King Geir said with a smile. Kavan was the first Elyri he had met, and he found everything about the bard to be honorable and respectable. "Captain Hiram will help you to the docks and onto the ship. He has a room set aside for you. Take this." He placed a vial in a leather pouch into Kavan's hand. "My father and I use a pinch of it with wine whenever we go to sea. It always rids us of the sickness. Should work as well in water for you, I hope. I suggest you give it a try."

"Anything would be better than that torture. Thank you, My Liege."

The King continued to smile and helped Kavan to his feet. When The Elyri was steady enough, Geir escorted him into the hall where Captain Hiram waited with Kavan's bag. They had, it appeared, planned to take him to the ships regardless of his condition. He would not have objected if they had. Unconscious, he might have been spared some of the forthcoming seasickness. He took up his bag, thanked King Geir once more for his thoughtfulness, hospitality, and the aid he was giving the prince, and then leaned on Captain Hiram all the way to the docks where the ships bobbed up and down in waiting. As much as he dreaded the upcoming journey, that movement and the feel of the wind on his face beneath the dark clouded night sky were welcome signs.

❧*❧

The healer was not surprised to find the gathering packed tightly outside of the tent in which he had been a prisoner for the past twenty-four hours. He did not want to face any questions but knew it was inevitable. He had nearly lost the prince, and, he suspected, his cousin with him, and was now exhausted and in need of fresh air, food, and sleep. No sooner had he stepped outside, when Bhríd held out a tin plate of stale bread and hard cheese, and Caol thrust a water-skin in his direction. Their thoughtfulness was appreciated and made their presence tolerable. He accepted the offerings and sank to the ground.

"It's not much," Caol started.

"Military rations rarely are," groaned the healer wearily.

There were several minutes of tense silence as those gathered watched Ártur eat; they wanted answers but managed to be respectful enough to allow the exhausted healer to have a moment's peace. Only when his sparse meal was complete did he sigh and look up without meeting anyone's gaze.

"He will live." There was a collective sigh of relief. "And he will walk again. The internal damage sustained has been healed, but for now, until I have a chance to rest, there will be scars. What he needs is at least two weeks of bed rest. What he'll get will be a few hours, I suspect; we shall have to see that he does not exert himself. He should be ready to ride by morning, but it will be uncomfortable. I suggest we get him a room in Kamin for as long as we are there to allow him proper rest."

Guthrie squatted before Ártur and squeezed the healer's hands. "I am pleased that Kavan is not the only miracle worker in your family. Praise k'Ádhá you were here to help him."

"There was no choice; I had to." He pushed to his feet, aided by the general's hands. To lose the prince would have been a greater loss than any around him realized. "Now…if you will excuse me, I need to sleep. I will sleep here in case he needs further tending." He pushed the tent flap open, hesitated, and then looked back. "How did we do?" In his push to save the prince, he had been unaware of anything else.

From the expressions around him and the darkening of the mood, he knew the answer would not be favorable. The healer regretted asking. Guthrie finally spoke, "We lost five hundred and seventy-two men, nearly one-half of our current force. Children and common folk, mostly…some of the cavalry…some horses. If we did not have reinforcements coming, I would be inclined towards retreat. But as far as we can tell, none of the King's force survived to report to him. It was one hell of a fight."

"Damn bloody massacre is more like it," Caol snorted, bitterness touching his normally youthful, animated voice. "All of those maimed and injured and…we lost Phaedr…"

With a start, Ártur met his kinsman's gaze and understood what he had been feeling in his gut over the last several hours. It also explained why Syl was not amongst this gathering. Bhríd nodded, accepted Ártur's unspoken sympathy and grief. No words were needed.

"How…he was not supposed to be out there…"

Bhríd shrugged. "We don't know how he got there. When the prince fell from his horse and the standard fell with him, I had to fight my way to his side. By the time I reached him, I found that Phaedr had retrieved the standard and was waving it over his head, swinging the prince's sword at anyone who came near. Took down a fair number of them too. I lifted the prince to get him out of further harm's way, handed him to Lord McHador, and then tried to lead Phaedr out. He lurched, I looked back as he pulled at my wrist…there was a spear through his chest. I broke it off…carried him out…but he was already gone…"

Phaedr was a hero. Ártur did not say it, not wanting to diminish the loss they each felt, nor did he try to hide the tears in his eyes and on his cheeks. "I am sorry...please..." He swallowed hard and wiped his face. "Relay my sorrow and sympathy to Syl."

He did not wait for Bhríd to confirm the request; without further words, he ducked into the tent, stood trembling for a few moments, and then fell to his knees beside the prince's cot. Instead of turning to prayer, his spirit opened instantly to Kavan's presence, hoping it was there to soothe him. It was. Despair, anguish, and loneliness flooded in both directions through the link, but neither knew whether it was a mirror of their own inner chaos or something more. The healer kept the link open until he fell into exhausted sleep.

On the other end of that link, Kavan did not sleep. The bard did not think he would ever sleep again.

The outside sounds of horses stirring and men breaking camp awoke Ártur several hours later. It was not yet light within the tent, but it never was when they pulled up camp. Stiff and sore from hours on his feet and a night spent on his knees, the healer groaned as he struggled to stand; his reward was to find the prince's eyes open at last.

"Good. Then I did not die," Prince Arlan murmured. "I was beginning to think I had, and that the afterlife was nothing more than the inside of a hospital tent on a battlefield."

With a hand on the young man's forehead, the healer forced a smile. "Your humor did not suffer any ill effects. How do you feel?"

"Miserable...but grateful to be alive. What happened? I recall falling...looking up into a very shocked face as I was pulled up by my hair..." Shuddering, he shook his head. "I thought I was dead."

"You might have been, but Phaedr managed to slaughter your attacker before he could slit your throat. Guthrie brought you back here."

"Phaedr? What was he...?"

"Saving you and the standard." The healer's voice caught but he managed to force the next few words out between clenched teeth. "He gave his life protecting yours."

Prince Arlan's face went white. When the healer tried to touch him, to ascertain if he was well, the prince pushed his hand away. "He should not have gone there. He asked before the battle how he could help; I told him the battlefield was no place for him, that he was to remain here and help you…" He paused, shaking his head. "What is the prognosis? Am I going to live?" He forced his thoughts on to other more immediate things in an effort to bury his feelings about Phaedr's death.

Ártur nodded. "It took work, but other than the scars and some bruising, you are in one piece. I will tend to the scars if you…"

"No…you will not. I insisted on going into that battle despite Kavan's warning. I deserve what I got. I am grateful you saved my life, Lord Healer, but I want the scars as a reminder. A reminder of my own impulsiveness, of your skill at saving lives, of Phaedr's sacrifice, and Kavan's foresight. Maybe next time he warns me, and I look at this in the mirror" he ran his fingertips along the burning red scar that marred his perfectly kept beard, "I will listen to him."

"And maybe," said Guthrie, his relief at seeing the prince awake lending itself to a touch of mirth, "I will become Queen. I thought I heard voices. It is good to see you, Arlan. Are you ready to move?"

The prince blinked in surprise. "I have been out that long?" That meant, he realized, that his injuries had been worse than he knew.

Guthrie stopped beside the cot to inspect the prince's well-being at closer range. "The fighting lasted into the second day, stopping only when we could no longer see but neither side was willing to relent. You were under Ártur's care for nearly a full night and day, and slept normally for the second night."

"Am I the only wounded then, or are the others able to travel?" Ártur turned away and gathered supplies from around the tent as Guthrie settled on the edge of the cot. The healer could not answer that question; the general knew it was up to him. Prince Arlan squeezed his hands. "How bad was it, Guthrie?"

There was no use in hiding the truth; Guthrie knew the prince deserved it, even if the news was not pleasant. He would know the extent as soon as he stepped out of this tent. "There were very few wounded to tend to. Such a massacre as...spread out over that amount of time..." He shook his head. "Mercifully, most of those who were wounded died in the field. The young ones...the peasants...even when wounded they continued to fight as if the future depended on their last ounce of strength and breath. Maybe it did. Most died before they could be treated. We lost five hundred and seventy-two men, Arlan..." He paused as the stunned prince collapsed backward. The cot groaned. "They died nobly; as far as I know, not one of King Owain's men lived to tell him of his defeat. Your followers did their duty to the end...they won this for you."

"Two thousand..." The prince closed his eyes as weakness overcame him. This carnage might have a dangerous effect on the kingdom in the years ahead. Restoring order to Enesfel was going to take a heavy toll. He listened to the silence of the tent, to Ártur's quiet movements, and when he opened his eyes several minutes later it was to sigh heavily. "It was not a dream. Very well, Lord General. Ártur...do I have permission to get out of this bed?"

The healer replied in a voice choked with emotion, "Since they are taking the tent down around us, yes. But please, be careful."

"I will be...I swear it." He slowly swung his feet onto the floor. "Today we ride. We will seek justice for those who have died for our cause and for those who had the unfortunate fate to die in the service of my nephew. We owe Enesfel that much."

❧Chapter 39❧

C aptain Wyndham glowered in General McLeu's direction but did not air his annoyance. The old man could not control his illness, of course. Since they had heard nothing from their last attack expedition against McHador and the forces of Hatu, it could only be assumed that the entire force either had been killed or had again defected to McHador's side. Neither possibility was to the King's advantage, as it meant that either McHador's force was stronger than anticipated, or else he had some tantalizing tidbit powerful enough to lure good men away from their duty to their King.

The general argued that McHador would never condone such a massacre of Enesfel's people, and that his meager troops could not have slaughtered the entire Enesfel cavalry. He omitted the possibility that the ex-general may have had many more men than they knew about, and that, for this particular cause, McHador might indeed do anything it took, including massacring Enesfel's military. The King's face was red with fury, his eyes bloodshot as he paced the State Room, listening to the arguments his advisors gave, seeking some bit of news or a path to act on.

"I suggest we wait no longer, Sire. If they are intent on reaching Rhidam, as it appears, we must rout them before they get closer. They are only a small cavalry…"

"Yet one obviously strong enough to defeat ours, Captain," the King snarled. "And what of those hundreds of Hatu infantry said to be waiting in Natrona? Waiting for what? Where are our support troops? You did send messengers to the estate lords for their promised support, did you not, General?"

The older man bobbed his head. It would have been too easy to claim he had forgotten, thus shouldering the failure himself. Instead, he spoke the truth, laying blame where it belonged. "I did, My Liege. They have sent what they can, but not the requested number. They claim to be undermanned because so many of fighting age joined one faction or another of those ruffians that went through the kingdom earlier this year…"

"And k'Ádhá only knows where they are. Shirking their responsibilities for some wild adventure in the desert, no doubt…"

The captain rubbed the back of his neck before voicing an opinion that he knew would be unpopular. "McHador was rumored to be involved in that too…perhaps there is a connection…"

"Our reports only rumored that he was involved initially but there was never any proof. Besides, his force is too small…and there are far more splinter groups rumored than one man could effectively control. He could not be in that many places at once…" argued the general.

"I know…but it is possible…" The King had latched on to the thought now and was for once actively considering it. "Perhaps they were not splinter groups at all but well-orchestrated splits…groups of men that will…or have…returned to aid him now that Hatu is behind him? Damn that man! What does he want from me?"

Regretting what he had started, undermining the King's position with doubts, the captain shrugged and attempted to find some way to soothe the agitated man. "We have no reports of any other groups moving from the north…or from the west or of anyone else coming into the kingdom. It is unlikely those men have returned to join McHador's force. As you say, they are likely away shirking their responsibilities…"

"Yes…yes…still…I wonder…" The King paused at the window, where his fingers tapped furiously on the frame. "Every day this drags on, my mother heckles me from her cell. It must be ended now. General Ferghus, if you cannot lead the remaining troops against McHador, Captain Wyndham shall. I want every available man…"

"Sire…might it be wise to keep reserves in Rhidam…to defend the castle? If…" he posed his suggestion as a question. His head weaved from side to side a few times as he coughed, and then he continued. "If they somehow get this far, wouldn't it be best to not leave the keep unmanned?" Captain Wyndham was again glaring at him, taking the mere thought of his losing, or defecting, as a personal affront.

Although it was an eventuality the King did not want to consider, he knew he had to. If nothing else, his life and Deidre's would be at stake, if enemy forces reached Rhidam. "Wise to the last, Lord General," he muttered. How could the old man be ill and infirm, he wondered, and yet still wise. After several moments of thought, he continued, "Gentlemen, determine the number of men required to effectively staff and guard the keep. Captain, you will take every other available man and lead what must be our final assault on Guthrie McHador. He must be stopped. You have to succeed. Winter is approaching and I do not want to spend it in the castle under siege. Act judiciously. If defeat looks imminent, retreat with what men you can and gather more…from anywhere you can. We have no more to spare on him…and no more seasoned leaders. You must win, Captain. McHador and his followers must be annihilated."

ᕥᕦChapter 40ᕥᕦ

The driving rain had prevented Prince Arlan's forces from traveling for the past two days. They had left Kamin after three days with another gain of three hundred and fifty, seventy of whom were nomads arrived from the desert who had been waiting for the prince's arrival for several weeks. Their presence, with their saw-toothed swords and lithe horses, took some of the sting out of the heavy losses they had sustained in their last battle, and lifted the prince's spirits, as did his own improving physical condition. The storm clouds they had feared would bring snow, produced only rain, but the temperature dropped enough that conditions were more unbearable than snow might have been. Everyone, man and beast, was soaked to the skin, cold and miserable. The healers feared what sickness would come as a result. The horses and foot soldiers plodded and sloshed through the mud until Guthrie ordered a halt. Guards were posted to look for opposing troops, but most doubted they would encounter anyone in this storm. It was too much of a hindrance to travel.

Ártur grimly watched the rain fall and tried to clear his head of dark thoughts. He had reluctantly stayed away from Syl during the journey to Kamin, knowing that she wanted to be alone with her grief. Only once, in Kamin, had he tried to approach her, but with a toss of her head, she had walked away. She needed more time. He could understand that, but it hurt more than he wanted to admit when she avoided his gaze, and when she did meet it, her eyes were filled with an angry pain that Ártur found troublesome. He could see without asking that it was directed at him as if he was to blame for Phaedr's death. Now, after wandering the camp in the rain for the better part of two hours, he found her sitting alone, staring in the direction they had come…the direction where Phaedr had been buried.

"Syl?" She looked at him sharply, stood, and started away. He caught her arm. "Please talk to me."

"I have nothing to say to you, Healer," she said bitterly.

He took an abrupt step backward. "Why? What have I done?"

"It is your fault he is gone."

Knowing whom she was talking about was different from actually hearing that blame. "My…" He shook his head. "I did not know he had been in the battle or was injured, until afterward, until it was too late…"

"Because you were too busy taking care of the foreign prince rather than your own kin. He would not have died if you had…"

"Bhríd says he died on the field; there was nothing I could have…"

"Bhríd lied. You could have helped him!"

He knew she needed to blame someone, needed to make sense of what had happened to her brother. The fact that he had been buried outside of Elyriá did not help. Still, her words stung. "He should not have gone there in the first place. He knew with his…"

"The blindness that you created!" she spat.

He fought to keep from losing his temper over that illogical accusation. "That is not true. You examined him the first time…before I did. You saw the damage. You also examined him afterwards. There was nothing anyone could have done. You accuse me falsely, Syl…"

"If Kavan could restore his psychic abilities, why could he not give back his sight?"

"Kavan is no healer, has no control over the 'miracles'. To blame him is to blame k'Ádhá. Would you stop blaming everyone else for Phaedr's death? He knew what he was doing enough to make his way through the battle to Prince Arlan's side, to retrieve the standard, to protect the prince until Bhríd and Guthrie arrived. He knew what his chances were. Do not mar his sacrifice with bitterness. I would have helped him if I could have, if he had lived long enough to make it to camp, if I had known..."

With narrowed eyes and one hand on her hip, she hissed, "No, you would not have. Prince Arlan was more important. To lose him is to possibly lose Kavan...you told me that. Go away, Healer. Leave me alone. Do not trouble me again; I do not want to talk to you anymore."

She stomped away through the rain, leaving Ártur with the deep despair of feeling he had lost her forever. He realized he had never given serious consideration to their relationship. He knew she felt responsible for her brother's death, as she had felt responsible for all of his scrapes and cuts when they were children. She had stayed with his body, diligently trying to restore life to it, until Bhríd pulled her away and made her tend other patients. Until her anger passed, Ártur would be forced to do as she asked. He would stay away, even if it hurt him to do so.

❧*❧

The lead warship lurched sideways as a burst of water sprayed over her sides, drenching Captain Hiram as he and his crew struggled to keep the vessel afloat. It had been many years since he had encountered a storm of this magnitude, but he was an experienced sailor and was thus unafraid as he waddled this way and that, barking orders to his crew. With black, ripe clouds blanketing the sky, pierced only by the occasional flickering forks of lightning, he could not see a trace of stars or sun and did not know when it had passed from day to night, and back to day again. He listened to the distinctive horns and klaxons of each ship over the roar of breaking waves, howling wind, and snaps of thunder. No more lightning, he muttered, signaling his first mate to operate the wheel so that he could slide and slip his way to the quarterdeck where a group of men battled to tie down loose riggings.

"Lord Cliáth," he bellowed over the din. One of the seven men holding fast to the rope looked at him. His pale hair clung to his face but he could not afford to let go of the rope to push it away until it was securely tied to the stanchions behind him. "What in hell are you doing up here?" The captain knew the Elyri had spent most of the voyage below deck combating seasickness.

"I came to lend a hand," was the hoarse reply. "I am not going to die below deck being useless."

"We are not going to die. I have been through worse. Long as we do not ram anything…damn!" He swore as he was tossed backward when a tall wave hit the ship. Kavan shot out one hand to catch him; Captain Hiram was surprised at the strength in his grasp and that he did not lose hold of the rope with that act. When he recovered both his balance and his wits, he shouted, "Stay and lend a hand if you must. I've got to get astern. Keep your eyes open, lads!" With strength like that, having Kavan up top to help could only be to their benefit.

Many weary hours later, the winds died down, the rain slowed to a drizzle, and patches of azure began to break through the inky clouds. With the sails furled now, the ships were nearly stationary in the open sea, but all nine were still afloat. There was no sun to guide them yet, but at least they knew there was daylight behind the clouds and the current was carrying them in the general direction they needed to travel. They had to rely on the water's movement until either the clouds cleared or night fell in order for Captain Hiram to attempt to fix their position by any visible stars. While they waited, the ships' crews inspected the vessels and repaired whatever damage was found. One craft had lost a portion of its mizzenmast. Another had suffered a hole above the water line that the sailors boarded with planks taken from benches and tables and sealed with pitch to keep her watertight. The rest of the sustained damage was minor and could wait until they found port.

Weak and unsteady, Kavan returned to his hammock during those hours of inspection. He tended his raw hands, drank another draught of King Geir's elixir, and tried to sleep. The concoction eased the discomfort but did not dispel it entirely, and though he thought his state of exhaustion would lend itself to sleep, he could not sleep for long without dreaming. As the sun set, he fled those dreams and forced himself above deck.

"Quite a storm, eh?" Captain Hiram did not lower the sextant as he spoke. "You did good...despite the sickness. Quite an arm too. Glad to have you aboard."

Kavan squelched the coming sentence before speaking it. The greater physical strength of most Elyri was one secret they rarely shared. Teren did not need another reason to fear them or feel inferior. "How much time have we lost?" he murmured instead.

"Storm lasted most of two days." The unanswered question did not trouble him. "We will need to alter our arrival date to account for the crippled lady back there. She'll have a hard time keeping up with that broken mast. And," he lowered the sextant and scribbled some numbers on his chart, "we have been carried off course a wee bit. I'll get the lads working at it and we'll make it to Káliel by tomorrow night."

"How much longer will the trip be?" Kavan asked as he studied the cloudy sky.

After some mental calculations, the captain replied, "Likely another five days to the original figure, milord."

The bard sighed. "Thirty-one days."

"Pardon, milord?"

"Two days storm delay, a day to repair, one to stop at Káliel, five days to account for the damage, fourteen of original travel time, six days delayed departure due to weather, and two days due to my...accident. Thirty-one days. Lord McHador calculated that, barring unforeseen events, it would take them thirty-five days to arrive in Levonne. Since we did not attempt to sail for twenty days to account for his schedule, they may already be in Levonne. Or, in any event, they will arrive before we do." That troubled Kavan, as the Sight had shown him nothing and he had not, in his state of unrest and melancholy, tried to contact Ártur. Thus, he had no idea how the prince and his men were faring. He needed to reach them soon.

The captain shrugged his shoulders. This was none of his concern; his job was to transport the soldiers to their destination as quickly and safely as possible. This unusual-looking Elyri had been intimidating at first; it took the captain many days to treat the bard as he did any other man, but he understood the bard was in command of the soldiers he carried and had business that Hiram did not know about. He did not know what he could say that would be of comfort. "We'll make it, laddie. Even if we get there a bit late, no one will oppose a..."

"Unless King Owain has defeated Prince Arlan's forces and is waiting for us."

Frowning, the captain grunted, "Then we put to sea again. Without a navy, King Owain won't come after us. But there's no point in fretting. Your prince will do his job; we will do ours. When we get to Levonne, someone can go ashore and find out how things stand. I suggest you eat and get some sleep, milord. I will call you when we are in range of Káliel."

೭౦*౯

"Troops ahead," Guthrie muttered to Bhríd who rode beside him in his usual position. The rain had ceased, and after allowing two days to dry out their gear and the rain-soaked earth, the prince and his followers continued their journey towards Levonne. The soil here was rich and black, mostly farmland, and after the extended heavy rain, the fields were thick with mud. With few areas of open land here through which to ride, and not wanting to destroy farms and crops, they had reluctantly taken to the road. Fortunately, they had come to a region with fallow, clear land to his right; if battle was to be joined, at least it seemed a good place for it. Though Guthrie disliked using peasant lands as battlefields, this time he had no choice, but at least there were no crops growing. "Send word back. Healers and those unable to fight take to the left field. We'll move forward as far as we can and pray they do not know we're here...or who we are..."

Unlikely, he knew. Reports of the previous battle had spread wide and drawn other men to their cause. If soldiers were approaching, they were likely the King's. If those men detected troops ahead, they would know those forces to be McHador's. There was nothing to be done about it.

The mass of people separated quickly, healers, women, and the infirm pulling back and beginning preparations for the injured to come should this confrontation turn into combat. On this day, the prince agreed to remain behind in safety. He was not yet up to full health and he did not want to risk dying this close to his objective. The wisdom of remaining behind won out.

Levonne was three days away; there, Kavan was due to rejoin them, along with Hatu's infantry, and then it would be the final leg of the journey to Rhidam. Prince Arlan's stomach twisted and lurched every time he thought about it. Messages had been sent to Luc McDermott, Oberon Cervasian, and Hewitt Colson; they would all arrive in Rhidam within days of each other, and then the final hour would be upon them. Lord Niall caught up to them in Kamin. So many men gave the prince confidence, but for the first time in many months on the road, Arlan admitted that he missed Brenna and wondered how baby Muir was growing. He was ready for this endeavor to be over.

Watching the soldiers move forward without him, he shook his head. For all of their strategy and planning, there was no way to know when or where they would meet this enemy, no knowing who would be its leader, and thus there was no way to set the traps and foils he and Guthrie and Bhríd spent many late nights devising. And, as Caol had bluntly put it, once the fanatical followers of Prince Arlan and the White Bard smelled blood, each battle became a massacre. Most did not have the well-honed military sense of trained soldiers. The prince worried how his men would fare today. They could not afford to fail.

Guthrie had insisted that the men from Hatu rid themselves of distinguishing marks or ornamentation. They rode at the front, Guthrie with them, keeping the line straight with the foot soldiers at the rear. He rode left of center to avoid being singled out as the leader by the opposing force. Despite this, he knew that one look at them and any force King Owain sent would know they had found their quarry. Once the two armies were close enough, he easily spotted the commander by focusing on a well-recognized family crest. Ternce Wyndham. He did not know whom he had expected, but he had not anticipated this man's rising into a position of command. Perhaps he should have. He spoke quietly to Bhríd, who nodded and rested his hand on his sword.

Captain Wyndham also heard the approaching army before he saw them; though he could not identify McHador in their midst, he knew he had found what he was looking for. He had not expected such a large force, however. Could his four hundred Cavalrymen and five hundred infantrymen defeat them…or even hold them? He stopped his troops and moved his horse forward. No one from the other side responded in kind.

"Who is your leader?" he called, his voice calm. "Send him forward."

The Elyri urged his horse forward a single step and spoke in his native tongue. "sumerthé aelá dhi; bhaeád phain ebh it? yháthibh dhi."

The men behind Captain Wyndham looked at one another in confusion. They were expecting cavalry from Hatu, with McHador in command, only to have the man who moved forward to speak be Elyri? Being unable to understand his words added to their bewilderment. Captain Wyndham momentarily wondered if King Ander's delusion of Elyri involvement was correct.

"Are you the leader?"

Bhríd switched to the Trade tongue, for the benefit of any men behind him who might not speak Enesi, the language of Enesfel. "I am the one given authority to speak. Your answers must come through me. We are on a mission of peace and good will."

"Yet you have killed mercilessly," challenged Enesfel's general. He was grateful his opponent spoke a language he could understand.

"Defense of one's self and one's own are the keys to happiness and honor. When one forgets who and what they are meant to serve in this life, that is the beginning of chaos."

"Whom do you serve? Hatu? Elyriá? McHador?"

"All and none. My allegiance is to a higher authority that will not be revealed unless you and your men lay down your arms and surrender."

Great, the captain thought bitterly. A holy war. "You think me a fool if you believe I will surrender. Others may have done so, but I will not. If it is Enesfel you wish to conquer, you must first conquer me."

The man nearest the spokesman raised a flag bearing the Lachlan standard. Lachlan? What insanity was this? A soldier beside this second man took the pennant and lifted it high above his head to allow men on both sides to see it. He cried out, "To conquer? No! To restore! For Enesfel!" The flag slashed forward as Prince Arlan's men took up the cry of "For Enesfel!" and rushed forward like a mighty wave crashing over a rocky beach. Captain Wyndham was not caught off guard by the action, but his puzzlement over the flag slowed his reflexes as he sent King Owain's troops into combat.

He tried to single out the Elyri spokesman but lost the dark roan in the crush of warring bodies around him. When he did catch sight of him again, he spurred his mount to the left, only to find his route cut off by the flag bearer, who brought the pole smashing down on his shield arm. The captain meant to strike but found his sword arm caught in the strong grip of an armored fist from his other side.

"Going somewhere, Captain Wyndham?"

"McHador." He would know that voice anywhere, even though it had been years since he had heard it. He turned his horse to face his new adversary, wrenching his arm free in the process. It throbbed where the metal-gloved hand tore away. He swung his fractured shield with his other arm, hoping to dismount the general, but his efforts failed. "What are you trying to prove?"

"I have nothing to prove, only my honor to protect. It was my last sworn duty to the House of Lachlan I served, and I will defend it to the death."

"And your death shall be here."

"Shall it?" Guthrie pulled his mount backward to open a gap between the two grappling men. The captain charged, only to find that struggling men quickly filled the space. He smashed into one of his own soldiers, sending the hapless fellow and the horse stumbling into the mud. By the time he looked up, McHador was nowhere in sight.

The sticky black mud provided an extra challenge as the horses found it difficult to maintain their footing. Soon, many of the men on both sides were forced off their mounts. Without the horses, Prince Arlan's forces had the advantage of numbers. Seeing that between the mud and the greater military strength of their opponents he could not hope to be victorious, Captain Wyndham signaled retreat. Those soldiers still mounted rushed to obey. Those on foot were less quick to untangle from the melee but many did succeed. Guthrie commanded

Bhríd to pursue but not to engage unless attacked; the Elyri took a mounted unit of soldiers and did so. Swinging through those left behind, the general led the rest of Arlan's forces in destroying those who insisted on fighting against him.

For such a short battle, there were entirely too many casualties. While Caol again took on the job of gathering and counting the dead, Guthrie rode among them. The late afternoon air was deathly still. There was no movement, no sounds of groaning men, no sounds of anything except the sucking of his horse's hooves in the mud. He watched Caol kick someone in the side. The general shook his head.

"Well?" he asked when Caol finally came in from the field.

"Nothing…absolutely nothing…seven hundred…"

"Total?" Guthrie asked, fighting the nausea.

"Of ours. I did not bother counting theirs…other than to make sure they were dead. Maybe two hundred…mostly infantry from the looks of it. They sure knew where to hit us."

Sighing Guthrie shook his head. "No. They knew nothing. Desperation was their ally. They have a King to defend and have already sustained heavy losses of manpower and morale. That, the cold, the mud…and our inexperience and self-assurance worked against us. We have had two battles in such a short time, and weeks of marching. Our men are exhausted. It could not have gone differently for us today, but it needed to be done. We survived. We have gained more horses, cut the King's army down a little more…"

"They have almost halved our numbers!" the redhead protested.

"Our current numbers. There are more in Rhidam, probably more in Levonne. We gain men every day. There are the other three regiments and King Geir's infantry. Meanwhile, we have destroyed most of Enesfel's cavalry and many of the men in our ranks would be his if they had not joined us. I do not think anything short of a miracle can save King Owain, but we can never fight with that belief in mind. We have to keep fighting as if we have everything to lose."

Caol grunted and kicked at the mud. "Because we do."

"Indeed."

"Sir," someone called. Guthrie watched the approaching soldier. "I found this on one of the men, sir."

Guthrie took the green and black pendant, turned it over in his palm as he realized that once again Neth had come to Enesfel's aid, and swore beneath his breath. "Let us hope this man was a mercenary, that the King has not called in foreign reinforcements." He knew their army, such as it was, might not stand a chance if they were pitted against the entire Nethite military. "Are there no wounded?" he muttered absently.

"None as far as I could tell," Caol muttered. "Just dead."

The general slid from his horse and pocketed the pendant he had been given. "Let us see to the dead and return to camp; I imagine the prince is waiting for our report.

⫷*⫸

A low, thick fog hung over the cove as the nine galleons waited dead in the water, with the captain and crew looking for an indication that the vessels they were to meet were here as promised. Perhaps they had been destroyed in the storm or suffered damage of their own, or had given up waiting when the Hatu ships did not arrive as scheduled. Kavan searched the horizon but saw nothing except fog. The thought of encountering Gabrielle Dilyn aboard one of those ships filled him with dread, but he knew the men with him desperately needed provisions. The storm had contaminated much of their reserves, and because each ship carried more men then cargo, there had been no room for surplus provisions. Seeing Gabrielle was a risk he was going to have to take.

"Are you certain this is the place?" he asked.

Captain Hiram scratched his beard as he tried to peer through the mist with his telescope. "This is the only fishing cove I know of on the east side of the main island. The only way to signal through this fog is by horn, but that would give away our presence to anyone else nearby…whether we want our arrival known or not."

That threat, and the suggestion of signaling the other boats, gave Kavan an idea. "We cannot risk that," he admitted as his hands gripped the railing. "I suppose all we can do is wait." Or rather, the captain needed to wait. Kavan could act, provided his head and body were not too exhausted to accomplish what needed to be done. "I am going below, Captain. Let me know if the mist recedes."

"Aye, milord," the captain said without looking at him. The Elyri had spent much of his time below deck combating illness, the request did not seem strange to Hiram.

Kavan left him as though to go below deck, but as he walked, he was already turning his thoughts inward, to the core of his being, the seat of his power. As soon as he knew he was alone and out of sight, he pushed his focus to the shape he wanted, relishing the tingle at the nape of his neck that spread along every nerve ending to the tips of his fingers, his toes, and the top of his head. Exhaustion and illness made the change more difficult than usual, but soon the gull was perched on the top of the cabin, preening its wings as Kavan delighted in the expenditure of energy he had not felt in too long. One of the sailors came around the corner, and the bird, as if startled, took to the air. He circled the galleons to get his bearings, and when he was satisfied with their position, he flew deeper into the cove. Not wanting to miss the boats, if they were there, he swooped low over the gentle waves, skimming the surface with his wings until he saw the dark ghost of a ship ahead. Only one, rather than two, but it was a large vessel, likely adequate to hold more supplies than the nine Hatu ships could use. The gull located an inconspicuous place to land and reluctantly resumed his own shape to approach the nearest sailor who appeared to be on watch as many on Captain Hiram's ships were.

"Pardon the intrusion…"

The sailor spun, startled, swinging the wooden pin he held, aiming for Kavan's head. The bard narrowly avoided the blow; if it had been one of the fellow's own crewmembers, the sailor probably would have knocked him to the deck.

Not recognizing the pale-faced man dressed in a white robe, the sailor growled, "Who are you? What are you doing on this ship?" He knew that Kavan was not a member of the crew and he knew all of the passengers on board.

"If you would take me to your captain, I will be able to complete my business…"

Snorting, roughly grabbing Kavan by the arm, the sailor said, "I'll certainly bring you to the captain, aye." With a yank, he pulled him towards the bow of the vessel where an older man strained his eyes in the direction of the open sea. He was having little luck seeing anything through the fog. "Sir? I found this stowaway portside…he claims to have business with you."

Eyes narrowed slightly, the captain looked the stranger over. Obviously Elyri, and thus not likely a threat, but he was not about to make assumptions. Having been sent here on a secretive mission that only Gabrielle Dilyn was to know about, the captain had to be careful. "What business is that, Elyri?"

"I am Kavan Cliáth. The vessels with which I travel were to meet someone here…someone sent by Lady Dilyn…"

He did not need to finish. The captain squared his shoulders. Lady Dilyn had not indicated that he would be waiting for an Elyri expedition. As most on the islands held great respect for their Elyri allies, he felt honored to have been asked to help her in a way he had not felt before. "We have supplies, aye. We've waited several days; I was beginning to fear you were not coming. Are your ships here?"

Kavan nodded and clasped the offered hand. "About five hundred yards to sea, yes. The storm and a damaged ship delayed our arrival, and we have spent several hours seeking you through this fog. May we begin the transfer?"

"Too risky to bring the ships closer; we risk ramming each other. But I've got rowboats that can be used. It will be a slow, tricky process, but I am eager to be home, so aye, we can chance it if you wish."

"I do wish it. Thank you, sir. I have my own transportation and will return at once to see that Captain Hiram is prepared for the transfers. Will you be seeing the Lady?" His gaze darted around them as he asked. Because she had not been summoned to the deck to greet him, he concluded she was not here. For that, he was both grateful and disappointed in equal measure.

"Once we leave here, I will report to her that her request has been honored. There are five of her personal guards on board. They are being placed at your disposal." He motioned to an unseen gentleman who approached from the shadow side of the ship. The man was massive, sable-haired, with a thick beard, and large sword at his side. Kavan vaguely remembered seeing him, during his stay but he had not gotten the man's name. He appeared to be roughly Kavan's age.

"This is Captain Wortham Delamo. Captain, this is Lord Kavan Cliáth…"

"Aye, I remember you, milord…"

Flustered, Kavan shook his head. "This must be a mistake. I did not request…"

Captain Delamo smiled, a look that did little to dispel what was otherwise an ominous appearance. After brushing his thick, wavy hair from his eyes, he extended his hand; he refused to drop it until Kavan shook it, and then did not immediately release his grip. "Lady Dilyn thinks that you and your prince might be in need of a personal guard. We are among Káliel's elite. Until recently, the Lady herself employed us, but when asked if we would be willing to serve her better elsewhere, the five of us accepted her offer. Effective now, we are no longer Káliel guardsmen, but Enesfel troops, if the prince will have us."

The talk of troops and a prince and Enesfel made the ship's captain nervous; he turned to give directions to the sailor who had brought Kavan to him. "Won't her father question your absence?" Kavan asked, hoping for some way out of this awkward situation. Not awkward for Prince Arlan; having Káliel guards to protect him would be a blessing. But Kavan found this man's gaze to be peculiarly unnerving and the thought of traveling with men who would probably not let him out of their sight unsettled him.

"Undoubtedly." The man laughed, a warm friendly sound that the bard liked. The sound eased some of his apprehension. "What excuse the lady gives her father is not my concern. Making excuses is one of her talents. We are doing as she bid…that is if you and your prince will accept us. Or shall we return to Lady Dilyn?"

The Elyri saw something in the man's eyes then, a touch of eagerness for adventure and some glimmer of understanding that recognized Kavan as different, something to be embraced rather than shunned. This man felt no fear of him and wanted to know more. Kavan was not accustomed to anyone showing no fear of him or to anyone not keeping him at a distance unless they were enamored by his music and religious fervor. The captain's grip was firm, his smile of offered friendship sincere. When he laughed again, still smiling, and released the bard's hand, Kavan knew that some connection had been made between them, though he did not understand it. He only knew that he liked this man and, despite his previous reluctance, wanted him to come to Rhidam.

"I am sure he would be honored to accept you, and I am equally certain you will be well-provided for. You must forgive my surprise…she said nothing of this before."

To his side, the ship's captain chortled. "Lady Dilyn does as she pleases. Should I send these five with you then, or with the supplies?" Kavan shook his head. "My transport will hold no more than myself, but I will be waiting for them and will prepare Captain Hiram for more passengers. When you see the lady, sir, please relay my gratitude."

The process of transport in the six small rowboats was slow and difficult, as the Káliel ship captain had indicated it would be, although it was obvious that all of these sailors were accustomed to working in such unfriendly conditions. Those ships that were restocked moved into the open sea to reduce the risk of being seen from the shore. By the time the fog started to burn away, it was approaching mid-afternoon and only Hatu's flagship remained. Captain Delamo and his four companions, who had helped load supplies onto the rowboats, were on the last one across. Empty of its final load, the last rowboat shoved away and Captain Hiram turned back to sea. The fog, at last, was lifted.

Kavan leaned on the rail, watching the cove retreat. If all went as planned, they would be in Levonne's harbor in nine days. Emptiness deepening within, despite the Káliel guardsmen, he stared as Káliel disappeared over the horizon. He would likely never see the islands again.

❧Chapter 41❦

The silence in Rhidam troubled Owain. It was not healthy, not right. The royal household was asleep and it was long past midnight, but the silence he sensed had less to do with the hour than with something intangible in the air that made him restless. Instead of sleeping, he paced the Grand Hall, staring at the banners, brooding. In the darkness, the colors could not be distinguished, all appearing no more than shades of gray, but he knew what they were, the burgundy borders, the amber background, and the black Lachlan eagle. There was no mirth in his faint smile as he perched on the edge of the low platform where the throne was situated. He recalled one late night at the age of five when he had come into this room alone to discover King Innis tottering the floor, pondering some problem of his own.

"Someday," the old man had said, "This could all be yours. Treat her as you would a beloved wife. Treat her kindly and she will reward you with prosperity and love. Abandon or mistreat her and she will either fall into sickness, wither and die, or else turn her back and betray you. There is nothing worse, boy, than the wrath of a woman scorned or deserted."

Odd, he thought, that was the clearest memory he had of the man other than his final rite. He wondered what Innis thought of him now, wherever he was, knowing what he knew of Owain's rule and the state of Enesfel. He looked once again into the small mirror he held, examining his face as though for the first time, and then in frustration hurled the object across the room and rubbed his damp forehead. The mirror shattered when it hit the floor but Owain did not react to the sound.

What is it mother will not tell me, he wondered. What does she have to hide?

He had never meant for things to turn out this way. He had hoped to bring into control the variety of things King Bowen had badly twisted during his short reign. Owain had never wanted to be King, at least not in the beginning. King Farrell's death had been an accident; he had sincerely loved his older brother. He had, more than once, admitted orchestrating Bowen's death, out of anger, out of a desire for revenge because the man refused to acknowledge him as his son...and for his mother. And the events that had precipitated Girvin's death had begun as a game, with Owain hoping the King would relent and allow him to marry Deidre. It never came to that. How could he have known that someone else would latch on to the game he had begun playing and take the threats too far? Girvin was not supposed to die.

And now he was alone.

Word had arrived from Captain Wyndham that evening regarding his first engagement with McHador. There had been relatively few casualties amongst the King's forces, compared to those suffered by the ex-general of Enesfel, but many men had been wounded in the muddy melee and would not be able to fight for some time. The captain had been forced to retreat but he believed he had dealt McHador a serious blow. If he could recruit more men, carry out a few more attacks, Captain Wyndham was confident McHador would no longer be a threat.

The King, however, was doubtful, particularly after learning that not only was Hatu backing McHador, but there had been at least one Elyri battling alongside them. If both Elyriá and Hatu were united against him, what chance did he have, unless he brought in King Ander's military? That was a door he did not want to open. He refused to expose Enesfel to the possibility of foreign rule, a return to Neth's stranglehold over the Sovereignties. It seemed there were no other men in Enesfel to be had, and without the advantage of an Elyri healer, by the time Enesfel's men recovered from their wounds, McHador would have overrun Rhidam. Instead of allowing Captain Wyndham to tarry, the King decided to summon him, and whatever troops were capable of travel, back to the castle. King Owain had a feeling he was going to need them.

He had tried to be a good ruler but admitted that there were things he could have done differently, or better, particularly if he had been able to keep the darkness of his childhood upbringing out of his decision-making. Now, McHador was doing his damnedest, it seemed, to take it away from him. In the overshadowing silence, he concluded that the kingdom had rejected him and was delivering him up for annihilation, as Innis had warned it would. Owain would not give up yet, not while there was even a slim chance of defeating McHador, but as he huddled in that unlit hall, he mourned the loss he could feel on the horizon.

In the corridor to his left, the figure that watched him clasped her hands together and allowed herself to cry. To see anyone aching that way upset her, but she did not try to comfort him. It was wisest, she believed, to keep an emotional distance from him, and physical distance as well, as often as she could. When he rose to his feet to pace once more, she fled the doorway for the safety of her room where she could lock both doors. Arlan, she thought with a sob as she wiped her eyes and cheeks. Please hurry. I cannot fight him much longer.

๛*๛

Prince Arlan looked northward, hand absently stroking the muzzle of the white horse he would ride for tomorrow's final journey. Before sunset tomorrow, if all went as planned, they would reach Rhidam. Home. It had been too long. He had never believed he would see the castle again, or his sister. He wondered what she looked like now, how much in Rhidam had changed in the long years he had been gone. Thinking about it made his stomach twist in undulating knots.

Hatu's ships had not been in Levonne when they arrived and there had been no indication that they would arrive anytime soon. The prince wanted to wait for Kavan, but as Guthrie rightly pointed out, sitting still this close to Rhidam could be suicide. That Enesfel's troops had retreated and not attempted to attack again only strengthened the need to keep moving. The closer they could get to Rhidam before another battle, the lower the chances there would be one; the closer they got to Rhidam, the higher their chances of success. Or thus they chose to believe.

The biggest surprise awaiting in Levonne had been a force of one thousand foot soldiers. Their leader, a young sergeant with thick red curls, explained that all of Rhidam and Enesfel was now alive with the story that Guthrie McHador was marching against King Owain. The sergeant, Yorick Zarkosta, had formed a covert unit within Enesfel's infantry. When Captain Wyndham had prepared to march, the unit of men refused to fight for the King. With McHador being seen as the larger threat, Captain Wyndham had been unable to spare any efforts to apprehend the defectors. The sergeant and his men fled to Levonne by an indirect route to await the renegade army and join them there. Between this unit and the one hundred and thirty-one Levonne townsmen, Prince Arlan's fighting force totaled almost four thousand men, most of who were, by now, at least marginally experienced in combat. The prince admitted he would feel better with Hatu's infantry behind him, and Kavan beside him, but for now, these men would suffice.

"You have not slept, My Prince," said Ártur as he approached. When the prince jumped in surprise, he chuckled, "My apologies. I did not mean to startle you."

"I was thinking…I did not hear you approach."

"About tomorrow?"

Prince Arlan shrugged. "That…and other things."

"Kavan." That was to be expected. The bard had been gone too long; Ártur imagined everyone missed him. He watched Arlan sit on his bedroll and the healer sat down beside him. Understanding how the prince felt, he murmured, "He is out there. I feel him late at night. He worries about getting here in one piece, after the storm…it seems he took it badly. But he is as well as a seasick man can be, and he has hopes of a swift arrival."

Prince Arlan continued to frown, an expression that reminded the healer more of a pout than a frown. "I wanted him here tomorrow, riding beside me. He should be here. If not for him, I doubt I would be. It was you, and he, and…all of you helped Guthrie and me pull this together, but it was Kavan who helped me understand where my duty lies…that I couldn't ignore that responsibility. He gave up his peaceful life in Bhryell to help me, although I have done nothing to warrant such loyalty." After a long pause, he whispered, "Do you miss him as much as I do?"

Miss Kavan? The healer uttered a melancholy sigh. "Very much. We may be cousins by blood, but we are brothers in spirit. We are sínréc. There have been many times…when your mother died…when Donal…if it had not been for Kavan's faith and support, I think I would have gone mad. He was young…too young to bear the burdens I placed on him, on top of his own. I wonder sometimes why he does not hate me. I try to understand him, but I cannot say I do."

"I do not think he is capable of hatred," the prince said with a nod, "maybe because he looks at things differently than we do. Strange…I do not even think he hates Owain, though k'Ádhá knows he has cause enough. I do not understand him either…but I want him back. If I could talk to him…let him know he will be missed tomorrow…"

"I believe he already knows, My Prince."

There was silence for several minutes as Prince Arlan stared across the sleeping camp and Ártur studied the starless sky. The healer's face suddenly brightened. "Perhaps you can let him know. I have never tried this...and I do not know if it will work..." He straightened, turned to face the prince, and said, "Put your hands palms up. Rest them on your lap if you must. This could take time."

Curious, having no reason to fear the healer, the prince did as instructed. "What are you going to do?"

"If I open myself up...and if Kavan is alert...I may be able to establish contact with him...a link between minds. He is close enough to us now that you may be able to feel him through me. If he can sense you, he may be able to detect your emotional state...though not likely your specific thoughts. I am not gifted enough for that."

Wide-eyed, as Ártur placed his palms on Arlan's, the prince nodded eagerly. "I am willing to try if it will put me in contact with him. Will it hurt?"

"It should not...although as I said, I have never tried. I know it would be impossible with anyone else, but with Kavan..." He shrugged. Kavan's strength and power created possibilities out of the impossible. "Close your eyes and concentrate on the images or emotions you want him to know. Yes...like that..."

Taking slow, deep breaths, Ártur opened his mind and touched the place within him that was always Kavan. Prince Arlan felt something, a static prickle crawling over his skin like a thousand tiny ants, but then he knew without a doubt that Kavan was there and the discomfort of that prickle melted away. It felt as if they were seated side by side once more. The prince was unable to contain his delight; it washed through the link and filled all three participants. It dissipated quickly, however, as Kavan's melancholy seeped in around the edges. Prince Arlan expressed concern, which Kavan brushed off. There was nothing the prince or anyone else could do for him and it would be futile for them to concern themselves with Kavan's troubles when they had matters of their own to contend with. When the prince pressured him for details, there was an angry flash, light, heat, and pain behind his eyes, and the contact was severed.

Dazed, the prince could only blink. His head hurt mercilessly and his eyes would not focus on anything but the spots of light and dark before him. "What was that?" he gasped as if coming up from beneath the water for air. "What happened?"

Recovering himself from the violent flash of anger that was unlike Kavan, the healer rubbed his eyes. Dully, the hurt in his heart stronger than what was in his head, he replied, "He broke contact."

"Why? Why won't he let me help him?"

Ártur shook his head. "There is nothing you could do through the link. I am not capable of projecting anything to him beyond basic emotion. Even if I could..." he rubbed the bridge of his nose, "whatever is troubling him...he does not wish to share it. With anyone."

"He is angry." The prince seemed as surprised by that emotion from Kavan as Ártur was.

"If he wants to confide in you, he will. Never demand intimacy from him, My Prince. He does not like to feel pressured into exposing himself. Let him come to you."

Clearly hurt by the thought of being left out of Kavan's life, Arlan muttered, "And if he does not?"

"Then he does not mean for you to know what is on his mind. Do not feel singled out; he does not share his innermost self with anyone most of the time."

The prince scowled. "Why must he be...I want to help him...repay him for the help he has given me."

Ártur clasped his shoulder warmly. "It is the way he is. You will have to accept it if you are going to accept him...I had to." His tone made it clear the subject was closed. The prince lay back and looked up at the sky.

"At least he is out there. He is alive, and he's coming back. It will be easier to ride into Rhidam and face Owain knowing that."

Ártur was glad to change the subject back to their present situation. "Which is what brought me to you to begin with."

"I thought you could not sleep either," the prince chuckled.

"Well, yes…that is true." He grinned and picked up the cloth bound item he had been carrying. "I think you should carry this with you tomorrow."

The prince took it, excitement on his face as he judged the item's weight and length as he took it, untied and unbuckled the straps, and rolled back the leather. Hands trembling, he took the pristine blade from the sheath within. "Ártur…where did you get this…?"

That reaction told the healer he had made the right choice in giving the sword to the prince now. "It was originally a gift from Kyne Mórne to your father when he became King. She was exceptionally fond of Innis, even before he took the throne; I suppose that was why she had it made for him. In turn, he gave it to Donal when Donal went to war the first time. Donal wrapped it and hid it away, refusing to take it into battle. It has never shed blood but has, by custom, come to stand for peace and justice in the Lachlan line. I was with Donal the night he died; he asked me to be sure you received it when the time was right."

"He knew I was alive?"

Ártur smiled wistfully, remembering his friend fondly, the sting of his death long faded. "He suspected it. He guessed that I would not let any assassins harm you if I could prevent it. And I think Kavan might have told him you were safe. Donal never told anyone what he suspected, except me…it was his way of protecting you. Your father would have wanted you to have this…to use it as an instrument of Enesfel's return to prosperity…"

The sword was returned to its sheath but Prince Arlan's fingers continued to stroke the hilt as if memorizing its details with his fingertips. "I will not shed blood with it either," he murmured. "I will not break that tradition. But I will wear it tomorrow…as a symbol of my place as a Lachlan. I'll wear it for Enesfel…for Kavan…and for my father."

⪻*⪼

That Prince Arlan had chosen tonight to wish for contact, and that Ártur had chosen to attempt it and succeeded, resulted in further agitating Kavan. For the first time in the voyage, he had come up to the deck for the sole purpose of gazing at the stars. The hammock had become equated with sleep, and what little sleep he could get was equated with dreams, dreams that always jolted him awake, filled him with shame and confusion, and deprived him of further sleep.

But it had not been a dream of her that awakened him tonight. Instead, it had been a dream of a silver wolf ripping away the lives of two men. Kavan had forced that memory far enough back within himself that he had not thought about it since the night it had happened. That it resurfaced now added to the humiliation he felt and further darkened his view of his existence. Prince Arlan's push for answers, a confession perhaps, had both angered Kavan and weakened him in a way he had not believed possible. Head throbbing in time to the beat of his heart, he returned to the hammock before he could accept the call of the swiftly moving waves that gently rocked the ship.

❧Chapter 42❦

Morning dawned crisp and cold; autumn had arrived in Enesfel at last. The year was drawing to a close, a year spent mostly on horseback traveling the whole of Enesfel in search of support for the step Prince Arlan was about to take. Great care was taken to adorn the horses with the royal banners and standards brought with them from Elyriá. The prince was grateful for the fur-lined burgundy cloak that protected him against the steadily blowing northeast wind. He shivered as Guthrie helped him mount up and adjusted his stirrups, and pulled the cloak tighter around his neck. The excitement he felt around him was almost tangible. His was not the only horse prancing nervously in reaction to the anticipation in the air. He patted its warm neck to soothe it and the horse whinnied. He waited, watching others fall into place, and as soon as everyone was ready, the procession began to move.

It was no longer their usual travel formation. There were no sloppy stragglers, no one wandered off the path or out of line. In Levonne, they had acquired ten wagons and traded the packhorses for sturdier draft animals to draw them with. Five contained a majority of the women who had been traveling with them as support, and those who had not recovered from the wounds of the last battle.

Caol Dugan rode point, radiant with the honor of what he deemed an important distinction. The thirteen unmarked horsemen who followed him were heavily armed and rode the largest horses available. Directly behind them, Minos Cornell led what had once been Enesfel's cavalry. They were marked as what they were; no one in Rhidam would mistake them for anything else. It would, Guthrie hoped, lessen the civilians' fear of being invaded. After all, this was Enesfel's own cavalry returning home, not as prisoners but with heads held high.

The ten wagons came next, sandwiched between Enesfel's cavalry and the cavalry that Guthrie had built as they traveled the kingdom. Hatu's cavalry brought up the rear, protecting the hundreds of foot soldiers who sang and chanted as they marched in straight ranks of eight men across. Before them, in the center of the procession, Prince Arlan was flanked by Guthrie and Ártur on his right, Bhríd and Syl on his left, and four soldiers fore and aft and two on each side. The eight men chosen to carry the pennants and standards and the six trumpeters traveled with that core group. The entire center unit displayed the royal colors. Prince Arlan did not believe that King Owain would interpret their arrival as anything other than what it was: the return of Prince Arlan Trebor Lachlan to the seat of Enesfel's power in the heart of Rhidam.

By noon, when they stopped to eat, the marching men had quieted their singing. A gaggle of local peasants and merchant carts had attached themselves to the end of the procession curious to see what would happen when they entered the city. The foot traffic was heavier as they drew nearer to Rhidam; many stopped to question them as they passed, or simply moved off the road to watch the seemingly endless group of soldiers march past. Lords Colson and Cervasian caught up with the Prince's forces, doubling the length of the parade, doubling Arlan's confidence. The prince did not see Caol during their stop to eat, but he was too excited about what the next several hours would bring to worry about the resourceful redhead.

He could see the náós spires, the dark gray towers of the castle, and the rise of houses and shops, while still some distance away from the city's edge. The prince could not remember seeing Rhidam from this view. Its grandeur, or at least the grandeur he saw in it, was like a dream. Guthrie smiled at his expression of wonder.

As they approached the bridge they would need to use to cross the Tegid, two more groups of men joined them. The first was small, no more than fifty men, but they were the most imposing figures in the procession, matched only by their fellow Cíbhóló nomads already in the ranks. After speaking briefly to the Elyri healer, they saluted the prince and fell in line. The second group, much grown from Guthrie's original eight recruits, was one hundred and forty-eight Cordashian men.

Prince Arlan could not sit still in his saddle and his horse grew fidgety as a result. How could this ever-increasing column of followers be real? How could a small core group of men have brought this many to his cause? He turned on his horse, about to say something to Guthrie, when music reached his ears from somewhere ahead. Curious, Guthrie sent Bhríd ahead to assess the situation at the front of the ranks. When the Elyri returned, he wore a wide smile as he fell into formation again.

"What is it?" Arlan asked anxiously when Guthrie too said nothing.

"The bridge, the field…the streets beyond…all lined with people singing, welcoming your arrival. dedhá Tythilius is among them…"

"My…" He reined in his horse, causing those behind him to skitter sideways or pull up short to avoid crashing into him. Guthrie grabbed the reins and started the white horse moving again. The prince cast him a sharp, scolding look and started to pull away. "I cannot do this…"

Guthrie chuckled but did not release the reins. "It is too late for nerves. They have known you were coming; now you are here. Their miracle is at hand. It is what we have spent all of these months working towards…what men have fought and died for. It is what the people of this kingdom want and need. Will you give up…deny them this?"

The prince looked away from Guthrie towards those who rode beside him, and then over the mass of men stretched out before and behind. He met Ártur's gaze and saw in his face the first characteristics that reminded him of Kavan. Kavan would not want him to give up, and he had to admit that, despite the anxiety, turning back did not interest him.

Squaring his shoulders, settling firmly into his saddle and lifting his chin, he took a deep breath. Fixing his eyes on the castle, he replied, "We ride into Enesfel."

The applause and cries of welcome greeted the lead horses as the crowd parted to allow them passage. It seemed an unending line of men and horses, but finally, when Prince Arlan's core group reached the bridge, gdhededhá Jermyn was waiting on the other side. He clasped the prince's extended hand with both of his own. "Welcome to Rhidam, My Prince. We have waited long for this day, and now k'Ádhá has seen fit to award our perseverance and faith. Tell us what you desire of your humble servants, milord."

"Join us, dedhá. All of you are welcome. You have done well; your work is appreciated. May k'Ádhá bless you for your aid and prayers."

"He already has. He has given us you, despite what travails you have endured. But…" The one-eyed man searched the gathering around the prince with disappointment.

Knowing who he was looking for, Prince Arlan squeezed his hands before releasing them. "Lord Harper will join us shortly. He was delayed at sea and we could not afford to wait for him. As soon as he arrives, I will send word." The roar of the crowd was growing louder as people further on waited for their chance to see their long-awaited miracle. "We must hesitate no longer. It seems they are waiting for us."

With a nod from Guthrie, the trumpeters began their fanfare. The cheers that went up as Prince Arlan crossed the bridge and touched outstretched hands, entering Rhidam at last, renewed his sense of purpose. Whatever doubts he still carried, Prince Arlan knew this was what he had been born, had been saved, to do.

❧*❦

"What is that commotion?" the King grumbled pushing away his untouched dinner. As distracted as he had been of late, he would not be surprised to learn he had overlooked some holiday or peasant festival. Faces around the table looked at one another, none of them having the answer to the question until a sentry entered the dining hall and bowed.

"They have arrived, Sire," the man said in a small voice.

"Who has?" From the weary, flat tone of his voice, it was obvious to the others around the table that the King had not jumped to the same conclusions they had.

Fidgeting with his hat in his hands, afraid to risk punishment by bearing bad news, the sentry replied, "McHador and his troops. They are in Rhidam…at the edge of the city near the river. They…he…is bearing the Lachlan standard…"

Each new word drained more color from the King's face until it was a stunned, gray slate. Heads around the table whipped wildly as they looked from one to another with alarm and concern. They wanted their sovereign to reassure them but all the King could do was stare, slack-jawed, at the sentry. When he did finally speak, his voice was little more than a squeak. "Mc…why are they people cheering the man who will destroy them? Why is he setting camp at the edge of the city? He cannot lay siege at that range…"

General Ferghus, who until that moment appeared to have fallen into another stupor as soon as the chaos outside had reached his ears, bobbed his head and muttered, "Maybe siege is not what he intends, My Liege…"

Finding a target for the struggling temper beneath the surface, the King spat, "Then what does he intend, General? Carrying the Lachlan standard? Does he think to wrest the throne from me? Even with Hatu and Elyriá behind him, he would have to be mad to think he can do that! He has no claim! You knew him. You served with him. What is he doing? What does he want?"

"Perhaps if you ask him…" started the frail man.

"If the King goes out there," Captain Wyndham snorted, "one of that rabble will slit his throat!" He and his troops had reached Rhidam earlier that day, but the weary, wounded soldiers had dispersed to take their rest. He had not expected to need them at the ready so soon.

"General Ferghus, I command you to learn what he wants. Why does he bear the Lachlan standard? What does he think he's doing? If you are still loyal to this crown," Owain added, his anger and anxiety peaking simultaneously, "do not come back to me until you know why he is here! I need to know! Tonight!"

The general slowly rose from the table without questioning the King's sincerity. That was obvious in his tone. Normally, the threat of dismissal would subside by morning, but as long as McHador was in Rhidam, Ferghus knew the King's position would not change. Without a word, he bowed and shuffled from the dining hall into the courtyard, waving off those who offered to either assist or accompany the ailing old man across town. This was one quest he had to complete alone. He knew the King was not angry with him, but rather at the situation they found themselves in, yet his tone and words cut to the general's heart. Was he loyal to the crown? Had he been loyal to Enesfel? He did not know anymore. It would be a long trek to where his old comrade was camped, but he suspected it would be an even longer walk home.

The cobblestone streets were unusually dark; even those taverns that remained open were sparsely populated. There were no campfires or singing from the náos tonight. Everyone, it seemed, had converged near the river, had flocked to Guthrie McHador. Ferghus shivered. They knew and they believed. Those pilgrims, all of those peasants and merchants and nobles who had followed McHador for months, all of those soldiers who had turned from their King; they believed, some without the slightest shred of proof. Why then, had he doubted?

Pausing where those gathered could not see him, he watched the gleeful commotion for a long time. There was a large pavilion erected in the center with the Lachlan standard in full view. That would be where McHador was. The general shuffled forward, surprised that no one stopped him as he drew nearer to that tent. How easy would it be, he wondered, for some assassin to sneak through? Yet there was a ring of guards around the pavilion that looked to be impassable, but pass he must, and thus he reluctantly approached them.

"Might I speak with General McHador?" He assumed the man was using that title.

The soldiers looked him over, determining him to be a nobleman at least, judging by his well-tailored clothing. Two of them looked at one another before one asked, "Your name?"

"Tell him…" What? He did not think it wise to reveal his identity, in case these soldiers had orders to kill any allies of the King. "I am a friend he met in Chantel, earlier this summer. I was told to seek him out when he came to Rhidam. He will remember me."

The soldier snorted and as he withdrew to the pavilion, the other soldiers he left behind slid sideways to fill in the gap his departure had created. Barely five minutes later, the soldier returned with Guthrie at his side. The two generals studied each other and then Guthrie motioned for Ferghus to follow without revealing his identity to the soldiers. Ferghus wondered if that was a wise choice or not.

"Come." They moved away from the perimeter of sentries before Guthrie spoke again. "Did the King send you?"

The old man shook his head. "No…not exactly. He asked me to find out what you want, why you bear the Lachlan standard as your own, but that is not the reason I came. I already know those answers. Take me to him, Guthrie. I must see him for myself. I did as you wished. I tried to deter the King; I refused to fight against you. Now, I beseech you, do this for me. Show me that my actions have not been in vain."

Guthrie did not like the desperate tone of the other man's voice, but he felt he owed proof of his claim. They passed through a second ring of guards nearer to the pavilion. General McLeu recognized the Elyri healer at a distance, and beside him, Hanford Weylin. The others around the fire he did not recognize or else had their backs to him. He swallowed the sick feeling in his throat and tried to steady his hands.

"Prince Arlan…?"

"Yes?"

The prince turned and watched the man with Guthrie come forward and touch his face with both hands. Many around the fire reached for their weapons, but Guthrie stayed them with a wave of his hand. The stranger knelt and bowed his head on the prince's knee. He needed no further proof. This could have been King Innis himself sitting there, so alike were they. "My Prince."

When Prince Arlan looked at Guthrie, the older man said, "General Ferghus McLeu."

The prince gently encouraged Ferghus to stand as he got to his feet. "Welcome to our camp, General McLeu. It is a pleasure to meet you. Guthrie speaks highly of you. Have you come to join us or at the request of the King?"

"He asked me to learn of Guthrie's purpose here; I already knew, but I had to see for myself if what I was told was true. It is a relief to know my old friend has not been deceiving me."

Though the prince did not understand, he smiled. "Will you stay? Join us for some wine? You are welcome, sir. All are welcome here."

Eyes darting around the circle, Ferghus asked, "Including the King?"

Prince Arlan bristled but did not otherwise show hostility. "My feelings for my nephew are complicated by many factors. I would welcome him, but I suspect he would not desire to be here, any more than I would be comfortable having him here. I do, however, desire to speak with him. If you would convey that Lord McHador wishes to meet with him before the gate towers tomorrow at noon, we would be grateful."

"I will tell him." Shaken, the general almost could not bring himself to move. "I cannot break my oath to the King to join you, milord, but nor will I betray you. I will allow you to confront him in your own time and way, and k'Ádhá will decide the outcome. My oath to the House of Lachlan will not permit me to do anything other than what I have done." He offered his hand to his friend. "Guthrie, when we meet again, I pray it will be under better circumstances."

Again, the general's tone of voice made Guthrie uncomfortable. "So do I, Ferghus. Mr. Dugan, please escort the general to the edge of camp and see that nothing unfortunate happens to him."

The redhead got to his feet. "Certainly, sir. This way, General."

Rhidam's streets seemed twice as dark and forsaken on the journey back to the castle, as Ferghus had known they would. The moment of revelation had passed; he knew the truth, one he should have believed all along, but he could not share it with his monarch. It was a heavy burden to carry, one he did not feel he could shoulder very long. He found the King alone in the darkness of the Grand Hall, seated on the edge of the throne, staring at the floor. When their eyes met, Ferghus realized sullenly that the King had begun to resign himself to his death.

"Well?" mumbled the King.

"The pilgrims...they are camped with McHador now...and the nomads...Duke Weylin...Captain Cornell...Yorick..."

This was what had become of so many men from his fighting force. The King seemed to grow smaller in both voice and body as he realized this. "Lieutenant Zarkosta?" Ferghus nodded his head, feeling honestly ill now. There was no pretending tonight. "What does he want? Why does he wave the Lachlan standard?

"He does have designs on the throne, milord...although he did not specifically say that. He has asked to meet with you before the gate towers at noon tomorrow; he will present his demands in full to you then."

The King snorted and stared into the darkness, his gaze seemingly fixed on some distant point in the room, or perhaps another point in time. "If I do not go?" he finally asked.

"I suspect he will wait."

Again the King snorted. "How long?"

Ferghus shuffled his feet. "As long as he must, I think. As long as he has the support of the people, he will not lack for provisions. May I retire, My Liege? I am not feeling well..."

Still looking elsewhere, the King dismissed him with an absent wave of his hand and did not watch him go.

The general went to his room in the guardhouse, took out a sheet of parchment, a stylus, and ink, and prepared to write his resignation. There was no other choice for a man in his position. He stopped, however, before he got a single word set down. He could not resign and live with himself afterward; he could not abandon the King like that. Yet nor could he help him in any meaningful way. The longer he pondered the quandary he was in, the more certain he was that there was only one fitting solution. k'Ádhá have mercy on all of us, he thought with a groan. This time, with a new surge of resolution, he put the stylus to the parchment and began to write.

❧Chapter 43❧

Daybreak brought no better news for the King, as he tried un-successfully to eat breakfast. After being unable to finish his meal the night before, he thought he should be famished, but he felt little desire to eat, especially now that the latest messenger had come to spoil his fragile mood once again.

"Nine of Hatu's ships? In Levonne's harbor?" Captain Wyndham nodded tentatively, uneasy about the tenor of the King's voice. It sounded like the tone of a man about to break.

"My source knows the difference between a trader and a galleon, milord. And knows the Harcourt standard. They did not dock but looked to be continuing up the Tegid."

The King's eyes narrowed as his finger's clawed through his hair. "They cannot reach Rhidam in galleons...those ships will never make it this far." Still, it would put them closer than he was comfortable with. "How many men could that mean?" If Hatu was set to deliver more men in the support of McHador, the King's plight was looking grimmer.

"Allowing for supplies and normal crew...just over three thou-sand."

"So many?" Having never seen a galleon himself except in paint-ings, the King had no experience by which to gauge their size. "We cannot hold off that many men, even if we can get past McHador and his followers to intercept them. He is still out there?" He sounded cautiously optimistic, although he knew it was foolish optimism."

"Aye, My Liege, he is. Another large regiment of men has arrived from the north to join him…and he has repeated his request to meet."

Another regiment. It was impossible now to judge how many fighting men Guthrie McHador commanded. The only number the King kept coming up with in his head was 'too many'. As the knot in his stomach tightened, defeating his attempts to eat, he mumbled, "We will meet on my terms, in my time. Has no one seen General McLeu?"

The captain shook his head. "No, Sire, not to my knowledge. One of the men indicated he was not feeling well last night; shall I see if he has taken to his bed?"

The answer did not particularly matter to the King, although he would feel more comfortable having someone with knowledge of McHador by his side. "Do that, please. And check on my mother. I seem to have forgotten her in the chaos." He cared even less for her welfare at this time than ever before but some niggling in the back of his mind suggested it was wise to keep an eye on her. After all, there was no telling what sort of hand she might have in these events.

Maybe he would blink and Neth's army would be there too. That was, he silently admitted, an even worse fate for him, and for Enesfel, then McHador's threat.

"Yes, My Liege. I will return when I have news."

"Please do…we need to decide what we can…and should…do about those ships." Not, he thought bitterly as Captain Wyndham bowed and left the room, that there was anything he could do now. He had a seed of an idea, but was it even worth the risk…and did he dare plant it in the Captain's head?

❧*❧

Shivering, Kavan waited on the rocky beach as the last of Hatu's soldiers disembarked from the galleons. Oh, to be on dry, solid, land again, even if his quivering legs could not easily support him. To be once more on Enesfel's soil almost lifted the edges of depression that clung to him, but he no longer believed anything could do that.

Captain Hiram waved from the bow of the ship in farewell. Upon reaching Levonne and learning that Prince Arlan and his troops had passed through the city four days earlier, the captain had chosen, after discussion with Kavan, to sail up the Tegid as far as they were able. It was late evening now, and Kavan knew he was not the only one who was having difficulty adjusting to standing on solid ground. They decided to set camp and march towards Rhidam at daybreak. After the last several days at sea, most of the men were looking forward to the next two or three days of marching. It would be a welcome change.

What Kavan wanted was a horse, but there were none to be had; each man would have to carry his own equipment. The Elyri was grateful he had allowed Guthrie to take his harp. Though the instrument was not heavy, anything beyond his own rations and clothing sounded like a larger burden than he felt strong enough to handle. Still, it would have been soothing to feel the brass strings beneath his fingers, to rest the firmness of its black wood against him. He missed his harp, his music, perhaps more than he missed any single person.

Sitting apart from the others, he gazed in the direction of Elyriá's craggy mountains. Home, he mused, though he realized that for him there was no home. There was his aunt's home, soon to be a home for Prince Arlan, Brenna, and baby Muir, but he did not consider either of those places to be home. As long as he had been gone, not even his own small house in Bhryell felt like home. And there was nowhere he could go where he would escape the blackness within himself. Nowhere he felt he could be welcome and at peace.

The men behind paid no heed as he stood and walked into the darkness, although one set of footsteps followed, always remaining a respectful distance away. The soldiers had labeled the bard eccentric, and all except Captain Delamo left him to his pursuits. Without looking, he knew it was the Káliel captain following him. But Kavan did not care, nor did he care what anyone thought of him tonight. He only desired to be alone.

ॐ*৯

Lady Ula de McCormick strained her gaze through the tiny, barred slit of a window that provided the only source of light and fresh air she could get. It was not always fresh, as soldiers and servants who knew where that small opening led, sometimes paused to urinate through it, or to push rotten food or offal through the bars. She wondered at times if her son's precious bride-to-be had endured such treatment, or if this happened only because she was his mother.

She had heard the commotion in the streets the day before, and the celebrating that lasted far into the night. Now there was little activity outside, nothing she could hear clearly. Captain Wyndham had confirmed her worst fears, however. Her plans for her only child had failed and there was nothing more she could do. Fear for her son barely outweighed fear for her own safety. Now, as the thud of the heavy wooden door at the top of the stairs told her that Captain Wyndham had gone, she struggled with the turmoil within. Only one word came to mind…her guards be damned.

Grasping the bars of the window to the outside, she cried in her loudest voice, "McHador!"

ॐ*৯

In the dimming candlelight of the library, the King fingered his quill, trying to read what thoughts were hidden behind Deidre's sea-blue eyes. Her emotions were, as always, plainly visible to him and he saw nothing but sorrow on her face. If there was anything else there, he would never know. "You will not marry me because I stand to lose the kingdom," he wrote finally. It was a logical assumption to make.

The princess shook her head; what she wanted to tell him, she knew she could not. Not without putting her brother in harm's way. "I do not think this is the time to discuss marriage, milord. There is a large army outside. We may all die soon. Until our future is secure, I cannot think about such things. After...if we live..."

He took the parchment and stylus back. "What if there is no after?"

For a few moments, her fingers stroked the back of his hand. It was a strong hand, one not afraid of work despite being a King's hand. His hand made her sad. "Then k'Ádhá grant us both strength and courage for whatever will come."

The King studied her, admiring her calm in the face of disaster; he clasped her hands, kissed them, and left the room. Of course she was calm. She might be afraid of death, but she had no idea of how bad the situation was.

Only when she was alone did she allow the tears she had held back to trickle down her cheeks. She had not wanted to hurt him, but postponing the wedding in this way had to be done. Hopefully, there would be no further chance to talk of marriage.

From the library window, she could not see the army she knew had arrived; too many buildings obstructed her view. But the changes in Owain, the frenzy of the staff and his advisors, the electricity in the atmosphere told her they were here. Though no one had told her, and she had not asked, she knew the army must belong to her brother. That knowledge filled her with the strength to face the King one last time. She prayed it would be enough to sustain her until whatever was to come was over.

❧*❧

He slid the sheet of parchment gently from the skeletal hand, trembling as he unfolded it. There was no blood, no wounds, no evidence of foul play, but the old general was clearly dead. His head rested on his folded arm, giving the appearance that he had fallen asleep at his desk and died in during the night.

"Milord," the parchment read, the letters shaky and barely legible. "I have come upon an obstacle that prevents me from adequately fulfilling the vows I took which require me to forever protect the House of Lachlan. In order to preserve my honor and dignity, I choose this. My secrets pass with me. May k'Ádhá's great wisdom resolve these events in a manner beneficial for the kingdom. All prayer and hopes go with you, my prince and my King. Protector to the House of Lachlan, Ferghus McLeu."

It was the old man's writing, weak as it might be. It was stamped with his personal seal that lay to one side of the desk near his hand. There was no doubting its validity.

Captain Wyndham knew this death placed him in the position of high command, but he discovered too late that he did not feel capable of fulfilling the position, and was not ready to assume the title. Particularly in the face of what lay ahead.

As he examined the room and the other objects on the desk, he wondered what might have driven Ferghus to seek his own death. It was possible the old man's ailment had finally caught up with him and that he had died while composing what was to be his resignation letter, but something in the choice of words suggested differently. To what secrets did he refer? What had the general known?

It had something to do with Guthrie McHador, that much the captain whole-heartedly believed.

He crumpled the parchment and tossed it into the remains of the fire. Let the King believe his general had died a natural death. Presenting more unanswered questions into the King's already troubled mind was not what Enesfel needed. Nor did he need to suspect that his general had taken his own life. What Enesfel needed was answers, but Ternce Wyndham did not have any. He could not even fathom what the questions were.

He wondered, as he made the decision he knew the King was unable to make, if anyone, other than Ferghus McLeu, did.

❧Chapter 44❧

The face drew nearer, her face, delicate and glowing and soft around the edges, and he felt the now familiar inescapable fire fill him as her breath warmed his skin. Thick, dark auburn hair hung over him, brushing against his face and he breathed deeply of her flowery fragrance. His hands found her waist and pulled her closer, relishing the way she moved as his mouth accepted hers. Closer, he thought, if only for one moment. Closer. One hand moved up his bare thigh. He shivered, moaned…

"Gabrielle!"

Kavan's cry echoed through the empty náós as he bolted upright, breath coming in quick, short, heavy gasps. He recoiled in horror at his body's condition and fled to the thóres, hoping to cleanse himself of the impurity of his dream. He had dreaded sleep, had meant to spend the night in prayer and meditation in this well-known place, but his exhausted body had demanded rest. Now that he was within a familiar place of sanctuary, his body had finally taken some of what it needed. He hastily changed into his second robe, as if that would erase the taint of what he had done, and then returned, not feeling any better, to kneel before the altar. His tormented mind refused to focus on anything save the tingle still coursing through his body, but he was spared the need to continue trying. The main door of the náós groaned as it opened and he spun, terrified of who might have entered. He could not even concentrate enough to touch the visitor's aura for recognition.

The shadow closed the door, not certain why he had come here. An intense psychic jolt had brought him wide-awake and he had followed its source to end up here. His mind reached out and touched one terrified point of light ahead of him in the room. "Kavan?"

The relief that flooded the younger man was intermixed with great anguish, loneliness, and shame. The healer hurried forward, lighting the lamp he had brought, and knelt on the steps at Kavan's side.

"By the saints…you look terrible…are you well?" He reached to lay a healing hand on his cousin, but Kavan eluded his touch.

"I am not ill if that is what you are asking." The rough whisper that came from the cringing man was hardly recognizable.

Ártur put his hand on his cousin's shoulder this time; the younger man was trembling badly but did not escape again. "Have you been eating? Sleeping? Is this a result of seasickness? Guthrie told me…"

"That is gone…mostly."

It seemed likely, but still the healer scowled. Something was wrong and despite what he had told Prince Arlan about not pushing Kavan for answers, he felt compelled to ask questions. This time, someone had to. "You did not answer the first two questions."

"I have been eating…when I can. As for sleep…" He shuddered and closed his eyes. "I cannot."

"Something is keeping you from sleep." It was tempting to try to probe his cousin's thoughts, but Ártur knew he would only find a blank wall. "What is it? kyá sínréc…I have spent many weeks feeling your pain. It grows worse each day. You felt isolated before; though I was not expecting you tonight, you are here now, amongst friends, and there is no longer need for loneliness. Or is it something more. Talk to me, dearest one, as we use to do. Allow me to carry your burden, or at least ease your pain, as you have often done for me." He took Kavan's hands within his own; they were shaky, cold, and moist and Ártur feared his cousin was going into shock. Perhaps there was an injury he could not see. Kavan would not meet his gaze.

There were many long minutes of silence, of Kavan drawing strength and a small measure of comfort from his cousin's touch without Ártur being aware of it. At last, when he realized his cousin would give him no respite until he said something…and feeling the need to unburden his soul to someone he could trust, he whispered, "I have been abandoned…He has abandoned me."

"Who has?"

The only reply Ártur received was a quick, almost unnoticeable, flicker of Kavan's eyes towards the image of Dhágdhuán on the wall. "I did not mean for it to happen. I cannot think what I could have done to avoid what transpired…and now…my soul is blacker than the night and k'Ádhá has turned his back on me. I have tried…but I cannot…"

There were tears. Ártur gasped and pulled Kavan into his arms, holding him for what seemed a blessed eternity, listening to the heartbroken sobs as the wetness of tears soaked through his thin shirt where Kavan's face pressed against him. Tears, he thought with a shiver. In all of the years he had known Kavan, there had never been tears.

The sensation of holding him was intoxicating and he wanted never to let go. Realizing that, he shuddered, but pushed the feeling away so that it would not interfere in the giving of comfort. When he could no longer bear it, however, he gently pulled away and tried to meet his cousin's gaze. "Look at me, Kavan. If not…tell me, from the beginning, what has happened to result in such a state. I cannot believe that you, of all people, could have done anything so heinous that k'Ádhá would not forgive you."

"You do not know." The bard brushed the silver-white strands from his face and stared at his hands on his lap. "I went to Káliel, as I was bid…to secure supplies for the ships. I met…" Something seemed to shake his whole body and he groaned.

"Yes? Go on."

"Please…do not make me continue. Do not make me talk about this."

But Ártur was not going to give in. Kavan needed to talk, he could see that. The healer wanted to get to the bottom of his heartache and help him heal. "Talking unburdens and restores one's soul. I may not be gdhededhá, but consider me a confessor if it helps. After all we have been through, if you cannot speak to me, I doubt very much you would ever tell a gdhededhá, even in confession. Talk to me, sínréc."

Kavan could not bring himself to slide away from his cousin despite wanting to. He had yearned for Ártur's companionship; now, despite the awkwardness and anguish, he knew he had to stay. He knew what his cousin said was true. If he was to ever hope for peace, he had to speak. When he began again, his voice was barely audible.

"Her name is Gabrielle. She is Ulstar Dilyn's only child."

Not wishing to judge his cousin prematurely, but rather encourage him to continue, Ártur asked, "Lord Dilyn, Prime Magistrate of Káliel?"

Kavan nodded. "Yes. She is…precocious. She enjoyed toying with me, not allowing me to come out of my bath to eat, opening the door when I was not dressed…things of that nature. It annoyed me greatly at the time," he shivered, "but it was oddly amusing…"

Chuckling, Ártur grinned. "I know what you mean. Elys use to do those sorts of things to me often."

The younger Elyri was genuinely surprised. "She did?"

"It is how some women…and some men…try to attract the attention and affections of someone they are interested in. It is part of courtship…"

"Courtship?" Kavan choked on the word. "I…did not know…" He wiped his free hand on the fabric of his robe, smoothing it. "She proved most useful; she arranged for a vessel to provide supplies to King Harcourt's ships though her father and the Council denied our request for aid. She sent five of her personal elite guards to serve

Prince Arlan. And she made it possible for me to avoid the sea voyage back to Natrona."

Casually, Ártur stretched and asked, "How did she do that?" as if their conversation was the most normal one in the world.

"There is a Gate on the premises. She is...her mother was Elyri. Gabrielle knows how to use the Gate and took me to it."

"I do not recall that Elyri settled on Káliel...though it seems they must have. I wonder how the Gate came to be there...when it was built." He pondered that for a moment before continuing, "Nor did I know an Elyri-Teren marriage could produce offspring with the talents. I've never heard of another such individual." He was still, imagining the implications of interbreeding as he waited for Kavan to say something. Thus far, he had heard nothing incriminating. "So? What is it about her that troubles you? That she saw you unclothed? What did you do?"

Kavan looked up abruptly with a look of near horror on his face. "Me? I did not do...she did not see..." He started trembling again and his hands grew colder. Ártur squeezed them to keep him from escaping.

"You must have done something if you believe k'Ádhá has forsaken you. What was it?"

Several times Kavan opened his mouth to speak, but no words came out. Finally, he croaked, "When we parted ways...she kissed me."

Ártur did not move. He waited. Nothing. "And?"

"And? Isn't that enough?" Kavan's face was etched with lines of confusion and shame as if he did not understand the healer's failure to react.

"What did you do?"

"I did not do...I allowed it. And...I touched her."

"Where?" the healer asked offhandedly.

"Ártur!"

Ártur pushed. "Where? How?"

Pulling his hands away, Kavan drew his arms close to his body and dropped his head. He was visibly appalled. His cousin's unresponsiveness and continuing questions only increased his anguish, and though he did not want to reply, he found the strength to speak. "I…" he whispered. "I put my hand on her waist…she was so…soft…"

The last few words came out so quietly that Ártur barely heard them. He leaned forward. "Is that all? What then?"

Kavan moved away from his cousin before he spoke again, his dejection and horror deepening. "I pushed her away, fled through the Gate, and returned to Natrona."

"That is all that passed between you?"

The bard's head bobbed once as he turned. Though tempted to laugh, the healer squelched the impulse. He had been expecting something more. That there was no more to Kavan's 'downfall' from perfection was both amusing and sad. "I do not see what you are distraught about…"

"We kissed!" Kavan squeaked, spinning back to stare at the healer.

"Yes. What of it? So have millions of other men and women throughout history. Do not tell me you have not seen others kiss. It is a normal, natural response to attraction and affection. Innis and Cordelia…Dháná and Tám…Arlan and Brenna…me and Elys…and every married or courting couple that has ever existed most likely…"

"You?" The bewildered silence that followed told the healer that not only had his cousin never been kissed, he had apparently never thought about it and had never considered the possibility of it happening to him.

"It is normal, Kavan, and hardly a mortal sin. There is nothing wrong with a kiss. A moment of passion does not damn you. If it did, no one would ever stand a chance of redemption."

"It is not just that…" How Kavan wished it were. Perhaps Ártur could explain away that act, but Kavan doubted he could excuse the rest. "When I got to Natrona…I sincerely wished she would follow…wished to go back…to hold her again…to…thyá Dhágdhuán…I do not know what I wanted. But since then, I have missed her…no…not her necessarily…but the feelings…things I never knew it possible to feel. I crave her…and I cannot…stop. Every time I sleep, there are dreams; there are always dreams. Tonight, I…" He covered his face with quaking hands. "I have defiled the steps of the altar with my thoughts, my dreams. Everywhere I look, I hear her, see her, smell her…feel her. I cannot…"

"Do you love her?"

"What?"

This time Ártur could not hold back the laugh of amusement. There should have been nothing funny in this, but Kavan's terror at such an innocent occurrence was beguiling. He caught his cousin's arms as Kavan tried to move further away, and pulled him back to the step. In a steady voice, no longer laughing, he asked again, "Do you love her?"

Still fighting shame and embarrassment, the bard weighed the question before replying. "I do not know her. I do not believe you can love someone you do not know…and I do not know her. I do not believe in the theory of love at first sight."

"So that is it then." Ártur shifted off his knees to sit. Carefully arranging his words, he smiled as he continued. "What you are experiencing, it happens to everyone…men and women, Teren and Elyri. When I first met Elys, I had dreams about her for many years. I have such dreams now, only they are about someone else. I have heard such stories from many…men on the battlefield, women around the fires. It is different for Teren; they experience this at a certain age, as they approach adulthood. It does not take another person to spark it. For us, it is brought on by the first person we meet who touches some primitive chord within us, someone with whom we share a kinship of spirit. For Teren, it is usually more about physical attraction, for us it is a psychic one. It awakens those impulses and desires we all have, that you have been experiencing."

"But we are taught not to give in to lustful thinking…"

Ártur rolled his eyes, seeing where this was going. "No one can control their sleeping dreams…or their body's reactions to them." He clenched Kavan's hands as his cousin tried to squirm away. He could not believe Kavan, so seemingly wise and learned, could be this naïve. The healer had never had to explain this to someone so late in their life, though he had explained it many times. And he had never thought he would need to bring morality into the discussion. He could not scoff, however, or he would hurt his cousin sorely and do more damage than good.

"k'Ádhá would never condemn a man for his dreams. Nor would He condemn anyone for the physical impulses of the body. We are made as we are, given these impulses, to bring us together, to create new life, to give each of us love and companionship. It is what we are meant to do. He never forbade us being attracted…"

"If gdhededhá are not supposed to…

Ártur shook his head. "They have taken vows that deter them from acting on those desires, from marrying or procreating. Have you made such vows?"

Sighing, Kavan lowered his head. "No. But what of Saint Kóráhm?"

The healer wanted to ask what the Heretic Saint had to do with this discussion. He knew that Kavan was quite enamored with the man after whom he had been named, but it seemed to have no bearing that Ártur could see. "What about him? We were not alive during his time. We do not have the intimate details of his daily affairs, only that which he wrote or was handed down through legend. But we do know he was not gdhededhá. He could have had a wife or someone of interest. What of the woman that reoccurs in many of his stories? Might his relationship with her be more than platonic?"

"We do not know," Kavan reluctantly conceded.

"Exactly. You cannot assume he never knew love, and because he was a man, you cannot assume he never experienced the same things you have been." When Kavan's expression did not change, he continued, exasperated, "k'Ádhá forgive me, but even Dhágdhuán was said to have experienced every temptation known to us. He did not act on them, and that is what set him apart. But you are not him. You are not gdhededhá, you have taken no vows. You did not act on your impulses, you controlled them, and that is admirable. Not everyone can do that, as you know. If we did not feel such things, if there was no attraction or love…you and I would not be sitting here discussing this, or we would all be the products of violence and rape."

The force of the words had a visible effect on Kavan. The tension began to ease out of his shoulders and his hands grew steadier. Softly, he asked, "Will these dreams ever go away? Will I ever be able to sleep?"

Ártur smiled. "It is always worst in the beginning. Until your psyche learns to process these new impulses, you can expect to experience pretty much what you have been. Berating yourself has likely intensified the dreams; your mind cannot learn to process something you are actively fighting against. But it will fade in time, particularly once you stop becoming upset over it. It will never completely leave you; once stirred it is part of us as long as we live. When…if…you meet someone, fall in love, then it will be strongest. If you marry, it will be a blessing to you both. In the meantime, there is nothing you can do to stop it. Do not condemn yourself needlessly, Kavan. It is not healthy…and I am sure k'Ádhá is not condemning you for it."

The náós was silent except for the hiss of the wind that pushed through the cracks in the rafters above them. The bard continued to stare at his hands, which his cousin was unconsciously stroking. When Ártur realized what he was doing, he released Kavan awkwardly and cleared his throat, shattering the silence. Kavan rubbed his eyes.

"You make it seem…"

"Normal?"

Kavan nodded.

"It is normal. Here…sit for a bit. I will let you think on these things…" He started to stand but Kavan caught his wrist.

"Where are you going?" He might have unburdened his soul, but he was not ready to be alone.

Ártur kissed his forehead affectionately. "I have something for you. Wait here. I want you to think about what I have said while I am gone; I will return quickly."

Reluctantly, Kavan inclined his head in acceptance and watched his cousin disappear into the darkness before kneeling again. Had he been wrong? Had it been his own naiveté that had brought this offensive shadow between himself and k'Ádhá? Ártur's words, as a healer who knew such things, made perfect sense now that he heard them spoken, and Kavan was ashamed that he had not considered this before. He had known, intellectually, all of what Ártur had said, and yet he had never thought to apply it to himself, as if he was somehow above mortal impulses and tribulations. Kóráhm had said he was wise, yet he did not even have the wisdom to face the simplest issues of mortality.

He lifted his head to focus on the dusty, carved image of Dhágdhuán. Was that why Kóráhm had sent him to Káliel? To teach him humility? To teach him that there were still many things he did not know? To remind him that he was not god-like but was, in fact, very corporeal and must come to terms with that? There was the faintest glimmer of hope and relief in his core by the time Ártur returned.

"My harp!" The case the healer carried could be nothing else. Kavan eagerly took it and lifted the small instrument from its velvet nest. Fingers caressing its smooth surface, he tuned it without making a sound, eyes closed in a way that lent a tender expression to his features. To Ártur, it appeared the reunification of two long-separated lovers and stirred deep happiness within him. This was a love Kavan never questioned. He could feel in the bard's aura that, while Kavan still had a long journey ahead to heal from the self-inflicted emotional trauma he had carried, he was more at ease than he had been when Ártur had found him.

"I thought you might want this. I do not think the two of you have ever been apart for this long. I would not doubt that some of your depression stems from that separation. You could not release your passions and questions through your music as you are accustomed to; they knotted up inside of you and made you miserable. Play for me, sínréc. I have missed your music."

"Not yet." He laid the harp across his lap and looked at Ártur. "While we are...there is something else..."

The healer sat once more, expression faltering as he vaguely dreaded what might come next. "More to the story?"

"No," Kavan sighed, thankful for that. "This is something else. Do you remember when I was apart from the men after we left Chantel?" Ártur nodded. "I knew that Prince Arlan was in danger, that something was wrong, but I did not know what. It troubled me, and I kept looking. It was...finally, before we reached Tarsee...the night I came back to camp...I found the source."

"I remember you saying something about it being done." Because Kavan had not spoken of it then, Ártur had given that night little thought since. He was surprised to have it come back now.

Kavan continued to stroke the wooden body of the harp, his eyes following the movements of his fingers. "There were seven of them, royal militia. They would have killed both Prince Arlan and Guthrie if I had not...dealt with them."

"Dealt with them how?" the healer asked with a scowl.

"I did not think…after what I Saw. I was angry, terrified for Arlan. I was in wolf form at the time the Sight came…and they were…" He shuddered. "I killed two of them before I realized what I was doing."

"You are…are you sure?"

Kavan nodded. "I was there. I remember. Technically, one died because he fell on his sword. But the other…his throat…I tasted his blood in my mouth…still do sometimes. I never told anyone. I did not intend for it to happen, it just…did."

This time when Ártur embraced him it was for his own comfort, not knowing how else to respond to this admission. That this far more serious moral affront distressed Kavan less than Gabrielle Dilyn's kiss confused the healer. The only explanation for it could be, perhaps, that the deaths had been in the defense of Prince Arlan, and thus Kavan had felt them justified. Perhaps they had been. The healer's oath would not allow Ártur to kill a man knowingly, and he had never believed Kavan to be capable of violence. He had, he realized, been wrong.

"I do not know what to tell you, Kavan. You did what you…what seemed necessary at the time. You saved Prince Arlan's life, and possibly an entire kingdom. Surely k'Ádhá understands that. Still, in this matter, I am not qualified to give advice or absolution."

Kavan nodded as he drew back. "Absolution is not what I seek. Forgiveness I have…there is no need to share this with anyone else. But you? Do you…?"

"kyá sínréc, you know me better than that. I could not hold such a thing against you. I am surprised, but you knew I would be. I will share this with no one if that is your wish." He put his hand carefully on the harp, knowing how treasured the instrument was. "Will you play for me? Please? Put your soul at ease, sínréc?"

"I will." Kavan settled onto his knees, facing the sculpture behind the altar, and knelt for many minutes with his hands clasped in prayer. Ártur let him take his time, understanding that Kavan needed that prayer as much as anything. He was beginning to think, however, that the music might not come tonight when the bard finally genuflected and touched his fingers to the strings. The notes that poured forth were at first desperately haunting, filled with longing, confusion, pain, and desire, a pouring out of all the questions and emotions he had needed to release. The healer closed his eyes and allowed himself to ride the music, to feel each note with his cousin, gaining some small degree of insight into how much pain Kavan had endured.

Slowly, however, the tone of the music began to change, growing more serene and calm, and the healer sensed an unusual tingle that started along his spine and slowly spread throughout his body until it surrounded him. And light. It felt as if he were in the midst of the brightest, purest of light on a warm summer's day. Increasingly joyous overtones began to creep into the song, but Ártur dared not open his eyes for fear the experience would end. This was for Kavan, not for him. The music was ecstasy, and he believed with all his heart that Kavan had found the answers he had been searching for.

The brass strings fell silent, though nothing else changed, and when they did not sing again, the healer opened his eyes to find his cousin standing at the base of the pyre figure, touching its feet. Kavan's hands were stained with red as the blood from those wounds trickled over them. Ártur came to stand at his cousin's side, awed to have witnessed this transformation a second time.

When Kavan's eyes met his for the first time, they were clear and steady, although tears coursed freely down his cheeks. But he was smiling, that faint, ecstatic, innocent smile Ártur had fallen in love with long ago. Wetting his lips, Kavan whispered, "I have come home."

Ártur put his hand on Kavan's sticky wet one, smiling with tender relief though he was not sure what Kavan's words meant. Still, he could tell that it was a good thing, and that pleased him. "Prince Arlan and the others will be happy to hear that. As am I."

⁊Chapter 45⁊

"Has anyone seen Ártur?" Prince Arlan asked as he accepted the plate of steaming ham and bread from the comely girl who delivered it. He smiled, wishing to be polite and respectful but not wanting to encourage her attention. There had been a steady stream of women surrounding them since arriving in Rhidam, women who either did not know, or did not care, that he had already taken a queen. Guthrie found the situation amusing since he knew that the prince had never dealt with this sort of devotion, and Caol was lapping it up, encouraging them to return. In the end, the prince could do nothing but endure the attention with smiles and kind words and try to live up to the nobility of his station. "His blankets were empty; it is not like him to wander away without telling someone where he is going."

Guthrie shook his head, his mouth full of food hindering his immediate reply. When he swallowed, he coughed and said, "Can't say I have, but this is a large camp. He could be tending someone's ailment from all of the food we had last night."

Wiping his mouth, Bhríd agreed. "I thought I would never want to eat again…and here we are." He laughed and held up his partially empty plate.

"Making up for months of travel rations," Caol added with a laugh. For such a small-bodied man, Caol could eat a great deal. Around them, the men were gathered in circles, eating heartily of the food brought by the townsfolk. There was little talking, just the sounds of hungry men greedily consuming what they were given. "Besides, doesn't he know this city? He could be visiting..."

The prince froze, head cocked. "Listen...do you hear that...?"

"Hear...?" Caol started, but there was a hush now drowning out even the sounds of eating, and over that, very faintly, came the tinkling chords of brass harp strings. "It sounds like..."

"Kavan!"

The prince dropped his tin plate into the trampled grass as he leapt up and looked hastily around. He spotted the white Elyri bard perched precariously on a crate with his harp resting on one knee, no more than ten feet away. The prince's first impulse was to run, to throw his arms around the man, but the need for dignity in front of his troops and the citizens of Rhidam kept him from it. It did not, however, remove the excited bounce from his step as he wove his way through the seated crowd. When Prince Arlan reached him, Kavan stopped playing to allow the prince to clasp his hand.

"Praise k'Ádhá you are here! You look exhausted, Kavan! Have you slept? Do you want breakfast? Hatu's troops...?"

Kavan squeezed the prince's hand in return. If he had received this greeting last night, he did not think he could have endured it. Now, however, he was sincerely glad to see the prince again. "They will arrive later today. I took the liberty of coming ahead." He looked at his cousin with a small, grateful smile. "There was something I needed to do."

Whatever passed between the cousins, Prince Arlan realized he was not meant to know about it. At the moment, however, he did not care. "It does not matter why you are here before them, but I am very pleased you are." Unconcerned with what the men around them thought, he embraced the bard tightly and murmured in his ear, "I have missed you."

"And I you, My Prince," came the flustered reply as Kavan awkwardly returned that embrace.

"I suppose you flew in?"

Prince Arlan's teasing grin brought a touch of mirth to the bard's face. "How else? What has happened to your cheek?"

"That is a long story, one I will tell you later," the prince said with a shrug. "Come, both of you. I shall have Caol find you something to eat." Tugging on his arm, Prince Arlan led the bard and healer into his inner circle where the others stood and smiled in welcome.

"Welcome back, Lord Harper," Bhríd smiled, having readied two plates for his kinsmen. "We are glad to have you back. Where are King Geir's troops?"

Kavan drank of the water he was given before replying. "They will arrive later today. We have had no military encounters, and I saw none of King Owain's men on the way; I do not expect them to encounter difficulties. Lady Dilyn has sent five of her personal guards to serve you, My Prince. They will arrive with the troops."

"Excellent," the general smiled. "Káliel guardsmen are exceptional swordsmen...and if they served the Magistrate's house, they will be at the top of their form. If nothing else, we can use them to train others. They will be a welcome addition."

Other voices joined in agreement as the bard scanned the camp. "We do not seem to be short of men..."

That observation brought a shrug and dark cloud to the general's demeanor. "We had three battles and lost many men. The young and common folk mostly. Fortunately, we gained several hundred more from defections of Enesfel's forces or we would be suffering now. It evens out in the end. And...we lost Phaedr..."

Kavan's eyes closed in mourning, but Prince Arlan, not wanting to discuss such poignant things today, quickly added, "He saved the standard and my life. I honor him for it. Owain may not have lost as many men, but he has lost a greater percentage of his force, particularly his cavalry."

"Have you spoken with him?"

"He's avoiding us. He lost many of his officers and most of his cavalry…I think he hopes the weather will drive us away." Caol indicated the cloud-laden sky. "Early Elcalum is always a fine time for rain."

Kavan groaned. "I do not want to see another rain storm for a long time. What are our plans?"

Done with his meal, Guthrie set his plate on the ground. It did not surprise him that Kavan was focused on the business at hand; the bard was rarely one to delay responsibility with frivolity. "We are waiting for the King to agree to a meeting…although I think it unlikely he will. We do not want to take any sort of military action until Hatu's infantry arrives. We might be able to hold our own with what we have, but I would rather not take the risk. We cannot afford to see Rhidam destroyed in our fighting. Once Hatu's men are here, and the King agrees to meet, we will present Arlan and give our demands. Since it is almost certain he will not give in to us, and may not meet with us at all, we have been working on contingencies to take the keep."

"Siege would be difficult and time-consuming," Kavan pointed out, "and getting across the bridge…"

"Hey," Caol scoffed with a laugh. "If my friends could capture the towers and bridge once, we can certainly do it again…though this time would not be as easy to orchestrate or accomplish. I doubt they will fall for kidnapping the princess a second time." He grinned at Kavan's amazed, questioning expression. "Don't worry, she agreed to go along with the plan and was not harmed. She is also willing to do anything to postpone marrying that monster."

"The princess…?" Kavan murmured, again surprised by the King's choices, although perhaps he should not be. He had been persistently trying to win her hand since King Girvin's reign many years ago.

Prince Arlan snorted. "Yes…on our birthday…which means I must get into the castle before then. I cannot allow her to marry him…"

"No," Kavan agreed, his voice trailing off and his face taking on a faraway thoughtful look. "You cannot…"

Leaning closer, the prince grasped his knee. "What? Do you have an idea?" He knew that expression.

The bard rubbed his temples. There were always possibilities, but how feasible were they? "I do not know yet. Perhaps. Let me think on it for a while. For now, I…"

"For now," interrupted Ártur, "Lord Harper needs to sleep. He has not had a decent sleep in weeks, and if he does not sleep of his own accord now, I shall be forced to make him." He shook his head at his cousin's consternation. "No arguments, cousin."

"You should sleep, Lord Harper. You look like you need it." The others around Bhríd agreed.

Prince Arlan stood and offered his hand. "Use my tent. No one will disturb you there. You are here and we are one again. We will talk later. Rest, my friend. That is an order from the prince."

Beaten, knowing they were right even if he did not want to admit it, Kavan picked up his harp and followed the healer towards the prince's tent. Once within the confines of those canvas walls, however, he said curtly, "You know I cannot sleep. The dreams…"

Ártur wagged his finger. "I can suppress them long enough to allow you a decent sleep and will make it possible for you to feel well-rested when you wake. I hope you are not going to fight me on this, cousin, because I do not think, after last night and what little sleep I got, I am in any mood to argue with you."

Although his expression and tone of voice told Kavan his cousin was teasing, the bard still felt responsible for that lack of sleep. "I am sorry, Ártur. So...you are going to rest too?"

Ártur scowled. His cousin was plotting something, he could tell. "That was my plan. Why? What do you need?"

"I need someone to find something for me if I am not allowed to find it myself."

"Dare I ask what?"

Kavan stretched out his legs on the King's bedroll. "bhydáni Tíbhyan told legends about how the Teren, in their first attempt to expel us from this land, discovered a secret entrance under the Rhidam palace which allowed them to sneak in and kill the Elyri ruler. That entrance was used later, I believe, during the Persecution as well. If such a passage exists..."

The healer sat beside him, eyes wide and sparkling with the possibilities that presented. He did not recall those stories, but he suspected they were not parts of history often taught to the average Elyri child. Kavan, he knew, had never been an average child. The unique educational experience he had shared with the bhydáni as his mentor had undoubtedly opened knowledge to Kavan not many could share. "We could get into the keep, surprise the King, and avoid mass bloodshed."

"Yes...perhaps," Kavan said. "Enough lives have been lost; I hesitate to risk more unnecessarily. Enesfel has suffered too much. There must be a book or document that suggests where such an entrance could be...or someone in Rhidam might know. If you could inquire around town, discreetly, learn what you can...I am willing to rest as you ask."

"And if I do not find anything?" asked Ártur, already committing to the quest against his better judgment.

"Then," Kavan replied as he lay back, "I will search tonight."

The healer knew what his cousin meant and he shook his head no. "You are not going into the castle…"

"You have done it. I have done it before. A bird, a stray cat, a rat…any number of creatures could get around without being noticed, and I am capable of defending myself."

Ártur groaned. "I don't like it…but you know that. You will do it even if I tell you not to…so…you want me to keep silent about this?"

"Until we know it is possible, yes. Prince Arlan still tends, I think, to rush into schemes without all of the details, and this must be dealt with carefully. This would not be information we want exposed to the world. It would be wise not to act too hastily against the King."

"I will see what I can find. Now…close your eyes and relax. Yes…think music. Good…"

Ártur tenderly placed his hands on both sides' of his cousin's face, feeling the notes that danced within the beautiful white head. He could almost hear the tune as he closed his eyes and located the points within Kavan that would allow his cousin a much-needed sleep. As soon as he touched them, the tension left Kavan's body and the bard slept. The healer remained there looking at him, his fingers tangled in the thick, white hair, tracing the lines of Kavan's face with his other hand, feeling again the perfection he always felt when he studied the bard's features. Before he slid away, he wrapped several blankets around the sleeping form to keep out the autumn chill and left the tent.

❧*❧

He had seen the General do it, had shadowed him to the fringe of the enemy camp and had skimmed around the edges of it, assessing it for weaknesses while Ferghus had met with whomever was in the heart of this encampment. There had to be weaknesses. Too many in that company were common folk, men and women with little training or skill. Common folk in common clothing with common weapons or none at all. It was easy, therefore to mingle, to feign their enthusiasm for the traitorous acts of Guthrie McHador.

Young enough to only know the man by reputation and the talk of his elders, he had no reason to think those tales anything more than exaggerated rumor built out of the myths of wars long fought. It took only one dissenting voice to spark the fire of determination, to under-cut the traitor and save the rightfully appointed King of Enesfel. Per-haps King Owain was not the best of kings, but he was Enesfel's king, a Lachlan by blood and crowned according to centuries of custom. A man with no royal blood in his veins would never claim Enesfel's throne. It would only take the act of a single daring, dedicated man, to see that made so.

A man who stood to gain acclaim, wealth, and favor if he could do what generals and captains and armies could not.

He threaded through the crowd, a smile, a mock oath, words of support all bolstering the appearance that he belonged here, that he was one more face among many who had given their loyalty to a cause that many did not entirely understand. That there was more to this ru-mor became increasingly obvious the further inward he delved, but he was resolute, the justification of his cause enough to push him deeper into the crowd.

As the ranks of the faithless closing behind him grew thicker, it began to gradually occur to him that, succeed or fail, he might not retreat from this alive. The adoration and reward he believed could be his might never fall into his hands. But success would stand his family in good political favor, grant his infant son rights that none in their family had ever held. That, and belief in the righteousness of his cause, held him true to course.

Not much further now. An inner ring of loosely scattered soldiers at arm, men less attentive as their confidence in the King's impotency to reach them grew heavy upon their shoulders and in their bellies full of rich food, sweet wine, and potent ale. A carefully chosen path would get him to a position where the deed could be done from a place of relative secrecy and safety.

When he found that place, hidden amidst horses, tents, and wagons that had transported all manner of support for these traitors, he crouched in a shadow that offered both protection and an unobstructed view of General McHador's inner circle. He knew his target from portraits revealed on the walls of the Guild Hall, where the city sheriff and his men, a number of physicians, legal counsellors, clerks and money lenders gathered to do business with heads of commerce and nobility alike. Those portraits, however, military and political in nature, had shown him more than the face of the man he was seeking to destroy.

They had also revealed the faces of kings.

Familiarity with those images laid bare the identity of the other in the general's company, one who was neither soldier nor commoner nor Elyri.

One who wore the burgundy and amber…and the posture and poise of a Lachlan prince.

He did not know what this meant. He did not know Lachlan familial politics, knew little of the history birthed when he had been a lad barely old enough to walk and speak on his own. Those long ago histories meant nothing. All that mattered was the duty he had been given.

But he was smart enough to understand in that moment that removing McHador was not going to be enough to put an end to this madness and save the King. If this unknown unfamiliar Lachlan was the root of this invasion, then he too must fall.

Resolve steeled, he crept forward.

Sharpening the knife of Elyri steel he carried with him at all time, ever prepared to lose his sword in battle or to be caught unaware even here within the relative safety of Prince Arlan's core camp, Bhríd listened to the debate between Arlan and Guthrie without participating. He considered himself well-schooled in the tactics of battle, would have been pleased to offer the prince his knowledge. But Guthrie had experience Bhríd did not, and thus the dark-haired Elyri was satisfied to listen and learn and speak only if spoken to. There was much to learn from that man and listening allowed Bhríd to concentrate his other senses on the atmosphere around them.

Arlan felt untouchable here, protected at the core of the company who had fought for him, fought beside him. The King's silence bolstered that sense of presumed security. Here, in the bright sun of midday, with Kavan asleep in the nearest tent and the newly arrived Káliel guardsmen clustered around it at the Prince's request, there seemed little to fear as they awaited a reply from Owain. Bhríd, perhaps because he was Elyri in the heart of a Teren conflict, perhaps because he had lost a brother to it, did not share that confidence. Being so near the castle where his kinsman had been held prisoner by the man housed within it felt to be cause enough for his uneasiness.

He lifted his head, that uneasiness spiking, raking through the hairs on the nape of his neck so that they stood on end. Thinking at first the sensation to be a result of the dark shift in his thoughts, a sympathetic reaction to what Kavan had endured that had served as the final call to action for Prince Arlan, he closed his eyes, his hands still and tense, to listen, to feel, to banish memories he knew only by the repetition of them from the healer. But the agitation would not leave, and the focus upon it quickly converged upon a point to his right, somewhere behind his shoulder amidst the skittish horses and a collection of water barrels and crates of goods offered by the citizens of Rhidam.

The hand upon his knife tensed, lifting the blade slightly from the whetstone. He could not turn to look without revealing his suspicion, without alerting the shadow that his presence had been noted. Turning would alert the prince and general as well and lead to an eruption of chaos and the possibility of success and escape for whatever the stranger had planned. Bhríd gauged everything, the stranger's line of sight, the possible trajectory of any projectile aimed into their circle, his own position and the likelihood of success or failure of the various actions he could take.

There seemed but a single solution, a single act, to be followed.

In that split second moment, when the air about him burst into life, when it crackled with electric tension of a sort only men in battle could gauge, or perhaps only an Elyri could gauge, he stood, turned, and side-stepped with an accompanying snap of his wrist. The air was sucked out of him as if to propel his blade in the straight line he saw in his mind's eye, and at the moment it struck home, drawing with it a cry of pain, Bhríd inhaled to refill the void in his chest. It was an aborted effort, however, as the short steel bolt ripped through the flesh below his ribs and tore clean though him. His interference was enough to alter the bolt's trajectory, enough to give Guthrie the opportunity to push the prince to the ground and lay upon him.

Bloody now, the metal shaft embedded in the wooden pole that served as the corner of the tent where Kavan slept.

The Káliel guards encircled the prince while others scrambled to drag the assailant from the shadows. Bhríd's knife had caught the young fellow, little more than a boy, in the throat, and though he lived still, blood gushed from the wound and from his mouth, turning to pink foam as his lungs filled with it and efforts to breathe failed. Ignoring his own heavily bleeding injury, Bhríd charged the man being dragged into their midst and locked his hand around the other's bare wrist. That wound was fatal; there would be no opportunity to question his motives, but there were ways, Elyri ways, of learning the truth.

Both fell to the ground, one stumbling, one wrenched from the hold of his captors by the drag of the Elyri's extra weight. The physical contact between them was brief, but it was enough.

Bhríd groaned and allowed himself the luxury of lying still while others rushed about him. He felt warm. He felt cold. He felt content. He felt restless. Someone needed to know, but his eyes would not open and his lips would not part. His injury was not that bad surely.

"Bhríd!"

That was his sister. Dear, sweet Syl who missed their brother so badly. Her hands, tender upon the edges of the puncture from which he bled. Through those fingers, energy flowed, replacing the haze of pain and blood loss with a clarity and vigor that kept him from slipping over the precipice of life into the eternal. When both were gone, the pain and the current of power, he was able to force his eyes open to focus on her face.

"Thank..." he began to murmur, closing his hand around hers.

"Bhríd? Are you well?" It was Prince Arlan's voice that interrupted, Prince Arlan's face that appeared, distressed and frightened, over the lady healer's shoulder. He did not need to ask what had just happened. Despite his false sense of security, he was no fool. Someone had tried to kill him, or perhaps kill Guthrie. It did not matter which. Either was the same crime in Arlan's eyes, and either intent deserved the fate Bhríd had meted out.

"I will live." He pushed himself up with his sister's help, gently fingering the tender bruised flesh beneath his ribs. "I am sorry he did not...but at least I know his intent." Looking up at the general who now stood behind Arlan, he said, "He was sent here for you, milord...but thought to be rid of you both upon seeing you, My Prince."

"Sent by whom? The King?"

Bhríd shook his head. "I do not know...a fellow soldier brought him the written command. Without access to that message..."

"We will never know...but it came from Owain. I know it did." Exasperated, Prince Arlan crossed his arms over his chest. Lack of proof did little to dissuade him from the belief that his nephew wanted him dead, which in turn fueled his desire to have Owain's head on a pike that had arisen when he had learned of the man's intention to wed Deidre.

"Well, Lord Champion, you have saved us both, for which I thank you. Please…sit with us…this demands immediate action. If this is how he wishes to conduct negotiations, we can no longer wait."

"Champion?" Bhríd humbly bowed his head. He had not joined this venture for title or wealth or even recognition. He had come for the adventure, and because it was a cause he believed in, without any thought given to what might come after, should they succeed. Taking up a title would demand certain sacrifices on his part, such as remaining in Enesfel instead of returning home, but it was also the sort of honor he felt compelled to accept.

The prince hesitated, his gaze falling upon the would-be assassin who lay dead and bloody at his feet. Did he have the right to appoint an Elyri to the post of King's Champion? Was it the proper thing to do? Would such a man as this, who had selflessly acted to sacrifice himself in order to save Arlan's life, from a race of people who espoused non-violence, even consider it?

His moment of revulsion at the site at his feet and his hesitant questioning of his own offer was buried beneath the act of pulling Bhríd's dagger free and handing it back to him. "If you would do me the honor, yes. I can think of no one better."

Bhríd paused only long enough to look at his sister and accept his dagger before bowing his head. "It will be my honor to serve you, milord…in whatever way I am able."

"Good." Arlan's smiled. "Join us then…and someone take this," he pointed at the deceased, "and put it somewhere my nephew will be sure to find it. I want him to know his efforts to be rid of us have failed."

◈White Pawn◈

❧Chapter 46❦

K avan emerged from Prince Arlan's tent in time for the evening meal, and as Ártur had promised, he felt more rested than he had in many weeks. After much cajoling, he agreed to play. Soldiers, townsmen, local peasants, all gathered thickly about the prince's core group so that Kavan could barely see beyond them. He could see that Hatu's infantry had arrived earlier in the day as expected and the five Káliel guardsmen had been welcomed into the prince's inner circle. Bhríd and the nomads were the only ones to match or surpass them in size. Captain Delamo, after an initial scolding look that suggested Kavan should have told him he was going ahead to Rhidam, took up a protective stance beside the bard and refused to move from it. The prince looked more at ease with them at his side, though Kavan wondered how much of that peace was due to his own presence, rather than that of the Káliel guards.

The thick tension in the air revealed that something had occurred during his rest, a ruckus directly outside of his tent that had not roused him from sleep, an attempt on a life, Arlan's or Guthrie's, that Bhríd had thankfully thwarted. The prince seemed disinclined to discuss it with Kavan, however, except to say that a plan was in the works that would bring Owain to justice for the attempt. Kavan saw enough in the general's expression to know the disinclination was due to a fear that the bard too might attempt to talk Arlan out of a hasty, brash decision, one Guthrie was doing everything he could to dampen and delay for as long as possible. The need for that hidden morsel of information, therefore, was all the more pressing and Kavan knew he had to seek it out, find it, tonight if he was to keep Arlan from doing something he might later regret.

He knew Ártur had not been successful in finding any useful information, although one old man had revealed that King Innis' great grandfather had confiscated most documents pertaining to the castle's history, which meant that if they had not been destroyed, they were likely inside the castle. Although Kavan enjoyed the much-missed adoration of his music and would have, under other circumstances, gladly played far into the night, tonight he wanted the crowd to disperse and everyone to sleep so that he could steal away and do what was needed. Several hours later, when his patience had worn thin, he graciously refused to play anymore and the crowd began to drift slowly apart.

"Milord," he said to the prince, "I am still weary…"

"By all means," the prince said with a smile that suggested he was glad the bard was not intending to press him for details of the unresolved matter between them. "Rest. We will soon be busy enough; take all the rest you need."

Kavan exchanged looks with Guthrie, hoping the general would speak with him later about events and plans he felt he should be aware of, and then got to his feet. No one tried to stop him as he chose, this time, to retreat to his cousin's tent for the proposed period of rest. Ártur would not question his absence, should he find him gone during the night. The prince, on the other hand, certainly would, and an argument would ensue about keeping secrets that Kavan was not interested in having. Captain Delamo insisted on following and settled outside the tent for the night as if to guard there. His presence meant Kavan would have to make a show of sleeping; he moved about within the tent as if preparing a bed and getting comfortable. When he felt the captain had relaxed his guard enough, Kavan would act.

Soon, no one was left at the fire except the healer, who had chosen to wait until the fire burned itself out. He knew he would try to stop Kavan from going to the castle if he followed him to the tent, and the attempt and subsequent failure would prove frustrating to them both; it seemed wiser to stay where he was. He could worry just as well here. It would snow soon. Maybe within days. Feeling that damp chill in the air, he pulled his dark green cloak closer around his body and stared at the dying embers, trying not to think about what his cousin was planning or the plans for conflict that were bandied about between the prince and general. After hearing about the day's earlier events, Ártur did not want any more bloodshed. He wanted this to be over.

"May I join you, milord?"

Startled, Ártur looked up at the beautiful round face and nodded, "Of course, milady…there is no need for you to ask permission to sit before one of the last fires in camp." He had barely seen Syl since they reached Rhidam and he had wondered often where she was. It struck him again, as she sat, how beautiful she was.

Syl pushed a stray wisp of blonde hair behind her ear. "Perhaps, but I would not blame you if you do not desire my company. I have been far from cordial of late."

"Understandable. We have all been busy and under great pressure…and you have suffered much. I think some of the tension has passed with our arrival in Rhidam but…"

"I think Kavan's return is what dispelled it. He is a blessing to all who know him. It is a pity he must always be disconsolate."

Ártur sighed. She was likely right about Kavan's arrival changing everything, but his cousin would never admit to that. "I know. I do what I can to give him happiness, but I do not think it is enough."

"You care for him very much, don't you?" She picked up a small bit of wood and tossed it into the fire.

He began to retort as if her words were some sort of accusation, but then he groaned and his shoulders sagged. Poking through the ashes with a stick to allow the new bit of wood to ignite, he said, "I have since the day I helped bring him into this world. It is almost as if he were my own son. He is more a part of me than he will ever know."

"Like Phaedr." Syl sniffed and clasped her hands together. "I think that is what angered me most…that you still have that one person who meant everything to you. I was always Phaedr's favorite; we use to do everything together as children. Though I was younger, I was his care-taker, his problem solver. This time, I could not solve his problems. I could do nothing for him…and now he is gone."

Though he did not think his words would offer comfort, Ártur offered them anyhow. "He died valiantly, Syl. There are few men who can see, and fewer who are blind, who would attempt what he did…or who would have succeeded. He saved Prince Arlan's life. I believe he knew what he was doing, and what the consequences of his choices could be. He had to know…in order to get onto the battlefield, to the prince, the way he did. He wanted to be important; he wanted his loss to mean something. He will be immortalized for what he did."

"I know…but that does not make losing him any easier. I was angry because…I am a healer, but I could not give him back his sight, or his life. There was nothing I could do. This time, when it mattered most, I could not help him." A sob wracked her body and she wiped her eyes. Ártur did not yet try to comfort her though he ached to. He did not want to upset her further by offering unwanted intimacy.

"I have wondered since then," he started, "if Kavan could have restored his life…but I realize that, if k'Ádhá had meant for that to be, Kavan would have been there. I wish there was something we could have done, Syl. I am sorry."

"I…know." It was hard to admit, but saying it aloud lifted a weight from her shoulders. "After fearing I would lose Bhríd today, and irrationally feeling that you should have been there to help him, I realized you cannot be in each place every time someone is hurt. You are only one man…and gifted as you are, I cannot blame you for everything. I am sorry. May we be friends again? I know you have Kavan, but I miss your friendship…your company."

Ártur edged closer to her, his heart hammering in his chest. The news about Bhríd's injury had been reported to him upon his return to camp, and he had inspected the site of the injury to reassure himself, despite his trust in Syl's ability. It too had made him think about Phaedr, and like Syl, he had needed to remind himself that he could not be in every place at once, that not all injuries were his to solve. Not all lives could be saved, despite his intentions and efforts. "Syl, you are not Kavan, Kavan is not you. It hurt to lose you, even for a little while, but I believed you would come back to me. I had to believe it. I think I…"

She looked into his face expectantly, the quiver of her lips suggesting something far different from grief. He swallowed hard, aware of the silly grin that was trying to cross his face. "Yes?" she whispered.

He liked what he saw in the soft green light of her eyes, liked what he felt radiating from her proximity, and he liked the way she made him feel. "I think I love you, Syl."

She lowered her gaze briefly, a matching silly grin spreading across her face. "And I you, Lord Healer. I think I always have." She slid into his embrace and stayed there.

❧*❧

The white raven landed on the sill of the open window he had found and glanced around the dark room with a ruffle of feathers. Kavan had chosen this shape in the hopes that anyone seeing him would know the superstitions and respond with anxiety and fear, particularly if that someone was the King.

But Owain was not in his chambers. Kavan took his own form, to make his search easier, listening with all of his senses for anyone's approach. The King's private rooms were a good place for important books to have been placed, particularly ones that might be best kept out of the hands of the general staff. He found nothing useful, however, and assumed the raven form once more to move to the second level of the castle. He did not think any of the other bedchambers on the third floor worth the time to investigate.

Other than patrolling soldiers, the second floor of the castle was empty. There were no guests, no tutors, and no reason for anyone to be in either the morning room on the east side of the castle or the drawing room at this late hour. He found no manuscripts, no books, in any of these rooms, but he had not expected to. If they were not in the King's chambers and had not been destroyed, then either the library, the State Room, or the storage rooms in the dungeon would be the most likely locations for them to be kept. And if there was a suspected secret entrance, it was likely on the first floor as well. He wanted to make that search before turning to the library where he would likely be lost in ancient texts for hours. The second level searched and secure, Kavan moved on.

There were guards occupying the billeting rooms, and the kitchen was cluttered with a group of servants discussing the army sitting at the edge of Rhidam. None of them could fathom why they did not attack, or why the King had not taken action against them. That was, even to Kavan, a peculiarity he hoped to gain an answer for. An assassination attempt had come, one these servants had no cause to know about, but who was to say whether it had been at the King's request or someone else's.

In the guise of a rat, he slid unseen past the servants and searched the well room, storage, and washrooms, and finally the dining hall. He found nothing, not even a draft that might indicate a hidden passage, thus he returned to the kitchen where the servants had at last gone off to bed. He found nothing there either, nor in the State Room or ballroom and, disheartened, he decided to make a pass through the Grand Hall, just in case, before he went to the library for the remainder of the night.

Entering the hall in rat form, he froze when he sensed, and then saw, the blond man seated on the platform near the throne, with scepter and crown tossed haphazardly onto the seat behind him. He wore only a pair of loose fitting black trousers and the black eagle pendant that signified the Lachlan dynasty. As a rat, Kavan knew he could never get close enough to judge the man, but as a cat, no one would be the wiser.

When the King looked down at the white feline that walked with its tail high and rubbed past his leg, he did not think twice about holding his hand to it. "Servants taking in strays again? Well, it is too late to put you out now, fellow. You are in for the night." The cat looked up at him, yawned, and then leapt into his lap. Seated there contentedly, it began to wash its paws. "A friend. Only a cat to support me. Perhaps I should keep you then. It is always good to have friends…one can never have too many." He sighed, scratched the animal's head, and then put him down to stand and pace before the throne.

"You know I never meant for any of this to happen, don't you? Mother always said I was meant to be the King my father should have been, and I worked hard to prove her right. I only wanted to correct the wrongs that Bowen…and now it has come to this." He stretched out his arms as if gesturing to the world around him and sighed. "I do not belong here. All I ever wanted was to belong somewhere. I know what my mother said…but I think my mother was wrong."

He paused in his pacing to lean his elbows on the arm of the throne and finger the scepter. "I wonder sometimes who my father was. Do you know? Of course not…you would not have been around then. Not

Innis, I know that. But I do not think I resemble Bowen, and he was so adamant about refusing to acknowledge me as his son that maybe he thought the same thing. But if not him, who? My mother is a whore…will sleep with anyone who will have her, even now. Maybe it was Farrell. Maybe a street vendor, or a stranger in a tavern. Hell…maybe it was her brother," he spat in disgust. The cat meowed as if in response, rubbing against his leg again. "Yes…you're right. Maybe it was Bowen and he was simply too much of a coward to admit to it. Maybe he regretted it…and me. I have to live with the doubt though. If I knew, maybe it would not be so difficult to give up the throne."

The cat leapt onto the royal seat of power and licked its rough tongue across the King's hand. Kavan was learning much about the King that he would not have learned otherwise, and it made him feel pity for the man. What he heard hurt his heart and gave him a lot to think about.

"That is the worst of it. Knowing that some foreign king will rule, defile this throne…ending the Lachlan dynasty with a whimper. It could be McHador, as Ferghus said, but I do not believe he wants to rule. He is doing this for someone else, but who? Elyriá? Hatu? Cordash?"

Yawning again, the cat stretched, and the King rubbed its ears with a dull chuckle. "I am boring you with my self-pity, aren't I? It is late, and I suspect tomorrow is going to be an exhausting day. Goodnight, little friend. Maybe we shall talk again before this story is played out."

The cat watched him go, considering every word he had heard, trying to match them to what he knew of past events. It made sense now. Too much sense. He felt reasonably confident that the King had not sent an assassin to kill the prince. Someone might have done it on his behalf, but Kavan did not believe Owain had it in him to make that order.

Certain he was alone, he continued mulling over the disheartening confession as he found his way to the library still in the form of the cat. He hoped before the night was through, he would get to confront the King one more time.

In his own form, he perused the library shelves and leafed through several volumes in a multitude of languages that initially looked promising, but he found nothing he did not already know about what he was looking for. The small light in his open palm was bright enough to read by but small and dim enough that it would be unnoticed by anyone who might pass by the library windows or doors. Only two volumes remained open before him before he paused to stretch and rub his tired eyes. He was beginning to despair of finding any keys that might circumvent the need for an attack on the keep. Nothing would be gleaned if he did not continue reading, and so he put the finished volumes back on the shelf and turned to those he had left.

In one he found the story he had been told about the Teren arrival in Rhidam; he read the differing account carefully, and then reread it several more times to better comprehend its meaning. Its version of the event was different from what bhydáni Tíbhyan had told him, and thus, the differences were worth noting.

Not passages in the castle, but rather below them? The dungeon?

If the passages below the keep had been secret, known only to the Elyri, how had the Teren found them? Tíbhyan always changed the subject when Kavan brought that question up in conversation, claiming to have no explanation or answer. But here, this could be the explanation Kavan sought. Not given in explicit detail, but implied nonetheless. The explanation he found was both fascinating and appalling.

From the position of the stars outside the window, Kavan realized it would be dawn soon. He could not afford to be found here, but he had to know the truth. If what he suspected was accurate, it would be most fortuitous for the prince, and perhaps devastating for the history of Elyri-Teren relations, at least from the Elyri perspective. He replaced the final two books on the shelves where they had come from, extinguished the handlight, and made his way to the staircase behind the Grand Hall that would take him into the cellar and dungeon.

There were sentries there, guarding whatever prisoners and valuables were kept below, but Kavan was not interested in either. It took only a few seconds of concentration before he was able to gather the keys from the now sleeping sentry and slip past him through the heavy oak door that barred the dungeon. Only two people were present there, the other sentry, sleeping in the bunk room, and a prisoner who slept in her cubicle at the opposite end of a row of cells. Not bothering to learn who she might be, Kavan flattened against the wall and made his way through the room to the farthest end of the dungeon.

Those ghosts of the past had not entered through the Gate Kavan had used before. They had come in elsewhere, somewhere long forgotten, unknown by anyone living.

Kavan was determined to change that.

Running his hands over the rough-hewn stone, he searched for a latch or a button, any means of springing the mechanism that must be there. It had to be, here next to the storage rooms. The account had clearly indicated that the invading Teren had entered near the cells in the dungeon, and had to pass the guardroom to mount the stairs. His fingers finally caught on a protruding edge and pried it eagerly. There was a snap and the twang of a spring. He listened, hoping he had not roused either guard or prisoner, as the smooth stone wall swung open on dusty, creaking hinges. No one stirred.

Only blackness lay beyond the reaches of his handlight.

After examining the back of the door to be certain it would open from both sides, he entered the musty catacombs and closed it behind him. He sensed nothing ahead that he needed to fear, and darkness had never frightened him. He took a single deep breath, intensified the glow of the handlight in his open palm, and cautiously started forward, down the carved stone steps deeper into the earth.

He moved slowly, not knowing what he might find as his senses continued to search around him in every direction. The tomb-like silence was chilling, causing him to wonder if he had trapped himself here. He had never been underground before and the possibility of a tunnel collapse burying him was frightening. He must have passed under the waters of the moat by now. One corridor after another, left or right, was passed; there were no residual energies left from the last people to pass through this place, nothing to guide him, only instinct which told him to continue straight ahead. Where did the other tunnels lead? What had this place been? With no marks on the wall, no obvious identification of his path, it was impossible to say. When the static sensation of power tickled his mind, it was a sign he chose to follow, to the left, through cobwebs, over the rubble of a crumbling portion of wall, until he found himself before a set of tall, iron double doors. He lifted the light and traced the High Elyri runes with his fingers.

High Elyri? Here? "k'dónár mályhag." Kavan shivered at the implications of those words. Sacred passage to where? Underneath those words were other runes he could not read but which reminded him of the inscription on the pendant he wore, the writing attributed to the phae k'kairá. If there were answers, Kavan suspected they awaited him inside. The door had no lock, no latch, and opened stiffly when he pushed, offering only a little of the expected resistance. Dust and bits of rock sprinkled down as he genuflected and stepped across the portal.

It appeared to be some sort of shrine, more ancient in construction than anything Kavan could remember seeing. The spacious room was carved directly from the black earth and mottled brown stone around it, polished smooth, sporting a single stone bench along the walls in what he guessed to be the fundamental directions. Though thick with dust, the scenes painted on the walls were mostly visible, if faded with age and wear, and religious in nature, confirming his belief that this had served as the site of some manner of religious ritual. The east wall depicted the creation, on the west wall the end of days. South and north depicted the officially held imagery surrounding the birth and death of Dhágdhuán. The nature of those images, the thoughts of mortality, made Kavan feel weak; despite his talk with Ártur, Kavan was unprepared to contemplate death and what might await him beyond the end moments of his life.

In each corner of the room stood a carved white figure, marble it seemed until he touched them to discover they were limestone. They were old saints lost to centuries past, and though there were names beneath them, and Kavan was well-versed in the histories of the saints, there was one name he did not know. Gíldás and Edhriá were two of the oldest names in the annals of the Faith, so old that there were no stories or myths accompanying their names. The third was called Llyr, bringing to Kavan's mind the individuals he had met during the journey to Rhidam, the ones who had been celebrating the Feast of Llyr. Was this the same individual? How had that one name been lost to the history books? Kavan did not know.

The fourth statue had no facial features, no identifying mark or symbol as many saints did. It stood in its featureless robe, holding nothing it is clasped hands. The inscription on its base read 'sányt k'málneag'. The unknown saint. As Kavan stared, almost eye to eye, there was something about it that sent an uneasy tremor up and down his spine.

Who had written that and when? Who were these men immortalized for eternity in a shrine long forgotten?

Breaking the spell the featureless statue had over him, Kavan returned to the center of the room and mounted the single step platform where he could inspect the rectangular, gold-inlaid marble altar. Something within the room was interfering with his handlight, something that grew stronger as he neared the altar; when he touched it, he jerked back in alarm. Yes, there was power there, as he expected, but something was wrong, wrong in a way he was unaccustomed to that had nothing to do with its long disuse. The power was raw, vicious, mostly unfocused, and radiating a mortal danger that could easily harm or even destroy any soul who foolishly tampered with it. Shaken, he rubbed his tingling palm, studying the altar with his psychic senses only. This must be corrected, somehow, but this was not the time. He could not stay to investigate it. It would be dawn soon, and he would be missed.

His extended senses drew him away from the altar, following a static trail of power that led back to the unidentified saint. He touched the cold stone with both hands, running them over the figure from top to bottom, not knowing what he sought but certain he would find something. When he reached the figure's hands, clasping them between his, he heard a loud click. To the left, a panel on the wall opened revealing a five by five room lined in musty, dark green velvet. He thought it might have served as a Purification chamber once, but it was its other use that was more valuable to him now. He had found what he had believed he would find.

A Gate. Far beneath the castle, where none would ever think to look.

Not concerned about the open panel since no one else would find this room when it had been hidden away for centuries, Kavan made the connection to the Gate in Rhidam's grand náós and was gone

❧*❦

The woman looked up from her bed, the chiseled lines of her face contorted as an unfamiliar fire coursed through her body. Her limbs appeared to shrivel before her eyes, her heart constrict to its smallest size, and her insides twisted in agony. It had never happened to her before, this pain, and it seemed to have no direct cause or source that she could locate. It came from outside herself, from somewhere far away, a place she had never seen. And though it came from outside, it struck at her core with a ferocious power of unimaginable strength. When it passed, an image appeared within her mind's eye and then faded as quickly as it had come. She did not know who he was, nor did she know where he was or what he could have done to hurt her. He had no cause to attack her, she knew that, but he was, without a doubt, the source of her pain. She also knew that he was the culmination of something that could not be permitted to continue. At last, her life had found its purpose. She knew what she had to do. That image within her mind had to be destroyed. Utterly. Completely. She would not rest until it was done.

❧Chapter 47❧

Men were starting to stir as Kavan returned to camp. Ártur was already awake, seated by the fire where he had been the night before, causing Kavan to look at him oddly. "I hope you have not been there all night," he chided as he sat.

The healer shook his head, smiling with relief that Kavan had returned unharmed. "I slept, but not well…with worrying about you. Did you have any luck?"

Though Kavan's face was passive, his expression mostly neutral, his green eyes sparkled with excitement. "More than I expected. Tíbhyan's tale was more than a history lesson…though he seemed to have left out some important details. I doubt he knows the truth."

If even the bhydáni, one of the most brilliant, educated, experienced minds in Elyriá, did not know something of Elyri history, Ártur was almost afraid to find out what details had been omitted. Still, caught in Kavan's contagious excitement, he asked, "What kind of details?"

Kavan leaned closer and lowered his voice. "I located a manuscript which alluded to catacombs beneath the castle which had but a single entrance…through the castle itself. No one ever found an outside entrance, though it seems many tried. Wondering how the Teren could have entered if there were no outside entrances, I went into the dungeon to investigate. I found the catacombs, Ártur…a maze of tunnels. I don't know where they lead, but I did find what I believe was a shrine or temple once. Incredibly ancient…older than Elyri construction I am certain…though the murals on the walls depict our holy stories. There were four saints there, old saints…only three were named…and an altar. But the altar's power was…wrong."

"Wrong?" Ártur had never known an altar to have power.

"Wrong, not like others I have encountered. Angry…malicious…" He shuddered. "But I found a Gate there, Ártur, concealed near the unnamed saint. Whoever attacked the ruling family…if they were Teren as the histories say, they had assistance. If there were no other entrances, they could not have operated the Gate if they had not had help."

"That is true," the healer murmured with a shiver. The implications of that were too horrific to think about. An Elyri traitor.

Fortunately, he was spared the chance to dwell on it. "You two are up early." The healer motioned for the other men to sit.

"Good morning, Guthrie…My Prince. Kavan has discovered something that might be of use to us."

Based on experience, the possibility of Kavan finding anything that he thought would be helpful caught the general's attention. "What is it?" He hoped it would be something to sway Arlan from the hasty course of action he was pressing for.

After catching Bhríd's eye, assessing his kinsman's condition for himself after not having seen him the evening before, Kavan waited until everyone was seated before speaking; he did not want to repeat himself. "I have found an entrance that will take us directly into the castle. If we are cautious, we should be able to use it without being detected until we wish to be. Below the keep are catacombs, tunnels, and rooms built centuries ago. In one of the rooms, I discovered a Gate. It would afford us an adequate position to assemble a unit of men with which we can infiltrate the fortress, paralyzing the King and apprehending him…"

"Apprehend?" snorted the prince, absently rubbing the spot under his ribs where Bhríd had been injured the day before. "I want that man killed…"

"That is not necessary, My Prince. I learned things last night…" Not wanting to debate the King's fate when there were pressing plans to be made, Guthrie interrupted. "Forget that for a moment. Tell me more about this passage. Where is it?" Avoiding discussion about Owain might help temper Arlan's actions, at least that was the general's hope.

Kavan sighed, fretting about how he could save the King's life if no one was willing to hear him. "Under the castle, beneath the dungeon. It can be accessed near the storage room…the panel can be opened from both sides. My excursions into the dungeon have indicated there are generally two to four sentries there, and there was only one prisoner last night. I do not know the number of soldiers on the grounds…"

"Our best men should be able to handle them," Prince Arlan exclaimed without thinking. "Kavan, you are a genius. Lord General, I suggest we move tonight…"

"Tonight? We need to make a plan. That is too soon…" It was better than the rush to action he had intended to make after breakfast, but only better by a number of hours.

"Owain will continue to ignore our requests and we cannot wait indefinitely. We cannot wait for him to send another assassin…"

"He did not…" started Kavan.

But Arlan continued without listening. "There are too many of us; Rhidam will be unable to feed us all once the snow arrives. The damp will bring disease and death. We must act at once. We can force his hand. We set the majority of our men in siege position outside, as intended, and inform him that we will not withdraw until he agrees to meet. If he capitulates, we continue with our original plan and keep this in reserve. I would think, however, he will choose to continue to stall, develop a strategy of his own before responding. If we move quickly, from the inside, he will not have a chance to avoid us and we can end this."

Guthrie leaned his back against the tree and crossed his arms over his chest. "There is a staircase and tunnel that can take him directly to a small building outside the city. It was built during the last war with Neth, I believe, to afford the King easy escape. It is connected to the same stairwell that leads into the dungeon. If he knows it is there, which I think he must, he will use it if he feels cornered."

"Then I expect there to be men there waiting for him, with specific orders not to harm him or my sister if she is with him. I want to destroy him myself. Is that understood, Lord General?"

Taken aback by the determination in the prince's voice and stance, Guthrie tried to hide the reluctant smile that threatened to cross his face. King Innis had used the same tone when giving commands, and it felt good to hear it from the prince. It pleased him to know that he had taught the boy well. All of his work was paying off. After months on the road, taking a back seat to the procedures and observing everything, Prince Arlan had seen enough. The time had come. The prince had assumed command, with a much sounder plan than laying an unending siege to the castle that they could not hope to quickly win.

The general was not sure, however, that Arlan was prepared to develop a fully functioning military strategy. Innis never had been, and Donal, while capable, had valued Guthrie's wisdom. As military advisor, it was Guthrie's duty to point out flaws and possibilities that the prince might not consider. He began to speak, but the prince continued.

"We will need a diversion outside…possibly more than a stationary siege as we discussed. You and Bhríd devise something appropriate; Bhríd, you will be in command of it if you feel able."

Bhríd nodded his head to indicate agreement but did not speak.

"I want you and Caol inside with me, Guthrie. If you think you can trust Captain Cornell, assign him to the secret exit point. He knows Rhidam better than many, and Owain might be less cautious with him. How many men do we take inside? Fifty? Seventy-five?"

Guthrie snorted. "That is largely a matter of how many men the Elyri can realistically transport through this Gate and how big that room is…not on how many we want to take."

Prince Arlan looked at Kavan expectantly. "What of it, Kavan? Ártur? How many can you manage?"

The healer frowned. "I have never done a mass move through a Gate; it is difficult to say. However…if Bhríd and Syl…" He did not even know if either knew how to use the Gates and so was disinclined to volunteer them. Again Bhríd nodded, willing to accept whatever duty was placed upon him. "How many will this room hold, Kavan?"

"It is difficult to judge a room's size by the glow of one handlight; I cannot be certain…"

Guthrie leaned forward with his elbows on his knees. "I think I have a better idea…though it might be trickier. Kavan, do you know if there are other Gates in the castle?"

Reluctant to disclose such information, Kavan replied in a strained voice, "If I speak of this, the details must never go further than those of us here. It would be detrimental to Elyri-Teren relations. That includes your heirs, My Prince. No one else must ever know of this."

Although the general agreed with a grave nod, Prince Arlan was not as quick to do likewise. Why should such important details of the castle's construction be withheld from his family? When he saw, however, that Kavan was not going to speak without his agreement, he reluctantly consented, knowing that Kavan was going to hold him to that promise.

"There are nine Gates, including the one I discovered. One in the guardroom in the dungeon, one in the kitchen pantry, one in each of the three oratories, one in the Grand Hall, one in the library, and one in the King's chambers."

Ártur was not the only one surprised. A more paranoid man would have seen them as potential points of invasion. Guthrie saw their large number, and the fact that they had never been used, to his knowledge, as proof that the Elyri were uninterested in conquering or harming the Teren.

"So many?" the healer murmured. "How do you…?"

"I have made it my business to know," was all Kavan said.

Steepling his fingers beneath his chin, Guthrie sat in silence, staring into the distance, until the prince nudged him. To his credit, though the prince was eager to hear the general's thoughts, he was also giving him time to think. "What are you thinking, Guthrie?"

The general cleared his throat. "With Bhríd overseeing the siege, we cannot rely on him to help us…he and Syl will be busy enough. It will be up to Kavan and Ártur. We cannot use the Gate in the Grand Hall; that would be too obvious. There will be men rushing all over in there if we lay siege to the castle. I think the kitchen is out of the question, as soldiers coming out of there, during a siege, will look peculiar. That leaves us seven, perhaps, to utilize. With the appropriate diversion outside and the proper attire for those inside, any soldiers we encounter would be too busy to pay attention to who is who. If we could take ten men into the oratories, the dungeon bunkroom, and the library, that would give us fifty men on the inside. The King will not likely be in his room, but a large group coming out of there might be noticed; perhaps we could send another five there at most. If we bring another five or ten with us through this new passage, it would give us sixty or sixty-five men on the inside." He glanced at the bard and the healer. "Do you think that is feasible…with just you and Ártur…?"

Before Ártur could speak, Kavan replied, "We will manage." The healer tried not to roll his eyes. Kavan might be able to transport so many men through the Gates, but Ártur was not certain he could.

"I hope you know what you are committing us to, cousin."

Kavan's response was a slight nod of his head.

Prince Arlan slid closer to the edge of the log. "Lord Harper must come because he knows the way from this Gate to the Hall, and I want Lord Healer on the inside, in case we need him."

To one side of the gathering, Hanford Weylin, who had been part of the prince's entourage since the prince's arrival in Rhidam many months ago, was listening to the conversation and chose that moment to speak. "May I join you inside, Prince Arlan?"

"I…" The prince hesitated. "You do realize that, if we fail, the King will likely have your head?"

The duke nodded. "I am no innocent boy, My Liege. I know the consequences of my actions, succeed or fail. I would rather fight for what I believe in than sit by and let my uncle gain all of the glory." He smiled impishly at Guthrie. "And my fate, if we fail, will be little different if I remain out here, or venture inside with you. I think I will be of more use to you at your side."

Those words made the prince smile. "Very well; your assistance is welcome."

"If you gain suitable attire from Captain Cornell, your forces would blend in with the soldiers inside," Kavan interjected. "Even in armor, however, neither I nor Ártur can pass as Enesfel soldiers."

"Then you can be our prisoners," Prince Arlan suggested with a grin. "How do you think Owain will like that?"

Guthrie cleared his throat again. "He will think he has gained a bargaining tool, particularly since he does not seem to be fond of Kavan and must suspect that Ártur and I were on good terms, strong allies, when we served Kings Innis and Donal. Bhríd, get our men in place outside the castle; you know what to do. I'll decide which men to take within. We will speak again at noon to hone our plan. There can be no errors, Arlan. If we go inside, we will not be able to get out unless we defeat him."

"Then we will defeat him. Is it agreed, gentlemen?" Those around the prince nodded, although Kavan, with his eyes closed, appeared to no longer be listening. Arlan lay his hand upon the bard's arm and felt the man shiver beneath his touch. "And you…I want everyone to conserve your energy and be prepared. I suspect it will be an eventful evening ahead of us."

How much of this plan hinged upon Kavan's ability to get him and his men inside undetected proved to the prince once more how valuable was the bard to his effort to regain a place in Rhidam. He could not do this without Kavan. Both he and the bard knew it, and likely many of those around them knew it too.

❧Chapter 48❧

King Owain watched from the dayroom as hundreds of enemy soldiers, mostly citizens of Enesfel and Rhidam, moved into position around the castle, sitting on the far side of the moat, awaiting his reply to their leader's repeated request. If this was a siege, it was the oddest one he had ever heard of. Instead of digging trenches or constructing a score of battlements, McHador's troops formed a thick ring of men around the castle. Not a tactic he would expect from a seasoned veteran like McHador. Then again, perhaps it was precisely that reasoning that led the ex-general to create such a haphazard-looking maneuver. It could be the sort of thing meant to throw a military novice off. After all, Guthrie McHador knew war. Owain Lachlan did not.

The body of a young soldier had been left before the gate to the moat bridge during the night, a body that none seemed inclined to explain to him. It was a message, he knew, but as he did not know if the soldier was one of his, killed by McHador's troops, or one of McHador's recruits killed by royal guards, no one knew. Or if they knew, they were not sharing the information with the King, as if the death was inconsequential or a secret he was not meant to share. The first option was negated by the fact that it had been left where it would be too obvious to miss, that made the second possibility more likely. But who would want to keep such a secret from the King? And why?

Echoes filled the castle halls, the sounds of men cutting wood, hammering stakes, forging iron into weapons. Those were the only men who looked to be preparing for battle, those men gathered before the outer gate constructing what the King supposed would become a ballista or battering ram. They intended to destroy the front gates, gate towers, and portcullis. Or at least they appeared as if they were preparing to try. The rest of McHador's men looked to be doing little more than setting camp as if they had grown bored of their location at the edge of the city and wanted a more crowded view of the castle. There was something odd about their actions, some ulterior motive behind what the King could see, but he had no idea what was. Still, he made a conscious decision not to be caught off guard by anything McHador attempted.

What he knew was that he did not intend to enter into discussion with the man on the bridge within the range of enemy archers. After the princess's kidnapping, the King was cautious about a proposed meeting on that bridge. Beside him, the princess watched the goings on, a mixture of horror and fascination on her face. He had not told her it was McHador preparing to attack them; he did not think it fair to steal the last of her childhood illusions, and he did not believe McHador would harm her. He had helped raise her, after all.

"Sire?" The newly appointed General Wyndham stood behind and to the side of him, also watching with a frown. The body left at the gates troubled him as well…but for entirely different reasons. "We cannot withstand a siege of more than a few weeks. They have most of the kingdom behind them; they will have enough supplies to last them indefinitely if they require it."

The King turned wearily to face his new general. He believed he saw guilt in the twitches at the corners of the other man's mouth and eyes, but Ternce had always been loyal. That perceived guilt was a product of his paranoia, nothing more. Or maybe the General felt guilty that his troops had been unable to prevent the situation from deteriorating this far. He could see that the man was as confused by McHador's tactics as he was. "What do you suggest I do, Ternce? Surrender?"

The man shook his head no, though the King thought his expression read differently. "Talk to him. He may desire something simpler than your surrender. Perhaps McHador merely desires the price off his head…some sort of retribution for his niece…or to return to active duty as you suggested before…"

"Would you be willing to give up your position to him?" the King asked skeptically.

The general cleared his throat and shifted his weight from one foot to the other. "If it would keep the peace…spare your life…"

The King grunted and shook his head before resuming his watch. "No…I think it is more than that, Ternce. I do not know what he wants, but he has gone to great trouble for more than his position, involving Elyriá, Hatu, the Cíbhóló. Ferghus said it was clear McHador has designs upon the throne. Why else ride into Rhidam under the Lachlan standard?"

Those were all very good questions, and ones the general repeatedly asked himself. He had no answers, and thus could only say, "Talking to him would answer those questions…and might gain you your life, Sire."

"And yours, I suppose." King Owain looked at the back of the princess's golden-trussed head. She was watching the proceedings thus not aware of their conversation. She seemed spellbound by what was going on outside, and who could blame her? There was a grim fascination with one's impending doom. Such beautiful children we could have had, he thought, desiring to touch her hair but refusing to. How could he allow her to die in a tomb of his making? He gave a final sigh and said, "Tell him I will speak with him tomorrow, Ternce.

Tomorrow. He may name the time and place, but I will not meet within the range of his archers."

He knew what an arrow's bite felt like. He was not willing to endure that pain again.

The general bowed, masking his relief. "I will tell him, My Liege."

Once the man was gone, the King glanced back at the princess to find her looking at him as if she had heard his order and did not understand it. Sometimes he wondered if her deafness was an act. "I am doing this for you, you know. I have nothing to gain from talking to him except your safety. Perhaps that will be enough to win your love."

If she could read the words on his lips, there was no indication she understood him, other than the faint, uncertain flicker of sadness that he believed he saw cross her eyes.

⊱*⊰

The sun settled over the horizon painting the sky a brilliant shade of crimson and violet when the small group of men reached the destination Guthrie had indicated. Captain Cornell slid from his horse, tethered her, and looked back at the city. What was the saying? Red sky at night, a sailor's delight? He wondered if the saying applied to soldiers.

He did not, however, think that anything delightful would come of tonight's events, though he had no idea exactly what Guthrie and the prince planned to do. He wondered why he had been sent to this little stump of a building with twenty armed men. Did the general honestly believe the King could, or would, somehow come this way, or was it the general's way of making sure that a man with uncertain loyalties did not interfere in what would transpire at the castle?

"Do you think we will attack tonight?" one of the men asked.

"No," Captain Cornell replied, though he had no actual knowledge to that end. He was not about to let his men know that the prince did not trust him enough to tell him what they were planning. "We are here as a precaution, to stop anyone who comes this way…spies, messengers, or the King himself."

"Guard duty?" asked another in barely disguised disgust.

Rankling at the man's tone, the captain snorted, "There is nothing dishonorable in our duty. If the general believes there is some threat we can stave off here, then it is our duty to see to that threat; that is what we will do. Is that clear, soldier?"

"Yes, sir," the man said with a bow and chastised tone.

Another asked, "What do you think will happen to the King, sir? When we do attack, I mean."

Captain Cornell shrugged, still wondering if he was doing the right thing by siding with McHador. That, he admitted bitterly, was precisely why he had been positioned here. With the rumor of a failed assassination attempt having been made upon Guthrie and Prince Arlan, an attempt that had surely come at the command of the King, it was increasingly unlikely the monarch would be allowed to live. Despite his shifting loyalty, however, the captain had little desire to see King Owain die. He was not certain that was the fate the man deserved, but the choice, unfortunately, was not his to make. Or perhaps it was fortunate that the choice was not his. He did not think he could have made it fairly if he tried. "That, I'm afraid, will be up to the King. If he comes this way, we will capture him first and there are specific orders that he be taken alive. After that, I do not know what will become of him."

❧*❧

Reining in his horse, Bhríd inspected the ballista that would hopefully break through the castle's main gate if they could get across the protected bridge. The ballista had been constructed more rapidly than he had thought possible, yet there were no apparent flaws in its construction. It bolstered his confidence to know that he had learned those childhood lessons and had retained that knowledge over the years. The true test, however, was yet to come.

He had always known the intellectual reasons for building a moat; now he understood the emotional ones. A moat provided both an extra feeling of security for those on the inside, and an extra level of frustration for those on the outside. They would need to take the gate towers first, before they could cross. He grinned within his newly acquired helmet; we can do that, he thought. The portcullis would be more challenging. He gave the orders to Sergeant Zarkosta and Captain Niall and watched them ride towards their units.

The cry of battle went up. There were few decent archers available, but all men were capable of throwing, and they had a single objective, burn down the gatehouse towers so that they could cross the bridge and break through the fortress doors. For now, Bhríd held the ballista back, nursing his bruised ribs as he watched. The night sky brightened as the first torches, oil casks, and pitch-tipped arrows were lit and propelled forward. Good, he thought, hearing the screams and shouts of men within the towers. We have your attention.

❧*☙

Kavan leaned his forehead against the náós wall, willing himself to catch a few moments of rest. Most of the soldiers were in place, except for Prince Arlan and the eleven men that were to start in the catacombs. Ártur could move no more; he did not know the location of their destination, and as far as Kavan was concerned, his cousin needed to conserve his energy in case healing was required. Everyone had been instructed to await the signal to act; the next step was up to Kavan.

"Two at a time," he said, rough voice cracking. "It will be quicker."

Ártur took his arm and held him back. "No more, Kavan. You are killing yourself."

"Hardly." Having spent hours in flight, Kavan did not see this expenditure of energy as any more difficult, although he knew, in truth, that it was. "You do not know the connection…"

"Then show me."

"We may need you to heal…"

"And we need you to lead us," the prince grunted, tired of waiting, anxious for action. He was ready for this quest to reach whatever conclusion awaited them. "You have transported most of our men with that reasoning and Lord Healer has done very little to assist. You cannot continue indefinitely. If I must order you to allow his help, I will…but I want to go in now."

Sighing, knowing there was no point in an argument he could not win, Kavan motioned Ártur into the k'dhín bhólibh. Palms together, Kavan sought and found the connection, but Ártur quickly broke away. "You barely have the strength to stand, sínréc. I admire your tenacity, but I felt how difficult…"

"No, it was…"

"It was difficult…you cannot hide that from me. I felt it. I saw the way. I will take everyone else through, and you can bring the prince. That should provide you with time to regain strength. Please…do not fight. You will regret it if you challenge me."

The bard nodded wearily and stepped out to allow his cousin to take the first two men. Five were the Káliel guards; the others included Duke Weylin, his Captain at Arms and Caol Dugan. Three of the Káliel men wore unmarked armor, as it was the only armor that would fit. The others, including Guthrie, Duke Weylin, Caol, and Prince Arlan wore the standard armor of Enesfel's militia. All covered their hands and faces to avoid recognition. Those already inside had done the same.

The healer returned and took two more, not meeting his cousin's perturbed gaze. He knew Kavan did not like to admit weakness, liked to think himself invincible in matters of power, but this time, they both knew Ártur was right. Kavan had been ill and exhausted for so long that he was not at full strength. Prince Arlan paced as he waited, Guthrie stood motionless, Duke Weylin toyed with the hilt of his sword, and Caol rocked back and forth on his heels. The duke and his captain were next, then Caol and Captain Delamo, who looked steadily at the bard with an expression that read he would rather have shared this first experience with the bard. Kavan was unable to meet his gaze. As soon as Kavan could detect that Ártur had gone through, the path through the Gate clear, he motioned Guthrie and the prince into the small chamber, made the connection after a brief mental struggle with his cousin, and then he too was through the Gate.

"I cannot see anything," the prince immediately grumbled to underplay the squeamishness he felt about using the Gates. His speaking gave Ártur no chance to chastise Kavan for his stubbornness and Captain Delamo's immediate return to Kavan's side discouraged scolding. Arlan's voice echoed in the small room despite the number of bodies packed tightly together for security.

Kavan asked, "Is a light source advisable, Lord McHador?"

"Perhaps you can find your way and lead us without it, but if these passages are as numerous and hazardous as you claim…and as deserted…I see no reason for not having one. It would make me feel better to see where we're going."

"But we did not bring torches…" Caol started.

"Torches would be excess weight." There was a flash, not blindingly bright, but the shock of going from total darkness to a lit room made most of the men squint and shield their eyes until their vision adjusted. Those who had not been expecting it, all except Ártur, stared at the flame in Kavan's open palm, though even the healer had not expected the strength and intensity from such a small point of light.

As the rest of the party adjusted to both the light and their discomfort and amazement, they made a show of straightening armor and weapons for the upcoming trek. Ártur, meanwhile, studied the statues of the saints and the altar that Kavan had told him about. He perceived no unusual energy from anything he saw, but the implied age of the room, and the knowledge that they were far below ground, made the healer uncomfortable. He shivered and rejoined the group, eager to be out of this place.

Nodding to his cousin, ignoring the reactions around him, Kavan said, "If we are ready...?"

The prince clutched at Kavan's arm, more like the boy the bard had known than the young man he had become. Captain Delamo grunted at being displaced but accepted it. "Are you sure you can do this Kavan?" This was no longer a game; there were few opportunities remaining for retreat. Not many more steps and there would be no turning back.

"I will be fine, My Prince. Come, we should proceed."

Guthrie's voice was shaky, though whether from surprise or a sudden burst of nervousness he was not sure. "Keep hold of the man in front of you," he instructed. "We cannot afford to be separated. If what Kavan describes is accurate, anyone lost here might be lost forever."

❧*❧

King Owain spun angrily towards the unexpected tug of small hand on his arm. His castle was under siege, Enesfel's people were trying to burn down the gate towers, and a few were actually attempting to swim the moat and scale the walls of the fortress rather than await the destruction of the portcullis. General Wyndham, whom Owain was more certain than ever was hiding something from him, was commanding the defensive countermeasures; the King knew his general was competent, but he believed, deep in his heart, that such efforts could not succeed. They were killing their own people. How could that come to good for any of them? From the dayroom windows, he could see to the ground below and beyond the moat towers to the host assaulting the castle. He had not moved from that vantage point all day except for a short respite to try to eat.

Now, as darkness tightened its grip on Rhidam, those men beyond the moat were little more than shadows scurrying between the glow of campfires. The largest amount of light was in front of the gatehouse, where the ballista launched its merciless tirade in sync to the throbbing in the King's head. A man fell with a scream from somewhere to his left, but there was too much commotion for the King to hear his end. One of theirs, he wondered absently, or one of mine? Aren't they all mine? With all of this before him, and a sense of betrayal burrowing in his belly, he was not in the mood for interruptions.

Princess Deidre flinched at his abrupt turn as if expecting to be struck, but she steadfastly held a piece of parchment out to him with a trembling, apprehensive hand. Not interested in a conversation, he tried to motion her away, to ignore her, but she stubbornly pulled him back and shoved the document into his hand.

That she had never been forceful with him before gave him cause to reconsider retaliation. Her desperate expression convinced him to read what she had to say. He scanned her handwritten message hastily.

'Milord,' it read, 'you cannot stay here. They will kill you. I do not want you to die. I know a way to escape this place. Come with me and you will have your life to fight again.'

The King's rage faded, touched by her concern for his welfare and the tears at the corners of her eyes. Perhaps she did care. If she was willing to escape with him, they might have a future together after all. He did not want to be perceived as a coward, for fleeing his throne, but if what she said was true, there might be a chance to survive, to fight again. He had no desire to die. Squeezing her hand, the decision was made in that instant and he summoned the two closest soldiers to join them. He nodded to the princess, agreeing to follow. With his large hand around her smaller one, she pulled him after her. Outside there was another crash of wood on wood. Another man screamed.

☙*❧

"Wait," Kavan whispered. The healer felt the surge of energy that built at the front of their column, slightly above where he stood, and ended just as abruptly. The others might believe the bard was merely listening at the walled dead end they had reached, but Ártur was curious about what his cousin had actually done. Each heard the pop of metal coils and the grating of stone against stone, and soon their passage was lit by outside torchlight as the panel slid away and Kavan led them up the stone steps and into the castle dungeon. The men they had brought here previously were dispersed elsewhere within the castle. One sentry slept at the end of a cell row, the other at the foot of the stairs; both appeared to have collapsed where they stood. Ártur's eyes widened. He had heard of such abilities, healers were capable of making others sleep, of course, but he had not known Kavan was capable of it…without even touching his subjects. He could not be certain if Kavan had done this now or if it had been done earlier when their soldiers had been brought inside. If it had been earlier, how long had these men slept? How long would they continue to do so? Kavan waited until everyone was out of the passage before closing the panel, masking their entry point from anyone else, and nodded at his cousin when the healer passed.

"Time to play prisoners," Guthrie grunted as he put his helmet back on his head and adjusted it. "You two ready?"

"Do we have a choice?" asked Ártur.

Indicating the bunkroom with a tilt of his head, the location of one of the castle's nine Gates, the one he had once used to escape certain execution, Kavan said, "It is not too late, sínréc."

☙ 767 ❧

"I am not backing out this close to the end," the healer said, managing an uneasy grin, "no matter how much I want to. You might need me. Besides, this should be extremely interesting."

"Interesting is not the word I would use," Captain Delamo added, his voice muffled as he lowered his visor.

Caol agreed. "Rather like entering a pit of poisonous snakes with only a dagger and a slingshot to protect you. If we are not very…"

Not wanting to waste time, or hurt their strained morale, Guthrie interrupted by clearing his throat. "Stick to the plan and we will succeed. Formation, everyone." He had to believe they would survive this, that they would win. Without that belief, they were doomed.

As each man moved into position and started up the stairs towards the dungeon door, a screech came from the row of cells to their right. Guthrie opened the door and allowed the others to pass, ignoring the wailing until he heard someone cry his name. He knew that voice.

"Ula." His expression hardened. He wondered why she was in the dungeon, imagining that her son had grown tired of her manipulations and interference. He chose to ignore her and the few questioning glances from others in his group. This was no time to deal with the King's traitorous mother. He was the last one through the door before it shut.

"No…Guthrie…Not…son…!"

He did not hear her words clearly over the creaking hinges as the door closed, but he stopped, hand on the latch, at what he imagined he had heard. No, he decided. He could not have heard correctly. Having known Ula for a long time, since the days when she hung on Prince Bowen's arm and tried to insinuate herself into King Innis' bed, he knew she would do and say anything to protect herself and her child. This time, however, she was helpless. He shook his head in disgust and started the men moving up the stairs, leaving her wailing behind them.

They climbed, listening to the sounds of the ballista in the distance. Kavan and Ártur were surrounded by men in armor as if they actually were prisoners; when Kavan stopped as they reached the first landing, Guthrie bumped into him and swore. He prepared to retort, but the sound of swords being drawn silenced him. None of them had thought the sound of footsteps from above would stop directly in front of them.

The King heard the sound too and looked past his two escorts to see ten soldiers and two men, one in white, one in yellow and green. One of the soldiers ordered, "Hold!" although why he was ordering their own men to halt, the King could not imagine. What he did not have to imagine, however, was the man whose gaze he now met, a man who sent shivers through his body in ways that confused and irritated him.

"You…" he snarled with surprise and frustration.

Guthrie did not recognize the man they faced as King Owain. In his mind's eye, he still saw Owain as the child last seen leaving Rhidam eighteen years ago. Now, however, he guessed from the behavior of the others, that this was indeed the King, and he struggled to quell the sick tremors that erupted in the pit of his stomach and spread through his body and into his hands. The King's features were uncomfortably familiar. The frightened woman behind the King was most likely Princess Deidre; Guthrie knew from Arlan's tension that he suspected the same. How much like Cordelia she looked. These realizations took only a second before Guthrie fell into the role he had chosen to play. The turmoil in his head would have to be sorted later.

He elbowed his way to the front of his group, muttering, "My Liege," in a way that made him sound out of breath and hopefully covered his awkward nervousness. "I have prisoners…" He could barely take his eyes off of the blonde King.

"You most certainly have. Where did you find them?" The King did not move other than to motion to his guards to put away their weapons, and to look the two Elyri up and down. The princess clutched his arm, unable to take her eyes from them either. He patted her hand reassuringly without looking at her and did not, yet, consider that she might recognized both Elyri.

"My men and I happened to be outside of the castle before the siege…hoping to gain intelligence about the body left at the gate. We got separated; those three," he pointed, "captured three of McHador's men. I believed them responsible for the body, but they unfortunately died under interrogation." He chortled darkly, a note of sincere apology in his voice. "We confiscated their armor, hoping it would help us infiltrate their ranks to learn more. Then we happened upon these two and apprehended them. I recognize this one as Healer MacLyr, a man known to be an ally of McHador's. The other refuses to state his name, and since neither will talk, I brought them here. We made it back before it was too late to get in and have been questioning them in the dungeon…"

The King rubbed his stubbled chin as he listened, the thundering of his heart almost overpowering the speaker's words. He did not recall requesting an intelligence raid, but perhaps General Wyndham had. If they had come in before the siege had been set, these prisoners had been here for hours without his knowledge. If they survived this night, Owain was going to have to have a serious discussion with General Wyndham about military protocols and rank. Or maybe someone had mentioned prisoners and the news had been lost on him during the day's events. He could not, at the moment, be certain. But prisoners, particularly these prisoners, gave him a bargaining position he had not previously held. He glanced at the princess. Perhaps there was no need for retreat.

"Bring them to the Grand Hall. I will talk with them in less constricting surroundings." Holding Deidre's hand, he led the way back up the stairs, keeping a cautious eye on those behind him and noticing that she was casting timid, frightened glances back over her shoulder.

Ártur touched Kavan's hand. 'Why do I feel like a pawn?' the unspoken communication passed between them. He felt sick, cold and less certain about this undertaking now that they were face to face with the King.

Though Kavan did not outwardly react, reading his cousin's underlying emotions as well as his thoughts, he silently replied, 'Because you are. We are.'

Behind them, both could feel the anger seething below Prince Arlan's tight composure. Kavan was concerned that the prince would break and ruin everything they had planned. Guthrie was also highly agitated, an emotion the bard understood. This night might not change only the future for Enesfel, it might bring about revelations that none of them expected. He tried to project a soothing aura to the others in their group, but the touch on his hand prevented him. Save your energy, the healer suggested with a quick glance at his cousin. We'll need it. Although Kavan did not want to, he relented.

At the top of the stairs, the King spoke to one of his attendants who broke off and left them. The King then led into the Grand Hall, leaned against the throne, and refocused his attention on the two captives led to stand before him with unworried expressions. He did not notice that one of the other men in the group had broken off and followed the first sentry into the adjoining corridor.

"It has been many years, Ártur MacLyr. General Wyndham told me there was at least one Elyri involved in McHador's scheme. I should have suspected it would be you, although you never struck me as the sort to ride into battle with a sword. Breaking your oath?" Ártur neither flinched nor looked away as the King waved the scepter under his nose.

Receiving no response from the healer, the King turned to Kavan, the bard he had imprisoned, tortured, and nearly executed once before. Although he regretted much of that now, he did not show it as he glared into the man's face and hissed, "I should have destroyed you when I had the chance. I do not know how you escaped your fate the first time, or what compelled you to come back, but it will take more than McHador's cooperation or a clergyman's sack of crowns to save you now."

Kavan glanced at Guthrie's armored figure without turning his head before speaking. The King was close enough that Kavan knew he could end this; he could bring the monarch to his knees and make him beg for his life without touching him. But that was not Kavan's way. He did not want to hurt Owain. He wanted only to set history aright.

"Your anger is not at me, though you believe it to be so. There is much pain in you, loss and resentment. You do not know what you desire, but you do know it is not this. It need not end this way, Owain."

For a moment, the two spirits connected. The King's thoughts flitted back to the previous night, to the cat he had bared his soul to, though why that cat came to mind he did not know. His expression softened, but because that memory confused him and he did not want to appear weak in front of his prisoners, his troops, or Deidre, he growled. "Enough, Elyri. How dare you address me in such familiar terms? Soft words will not sway me. I should kill you, be done with you, but I would rather wait until McHador can see that he cannot defeat Owain Lachlan so easily."

The commanding soldier hesitated, squelching back the knot in his stomach, and held his breath as he removed his helmet. "Then perhaps you should consider proving yourself now."

Gasps sounded around him, including from his own comrades who had to pretend that they had not known the enemy general was in their midst. No one in the room, however, appeared more shocked than the King, whose hand when to his face in a panic of recognition. Both men stood frozen as they stared at one another.

The King appeared to be the first to regain his wits. "Seize him!" he cried. Two of Káliel's men, both in ill-fitting Enesfel chain armor, grabbed Guthrie, wrestling the general's sword, dagger, and shield away from him. He resisted, fighting back convincingly in an attempt to reclaim his weapons, but in the end, they overpowered him and held his arms to prevent escape.

"I guess this explains things..." Caol remarked.

Shaking and cold, the King snorted. "This explains nothing, soldier, unless you know something you're not sharing."

Caol bowed. "As he said, Sire, we were separated during our mission. We brought these prisoners to the rendezvous and when our commander, Captain Doulbirt, was not there, we returned to the castle. We met this man at the gate as we came in...in the commander's armor. There was much noise and commotion as McHador's forces began to move into place...and he did sound like the captain...we did not ask questions...even though he was behaving...oddly. General McHador must have waylaid the captain and stolen his armor. I am sorry, Sire, if we behaved incorrectly by bringing him..."

"Behaved incorr..." The King scoffed, hoping he sounded more confident than he felt. He could not recall any officer named Doulbirt, but there had been many military losses recently; this captain could have been a recent replacement. "Soldier, you have brought me a prize better than these two insignificant Elyri." Even as he said the words and glared in Kavan's direction, there was a flicker of emotion in his eyes that suggested his thoughts did not match his words. "Their army will have to withdraw if they want him alive."

Guthrie snarled. "They will never retreat! My life is nothing to them. Do you think I was caught by chance? What they want is more important than my life..."

"And what do they want?" demanded the King, pushing aside the anxiety McHador's words birthed within him.

"You wanted to see me, Sire?"

General Wyndham entered the Grand Hall with ten soldiers behind him. He had not wanted to take any of them away from defending the keep, but when the messenger expressed concern for the King's safety and indicated that the King had summoned him, the captain deemed it necessary to bring reinforcements. But ten was the most he felt he could spare. He did not immediately notice Guthrie McHador or Ártur MacLyr standing before the King until after he spoke, and when he did recognize them, he was as surprised as everyone else.

Guthrie whistled. It was now or never. The presence of other soldiers in the room made the action a necessity before more were summoned. The men who held him let go and returned his shield and sword to his hands. The King drew back in horror as those men he believed to be his own charged to intercept General Wyndham and his ten. Ártur broke free and rushed to grab the King's arms, intending to pull him out of harm's way as Kavan wished, but the King pushed him back, grabbed the princess's hand, and prepared to flee the room. He had only a short sword and thus could not adequately defend himself, or her, against soldiers in armor with longswords and polearms. One soldier, however, the boy who had spoken convincingly against McHador moments before, leapt forward, pulled the princess from the King's grasp with a warning flash of his sword that knocked the King's blade from his hand.

Unarmed, unable to defend himself or retrieve the princess, the King let her hand slip from his when Caol pulled, and he turned to run, intending to go back to that secret passage she had been leading him to. He did not know precisely where it was, but it had to be there somewhere…didn't it? He saw the bard out of the corner of his eye and took no more than three steps before coming face to face with the largest hart he had ever seen. It was snowy white. He squeaked in horror and looked frantically for help as the creature lowered its head and forced him against the wall, pinning him there between its great silver antlers.

There was no one available to assist him. The healer and one soldier were on the platform near the throne, the healer wielding the royal scepter as a club and the soldier wielding a well-polished sword. Before them, McHador was defending them as if a man half his age, while the other soldier still held the princess with one arm and fought off any who dared approach with the other. The princess looked as if she would faint but was too afraid to. The appearance of the hart in the midst of the Grand Hall caused the King's men to pause their attack.

Still, Guthrie and his men were outnumbered. Two fell, and five others, except for Guthrie and the two on the platform, raced for the doors to the Grand Hall. The King dared to hope that he had another chance at victory, despite the fact the princess was being dragged away and the hart continued to hold him fast to the wall as if the combat behind it did not matter. It pawed the floor with one silvery hoof, snorting hot breath in his face, staring at him with brilliant green eyes. No, the King begged silently, still not believing what his senses were telling him. Not you. All along…not you. It cannot be you…

His heart sank one last time, however, as McHador's fleeing supporters opened the doors and soldiers wearing Enesfel armor but bearing the standards of King Geir of Hatu entered the room. In the midst of chaos, the King had not heard the portcullis collapse to allow these men entry. It must have collapsed. How else had they gotten inside? The fleeing five men turned on their pursuers with a vengeance. General Wyndham saw that he was outnumbered, but he would not give up. He had a King to protect, even if he was being prevented from reaching the trapped man.

Near the throne, the healer let out a shriek as a sword bit into his thigh. He slid to the floor, clutching his leg. The hart turned its head abruptly towards the sound, its antlers raking bloody lines across the King's chest, leaving Owain free to run. He tried to flee, but the young man who had pulled Princess Deidre away from him lunged and drove his sword deep into the King's abdomen, despite every previous admonition not to harm him. The King staggered backward, too stunned to make a sound. His attacker released his sword, allowing the man to stumble to the floor. The King's sight was dimming but he knew it was no hallucination when he watched the great hart transform back into the white Elyri harper. With McHador distracted by the commotion of the fallen King, General Wyndham raised his sword to strike.

"I command that all of you halt!"

General Wyndham froze and lowered his sword; the command had been spoken with the authority of nobility and he was conditioned to respond to such tones. All eyes except Kavan's turned to the soldier who unceremoniously stood on the throne with one foot on the carved arm. This soldier, they knew, was no commoner. Attention began to shift to the fallen King of Enesfel and the Elyri who knelt over him. Captain Delamo marched across the room, dropping his helmet along the way, and stopped beside Kavan, looking from the King to the bard expectantly. The princess was crying, nearly hysterical, and refused to let anyone touch her, though she did not attempt to move towards the fallen King.

"Leave him, Kavan," said the soldier on the throne as Ártur pushed to his feet, intending to help the wounded king in spite of his own injury. Reluctantly, the healer sat again in response to the order. Guthrie looked as if he would be sick and leaned on his sword to remain standing.

Kavan neither looked up nor acknowledged the command. His eyes were on the barely conscious King. The man was in shock, the pain in his eyes a reflection of the pain in his soul as much as from the mortal wound. He reached for the man's hand, wanting to offer comfort and friendship in his dying moments, since, unless the healer disobeyed Arlan, there would be no healing for the King.

Before his fingers made contact with Owain's skin, Kavan shuddered, feeling the surge of tremendous warmth that showered down upon him like fire from the heavens, engulfing him, soaking into his core through his skin before coming to rest in his hands. That warmth lasted only a few moments, however, and dissipated quickly across the surface of his body, but the tingle of raw power remained in his hands. Kavan knew this feeling. He knew what it meant. Trembling, he glanced at Captain Delamo whose rich brown eyes were wide with expectation as if he knew something important was about to transpire. The faith the captain exhibited, the willingness to accept and not condemn him, was enough to ease the constriction in the bard's heart and soothe his fear. Kavan touched his Kílyn cross to his lips in prayer.

"Leave him, Kavan," the command came again, more insistent this time. The prince may have wanted to be the one to kill Owain, or at least punish him, but if the man was dying, Prince Arlan saw no reason to express regret. Those in the room knew the King's fate was decided. Guthrie looked elsewhere unable to bear to watch that life slip away.

Again, Kavan refused to acknowledge the words. He knew what he had to do. The King would die if he did not, and his was not the place to withhold something that k'Ádhá was willing to impart. To refuse that gift would have been an even blacker stain on his soul than that kiss with Gabrielle had left. This was the opportunity, he believed, to make up for the two lives he had once taken by giving one back.

He turned both palms upwards in a gesture of supplication before pulling the sword free. The King's body convulsed as blood began to trickle from his mouth and the light in his eyes grew dimmer. With one hand, Kavan struck the short sword against the stone floor, causing it to splinter unnaturally as if it were ice. Every person in the room jumped. The soldier on the throne stepped down in anger, but Kavan threw him a wrathful, threatening glare before turning his attention to the dying King. The Káliel Captain waved his sword making it clear he would defend the Elyri at all costs, even against his new employer.

Prince Arlan stopped mid-step.

Placing his hands over the wound, Kavan murmured, "You are exonerated, milord. Live…and show the world who you truly are."

Though no one could see what was happening, Kavan could feel the wound heal, muscle reforming within, the flesh closing beneath his hands. The weak body twitched and convulsed, gasping for air, grasping at the last threads of life that touch unexpectedly offered. Owain's blue eyes searched the bard's face, seeking answers he could not find, his mouth opening to ask questions he did not have the strength to voice.

Wortham was the only one to see any of it. The others in the Grand Hall only knew that, when Kavan removed his hands and helped King Owain to his feet, there was no trace of injury other than the blood staining the King's royal garments and the bard's hands. With a gesture from Kavan, Captain Delamo and another of his compatriots supported the King between them while Kavan trudged to the platform and sagged limply down beside his cousin, removing himself from a position of central attention in favor of a side location where he would be harder to see. There were several tense minutes of reverent silence. Gazes darted between King Owain, the soldier in front of the throne, and the Elyri-miracle worker who had spared the King's life. The King's gaze, however, confused, bereft, and desperate, was solely upon Kavan.

The moment passed. The soldier in front of the throne handed his sword to Duke Weylin who stood on his other side. He did not look at Kavan. What had happened, miracle or not, should not have, but this was not the time to deal with it. Savoring the moment of delicious tension in the room, Prince Arlan removed his helmet. Astonishment was his reward. Nearby, the princess fainted and Caol caught her before she hit the floor. He knelt there, holding her on his lap, tossing his helmet aside, as the tableau unfolded. King Owain, shaking from blood loss and shock would have collapsed if he had not been held securely in place.

"Prince Arlan."

It was the only words he could utter. Despite not having seen the youngest Lachlan prince since shortly after his birth, the King knew the truth. The portraits of Kings Innis and Donal that adorned the castle walls could have been this same man. He should have known. In a way, he realized, he had always known.

"I do not believe this fighting is necessary any longer, nor do I wish to continue this charade. If you would lay down your weapons…you too, General Wyndham…or must I have them taken from you?" The general bristled but obeyed after briefly pondering the possibility and chances of rescuing the King. The prince sat on the throne and looked around him. "Lord MacLyr, when your wound has been tended, please see to our comrades." He indicated Hanford's captain and one of the Káliel guards. The healer nodded in agreement.

The prince cast one sharp glance at Kavan, who was staring at his bloody hands, and then turned his glare to the King. "I desired nothing more than to return as the rightful prince I am; if you had agreed to meet with us, all of this could have been avoided. As it stands, you forced my hand. I would have let you die for your crimes, should have let you die. Fortunately, for you, Lord Harper had other plans. Be grateful I do not kill you now." He caught the wounded sagging of the bard's shoulders and felt chastised, although he was still displeased with the outcome of this situation. "For his sake, I shall not." At least, he mused, not yet.

Duke Weylin began to gather the weapons from each of the King's men present in the Hall. Sporadic fighting could be heard elsewhere in the keep as members of the prince's force encountered King Owain's guards. Outside, the sounds of the siege continued. "Mr. Dugan…" He watched the man tend to his sister whose eyes now fluttered open. Not wanting her left unattended, the prince motioned for one of the Káliel guards to see to her as he continued, "please signal Lord Caner to halt the siege. Destroying the towers and gates is no longer necessary." Caol bowed, and as he bounded out of the room

with a look back at the princess, Prince Arlan looked towards his prisoner. "Kneel."

The King had no choice. His legs would not support him; when
the two men holding him allowed him to drop to his knees, that was
where he stayed. Princess Deidre's eyes flashed back and forth between Owain and the young man she knew must be her brother, barely
believing he was here. The healer had bound his leg until he could tend
to the wound properly and was moving through the room, tending to
any injured man he found. The Káliel guard beside her offered to help
the princess to her feet. Reluctantly, she accepted the offer.

"I never believed you to be dead, Arlan," the King forced himself
to speak, his voice shaky and weak, his words uncertain. He had not
been asked to speak and expected to be struck down for doing so.
"Though my mother desired your death, she thankfully never has been
able to do anything well. I have never wished you harm." His eyes met
Guthrie's and both men quickly looked away from each other.

"Then it was not Bowen who orchestrated the attempts on Prince
Arlan's life," the healer remarked in a low voice, relieved that his long
ago assessment had been accurate. Caol came back into the Hall and
indicated with a bow that he had done as instructed. Deidre stared at
the young man with familiar red hair in surprise.

The King nodded. "I did not learn about any of it until much later,
until after I returned to Enesfel…and I do not know why she felt it
necessary. She is in the dungeon if you wish to question her."

"We know where she is." Guthrie's tone was bitter. "What of Farrell, and Bowen, and Girvin?"

"Bowen deserved to die," was all King Owain said, his eyes downcast.

Prince Arlan rose from the throne, sword hissing from its scabbard
as he moved. "And what of Farrell and Girvin, my nephew?"

"No!" Kavan's bark was adamant, previous weakness leaving him
as the princess darted forward and threw herself between her brother

and the King. She shook her head, crying with a hand raised as if to stop the blade from falling. She might not hear the words being said, but she understood the intent of her brother's action.

"Do not kill him, Arlan." Owain looked from the princess to the bard, puzzled by this show of support and the audacity of the Elyri to challenge a prince's acts.

Guthrie too took the fallen King's side though he did not move any nearer. "Enough, My Prince. His death would be meaningless. He is not your nephew; he has no claim to this throne. I know that," he again met Owain's gaze, "as does he."

Kavan looked at Guthrie with an expression of tenderness, sympathy, and understanding. Yes, the general realized, the harper knew the truth too. Had known since last night and had tried to tell him this morning, when he had been unwilling to listen. Having the bard's support made the awkward burden easier to bear.

The prince reluctantly lowered his sword. "Not my…" As neither Guthrie, Owain, nor Kavan seemed likely to answer questions, the prince chose to drop the matter. "Very well, Lord General, Lord Harper. At your requests, and for the sake of my beloved sister, I will spare his life. But pray tell, what do you suggest I do with him?"

It stung to be talked about as if he was not in the room, and the King cleared his throat, pride demanding he be heard though it could not demand anything more. "He speaks the truth. The throne is not mine, should never have been mine, except at my mother's insistence. I have not done as well by Enesfel as I had hoped. You are the rightful heir to the Lachlan throne, and I surrender it to you. It is the proper thing to do, the only thing I can do. I do not think we can live in the same kingdom…I ask only to live, to be sent away if you feel it fitting."

"Sent away?" Arlan scoffed. "To Neth? Where my brother sent you?"

"It might have been best if I had not returned…or had not stayed on after Bowen's death. But that is the most logical place. I will return to my mother's people, if you agree, and make my home there." He did not look forward to such a move, to living in that hate-infested land where his kin might, at any time, seek his death, but it was better than the death he believed Arlan would mete out if he remained in Enesfel. He lifted his chin and looked at Kavan with a gentle expression. "I shall never again, however, share their convictions."

With a bowed head and his closed bloody fist over his heart, Kavan accepted the apology intended to wipe the slate clean between them. He held no animosity towards Owain any longer.

"What guarantee do I have that you will leave peacefully and cause no further grief to Enesfel?"

Before Owain could speak, Guthrie said, "You have it on my life, My Prince." Heads turned and Owain hung his head, feeling a surge of something he had never felt before. The closeness of something akin to friendship, perhaps, or at least the selflessness of someone giving something to him, as Kavan had given him his life back, without having been asked, without seeking anything in return.

Prince Arlan was astute enough to realize that he was missing an integral part of the dialogue taking place before him. He was not comfortable with the invisible undertones, and though he doubted he would get answers tonight, he intended to get them soon. "What of his mother?" he asked, still speaking as though Owain was not in the room.

The blonde man grunted. "She is a liar, a conspirator against the Crown, a murderer, and a whore. She might be my mother…but even I know that to send her back to Neth, to her brother, will mean no peace for anyone."

Guthrie agreed. "No one will lay down their life to vouch for her. That would be suicide. If the choice were mine, I would demand her execution." He watched Owain's shoulders twitch but did not regret the bitterness in his voice. "She has caused too much grief to too many people. I think many would argue that she deserves to die."

"Yes," Owain agreed weakly, "she does."

The prince looked around him, gauging the expressions of every person. Most seemed in agreement that the woman was best not allowed to propagate further disharmony, but the prince did not particularly want to start his reign with an execution unless that execution was Owain's. Clearing his throat, he waved his hand dismissively and said, "We will tend to her later; she is not going anywhere. Mr. Dugan?"

The redhead came to attention. "Yes, milord?"

"Take some men. Spread the word through the castle that as of now I am…" He stopped and his bravado slipped. He had spent his entire life preparing for this day, had spent over a year struggling day-by-day, hour by hour, to reach this moment. Now that he was here, with the scepter lying at his feet and the throne behind him, he could barely believe it was real. With his sword once more sheathed, he approached Owain and carefully removed the circlet from his head, the informal band of gold that Lachlans had worn for generations when ceremony did not demand something more formal. "King…" he whispered under his breath, turning to look at Kavan and then down at the object he held. Suddenly he grinned like the boy Kavan had known, rushed back to the throne and hugged his sister tightly. "I am King!"

Caol grinned. "Right away, My King!"

"And Mr. Dugan, see what you can do to arrange a celebration. There is cause to celebrate, don't you agree?"

"Unequivocally, My King." Caol bowed again and raced from the Hall.

General Wyndham had not moved during the entire proceedings. While he did not understand Owain's willingness to capitulate without fighting, he did understand what had transpired. The King he had served had been deposed, the throne claimed by another Lachlan…a true Lachlan it appeared, without further bloodshed. Owain had been spared, the kingdom given back its peace. "If it is the same to you, milord," he said stoically, "I do not think I should be…part of the celebration. I think I should inform the palace staff…and the castle troops. They may not be willing to believe the word of your man."

"Yes…of course. See to it, General…then you and I will need to talk." The new King, with the circlet placed at a slant on his head, pointed to two of the Káliel guards, "Go with him." He wanted to trust the man, but at this precarious moment, he knew he could not afford to take chances. Someone had ordered his assassination after all, and he still did not know if it had been Owain, General Wyndham, or someone else. "Guthrie, what shall we do with…?"

"Please do not place me in the dungeon with my mother. I have no desire to see her again." Owain's tone was that of a man broken and defeated, but also one grateful to be alive. Kavan began to speak, but Guthrie beat him to it.

"I will take him to a room and see that he is guarded."

"Very well. But hurry back, Lord General. I do not want you to miss the celebration you have valiantly and steadfastly earned," said the young King. General Wyndham had not yet moved but watched his former King and the Lord General leave the room with only a handful of attendants. He hoped, for a moment, that Owain would find the strength of will to overthrow them, but judging by the weak slump of his shoulders and the way he continued to lean on the two men who propped him on either side, the general realized there would be no more overthrowing tonight. Arlan Lachlan was here to stay.

The new King turned to Kavan. Whatever anger he felt over Owain had been displaced by the joy and relief of success and the crown on his head. "Lord Harper, a song or two?"

Kavan, however, was less quick to let go of that hurt and the angry indictments. He knew that, when Arlan's euphoria faded, the accusations would return. He wanted none of it. "I do not have my harp." His words were clipped and strained as he and Arlan stared at one another.

But Arlan was not going to be deterred. He was brimming with the newfound self-assurance this night had brought, and he wanted others to share in his fortune and to be as happy as he was with the outcome of their efforts. "I will send someone to fetch it. You did whatever you did for a reason, Lord Harper, and I shall hear you out later. Right now, we have accomplished more than we came for; we are owed a night of celebrating before we get back to work. I would not be here if it weren't for you; you can either join me or not…but I pray you will. Please, Kavan…"

That youthfulness and pleading were difficult for the bard to deny. "My hands…" he said in half-hearted protest.

"Wash them. Then I expect you to play." He paused, softened his voice, and put his hand on his friend's shoulder. "Will you? For me?"

Though his expression did not change, inside, Kavan's resolve crumbled. "I will," he agreed. If nothing else, music would be a welcome escape from the weight in his center.

"Good." The King gave Kavan his typical boyish grin before turning to the healer. "It is time, I think, that Brenna joins us. Is that possible, Lord Healer?" He could send Kavan, but he did not want to give the bard any chance to slip away tonight. He might have won the throne of Enesfel, but Arlan still needed his friend and mentor.

Finished tending the wounded soldiers in the room, Ártur looked up from healing his own leg. "Certainly, milord…but shouldn't we see to any other wounded first?"

For a moment, Arlan looked confused, as if those in the room would be the only injured to contend with, but then he nodded. "Of course…do that…but set the other physicians to the task. We have all the time in the world. I am the King of Enesfel, and I have no intention of going anywhere." He collapsed, laughing gleefully, onto the throne and held his hand out for his sister to take. It was good to see her again!

Men rushed to obey. There was a flurry of activity in the Grand Hall and throughout the rest of the castle, and Rhidam, as the news spread that Arlan Lachlan had claimed the throne. The gates were opened, allowing men inside, though Bhríd remained on the outside with his regiment to douse the fires that burned in the towers.

When the wounded men were tended, and the dead collected and taken to the náós where they would be attended in the light of day, Ártur did as asked and brought Brenna and young Muir to Rhidam. The new Queen tearfully embraced first her husband, then the princess she had dearly missed, and finally her uncle, before returning to the princess. Laughing through their tears, the women nestled on the edge of the platform, passing Muir between them, reveling in each other's company. Within hours, the Grand Hall was filled with people, supporters, and soldiers, merchants, and peasants, nobility and friends. Caol returned, Kavan's harp in hand as though he had known it would be wanted, and then he found a seat on the platform as near to the princess as he dared, watching her from the corner of his eye as he remained attentive to the King.

"Play, Lord Harper," the King instructed with a clap of his hands. With the royal circlet on his head and scepter in hand as he sat on the throne, no longer dressed in armor, he looked more the part of a king than ever before. Beside him, his sister pulled something from her pocket and then hesitantly touched his hand. In her outstretched palm was the royal amber ring that King Donal had given to Ártur for safe-keeping so that it could be returned to the hand of Enesfel's rightful ruler. The ring slid easily into place and Arlan kissed his sister's palm in return. The royal ring had come home.

The ancient black harp sang out, leading to a frenzy of dancing and drinking from the jubilant followers of Arlan Lachlan and Guthrie McHador. Captain Delamo stood next to the bard, his feet tapping in time to the music but he was apparently not planning on moving since he stood with his sword clenched tightly in both hands, its tip touching the floor between his feet. The room was a kaleidoscope of colors as people moved in and out of the dance for hastily prepared food and drink brought up from the kitchen and royal stores.

At some point during the revelry, the King and his queen were pulled into the whirling chaos. The bard lost sight of him but knew he was unharmed. There might be Enesfel soldiers here, but now they were Arlan's soldiers, and Kavan knew the young man was safe. There would be no assassination attempts tonight. From outside the castle, rupturing the city's darkness, sang the peeling of long silent náós bells. The music stopped to allow the revelers to appreciate the sound and what it meant.

"To dedhá Jermyn!" shouted the newly crowned King.

Cheers and drinks went up around the room and Arlan worked his way back to the throne with Brenna's hand clutched firmly in his.

When the bells fell silent, he continued, "And to all who placed themselves in my trust, particularly my sister, my queen, and those who died on behalf of this great cause. We shall erect a monument to commemorate this day, to remember all who gave their lives to see justice done in Enesfel. With all sincerity, I thank each of you. I would not be before you, here to dedicate my life to your service and to this kingdom, if not for each of you. I will strive to never let any of you down, but to rule with justice, fairness, and honesty. Enesfel deserves it."

The second rupture of cheering and applause rose up and the harp remained silent. Kavan met Guthrie's eyes when the general at last entered the Hall; he appeared much older, although only Kavan seemed to notice. Both men nodded in understanding. Guthrie took his place on a stool near his niece and did not move from it. He drank a great deal but said nothing. No amount of coaxing could cause him to join the merrymakers on the dance floor, to laugh, or to sing.

At the edge of the gala, near an open doorway to his left that led out of the Grand Hall, Kavan glimpsed a gray-cloaked figure. The man lowered his hood, looking at the bard with undisguised fondness and appreciation. Kavan's tension faded and his melancholy transformed into reverence with a small joyfully relieved smile that he had not managed to produce in several weeks. Thank you, he thought. There was no chance to speak together, but it was enough to have the auburn-haired man there.

No, echoed the reply in his mind, thank you. You saved a man's life and soul tonight. You are truly blessed. k'Ádhá be with you, átae-lás mai. Play. The King is waiting.

The healer, noticing Kavan's sidelong stare, followed it, and this time saw the man for himself before the Heretic-Saint slipped into the fullness of the crowd and disappeared from sight. Perhaps he was celebrating as well. Perhaps he had departed. Ártur touched his cousin's shoulder to let him know that he too had seen Kóráhm. He could doubt those visitations no more.

Unexpectedly, King Arlan turned and embraced the bard before lifting his glass and crying, "To the true hope of Enesfel!" Without Kavan, he knew he would not be here tonight.

The cheer that surrounded Kavan was like a warm wave unexpected as it was. None of this was his doing. He had done no more than his destiny had intended. He did not want their gratitude. He wanted only peace. He blushed with his head bowed, the harp quiet in his hands.

"You know, Lord Harper," Arlan said with a mirthful smile, "you do blush well." The nearest friends and comrades laughed affectionately; Kavan's blush deepened, but this time he did not turn away.

❧Epilogue❦

The dark halls of Rhidam's castle were quiet at last when Kavan made his way to the courtyard. It was not yet light outside, but the late autumn warmth of the sun was not far off. During the night, as the victory celebration continued, a light blanket of snow had fallen. Now, there were scattered footprints marring the pristine mantle, most of them going back and forth to either the guardhouse or the main gates. The gate towers were badly scorched and the gates had been splintered, but it was damage easily mended. There was other damage done, however, that would not be so easily repaired or healed.

In the doorway, Guthrie leaned against the side of the entry, watching the group of horsemen cross the bridge, bound for Neth. Kavan stopped beside him. The blonde rider at the center looked back. His gaze traveled over them both, locking with the Elyri's before he lifted his chin and passed over the bridge. Kavan and Guthrie watched until the riders were out of sight and then stood in companionable silence.

"Have the last of the merrymakers retired?"

"Finally, yes." Kavan looked at his fingertips. "I was beginning to believe they would never allow me to rest." Again, it was quiet for many minutes, each absorbed in their own thoughts until the general cleared his throat. His eyes were still on the empty gates.

"Thank you for saving his life."

"I could not have done otherwise. I was given the chance to spare him for a higher purpose. To deny that power, to allow him to die when I could prevent it would have been a great sin. I could not have endured such a burden." Kavan sighed and raked his hair away from his face. "Besides...I sincerely had no desire for him to die."

"I know. You are the only one...and the only other who came to see him off." Guthrie was not surprised by this, only saddened. The bard lowered his gaze as though embarrassed.

"Despite his initial dislike of me...and what he has done...I understand him. We have come to a place of agreement, I believe. Knowing what I know...I bear him no ill will. He is a lonely, troubled man, but there is good in him. Perhaps now it will be allowed to flourish, now that things have been set right. For my part, all is forgiven."

The general smiled a little, amazed at the bard's unfaltering ability to forgive. "Still, I thank you. I think it meant much to him to see you here."

A bird chirped in the distance as the first fingers of light painted the sky. There had been no need for words between Owain and Kavan; they had reached a silent understanding of the past and forgiven the others' actions. To forgive the enemy, Kavan thought with a sigh, though he did not view Owain as an enemy. Only a pawn in some greater game in the annals of history, as Kavan had been a pawn the previous night. Perhaps there had never been an enemy, only the need to set the kingdom in its proper order. Chaos and order often seemed all there was.

He felt Guthrie's desire to talk but the general did not know how to begin. Finally, as the older man began to shift nervously, Kavan asked, "How did it happen?"

There were several tense minutes before Guthrie spoke, and Kavan thought at first he would not. "I went through a period of great mourning after Jezeel died. I drank too much and acquired many of the usual vices. Ula had been after me for months, even before Jezeel's death, during one of the many periods when she and Bowen were estranged. There was a night…I did not remember it until last night, and I had been drinking heavily then and was never certain it was real. She never spoke of it, stopped pursuing me…and I assumed it had been a drunken dream. She attached herself to Bowen again within a matter of days, knowing, I presume, that I wanted nothing to do with her. There was some sort of banquet shortly thereafter; I do not recall the occasion…but that is when she claimed to have bedded Innis. He had been drinking that night as well and could not remember being with her, but we all knew he had not spent it with Lady Cordelia who was in Kamin at the time. Once the assertion was made, Innis refused to entertain the possibility that her child was anyone else's. I never believed her, of course, as I was with him much of that night. But I did leave him eventually…and with Bowen the only supposed witness to their assignation…" He shrugged. "I assumed, like many others, that Bowen was his father, but he did not want to marry her and knew the child would have a better chance of ruling if Innis accepted him. I never imagined that he might be…"

"And now?"

Guthrie sighed. "Do not speak of this to anyone. I might still be wrong…but I do not believe I am. If I am right, I do not believe others need to know. He knows, I know. That is enough." He stared at the sky, watching the light creeping slowly higher, and then continued, "It is as you suspect. Owain has no claim to the throne of Enesfel. He is, in all likelihood…my son."

The general accepted Kavan's supporting touch and then turned back inside, heading down the long corridor to the stairs. Kavan did not pursue him. Instead, he took Guthrie's place at the doorpost and stared into the pale blue-gray sky.

They had done it. They had restored Enesfel to the Lachlan house, restored Arlan Lachlan to his proper place. Gabrielle's face flashed through his thoughts unexpectedly, without the usual accompanying surge of fire and pain. Yes, he decided, he would have to let her know of their success. She deserved that after the risks she had taken. Owain's face appeared to him next. Kavan clasped the silvery Kílyn cross and raised it to his lips. Despite the words that had passed the night before, he knew he had not seen the last of Owain Lachlan. That thought pleased him immensely as he closed the heavy door against the morning cold. It was time to rest.

The End

Brigham ❧*❧

❧White Pawn❧

Character Index Book 1

Affrid Niall, Duke--An adviser of Kings Innis and Donal who signed Prince Owain's ineligibility documents; he is Duke of Dorshur and assists Guthrie McHador and Prince Arlan with troops in overcoming King Owain.

Ahern Valdis--The King of Cordash during the reigns of Kings Girvin, Owain, and Arlan.

Ander de Corrmick--The King of Neth, brother of Ula, uncle to Owain Ustes.

Antony--Master of the hounds during King Farrell's reign.

Arlan Trebor Lachlan--The youngest son of King Innis of Enesfel.

Ártur MacLyr--The Elyri healer employed by King's Innis and Donal then again by Prince Arlan; he is the cousin of Kavan Cliáth.

Bhílári, gdhededhá--Head clergy of Hes Índári, Bhryell who witnesses many of Kavan's "miracles."

Bhríd Cáner--An Elyri merchant's son who fights for Arlan's cause; he is a distant cousin of the MacLyr's and Cliáth's.

Bowen Ellard Lachlan--The 3rd son of King Innis; the 22nd King of Enesfel.

Brenna Weylin Lachlan--Guthrie McHador's niece, mother of Muir Innis, wife of Prince Arlan Lachlan.

Caol Dugan--A youth from Durham who assists Prince Arlan in his quest for the throne.

Cocidius--A palace guard during King Donal of Enesfel's reign, friend of Prince Bowen.

Cordelia Lachlan--The 3rd wife of King Innis of Enesfel, mother of Girvin, Deidre, and Arlan.

Deidre Agnes Lachlan--The only daughter of King Innis of Enesfel, twin to Arlan.

Delia--The maidservant to Prime Magistrate Ulstar Dilyn of Káliel.

Dháná MacLyr--The wife of Tám MacLyr, mother of Sámel and Ártur MacLyr, Kavan Cliáth's aunt.

Donal Malin Lachlan--The 1st son of King Innis of Enesfel; the 20th King of Enesfel.

Dórímyr, k'gdhededhá--The highest religious leader in the Faith of Elyriá.

Doulbirt, Captain--A fictitious soldier created by Caol Dugan.

Edard Transk, Sir--King Innis' chamberlain and an ally of King Donal.

Elys Phryádá--The fiancé of Ártur MacLyr.

Edhriá, málneag--An ancient saint

Farrell Rasmus Lachlan--The 2nd son of King Innis of Enesfel; the 21st King of Enesfel.

Ferghus McLeu--The second in command or Enesfel's military under King Innis, who replaces Guthrie McHador as general during King Donal's reign and remains as Lord General until Arlan Lachlan claims the throne.

Gabrielle Dilyn--The only child of Ulstar Dilyn, Prime Magistrate of Káliel.

Geir Harcourt--The single heir of King Perren Harcourt of Hatu, he becomes King during Girvin Lachlan's reign.

Gíldás, málneag--An ancient saint

Girvin Alaric Lachlan--The 4th child of King Innis, first child of Cordelia; the 23rd King of Enesfel.

Gratz Durbin--A harbor patrolman for Káliel.

Guthrie McHador--Page, friend, and then Lord General for King Innis, and general and military advisor for King Donal, who assists Prince Arlan in his bid for the throne.

Gwenyr Tresa Lachlan--A daughter of Donal Lachlan, 1st twin, who died of plague at age 2.

Hanford Weylin, Duke--Brenna Weylin's brother, the duke of Alberni, who sides with Prince Arlan against King Owain.

Hewett Colson--A captain in King Owain's ranks who defects to Prince Arlan's cause. His father is the duke of Seres.

Hiram--The captain of Hatu's naval fleet.

Hwíletá MacLyr--Ártur MacLyr's deceased sister who died during the last plague.

Ilka Lisbet Lachlan--A daughter of Prince Donal, 2nd twin, who died of plague at age 2.

Innis Trebor Lachlan--The 19th King of Enesfel and one of the most popular Lachlan kings, he is the father Kings Donal, Farrell, Bowen, Girvin, and Arlan.

Jermyn Tythilius--A brother in the Order of Saint Kóráhm in Clarys, Elyriá. He leaves Elyriá to assist the search for a purpose to his life and ends up supporting Prince Arlan's bid for the throne of Enesfel.

Jezeel McHador--The deceased wife of Guthrie McHador, who died of the plague during King Innis' reign.

Johanna, Lady--Nursemaid, nanny, and attendant for Cordelia Lachlan and her three children.

Jon Bottrili, Duke--One of the dukes created by King Girvin who retains his status when Prince Owain assumes the throne. Because of this, he is loyal to King Owain; Prince Arlan's forces avoid him. He is the duke of Nelori.

Kavan Kóráhm Cliáth--Last of the Cliáth's, he is the only child of Rístyrd and Llyárá and is cousin to Ártur MacLyr. He is an admired harper, possessor of llánec, and holder of great psychic abilities.

Konsíl, ílMairós--A healer in Bhryell.

Kóráhm, málneag--The Elyri saint for whom Kavan was named, who is also known as Kóráhm the rón, or heretic, by many because of some controversial writings made before his martyrdom. Few of his writings are available and he is not commonly discussed.

Laird Valdis--The father of King Ahern. He was the King of Cordash during the reigns of Kings Innis, Donal, Farrell, and Bowen.

Llyárá Cliáth--The wife of Rístyrd Cliáth, mother of Kavan. She died during the plague.

Llyr, málneag--An ancient saint.

Loring Gottfrid, Duke--The duke of Erleta who, while he does not fight against King Owain, provides supplies to Prince Arlan and does not report his activities to the King.

Loris de Corrmick--The son of King Ander de Corrmick of Neth.

Luc McDermott--An officer who served with Guthrie McHador during Kings' Innis and Donal's reigns, and retired with the ascent of Farrell to the throne. He joins Prince Arlan's forces in their march against King Owain.

Mátán, málneag--An Elyri saint, popular for advocating wise and judicious use of Elyri abilities. He was a scholar and a teacher who was in Enesfel when the first Lachlan became King. Though he personally denied involvement, and Teren chronicles do not mention his name, many believe that Mátán was at least partially responsible for the Lachlans gaining the throne. He is the patron of scholars, students, and those seeking political change.

Meara Lachlan--The wife of King Donal Lachlan.

Medhyr--A legendary Elyri who possessed llánec; he is said to have been blind from birth. He made many "prophecies" about the arrival of the Teren.

Minos Cornell, Duke--The 3rd in command of Enesfel's military under King Owain. He is the duke of Theron, though his wife and a cousin run the estate.

Mormer Nelsen--The Teren physician for the house of Lachlan under Kings Innis and Donal.

Mórne, High Mother (Kyne)--The matriarchal ruler of Elyriá; head of the k'lómesté.

Muir Innis Lachlan--The bastard son of King Owain by Brenna Weylin, raised as Prince Arlan's son.

Muriel, Lady--A lady in waiting for Princess Deidre Lachlan and Brenna Weylin after King Bowen dismisses Lady Johanna from the Lachlan court.

Nevin Drantz--A suitor of Gabrielle Dilyn.

Oberon Cervasian--He served as a captain in Enesfel's military under King Donal but retired shortly after Guthrie McHador left service. He joins Prince Arlan's quest for the throne.

Owain Ustes Lachlan-- Believed by many to be either the 5th child of King Innis or the only son of King Bowen, he is the son of Ula de Corrmick of Neth. He is the 24th king of Enesfel.

Perren Harcourt--The King of Hatu during Kings' Innis, Donal, Farrell, and Bowen's reigns, he is the father of King Geir.

Phaedr Cáner--The brother of Bhríd and Syl Cáner, who joins Prince Arlan's forces.

Phyóná Térari--A distant relative of the MacLyr's and Cliáth's who dies during childbirth; her funeral is Kavan's first service as an altar attendant.

Rístyrd Cliáth--An Elyri harp maker of the historical & legendary Cliáthans, he is the father of Kavan. He died in a fire when Kavan was an infant.

Robret--A clerk under King Owain.

Sámel MacLyr--Ártur MacLyr's older brother, Kavan's cousin. He is a harp maker in the Cliáth tradition like his father.

Syl Cáner--The sister of Bhríd and Phaedr Cáner, she is a healer and a distant cousin of the MacLyr's and Cliáth's.

Tám MacLyr--An Elyri harp maker in the tradition of the Cliáths, he is the father of Sámel and Ártur; he was the half-brother of Rístyrd Cliáth.

Ternce Wyndham--The 2nd in command during King Owain's rule; he replaces Ferghus McLeu as General.

Tíbhyan--Elyri bhydáni who becomes Kavan's private tutor. He is the oldest man in Bhryell and one of the top 10 sages in Elyriá.

Tymm Revaugn--A young captain sent to battle Guthrie McHador.

Ula de Corrmick--The sister of King Ander of Neth, mistress of Prince Bowen, mother of King Owain.

Ulstar Dilyn--The Prime Magistrate of Káliel.

Wortham Delamo--Captain of the five elite Káliel guards sent by Gabrielle Dilyn to assist Prince Arlan in his cause.

Yorick Zarkosta--A young sergeant in King Owain's army who defects to Prince Arlan's cause with one thousand of the King's infantry.

Elyri Phonetics

á--ä (as in m<u>o</u>p)
a--ă (as in c<u>a</u>t)
ae--ā (as in <u>a</u>ce)
ag--ä (as in m<u>o</u>p) (HE**)
ai--ī (as in <u>i</u>ce)
au--aù (as in <u>ou</u>t)
é--ŭ (as in b<u>u</u>t)
e--ĕ (as in b<u>e</u>t

i--ē (as in b<u>e</u>)
í--ĭ (as in s<u>i</u>t)
ó--ō (as in g<u>o</u>)
o--ŏ (as in m<u>o</u>p)
u--ū (as in bl<u>ue</u>)
y--ē (as in b<u>e)</u>
yh--y (as in <u>y</u>es)

b--b
bh--v
c--k
ch--ch
d--d
dh--j
gae--gwā
gdh--zh (as in vi<u>si</u>on)
gh--g (as in go)
gk--<u>k</u> as in loch (HE)
h--h
hw--w (breathy, as in whale)
k'--k
k--k

l--l
Ll-- l
m--m
mh--m (slightly breathy)
n--n
ne--nyä
p--p
ph--f
r--r
s--sh
t--t
th--th (as in thistle)
z--z

· C is always pronounced **K** but the letter **K** is most often used to designate this sound. **C** mainly appears at the beginning of some proper surnames and place names and occasionally in the center or at the end of a word. This is believed to be a carryover from the earliest days of the Elyri language, or to have been influenced by the Teren languages, but Elyri linguists and scholars have not yet determined its significance. However, in keeping with this unspoken, unexplained rule, no Elyri have first names, or middle names, starting with **C**.

- The combination **gk** (pronounced as in the German ich) occurs only at the end of words unless there is a verb suffix or plural suffix behind it, and only in those words of High Elyri origin.

- The letter combination **ag** occurs at the end of words of High Elyri origin. If the combination appears elsewhere in a word, it will either be as a product of two words having been combined or will be the result of a suffix having been added. Though some Standard Elyri words have retained their **ag** ending, most words carried into the standard will have the **ag** combination replaced with **á** when written, though they sound alike when spoken.

- The **H** sound only appears in High Elyri words and in some names carried over from ancient sources; Standard Elyri derivatives will normally drop the **h** from the original word but there are exceptions to the rule

- Double **L**'s are found at the beginnings of words, single **l**'s in the body or at the end. When words do have the double **L** in a location other than the beginning, it is always the result of two words being combined into one.

- In High Elyri, there were no naturally occurring **B, P,** or **ow** (as in cow) sounds. These did not get introduced until Elyri acquired their current religious faith. Even then, the sounds were not commonly used until the standard Trade tongue influenced everyday life. These sounds mainly appear in proper names or religious settings.

- The combination of the letter **ne** occurs almost exclusively at the end of a word and is always pronounced **nya**, regardless of where it occurs.

· The **ee** sound at the beginning or end of a word is always represented with an **I**. In the center of words, it is represented by a **Y**. When the **ee** sound is represented in the center of a word by the letter **I,** it is a result of two words being combined into one. In some cases, as with the name Cliáth, the original words may no longer be known. The few exceptions where Standard or High Elyri words begin with a Y for the ee sound are believed to have originated as intentional misspellings.

· There is no **S** sound in the Elyri language. **S**'s are always pronounced **sh**.

· The letter **Z** appears only in the High Elyri or in words derived from the High Elyri or originated as misspellings in one of the Teren languages and were absorbed back into Elyri in the aberrant form.

Elyri Grammar

In most Elyri words, the stress falls on the second to last. Words where the stress fall on the final syllable (or on the first syllable in words with more than two syllables) are either names, the result of an Elyri translation of a Teren word, caused by the addition of a prefix or suffix, or the result of a word being truncated, having dropped the last syllable over time.

The **k'** at the beginning of a word signifies importance or singularity. It is applied to a word that can have a common meaning and a special meaning: k'tyne would be a favorite niece or female cousin, whereas tyne is simply a niece or female cousin. In the case of the phae k'kairá, when the Teren translated the term into "the Others" it is the **k'** that indicates the O to be capitalized; not just any others but the Others.

The Elyri written language does not have additional characters for capitalization. The first letters words may carry a dot beneath them to signify that the word is a proper name, a place, or a title, but first letters of sentences are not capitalized.

Sentence breaks are characterized by either a new line of text or by a symbol that looks similar to an s. This has resulted in many mistranslations from Elyri into other languages.

Nouns

Noun forms of verbs do not have gender. When these nouns are made plural they take the plural inclusive suffix sur.

The prefix **íl** added to a verb makes it into a noun; the word then means "one who" as in "ílDaeni"-one who instructs, i.e.: teacher.

Some nouns are formed by adding the prefix **ai** to a verb; the verb dhesá means touch, aidhesá also means touch but is a noun. Not all verbs can accept the **ai** prefix.

-thé: the standard plural suffix

Nouns ending in **I** are both singular and plural and do not take the -**thé** ending

Elyri monetary denominations are both singular and plural.

There are other exceptions to the singular/plural rule, most being words carried over from the High Elyri. High Elyri contains very few words that are NOT both plural and singular. Any exceptions to the rule are noted.

Some words have gender. A word ending in **ne** is feminine and a word ending in **dhá** is masculine. Both are made plural in the same way (with the **thé** ending). Some gender neutral words that have been altered from their original form may have either ending.

Some words in Standard, those referring to a group that includes both male and female individuals, require the -**sur** ending, creating the plural inclusive form of the word. The same ending exists in High Elyri.

Adjectives

There are few adjectives in the Elyri language. Instead of saying someone is beautiful, or wise, and Elyri would say they possess beauty
or they possess wisdom.

To modify such qualities, an Elyri speaker would say:
> bhykólé aelá shwyth: She possesses wisdom. Teren: She is
> wise.
> ochbhykóle aelá shwyth: She possesses more wisdom. Teren:
> She is wiser.
> utbhykólé aelá shwyth: She possesses the most wisdom.
> Teren: She is wisest.
> naimbhykólé aelá shwyth: She possesses no wisdom. Teren:
> She is not wise; or She is a fool.

The few adjectives that do exist come through the High Elyri and are
believed by most linguists to have their origins in some language
other than the Elyri.

Verbs

When **ibh** modifies a verb (ie: is singing, is looking) it is attached as
a suffix to the verb. In all other instances, it is a separate word
(bhydáni ibh gaeth: He is bhydáni.)

When **im** modifies a verb (ie: was singing, was looking) it is attached
as a suffix to the verb. In all other instances, it is a separate word
(ílDaeni im gaeth: He was a teacher)

There is no "be" in the Elyri language. Whereas a Teren would say,
"He will be singing" the Elyri would say "He will sing." Instead
of "I will be there" it would be "I will come" or I will go"; instead
of "I will be here" it would be "I will stay", "I will attend," or "I
am here."

Rather than using verbs such as "strengthened" or "beautified", in
Elyri they would say "given strength" or "given beauty"

Verb Tenses

(present) do, does	(past) (ár) did, have done	(present) (ibh) am, are, is doing	(past) (im) was, is, were doing	(future) (ád) will do, to do, be done
aelá	aelár	aelibh	aelim	aelád
ándás	ándásár	ándásibh	ándásim	ándásád
árá	árár	áráibh	áráim	árád
bhaeá	bhaeár	bhaeibh	bhaeim	bhaeád
bheken	bhekár	bhekibh	bhenim	bhekád
bhair	bhairár	bhairibh	bhairim	bhairád
bhólon	bhólár	bhólibh	bhólim	bhólád
chóne	chóneár	chóníbh	chónim	chónád
daeni	daenár	daenibh	daenim	daenád
dhesá	dhesár	dhesibh	dhesim	dhesád
dhys	dhysár	dhysibh	dhysim	dhysád
donai	donár	donaiibh	donim	donád
ghlaiph	ghlaiphár	ghlaiphibh	ghlaiphim	ghlaiphád
ghytae	ghytár	ghytibh	ghytim	ghytád
kelém	kelémár	kelémibh	kelémim	kelémád
mairós	mairár	mairibh	mairim	mairád
naeth	naethár	naethibh	naethim	naethád
yháth	yháthár	yháthibh	yháthim	yháthád
zene	zenár	zenibh	zenim	zenád
zólágk	zólágkár	zólágkibh	zólágkim	zólágkád

Verb/Noun Tenses

	noun form 1(íl)	noun 2(ai)
aelá	ílAelá (one who owns)	
ándás	ílAndás (one who honors)	aiándás
bhaeá	ílBhaeá (one who asks)	
bheken	ílBheken	
bhair	ílBhair (one who accepts)	aibhair (acceptance)
bhólon	ílBhólon (one who purifies)	
chóne	ílChóne (one who brings)	
daeni	ílDaeni (one who instructs)	
dhesá	ílDhesá (one who touches)	aidhesá
donai	ílDonai (one who endures)	aidonai
ghlaiph	ílGhlaiph (one who sleeps)	aiglaiph
ghytae	ílGhytae (one who threatens)	aighytae (threat)
kelém	ílKelém (one who passes)	
mairós	ílMairós (one who heals)	aimairós
naeth	ílNaeth (one who finds)	
zene	ílZene (one who gives)	
zólágk	ílZólágk (one who reveals)	

Verb Tenses (High Elyri)

(present)	(past)(-ár)	(future)(-es)
aelás	aelásár	aeles
bhánys	bhánár	bhánes
dytae	dytár	dytes
ghai	ghaiár	ghaies
síndóbhaene	síndóbhaenár	síndóbhaenes
zugdhu	zugdhuár	zugdhues
tyreth	tyrethár	tyrethes
pháló	phálóár	phálóes
scenyhur	scenyhár	scenhyures
elzen	elzenár	elzenes

Verb/Noun Tenses (High Elyri)

(noun 1) (bhe-)	(noun 2)(ae-)
bheaelás (one who owns)	aeaelás (possession)
bhehánys (one who makes music)	
bhedytae (one who obeys)	aedytae (obedience)
bheghai (one who does)	
bhesíndóbhaene (one who forgives)	aesíndóbhaene (forgiveness)
bhezugdhu (one who protects)	aezugdhu (protection)
bhetyreth (one who knows/scholar)	aetyreth (knowledge)
bhepháló (one who buries/gravedigger)	aepháló (grave)
bhescenyhur (one who names)	aescenyur (name)
bhelzen (one who gives)	aeelzen (gift)

Foreign Phrase Index

ELYRI WORDS

HE: High Elyri	SE: Standard Elyri	
n--noun	v--verb	adj—adjective
adv--adverb	prn--pronoun	prp--preposition
pl--plural	sng--singular	psv—possessive
pl in--plural inclusive		

á (ä) (prp)--HE/SE; and, also, together with, together

ádhá (Ä-jä) (n)--HE/SE; god; k'Ádhá-supreme deity in the Elyri monotheistic religion

aelá (Ā-lä) (v)--SE; Have (has), possess, own

aendhá (ĀN-jä) (n) (pl: aendáthé)--SE; A father's male relatives, including his father, grandfathers, uncles, brothers, and cousins.

aene (Ā-nyä) (n) (pl: aenethé)--SE; A father's female relatives, including his mother, grandmothers, aunts, sisters, and cousins.

aidóbhae (ī-dō-VĀ) (n) (pl: aidóbhaethé)--SE; compassion, mercy, forgiveness.

aimairós (ī-MĪ-rōsh) (n)--SE; healing

aitaethó (ī-TĀ-thō) (n) (sng and pl)--SE; suffering

árá (Ä-rä) (v)--SE; do

át (ät) (prn)--SE; I, me, myself

átaelá (ä-TĀ-lä) (prn psv)--SE; mine, my

átaelás (ä-TĀ-läsh) (prn psv)--HE; mine, my

bhaeá (VĀ-ä) (v)--SE; ask, request

bhaeád (VĀ-äd) (v)--SE; will ask, will be asked, will seek

bhair (vīr) (v)--SE; accept

bhekád (vĕ-KÄD) (v)--SE; will strive

bheken (vĕ-KĔN) (v)--SE; strive

bhelts (vĕltsh) (n) (sng and pl)--SE; Elyri gold currency.

bheturbhae (vĕ-TŪR-vä)(n) (sng and pl)--HE; traitor

bhólon (vō-LÄN) (v)--SE; purify, purifies

bhydáni (vē-DÄN-ē) (n) (sng and pl)--HE; This is both a title and a social standing. It can be translated teacher, master, sage, or wise one, though it actually encompasses all of these meanings. The title is given to those who, through their exceptional psionic capabilities, wisdom, and intelligence, have demonstrated their worth. Psionic ability is the key to the title, though great ability without wisdom and intelligence will not gain the title. With the title comes the privilege of teaching their knowledge to the children, particularly their psionic knowledge. Each city, town, or village will have at least one bhydáni. Either the bhydáni will ask another into their ranks, or, in the event that a location has no functioning bhydáni, the inhabitants will select someone to fill the position. In extremely rare cases, someone can become bhydáni by accident; they accept mentorship of someone and others begin to ask for the privilege of learning from them. By becoming an official teacher, the individual has become bhydáni. A little less than 2/3 of all bhydáni are female.

bhyne (VĒ-nyä) (n) (pl: bhynethé)--HE/SE; Mother.

chellé (CHĔL-ŭ) (n) (sng and pl)--HE; home, house, dwelling, residence; also frequently used to as the shortened form of chellé hábhai, or Seeking House, the residences of various religious orders.

chóne (CHŌ-nyä) (v)--SE; bring

Cliáthan (klē-Ä-thăn) (n)--HE; A harp made by the Cliáth family and their associates. It is assumed that such an instrument is of the highest quality and will have the Cliáth emblem etched on its base. No one has been able to duplicate the quality of these craftsmen.

dást (däsht) (n)--SE; all, everything, every

dedhá (DĚ-jä) (n) (sng and pl)--SE; priest or monk; the term makes no distinction between the two. The shortened form came into use after the Teren came into the lands and adopted the Faith as their own.

Dhábhyne (jä-VĒ-nyä) (n)--HE; Honored Mother, nurturer. While this term can apply to one's biological mother, it is mainly used to address any woman who is clearly one's elder or superior, or as a term of respect to any woman (not a young girl) with whom a person is not familiar.

Dhágdhuán (JÄ-zhū-än) (n)--HE; the Intercessor, considered to be the founder of the Faith because his death is said to make it possible for mortals to reach the divine

dhek (jĕk) (n)--SE; one

dhi (jē) (pn) (pl: dhithé)--SE; You.

dhín (jĭn) (n) (pl: dhínthé)--SE; a chamber or small room

donai (dä-NĪ) (v)--SE; endure, put up with, tolerate

dónár (dō-NÄR) (n) (pl: dónár)--HE; passage, hall, entranceway

donaiibh (dä- NĪ -ēv) (v)--SE; enduring/tolerating

ebh (ĕv) (pn)--HE/SE; we, us

ergothé (ĕr-GÄ-thŭ) (n) (sng and pl)--SE; strength, fortitude

Ethenae (ĕ-THĔN-ā) (n)--HE/SE; the peaceful afterworld where the blessed and holy reside after death.

gaeth (gwāth) (prn)--HE/SE; he, him, himself

gaethaelá (gwāth-Ā-lä) (prn psv)--SE; his

gdhededhá (zhĕ-DĔ-jä) (n) (sng and pl)--HE/SE; priest or faith teacher or disciple; the term makes no distinction between them.

hes (hĕsh) (n) (sng and pl)--HE; heart

hwonághk (hwän-äk) (n) (sng and pl)--HE; any Elyri who has never received training in the ways of Elyri power. Generally, this term is used in a derogatory manner since those who are untrained are viewed as dangerous renegades, but the term is actually benign and unassuming.

ibh (ēv) (v)--HE/SE; Is, are, am; its translation is dependent on the rest of the sentence.

ílDaeni (ĭl-DÄ-nē) (n)--SE; one who teaches, one who instructs, teacher

ílMairós (ĭl-MĪ-rōsh) (n)--SE; healer, physician.

im (ēm) (v)--HE/SE; Was, were; its translation is dependent on the rest of the sentence.

índári (ĭn-DÄ-rē) (n) (sng)--HE; peace

it (ēt) (pn)--HE/SE; this/that. The rest of the sentence implies its translation.

íth (ĭth) (prp)--HE/SE; the

ithé (Ē-thŭ) (n) (sng and pl)--SE; grief, sadness, emotional pain, sorrow

k'Ádhá (k Ä-jä) (n)--HE/SE; god; Ádhá-supreme deity in the Elyri monotheistic religion

k'dhín bhólibh (k jĭn-vō-LĒV) (n)--HE/SE; Purification Chamber, a small room within a thol where the faithful come to purify their souls via confession to the clergy

k'gdhededhá (k- zhĕ-DĔ-jä) (n) (sng and pl)--HE/SE; The Elyri designation for the male individual who is elected as the head of the Faith.

k'rylag (k-RĒ-lä) (n) (pl: k'rylagthé)--HE; Once Kóráhm chose the word rylag for his method of travel, k'rylag was carried over into standard Elyri and came to refer strictly to the Gates, not a standard gate.

kóh (kō) (pre)--HE/SE; in, within, inside

kóhá (KŌ-hä) (prp and adv)--HE/SE; out; without; outside

kyá (KĒ-ä) (n) (pl: kyáthé)-- SE; Beloved, dearest one

Kyne (KĒ-nyä) (n) (sng and pl)--HE/SE; The High Mother, the Matriarchal ruler of Elyriá. It includes the translation "Mother ruler", "Mother protector", and "exalted mother". Since nearly all Elyri families can trace some familial link to the Bhíncári, the Kyne is both a figurative, and near literal, mother of all Elyri. This position is both hereditary and elected, chosen from among all of the women in the Bhíncári family.

Llaethlágárá (LĀTH-lä-gär-ä) (n)--HE; The mountains separating Elyriá from Neth and Enesfel.

llánec (LÄ-nyäk) (n)--HE; the occasional Elyri "ability" of being given insight into the future. Unlike other Elyri abilities, this one cannot be learned or controlled; an individual must be born with it. One who possesses it endures periodic "blackouts" as events are revealed but they cannot summon visions. Generally, the things they "see" are vague in nature, and rarely involve the seer. It is often translated into the Trade language as "the Sight." Literally translated as "bitter sight"

Llyr (lēr) (n) A figure in connection with the Feast of Llyr; nothing else is known about this individual.

lochi (LŎ-chē) (n) (pl: lochithé)--SE; one who consorts with demons and practices evil arts.

lómesté (lō-MĔSH-tŭ) (n) (pl: lómestéthé)—HE/SE; translated in the Trade tongue as council, it is a unit of 5 to 9 elders and bhydáni that govern a single town or region; k'lómesté is the Elyri High Council in Clarys. All bhydáni in the region will be a member of the lómesté, but the lómesté need not consist solely of bhydáni.

mai (MĪ) (n) (pl: maithé)—HE/SE; child; used in the Standard as a term of endearment

mairós (MĪ-rōsh) (v)--SE; heal, healing

málneag (mäl-NYÄ-ä) (n) (pl: málneagthé)--HE; it can mean one who possesses a quality of blessedness, sacredness, or holiness; its most common translation into the Trade languages is saint.

mályhag (MÄL-yä) (adj)--HE; sacred, holy, blessed. This is one of the few adjectives in the High Elyri and it (as well as all other such adjectives) is believed by some linguists to have its origins in some language other than Elyri though in this case there does appear to be a common root with the term saint which is believed to be a true High Elyri term.

monás (MÄ-näsh) (n) (pl: monásthe)--SE; physical pain

náós (nä-ŌSH) (n) (sng and pl)--HE/SE; a place of worship, temple; also occasionally used to refer to the altar.

phae k'kairá (fã k KĪ-rä) (n) (sng and pl)--HE; The name given to the race of beings who inhabited the territory of the Five Sovereignties before the Elyri arrived. By the time the Elyri came, all that remained of the k'kairá (as they are sometimes called) were crumbling stone circles, mounds, huts, some of which bore written symbols on them. Unlike most High Elyri words which end with the ah sound, this one does not end with the letter combination ag.

phain (fĩn) (prp)--HE/SE; of

phyróth (FĒ-rōth) (n) (pl: phyróthé)--HE; demon, evil spirit, devil

raeyth (rā-ĒTH) (adj)--SE; best

redh (rĕj) (n)--HE grace, sometimes used as forgiveness in a religious sense

rón (rōn) (n) (sng)--SE; one who's beliefs run contrary to the teachings of the Faith; a heretic

sányt (SHÄ-nēt) (v)--HE; prophesied, will come, to come to pass; pertaining only to prophesied events

serbháló (shĕr-VÄ-lō) (n)--SE; A form of Elyri wine with almost no alcohol content, used only for the purposes of religious ceremony.

sídysá (shĭ-DĒ-shä) (n)--HE; A seldom taught Elyri discipline in which one practitioner sends forth a single, brutal cohesive burst of energy which explodes within the skull of his opponent. An unprepared opponent (particularly a Teren) could experience pain, brain damage, or even death depending on the skill of the attacker.

sílai (shĭl-Ī) (n)--HE; sacrifice.

sínréc (shĭn-RŬK) (n) (sng and pl)--HE; This word has no direct translation. Blood kin with a special bond is about the closest it can be described. Any blood kin can be sínréc, but saying "he is my cousin," is different from saying "he is my sínréc" (or "he is sínréc."). It is sometimes used for non-relatives who are extremely close.

só (shō) (adj)--HE; Small, little, tiny, not much, a small amount.

sónás (SHŌ-näsh) (n) (sng and pl)--SE; Elyri silver currency.

sulás (SHŬ-läsh)--HE; so be it, so it is, so shall it be; used only in prayer and prayer song

sumerthé (SHŪ-mŭr-thŭ) (n)--SE; rights, claim, permission

sun (shūn) (prp)--HE/SE; to/from

taene (TĀ-nyä) (n) (pl: taenethé)--SE; sister.

thae (thā) (prp)--SE; by, according to, because of

thóres (THŌ-rĕsh) (n)--SE; the room or rooms in a náós that serves as clergy offices and residences.

thyá (THĒ-ä) (adj)--HE; cherished, treasured, adored

udhan (ū-JĂN) (n)--HE; watch, guard

uhwlth (ūwlth) (prp)--SE: now, immediately, at once. A command of urgency.

yháth (yäth) (v)--SE; outnumber

yháthibh (yäth-ĒV) (v)--SE; am outnumbered, is outnumbered, are outnumbered, outnumber

záryph (zä-RĒF) (n) (sng and pl)--HE/SE; winged beings connected to the realm of the holy; angels

zenár (zĕ-NÄR) (v)--SE; gave, have given, did give, gave

zene (ZĔ-nyä) (v)--SE; give, gives

zíthrós (ZĬ-thrōhsh) (n) (sng and pl)--HE; hypocrite

zólágk (ZŌ-läk̲) (v)--SE; reveals, shows, begins, starts

Translations

Hes Índári Náós
Heart (of) Peace Church

bhair íth sílai phain Dhágdhuán
Accept the sacrifice of Dhágdhuán
ebh ibh k'dhek thae k'dhek
We are One because of Him
k'gaeth chóne ebh sun k'Ádhá
He brings us to k'Ádhá

kóh dást át árá
In everything I do
át bhekád sun átaelá raeyth
I will strive to do my best

Chellé Udhan
House of the Watch

Hes Dhágdhuán Náós
Dhágdhuán's Heart Church

"ithé donaiibh, ergothé ebh zenár
Enduring grief, we are given strength;
monás donaiibh, aimairós ebh zenár;
Enduring pain, we are given healing;
aitaethó donaiibh,
Enduring suffering,
zólágk k'gaethaelá aidóbhae."
Reveals His compassion

sumerthé aelá dhi; bhaeád phain ebh it? yháthibh dhi.
What rights do you have to ask this of us? You are outnumbered.

thyá Dhágdhuán
Cherished Dhágdhuán

k'dónár mályhag
Sacred Passage

sányt k'málneag
The Saint who is prophesied.

Pronunciation of Elyri Names

Ártur (är-TŪR)
Bhílári (vĭ-LÄR-ē)
Bhíncári (vĭn-CÄ-rē)
Bhríd (vrĭd)
Bhryell (bhrē-ĔL)
Cáner (KÄ-nyär)
Cíbhóló (kĭ-VŌ-lō)
Clarys (klär-ĒSH)
Clebhest (klĕ-VĔSHT)
Cliáth (klē-ÄTH)
Derkun (DĔR-kūn)
Dhágdhuán (JÄ-zhū-än)
Dháná (JÄ-nä)
Dórímyr (DŌR-ĭ-mēr)
Edhriá (ĕ-JRĒ-ä)
Elyri (ĕ-LĒR-ē)
Elyriá (ĕ-LĒR-ē-ä)
Elys (ĔL-ēsh)
Gíldás (gĭl-DÄSH)
Hwíletá (hwĭl-ĔT-ä)
Káliel (kä-LĒ-ĕl)
Kármár (KÄR-mahr)
Kavan (KĂ-vän) (in Elyri his
    name is spelled Kabhan)
Kílyn (kĭ-LĒN)
Konsíl (KÄN-shĭl)
Kóráhm di Curnydhá (KŌR-
    äm DĒ kūr-NĒ-jä)
Llyárá (lē-ÄR-ä)
MacLyr (mäk-LĒR)
Mátán (mä-TÄN)
Medhyr (mĕ-JĒR)
Mórne (MŌR-nyä)
Phaedr (FÄ-dŭr)
Phryádá (frē-Ä-dä)
Phyóná (fc̄-Ō-nä)
Rístyrd-(rĭsh-TĒRD)
Sámel (SHÄ-mĕl)

Syl (shēl)
Tám (täm)
Térari (tĕ-RÄR-ē)
Tíbhyan (TĬ-vē-ăn)
Turyn (tū-RĒN)

The Five Sovereignties - City Legend

Enesfel	Cordash	Elyriá
1-*Rhidam	1-*Aralt	1-Clarys
2-Alberni	2-Anzet	2- Ánásair
3-Bryn	3-Ediug	3-Bhastyán
4-Chantel	4-Eleva	4-Bhórdh
5-Dorshur	5-Jassett	5-Bhryell
6-Durham	6-Kakkoris	6-Cármycá
7-Erleta	7-Korr	7-Cylleá
8-Jardin	8-Liatti	8-Dhánthes
9-Kamin	9-Lindumn	9-Ibhórys
10-Kilmacud	10-Matina	10-Káská
11-Levonne	11-Pesek	11-Khwíncanon
12-Nelori	12-Sebring	12-Rísóri
13-Seres	13-Trallan	13-Sábhóne
14-Talladegah	14-Verbier	14-Sídhári
15-Tarsee	15-Vioe	15-Turyn
16-Theron	16-Vron	
17-Wexel	17-Wynett	

Hatu	Neth	Káliel
1-*Natrona	1-*Glevum	1-*Káliel
2-Avarrou	2-Fiara	2-Jaffe
3-Cran Ufa	3-Gorea	3-Mara Qin
4-Drisoge	4-Mawr	4-Pháne
5-Enda	5-Nogero	5-Shola
6-Fa Ruqi	6-Pravek	
7-Furr Katio	7-Ruidoso	
8-Kílyn	8-Venago	
9-Palil		
10-Wasilla		
11-Yd Haszafni		

The Five Sovereignties

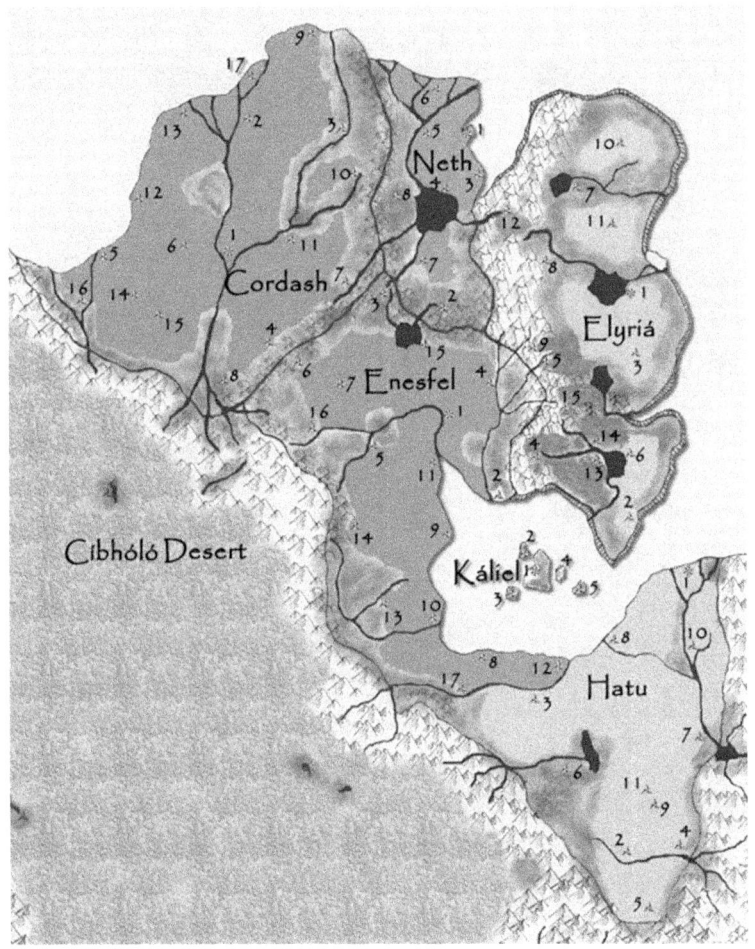

≈White Pawn≈

About the Author

Unsatisfied with 'how the story ends' as a young reader, Tamara took on the challenge of crafting endings to the tales of others to better suit her vision of the world. That desire to mold reality into how she imagined it should be gave birth to a life-long fascination with the written word, and its capacity, particularly through realms of fantasy and science fiction, to foster an understanding of the people, events, thoughts and emotions that make us who we are.

A long-time resident of Clearlake, California, after a life that took her back and forth across the country, Tamara is owned by a pack of papillions, a pride of cats, and an eclectic arsenal of films she enjoys in her off-moments.

formatting:❧White Pawn❧

White Prophet
Kestrel Harper Saga Book 2
(excerpt)

S he stood rigid against the side of the door, under the rough-hewn tavern awning as he had been told she would be. He had only seen her one other time, the day he met her two months prior when she had freed him from his tormentors. It had been a simple misunderstanding, but one that had gotten him on the wrong side of the king and landed him in that swampy hole of a prison for more than ten years. Most did not live that long in such conditions, but he had been determined to survive, survive and escape. He did not know her, did not know why she had picked him for rescue and had not seen her since that overcast, thundering night; she had been no more than a shadow then, and he had not expected to see her again. Whatever she wanted him for would likely be revealed through an intermediary, not in person. That assumption had been wrong.

He had moved on, barely giving her thought after that. He had a lot of catching up to do, and survival was his number one interest. When her messenger had caught up with him, to request this meeting, he had been surprised. He could have ignored the summons, but he was no idiot. She had paid his ransom and freed him; only a foolish man would refuse someone with as much clout and resources as she seemed to possess. He was curious to meet her, to find out why such an elegant woman had gone to the trouble of securing his freedom. She wanted something from him, and he was not going to learn what that might be if he refused to meet with her. There was no harm in a meeting. His instructions had brought him to this distant place, where he had expected to be kept waiting for her arrival. That she had arrived here before him told him that whatever she wanted, it had to be important.

"So…what do you want with me?" he asked, a bit more snappishly than he intended. He did not want her to think he was easily manipulated as to jump to her beck and call. "You expect something for getting me out of that place. What is it?"

Pushing her short dark hair behind her ear, she blinked as she stared at him, and he almost believed she had not heard him or did not understand his words. Her face was unresponsive and blank. Great. A foreigner who did not speak Trade. Everyone spoke Trade, didn't they? She blinked again, her hand still lingering at her ear. He started to speak but she cocked her head, waited a few more seconds, and then said, "There is a woman inside. Elyri. I want you to follow her."

He stared back. Of all the requests she could have made, that was it? Or was this some sort of test? He scowled, shook his head. "Simple enough…but why me? There are hundreds of people who would do that for a lot less than I'll ask of you." Smirking as he folded his arms over his chest, he added, "You might have sprung me, but I can't live off the air. What does she have that you want? What has she done?"

His benefactor shook her head, seeming to match his smirk although her expression did not change, and then drew a pouch of coins from inside her worn leather vest. "My interest in her is not your concern. Your expenses will be covered, but know this…you are in no position to make demands of me…unless you wish to return to your last place of permanent residence."

That was a distasteful thought, but rather than show it, he merely shrugged and said, "I could simply refuse the job…go my own way…" He did no more than glance at the pouch of coins.

Her expression changed at last, the smile melting over it a disarming, seductive and vaguely menacing one that made his blood run cold. Very few people had that effect on him. "Yes…you could…but you won't." Her arm dropped to her side and the pouch slipped from her hand, clinking and jingling as it hit the dust at her feet. "I chose you because of your connections. You have access to what I want."

"And that is?" Something seemed to distract her, or she was bored; her narrow face turned and her gaze wandered away from him and fixed on some point further down the street, on something he could not see. Growing frustrated with her avoidance, he hissed, "Listen, lady…"

"I want the Káliel Serpents," she said softly.

&white Pawn&

www.ingramcontent.com/pod-product-compliance
Lightning Source LLC
Chambersburg PA
CBHW070922100726
47908CB00001B/60